Praise for

THE LION OF SENET

"*The Lion of Senet* is one of those rare hybrids, an SF plot compounded with the in-depth characterization of a good fantasy tale. It is a book that recognizes the old saw, any sufficiently advanced science is indistinguishable from magic, and makes good use of the premise. Jennifer Fallon mines the rich borderland between fantasy and SF to produce a tale of deception and ambition in a battle between science and religion. Well-rounded characters and conflicts that are ethical as well as adventurous make for an intriguing read."
—Robin Hobb

"In *The Lion of Senet* Jennifer Fallon has created a fast-moving and exciting fantasy saga of betrayal and deceit, peopled by an engaging cast of characters. I can't wait to see what new twists she will bring to the plot in Book Two!"
—Sarah Ash, author of *Lord of Snow and Shadows* and *Prisoner of the Iron Tower*

ALSO BY JENNIFER FALLON

The Lion of Senet
Eye of the Labyrinth

LORD
of the
SHADOWS

BOOK 3
OF THE SECOND SONS TRILOGY

JENNIFER FALLON

BANTAM BOOKS

LORD OF THE SHADOWS
A Bantam Spectra Book / June 2004

Published by Bantam Dell
A Division of Random House, Inc.
New York, New York

Bantam Books and Spectra are registered trademarks of Random House,
Inc. and their colophons are trademarks of Random House, Inc.

ISBN 0-553-58670-X

Manufactured in the United States of America
Published simultaneously in Canada

OPM 10 9 8 7 6 5 4

For David,
and as always, Adele Robinson

Acknowledgments

We have some interesting discussions in my house, usually late at night and frequently incomprehensible to the casual observer. We talk, argue and agonize over worlds that don't exist and the people who populate them as if they are real. It is not possible to quantify the value of these discussions when it comes to populating the world of Ranadon.

I wish to thank my son David for the idea of diamond blades and for reminding me that sometimes you have to take a risk to change the world you live in. I cannot thank my daughters enough: Amanda, for being my sounding board and for providing so many bright ideas that it would be impossible to list them all; and TJ, for her constant reading of draft after draft of this series and for reminding me that some stories are too big to tell in a single volume.

I must also thank Peter Jackson for his help in defining the world of Ranadon, and Doug Standish for working out the physics of Ranadon's solar system. If there are mistakes or inconsistencies, they are totally mine, because I kept rearranging the universe to suit my imagination instead of the other way round.

Special thanks must go to the gang from Kabana Kids Klub, especially Ella Sullivan for keeping me on the straight and narrow regarding the geology of Ranadon, and Erika Rockstorm, for her assistance in ironing out some details of this world. I must also thank Ryan Kelly for his advice, his mathematical prowess, and for helping Dirk appear so clever, and Stephanie Sullivan, Analee (Woodie) Wood, Fi Simpson and Alison Dijs for being such economically viable (it sounded better than cheap) proof-readers.

Once again, I have Dave English to thank for helping me look like I know something about ships and sailing, and my good friends John and Toni-Maree Elferink for knowing way too much about the human body and what happens when you do terrible things to it.

I would also like to acknowledge Fiona McLennan and the Phantophiles from the Voyager Online community for their enthusiasm and support, for keeping my spirits up and for providing quite a few of the names that crop up throughout the series.

Last but not least, I wish to thank Lyn Tranter for her help and support, and the staff at ALM for being so wonderfully patient with my eccentricities and Stephanie Smith for giving me so much leeway with the story, when all she wanted was for me to "tidy up the last chapter a bit..."

'Tis all a Chequer-board of Nights and Days
Where Destiny with Men for Pieces plays...

THE RUBÁIYAT OF OMAR KHÁYYAM

(translation by Edward J. Fitzgerald, 1859)

LORD
of the
SHADOWS

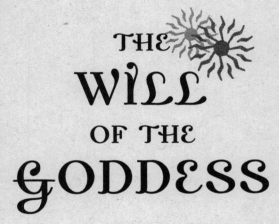

PART ONE

THE WILL OF THE GODDESS

Chapter 1

Neris Veran was waiting as Tia climbed the goat path up to his cave overlooking the pirate settlement of Mil. His eyes were bright and he was unnaturally alert, a sure sign he'd recently taken another dose of poppy-dust. He must have been waiting for her since he spied her crossing the bay. It was raining, but it didn't seem to bother the madman. His thin shirt was soaked, his ragged, unkempt hair plastered to his head.

"Where's Dirk?" he asked as soon as she stepped onto the rocky ledge.

"Can't we go inside, Neris?"

"Where's Dirk?" he repeated stubbornly. "And why is everybody suddenly back in Mil?"

Tia glanced over her shoulder through the rain at the ships anchored below them. It was an unusual sight, all the pirate ships in port at the same time. She hadn't thought Neris would realize it, though.

"Let's go inside, Neris," she insisted. "I'm not going to stand out here in the rain being interrogated by you."

"It's only water," Neris said, turning his face upward. He let the rain fall on his closed eyes for a few moments, and then he looked back at Tia and grinned. "You're always complaining I don't wash often enough."

"Come on, Neris," she urged. "You'll catch your death if you stay out here."

"How do you know?"

Tia hurried across the ledge. He turned to watch her sheltering in the entrance of the cave, looking quite irritated. "You row across here in a downpour and that's perfectly all right for you, but if I stand in it, I'm being foolish! Suppose I *want* to catch my death? Suppose I'm too cowardly to take my own life so I'm standing here in the rain, tempting fate, daring her to take me?"

Tia sighed impatiently. There was no reasoning with him when he started asking questions like that.

"Did you want to hear about Dirk or not?" she called to him over the steady patter of raindrops, hoping that would entice him to come in out of the rain. She didn't wait for his answer. Instead, shivering a little in her wet clothes, Tia hurried over to the small fire in the cave and began to coax it back to life.

"So where is Dirk?" Neris asked her again as he stepped into the cave, shaking his head like a dog, showering everything within reach with a fine spray of raindrops.

"In Avacas," Tia replied shortly as she tended the fire. "He's joined the Shadowdancers."

Neris didn't reply.

Tia turned to look at him. "Did you hear what I said? Dirk Provin has betrayed us. He's joined Belagren and Antonov. He made a deal with the High Priestess, handed me over to them as part of it, Neris, just to save his own stupid neck."

Neris nodded, walked to the bed and sat down, oblivious to the fact that he was soaking the bed with his wet clothes.

"He betrayed me without so much as a flicker of remorse, Neris."

Her father's expression was thoughtful, rather than upset. He was taking the news far better than she anticipated. Where was the rage? The feelings of grief and torment over Dirk's unconscionable betrayal? Tia had felt little else since Omaxin, when she'd heard Dirk inform the High Priestess Belagren that he was ready and willing to join her.

"Aren't you going to say something?"

"I'd like some tea."

"I meant about Dirk."

"I know. But I'd still like some tea. What did you do?"

"When he betrayed me? I shot him."

"Well, you never did have much of a sense of humor."

"*Neris!* This is nothing to joke about! He sent a message to Reithan. He told him he was going to tell Antonov the route through the delta."

"That would be logical."

"Logical! Are you—" Tia was going to ask: *Are you crazy?*

As her father's insanity was a well established fact, it seemed a rather pointless question. "Neris, are you listening to me? Don't you understand what he's done?"

"Better than you, probably."

"Dirk Provin has betrayed us. He handed your only daughter over to the High Priestess to be tortured and killed. I thought you'd be upset."

"I'm a little surprised," Neris conceded. "But why would I be upset? Anyway, as you obviously *haven't* been tortured and killed, why should I waste time worrying that you might have been?"

Tia cursed under her breath as she moved the kettle over the fire. "I don't know, Neris. Why *would* I think you might be upset? Perhaps because, thanks to Dirk Provin, we're all likely to be dead in six weeks?"

"Is that supposed to frighten me? I've been trying to work up the courage to kill myself for more than twenty years, Tia."

"And that's all you can say?"

"What else did you want me to say? I'd actually like to say 'I told you so,' but I didn't, so there wouldn't be much point, would there? Or I could say 'Naughty Dirk,' but you've undoubtedly called him far worse. Or I could say..."

"Just forget it, Neris."

"Now you're mad at me. Still, I suppose with Dirk gone, you have to find someone to be mad at."

Tia rose to her feet, fighting back the urge to take him by his thin, wasted shoulders and shake some sense into him.

"We're evacuating the settlement."

"That's probably a wise move."

"You won't be able to take much with you, but—"

"I'm not leaving," he cut in, quite indignantly. "I'm staying right here! I'll get the best view from up here. Do you think they can get the *Calliope* through the delta? I've heard she's a magnificent sight under full sail."

"Is that all you care about? Seeing the *Calliope*?"

"I suppose I'd like to see the other ships, too..."

"There is no *Calliope*, Neris. Reithan burned it in Elcast when we tried to save Morna Provin."

"What a shame," Neris sighed.

Tia wanted to scream at him. "Neris! Concentrate, *please*! We're evacuating Mil. You can't stay here when we leave."

"Why not?" He seemed genuinely puzzled.

"Because you'll be killed or..." She didn't finish the sentence, not wishing to remind her father an even worse fate awaited him. It would be far better for all of them if he were dead, if the only alternative was Neris in the clutches of the Lion of Senet or the High Priestess of the Shadowdancers.

Neris's eyes narrowed cannily. "You think Dirk will have told Antonov and Belagren I still live, don't you?"

"Why not?" she replied. "He seems to have told them everything else."

"He won't tell them about me."

"How can you be so certain?"

"Because if Dirk wants to secure his position in Avacas with the High Priestess, then he needs her to believe I'm dead. While Belagren thinks Dirk is the only man alive who can tell her when the next Age of Shadows is due, he's indispensable. If she knew that I lived, it would reduce his value to her significantly and he's too smart to let something like that happen."

Tia stared at her father, surprised to hear him make such an astute observation.

"Neris, did Dirk say anything to you before he left?" she asked suspiciously. "Did he give you any hint about what he was planning?"

"Why would he tell me what he was up to?"

"He told you lots of things, didn't he?"

"Tia, Dirk's a very smart boy. The last thing he'd do if he was planning to betray us would be to confide in a madman."

Tia stared at her father, trying to decide if he was telling the truth. He might be. Or he might be telling her what he *believed* to be the truth, which in Neris's tortured mind was quite often the same thing.

"What did you tell him, Neris?"

"I'm sure I don't know what you mean." He looked away, quite offended by what she was implying.

"Why now? Why did Dirk choose to do this now? Why

didn't he do it months ago? Or wait another year? Did you tell him something important? Something that would give him the ammunition he needed to set himself up as the Lord of the Shadows? Something important enough for Belagren to appoint him her right hand?"

Neris grinned. "Lord of the Shadows? Is that what he's calling himself now? Our boy is demonstrating a previously unsuspected flair for the dramatic, isn't he?"

"What did you tell him, Neris?"

"Nothing."

"What about this eclipse that's coming?"

Neris looked puzzled for a moment and then he smiled. "So he told them about the eclipse, did he?"

"He sent the message to Belagren before we even got to Omaxin. How could he have known about this coming eclipse, if you didn't tell him?"

"He told them about the eclipse?" He began to laugh. "Oh, that wicked, wicked boy!"

"Neris? I don't see what's so funny about this. He's going to consolidate Belagren's power for years to come. And if I find out it was you who told him about it..."

But he wasn't listening to her. Neris was laughing so hard he toppled sideways on the bed, holding his sides as tears streamed down his face.

"Neris..."

"I never thought he'd do it!" he gasped between great heaving guffaws. "Oh, that's just too much!"

"Neris!"

It was no use. Whatever Neris found so funny, it totally consumed him. Tia glared at him as he sobbed with mirth, furious he would react to something so devastating with hysterical laughter. She glanced down to find the water bubbling in the kettle. Snatching an old shirt of Neris's from the floor, she lifted the kettle clear of the flames and dumped it on the floor beside the fire.

"Get your own damned tea!" she snapped before stalking out of the cave and back into the rain, wishing that just once, Neris would act like a sane man.

Chapter 2

In death, the High Priestess was not a pretty sight. Belagren had fallen against the wall and lay slumped beneath the window of her sitting room, her jaw slack. Only the whites of her eyes showed beneath her partly closed eyelids, as if she was staring blindly into the afterlife. Dirk Provin gagged on the sharp aroma of urine as he entered the room.

Why don't people die with beatific smiles on their faces?

Instead, the High Priestess's bladder had relaxed when she died and it had stained the red silken robes bunched up beneath her, revealing ankles and lower limbs swollen with the body fluids that had pooled there when her heart stopped beating.

If there really is a Goddess, and if death is her reward, then why is the transition to the afterlife such an ugly, degrading thing? Dirk wondered.

Yuri Daranski, the palace physician, was bending over the corpse and looked up when he heard the door open, his ferrety eyes guilty. He seemed relieved when he saw who entered and beckoned Dirk forward. Somewhat reluctantly, Dirk crossed the room, noticing a tray with a cup and saucer resting on the table beside the settee. He hesitated for a moment, picked up the cup and sniffed the familiar scent of peppermint, and then without changing his expression he walked to the window and squatted down beside the physician.

"She's been dead for a little over two hours," Yuri told him. "See, rigor mortis has begun to set into her fingers and toes."

"Do you know how she died?" He declined to touch her and confirm what Yuri told him. The Shadowdancer knew his trade.

Yuri glanced at Dirk with a frown. "A stroke perhaps...or something else."

"What kind of something else?" Dirk asked carefully.

The physician hesitated before answering. "Poison."

"You think she was murdered," Dirk said, knowing she almost certainly had been—and who the likely culprit was.

"I seriously doubt she took her own life." Yuri shrugged.

There was a moment of silence—a moment of suspicion and uneasiness as the youth and the old physician sized each other up, debating how far each could be trusted.

"Have you told Antonov of your suspicions?"

Yuri let out a short, skeptical laugh. "If anyone is going to tell the Lion of Senet the High Priestess has been murdered in his own palace, it won't be me, Dirk Provin. I'm rather fond of my head right where it is, thank you."

"You expect *me* to tell him?"

Yuri shrugged. "You're the Lord of the Shadows, aren't you? The right hand of the High Priestess of the Shadowdancers? That puts you in charge now, my lad—temporarily, at least. I suppose it'll be up to old Paige Halyn to appoint her successor." Yuri stood up and wiped his hands on a towel. It was a symbolic gesture, Dirk thought. As if he were wiping his hands of the whole affair. "What are you going to tell him?"

Still squatting beside the corpse, Dirk studied Belagren for a moment longer, and then glanced up at Yuri. "I'm not going to tell him she was murdered, that's for certain. Not without a culprit I can hand him on a platter."

"You're going to *lie* to him?"

"I'm going to make certain the Shadowdancers aren't destroyed by Antonov in a fit of rage," Dirk corrected. He hesitated for a moment and then added, "Will you back me up on this?"

Yuri thought about it and then nodded. He hadn't gotten to the position of trust he held in the Shadowdancers without being a realist. "Aye. I'll say it was a stroke." He tossed the towel aside and looked at Dirk approvingly. "You've a level head on your shoulders, boy."

"And like you, I prefer it where it is." Dirk stood up and glanced around the room. "Has he seen her yet?"

"Briefly, I believe. Apparently he sent for the High Priestess to attend him in the temple and when she couldn't be roused the guard fetched a servant to wake her. It was the laundry maid, Emalia, who found her. She told the guard, he told Antonov, who raced into the palace, took one look at her body and then stalked off. I suppose he's back in the temple."

Dirk knew for a fact that he wasn't. The Lion of Senet had not returned to his private temple. He'd been watching for Antonov from the window in his room and had seen no sign of him since the Lion of Senet had hurried back to the palace in response to the guard's summons.

"We need to get her cleaned up. He'll want to see her again, but not like this."

Yuri nodded. "I'll get Ella and Olena to see to it. What are you going to do?"

"First, I'm going to send a message to the Hall of Shadows and get Madalan Tirov back here. I can't deal with this on my own. Then I'm going to find Antonov and try to convince him this was the will of the Goddess."

Yuri nodded. Like most Shadowdancers in Belagren's inner circle, Yuri knew there was no Goddess, or if there was, she certainly hadn't spoken to the High Priestess and told her anything of value. Yuri knew about Neris. He knew about the Milk of the Goddess; he knew about many other things Dirk would dearly like to know about, too.

"I don't envy you that task."

"I'm not looking forward to it, either," Dirk agreed. "Will you take care of things here?"

"My task is by far the easier one," Yuri replied. "Good luck with yours."

Dirk pushed through the curious crowd gathered outside Belagren's room, grateful for the escort Antonov had appointed to watch over him. His guards bullied a path through the servants and courtiers, making it easier for him to avoid the questioning looks that followed him back to his room.

Once he reached his own suite, he slipped inside, locked the door and then leaned against it, closing his eyes against the horror of what he had just witnessed. What made it even worse was the knowledge that he was responsible.

Marqel had killed her. There was no question in Dirk's mind about it. *That stupid, shortsighted, murderous little bitch!* She was too self-absorbed to understand the ramifications of what she had done and Dirk was a fool for not realizing it. They'd argued on a number of occasions about it in the past few weeks. Dirk had tried to explain to Marqel why Belagren had to live, but she had obviously only listened to the part about becoming High Priestess. *Stupid, stupid girl!* Did she have any idea how much harder she had made things?

Dirk did not grieve for Belagren. A part of him was glad to see the end of her. Nor was he particularly concerned about the manner of her demise. But the timing was everything. The chances were quite good Marqel had ruined everything with her meddling.

Why couldn't she have just done what I told her?

Dirk would have little chance to take Marqel to task for it, either. Now that he had set this plan in motion, he would have little private contact with Marqel, or it might begin to raise suspicion. Dirk opened his eyes and reached into his pocket. He withdrew the delicate porcelain teacup he had taken from Belagren's room. He sniffed it again, smelled the peppermint, the proof of Marqel's guilt.

I'm insane for thinking this would work.

Then he walked into the bathroom, held the cup high and let it go. It dropped to the tiles and smashed to pieces.

Dirk gathered them up carefully and threw them down the garderobe before he walked back into the main room. He sat down at his desk, took a deep breath, picked up a pen, and taking a fresh leaf of paper, he began to compose a note to Madalan Tirov, Belagren's former right hand and closest confidante, informing her the High Priestess was dead and she was required urgently at the palace.

With the letter to Madalan on its way to the Hall of Shadows, Dirk went looking for the Lion of Senet. He found Antonov on the terrace outside his study, standing near the marble balustrade, staring up at the second sun.

"Your highness?"

The Lion of Senet did not answer immediately. Dirk wondered if Antonov had heard him.

"Sire?"

Slowly, he turned to look at Dirk. His expression was thoughtful rather than grieving. Perhaps Marqel had managed to convince him her visions were true before he learned about the High Priestess. Or he was still in shock. Whatever Antonov was feeling, Dirk knew he would have to tread very, very carefully.

"You've heard the news then?" Antonov said tonelessly.

"I've just come from the High Priestess's room, your highness. Yuri is with her. He seems to think she died of a stroke."

"A sign from the Goddess."

"Sire?"

"You'll do well out of this," he replied, not answering Dirk's question. "You're the High Priest of the Shadowdancers now, aren't you?"

Dirk shook his head. "No, your highness, nor do I wish to be. The Lord of the Suns must appoint the High Priest or Priestess. I've sent to the Hall of Shadows for Lady Madalan. She can take care of things until a successor is found."

"Your humility does you credit, Dirk."

Dirk considered his decision practical, rather than humble, however, if Antonov wanted to think that of him, it would do no harm. But Antonov's calm demeanor worried him. The Lion of Senet had been very close to Belagren. He'd been her lover for more than twenty-five years.

He was taking her sudden death very well.

"It's good you've sent for Madalan," Antonov added. "She'll know how to deal with all the finicky little details that must be attended to at a time like this. Besides, I have another task for you."

"I'm at your disposal, sire." Dirk sounded much less concerned about the prospect than he felt. But he was getting good at this. Neris had once told him that he needed to be a better liar. And he was. Dirk was not sure if he should be proud of the fact, though. There was something unwholesome about being a good liar. Something inherently wrong with it.

"I want you to go down to my temple," Antonov said. "There you will find a Shadowdancer waiting. She claims to have had a vision. She claims the Goddess told her she would send me a sign to show me the vision was true. I want you to find out if she's lying."

"*Me,* your highness? Wouldn't you be better asking someone more qualified?"

"You have felt the presence of the Goddess, Dirk. You can read her writings in the ruins at Omaxin. Belagren thought you good enough to appoint you her right hand. There is no one more qualified."

"But, sire..."

"Do not argue with me, boy. Do as I say."

"How do you expect me to know if her vision is real?"

Antonov studied Dirk for a moment before he answered. "She claims the Goddess revealed the way through the Spakan River delta."

Dirk hoped he looked suitably stunned by the revelation. "That's...astonishing."

"It is," Antonov agreed, apparently convinced that Dirk's shock was genuine. "And given the sudden and unexpected demise of the High Priestess, it's either the most significant event since the return of the second sun, or the most heinous crime in Senet's history."

"You suspect foul play?" Dirk asked, aware his own life was at just as much risk as Marqel's. He had no doubt Marqel would betray him in a heartbeat to save her own neck.

"I suspect nothing, Dirk. I'm leaving that up to you. Find out if she's lying. Make her give you the details. You should know enough about the delta to tell if what she claims is true. Test her. Challenge her. Find out if the Goddess really spoke to her or if she's simply deluding herself."

"I think, your highness, perhaps if Madalan, or even Ella, were to speak to her..." It wouldn't do to appear too eager.

"I want you do it," Antonov insisted. "In this case, I trust you to uncover the truth with a vigor nobody else would bring to the task."

"Why is that?"

"Because the Shadowdancer who would have me believe she is the new Voice of the Goddess is your old friend Marqel. The thief from Elcast who claims you raped her at Kirsh's birthday party. I'm quite certain she lied about that, so I'd not put it past her to lie about this. Given what I will do to her if I find out that she *is* lying, I trust you as I trust no other to expose her."

"And if she's telling the truth?" he asked cautiously. On Antonov's belief in that, hinged his entire future.

"Then we will honor Belagren for her piety and wisdom, and after her funeral, we will announce we have a new Voice of the Goddess." Then for the first time, Antonov allowed a hint of his grief and anger to surface. The Lion of Senet was not taking this nearly as calmly as he would like Dirk to believe. "And," Antonov added with quiet menace, "when we have given thanks to the Goddess for this boon, we will sail into Mil and wipe that pestilent outpost and all who inhabit it from the face of Ranadon."

"And bring back your son?" Dirk asked, wondering how far down Antonov's list of priorities the Crippled Prince ranked.

"Of course," Antonov replied, almost as an afterthought. "We will bring back my son."

Chapter 3

Marqel heard someone approach and hurriedly scrambled to her feet. She'd been sitting on the floor with her back to the altar, chatting in a low voice to the guard Antonov had left behind to watch over her. He wasn't able to tell her much, but it was better than pacing the temple, burning up with curiosity. Better than praying. The temple was guarded outside, too. The men did not challenge the newcomer as he approached. They merely bowed in acknowledgment of his rank and stood aside to let him enter.

The guard inside hurriedly stood to attention as the Lord of the Shadows walked in.

"Leave us," Dirk ordered.

Marqel studied him warily but it was impossible to gauge Dirk's mood. The guard saluted and hurried from the temple, leaving them alone.

She smiled as he approached her, her uncertainty giving way to a smug feeling of one-upmanship. Dirk would learn, soon enough, that she was not to be trifled with, that she was just as capable as he was of coming up with a clever plan. He stopped in front of her. Before she had time to defend herself, he raised his arm and backhanded her across the face.

Marqel staggered backward under the force of the blow. She glared at him, rubbing her stinging face.

"What was *that* for?"

"Belagren."

"Oh," she said. "So you've heard about that." In truth, she was more surprised that Dirk had guessed she was responsible than guilty over the actual murder. "You didn't have to hit me."

"After what you did, I should think it a small price to pay. With my help, you're going to get away with murder. I *should* have you burned at the stake."

"But you won't, though," she predicted, a confident smirk covering her relief. "You need me."

"Defy me one more time, and I'll find another way, Marqel," Dirk warned. "Make no mistake about that. I told you Belagren wasn't to die."

"She would have killed me the moment she found out I was claiming to be the Voice of the Goddess."

"Belagren would have *verified* you were the Voice of the Goddess, you shortsighted idiot! If you hadn't interfered, she would have had no choice. Once Belagren realized I'd told you and not her what she wanted to know, she would've had no option but to support you, or lose Antonov's faith completely.

You've thrown everything into doubt. Antonov doesn't believe you."

"Yes, he does!" She was sure of that one thing, if nothing else. Antonov had held her, comforted her.

"He sent me here to prove you're lying."

"Then we have nothing to worry about, do we?" She shrugged. "You'll just go back and tell him I'm not lying, I'll be High Priestess and everything will be fine."

"Everything will *not* be fine, Marqel," Dirk corrected. He sounded angry, which worried her a little. Dirk's normal state was coldly dispassionate. "The Lord of the Suns must appoint the High Priestess. When he gets here, who do you think he's going to choose? An experienced Shadowdancer with some proof of leadership ability or some nameless acolyte who claims she's had a vision?"

"You said *you* could make me High Priestess," she accused. "And you said the Lord of the Suns wouldn't be a problem."

"If you'd done exactly what I told you to do, he wouldn't have been. He would have had no choice but to make you High Priestess, because Belagren would have agreed to it. Now it's going to be a real problem."

For the first time Marqel began to feel a little uncertain. "What are we going to do?"

"You and I are going to spend the next few days going over your story, so I can convince Antonov I've interrogated you sufficiently. If we don't, he's likely to hand you over to the Prefect of Avacas, and trust me, you don't want that to happen. In the meantime, I've arranged for Madalan Tirov to take over until Paige Halyn can get here from Bollow."

"Madalan? But she hates me!"

"A sentiment I'm extremely sympathetic to right at this moment."

Marqel scowled at him. She'd thought Dirk's reluctance to kill Belagren was because he was squeamish, not because he had other plans. "You didn't tell me I'd have to deal with Madalan," she sulked.

"And whose fault is that, Marqel?" he replied unsympathetically. "Exactly what did you tell Antonov about Belagren, anyway? I assume you told him something to explain her sudden demise."

"I said what you told me to say. I told Antonov I wanted to see the High Priestess, because she would make everything right again. I was very convincing."

"What else?"

"I told him the Goddess would give him a sign to prove I wasn't lying."

"And your sign was Belagren's corpse?" He swore under his breath as he shook his head. "You don't think about anything but yourself, do you? You could have ruined everything."

"But I didn't," she pointed out in her own defense. "Everything is fine."

"We don't know that yet."

"Well, you're the brains behind this plan, Dirk Provin. Find a way to fix it."

"I wouldn't *have* anything to fix if you'd done what you were supposed to do."

He was taking this far too seriously. She smiled. "Honestly! The way you're carrying on, you'd think I'd done something really dreadful."

Dirk stared at her for a moment before he answered. "Do you have any concept of the difference between right and wrong, Marqel?"

"Don't you preach to me about right and wrong! You're far worse than I am, Dirk Provin. You're highborn. You were brought up learning all that stuff about honor and nobility and look what you're doing!"

"What I'm doing is not killing people just because they stand in my way."

"Aren't you? Your body count is far greater than mine."

"What are you talking about?"

"You killed Johan Thorn, didn't you? I heard you even killed your own mother. And what about those men who died when you told Antonov the best way to interrogate Johan Thorn? Don't look down your righteous nose at me, Dirk Provin. I'm not the one they call the Butcher."

For once, Dirk didn't seem to have an answer.

Marqel smiled, finally beginning to feel as if she had gained the upper hand again. "Belagren is dead, Dirk. Your job is to deal with it. Make Antonov believe I'm telling the truth. Make the Lord of the Suns appoint me High Priestess. I've proved I'm the Voice of the Goddess. Once we sail into Mil and rescue Misha, even you won't be able to touch me. So just do your job, Lord of the Shadows, and I'll do mine."

Dirk was silent for a moment longer, and then he shrugged. "Go back to the palace for now. I'll set a guard on your room and order them to keep everyone out, including Madalan. That should keep her off your back for a while and give me time to think up a reasonable explanation for her."

"There! That's better, isn't it?" she declared as she headed for the temple's entrance, glad to be finally allowed out of there. "Things are so much easier when we work together, aren't they?"

"Things are better when you do what you're told, Marqel."

She didn't bother to answer him, fed up with his disapproval. If he wanted someone to grovel to him, why didn't he pick somebody else to do his dirty work? Like that spineless little cousin of his he was so fond of? Alenor would probably lick his boots clean if he asked her to.

"Marqel."

She turned to look at him.

"Don't get too cocky. You know enough to tell Antonov how to get through the delta, but you have no idea when the eclipse is due. You might find that a little hard to explain away if I'm not there to help you."

"You'll keep helping me, Dirk," she told him confidently. "After this, you have no choice."

Chapter 4

For several days, Misha Latanya remained confined to a small hut near the black sandy beach lapped by the waters of the hidden cove in the legendary pirate stronghold of Mil. He saw nobody other than Petra, the herb woman, and Master Helgin, the old physician and Dirk Provin's boyhood tutor from Elcast.

Misha spent a good part of his days talking to Helgin while he waited for his fate to be decided. The physician's journey to Mil had been almost as strange as his own. Helgin's rise and fall was a story in itself. He had gone from a young man full of ideals and hopes, the personal physician of the Dhevynian king, to an exile and an outcast, first on Elcast and now here in Mil. Listening to Helgin, Misha realized how little he knew about the lives of the ordinary people on Ranadon; how little he knew of the truth about the War of Shadows. It was disturbing to think someone in his position was raised in such ignorance.

The old man did put his mind at rest on one point. Helgin was of the opinion the Baenlanders were essentially decent people and were unlikely to execute him out of hand. Other than that, he could offer no comfort regarding the prince's eventual fate. Misha had not seen Tia since they landed.

The pirate settlement was crude, but in some ways, it was disturbingly ordinary. There were children aplenty here who laughed and played in the murky shallows, and even a small schoolhouse manned by a thin, tall woman who smiled at her errant charges like an indulgent grandmother. Herds of goats roamed the hills above the settlement, tended by boys too young to be apprenticed to the sea. A smith with a well-built forge wielded her hammer with a rhythm that echoed off the cliffs, filling the whole settlement with its metallic song. The lives of these people were so unremarkable, so normal; it was easy to forget they were outlaws.

The reputation of the pirates of Mil had never really been

romantic nor particularly noble. Until he was captured on Elcast, Johan Thorn and the pirates of Mil had been little more than a legend to Misha—vicious brigands who plundered shipping around the Bandera Straits and the Tresna Sea, attacking anything with sails, particularly if it was Senetian, able to stay afloat long enough for the pirates to throw their lines across. To find such common, everyday things as goats and fishing nets here made it somehow seem less real. Misha had to remind himself of the danger he was in. He could not risk seduction by the air of domestic harmony that permeated this place.

The Baenlanders seemed in no hurry to decide his fate. Master Helgin told him there were other things going on in the settlement, more important even than having the Lion of Senet's heir as a guest.

He finally received word he was to meet officially with his captors for the first time almost a week after he arrived in Mil. They weren't supposed to be his captors. Misha had come here willingly enough, but he wasn't so foolish to think the Baenlanders would welcome their worst enemy's eldest son into their midst without a great deal of suspicion. Still, he was only lightly guarded. And there was nowhere for him to run to, even if he could. Generally, the villagers gave his small hut a wide berth and Petra cooked his meals. The only other sign he was a prisoner was the guard outside the hut wearing a sword and a sullen scowl, to remind Misha of the futility of trying to escape.

Helgin arranged for two sailors to carry Misha to the longhouse the pirates used as a communal meeting place. The men said little on the short trip from the shack to the longhouse, merely placing him in a chair near the table at the other end of the hall and leaving him alone. There was no guard left to watch him. Misha could barely walk. Where would he run to?

A few moments after the sailors left, two girls entered the hall carrying trays of food. Apparently, the Baenlanders thought this was going to be a long meeting. The smaller of the two girls was dark-haired and petite and looked to be about fourteen. Her taller, more voluptuous friend was as fair as the smaller girl was dark. The girls looked at him curiously as they placed the trays on the table, but said nothing.

Misha smiled at them, hoping he appeared friendly. Master Helgin had just given him another dose of poppy-dust, so he wasn't shaking, nor in danger of having a fit and scaring the girls witless. The blond girl frowned at him, but the dark-haired one seemed more receptive.

"Are you really the Crippled Prince?" she asked.

"Mellie!" the blonde hissed. "Come away from him!"

Misha met her eye evenly and nodded. "That's what they call me."

She looked him over with a critical eye. "You look all right to me."

"Mellie!"

"Oh, don't be such a bore, Eleska!" Mellie scolded, before turning back to the prince. "What's wrong with you?"

Misha smiled. Nobody had ever asked him that question so bluntly before. "My left side is withered." He decided not to volunteer the information he was also a poppy-dust addict. That was something he'd still not come to grips with himself.

"Why?"

"I had a stroke when I was a baby."

"I didn't know babies could have strokes."

"I can assure you they do," he replied with a thin smile.

Mellie thought about it for a moment, and then she shrugged and thrust her hand forward. "My name is Mellie Thorn. Should we call you your highness, or something?"

Misha accepted her unexpected handshake, somewhat bemused. "It's nice to meet you, Mellie. And you can call me Misha. I've a feeling you don't stand on ceremony much here in Mil."

"I know," she agreed with a smile. "It drives Mama mad, sometimes. The snarly one by the door is Eleska Arrowsmith."

"It's nice to meet you too, Eleska."

"We have to go, Mellie!" her friend insisted. "Lexie's going to be really mad at you if she finds out you stayed here chatting to ... *him*."

"So don't tell her about it," Mellie shrugged, and then she smiled at Misha again. "What's it like being a prince?"

Just wonderful, he was tempted to reply. *I get to live in a palace and have someone poison me on a regular basis...* He forced himself not to follow that train of thought, and put on a cheerful face for the benefit of the girls. "What's it like being a pirate?"

The girl laughed delightedly. "I wouldn't know. They never let me sail farther than the end of the delta."

The girl's resemblance to Alenor when she laughed was uncanny. "Did you say your name was Mellie *Thorn*?"

She nodded. "Johan Thorn was my father."

Johan Thorn's daughter? Dear Goddess, what would my father do if he ever discovered Johan had left a legitimate heir? Would he become as fascinated by Mellie Thorn as he was by Dirk?

"So that means Dirk Provin is your half-brother...," he said thoughtfully.

Mellie's expression darkened. "He's not my brother anymore. He's a traitor."

Before Misha could say anything to that, the door at the end of the longhouse opened and a small, well-rounded woman stepped into the hall. "Mellie!" she said sharply. "Go and help Eleska with the rest of the food, please."

"Yes, Mama," Mellie said. She turned to the door, giving Misha a wink as she passed him. Misha quickly covered his smile as Mellie's mother crossed the hall to stand before him.

"The last time I saw you, your highness, you were just a babe," the woman remarked, looking him over with the same undisguised curiosity her daughter had.

"We've met before?"

"In Avacas. During the Age of Shadows. I was the Duchess of Grannon Rock in those days. You'd be too young to remember, I suppose."

"You're the Lady Lexie? Drogan Seranov's wife?"

"His widow," she corrected.

"And Mellie?..."

"Is the child of my second marriage," she explained. "To Johan Thorn."

"You are wise to have kept her existence a secret, my lady," Misha said, nodding in understanding. "News Johan had a legitimate heir would be even more disturbing than the news he sired a bastard."

"I'm glad you understand that, your highness."

The door opened again and a tall, dark-haired man walked in. He was a little older than Misha, his features vaguely familiar, although Misha was sure he'd never met the man before. Lexie beckoned the newcomer forward. "Prince Misha, this is my son, Reithan."

Misha smiled, and held out his hand, guessing that was the way of things here in the Baenlands. "The notorious Reithan Seranov, I presume. I'm honored, sir."

Reithan looked down at Misha's outstretched hand for a moment, and then somewhat reluctantly he accepted the handshake. "The notorious Crippled Prince, I presume."

"Your reputation is far more adventurous than mine, my lord," Misha said with a smile.

"You can call me Reithan," the pirate shrugged. "I've no title I can claim. Not since your father had my father declared a traitor and stripped him of his estates." It was a simple statement of fact. There was no reproach or bitterness in Reithan's voice.

"There is much between our countries to be forgiven," Misha agreed.

"Actually, I think you'll find they'd rather be compensated," Tia remarked as the longhouse door swung shut behind her. She strode the length of the long room and came to stand beside Reithan, and then looked down at Misha. "You're looking better today."

"An illusion of well-being created by poppy-dust, I fear," he admitted. "Although at least now, I'm able to eat regularly. Helgin tells me I have a 'manageable addiction,' whatever that is."

"It probably means you won't die from it," Tia suggested.

As she was speaking, several other people entered the longhouse, including Dal Falstov, the captain of the *Orlando,* the ship that had brought him to Mil, and a badly scarred man.

Lexie introduced them as Porl Isingrin, the captain of the *Makuan,* Lile Droganov, Novin Arrowsmith and Calla, the village blacksmith.

"This makes up our village council, such as it is," Lexie explained as everyone took their seats. "As you can imagine, your highness, the problem of what to do with you is rather vexing."

"It was never my intention to cause your people trouble, my lady," Misha assured her.

"Tia claims you actually *asked* to come here," the scarred captain of the *Makuan* said. He posed a truly daunting figure with his puckered, shiny flesh that had burned his features into a permanent scowl.

"When I realized I was being systematically poisoned, Captain, I asked Tia where she thought I would be safe. It was she who suggested I come to Mil."

"How generous of her," Calla remarked. She was a big woman, with cropped gray hair and well-muscled arms. Misha could well believe she was a blacksmith by trade.

"What was I supposed to do, Calla?" Tia objected. "Just leave him there to die?"

"Well, yes, actually," the blacksmith replied with cold practicality. "That's exactly what you should have done. What Senet does to their own is none of our concern."

"I thought it might help us."

"If you wanted to do something to help, Tia," Novin Arrowsmith snorted contemptuously, "not letting Dirk Provin betray us would have been a good start."

"That's not fair, Novin," Lexie scolded before Tia could respond to the accusation. "We were all taken in by him. You can't single out Tia to ease your own guilt. Besides, we did not come here today to apportion blame. We're here to decide how to proceed from this point."

Lile Droganov coughed uncomfortably and looked at Misha. "No offense, your highness, I've got nothing personal against you, mind..." He turned to the rest of the council. "What we probably *should* do is send his body back to the Lion of Senet in little pieces with a note saying his second son is next if he doesn't withdraw immediately from Dhevyn."

The suggestion wasn't met with howls of protest, which worried Misha a great deal.

"I fear Antonov may not be so easily bluffed," Lexie warned.

"Who said anything about bluffing?" Novin suggested with a malicious grin.

"Don't be an idiot, Novin," Calla snapped. "That would just bring Antonov's wrath down on us like an erupting volcano."

"Well, that's going to happen whatever we do," Lile pointed out. "Why not at least strike the first blow?"

The direction this conversation was heading was making Misha very nervous. "You can't afford for me to die," he hurriedly told the gathered Baenlanders.

"Why not?" Novin shrugged. "I can't see it makes much difference one way or the other."

"Because if Misha dies, Kirshov Latanya will become the heir to Senet," Tia reminded them impatiently.

"He's just married Alenor D'Orlon, remember?" Reithan Seranov added, surprising Misha with his support. "And that means any issue of theirs will be the heir to both Senet and Dhevyn. Within one generation, Dhevyn will be absorbed into Senet and you can kiss all your dreams of freeing Dhevyn goodbye forever."

Misha nodded. "They are right. If I die, you might as well forget everything you've fought for. It will become irrelevant."

"What would you do in our place, Misha?" Lexie asked.

"I'd make a deal."

"With whom?" Porl Isingrin scoffed. "The Lion of Senet? Your father thinks negotiating and giving in to him are the same thing."

"I'd make a deal with *me*," Misha suggested, ignoring the little voice in the back of his mind suggesting making a deal with the Baenlanders was akin to treason against his own people.

His own people had tried to kill him.

"You're not much more than a prisoner, your highness," Lexie reminded him. "What could you possibly offer us?"

"Dhevyn," he told them, the plan forming in his mind as he spoke. He leaned forward in his chair, a little too eagerly perhaps, but he couldn't help it. For the first time in his life, Misha saw a future ahead of him not filled with humiliation and despair. The people who had poisoned him had perpetrated the treason, he reasoned. He was not the guilty party.

"Keep me alive," he suggested. "Keep me safe from those in Senet who would see me dead, and when my father dies and I ascend to the throne, I will withdraw every Senetian governor, every Senetian soldier, from Dhevyn as my first act as Lion of Senet."

His offer was met with contemptuous silence.

"I give you my word," he added, praying the Goddess would make them believe him. "Aid me and I will guarantee Dhevyn independent sovereignty in perpetuity."

Chapter 5

The council meeting dragged on well past first sunrise. When Misha made his startling offer, the council had reacted with stunned disbelief at first. Then Novin Arrowsmith had burst into derisive and disbelieving laughter. After that, the meeting had erupted into chaos and Lexie had asked Reithan and Lile to carry Misha back to Petra's house, while they discussed their options.

He'd not heard from anyone in the longhouse since.

"What's taking them so long?"

"It won't be much longer now," Helgin assured Misha, guessing the reason for his growing apprehension.

It was odd, but here in Mil, where they knew and seemed to accept he was an addict, nobody assumed if he got a bit jittery it was because he was about to have a seizure. These people knew the symptoms of poppy-dust addiction well, and could tell the difference between a man frustrated by impatience and a man about to start foaming at the mouth.

No sooner had the physician spoken than the door opened and Tia stepped into the cluttered little cottage Helgin shared with Petra. He'd not seen the old herb woman all day. She was busy delivering a baby, so Helgin had informed him.

Helgin smiled. "There! What did I tell you?"

"What did they decide?" Misha demanded of Tia, ignoring the old man's smug look.

"Nothing yet," Tia shrugged. "You don't happen to have any tea, do you, Master Helgin? I'd kill for a hot cup."

"Not a fresh batch," Helgin told her. "But it's no trouble to make it. Would you like some tea, Misha?"

"Thank you," he replied with a nod, watching Tia closely as she took a seat at the scrubbed wooden table opposite him. "What's taking them so long?"

"They don't know if they can trust you," she shrugged.

"But I gave them my word."

Tia smiled thinly. "The word of a Senetian doesn't mean much around here, Misha. Particularly a Senetian with your rather dubious pedigree. There's also the question of your addiction. Novin Arrowsmith is trying to convince everyone you won't even remember what you said as soon as the poppy-dust wears off."

"I will remember my promise," he assured her. "And keep it."

"I believe you. But unfortunately, it's not me you have to convince."

Misha cursed silently, both his own weakness and the unknown parties who had done this to him. He glanced over at Master Helgin, who was bustling around the stove, preparing the tea. "How long will it take me to get free of the poppy-dust?"

Helgin turned to look at him with concern. "I'm not sure."

"But you have some idea, don't you?"

Helgin brought the teapot to the table and took a seat beside Tia. "Have you considered, your highness, that you might be better simply managing your addiction, so that—"

"I don't want to manage it, Helgin! I want to be free of it!"

"Perhaps I should explain," the physician said. "If what

you've told me is correct, then you've been unknowingly taking poppy-dust since you were eight or nine years old. Every pore in your body is steeped in it. Your body simply doesn't know how to function without it. If you were to stop taking the drug... well, you've seen the results for yourself. It's liable to kill you."

"Are you telling me I *can't* get free of it?"

"No. I'm telling you it will be hard, painful and possibly fatal, and even if you do manage to survive the withdrawal process, it will take up to seven years before your body is totally free of the drug. And I'm just talking about the physical addiction. You have a dependence on the drug your mind will find hard to let go. That may last a lifetime. You'll need more than physical strength to get through it. It will require a strength of character that few men have."

"That's why we never tried to make Neris shake his addiction," Tia added, sympathetically. "It was kinder to let him keep taking the drug than put him through the agony of withdrawal."

Misha stared at both of them with a frown. "You think I'm too weak to do it?"

"You're certainly too physically depleted to attempt it at the moment," Helgin informed him. "As for your strength of character? Well, only time will tell on that score, your highness. Nobody really knows what they're capable of until they try."

"And I have to try," he insisted.

The old physician looked extremely doubtful. "You can still lead a fulfilling life with a manageable addiction," he tried to assure him. "Your problem has been that you weren't in control of it. The doses you received—be they too little or too much—were controlled by Ella Geon. Now you know what you are facing, you can deal with it yourself and—"

"No!" he declared. "It's not an option. I have to get free of this or I might as well die. I will always be vulnerable while my life revolves around my next dose of poppy-dust. If I can't rule my own life, what hope do I have of convincing anybody I'm capable of ruling Senet?"

"I think what Helgin is trying to say is you will always be vulnerable to it, no matter what," Tia told him. "Even if you manage to survive withdrawal, even if you're strong enough to deny the mental cravings, you'll always be at risk. It would take something as simple as a bad headache to bring you undone. One well-meaning courtier bringing you something to relieve the pain might be all it takes to put you right back where you are now."

"Then I will surround myself with people I can trust," he replied. "But I have to try. If I don't, then I have no future."

Tia nodded in understanding. She at least seemed sympathetic to his plight. But the old physician tut-tutted under his breath.

"I will be free of this, Master Helgin, or I will die trying," he announced with quiet determination.

"I'll help you, if that is truly what you want," Helgin said unhappily. "But in my opinion, you would be far better learning to live with the hand you've been dealt than trying to fight it."

"How can I?" he asked. "How can I claim clear judgment if everyone knows I'm an addict? How can I condemn a criminal for trafficking in the very thing that allows me to make it through the day? Don't you see I have no choice?"

"Well, before you get too carried away condemning the criminals trafficking in poppy-dust, Misha," Tia reminded him with a scowl, "just remember, it's those same criminals who are currently giving you asylum from your own people, who seem intent on killing you."

"That wasn't what I meant, Tia..."

"I know," she shrugged, "but you can see the council's problem with you."

"If you're planning to do this, then you must regain your strength," Helgin warned. "And that means stabilizing your addiction. You need to gain some weight, for one thing. And I'd like to see you up and about, walking."

"Wouldn't we all," Misha sighed.

"You were riding a horse when I first met you, your highness," Helgin reminded him. "You walked into Elcast Keep."

"My good leg was stronger then. But my left side has been weak for as long as I can remember."

"If you could walk then, you can walk now. All you need to

do is start using the muscles again. Whose idea was it you should be bedridden, anyway?"

"I'm not sure if it was a conscious decision on anyone's part. The worse my condition got, the easier it was not to venture from my bed."

"I thought what they did to Neris was bad," Helgin lamented. "But what has been done to you—Antonov's own son—defies belief."

"I will make them pay, Master Helgin. But I can only do that if you help me."

"You'll need more than my help, I'm afraid."

"Can I do anything?" Tia volunteered.

"I can't ask you to do any more for me, Tia."

"I could help you walk. There's plenty of sand around Mil, which will help build up your muscles, and when you're ready, we could tackle the goat tracks in the hills. At least I can help you until we leave."

"You're going somewhere?" Helgin asked.

"We all are. Dirk's told Antonov the way through the delta. Or at least he's planning to. We have to evacuate Mil."

"Then the rumors about him are true?" Helgin sighed.

Misha sympathized with the old man. Dirk had been his protégé, his pride and joy. He loved the boy like a son. Dirk had rescued the physician from Elcast. Helgin couldn't believe Dirk had turned on them. Misha had trouble believing it, too; he was more inclined to think Dirk was up to something than simply accept he'd just changed sides with no warning.

"Yes," Tia confirmed in an unexpectedly savage tone. "They're true."

"I can't imagine what would have driven him to do such a thing," Helgin said, shaking his head.

"Greed?" Tia suggested. "Ambition? A lust for power? Take your pick."

"The boy I helped raise was not like that," Helgin objected.

"The boy you helped raise, Master Helgin, is a traitorous, murderous, power-hungry, selfish little bastard."

Helgin shook his head. "You've not seen the other side of him..."

"I've seen sides of Dirk Provin you can't even imagine," Tia snapped, rising to her feet. "And they all look the same to me—just pure, unadulterated evil."

With that, she stalked out of the small cottage, slamming the door behind her. Misha turned to look at Helgin. The old man seemed as surprised by Tia's vehemence as he was.

"I think, your highness," Helgin remarked, "it might be prudent not to mention Dirk Provin's name in Tia's hearing. She appears to feel very strongly about him."

"Very strongly," Misha agreed thoughtfully as he stared at the closed door, wondering if there was more to Tia's reaction than simple anger over Dirk's betrayal. He turned to Helgin. "Do you think he simply betrayed the Baenlanders out of greed or selfishness? Or is there more to it than that?"

"I'm an old man, your highness, and I've seen more than my share of strife and pain. But if I've learned anything in this life, it's that there is *always* more to it than what we see or what we think we know." He lifted the lid on the pot and sighed. "Damn, it's gone off the boil." Helgin rose from the table and walked back to the stove to boil the kettle again. "I'll tell you something else, lad. That girl's hurting from more than just a feeling of being betrayed."

Misha looked up in surprise. "You mean Tia and Dirk? . . ."

Helgin shrugged. "I don't know anything for certain, Misha, but I'll tell you this much. Tia Veran's not just angry at Dirk. I suspect she's angry with herself."

Chapter 6

Dirk was able to stave off the inevitable confrontation with the Lady Madalan, Belagren's closest confidante, for nearly two days before she finally cornered him. In that time he'd made a great show of interrogating Marqel to determine if her vision was true, while Avacas reeled from the news the High Priestess of the Shadowdancers was dead.

Although she had never been as daunting as her good friend Belagren, Madalan Tirov was sufficiently riled to bluff her way through his guards and gain admittance to his rooms, even though Dirk had left strict instructions that he wasn't to be disturbed. He could have had her thrown out, but facing Madalan and securing her cooperation was something he could not afford to put off for much longer.

"What the hell are you playing at?" Madalan demanded, as soon as they were alone.

"My lady?" he asked innocently.

"Belagren is dead and that sly little Dhevynian slut is claiming she's now the Voice of the Goddess."

"Interesting coincidence," Dirk agreed. "Can I offer you some wine?"

"You can offer me an explanation!" she growled, her voice gaining volume with every word she spoke. "There's only one way Marqel could be speaking to the Goddess, Dirk Provin, and you and I both know how that is. *You* must have given her the information."

"Maybe you should speak a little louder, my lady. I'm sure there's a sailor or two in Paislee who can't hear you."

"You murdered Belagren!" Madalan accused, albeit at a much lower volume.

"No, I didn't," Dirk corrected. "She died of a stroke. And unless you want to explain to Antonov why anybody would want to murder his beloved High Priestess, you will quash any rumor to the contrary as soon as it rears its ugly head."

His words seemed to quell Madalan's anger a little. Despite her shock and fury over Belagren's death, she knew Dirk was right. For Madalan to go to Antonov with her suspicions would mean she would have to offer a motive, and that would mean explaining a few things to the Lion of Senet that Madalan had helped Belagren conceal from him for more than a quarter of a century.

"If you didn't kill her, who did?"

"Marqel."

"And you expect me to let her get away with it?"

"You have no choice." Dirk shrugged. "It's not your fault Belagren's plan backfired on her."

Madalan was instantly suspicious. "What do you mean?"

"You didn't know about it?" Dirk asked, feigning surprise. "I thought you and Belagren shared all your secrets?"

"Apparently not," Madalan retorted. "What plan are you talking of?"

"Belagren was concerned Antonov was slipping through her grasp," Dirk explained, watching the older woman closely. Madalan nodded unconsciously in agreement, which relieved Dirk a great deal. It had taken quite a while to come up with a feasible explanation for what had happened and Madalan had sufficient rank to expose him and be believed if she doubted his version of events.

"She decided it was time to 'pass on the torch,' as it were," he continued. "She wanted to make Antonov believe the Goddess now spoke through another Shadowdancer, one who was young, attractive and would do whatever Belagren told her to do. She noticed Antonov eyeing his son's mistress one day and decided the new Voice of the Goddess would be Marqel."

"That's ridiculous!" Madalan snorted. "Belagren would never trust Marqel with anything so important."

"I believe, my lady, her decision was made mostly out of lack of trust in me."

"I don't see the connection."

"Belagren was distrustful of my defection and remained so right up until her death. I believe she reasoned if I was lying to her and gave her false information, if it was proved to be a lie, she could disown Marqel and let Antonov vent his wrath on someone who was essentially disposable."

"Absolving her of any blame in the affair," Madalan concluded thoughtfully. It was something Belagren would do. "But what if you weren't lying? What if your information proved correct?"

"Then she still owned the Lion of Senet through Marqel and as an added bonus, she was spared the necessity of catering to his...carnal needs. I believe she's found intercourse quite painful since her menses ceased."

Dirk knew Belagren often procured young women for Antonov, but he was only guessing about the menopause. Given Belagren's age, he figured he was on safe ground. Back in another lifetime, while he'd been an apprentice physician on Elcast, he'd heard one of Master Helgin's patients complain endlessly about her insatiable husband and the pain he caused her once she'd passed childbearing age. Helgin had quite seriously suggested the woman encourage her husband to find a younger mistress, which is what had given Dirk the idea in the first place. If Belagren had ever confided such a thing to her closest friend, however, Madalan gave no sign.

"So you told Marqel, and not Belagren, how to get through the delta," Madalan said.

"No, I told Marqel *and* Belagren. The High Priestess would never have trusted me to impart such important information to Marqel without knowing every detail herself."

Madalan nodded. That was also something Belagren would do.

"Of course," he sighed, "none of us counted on Marqel being so ambitious. She killed Belagren and then told Antonov her death was a sign Marqel should become High Priestess."

"I warned Belagren that little bitch couldn't be trusted. When I get my hands on her ..."

"You will bow and smile and proclaim her Belagren's natural successor," Dirk finished for her.

Madalan stared at him in shock. "Are you mad?"

"Antonov believes Marqel is now the Voice of the Goddess, and if you even *hint* Belagren's death was anything other than the will of the Goddess, we'll all be destroyed. We have no choice but to play along with it."

"I will never let that murderous whore profit from what she's done! I'm certainly not going to bow to the smug little slut and offer her my loyalty. If anyone should succeed Belagren, then it should be me." Her eyes narrowed suspiciously. "Or are *you* planning to step into her shoes now that you've removed me from my position as the right hand of the High Priestess?"

Dirk shook his head. "I don't want the job, Madalan. I never did. I wanted to be Belagren's right hand to protect myself from Antonov, that's all. Anyway, you mustn't become High Priestess. The Lord of the Suns named you his successor. When Paige Halyn dies, you're to become the Lady of the Suns. Then you will outrank Marqel and we will have some hope of controlling her."

"How do you know about that?"

"Belagren told me."

Madalan was still doubtful, but everything Dirk had told her fitted in with the way Belagren did things. His story was *plausible* and it was always easier to believe a plausible lie than go digging for the truth, especially when you stood to profit from it.

"Paige Halyn may live for years yet," Madalan pointed out. "How do we control Marqel in the meantime?"

"Keep her away from Antonov, for one thing," Dirk suggested. "Take her back to the Hall of Shadows and bury her in paperwork. She's going to need training, even Antonov will accept that, and it's perfectly reasonable you assume the duties of the High Priestess, and the role of training her successor, until the Lord of the Suns can get to Avacas to appoint Belagren's replacement formally. Between the two of us, I'm sure we can find any number of ways to delay Paige's decision to appoint Marqel until it suits our plans. You will effectively be High Priestess until then, anyway. Paige Halyn is dying, so Belagren informed me. If we manage it right, there'll be little time for Marqel to do any real damage before you succeed him and then you can curb her excesses all you want and not even Antonov will be able to stop you."

Madalan was still not convinced. "It feels wrong, letting Marqel commit murder and receive nothing for it but a slap on the wrist."

"If it's any consolation, she's had a slap on the face."

"I do not appreciate your attempts at levity, Dirk Provin. Have you told Antonov you believe Marqel's vision is accurate?"

"Not yet. I thought it would sound better if you were there to back me up."

Madalan shook her head doubtfully. "This is fraught with danger..."

"Then as an added precaution, might I suggest you start looking for a replacement for Marqel?"

"Why?"

"The Goddess has just chosen a different voice, my lady. If she can do it once, she can do it again. Let's find another Shadowdancer we can groom for the role of Voice of the Goddess. That way, if Marqel proves too much trouble, we can simply announce the Goddess has found a more worthy vessel and the Goddess can take Marqel to her bosom anytime we decide she's no longer useful to us."

Madalan nodded slowly, apparently not in the least bothered by the suggestion they might have to kill Marqel. "That may work."

Dirk watched her closely for any sign she doubted him. But Madalan had followed Belagren for years. He was counting on that habit surviving her death.

"You knew the High Priestess better than I, my lady," he pointed out, with a touch of convincing humility. "This is her plan, not mine. Despite the alteration Marqel took upon herself to make to it, I feel we should be guided by Belagren's wisdom and follow it through."

"Has the Lord of the Suns been informed of the High Priestess's death yet?"

"I thought you should do that," he replied. "In your role as acting High Priestess."

Madalan thought about it for a moment and then nodded slowly. "Does anyone else know what really happened?"

"Yuri knows. We talked about it. He understands the wisdom of not revealing the true circumstances of Belagren's death."

"Yuri would," Madalan agreed. "He's been around long enough to know the way the land lays. What about Marqel?"

"She's riding a wave of euphoria," he told her. "She thinks she's gotten away with murder and is about to become High Priestess of the Shadowdancers. She won't say or do anything that might jeopardize that."

"We need to keep a close eye on her. If she can murder Belagren, she can just as easily murder one of us."

Dirk smiled. "She won't kill me, my lady. Without my help, she is no longer the Voice of the Goddess."

"That's little comfort for me, Dirk."

"When you're Lady of the Suns and hold power over every Sundancer and Shadowdancer on Ranadon, you should find plenty of comfort, my lady."

The Shadowdancer studied him thoughtfully. "You know, if your father had had even a fraction of your wit, Belagren would never have gotten as far as she did."

"Then you should be grateful I'm on your side, my lady."

Madalan scowled at him. "You'd better be on my side, Dirk Provin. Because Belagren's fate will seem like a blessing if I find out you're not."

After Madalan left, Dirk closed the door behind her and locked it, but not before reminding the guards outside that not wanting to be disturbed meant exactly that. He turned his back to the door and leaned against it with his eyes closed for a moment, and then he opened them and held out his hands.

He was not surprised to discover they were shaking.

Chapter 7

The force gathered in the courtyard outside the Avacas palace was as much for show as anything else. Kirsh knew that, just as he knew the chances of finding anything useful about his brother's disappearance in Tolace were slim. But the Crown Prince of Senet had been kidnapped. It was important something was seen to be done, even if it was fruitless.

He had two hundred men ready to ride out with him. One hundred and fifty of them were Senetian troops, part of his father's Palace Guard, and the other fifty were Dhevynians, members of the elite Queen's Guard of which Kirsh was, until recently, a member and who were now his—as Dhevyn's regent—to command.

Given a choice in the matter, Kirsh would have preferred to leave the Senetian troops behind. Their numbers would slow him down, for one thing, and he didn't really trust their discipline. The Dhevynians, on the other hand, were much better trained, even if their first loyalty was to the Queen of Dhevyn and not to her regent. He'd managed to get Sergey appointed captain of the Senetian Guard, and with Alexin leading the Dhevynians, he was at least confident his commanders were capable and would only question his orders if they had a genuine concern.

Kirsh had been afraid the news of Belagren's death would delay his expedition, but his father was adamant they leave as scheduled, insisting the living were more important than the dead. Antonov seemed to be taking Belagren's sudden demise very well. Although he had respected the High Priestess, Kirsh had never been as close to her as his father. He mourned her passing but he wasn't actually grieving over it. There were too many other things going on in his life; too many other problems he wasn't sure how to deal with. He anxiously cast his eyes over the crowd come to watch their departure, looking for Marqel again, but there was no sign of her. She hadn't been in her room when he went looking for her earlier. It was unlike her to let him leave without saying good-bye.

The Lion of Senet came to see them off, with Alenor beside him. Kirsh was surprised she had come to bid him farewell. The queen was still pale and gaunt from her miscarriage and she clung to Antonov's arm for support. The effort of descending four flights of stairs from her rooms had exhausted her. She shouldn't have come. It was both a foolish gesture and a pointless one. *Still, one must keep up appearances,* Kirsh thought sourly as he rode forward with his two captains to greet his father and his wife.

"Spare nobody, Kirsh," Antonov ordered. "Find those who did this and punish them."

"I will, sire."

"Good luck, Kirsh," Alenor added.

"Thank you." He said nothing more to his wife.

There was nothing else to say.

"I'll have the fleet ready to sail for the Baenlands within two weeks," Antonov informed him. "You have until then to find out what happened in Tolace. We'll pick you up on the way to Mil."

"I'll get him back, Father," Kirsh promised.

A fleeting smile, full of pride, flickered over Antonov's face. "It will be as the Goddess wills it, son. And in this, I'll soon know if she is with us."

The comment puzzled Kirsh a little, but he was too used to his father's devout belief in the Goddess to question it. He saluted the Lion of Senet and the Queen of Dhevyn and wheeled his mount around. Sergey and Alexin followed him to the head of the column. Kirsh gave the order to move out and the force headed toward the gates, their pennons snapping in the brisk breeze, their uniforms smart and fear-inspiring in the bright light of the second sun.

Kirsh glanced over his shoulder when they reached the gates. Alenor stood there with his father, a small, fragile figure leaning on the powerful strength of the Lion of Senet.

There was still no sign of Marqel.

They traveled the 120 miles to Tolace in two days. Kirsh pushed the troops hard, but nobody complained. Every man knew they were on a mission to rescue the Crippled Prince, and if some of them thought him not worth the effort, there wasn't a man among them foolish enough to voice his opinion in the hearing of the prince's younger brother.

Kirsh commandeered the Hospice when they arrived in the seaside town and ordered everyone involved in the affair brought before him for questioning. He had quite deliberately left Barin Welacin back in Avacas. Despite the Prefect's assurances that nobody could get information out of a reluctant witness as fast or as efficiently as he could, Kirsh still remembered what had happened to Dirk when he foolishly made a comment about the best way to interrogate Johan Thorn. That one careless remark had earned the unsuspecting boy from Dhevyn the nickname "The Butcher of Elcast." Kirsh had no desire to earn an equally brutal title for something even less substantial.

Anyway, if it turned out he couldn't learn what he needed to know, he reasoned, there was always the threat of sending for the Prefect of Avacas. For some, just the thought of attracting Barin's attention would be enough to loosen their tongues. Kirsh wanted to do this on his own. He wanted to be the one who discovered the truth.

He wanted to be the hero.

The first person they brought before him was Sonja, the Shadowdancer who had been nursing Misha at the Hospice and the one who had allowed him to meet with Lady Natasha Orlando, the impostor later identified as Tia Veran.

Kirsh had taken over the administrator's small, cluttered office. He sat behind the wooden desk, flanked by Sergey on his right and Alexin on his left. The woman was visibly shaking when they admitted her. She stopped and looked at the three of them nervously. There was no chair for her to sit on. She stood before them like a prisoner awaiting sentencing.

"I am reliably informed it was you who arranged for my brother and Tia Veran to meet," Kirsh began, looking at her coldly.

"We didn't know it was Tia Veran, your highness," she protested. "Prince Misha seemed to know her. He said nothing about her true identity."

"You were one of the people responsible for the protection of the Crown Prince, my lady. Don't you think part of your duties was checking the credentials of anyone seeking an audience with him?"

The Shadowdancer shook her head. "It wasn't like that, your highness. Lady Natasha never sought an audience with the prince. He sought *her* out. He made us find out where she was staying and had us take him to her cottage. They met several times, your highness, but it was always your brother who instigated the meetings, not Lady Natasha."

"Are you telling me Misha *deliberately* sought her company?"

"I swear, your highness, I speak the truth!" The woman looked on the verge of tears. Perhaps it was his threatening scowl, or the knowledge that the red robes of her order would do little to protect her if she were blamed for this. "As the Goddess is my witness, your highness, your brother willingly met with Tia Veran! If he was in fear of his life, he gave no sign of it. They seemed to be friends. Good friends."

Kirsh glared at her. "Be careful what you say, woman. You're implying the Lion of Senet's heir and the daughter of the worst heretic ever to walk the face of Ranadon were conspiring together."

"Maybe they were," she suggested defiantly. "He certainly never asked for poppy-dust until he started meeting with her."

"Poppy-dust?" Kirsh asked in confusion. "What are you talking about?"

The Shadowdancer looked at the floor, suddenly unable to meet his eye. "The day before Prince Misha met with Lady Natasha in her cottage the first time, he asked for some time alone, so we left him in one of the gardens. We were nearby, but not so close we could overhear anything said. I heard him talking to someone so I went to investigate. When I arrived, he was alone and asked to go back to his room. When we got back he asked for two things: to locate a young woman with short red-blond hair who was currently staying at the Hospice and that he be given a dose of poppy-dust."

"He *asked* for it?"

"He insisted, your highness."

"And you gave in to him," Kirsh concluded. "Your job was to care for my brother, woman. Not turn him into an addict."

"If your brother was an addict, your highness, he was one long before he came to this place. His symptoms disappeared quite rapidly once he'd taken the dust, and after that, he began to meet with Lady Natasha on a regular basis. It was only a few days later he disappeared during the fire."

Kirsh sagged back in his chair, stunned by what the Shadowdancer had told him. It all made sense in his mind. The first time he'd seen Tia Veran she was in Misha's rooms, posing as a servant, leaning over his brother who was in the throes of a violent seizure.

Was that how it had happened? Had she slipped an illicit dose of poppy-dust to him then? If she'd given him a large enough dose, it might have caused the seizure—and it might have addicted him almost instantly. But how had he been getting hold of it since then? That first meeting between his brother and Tia Veran was almost three years ago. Maybe she'd been bribing the servants to bring it to him. Perhaps the Baenlanders had someone else working in the palace who was able to smuggle it to him.

The implications were frightening. Even worse was the effect such news would have on his father. Antonov despised poppy-dust, those who traded in it and more important, those who were addicted to it. It would kill him to learn Misha had fallen into its trap.

And because of a stupid promise I made as a boy to Dirk Provin, I was the one who let her escape . . . If he'd known then what he knew now about Tia Veran, he would have killed her himself before letting her go.

And then another thought occurred to him. If Antonov learned the truth, the Lord Chancellor's suggestion they simply leave Misha to die in the hands of the Baenlanders might look very attractive to his father.

"Who else knows my brother was a poppy-dust addict?"

"I don't think anyone else knew but me, your highness," she hurried to assure him. "I would never repeat such a thing."

Kirsh nodded thoughtfully. "You may go."

Sonja looked at him in surprise. "Your highness?"

"You may go," he repeated. "Or did you have something else to tell me?"

"No, your highness."

"Then get out of my sight."

Sonja fled the room, bowing several times on the way out. When she was gone, Kirsh leaned back in the chair and closed his eyes for a moment, and then he glanced over his shoulder at Sergey.

"Take care of it, Captain."

Sergey nodded without question and left the room. Alexin looked a little confused. "Take care of what?" he asked.

"It's none of your concern. Who's next on the list?"

Alexin didn't answer immediately. Kirsh turned to look at him and caught the look of dawning comprehension as it crossed the Dhevynian captain's face.

"You're going to have Sergey kill her!"

"I said it was none of your concern, Alexin."

"She's done nothing but tell you something you didn't want to hear," he objected.

"That woman knowingly supplied poppy-dust to my brother. Trading in poppy-dust is punishable by death."

"After a trial, perhaps. You've just ordered her to be summarily executed."

Kirsh looked away, uncomfortable with the censure in Alexin's eyes. "I will not have a rumor spread that the Crown Prince of Senet is a poppy-dust addict."

"And you'd murder a Shadowdancer just to stop it?"

"I'd murder every man, woman and child in Tolace if it meant stopping it," Kirsh replied. He glanced up at Alexin, hoping for some hint of sympathy for his plight. "Don't you understand? If my father learned of this, he'd leave Misha to rot in the hands of the Baenlanders. I can't—I *won't*—allow that to happen."

"So you're going to slaughter everyone who knows about it? I thought we taught you better than that in the Queen's Guard, Kirshov."

"You taught me the meaning of honor, Alexin," Kirsh agreed. "Which is why I want your word you'll say nothing about this. To anyone. Once I have your oath, I know you won't break it."

"You want me to swear an oath I'll not speak the truth, no matter how barbaric your behavior is? You ask a great deal, your highness."

"You're my friend, Alexin, and I hold your opinion in high regard. But when it comes down to it, you're nothing more than an officer under my command and that puts you a long way below my brother on the list of those I care about. Give me your word, or suffer the same fate as Sonja."

Kirsh was afraid Alexin would call his bluff. He was fairly certain he didn't have the will to order a captain in Alenor's guard killed. Even if he could command a friend's death, he was certain the political consequences of such a foolish order would be devastating. But Kirsh had a reputation for not thinking about the consequences of anything he did, and he was relying on that as much as his manner to convince Alexin he meant what he said.

The captain debated the issue for a painfully long time before he nodded slowly. "You have my word."

"Thank you, Alexin."

"Don't thank me, your highness," Alexin said with icy disapproval. "I'm doing you no favor, believe me. And don't expect me to be a party to it, either. You may have my silence on this matter, but not my sword. If you want to go around murdering innocent people to protect your brother's reputation, you can do it without any help from me."

Fed up with the Dhevynian captain's condemnation and the guilt it was forcing him to confront, Kirsh turned back to the list of names in front of him.

"Bring the next witness in," he ordered coldly.

"Should I ask them what they'd like for their last meal first, your highness?"

"Don't push it, Alexin."

The captain looked like he might say something further but in the end, Alexin simply walked to the door to call in the basket maker's wife who'd claimed she'd been hired by parties unknown to act as chaperone for Lady Natasha Orlando.

Chapter 8

Jacinta D'Orlon used the excuse of a shopping trip into the city to meet with Porl Isingrin, the captain of the Baenlander ship the *Makuan*. The Kalarada markets were busy this morning, and with her escort of only one Guardsman, she was able to make her way through the markets to the tavern without attracting any undue attention. The Guardsman at her side was Pavel Darenelle, the second son of the Baron of Lakeside on the island of Bryton and a good friend of her brother's. He was also a member of the growing underground among the Dhevynian nobility who were trying to undermine the Senetian occupation of Dhevyn, which was why Jacinta had chosen him for this expedition.

The inn where they arranged to meet was near the markets, a rather expensive establishment that offered private dining rooms; it was a favored resting place for visiting nobility not important enough to rate accommodation in the palace. Jacinta was met by the innkeeper, who showed her to the room where Porl was waiting for her. Pavel took up guard outside the door as she slipped inside.

"My lady," Porl Isingrin said with a bow, as she closed and locked the door behind her.

"It's good to see you safe, Captain," she replied. "With everything going on, I feared the worst for you and your people in Mil."

"The worst is yet to come, my lady," he warned. "It's the reason I'm here. We need your help."

"What can I do? With Alenor away in Avacas, my power is limited to hiding the royal seal so those Senetian lechers infesting the palace can't issue any new laws in her name."

Porl smiled, making him look quite fierce. "You're involved in a dangerous game, my lady."

"No more dangerous than the game you're playing." Jacinta didn't feel terribly brave or noble for hiding the seal. Mostly, she

felt powerless and she didn't like the feeling very much, at all.
"How can I help you, Captain?"

"I have a ship full of refugees, my lady. I need somewhere
safe for them to hide."

"How many are there?"

"About eighty. The *Orlando* is in Mil collecting another
load even as we speak."

"Why are you evacuating Mil? Surely the delta is protection enough for your people?"

Porl shook his head. "Antonov has been given the route
through the delta. Or at least he will have it very soon. Mil is no
longer the safe haven it once was."

"By whom?" Jacinta asked, her eyes narrowing with anger.
"Who betrayed you?"

"Dirk Provin."

"Duke Wallin's second son?"

Jacinta had studied the Dhevynian noble families in some
detail, mostly to keep one step ahead of her mother in her
never-ending quest to find a suitable husband for her only
daughter. Being the right age and of an impeccable lineage (he
was descended from the Damitian royal house on his mother's
side and was related by marriage to the Lion of Senet), Dirk
Provin had been quite high on the list, she recalled, until he
vanished from Avacas a wanted man. Lady Sofia had struck
him off rather forcefully after that.

"Aye," Porl agreed heavily. "But here's something you may
not know about him. He's not Wallin Provin's son. He's Johan
Thorn's bastard."

That news left her speechless.

"He spent two years with us in Mil," Porl added. "After
Morna Provin was executed we sent him to Omaxin to see if he
could learn anything about the next Age of Shadows. He betrayed us to Belagren, joined the Shadowdancers and bought
himself the position of Lord of the Shadows and right hand of
the High Priestess with what he knows about us. Then the arrogant little prick even sent a message boasting he was going to
tell Antonov the route through the delta."

"He sent you a message?" she asked with a frown. "Why would he do that?"

"I've no idea, my lady. The consensus is that he wanted to make certain we knew who had betrayed us. But he won't gloat for long. We've hired the Brotherhood to take care of him."

"You paid for a Brotherhood assassin? I'm surprised you're not here asking me for money. I dread to think what that will cost."

"It's worth every dorn, my lady."

Jacinta fell silent, wondering what was really going on in Avacas. She would find out soon enough, she supposed. Alenor had sent for her and she was due to leave for the mainland the following morning. In fact, Porl Isingrin was lucky she had been in Kalarada at all.

"These people you need to hide," she told Porl. "Take them to Bryton. My family has estates near Oakridge. They are orchards mostly and the fruit-pickers' cottages will be empty at this time of year. The caretaker's name is Lon Selorna. He's a loyal Dhevynian and he'll help you if you tell him I sent you. Your people can hide there until it's safe to return."

"Thank you, my lady."

"It's little enough help, Captain," she lamented. "I wish I could do more."

"Keep our queen safe," he suggested. "Bring her home to Kalarada."

"I'll do my best. But the news we have is not good. She's been desperately ill since losing the baby."

"I'd never wish her harm," Porl said, "but I can't bring myself to mourn the loss of a child that might one day inherit both Senet and Dhevyn."

Jacinta nodded sympathetically and said nothing. Only she, Alenor, Alexin and—by now—Kirshov Latanya knew Alenor's lost baby had not been the Lion of Senet's grandchild.

"I mustn't keep you, my lady," Porl added. "I've no wish to endanger you."

"Don't fear for me, Captain. I can take care of myself."

"We won't forget your aid, my lady."

Jacinta smiled thinly. "If you ever get caught, Captain, the nicest thing you could do for me would be to forget you even know my name."

Jacinta spent the rest of the morning shopping, loading Pavel up with so many packages he had to send for a cart to return them all to the palace. She then took a detour on her way home to the barracks of the Queen's Guard, on the pretext of visiting Alenor's colt, which she had promised the queen she would keep an eye on in her absence.

The Lord Marshal was busy with Dargin Otmar and a new batch of recruits when she arrived, so she was able to slip down to the stables without having to deal with either of them. Pavel left her with the colt and vanished for a time, returning with Tael Gordonov. The captain bowed as he stopped by the railing, and then glanced over his shoulder to make certain they were alone.

"We got word this morning Kirshov has taken Alexin and his guard to Tolace with him," he told her. "I've been placed in command of the guard going with you to Avacas to replace them."

"Why Tolace?"

"Haven't you heard? The Baenlanders abducted Prince Misha. Avacas is a very dangerous place to be a Dhevynian, right now."

"And by involving the Queen's Guard and Dhevyn's regent, Antonov manages to make it appear we're complicit in whatever tyranny he chooses to inflict as a punishment," Jacinta concluded with a frown. "Did you know they're evacuating Mil?"

He shook his head. "Why?"

"Antonov knows the way through the delta. It seems Dirk Provin has changed sides."

Tael swore under his breath. "I warned Alexin to be wary of him."

"Do you know him?"

"I know *of* him. They say he's as smart as Neris Veran was."

That was something Jacinta hadn't known. And it puzzled her. Why would someone as smart as Neris Veran betray the Baenlanders and then destroy the element of surprise by warning them of his intentions? That wasn't smart. It was stupid.

"Will you ask someone to keep an eye on Alenor's colt while I'm away?"

"Of course, my lady."

"And can you make certain the men you take with us to Avacas are trustworthy?"

He smiled. "There is no other kind in the Queen's Guard, my lady."

Jacinta had one other thing to take care of before she left for Avacas to join Alenor. She waited until long after first sunrise before making her way through the labyrinthine halls of Kalarada Palace to the rooms occupied by the Palace Seneschal, Dimitri Bayel. She hoped nobody saw her making such a strange late-night visit to his rooms. Jacinta seriously doubted anyone would believe she was sneaking into the old man's bedroom this late for a lover's tryst.

Dimitri opened the door himself, dressed in his nightshirt.

"I'm leaving for Avacas in the morning, my lord," she said as she slipped inside. "I wanted to speak to you before I left and beg you to watch over things while I'm gone."

Dimitri shrugged forlornly. "How can I stop the Senetians doing whatever they please, my lady?"

"Not letting them get their grubby paws on this would be a good start," she suggested as she reached under her skirt and produced the heavy seal of Dhevyn Alenor had entrusted to her care before she left for Avacas.

The old man stared at it in shock. "Lady Jacinta! They've been turning the palace inside out looking for that!"

"I know," she said with a smile. "I can't risk taking it with me. Will you keep it safe until Alenor returns?"

He accepted the seal with a solemn nod. "Of course. I will guard it with my life. They've already searched my rooms twice, so it should be safe enough here."

"Thank you." Impulsively, she hugged him.

"You favor your uncle, you know," he remarked, a little uncomfortable with her embrace.

"My uncle?"

"Fredrak D'Orlon. Alenor's father. I often wonder if Antonov would have been so keen to put Rainan on the Eagle Throne after Johan fled, had her husband still been alive to advise her, just as I often wonder if the hunting accident that killed him was really an accident."

"The Senetians have much to atone for, my lord," she agreed. "But one day we'll be free of them. I promise."

Dimitri sighed wistfully. "Ah, the eternal optimism of youth. I can remember thinking as you do once, my lady. I hope you are not disillusioned too savagely when you get to Avacas and you begin to fully appreciate what we're up against."

Jacinta smiled mischievously. "You should be more worried about the people in Avacas, my lord. They haven't met me yet. It's the Lion of Senet who doesn't fully appreciate what he's up against."

Chapter 9

The walk down to see Kirsh off exhausted Alenor so she kept to her room for the next few days. It was good to have such an excuse. With news of the High Priestess's death so close on the heels of the news about Misha, the Queen of Dhevyn was more than happy to stay hidden in her room, out of the way of the hysterics that were undoubtedly going on in the rest of the Avacas palace.

Her confinement had a downside, though. She had no idea what was really happening, no reliable source of information and no way to sort the truth from the rumors. She trusted nothing Dorra, her lady-in-waiting, told her and with Alexin gone, there was nobody else she could turn to—except, perhaps, her cousin Dirk Provin. But he was playing his own games, and she wasn't sure any longer how much she could rely on him, or if she could rely on him at all.

Alenor sent for him, however, as he was still the closest thing she had to a friend in Avacas. It took him four days to answer her summons, which concerned her a great deal. Was Dirk busy with other things, or was she so low in his estimation he could simply ignore her?

When he arrived, he left his guards at the door and crossed the room to her. She was out of bed, dressed and sitting on the settee by the unlit fireplace, looking much better than she felt. Dirk bent down and kissed her cheek with a smile, but she was in no mood to be friendly.

"I sent for you days ago."

"I've been busy." He turned to Dorra then and waved his arm carelessly. "You may go."

Her lady-in-waiting bowed and left the apartment without so much as a whimper of protest. Alenor watched her leave in shock and then turned to Dirk. "How did you manage that? I can barely force her to leave me alone to use a chamber pot!"

"She probably knows by now I was the one who arranged to have her removed from your service," he shrugged. "Maybe she doesn't want to antagonize me."

Alenor's eyes narrowed. "What are you up to, Dirk? A few weeks ago, you were under house arrest. Now you're acting like you own the place."

"I'm still under house arrest," he informed her. "Didn't you see my escort?"

"I saw them. But they act like a bodyguard, not your jailers."

"Perhaps Antonov thinks I need both."

Alenor shook her head with a frown. "Tell me what's happening while I've been shut up in here."

"The weather's been nice," Dirk told her, taking the seat opposite. "Although it did rain yesterday, and that put a bit of a damper on—"

"Dirk!"

"Oh, did you want to know something else?"

"What's the matter with you? Of course I want to know! What's happening out there? What did Belagren die of?"

"A stroke."

"What's Antonov going to do now that his precious Voice of the Goddess is no longer with us?"

"I believe the Goddess has chosen a new mouthpiece," Dirk told her.

"Who? Madalan?"

"Marqel." Dirk smiled at her stunned expression. "Not what Antonov was expecting, I can tell you. Poor Kirsh is in for a bit of a shock, though, when he gets back and learns his mistress has moved on to bigger and better things."

"Dirk...did *you* have anything to do with this?" She couldn't imagine it happening any other way. Alenor knew exactly how Belagren had fooled the world into believing she was the Voice of the Goddess. "Did *you* kill Belagren?"

He looked rather irritated by the question. "Why does everyone keep asking me that? No! I did *not* murder the High Priestess. She died of a stroke, Alenor, and Marqel now speaks for the Goddess. That's all you need to know. Or believe."

"Why are you helping Marqel?"

"Who says I'm helping her?"

"If you're supporting her contention that she speaks for the Goddess, what else do you call it?"

"I call it surviving," he said. "That's all. I'm the right hand of the High Priestess of the Shadowdancers. I'm *supposed* to believe all this shit."

"And how long can you keep up the lie, Dirk?" she asked with concern. "Listen to yourself! You call it shit, yet you expect everyone in Avacas to believe you're one of them."

"They believe, Alenor, and provided you don't tell them anything to the contrary, they'll keep on believing."

"What did Belagren really die from, Dirk?"

"A stroke," he insisted, rising to his feet. "Was that all you wanted to know?"

"Dirk..."

"Don't start on me, Alenor," he warned. "I'm not the only one around here living a lie. Instead of worrying about what

I'm up to, you might like to spare a thought for your husband and your lover, both of whom are in Tolace as we speak, indulging in a spot of mindless slaughter to scare the townsfolk into telling them what really happened to Misha."

That was news she'd heard nothing of. It didn't seem possible. "I don't believe you!"

"Kirsh has executed a Shadowdancer, three Senetian Guardsmen and an herbalist so far, and from what I can tell from the reports he's sending his father, he's just warming up. Your boyfriend is right there alongside him. Sergey's doing the actual killing, I hear, but then, Kirsh always was good at getting somebody else to do his dirty work for him."

Tears filled Alenor's eyes, as much from Dirk's harsh tone as from his words. "Alexin would never allow—"

"Alexin has no choice, Alenor," he reminded her. "He can't argue with Kirsh, he can't disagree with him. He can't do the slightest thing to betray *you*. I warned you to send him away. And what do you think will happen when they get to Mil? Suppose in the heat of battle Kirsh's life hangs in the balance and it falls to Alexin to save him? What do you think will be going through his mind, Alenor?"

"I never thought about..."

"You never thought about anything," he accused.

Alenor struggled to maintain her queenly composure. "Are you going with them to Mil?"

Dirk sat down again, as if he no longer had the energy to be angry at her. "Maybe. Antonov is convinced I'm the only one who'll be able to warn him if Marqel is lying. But I should be able to talk him out of it."

"Marqel? What has *she* to do with invading Mil?"

"The Goddess gave her the instructions to get through the Spakan River delta."

"But you told Alexin you would—" She stopped abruptly as she realized what his words meant. "Goddess! You told Marqel, didn't you? You told Alexin you were going to give Antonov the information, but you gave it to Marqel instead! Do you realize what you've done! You've made it seem as if the Goddess..."

"The Goddess *has* spoken to Marqel, Alenor," he insisted. "And if you have any brains at all you'll never even hint you suspect any different."

"Are you really going to do this, Dirk?" she asked, stunned by the depth of his treachery. "Are you really going to stand in the bow of a Senetian ship and lead Antonov into Mil to destroy your...*our*...friends?"

"Yes."

"But you told them they had weeks to evacuate! They'll be trapped."

"At the time, I thought they *would* have time to get away. Misha's kidnapping forced a change of plans. I'm sorry, but it's unavoidable."

"Can't you get another message to them?"

"Alexin is in Tolace with Kirsh and the rest of your guard. What do you suggest I do, Alenor? Issue a general bulletin asking if any Baenlander spies currently in the palace could please make an appointment with me to learn something to their advantage?"

"Why are you being so cruel?"

"I'm not being cruel. I'm being practical, which is more than I can say for you."

"You're supposed to be my friend."

"I am your friend, Allie," he sighed. "But the one piece of good advice I offered, you ignored."

She wiped away unshed tears and looked down at her hands. "I know. You were right. I should have sent Alexin back to Kalarada." She looked at him, searching his eyes for an answer she knew would not be there. "What am I going to do, Dirk?"

"Get well, Alenor," he advised. "As fast as you possibly can. Then get the hell out of Avacas. You're not safe here. Your guard isn't even here to protect you; they're off in Tolace helping Kirsh with his little reign of terror. As soon as your own people get here from Avacas, start making arrangements to go home."

"But Antonov won't let me leave. I asked him about it yesterday and he gave me some excuse about caring for my health. I'm starting to fear I'm a prisoner here, Dirk."

"He'll be gone by the time your people get here, heading for Mil. I'll make sure nobody else in the palace stands in your way."

"Can you do that?" she asked doubtfully. "Have you that much power, Dirk?"

He smiled wanly. "I got rid of Dorra for you, didn't I?"

Alenor looked for some hint he spoke the truth, but she had no more chance of reading his thoughts than anybody else. "Dirk, promise me that what you're doing isn't going to hurt Dhevyn."

"I promise, Allie. You just have to trust me."

"Nobody else does."

"That doesn't matter if *you* still believe in me."

Alenor smiled faintly. She did trust him, and with good reason. He hadn't betrayed her secret. If Dirk had meant to do her or Dhevyn harm, he could have destroyed her weeks ago. He certainly had enough ammunition to ruin her. "I believe in you, Dirk. I just wish you'd make it a little easier for me."

"I wish I could make it a little easier for all of us," he sighed.

"Be careful."

"You're a great one to talk." He rose to his feet and looked down at her with concern. "*You* be careful, Allie. Go home and keep Dhevyn safe."

"And what will you be doing in the meantime?"

"Trying to stay alive," he said with an unconvincing laugh.

Alenor would have laughed, too, but she understood all too well that Dirk wasn't joking.

Chapter 10

Dirk's visit with Alenor disturbed him more than he let her know. It was dangerous for her in Avacas, but not for the reasons she imagined. Alenor feared Antonov would learn her secret. She was frightened Kirsh might tell his father the child she lost was not his. But that danger paled into insignificance against how close Marqel had come to killing Alenor. And Dirk was still worried Marqel would try something else to harm her. The Shadowdancer's jealousy had already cost Alenor her child.

Dirk could do little to solve the problem, however, other than warn Alenor to be on her guard, and keep Marqel confined. The latter was becoming increasingly difficult as Antonov demanded an answer to whether or not the Goddess had truly spoken to her.

Dirk walked down the stairs to the third floor, where Marqel's room was located, thinking he would have to speak to Antonov soon. Belagren's funeral would take place the day after tomorrow. Antonov had to know by then if the Goddess had taken Belagren from him so Marqel could step into her place. Or if another, more sinister hand had intervened.

Dirk was still furious that Marqel had killed Belagren, but made a point of not letting Marqel realize it. His only lapse had been on the morning Belagren died, when he had slapped that thoughtless, murderous little bitch for what she'd done. He'd never hit a woman before; never even wanted to. But for Marqel, he found himself willing to make an exception. It was hit her or strangle the breath out of her, so in his view she'd actually gotten the better part of the deal.

Marqel still had no concept of what she'd done. No inkling of how close to ruining everything she was. Dirk's whole plan relied on Belagren's disgrace. He needed to prove she was human, flawed and culpable. All Marqel had done was raise the late High Priestess to the status of a deity. It was going to be next to impossible to destroy that image in Antonov's mind. Were it not for the fact that killing Marqel now might bestow on her the same divine aura, he might have been tempted to give in to his desire to strangle her after all.

The guards on Marqel's room admitted him without question. She was reclining on the bed when he entered, her hand held by a servant who was polishing her nails while Marqel relaxed against the pillows with slices of cucumber over her eyes. When she heard the door close, she lifted one of the slices with her free hand and glared at him with one eye.

"Oh, it's you."

"Leave us," Dirk ordered the servant.

The woman put down her towel and file and hurried out of the room. Marqel removed the cucumber slices and sat up, not at all pleased she had been disturbed.

"You can't just come in here and order my servants about," she complained.

"Actually, Marqel, I can," he reminded her. "And they're not your servants. Not yet, anyway."

"Have you spoken to Antonov?"

"Tomorrow. I want Madalan there when I tell him we believe your visions are genuine."

"I still can't believe you got that old hag to agree to this."

"I told Madalan it was Belagren's idea," he explained, taking a seat on the edge of the bed. The rooms on the third floor were much less grand than the royal apartments on the floor above.

Marqel smiled. "Then it's a good thing Belagren's not around to disagree with you, isn't it?"

She was constantly seeking reassurance that what she had done was for the best. Dirk doubted it was because she felt any guilt about committing murder. It seemed more likely she was just trying to convince herself she knew better than he did. Dirk was beginning to suspect Marqel was not entirely sane. She wasn't insane the way Neris was. But there was something missing, however; some attribute of decency or conscience others possessed simply didn't exist in Marqel. It made her dangerous and unpredictable. Both were traits he could ill afford now.

"I also told her the reason Belagren chose you was because you were disposable," he added, taking a degree of malicious satisfaction from her shocked expression. "You have no family to protect you. Nobody to object if you suddenly disappear. *That's* what she found so easy to believe, Marqel. For all I know, Madalan's already grooming your replacement. Just remember that before you start getting creative again."

"That's not fair!"

"Maybe not," he shrugged. "But it wouldn't have been a problem if you'd done what you were told. You'd have Belagren protecting you. Now you're going to be constantly fending off Madalan's attempts to remove you."

"You won't let her kill me, will you?"

Dirk smiled.

"Dirk!"

Finally, he shrugged. "For the time being, I'll see she doesn't kill you."

"For the time *being*?"

"This is a risky game we're playing, Marqel. Who knows what the future will bring."

"You bastard! You cross me and I'll tell Antonov everything!"

"Do that," Dirk told her, unconcerned. "You go to the Lion of Senet and tell him how you killed Belagren because there really isn't a Goddess and that I offered to tell you what he wanted to know so you could become High Priestess."

"He'd burn you alive," she hissed at him.

"No," Dirk replied calmly, "the first thing he'd do is ask me if it was true. I would deny it, of course, and Madalan would back me up, as would every other Shadowdancer on Ranadon. Whose word do you think Antonov would believe then?"

"You think you're so damn smart, don't you?"

"I'm thorough, Marqel. There's a difference."

She thought about it for a moment, and then shrugged, as if she realized she couldn't win the argument. "What are you going to tell Antonov?"

"I'm going to tell him your visions appear to be true, but we won't know for certain until he invades Mil."

"You're supposed to vouch for me," she objected. "That's as good as saying I'm lying."

"It's a tentative assurance you're telling the truth," he corrected. "I'm supposed to hate you, remember? Antonov will expect me to be doubtful."

"*Supposed* to hate me?" she scoffed. "That's pretty much a given. What do you want me to say to him?"

"I want you to keep acting as if you're devastated by this unwanted honor. Make him comfort you. Make *him* convince *you* that you're the Voice of the Goddess."

Marqel smiled suddenly. "You really are quite good at this, aren't you? Do I get to do anything at the funeral?"

"That will be up to Antonov."

"When do you want me to sleep with him?"

"Not until your vision is proved true."

"You want me to wait until he's invaded Mil? That's ridiculous! I could have him eating out of my hand long before then."

"Try it any sooner and he'll think you nothing more than a grasping little slut," Dirk warned her, then added coldly, "not an unreasonable assumption in your case."

She scowled at him. "I don't understand why you want me to wait."

"Because you're the Voice of the Goddess, Marqel," he explained. "Sleeping with her voice is akin to sleeping with the Goddess herself in Antonov's mind. He has to initiate it, or the first thing that will pop into his mind isn't that you're the living embodiment of his Goddess, but that you are a thief and whore who was, until very recently, his own son's mistress."

His explanation seemed to satisfy her, but Dirk could never really tell with Marqel. He thought she'd understood why Belagren had to remain alive, too.

"I suppose," she conceded. "It might be a bit awkward though, if Kirsh is around."

"I'll deal with Kirsh," he promised. "He won't be a problem."

Marqel nodded, and then she looked at him with a curious expression. "If I had a baby to Antonov, would my child be in line for the throne?"

"*What?*" Dirk asked in astonishment.

"Well, suppose I had a baby? I mean, Misha's as good as dead, and Kirsh will probably get himself killed doing something foolish long before Antonov dies of old age...doesn't that mean my child would become the next Lion of Senet?"

Her question appalled him. It also gave him an insight into the depth of her ambition. He understood now why she had aborted Alenor's child. She had visions of herself as the mother of a king or queen.

Dirk was starting to wonder what he'd unleashed.

"Your child would be a bastard," he told her. "The next Lion of Senet would be Antonov's closest legitimate relative."

"Who's that?"

"Even if I knew, Marqel, I wouldn't tell you. I've a feeling I'd be marking the poor sod for death."

She smiled. "You don't trust me much, do you?"

"Give me one reason why I should?"

Marqel decided not to answer that. She straightened her red robe and made a great show of examining her newly polished nails. "You just keep up your end of the bargain, Dirk, and then you won't have to worry about me."

"I worry about you constantly, Marqel," he told her. "So before you decide to make your own modifications to my plan again, just remember, at some point, I may get *so* worried that I decide I can do without you."

"You can't do this without me," she told him confidently.

"How do you know?"

"Because you despise me and you don't trust me. If you could have found *any* way to do this without involving me you would have, Dirk Provin."

Dirk shrugged off her accusation as if it meant nothing. Marqel wasn't fooled, however.

She knew as well as he did that she was right.

Chapter 11

Dirk and Madalan met with Antonov on the terrace outside his study the day before Belagren's funeral. Dirk hated the terrace, and suspected that Antonov knew it, which was why he seemed to conduct all his meetings with Dirk here, just to keep him off balance. It didn't work. Dirk had come too far to let emotion stand in his way. If Antonov wanted to rattle him by making him stand on the very spot where he'd killed Johan Thorn, then Dirk would do it and bear the torment. If anything, rather than upsetting him, it strengthened his resolve.

The day was overcast and threatening rain when they arrived. Antonov studied them closely as they emerged onto the terrace from the doors leading into his study, as if he could learn what he wanted to know simply from the expressions on their faces. Madalan curtsied politely to Antonov, who reached forward to take her hand.

"You've no need to bow to me, my lady," he told her, helping her up. "It is I who should bow to the Goddess's representative here on Ranadon."

"I appreciate the sentiment, your highness," Madalan replied. "But I fear that role is reserved for another."

Antonov's eyes immediately turned on Dirk. "Marqel speaks the truth?"

Dirk shrugged uncomfortably. "It would appear that way."

"You don't sound convinced."

"I'm not," he agreed. "But neither can I fault her testimony nor shake her story."

"And what of you, Lady Madalan?" he asked the Shadowdancer. "Are you also convinced Marqel is now the Voice of the Goddess?"

"Like Dirk, I was extremely suspicious of her claim, your highness. But I was there when Belagren received her first words from the Goddess in Omaxin during the Age of Shadows. Marqel displays the same...symptoms, I suppose you could call them, for want of a better word. Whatever happened, it has had a profound effect on the girl. I'm inclined to believe her. I certainly believe *she* believes the Goddess has visited her."

Dirk mentally breathed a sigh of relief. Madalan sounded as if she truly believed what she was telling Antonov. He wondered, though, what Belagren had really done when Neris told her he knew when the second sun would return. He suspected her reaction had been more akin to rubbing her hands with glee than being humbled or upset.

"And yet Dirk remains unconvinced," Antonov noted with a frown.

"Our newly appointed Lord of the Shadows has little reason to welcome the notion Marqel is now the Voice of the Goddess, your highness."

Antonov nodded thoughtfully, turning to Dirk once more. "Did you question the route through the delta she now claims to know?"

"From what little I know of it, your highness, her directions seem genuine," he confirmed. "They're a little obscure. She speaks of things like 'turning east in the lee of the broken island,' which I'm guessing refers to the place the Baenlanders call Split Rock. It's a massive monolith protruding into the delta. I think it's the peak of a submerged mountain. The hidden rocks surrounding it are perilous."

"Would you take a fleet into the delta based on the information she has?"

"That would depend on what I wanted to achieve." Dirk shrugged. "If I merely wanted to confirm the veracity of Marqel's directions, I'd send in a small force—one that could get in and out of the delta quickly and stealthily. If I was planning to destroy them, I might risk sending a whole fleet in. But if she's wrong, it's an expensive way of exposing her lies."

Antonov was silent as he thought about it. Dirk could well imagine the argument going on inside his head: should he refuse to believe Marqel and risk offending the Goddess? Or should he risk an invasion fleet, only to be exposed as a fool when his ships finished up shattered and decimated on the hidden reefs and rocks that protected the Baenlands?

Dirk was hoping his suggestion about sending in an advance scouting party would appeal to Antonov. That would give the Baenlanders a little more time. It was bad enough that he had betrayed them, but he'd made the situation infinitely worse for them by sending a message telling the pirates they had time to get away, and then reneging on his own promise. The six weeks they thought they had to get everyone clear was now down to less than three. By the time the lookouts spied Antonov's fleet heading for the delta, their ships would be trapped in the bay.

Antonov was still mulling over his decision when a servant stepped onto the terrace and announced the Lord of the Suns had arrived from Bollow.

The old man stepped onto the terrace as the servant announced him, his long gray beard brushing the jeweled sun clasp on his belt. He bowed stiffly to Antonov and Madalan, and then caught sight of Dirk. He was unable to hide his surprise.

"Dirk Provin!"

"My lord," Dirk replied, bowing respectfully. "Welcome to Avacas."

The Lord of the Suns stared at him with rheumy eyes. "It's a pity we meet again under such tragic circumstances."

Dirk met his gaze evenly. *He's angry with me,* Dirk realized. *He thinks I murdered Belagren. And he thinks I've made him my accomplice by asking him to send that letter to her.*

"It was my hope, too, that our next meeting would be under happier circumstances, my lord," Dirk replied, hoping Paige would understand what he meant. There was little hope of getting the Lord of the Suns alone to explain things to him, and certainly not before the funeral tomorrow.

"The death of the High Priestess is only a tragedy if you lack faith, Dirk," Antonov remarked. "When a soul is called to the bosom of the Goddess after a lifetime of exemplary service, one should rejoice. It is selfish of us to grieve for our own loss. Rather, we should be celebrating Belagren's life."

Dirk nodded in acknowledgment of Antonov's wisdom,

privately marveling at his logic. *Is that how you're coping with the loss of the woman you presumably loved for most of your adult life? By telling yourself the Goddess has taken Belagren from you as a reward for her faithful service?*

His reasoning scared Dirk a little. Antonov's faith was so unshakable, so adaptable to the vagaries of day-to-day living, Dirk began to wonder if he could ever succeed in bringing the Church of the Suns down. Would Antonov ever see the truth, or merely assume the Goddess was testing his faith and deny the evidence of his own eyes? As Dirk watched the Lion of Senet smile serenely, comforted by the thought his High Priestess was called to the Goddess, rather than torn away from him in a cruel twist of fate, Dirk began to doubt *anything* he did would make a difference.

"And there is even more reason to celebrate," Antonov told the Lord of the Suns. "The Goddess has given us a new voice."

Paige glared at Dirk for a moment before recovering his composure and turning to face Antonov. "She *has*?"

"She has chosen a young Shadowdancer named Marqel," Madalan explained. "You may have met her when we stopped in Bollow on our way to Omaxin."

"I don't recall her," Paige replied, obviously unsettled by this new revelation. "Are you certain about this?"

"Dirk is doubtful," Antonov told him. "But he has personal reasons for not wanting to see this young woman elevated to a position of honor. The Lady Madalan appears convinced. Perhaps after you have spoken to Marqel, we can settle the matter once and for all."

"I will do as the Goddess guides me, your highness."

Antonov nodded and waved his hand dismissively. "Then if you will all excuse me, I have many things to arrange before the funeral tomorrow."

Dirk bowed to Antonov and then turned to the Lord of the Suns. "May I help you to your room, my lord? It's a long way to the top floor and I'm sure your journey must have been exhausting."

"Thank you, Dirk," Paige said, leaning on the arm Dirk offered him. "Your highness."

Antonov barely acknowledged the Lord of the Suns's farewell, his mind already on other things. Dirk helped Paige Halyn through the study and back into the palace hall, where Madalan left them, heading off on her own business. She spared Dirk a glance that spoke volumes before she departed, but he was satisfied she would not betray him.

Not yet, anyway.

Dirk's guard fell in behind them as soon as they stepped into the hall. The old man looked over his shoulder at the armed men who now accompanied them, and then turned to Dirk questioningly.

"I'm under house arrest," Dirk explained.

"For what?"

"For being who I am."

Paige nodded in understanding. "Things in Avacas are not as I expected," he said, as they headed down the hall toward the grand staircase that dominated the foyer.

"There have been some . . . unexpected events," Dirk agreed cautiously, aware his guards could hear every word, and would probably report it to either Antonov or Barin Welacin.

"We must talk, you and I," the Lord of the Suns announced.

"I'm sure we'll find time," Dirk agreed, as if there was no urgency at all. "If not before the funeral, then maybe afterward we can arrange something."

The old man searched his face carefully. "There are some . . . matters I wish to discuss with you, Dirk."

"Then I will be certain to make the time," Dirk promised.

"They are matters I am convinced only *you* can explain clearly," Paige ventured in a voice laden with hidden meaning.

"Perhaps after the funeral," Dirk repeated, wishing the old man would just leave it be. But the Lord of the Suns wasn't going to be dismissed so readily.

"They are very *important* matters, Dirk."

Why not just come right out and tell everyone what's really going on! Dirk wanted to shout at him. He glanced at the guard pointedly and then looked at Paige Halyn.

"I promise, my lord. As *soon* as I can, we will meet and I'll give your *matters* my undivided attention." Then he added meaningfully, "I hope I can provide you with the satisfactory explanation you're looking for."

Finally taking the hint, the old man nodded his agreement. "I will look forward to it, Dirk."

Paige Halyn said nothing further on the matter as they turned and headed up the broad sweeping stairs leading to the royal apartments on the fourth floor, Dirk's guard following close behind.

The Lord of the Suns was puffing and wheezing by the time Dirk delivered him to the door of his guest apartment. He excused himself hastily, before Paige could say anything else liable to implicate them both, and returned to his own rooms farther along the hall. The guards stopped at the door, leaving him to enter alone.

Dirk locked the door and walked through the sitting room to the bathroom, where he splashed himself with water to cool his fevered face. He was quite sure his close brush with exposure, not the heat of the afternoon, had caused the sweat on his brow.

What was Paige Halyn thinking, acting as if we're old friends?

If the Lord of the Suns had any wits at all, he would not have asked Dirk to meet with him so openly. They were supposed to barely know each other. He should have done little more than acknowledge Dirk's existence.

Dirk glanced in the mirror with a sigh.

"I'm surrounded by fools," he told his reflection.

It didn't help that Dirk was starting to suspect the biggest fool he was dealing with was himself.

Chapter 12

Belagren had always had a flair for the dramatic. It was one of the things that had made her successful as High Priestess. Her funeral proved to be no exception. She had long ago drawn up quite explicit instructions about how the ceremony should be conducted. Belagren planned to go out in such a grand manner people would remember the event for years to come.

One way or another, she intended to achieve immortality.

Marqel was rather put out to discover she was not to have a prominent role in the ceremony. As the new Voice of the Goddess, she felt she deserved to be in the front ranks of the mourners, or better yet, in the small select group that stood with the Lion of Senet. She should be up there, honored as Belagren's successor, not forced to traipse along in the heat like a dog sniffing the back of a butcher's cart for a bone. They wouldn't let her say anything or do anything. Dirk wouldn't even let her speak to Antonov. That really irritated her. She was certain that if she could speak to the Lion of Senet again, if she repeated her story about hearing the Goddess, then he would be convinced of her divine calling and Marqel could finally take on the role she was destined for. But Dirk and Madalan had made sure that wouldn't happen until *they* were ready.

She was sick of doing what other people wanted.

The second sun had set. Marqel walked behind the carriage, merely one of the scores of faceless Shadowdancers, bathed in the scarlet light of the first sun. They trailed the High Priestess in a long line, three abreast on the road in their red robes, as if her funeral carriage was leaving a thin trail of blood in its wake.

Belagren's body had been taken back to the Hall of Shadows to be prepared for the funeral, so the procession to bring her body down to the harbor was a long one. It took nearly three hours for the flower-laden carriage bearing her remains to wend its way through the narrow streets of Avacas. A large, solemn crowd had gathered to witness the passing of a legend, some of them genuinely grieving the loss of the woman they believed to be the Voice of their Goddess, others merely curious, hoping for a glimpse of the fabled High Priestess, even if she was dead.

Marqel had joined the procession of Shadowdancers who walked in the wake of the carriage, doing her best to look like she was mourning the old bitch. The men and women around her walked with their heads down, some of them muttering silently to themselves. *Were they praying? Or just running through tomorrow's laundry list?* she wondered. Perhaps they *were* praying. Somewhat to Marqel's surprise, she had discovered that despite the fraud on which their cult was based, many Shadowdancers honestly believed in the Goddess.

Still, Marqel mused, *I suppose Belagren didn't keep her secret all these years by broadcasting it to all and sundry.*

Fools, she sneered silently. *If only you knew what I know ...*

There was a roped-off area near the docks, where Antonov and his closest advisers stood on a podium decked out in the gold-and-white colors of the Latanya family, waiting for the funeral carriage to arrive. Alenor sat beside the empty chair reserved for the Lord of the Suns, looking pale and gaunt. Marqel recognized the chancellor, Lord Palinov, and a few other familiar faces from the palace. Dirk was with them, too. He might be Lord of the Shadows and the right hand of the High Priestess, but he stubbornly refused to wear the red robes of their order, and was dressed in dark trousers, calf-high boots and a jacket that was well cut, expensive and suited to his lean frame. He hardly posed a daunting figure, though, standing beside Antonov. *You had to get to know him,* Marqel decided, *to appreciate how intimidating he could be*.

She wondered why he wasn't walking with the rest of the Shadowdancers, until she remembered Dirk was the nephew of Antonov's late wife, the Princess Analee of Damita. Marqel frowned at the thought. It reminded her that no matter what she did, she would never be family. Dirk had committed murder. He had destroyed Antonov's favorite ship. He had spent two years living among the Lion of Senet's enemies—a criminal running drugs with Reithan Seranov and doing Goddess knows what else... Yet there he was, standing on the podium next to his uncle in a position of honor because he was *family,* and being family gave him a level of protection Marqel could never hope to aspire to.

For a moment she scanned the faces of the other people standing with Antonov. Was there a distant cousin up there, she wondered? Was there another member of the Latanya family on that podium? Was the heir to the throne after Misha and Kirshov up there now, waiting for his chance at power? If there was, Marqel silently wished him luck. With Dirk Provin in Avacas, she doubted anybody else had much of a chance at anything.

Still, she supposed. *He might hate me, but Dirk needs me. And a child by Antonov will make me family, too...*

She was still a little concerned about her ability to bear a child, but had decided not to worry about it for now. Once she was High Priestess, Marqel was certain there would be other herbs, other drugs she could use to ensure a baby. There were many secrets she would become privy to, once her position was confirmed. She was confident that among them was the solution to her dilemma.

In the meantime, Marqel resolved to bide her time and do as Dirk ordered, although she was honest enough to admit it was not just his plan that appealed to her. She was beginning to develop a healthy respect for his influence. That he stood beside Antonov today, unpunished for all that he had done, drove home forcefully that she was a long way from being able to defy him. She didn't have Kirsh to protect her anymore and until she had Antonov utterly convinced she was the Voice of the Goddess, until he believed her—even above his precious nephew—she was in no position to challenge Dirk on anything.

It came as something as a shock to Marqel to realize that she had been so engrossed in her own thoughts that the Lord of the Suns had almost reached the end of his eulogy without her even noticing. The old man had finished chronicling Belagren's remarkable life—*that must have really stuck in his throat,* she thought—and now beseeched the Goddess to take Belagren into her embrace for eternity.

And I'll bet he doesn't mean a word of it.

When the Lord of the Suns was finished, he returned, slowly and painfully, to the podium and gave a signal. The honor guard stepped forward to lift Belagren's body from the carriage and carry it down to the elaborate floating bier tied up at the end of the wharf. Antonov stepped down from the podium and followed the small procession, waiting as the honor guard secured the High Priestess to the pyre. There were two longboats attached to the pyre, waiting to tow it out into the harbor. In the prow of each boat sat a drummer, who would pound out the mournful beat so the oarsmen could draw the float away from the wharf with a degree of solemn dignity.

That, and to make sure the wharf doesn't catch fire, Marqel thought with a sly little smile.

Antonov moved forward as the honor guard stepped back. Somebody appeared with a torch and handed it to him. He held the flaming baton on high for a moment and then touched it to the pyre. A wall of flame immediately obscured Belagren's body. The drummers in the longboats took up the beat and the pyre began to move out into the harbor. Marqel watched it burn, fascinated by the flames.

"I wonder how long it's been since he set fire to a body that was already dead?" a sour voice in the crowd muttered. Marqel looked around in surprise, but whoever was brave enough to make such a remark was smart enough to draw no further attention to himself.

Marqel looked back at the pyre, wondering idly if the voice was simply a lone dissenter or if such sentiments were common among the people in Avacas. She'd had little to do with the general population in Senet since becoming a Shadowdancer, and her life as a traveling performer before that had always marked her as an outcast. Marqel had no real understanding of the lives of ordinary people.

It didn't matter anyway. She was never going to be *ordinary,* so what ordinary people thought meant nothing to her. She was going to be High Priestess of the Shadowdancers.

Antonov stood at the end of the wharf, a lone, poignant figure silhouetted by the flames, as the High Priestess burned. Marqel studied him closely. He was a powerful, well-built man, still fit and good-looking, considering he was old enough to be her father. She'd been shocked by the suggestion that she should become Antonov's mistress when Dirk first proposed it, but as she watched the Lion of Senet now, she realized it wasn't going to be such a chore. Kirsh was young and good-looking and he adored her, but Antonov wore an aura of power Marqel found much more seductive. All Kirsh could offer her were furtive kisses and second place to his wife.

Antonov could give her the world.

Marqel glanced back at Dirk and smiled to herself. *And when he does,* she told him silently, *I won't need you anymore, Dirk Provin.*

Then we'll see who the clever one really is.

Chapter 13

Misha's health improved rapidly once Master Helgin and Petra taught him how to deal with his addiction. Taken in the right quantities, poppy-dust made him alert, stronger and more confident. He was eating regularly and had already gained weight, although Helgin wouldn't be happy until he gained a lot more. The physician speculated that Ella had been varying the dose she gave him just to keep him off balance, but once he was in a position to regulate his own medication, he found he had some chance of living a normal life. He also began to understand what Helgin meant when he referred to a "manageable addiction."

But Misha wasn't interested in managing anything. He wanted to be rid of it, once and for all, and were it not for his experiences in Tolace he would have refused the drug out-right.

Helgin assured him that once he was stable and had re-gained some strength he could begin to taper the dose gradually, which would give his body time to adjust. While such a course of action was eminently reasonable, it might take months—even years—before he was completely free of it. Misha didn't have years. Dirk had betrayed the Baenlanders and told Antonov the way through the delta. Misha would be lucky if he had weeks before they came for him, and once he was back in the clutches of Belagren and Ella Geon, he wasn't sure he would have much longer to live, regardless of whether he was an addict or not.

He was walking again—painfully—but at least he could hobble a short way along the beach. Calla had paid him a visit several days before and then returned the following day with a metal crutch she had made for him, which made it easier for him to get around. Misha was dismayed by his weakness, but somehow, he had to survive this. He had to free himself of the poppy-dust and return to Avacas, strong enough to confront his father and tell him what was going on.

Misha had learned much more than how to manage his addiction in the short time he had been in Mil. With no reason to doubt the High Priestess's version of events, he had always believed Neris Veran was the heretic who had corrupted the King of Dhevyn, which led to the War of Shadows. Since he'd been in Mil, since he'd had Neris's supposed "heresy" explained to him in detail, his whole world had turned on its ear. A few months ago, he would have denied the story about Neris discov-ering the truth about the return of the second sun in the ruins of Omaxin and sharing it with Belagren, who then announced the Goddess had spoken to her. But then, a few months ago, he would have scoffed at the suggestion he was a poppy-dust ad-dict, too.

Once he had accepted that brutal truth, it wasn't very hard at all to accept the rest of it.

"Misha!"

He turned at the call and discovered Mellie Thorn skipping along the beach toward him. He stopped and looked at the ground he had covered, disappointed by the short distance he had traveled. He felt like he'd just run a marathon.

"Hello, Mellie," he said, when she caught up with him.

"I saw you from the house. Are you supposed to be out here on your own?"

"No," he told her with a smile. "Can't you tell? I'm trying to escape."

Mellie laughed. "I really like you, Misha. It's such a pity you're a Latanya."

"Isn't it," he agreed wryly. "And what about you? Are you allowed to be talking to me?"

"It's all right. Mama's decided you're harmless."

"Really?"

She smiled at the expression on his face. "You know what I mean."

"Well, I hope it means she thinks I won't do you any harm."

"I think so. Anyway, Tia thinks you're all right, and Mama always listens to her." A frown darkened her warm brown eyes. "Everybody does now, since that awful business with Dirk."

"Why is that?"

"Because Tia always insisted we shouldn't trust him and nobody listened to her until it was too late."

"Did *you* trust him?"

She looked away. Dirk's betrayal had obviously broken Mellie's heart.

"I'm sure he had a good reason for what he did, Mellie," Misha told her gently.

"Tia says it's because he's selfish and power hungry."

"And what do you think?"

Mellie shrugged uncomfortably. "I don't know. I want to think he's doing something good, something he hasn't told anybody about, and I know Mama hopes the same thing, but it's just...well, why would he *do* such a thing and not tell us about it?"

"Perhaps he had his reasons," Misha suggested, realizing

his words were little comfort. He understood how she felt. Belagren probably had eminently good reasons for having him poisoned.

"He has plenty of reasons," Tia announced, coming up behind him. Misha hadn't heard her footfalls on the soft black sand. "Mostly they're about what's best for Dirk Provin."

He turned to look at her. She wore the same look of icy rage she always wore when anybody foolishly mentioned Dirk's name in her presence.

Mellie sensed Tia's fury and quickly changed the subject. "Misha's trying to escape. Do you think we should stop him?"

Misha watched curiously as Tia visibly forced aside her anger and smiled at Mellie. "Think you can handle it, Mel?" she joked. "He's getting pretty good on that crutch. Are you sure you'd be able to catch him?"

"I'll need a head start," Misha warned. "Of about...a *week*."

Mellie laughed. Misha suspected her merriment had as much to do with the fact that Tia was prepared to put aside her anger and join in the game as it did with their rather lame attempts to make light of his disabilities.

"Well, I'll take over guarding this dangerous prisoner for now," Tia offered. "Lexie wants you back at the house."

"Did she say why?"

"No, but I wouldn't drag my heels if I were you. She seemed a bit miffed you'd disappeared."

"I'd better go then. You won't tell her I was consorting with the enemy, will you?"

"Not if you leave right this minute."

"I'm *going*!" she promised, and then she turned to Misha with a smile. "Bye, Misha."

"Good-bye, Mellie."

As she turned and hurried up the beach toward the steep path leading to the stilted house overlooking the bay, Tia turned to him with a frown. "Please don't talk to Mellie about Dirk. She's hurting enough without you reminding her about it constantly."

"It was Mellie who brought it up, Tia."

"Well, the next time she brings it up, just ignore her."

"I think she *wants* to talk about Dirk," he suggested, aware he was treading on very thin ice. "Sometimes talking about these things can help ease the pain."

She glared at him. "For you, maybe. Personally, the news somebody has slit his throat would suit me just as well."

"Is that what you're hoping for? News that your assassin has been successful?"

"How did you know about that?"

"Petra mentioned it. She was complaining about what an assassin would cost. I think she was rather put out you didn't ask *her* to go to Avacas to poison Dirk, actually. Sort of a professional pride thing."

Tia managed a thin smile. "She's not the only one who volunteered for the job."

"I'd not like to be in Dirk's shoes," Misha remarked. "I think if he'd known how many angry women he would have dogging his heels, he might have decided it was easier to live with my father's wrath, after all."

"If that was a joke, it was in very poor taste, Misha."

"I'm sorry," he said. "I don't mean to trivialize the trouble he's caused you."

"Let's just stop talking about it," she suggested testily. "Anyway, I have some news you might be interested in."

"What news?"

"Belagren is dead."

Misha stared at her in shock. "The High Priestess?"

"How many Belagrens do you know?"

"But...I mean...how did it happen?"

"Officially, she died of a stroke, according to the Brotherhood," Tia shrugged. "My money's on Dirk, though. It seems a little bit too convenient that no sooner is he confirmed as her right hand than she suddenly keels over. Care to wager on who the next High Priest of the Shadowdancers will be?"

"You think *Dirk* killed her?"

"He's pretty good at it, Misha. I know. I've seen him at work."

"I can't believe it!"

"If you can't believe that, you're going to have even more trouble accepting the rest of it."

"The rest of what?"

"Your brother's been in Tolace investigating your disappearance. The word is he's being very thorough. The body count has almost reached double figures, I hear."

"*Kirsh*? What are you saying, Tia? That he's killing people just because I left the Hospice?"

"He's killing people because they think you were *kidnapped* from the Hospice, Misha."

He shook his head in disbelief. "That doesn't sound like Kirsh. You must be mistaken. Barin Welacin must be responsible..."

"The Prefect is still in Avacas," she told him. "Your precious little brother's doing this on his own initiative. I don't know why you look so surprised. Your people have being doing things like this in Dhevyn since the Age of Shadows. Is it Kirshov wielding the sword that shocks you, or that such brutality has finally reached Senet's shores?"

Misha stared at her, stung by her harsh words. "What are you talking about? Senet came to Dhevyn's aid during the Age of Shadows..."

"Senet *invaded* Dhevyn, Misha," she corrected. "When the people of Dhevyn started rioting because there was no food, Johan Thorn asked your father for help. What he got was soldiers—on every island in Dhevyn. And they put down the riots, I'll grant you that. But they didn't do it by helping distribute what little food there was in an orderly manner. They did it by imposing martial law, by killing anyone who stepped outside after curfew. And then, when they had the entire kingdom too afraid to move outside their doors, they imposed their religion on Dhevyn, and then the killing was justified because people refused to worship your damned false Goddess."

"That's not the way I was taught it happened, Tia."

"Of course it's not what you were taught," she scoffed. "History is always written by the winners, and they always paint themselves as heroes. That way, they don't have to acknowledge the unpleasant details."

Tia turned on her heel and began walking away from him, leaving Misha shocked and very disturbed by what she had told him. He wanted to deny it, but in light of everything that had happened to him recently, her story seemed more than just rebel rhetoric. In fact, it seemed quite plausible. *How much of it was my father's will,* he wondered, *and how much Belagren's?*

"Tia!" he called after her.

She stopped and turned back. "What?"

"There's nothing I can do to change the past," he told her with genuine regret. "But I might be able to help change the future."

"How?"

"By giving you some advice."

"That's just what we need," she said. "Advice from the Crippled Prince."

She was angry, and perhaps with good cause, so Misha chose to ignore the insult.

"Get Mellie out of the Baenlands while you still can."

Tia looked confused. That was the last thing she was expecting him to say. "Why?"

"Because she's Johan Thorn's only legitimate child. She has more right to the Eagle Throne of Dhevyn than either Alenor D'Orlon or Dirk Provin; more right to it than any living soul. If my father ever learned of her existence he would hunt her down, take her back to Avacas and try to mold her into a puppet monarch just as he did with Alenor and Dirk."

"Mellie would never become Antonov's creature," she objected.

"I know," Misha agreed. "Which is why you must protect her. The Lion of Senet has only two types of people in his world, Tia: his friends and his enemies. If Mellie won't be his friend . . ." His voice tapered off, not sure he wanted to admit aloud the type of man his father was. He was still coming to grips with it himself.

"You mean he'd kill her?" Tia asked. She didn't sound surprised.

"That's exactly what I mean."

She thought about it for a moment and then nodded. "I'll mention it to Lexie."

"I wish I could do something to redress the pain we've caused your people, Tia."

"Be a better man than your father," she suggested bluntly, and then turned and walked back along the beach, leaving him alone with his newly forged crutch and a sudden feeling of overwhelming guilt for being the son of the Lion of Senet.

Chapter 14

Antonov waited a long time before he turned and headed back along the wharf toward the podium where Dirk and the other dignitaries waited. He stood watching the High Priestess's body burn, a lone figure dressed in white, bathed in the scarlet light of the second sun. He seemed lost in thought. *Or maybe he's praying,* Dirk thought. *Maybe he's asking the Goddess what he should do, now that his anchor in life is gone.*

Paige Halyn returned to the podium once he finished his eulogy and sat just behind Dirk, in the gilded chair next to Alenor, wheezing heavily from the effort. He had delivered his speech in a dry, toneless voice; the words of praise for his nemesis had little meaning for him. He'd not composed them himself, but had read the speech from a document Belagren had left behind. Apparently, the High Priestess had given a great deal of thought to the way she wanted to be remembered, and had long ago prepared the eulogy herself. It painted a picture of a humble and devout woman who'd made every move in her life guided by the hand of the Goddess. It was actually quite a moving account, if you didn't know she'd written it herself. Dirk was certain, however, she never expected it would be Paige Halyn who delivered it.

The crowd waited in silence, nobody game to move until Antonov did. But they were getting restless. They had seen what they had come to see and were starting to fidget with boredom. Dirk glanced around at the mourners, wondering how many of them had any idea of the impact the death of the High Priestess would have on their lives.

Times were about to change. Perhaps only he knew how much.

Dirk looked down the wharf at Antonov, but he still showed no sign of moving. Across from the podium, on the other side of the street behind a wall of soldiers, a commotion started as a child broke through the lines. She was about six or seven, and neatly—if plainly—dressed, clutching a small posy of flowers.

The little girl ran toward the podium as her mother, held back by the guards, hissed loudly at her to return. But the child ignored the call and kept on toward the podium. As she approached, two of the palace guards stepped forward to prevent her coming anywhere near the royal enclosure.

"She's only a child!" Alenor objected as the guards moved in on the little girl.

"Stand down," Dirk ordered in a low voice.

The guard closest to him heard the order and signaled to his companion to allow the child through. She was a scrawny little thing, with large blue eyes and thin blond hair braided tightly against her head. The girl stopped in front of the podium and thrust the small posy forward at Dirk.

"These are for the High Priestess," she said.

Dirk squatted down to accept the posy.

He felt a stinging pain in his left ear, but didn't realize he'd been hit until the little girl started screaming. Then he heard Paige Halyn cry out. He spun around to find the Lord of the Suns pinned to his gilded chair, his yellow robe covered in a rapidly spreading red stain.

A black-painted bolt protruded from his neck.

Dirk's first thought was for Alenor. Even before the panic started, he pulled Alenor from her seat to the podium floor to shield her from a second shot. Chaos erupted in the street as the terrified mourners closest to the podium realized what was happening and tried to flee. Dirk suspected they were more frightened of being caught up in the aftermath of an assassination attempt than they were of actually being harmed by a stray arrow. Guessing the direction of the bolt from the angle it had hit Paige Halyn, his eyes flew to the roofline across the street.

"Up there!" he shouted at the nearest guard as he caught a flash of movement. "On the roof!"

The man nodded and ordered several guards to follow. They shoved their way through the fearful crowd as the rest of the soldiers moved in with drawn swords to surround the royal podium.

"Are you all right?" he asked Alenor.

She nodded shakily, too terrified to speak. Dirk ignored the screams coming from the crowd and turned to the Lord of the Suns. The blood seeping from his pierced throat already covered his shoulder and his chest. He was pale and breathing shallowly, on the brink of losing consciousness. Dirk reached up and tried to jerk the bolt free, but it was embedded in the chair. He put his arms around Paige Halyn and lifted him forward, surprised at how light he was. Lord Palinov pushed his way through the equally terrified and confused dignitaries on the podium as Dirk freed the Lord of the Suns from the bolt that had nailed him through the neck, and lowered the old man to the deck.

"Find Yuri!" Dirk shouted, as he pushed Paige's impressive, blood-soaked beard out of the way and covered the wound with his hands, trying to apply some pressure to stop the bleeding.

Palinov stared at the unconscious old man in shock.

"*Quickly!*"

The chancellor shook himself and hurried off. Dirk turned his attention back to Paige Halyn. *Don't you die on me!* he wanted to scream at the old man. *Not now! Not like this!* The blood seeped through his fingers as Paige lay beneath him, ashen and barely breathing. Dirk guessed the bolt had hit the jugular vein. That in itself was potentially fatal. But even if the bolt hadn't hit anything vital, the shock or the blood loss might kill a man as old and frail as Paige.

Dirk pressed harder, determined not to lose him. The screams in the streets had changed their tone from panic to fear. Soldiers beat the people back. Dirk looked over his shoulder for Yuri. Antonov approached, his expression thunderous.

"Does he live?"

"Barely," Dirk told him. "But this is way beyond my skill. We need Yuri."

Before Antonov could answer, the line of soldiers opened and the physician pushed his way forward. He fell to his knees beside Dirk. Yuri examined Paige with a frown and then nodded with approval. "Keep the pressure on. We can't move him until we stop the bleeding."

Dirk barely heard him over the din. Antonov turned and bellowed "Clear the street!" which seemed to galvanize both the soldiers and the crowd into action. Before long, the press of people eased. Dirk had not moved. He knelt beside the dying Lord of the Suns, bloody to the elbows, too afraid to ease the pressure on the old man's neck for fear of him bleeding to death.

Yuri checked Paige's pulse, then looked at Dirk. "His pulse is weakening, but that's not actually a bad thing. We've more chance of a clot forming, which may halt the bleeding." He glanced over his shoulder in the direction of the roof. "That bolt was meant for you, I think." The physician rose to his feet and began to issue orders, demanding a carriage from the palace and the streets cleared to allow it through.

Dirk pressed even harder against the jugular. The Lord of the Suns was not going to die, he vowed, not from an arrow meant for him. And certainly not by the hand of an assassin. More was at stake here than Dirk's already overburdened sense of guilt.

A red-robed figure appeared through the chaos on the other side of the Lord of the Suns. He looked up to find Marqel standing over him. For once, she looked genuinely concerned.

"Can I do anything?" she asked.

He nodded. "Come down here."

Marqel knelt beside the old man and looked to Dirk for further instruction.

"Put your hands over mine."

Marqel frowned disdainfully at Dirk's blood-soaked fore-arms.

"He *mustn't* die, Marqel," he warned in a low voice. "We need him."

Even Marqel did not miss his meaning. She nodded in understanding and, with some reluctance, placed her hands over Dirk's. "I'm going to take my hands away. The moment I do, I want you to press down. Hard. And don't let up. If you do, he'll bleed to death."

"Dirk!" Antonov barked at him from the street.

Marqel pressed down forcefully as Dirk slid his blood-slick hands out from under hers. Yuri came back to check on the patient as Dirk rose to his feet. He knelt down beside Marqel and nodded when he saw she was now stemming the flow as effectively as had Dirk. But the old man had lost a lot of blood. It pooled beneath him and ran in rivulets across the deck of the podium. Dirk discovered his knees were drenched where he'd knelt in it.

"Dirk!" Antonov called again, with growing impatience.

"I won't let him die," Marqel promised, looking at him earnestly.

Dirk hoped she meant it, but with Yuri watching over her, she probably couldn't do much harm. The street had opened up a little, at least around the podium, and he could see Antonov standing with several guards. Someone had helped Alenor to her feet and led her away from the carnage. Covered in blood, he stepped down from the podium and crossed to where Antonov was waiting for him.

The guards behind Antonov held a slender man of about thirty-five, dressed in a dark red shirt and trousers, no doubt designed to blend with the red roofs of the city and the dull light of the first sun. The man slumped between the soldiers who held him, apparently beaten senseless. The guards must have caught him quickly, if they'd had time to do that much damage.

One of the soldiers following them carried an expensive-looking crossbow.

"You're wounded."

"The blood isn't mine, your highness."

"Some of it is," Antonov disagreed, pointing to Dirk's ear.

He reached up and touched his left ear gingerly, wincing as he discovered he was bleeding profusely.

"Do you know this man?" Antonov asked, grabbing the assassin by the hair and lifting his head so Dirk could examine his face.

Dirk shook his head. "I've never seen him before, your highness."

Antonov let the man's head drop and held his hand out for the crossbow. The guard handed it to him and Dirk watched as Antonov examined it with a thoughtful expression.

"This is not a poor man's weapon," he remarked. "It's the tool of a professional killer. Your enemies must be rather well off, Dirk. Or very desperate."

"You're assuming it was meant for me, your highness?"

"Aren't you?"

Dirk shrugged. "I haven't really had time to think about it, sire."

"We'll know soon enough who his intended target was," Antonov assured him, handing the crossbow back to the guard. "Take him to the Prefect."

He turned back to Dirk as they dragged the man away to face what was undoubtedly going to be a fate far worse than death in the hands of Barin Welacin. Antonov studied Dirk for a moment in silence, taking in his blood-drenched clothes and hands. "If he'd been aiming for your chest, you'd not be standing here now, you know."

"Maybe it was simply meant as a warning," Dirk suggested.

"More than likely the man was showing off," Antonov shrugged. "Assassins are arrogant creatures. A head shot is far more impressive than a body shot."

Dirk wondered how Antonov knew that. Had he employed assassins in the past to deal with his enemies?

"Yuri says your quick thinking may have saved the Lord of the Suns's life."

Dirk glanced over to where Yuri was leaning over Paige's body with Marqel. "He's not out of danger yet, your highness."

"I see Marqel is aiding him. Perhaps, if the Goddess is truly with her now, her presence will be enough to tip the scales in his favor."

Dirk nodded, thinking things could just as easily go awry if he died.

"You should go back to the palace," Antonov added. "You shouldn't be standing out in the street in such a state, or so exposed. When the carriage arrives for the Lord of the Suns, make sure you and Alenor are in it with him."

"Yes, your highness."

"And Dirk," Antonov said, as he turned away.

"Sire?"

"Be certain to give thanks to the Goddess for this. She has obviously spared you for a reason. Don't let her generosity go unacknowledged."

Dirk accepted his advice with a solemn bow. "Perhaps it was the High Priestess who was watching over me."

Antonov smiled. "You could be right. It would be like her to do that."

Actually, it would have been more Belagren's style to have *hired* the assassin, but Dirk didn't think it wise to point that out. He bowed low again to the Lion of Senet and returned to the podium to see if there was anything more he could do to help.

Dirk's ear stung and the blood trickled annoyingly down his collar, but his close brush with death had not really hit him yet. He was far too concerned that Paige Halyn might die and ruin all his plans.

And that was the least of his problems.

He had expected the Baenlanders would send someone after him, but he thought Reithan, or even Tia, would take on the job of ridding the world of Dirk Provin. But they'd hired a Brotherhood assassin, and that meant he was still in danger.

The Brotherhood offered a guarantee when they contracted a hit. The job would be done, no matter how long it took.

This wasn't just an attack on his life, Dirk realized with a sinking heart. It was probably the first of many.

Chapter 15

Misha's suggestion they get Mellie out of the Baenlands met with a much more agreeable response than Tia expected. She had thought Lexie would scoff at the idea, or at the very least refuse to send her daughter away. But Lexie's reaction was thoughtful and pensive, and she said nothing more about it for a day or two, then called Reithan and Tia out on the veranda after dinner to discuss it.

"Misha Latanya makes a very valid point," Lexie began, glancing over her shoulder to ensure her daughter was out of earshot, "when he warns us to be cautious about Mellie."

"You don't seriously think Antonov would try to put Mellie on the Eagle Throne, do you?" Reithan asked. He sounded amused, not concerned.

"Perhaps not." Lexie shrugged. "But I *am* certain he would not permit another potential claimant to the throne to exist if he knew about her."

"So you think we should send her away?" Tia asked.

Lexie nodded. "Mellie's protection has always been her anonymity. While Antonov had no idea she lived, she was safe from him. But I fear what might happen if we can't get everyone away from Mil before the Senetians arrive. It would only take one inadvertent slip on the part of a delirious, wounded prisoner for her existence to be revealed."

"Would he really be that interested in her?" Reithan scoffed. To him, Mellie was his annoying little half-sister. He had probably never thought of her as a future queen.

"You need only to look as far as Dirk Provin to realize how obsessed Antonov is with all of Johan's progeny, Reithan."

"Dirk's a boy after his own heart," Tia grumbled. "That's why Antonov is so enamored of him."

"I don't think you fully appreciate the lengths Antonov is willing to go to, Tia," Lexie said, shaking her head. "This is not a sudden obsession of his. It goes back before Dirk was even born."

"What do you mean?"

"Morna had already made her plans to leave Mil when she learned she was pregnant with Dirk. She would have been only two, perhaps three months gone when she arrived back on Elcast, so her condition would not have been obvious. But it doesn't take someone like Neris to do the sums, and Antonov is no fool. When Dirk was born, he must have guessed the truth. He must have known all along whose son Dirk was, yet he left him unmolested on Elcast for nearly sixteen years, just biding his time, waiting for the right moment to take Dirk under his wing."

"Then why didn't Johan know Dirk was his son? *You* obviously knew."

"I suspected, Tia, that's all. Morna kept a very low profile after she returned to Elcast, so Dirk's birth wasn't exactly trumpeted across the length and breadth of Ranadon. By the time we heard about it here in Mil, it was nearly two years after Morna left. Johan wondered about it, I suppose, but we never knew for certain. And think about it from his point of view: he and I had just begun to get close. I suppose it was easier for him not to confront the possibility Morna's child might be his."

Lexie's explanation reminded Tia of something she didn't like to think about. The Johan Tia wanted to remember was afraid of nothing. It hurt to realize her beloved king preferred to avoid conflict; that, given a choice, he opted to walk away, rather than fight. The golden memories of Johan she cherished in her mind were gradually tarnished by the truth.

Reithan nodded in agreement with his mother's words. "Johan was truly stunned when he learned he had a son. I remember that night in Avacas when Antonov told him who Dirk was. Antonov was positively gloating about it."

"I remember that, too," Tia agreed bitterly. "That was

right before Dirk drove a knife into Johan's throat, wasn't it? That's why he was gloating, Reithan. Because Antonov knew he'd found someone as evil and ambitious as he was. It was just a bonus that he turned out to be Johan's son."

Lexie sighed. "Whatever the reason, Tia, I think we would be wise to take Misha's advice."

"But where do we send her?" Reithan asked with a frown. "She'd be no safer in Dhevyn than she would be here in the Baenlands. And we might as well surrender her to Antonov ourselves as try to hide her in Senet."

"I was thinking of Oscon in Damita," Lexie said.

"Can he help us?" Tia asked doubtfully. "He doesn't even rule his own country anymore. He leaves that to Baston, and he's such a puppet of Antonov's he might as well *be* Senetian."

"Oscon's isolation and disgrace are what make him safe," Lexie explained. "Damita has done very nicely under Antonov's patronage since the War of Shadows, but Oscon remains a major embarrassment to his son. It suits everyone to forget the old man still lives. Baston hasn't even visited his father in a decade."

"It must irk that slimy little weasel no end to think his father and sisters rebelled against his good friend the Lion of Senet."

"It does," Lexie agreed. "That's why he's spent his every waking moment since his father surrendered at the end of the War of Shadows trying to prove to Antonov he is loyal to both the Goddess and to Senet."

"Then Damita is just as dangerous as Senet," Tia objected.

"Oscon lives on the coast in the north, several hundred miles from the capital, Tanchen. There's little danger she would be discovered there."

"What if Baston has spies among Oscon's household staff?"

"It's unlikely," Lexie told her. "We've remained in contact all these years, and he's sheltered our people in the past in an emergency without a problem."

"I could take her on the *Wanderer*," Reithan suggested. "We could slip in and out of Damitian waters without anybody knowing we'd landed."

Lexie nodded in agreement. "Can you find room for Misha as well?"

"What?" Tia cried. "Why Misha?"

"Because if we leave him here the chances are strong he will be rescued by his own people, and that could be as good as signing his death warrant."

"When it comes down to it," Reithan shrugged, "do we really care?"

"I think we should. I think we would be well served by seeing to it that Misha Latanya lives to inherit his father's crown."

"I think we're fools to be buying into Senetian politics," Reithan warned.

"Maybe so." Lexie shrugged. "But we've bought into it, like it or not. It seems a pity to let such an opportunity slip through our grasp."

"You believe his promise about withdrawing Senetian troops from Dhevyn, then?"

"Yes, I do. And so does Tia."

Reithan frowned at her. "Is that true?"

"He seems pretty genuine," she replied. Her assurance sounded so inadequate when said aloud.

Obviously not happy with the idea, Reithan shook his head. "And how is Oscon going to react, do you think, if we arrive on his doorstep—unannounced—with the heirs to both Dhevyn and Senet, looking for sanctuary?"

Lexie smiled. "You've never met Oscon, have you? Don't worry. I think you'll find him quite enchanted by the idea."

"Do you know him well?" Tia asked curiously.

"Oscon and Reithan's father were close friends. He's abrupt, brusque and irritable, but he's a true and loyal friend."

"But he surrendered to Antonov."

"He put an end to what was, by that time, a pointless slaughter, Tia," she corrected. "And he gave Johan and most of the people now living in Mil a chance to get away. For that, he was forced to abdicate his throne and bear the shame of being an exiled king. He's lost his crown and both his daughters to Antonov. He has much to be bitter about."

"Shouldn't we send him a message first?" Reithan suggested. "Just to sound him out?"

Lexie shook her head. "By the time we got a message to him, you could already be in Damita. Besides, I have an uneasy feeling about all this. The Brotherhood seems to think Antonov is already gathering his fleet."

"Are they certain?" Tia gasped.

"No, but there's an unusual amount of activity going on in Paislee and Avacas at the moment, and then there's that terrible business in Tolace."

Tia glanced at Reithan for a moment and shrugged. "Well, if you think it's for the best…"

"I want you to go with them, Tia."

"I have to stay here," she stated flatly. Running away was not an option.

"I need you to watch over Mellie. There is nobody I trust more than you to do that."

"Don't try to flatter me, Lexie…"

"I wish it were simple flattery, my dear," Lexie said. "But the truth is, Mellie has led a very sheltered life here in Mil. She is totally unaware of the danger she is in. You *do* appreciate it, though, and I'm quite sure you'd give your own life if it meant saving hers. I can't imagine sending anyone else to protect her."

"Mother's right, Tia," Reithan agreed, adding his weight to the argument. "If we're going to do this, you're the logical one to send. Besides, Misha trusts you. If we're sending him along, you're the best one to watch over him, too."

Tia shook her head. "I can't watch over them both. Misha's determined to defeat his poppy-dust habit. I can't protect Mellie and help him at the same time."

"Can you fit in another passenger, Reithan?" Lexie asked.

"Who did you have in mind?"

"Master Helgin."

He shrugged. "It'll be crowded, but I suppose I can squeeze him in."

"The *Wanderer* will sink before we get through the delta," Tia warned.

Reithan smiled. "Then you'd better bring a bucket along so

you can keep bailing." He turned to his mother then, his smile fading. "When did you want us to leave?"

"As soon as you can," Lexie replied. "I don't want to give Mellie too much warning. She's likely to spend the next three days just saying good-bye to her friends. I'd rather you just slipped away, unnoticed. The fewer people who know where you've gone, the better."

Tia smiled briefly. "The three fastest forms of communication in the Baenlands: carrier pigeon, the *Wanderer* and telling Eleska Arrowsmith about it."

Lexie nodded ruefully. "That's exactly what I'm afraid of."

"We'll leave tonight then," Reithan confirmed. "Now that the decision is made, there's not much point in waiting."

"Are you sure about this, Lexie?"

Lexie sighed heavily before she answered. "Am I sure I should be sending Mellie away? No, I'm not. But I *am* sure I want her kept out of the clutches of the Lion of Senet, and if that means I never see my daughter again as long as I live then I will do it, and sleep soundly at night, knowing I made the right decision."

Chapter 16

Dirk asked for, and received, permission from Antonov to visit the assassin who tried to kill him, three days after Belagren's funeral. The Lord of the Suns still lived, if only barely, but he was critically ill and Yuri was not hopeful.

With Paige Halyn at death's door, Dirk was able to delay Antonov's demands that the Lord of the Suns verify Marqel's vision a little longer, which gave the Lion of Senet more time to grow accustomed to the idea. It also meant the attack on the Baenlands would be delayed, even if only by a few days. Marqel had been on her best behavior and, mindful of the fact that she needed the Lord of the Suns to confirm her as High Priestess, was doing all she could to aid Yuri in caring for him, to make certain he lived long enough to do it.

As for Dirk, he felt like he was juggling fireballs.

Between Belagren's death, the attempt on his own life, and trying to keep Marqel under control, Madalan on his side, Alenor safe and Antonov convinced that all of this was the will of the Goddess, he was exhausted. He had barely slept since Paige Halyn was wounded, partly out of worry over the old man's fate, and partly because he was terrified that the next assassin would somehow manage to slip past his guards. He was afraid that if he did fall asleep, he might never wake again. He took all his meals in the dining room now, eating the same food as the other residents of the palace rather than risk poisoning. He would only drink water or wine poured from a jug others were also drinking from, and he was constantly looking over his shoulder, waiting for the next attack.

At this rate, the Brotherhood wouldn't need to make another attempt on his life. If he kept on like this, he would *worry* himself to death.

The Lord of the Suns' condition had not improved, but neither had it deteriorated. Dirk's fear now was that even if he survived the shock and blood loss of his wound, infection might set in. The bladed bolt that had taken a slice out of Dirk's ear and then lodged in Paige Halyn's neck would have been sharpened on an oilstone, he knew, and more than likely lubricated with spit. Essentially, it may as well have been poisoned.

There was a time limit, fortunately. Sixty days was all he needed. Paige Halyn *had* to live for sixty days.

The sixty-day law had come about to protect members of the nobility who foolishly got themselves into duels over points of honor. Antonov had outlawed fighting to the death, but it was perfectly acceptable to wound your opponent to redress an insult. But a serious problem arose when a minor wound turned septic and killed the unfortunate dueler. Antonov had decreed that if a man lived for sixty days after receiving a wound, then even if he died on the sixty-first day, his assailant was not responsible. Dirk was counting on that fine point of law working in his favor. But he was afraid it was going to take more than

Yuri's expertise and Marqel's tender care to keep the Lord of the Suns alive for the next fifty-seven days.

He was afraid it was going to take a miracle.

Dirk entered the dungeons beneath the garrison in the center of Avacas accompanied by six men handpicked from Antonov's Palace Guard. Antonov had trebled their number after the funeral. They were charged with protecting the Lord of the Shadows, as much as guarding him.

Dirk had gone out of his way to befriend the men assigned to enforcing his house arrest and they were becoming more and more relaxed in his company. The ride through Avacas to the garrison was tense, though. Every bough of the tree-lined avenue leading from the palace might be harboring another assassin. Every shady alley, every dusty window, every looming rooftop offered a place of concealment. Dirk was living on tenterhooks, waiting for another attack, quite certain the next one would succeed.

To his surprise, Ella Geon was with the Prefect when Dirk entered the lower levels of the vast barracks where Barin Welacin ruled the murky underworld of his spy network. They were in one of the cells set aside for interrogations, but it was not what Dirk was expecting. There were no chains on the walls or wicked implements of torture in evidence; no glowing coals or hot branding irons. There was simply a flat metal table in the center of the bare-walled room, to which the assassin was tied. The man appeared to be unconscious. Dirk seriously doubted he had simply nodded off while he waited for his torture to begin.

"You look disappointed, my lord," Barin said when Dirk entered the room. His pleasant, grandfatherly face was creased with amusement.

"I was expecting something a little more . . . sinister," Dirk admitted.

"You suffer the same misconception as most people," Ella told him. "You think physical torture is the only way to extract a confession."

"Actually, my lady, I try not to think of things like that at all," he replied. "I admit I'm surprised to find you here. I thought you were trained in helping the sick and wounded. Still, I suppose things must be a little slow with Misha gone. How creative of you to come down here to drum up some business."

Ella glared at him, but did not reply. Dirk had taken only Madalan and Yuri into his confidence among the Shadowdancers, and mistrusted Ella just on principle. This woman had turned Neris into an addict. This woman gave birth to Tia, simply so she would have something to hold over Neris when she began to fear the poppy-dust was losing its effect.

"Has he said anything yet?" Dirk asked Barin.

"We've only just started. The honey-dew affected him quite badly. We'll know more when he comes around again."

"Honey-dew?" Dirk asked. It seemed such an innocuous name for something sufficiently powerful that Barin felt no need for any other method of persuasion. Other than the ropes that bound him, there wasn't a mark on the unconscious assassin.

"It's a type of fungus," Ella explained. "It comes from the flowering head of rye when the crop has been exposed to too much moisture."

"You mean ergot?" he asked, his natural curiosity for a moment winning out over his determination not to become involved. Sometimes it was painful to recall he once planned a career as nothing more menacing than a physician. "But that's used to control bleeding after labor. At worst it's an abortifacient."

Ella smiled at him coldly. "You know your herb lore, my lord."

"You forget I was apprenticed to Master Helgin, my lady."

"Then you should find this morning's proceedings most enlightening," Barin declared, sounding positively delighted by the prospect of sharing his expertise with someone who could fully appreciate his skill. "A few grains will speed up the contractions of a woman in labor, certainly, but increase the dosage and it causes the contraction of every muscle in the body, even the muscles that make up the walls of veins and arteries, as well as the internal organs."

"You mean it will give him cramps?"

"Cramps so bad his bones will break," Ella confirmed. "And hallucinations. Violent muscle spasms, vomiting, burning sensations, delusions and crawling sensations on the skin...it's amazing."

"Handled correctly, we can even force gangrene to develop in the extremities," Barin added with relish. "A man's tongue loosens very quickly when he's facing the prospect of his fingers and toes dropping off."

Dirk stared at the two of them, wondering how such people could live in this world and still think themselves a part of humanity. Their detached, clinical interest in watching a man cramp so violently he snapped his own bones made Dirk physically ill.

"If he's delusional, how do you know he's telling the truth?" Dirk asked, sorry that he had come here now, but at the same time, glad he had. It was good to be reminded why he was doing this.

"It's not what he says while he's having the delusions that is important," Barin explained. "It's severing his link with reality that makes this type of torture truly effective. Physical pain gives a man something to cling to. But make him lose touch with everything he knows or thinks is real; make him think the chair he's sitting in has just turned into a mass of writhing snakes, or he's being eaten alive by invisible spiders, and he loses the will to fight very smartly."

"An interesting theory, Master Prefect," Dirk replied tonelessly. He wanted to flee this place so badly he consciously had to stop himself from stepping backward. But the Prefect of Avacas had been there the night Johan Thorn died. Both he and Ella Geon had watched him kill his own father, which made it easier for them to believe he was unaffected by what he was hearing now. "And truly, I wish I had the time to stay and witness this remarkable...effect you describe. But I just came down to see if you'd broken him yet. His highness is most anxious to learn who it was that hired this man."

"It takes a little time, my lord. We do know he's a Brotherhood assassin."

"I could have told you that the day he attacked me," Dirk told the Prefect disparagingly. "If that is all you've discovered in three days, then I find your methods unnecessarily complicated and barbaric. Are you sure you're doing this to find out what he knows? Or simply because you enjoy it?"

Barin's smile faded into a frown. "Prince Antonov has never seen fit to question my methods before, my lord."

"Perhaps because he's unaware of how inefficient you are, Master Prefect."

"I am answerable only to the Lion of Senet," Barin reminded him. "Your opinion of my methods is really not the issue."

"Don't be too sure of that," Dirk warned him coldly. *I'm turning into quite an actor. If I live through this nightmare, I should run away and join a theatrical troupe,* he told himself. *But how much longer can I keep pretending I don't feel anything?*

How much longer before I lose my nerve?

Nothing of what Dirk was thinking reached his eyes. He looked down at the assassin with a disapproving frown. "Perhaps, if you ever finish the job, you could inform me when you've learned something useful?"

Barin studied him closely for a moment, debating the advisability of challenging Dirk's authority. Dirk unconsciously held his breath, relying on his manner as much as his rank in the Shadowdancers and his relationship to Antonov to convince the Prefect he was a force to be reckoned with.

After a small hesitation, Barin bowed obsequiously. "Of course, my lord. I will have a messenger dispatched to the palace as soon as we learn anything."

"You do that," Dirk said, and then turned on his heel and walked from the interrogation chamber, forcing himself not to run.

Chapter 17

When the Lord of the Suns regained consciousness the following day, Marqel sent for Dirk, rather than Yuri. They needed to get this High Priestess business out of the way, and she wasn't going to wait for Yuri to fuss over the old man for hours before they did it.

Marqel hated sickness. She hated old age, too. It had a smell about it, as if somehow the body was already rotting, even though it had yet to die. Tending the Lord of the Suns was a chore she loathed, but she aided Yuri willingly, sharing the watch over him with the Shadowdancer Olena Borne. The only reason she nursed the old man with so much dedication was to ensure the old fool didn't up and die on her before he could make her High Priestess. Ella Geon had not been around the palace much lately to help. She was doing something with the Prefect down in the garrison in town. Marqel hadn't seen her since the funeral.

Marqel was alone with Paige Halyn when he began to stir. She hurried out into the hall and grabbed the nearest servant, ordering her to find the Lord of the Shadows, and then made her way back to Paige Halyn's room to resume her vigil.

A few moments later, Marqel stood up from her chair by the bed as Dirk hurried into the room. "He woke up about ten minutes ago."

He pushed past her wordlessly and knelt by the bed. "My lord?"

Paige Halyn turned his head painfully toward Dirk. *"Dirk?"*

"Gently, now," Dirk advised. "You don't want the bleeding to start again."

"What happened? Have I been ill?"

"You took a crossbow bolt in the neck meant for me," he explained.

A frown flickered over the old man's face. "I seem . . . to be doing you a lot of favors . . . lately."

"Don't die on me," Dirk suggested with a hint of a smile. "That would be the biggest favor you could do me right now."

"Things...are not going as you expected..." It was taking Paige Halyn every ounce of his strength to speak. And the Lord of the Suns was not asking Dirk a question, Marqel thought curiously.

"All the more reason for you to live, my lord."

"I'll try...not to inconvenience you..."

Dirk looked up at Marqel and beckoned her closer. "This is Marqel, the new Voice of the Goddess."

The Lord of the Suns glanced at her, but his face was etched with so much pain it was impossible to tell what he thought.

"You wish me to lie to Antonov?"

"You've been lying to him for decades, my lord," Dirk reminded the old man gently.

"Those were lies of omission," Paige replied, as if that excused his dishonesty. "They were lies of inaction, not intent. What you ask is...deliberate deceit."

"But it's deceit for the greater good."

"And the end justifies the means, I suppose?" Paige gasped bitterly. He closed his eyes for a moment as the pain became too much to bear. After a time, he opened them again and looked at Marqel. "Do you know what you're doing, young lady? Or are you simply blinded by ambition...as Belagren was?"

Marqel glanced at Dirk, not sure how to answer him. Dirk nodded encouragingly, but offered her no advice about what she should say.

"I'm just doing what Dirk tells me, my lord," she told him, honestly enough. "He's the one with all the ambition."

That last part wasn't strictly true, but there was no need to burden the old man with details. If her answer satisfied him, there was no way of telling.

He turned his attention back to Dirk. "You place me...in an untenable position, Dirk Provin. I'm left with a choice between allowing the old lies to continue or endorsing a whole raft of new lies."

"But they are lies that will eventually lead to the truth," Dirk pointed out.

Marqel bit back an exasperated sigh. She had no idea what they were talking about. All she wanted was for Paige Halyn to hurry up and announce that she was the new High Priestess. Then he could die.

The Lord of the Suns closed his eyes. He was silent for a long time. Marqel was just beginning to wonder if he had dropped off again, when suddenly he spoke.

"I have your word on this?" he asked.

Dirk nodded. "I'll not let you or the Goddess down, my lord, I promise."

"Very well."

Dirk smiled at the old man briefly then turned to Marqel. "Fetch Antonov," he said.

A short time later, they all gathered in the Lord of the Suns' room. Antonov arrived, looking concerned. Madalan came in a few moments later, but her expression was harder to read. Yuri was bending over his patient, tut-tutting impatiently, and making noises about overexciting the old man. Dirk stood in the background, a spectator rather than a participant. He was supposed to be opposed to this, and once Antonov arrived, that was exactly the impression he gave.

Antonov stepped up to the foot of the bed and looked down on the Lord of the Suns for a moment before turning to Yuri. "How does he fare?"

"He's desperately ill, your highness," Yuri told him. "Much too ill to be entertaining so many visitors."

The Lord of the Suns reached out a clawlike hand toward Antonov. "I'm well enough...to speak, your highness."

"I've no wish to endanger your health further, my lord."

"The Goddess will take me when she's ready, sire, and not before. She works in her own ways...and in her own time."

"It would be greedy of her to demand the High Priestess and the Lord of the Suns at her side so close together."

"The Goddess never takes something from us without giving something in return, your highness." He closed his eyes, marshaling his strength before continuing. "For all things there comes a time when younger blood is called for."

Antonov's eyes suddenly fixed on Marqel. "Are you saying this girl speaks the truth? That the Goddess truly has spoken to her?"

"The Goddess gives without fear or favor, your highness, and it is not for us to judge the worthiness of the recipient..." He stopped for a moment, as if gathering his thoughts. "She called the High Priestess to her, and gave you another voice in return. When I die, she will do the same with me."

Marqel discovered she was holding her breath. She looked down at her hands, which fortunately gave the impression she was humbled by the responsibility she now faced.

"Trust in the Goddess, your highness," Paige Halyn continued painfully. "Haven't I always advocated that?"

"There was a time when you doubted the High Priestess, my lord," Antonov reminded him. "I recall a time when you were loudly opposed to everything she stood for."

"It can be difficult to accept change, sire. But I know the truth in my heart, now." The old man smiled wanly. It was a serene, accepting smile, as if he had finally made peace with himself. "I have lived to see the Goddess bring me a ray of hope for the future. It is my fervent wish that you, too, will achieve such clarity of vision before you are called to her embrace."

Marqel listened to the Lord of the Suns sprouting his flowery rhetoric, desperately fighting the urge to giggle. *It is my fervent wish that you, too, will achieve such clarity of vision* ... Why didn't he just come right out and say it? *Hey, Antonov, I hope one day you'll realize you've been had.*

She glanced over her shoulder at Dirk to see what he thought about all this, but as usual, his expression betrayed nothing.

"Marqel."

She started a little to hear her name and turned back to look at Paige Halyn.

"Come here, child."

Marqel walked to the bed and took the hand the Lord

of the Suns offered her. His skin was as dry and fragile as tissue paper someone had wrinkled up and thrown into a forgotten corner.

"I name you High Priestess of the Shadowdancers," he announced with an effort. "You are ... the Shadowdancers' Voice of the Goddess. I charge you with bringing her truth to the world."

"I will," she whispered in a choked voice, deciding a few tears might be appropriate at this juncture. She risked a glance at Antonov out of the corner of her eye. For the first time he looked at her with more awe than suspicion.

"You must swear to this," the Lord of the Suns insisted, his skeletal grip tightening on her hand. "And you must swear you will listen to my guidance and the guidance of my successors."

"I swear," she promised, thinking there wasn't a chance in hell she was going to do a thing Madalan Tirov told her to do, when the Shadowdancer replaced Paige Halyn and became Lady of the Suns.

The Lord of the Suns closed his eyes, exhausted by the effort of sustaining such a long conversation. Yuri hurried forward and bent over the old man to examine him, and then he turned to Antonov.

"Really, your highness, this is too much for him. I must insist you finish your business with him later, when he's stronger."

Antonov nodded his agreement. "We'll leave him in peace." He looked across the bed at Marqel. "We have other things to take care of at present."

They filed out of the bedroom and gathered in the sitting room. Antonov turned to Madalan first, his manner businesslike and brusque. "We need to issue an announcement, my lady, informing the world that the Goddess has seen fit to give us another voice. We must also announce the news that we have a new High Priestess."

"I'll see to it, your highness," she promised with a low bow. Madalan glanced at Dirk for a moment, but Marqel couldn't see the expression on her face. The Shadowdancer left the apartment, closing the door softly behind her.

"Dirk."

"Your highness?"

"I'm giving the order for the fleet to leave today. I want you to set sail for Tolace and pick up Kirsh and the men he has with him there before you set course for the Baenlands. He'll be in command after that, but until then, you will be in charge."

"Me?" Dirk asked in shock.

Marqel liked it when things didn't go the way Dirk planned. It proved he was human.

"I'm no admiral, your highness," he protested.

"Organizing and dispatching the fleet to Tolace doesn't need an admiral, Dirk, it needs someone with a good brain and an eye for detail, and you're more than capable of both. Kirsh will take care of the military side of things once you've picked him up. Anyway, he'll need you to help him through the delta."

"The new High Priestess can do that, your highness," Dirk pointed out.

"Marqel is staying in Avacas," Antonov decreed. "We have just lost one High Priestess, Dirk. I'll not risk her successor by sending her into battle. Anyway, you're by far the more logical choice to send. You've spoken with Marqel at length and know the instructions the Goddess gave her about the delta, probably better than she does, because to you, they actually mean something."

It was all she could do not to openly gloat. Dirk had never planned for her to be left alone in Avacas with Antonov while he went off to war. *Oh, this is just too perfect . . .*

"But what about my studies . . . the Goddess's writings in Omaxin?"

"Omaxin has been there for thousands of years, Dirk," Antonov shrugged. "It'll still be there when you get back."

"The new High Priestess needs me here."

Marqel smiled. "But the Goddess needs you in Mil, my lord," she said humbly, as if it cost her a great deal to be denied his help. "I believe you could do more for the Goddess's cause by cleaning out the rebels in Mil than by staying here with me.

And I will have Madalan to aid me until you return." *Try to get out of it now that the Voice of the Goddess has spoken.* It was all she could do to keep her delight hidden.

Antonov nodded in agreement. With the support of the Goddess, there was no chance he would change his mind now. Dirk didn't even glance at her, but Marqel could imagine how angry he must be that she hadn't sided with him. *Serves him right.*

"But I thought you were planning to lead the attack yourself, sire."

Dirk sounded quite reasonable. Not angry. Not even concerned. Either it really *didn't* bother him or he was a very good actor. The latter, she suspected.

"Kirsh needs an opportunity to prove himself in a real conflict," Antonov shrugged. "It's the symbolism, Dirk. It will send a loud message to the Dhevynians if the Regent of Dhevyn leads the attack on the Baenlanders, with Thorn's bastard at his side. Those damned pirates have far too much support among the general population in Dhevyn."

"I'm under house arrest," Dirk reminded him.

He's really getting desperate, Marqel thought delightedly.

"I'm releasing you from it. The guard will stay with you while you're still in Avacas for your protection. Besides, you'll be much safer from an assassin at sea than you will be here in Avacas."

"But, *sire* . . ."

Antonov looked at him curiously. "You're not reluctant to do this because you still sympathize with your old friends, are you, Dirk?"

"No, sir."

"Then the matter is settled. You will leave with the fleet on tomorrow's tide."

Before Dirk could object further, Antonov turned to Marqel. He took her hand and gently raised it to his lips. "I trust you will forgive me for doubting you, my lady."

"Your doubts were no more than those I had myself, your highness," she assured him modestly.

Antonov smiled at her and, at that moment, Marqel felt a warm rush of satisfaction.

The Lion of Senet was hers for the taking.

Chapter 18

The Hospice in Tolace had taken on the air of an armed camp, and the feeling in the small coastal town was little better as Kirsh sought to uncover the truth behind his brother's disappearance.

The number of people who seemed to know that Misha was a poppy-dust addict had grown alarmingly and, as he had each one put to death to prevent the secret from slipping out, he had to suffer the silent accusation in Alexin's eyes. True to his word, the Dhevynian captain had said nothing further about what the prince was doing. He didn't have to. His unspoken disapproval was enough.

Kirsh should have known it wasn't going to be as easy as simply killing the Shadowdancer who was nursing Misha. One could not acquire a substance like poppy-dust without involving others. There were the guards watching over him—Kirsh thought them deserving of death anyway, considering it was they who let Misha slip through their fingers—and the Hospice's herbalist, who had actually provided him with the drug. The servants who delivered the drugs to his cottage. The friends they gossiped to in the local tavern. All of them deserved to die.

Containing the rumor was proving almost impossible. People were already speculating about the executions, and it wouldn't take long, Kirsh guessed, before people started putting the pieces together. Once a good rumor took hold, there was no way of stopping it; no way of preventing it reaching Avacas, and eventually, his father's ears.

He still had another dozen people in custody, and it was his unenviable task to decide which of them was to die next. He was leaning toward the basket maker and his wife. Although they continued to protest their innocence, it seemed a little too coincidental that it was Gilda Farlo who had brought Tia Veran into the Hospice, and Boris Farlo who happened to pay a late night visit on the flimsy pretext of finding a special basket the same night Misha disappeared. They were not directly involved in Misha's addiction, but that didn't really bother Kirsh. They had helped Tia abduct his brother, and that made them guilty enough for him.

Their deaths were more about vengeance than justice.

How they had gotten Misha out of the Hospice remained a mystery. It seemed logical to assume that Boris Farlo had hidden Misha in his cart, but how had they spirited him out of his room without his permission? Had they drugged him and carried him off? How had they managed such a feat without disturbing the guards in the next room? The alternative—that Misha willingly left the Hospice with Tia Veran—was inconceivable.

Or was it? Kirsh wondered. *If Misha were an addict and feared discovery, would his fear be enough for him to consider fleeing Senet? Was he so far gone in the drug he would prefer to abdicate his responsibilities as the crown prince, rather than be without it?* Kirsh could not believe that of Misha. But then, neither could he believe his brother was nothing more than a pitiful addict.

It just seemed easier to keep killing everyone who might have been involved.

He tossed the list of captives onto the desk and turned to look out over the Hospice gardens. Hidden among the beautifully landscaped grounds was such a conspiracy of silence and deceit, Kirsh thought his head might explode from trying to unravel it. He had a hangover, which wasn't helping his thought processes much. He had been drinking a lot lately, and mostly alone. His rank and tendency to execute anybody who even hinted he suspected Misha was an addict isolated him from both his men and his captains.

A knock on the door disturbed his rather jerky train of thought. He called permission to enter, hoping it was not

Alexin. He didn't think he could face the look of wordless condemnation Alexin usually wore.

It was not Alexin who entered, however, but Sergey. The Senetian captain was one of the few who did not seem bothered by what Kirsh was doing. In fact, Kirsh had a sneaking suspicion the man enjoyed it.

"What is it, Captain?"

"The ships have arrived from Avacas, your highness. There's been a longboat lowered from the command vessel. It's the *Tsarina,* I think."

The *Tsarina* had been his father's flagship before the *Calliope,* reinstated after the loss of his new ship in Elcast.

"Do we know who's in command?"

Kirsh knew most of the men his father was likely to send in command of the fleet, and he wasn't particularly looking forward to having any one of them looking over his shoulder.

Sergey shook his head. "I suppose we'll find out as soon as they land. I've sent a party down to the beach to wait for them." Tolace did not have a dock to speak of, certainly not one large enough to cater to the *Tsarina.*

"Well, whoever he is, make sure you bring him straight here as soon as he lands. We've wasted enough time here in Tolace."

"Of course, your highness," Sergey promised, with a sharp salute.

Kirsh picked up his half-empty cup of wine—his third since breakfast—and turned to stare out over the gardens as Sergey departed. With a heavy sigh, he went back to wondering if he should order the execution of Boris and Gilda Farlo.

A little over an hour later Sergey returned with the fleet commander. He opened the door and stood back to let the man enter.

Kirsh rose to his feet to greet his father's admiral. He was prepared for almost anything but the figure that appeared in the doorway. The man who stepped into the Hospice administrator's office was Dirk Provin.

The two young men stared at each other for a moment, and then Kirsh glanced at Sergey. "Leave us."

The captain saluted and closed the door behind him on the way out. Kirsh turned his attention to Dirk. "What the hell are you doing here?"

"Delivering your fleet."

Kirsh hurled the pottery goblet he was holding at Dirk, who ducked the missile nimbly. He glanced at the spreading stain on the wall for a moment before turning to look at Kirsh.

"It's nice to see you, too, Kirsh."

"You smug little bastard. This is your fault."

"My fault?" he asked. "What's my fault? I only just got here."

"You made me let her go. You knew what she planned."

"Ah," Dirk said, with dawning comprehension. "You think I asked you to let Tia go so she could kidnap your brother? Is that it?"

"Don't treat me like a fool, Dirk."

"Then stop acting like one, Kirsh."

"You *knew*," he accused, in a slightly more reasonable tone, his anger spent for the moment. "You must have known."

"How must I have known? I didn't even know Misha was here in Tolace until I got to Avacas. Neither did you. Tia escaped days before then."

"You probably put her up to it," Kirsh insisted, determined to pin the blame for this on someone.

"I had no idea what Tia Veran was going to do when she escaped," Dirk repeated patiently. "And if I had known what she was planning, I would have told her not to do it."

"Really?" Kirsh scoffed. "Why?"

"To avoid exactly what's happening here now, Kirsh. I hear you're having a high old time executing innocent bystanders."

The accusation shocked Kirsh. It wasn't like that at all. He was doing this to protect Misha. But how could he explain without revealing the truth? And who was Dirk to censure him, anyway? Despite his protestations of innocence, Kirsh would go to his grave thinking that somehow Dirk was involved in Misha's abduction. There was just no way to prove it.

"Don't you dare stand there and accuse *me* of being dishonorable, Dirk Provin."

"I wasn't accusing you of anything," Dirk said. "I was just curious about the executions, that's all. You had a Shadowdancer put to death. I am the right hand of the High Priestess. She deserves an explanation."

"Sonja was lax in her duties."

"So you killed her?" Dirk asked with a raised brow. "That's a little harsh, don't you think?"

"If she had been more vigilant, Misha wouldn't have been abducted."

"You're sure of that, are you?"

Kirsh sat down and made a show of picking up his quill to continue his work. "I don't have to explain myself to you. Aren't you supposed to be under house arrest?"

"I've been seconded to the navy." Dirk shrugged. "Not that it actually required much effort on my part. Your father's sea captains are more than competent. I just had to stand on the foredeck looking aristocratic and nod in agreement when somebody asked me to confirm an order they were going to carry out anyway, whether I agreed with it or not."

"What did you do to get the job, Dirk? Who did you sell out this time?"

Dirk shook his head ruefully. "You wouldn't believe the lengths I went to in order to get out of this, Kirsh. I have no desire to be here, and if you want to send me back to Avacas, then do it. I'll gladly leave right now."

Kirsh frowned. "I don't think so. If my father sent you here, then he had good reason to send you away from the city."

"It might have something to do with the Brotherhood assassin who took a chunk out of my ear."

"There's a Brotherhood contract out on you?"

"Apparently. You didn't hire them, did you?"

"No," Kirsh snapped. "But only because it never occurred to me."

"We'll know soon enough who's paying them," Dirk said. "Barin Welacin and Ella Geon were having a high old time, too, last I saw of them, figuring out ever more imaginative ways to torture the information out of the assassin they caught."

"I hope they have more luck getting the truth out of him than I'm having here," he muttered unhappily.

"Is there anything I can do to help?"

Kirsh looked up, surprised by the offer. "Like what?"

"Maybe I could talk to the prisoners," Dirk suggested. "See if I can learn anything."

"What makes you think you could get anything more out of them than I could?"

"You're still pretty new at this, Kirsh," Dirk reminded him. "I, on the other hand, am the Lord of the Shadows, the right hand of the High Priestess. And the Butcher of Elcast. Perhaps having their immortal souls threatened will work where mere physical pain has failed."

Kirsh wasn't sure he trusted Dirk's offer of assistance, but he could see no harm in it. At the very least, it would get him out of Kirsh's sight for a while. He was in no mood for Dirk and his glib answers for everything. "Very well, you can start with these two," he told him, handing him the list he had been going over earlier.

"Gilda and Boris Farlo," Dirk read. He looked at Kirsh. "Who are they?"

"The local basket maker and his wife. She claims she was simply hired by an anonymous man she conveniently can't identify to bring Lady Natasha to the Hospice, and the night Misha disappeared, her husband made a late night visit to the Hospice in a cart on the pretext of looking for a basket that had been delivered by mistake."

"Coincidental, but hardly enough to condemn them," Dirk said.

"There's a rumor around town they're both well placed in the Brotherhood, too," Kirsh added.

Dirk nodded thoughtfully. "I'll talk to them. We don't want to waste too much time on them, though."

"Why not?"

"Don't you want to invade Mil?"

"We have to find out how to get through the delta first."

Dirk looked at him in surprise. "Your father didn't send you a message?"

"A message about what?"

"We know the way, Kirsh. The night Belagren died, the Goddess chose a new voice and gave the instructions to her."

"You have the route?" he gasped in surprise. Suddenly his anger at Dirk was forgotten. This changed everything. Now he could do something really useful. Now he could actually do something to get Misha back.

"Every little tack and turn," Dirk confirmed. "I don't know about you, but I'd rather be on my way to Mil than stay here tormenting the local basket maker."

"So would I. We'll leave at second sunrise tomorrow," Kirsh agreed, glad to be given an escape from his current, thankless task.

Dirk nodded and smiled thinly. "I thought you might see it that way. I'll have a little chat with your basket maker anyway, just to see if I can learn anything useful, but I suspect it'll be a moot point once we reach Mil."

He turned to leave, but something occurred to Kirsh that he had not thought to ask earlier. "The new High Priestess, Dirk? You didn't say who it was."

Dirk hesitated his hand on the doorknob before he turned back to look at Kirsh. "You haven't heard?"

"Would I be asking if I had?"

"I'm sorry..."

"You've no need to apologize, Dirk, just tell me who I'll have to suffer across the dinner table for the next decade or so. I hope it isn't Madalan Tirov. She's a sour old hag." He smiled. "My father might find himself suddenly otherwise engaged on Landfall if he has to take her to his bed."

"It wasn't Madalan, Kirsh."

"Then who was it, Dirk?"

Dirk remained silent. His reluctance seemed rather odd.

"For the Goddess's sake! I'm beginning to think you don't want me to know."

"You'll find out soon enough, I suppose, when they make the announcement."

Dirk's unwillingness to divulge the identity of the new High Priestess was making Kirsh suspicious. Maybe it was because a new High Priestess had not been appointed, but a High *Priest*.

"It's you, isn't it? Is that why you're here? Because you know the way through the delta? Because the Goddess supposedly gave *you* the information?" Kirsh shook his head in disgust. "Did you murder Belagren, too, just to make it look good?"

"It's not me, Kirsh." He was a long time adding: "It's Marqel."

Kirsh stared at Dirk uncomprehendingly.

"Marqel is the Voice of the Goddess. The High Priestess of the Shadowdancers."

"It can't be!"

"It's true, and believe me, I'm no happier about it than you are. The Lord of the Suns has confirmed it. I'm sorry, Kirsh..."

"Get out!"

Dirk did as Kirsh ordered and the prince sagged back in his chair, closed his eyes and let the fantasy world he had been living in come crashing down around him.

Chapter 19

The Hospice was not equipped with prison cells, so they had had to make do with the isolation rooms where the mentally disturbed patients were confined during psychotic episodes. With the growing prevalence of poppy-dust addiction, the rooms were in demand more often than the Shadowdancers liked to admit.

Boris Farlo proved to be a rotund, jolly little man, who

jumped to his feet and immediately began protesting his innocence as soon as Dirk stepped into the padded room. Dirk dismissed the guard, heard the cell door lock behind him and then
turned to the basket maker. He had been roughed up a bit and
sported a rather spectacular black eye, but other than that, he
seemed none the worse for his incarceration.

"Shut up," he ordered impatiently.

"But, my lord . . ."

"I'm not interested in listening to your lies," Dirk told him.
"In fact, I'm quite disgusted by them. Surely, you could have
come up with something more convincing than a misplaced
basket? I always thought the Brotherhood was smarter than
that."

Boris met his eye with an innocent shrug. "I'm sure I don't
know what you're talking about, my lord."

"I'm sure you *do*."

The basket maker studied him curiously. "I've not seen you
around Tolace before. Who are you?"

"My name is Dirk Provin."

Boris hesitated, and then dropped all pretense of innocence. "What do you want with me?"

"I want a deal. With the Brotherhood."

"Then perhaps you should speak to someone from the
Brotherhood, my lord," Boris suggested with a sly little smile.

"I'll take my chances with you."

The fat man shrugged, as if it made little difference to him.
"You can tell me of the deal you wish to make, my lord, but I
can't guarantee it will reach the ears of those who might want to
hear it."

"I'm sure if I arranged for you and your wife to be released,
they'd get word of it somehow."

Boris looked at him with new respect. "You can do that?"

"I'm the Lord of the Shadows, Master Farlo," Dirk told
him. "I can do pretty much anything I want."

Boris considered his offer silently, and then nodded.
"What's the deal?"

"I want them to call off the assassins they've set onto me."

"Once a contract is accepted, the Brotherhood does not

renege on its promises, my lord," Boris warned, and then he added with a smile, "At least, that's what I've heard."

"I can make it worth their while."

"Money is not the issue, Lord Provin. It's the principle of the thing. How would it look if we...*they*...were bought off so easily? I mean, what would be the point of employing an assassin at all, if all your target had to do to get rid of the threat was to offer more money?"

"Your moral dilemma truly breaks my heart," Dirk said. "But I wasn't planning to offer money."

"Then what were you planning to offer?"

"Information."

Boris frowned. "What sort of information?"

"When I returned to Avacas, Antonov asked me for the names of every man and woman connected with the Brotherhood I could identify. After two years in the Baenlands, it was quite a list. Even I was surprised by the length of it."

"And you gave it to him?"

"Of course I gave it to him."

"Then the damage is done." Boris shrugged. "What can you possibly offer the Brotherhood that would make them withdraw the contract on a man who has so comprehensively betrayed them?"

"I can give them the names on that list."

"To what purpose? If Antonov already has them, then it's too late to save anyone."

"The High Priestess has just died," Dirk reminded him. "His eldest son has been kidnapped and the Lord of the Suns lies in Antonov's palace on the brink of death, thanks to your bumbling assassin. He has other things to occupy him right now, and there is a limit even to the Lion of Senet's resources. Your people are probably safe until we get back from Mil."

"And if the Brotherhood refuses to consider your offer?"

"Then I'll let Kirshov kill you and your wife, Barin Welacin can have a free hand with the names on that list, and I'll just have to take my chances with your assassins."

"You drive a hard bargain, my lord. Perhaps, if you ever

tire of a career with the Shadowdancers, you should consider becoming a merchant."

"I'll keep it in mind," Dirk promised, with a thin smile. "Do we have a deal?"

Before Boris could agree, there was a knock at the door. Dirk called permission to enter and heard the door unlocking. It swung open to reveal a short, dumpy and very irate looking woman and a buxom blond girl of about eighteen. The women rushed into the cell and threw themselves at the basket maker, the three of them gushing over each other, checking to ensure each was unharmed.

Dirk smiled at the warmth of the reunion and then turned to the guard. "They'll be all right with me, for the time being. I'll call you when we're done."

Boris looked up as the door closed and glared at Dirk suspiciously. "Why have you brought them here?"

He did not answer the basket maker, but turned to the older woman. "You must be Gilda, Master Farlo's wife. And this is one of your daughters?"

"Her name is Caterina," Gilda told him. "And she has nothing to do with any of this."

"I'm sure she doesn't," Dirk agreed. "As for the reason you're here...I brought you here to release you, Mistress Farlo."

"Why?" Gilda asked skeptically.

"Because Master Farlo and I have struck a deal."

Gilda turned to her husband questioningly. "What have you done, Papa?"

"Nothing!" he protested. Dirk thought he was more frightened of his wife than anything else he had been threatened with recently. "Lord Provin simply wants me to take a message to someone."

Gilda turned to Dirk with a scowl. "Lord *Provin*? You are Dirk Provin?"

"Yes."

She spat on the ground at his feet. "That's what I think of you and your offers, boy. We'll have no part of them."

Dirk wasn't really surprised by her attitude. In her place,

he would probably feel the same. "I'm sorry you feel that way, mistress. I was going to accept your husband's word on this, but I see now it would be foolish in the extreme to trust him to carry out my instructions if you plan to undermine them. You force me to take more drastic action."

"What drastic action?" Gilda sneered.

In reply, Dirk knocked on the door and waited for the guard outside to unlock it. Three heavily armed Senetian Palace Guards stepped into the small cell, filling it with their looming presence.

"Take the girl," Dirk ordered.

Boris and Gilda tried to protect her, but they had no chance of fending off the soldiers. Caterina screamed as she was torn from her parents and dragged from the cell by two of the guards. The third remained to await further orders.

"Have her taken down to the longboat," Dirk told him. "She'll be going back to the *Tsarina* with me."

"No!" Gilda cried in protest, lunging at him. The guard beat her back effortlessly, knocking her to the floor. Boris bent down to help his wife up, glaring at Dirk.

"The tales about your cruelty hardly do you justice, Dirk Provin."

Boris managed to make his name sound like an insult. Dirk dismissed the guard and then turned back to the basket weaver and his wife.

"Do as I ask and your daughter will be returned to you, whole and unharmed," he said. "Cross me, or try to have me killed, and I will leave instructions that she is to be handed over to the crew for their amusement before she is killed. Is that clear?"

The rotund little man wasn't looking nearly as jolly as he had been when Dirk first entered the cell. "How do we know you'll keep your end of the bargain?"

Dirk noticed that Boris said "we." The basket maker had given up pretending he was not a member of the Brotherhood, which relieved Dirk a great deal. It was bad enough having to threaten these people. It would have been even worse if it had all been for nothing.

"You'll get the list before I sail," Dirk promised.

"But Caterina . . ." Gilda began desperately.

"Will be safe as long as I am," Dirk assured her.

The woman glared at him. "If you harm one hair on my daughter's head you'll be begging for death before I'm finished with you, Dirk Provin."

"If any harm comes to your daughter, I'll already be dead, Mistress Farlo," he replied, sounding much more careless of her threat than he actually felt. Without giving her a chance to answer, Dirk turned and knocked on the door again. The guard opened it and stepped inside, waiting for his orders.

"Master Farlo and his wife are free to go."

The guard looked at him doubtfully. "My lord?"

"You can release them, Sergeant."

"But his highness said . . ."

"His highness asked me to come here and determine the innocence or guilt of these people. While I've no doubt they're guilty of something, they are innocent of anything connected with Prince Misha's abduction. Now do as I order, or would you prefer I had Prince Kirshov called down here to give you the order himself?"

After a moment's hesitation, the man nodded and stepped back. "As you command, my lord."

Dirk turned back to the basket maker and his wife. "Go," he said sternly. "And don't let me hear anything unsavory about either of you ever again, or you *will* taste Prince Kirshov's justice."

Although Gilda obviously wanted to stay and argue, Boris grabbed his wife's hand and dragged her from the cell.

Dirk watched them leave, thinking all the people who thought he was a mathematical genius were wrong. His genius was not figures; his genius was getting himself embroiled in plots so complex not even he could be sure how they would end.

And to top it all off, he was now lumbered with the unwelcome and unwilling company of Caterina Farlo.

It was days like this Dirk was sorry that when Tia tried to kill him, she missed.

Chapter 20

Marqel had given very little thought to what was involved in being High Priestess beyond the prestige and power she imagined she would wield. The reality of her position proved to be rather less glamorous than she expected.

One thing Marqel had not been counting on was that the official residence of the High Priestess of the Shadowdancers was not Antonov's palace, but the Hall of Shadows. Madalan took great delight in pointing out this awkward fact to her the day after Dirk left Avacas with the fleet. The Shadowdancer arrived at her door with a bevy of aides in tow, and announced that, as Marqel was now the High Priestess, she must return to the Hall of Shadows to assume her duties formally.

Marqel was escorted out of the palace with a great deal of pomp and ceremony. She was driven back to the Hall of Shadows in Belagren's coach, with Madalan sitting opposite her the whole way, smiling at her like a spider that had just discovered a particularly juicy fly had landed in its web. It began to rain as they turned out of the palace gates and the drops pounded on the taut leather canopy.

"You'll need to address the Shadowdancers as soon as we arrive," Madalan informed her loudly over the downpour as they jolted along the slick cobblestones toward the Hall of Shadows. "Have you given any thought to what you are going to say?"

"Why do I have to say anything?" Marqel looked down at her gown. A few stray raindrops had splashed into the coach. They would probably stain the red silk. But it didn't really matter, she supposed. She was High Priestess now. Marqel could afford all the gowns she wanted.

"It is expected of you."

"Can't *you* say something to them?" she asked, not wanting to confront that sea of hostile faces. Marqel knew her elevation to High Priestess would be unpopular among the other Shadowdancers. It was the reason she wanted to stay at the palace, where she had Antonov's protection.

Madalan wasn't interested in making this easy for her. "What would you have me say to them, Marqel? *I'm sorry, but your High Priestess couldn't be bothered with you right now?*"

"That's not what I meant," she said, guessing Madalan would really get angry if she didn't at least give the impression she cared. "Can't you just tell them I'm so overwhelmed by the honor of speaking to the Goddess that I can't bring myself to face them...or something like that?"

"And what will be your excuse the next time?" Madalan asked impatiently. "No, Marqel, you can't and shouldn't put this off if you expect to hold onto your rather tenuous grasp on the position of High Priestess."

"It's not tenuous," she objected. "I'm the Voice of the Goddess."

"You are a pawn, Marqel," Madalan told her harshly. "And a highly disposable one at that. Until Kirshov returns from Mil, your position is *very* tenuous."

"What do you mean?"

Madalan looked at her for a moment, and then laughed. "You have no idea, do you? Foolish girl! Why do you think I agreed to this preposterous arrangement? Because I thought you were worthy of replacing Belagren? You're not usually so stupid!"

"You've got no choice but to go along with it," Marqel pointed out with a pout, rather hurt by Madalan's attitude. "Dirk told *me* the way through the delta, not you."

"And have you considered the possibility he's lying to you, Marqel? That boy can't be trusted as far as you could spit him into a headwind. For all you know, you are simply a puppet in some twisted game he's playing to get back at Antonov for killing his mother."

Marqel hadn't actually thought about it like that. "Why would he lie about it?"

"If the instructions he gave you are false, Marqel, then Senet's entire naval capability will be destroyed in one hit, trying to get through the delta. How much do you think the pirates in the Baenlands would enjoy seeing that happen?"

"But if he's lying, then Antonov will—"

"Blame you," Madalan finished for her bluntly. "As far as the Lion of Senet is concerned, *you* are the voice of the Goddess. Dirk Provin will remain blameless. You really shouldn't underestimate that boy, Marqel. It may end up costing you your life."

"Do *you* think Dirk is lying?"

"Ask me again, if and when the fleet returns from Mil."

Marqel was silent for a time, considering what Madalan had told her. It made a frightening amount of sense that Dirk would use her in such a fashion. All his promises about making her High Priestess...she thought they'd seemed too good to be true. Perhaps they were.

"What should I do?"

"Start thinking up a reason why the fleet was destroyed," Madalan advised. "And make it a good one, because if you have to stand before Antonov explaining why the Goddess sent his ships to be wiped out in the Baenlands, it had better be convincing."

Now she was really worried. "Do you think he'd have me dismissed as High Priestess?"

"You should be so lucky," Madalan snorted. "He's more likely to have you disemboweled with a spoon, girl, and then strung up by your intestines."

"But what if Dirk is telling the truth?"

"Then I have misjudged the boy and I will beg his forgiveness. I'll even do something nice for him, once I'm Lady of the Suns. Speaking of which, you might recall you swore to Paige Halyn in front of a number of witnesses you would be guided by him. And by his successors."

Marqel remembered the promise and had no more intention of keeping it now than she had when she made it. But she realized something else, too: for the time being at least, she needed to keep Madalan Tirov on her side.

"I'm glad you're here to guide me, my lady."

Madalan looked at her suspiciously for a moment and then

shrugged. "We'll see." She leaned forward as the carriage came to a halt outside the Hall of Shadows. "We've arrived. For now, Marqel, you're High Priestess. So you'd better start acting like one."

Marqel got through the address to the Shadowdancers with some nonsense about believing in the Goddess and being guided by her words. She couldn't later recall what she said, but even Madalan had not been able to fault her, so she must have said the right things.

After they left the main temple, she was led not to the High Priestess's luxurious suite, but to her office. Marqel wasn't really paying attention to their destination. She was remembering that Belagren had owned an awful lot of jewelry. *I wonder what happened to it. It really should come to me. I'm her successor.* There had been a particularly pretty bracelet she had always coveted, made of gold inlaid with diamonds. *Perhaps it's waiting for me in her rooms, along with all of Belagren's other stuff.*

If Marqel thought delivering a speech was the worst that could happen to her, she was sadly mistaken. Four secretaries awaited her in the office with a pile of documents. She would be lucky to find her bed before tomorrow's second sunrise.

Madalan stood beside the new High Priestess, gloating over the look on Marqel's face, positively relishing the prospect of Marqel having to deal with even half of the business laid before her. There were requests for money from Shadowdancers from all over Senet and Dhevyn; for personnel to be sent or transferred, from various duchies for assistance, demands from Omaxin for more scribes and better accommodation now that it seemed they were to be stationed there permanently...the list went on and on...

"How did Belagren deal with all this?" Marqel asked, throwing her hands up in despair. She had dismissed the secretaries before they could dump any more work on her.

"By being conscientious," Madalan told her. "You don't

think Belagren stayed in power as long as she did by swanning around making proclamations, do you? She kept her position because she was good at what she did, Marqel. She was a brilliant administrator and a clever politician. And she kept her eye on things. Nothing happened in the Hall of Shadows she wasn't aware of. She could walk through these halls and greet every Shadowdancer she met by name. She remembered the names of their families, too. Even the debtor slaves who clean the privies weren't beneath her notice."

"I thought she kept her position because she was screwing Antonov," Marqel remarked.

Madalan's slap caught her by surprise. "Don't you dare belittle her memory, you grasping little slut! You still live only because I need to find out if Dirk Provin is lying to us. And make no mistake, that's the *only* reason you've gotten away with Belagren's murder. Make one more comment like that, my girl, and Voice of the Goddess or not, I will kill you myself."

Marqel rubbed her face and scowled at Madalan, but said nothing. The news Madalan knew what had happened to Belagren had taken her by surprise. She thought Dirk had covered it up. She certainly had not expected him to tell Madalan what had happened. Nor had he even hinted he *had* told her. It made her wonder what else he had neglected to mention. It also, for the first time, drove home how dangerous a situation she was in. The gloss of her new position was being rapidly sanded away by Madalan's abrasive manner.

"I'm sorry, my lady," she muttered, mindful of the need to retain Madalan's support.

"You will be, Marqel," Madalan promised.

"I'd better get to work," she added meekly, turning back to face the pile.

Madalan glared at her, trying to detect any hint of mockery in her tone. When she found none, she seemed satisfied that Marqel was sufficiently chastised. Madalan took the seat on the other side of the desk and began to sort through the papers.

"You're going to have to refer this one to Antonov," Madalan said, thrusting a document at her.

"What is it?"

"A request for troops. The Sidorians have taken to raiding the camp in Omaxin again. We had the same problem with them a few years ago. You'll have to draft a letter to the Lion of Senet and ask him to send some soldiers north to put down the trouble."

"Don't we have our own guard?"

Madalan sighed heavily. "Yes, Marqel, we do. But they are almost entirely ceremonial. Besides, why should we bear the cost of such a venture when it's the Lion of Senet's responsibility to protect his borders?"

"I never thought about it like that," Marqel replied. "Suppose he says no?"

"He never says no."

Marqel looked up from the letter with a frown, realizing just how far out of her depth she was. "Will you help me write the letter, my lady? I don't think I can deal with any of this without you."

Madalan nodded her agreement and continued to sort through the pile, and the new High Priestess got her first lesson in the art of governing the Shadowdancers.

Chapter 21

Dirk forgot about the basket maker's daughter until he returned to the *Tsarina* with Kirsh just after first sunrise. One of the sailors informed him that his "lady friend" was installed in his cabin, awaiting his return.

"Your *lady* friend?" Kirsh asked, looking at him oddly.

Dirk swore under his breath before he answered. "I took the basket maker's daughter hostage as a condition of his and his wife's release."

"I see," Kirsh replied thoughtfully. "Is she pretty?"

Dirk rolled his eyes with exasperation. "That's not why I brought her here, Kirsh. I thought it would be easier to get the father to admit he had something to do with Misha's escape if he thought his family was threatened."

"And did he confess?"

"Not yet."

"You mean he called your bluff," Kirsh shrugged, coldly indifferent. "Well, just don't let your ... off-duty activities ... interfere with your other duties."

The prince was angry with him, Dirk knew. And still blaming him for Misha's disappearance. If any harm came to Misha in the Baenlands, Kirsh might never get over it. There was nothing to be gained by telling Kirsh why he had taken Caterina Farlo as his hostage, though, so he didn't bother. He was in no mood to explain himself to a man who had summarily executed nearly a dozen innocent people for no good reason, anyway.

"I'd better go see to her."

"I want to meet with the fleet captains after dinner," Kirsh announced. "I'll expect you to be there."

"Of course, your highness," Dirk agreed, and then made his way below, wondering what he was supposed to do with Caterina Farlo.

When he opened the cabin door, the girl backed up against the bunk, holding a fruit knife out in front of her with a snarl.

"Take one step toward me and I'll cut off your balls," she declared savagely.

Like mother, like daughter, Dirk thought with a sigh. He closed the door and approached her. She waved the knife at him threateningly.

"I mean it!"

"I'm quite sure you do," he agreed, snatching the knife from her grasp. She stumbled backward and landed on the bunk.

"I'll scream!"

"In your position, I probably would, too," Dirk agreed.

"But as I have no intention of raping you, it'd be a bit of wasted effort, wouldn't it?"

Caterina Farlo glared at him suspiciously. She was quite plump, and not very tall, but she was endowed with a flawless complexion and thick, wavy blond hair.

"What do you want with me then?"

"Actually, I don't really want you at all," he answered. "Your father was supposed to agree to my offer without any other sort of persuasion. But your mother put paid to that idea. What *am* I going to do with you?"

"You're not going to give me to the sailors, are you?" she asked. Something in her voice made him look at her askance.

"*No.* Did you want me to?"

"Of course not!"

"I was just asking," he said with a faint smile. "I suppose I could find you something useful to do. Can you cook?"

"Can I *cook*?" she snapped, insulted by the question. "What sort of well-bred woman can't cook?"

"I could name one," Dirk replied, thinking of Tia. He also thought Caterina was repeating her mother's words, rather than expressing her own opinion. Gilda Farlo obviously left a considerable influence on her daughters.

He considered the problem for a time as he pocketed the fruit knife.

"I suppose if I'm not to send you belowdecks to be ravished, you might be able to help the cook. You're not going to do anything stupid like jumping overboard, are you? We're really in a bit of a hurry, and we'll be too far from the coast for you to swim back to Tolace by tomorrow." He glanced around the cabin with a frown. "We'll have to find you somewhere to sleep, too, I suppose."

Caterina watched him closely, her expression confused. "You're not anything like I was expecting," she said.

"And just what were you expecting?"

"I've heard all sorts of horrible things about you. I thought you'd be older, though. And nastier."

"I'm sorry if I disappoint you," he said, wondering what

else the rumors said about him. "Perhaps before this voyage is over I can do something brutal enough to restore your opinion of me."

For the first time, Caterina smiled. "My sisters are going to be *so* jealous."

"Why would they be jealous?"

"Because I was the one who got taken hostage. I've been kidnapped! And not just by anybody, but by the Butcher of Elcast, no less. I'm on the Lion of Senet's flagship. I'll get to meet a real prince. And I get to go on a sea voyage without Mama around. I've never been out of Tolace before." Caterina sounded as if she was rather warming to the idea of being carried off by an evil nobleman bent on ravaging her. "Where are we going, anyway? Somewhere exotic? Kalarada? Or maybe the islands of Galina? I hear the woman there don't wear any clothes at all." Although she acted scandalized, Caterina had obviously decided to treat this interesting change in her circumstances as if it were a grand adventure.

Dirk shook his head. "I'm sorry to disappoint you, but we're going to the Baenlands."

"Why? There's nothing there but pirates and poppies."

"How do you know that?" Dirk asked, rather bemused by her attitude.

"I know someone from the Baenlands," she announced smugly. "She told me all about it."

"Really?"

"She did!" Caterina boasted. "She was staying at our house before... well, before all that trouble started at the Hospice." Caterina shut her mouth abruptly, realizing she had said too much.

Dirk stared at her in surprise. "You spoke to *Tia*?"

"Who?"

"I mean Tasha," he corrected, guessing Tia had not used her real name.

"Will I be in trouble if I say yes?" she asked doubtfully.

"You've already been taken hostage, Caterina," he pointed out. "I've released your parents and I've promised you won't be harmed. What more can I do to you?"

She thought it over for a moment, then nodded. "She borrowed some of my clothes. They didn't fit her very well."

"How did she seem?" *Was she angry? Hurt? Was she the one who told you about the vicious reputation of the Butcher of Elcast?* There were so many questions Dirk wanted to ask. So many things he could *never* ask, for Tia's protection as much as his own.

"She seemed all right, I suppose, why?"

"No reason." Dirk shrugged. "Although you might want to forget you saw her. I had a lot of explaining to do when I let your parents go free. It rather negates all my hard work if you start bragging you and Tasha were swapping clothes."

"We weren't *swapping* clothes," she objected. "It was raining, that's all, and her clothes were wet."

"Whatever the reason, do us both a favor and just pretend you never heard of her. I can only protect you up to a point, Caterina. If Prince Kirshov learned you'd been consorting with Tia Veran, there'd be nothing I could do to stop him doing whatever he chose with you."

Caterina appeared to take the warning seriously. She nodded and looked around the small stateroom. "I could sleep on the floor in here."

"Wouldn't you rather somewhere more comfortable?"

She shook her head. "I don't know anybody else on the ship."

"You don't know me, either."

"Maybe." Caterina shrugged. "But you've said you won't hurt me."

"I might be lying," he suggested, wondering what he'd done to engender such trust. Then it occurred to Dirk her willingness to remain probably had little to do with trust. Caterina's adventure would not be nearly so exciting if she couldn't tell her sisters how she had been held prisoner in the cabin of the wicked Butcher of Elcast. *Why couldn't Boris Farlo have had five sons?* Dirk thought wistfully. Then he could have sent the young man to work belowdecks and not spared him another thought for the rest of the voyage.

Why do I keep complicating my life by doing these stupid, stupid things?

Caterina shrugged. "I'm your prisoner now, my lord. It's not like you'd have to seduce me, or anything, if you wanted to . . . you know . . . take advantage of me . . ."

A little alarmed, Dirk studied her for a moment. Apparently, Caterina's adventure was not going to be complete without a little romance. She had shifted slightly on the bunk so her more than ample cleavage was all he could see when he looked down at her. And she was smiling at him. Dirk had a bad feeling she was trying to be alluring.

"I have to go," he said brusquely.

"When will you be back?"

"I don't know."

"Did you want me to wait up for you?"

Dirk stared at her, shaking his head in despair. "*No.*"

Caterina settled herself back onto the bunk. She looked far too comfortable for his liking. "I'll probably wait up anyway. Then you can tell me all about your day when you get back."

Dirk fled the cabin, still cursing under his breath as he slammed the door behind him and went to meet with Kirsh and the fleet captains to discuss the invasion of Mil.

Chapter 22

Kirsh still suspected that Dirk had tricked him into letting Tia Veran go free so she could kidnap Misha and draw them into an ambush. The notion refused to go away. Dirk denied it, of course, and Kirsh couldn't bring the matter to his father's attention without implicating himself in the affair, so he had no choice but to live with the uncertainty that went with his guilt, hoping against hope that he was wrong.

The fleet slowed as they reached Daven Isle, the ships reducing their sail and tacking against the wind as they prepared to enter the Bandera Straits. The small rocky island was home to so many roosting birds the cliffs were stained white with their droppings. It was still some distance away, but the faint screeching from its thousands of winged residents drifted clearly across the water. Here the pirates awaited their prey, catching Senetian traders as they readied themselves for the tricky currents and fickle winds of the narrow Straits. With smaller, more maneuverable craft, their intimate knowledge of the hidden rocks around Daven Isle, and their ability to flee into the Spakan River delta, the pirates were unstoppable.

But not today, Kirsh mused as Dirk came to stand beside him on the foredeck. There was no sign of any pirate ships in the Straits. He thought that meant they were still in the bay farther upriver, beyond the delta. At least he hoped they were. Once his fleet entered the delta, there would be no escape for the pirates.

"Captain Clegg was wondering if we should heave to and wait for second sunrise tomorrow before we proceed," he remarked to Dirk.

"I'd recommend waiting," Dirk advised. "The instructions we have refer quite specifically to the position of the second sun. I don't think we should tackle the delta with only the first sun to light our way."

Although not happy about the need to wait, Kirsh nodded in agreement. Since hearing the instructions the Goddess had given Marqel, he had suspected they could only safely be followed during the day. As for the other implications of his beloved now being the High Priestess of the Shadowdancers and the Voice of the Goddess—he was trying very hard not to think about them at all.

"I think I'll have the *Hand of Fate* and the *Azure* take up position near the entrance to the delta anyway," he decided. "I don't want any pirate ships slipping by us before second sunrise tomorrow."

Dirk glanced back at the two following ships and the half-dozen more spread out behind them. "Are you planning to take all these ships through the delta? The bay of Mil isn't that big, you know. It's going to get awfully crowded in there, and you'll have precious little room to maneuver if you need it."

"I'm glad you brought that up," Kirsh told him. "We need to discuss how we're going to attack their defenses."

"What defenses?" Dirk scoffed. "It's a village smaller than Tolace, Kirsh."

"So you keep telling me," he said, his tone leaving no doubt about how unreliable he considered that information. "I can't believe they have no defenses at all."

"Up until now, the delta has been all the protection they needed."

Kirsh was still not sure he believed Dirk. He had a sneaking suspicion he was sailing into a trap. Would Mil prove to be as defenseless as Dirk promised? Or was there a whole army hiding in there, waiting to wipe out his invasion force? Was that why Dirk was advising him not to take all his ships through the delta? Was he trying to help, or was he trying to even the odds a little for his friends?

"How many fighting men do they have?"

"I couldn't really say," Dirk shrugged.

"You can't or you won't?"

"I can't," Dirk assured him. "There are simply too many variables, Kirsh. Their ships may not be in port, which will significantly reduce the number of men they can throw into a fight. Or they may have gotten word we were heading for the delta and fled the settlement."

"How could they know something like that?"

Dirk shook his head. He seemed amused. "Look around you, Kirsh. You don't think you can sail out of Avacas with a fleet this large without somebody working out where it's headed, do you? Senet isn't at war. The only logical place a fleet this big *could* be heading is Mil. And, whether you like it or not, there are plenty of Dhevynian sympathizers in Senet who could have sent them word."

"Including you?"

"Sure," he agreed. "I sent word to the Baenlanders to warn them of the attack. That's why they hired an assassin to come after me. Out of gratitude."

"It could have been a feint. An attack simply to convince us you really had betrayed them."

Dirk looked at him for a moment and then shook his head in amazement. "Have *you* ever used a crossbow, Kirsh?"

"Yes."

"And you honestly believe I arranged to have a Brotherhood assassin nick my ear, just to make it look good?"

Kirsh looked away, annoyed by Dirk's amusement. Admittedly, the chance of such a thing was remote, and it would make Dirk courageous beyond imagining if it were true. What had he heard Belagren say once? *When all other explanations had been discarded, the one left, no matter how unlikely, was probably the truth.* Which meant Dirk had betrayed the Baenlanders and joined the Shadowdancers because he really *had* seen the light, and not for a more sinister reason. But Kirsh wouldn't know for certain until they sailed through the delta. Until then, a core of distrust lay heavy in his stomach, like the remnants of a bad meal.

"Let's assume the worst, then," he said, pushing away his irritation to concentrate on the problem at hand. "If their ships are in port, how many men do we face?"

"Men? More than a hundred, maybe two hundred. Not all their ships berth in Mil, though. Quite a few simply call in every now and then, to bring supplies and news. Not every ship sailing the delta is crewed by brigands, Kirsh."

"If they're in Mil when I get there, that's exactly what they are, Dirk."

"Then be prepared to face every man, woman and child in the settlement who can pick up a weapon. They won't give in easily."

"What about escape routes? Can they flee upriver?"

"Some of them might try, but it will only mean they'll take a little longer to die. There's nothing upriver but barren lava flows."

"Where are they likely to be holding Misha?"

"Either down in the village or up at Johan's house."

"What sort of fortifications does the house have?"

Dirk smiled. "Ah...now that's going to be a *real* challenge.

There'll probably be at least two, maybe as many as *three* women in there protecting it, and then there's that nasty, wide-open veranda that goes all the way around. Are you sure you have enough men to handle it, Kirsh?"

"If you're going to be so cynical about this, Dirk, why did you bother coming?"

Dirk leaned on the railing and studied the horizon thoughtfully. "I wasn't given a choice, remember?"

"You could at least pretend to have some enthusiasm for the task."

"I'm brimming with enthusiasm, Kirsh," Dirk said. "But the word *overkill* leaps to mind. You're taking a thousand men into battle to round up a couple of hundred women and children. It's not that I lack enthusiasm for your cause. I'm simply overwhelmed by your Senetian tendency toward excess."

"Then why do I get the feeling you're always laughing at us, Dirk?"

"I don't know," his cousin shrugged. "Maybe it's because deep down, even you think your methods are laughable sometimes, and if *you* think that, then you assume everybody else must think the same."

Kirsh had been acquainted with Dirk long enough to know better than to get into an argument with him about... *anything*. He could twist things around worse than a Tribunal Advocate, but somehow, Kirsh never seemed to learn.

"When we land tomorrow, you're not to go ashore until I tell you it's safe."

"I'm touched by your concern."

"I'm *concerned* you'll have a change of heart when the killing begins."

"It won't be a change of heart, Kirsh. You know quite well how I feel about needless killing."

"I abhor needless bloodshed as much as you do, Dirk," Kirsh reminded him. "It's in the definition of *needless* that we differ."

"A few hundred corpses aren't going to bring Misha back if he's already dead," Dirk pointed out.

"If Misha is dead, Dirk, you won't need to count the corpses. I'll reduce Mil, and everyone in it, to ashes."

When Dirk didn't reply, he turned to look out over the blood-red sea.

"You should go below and get some rest. And get rid of that girl for the night. I don't want you running us aground tomorrow when we enter the delta because you're too tired to concentrate on the route."

Dirk smiled ruefully. "I'll send Caterina to *your* cabin then, shall I? She'd probably get a bigger thrill out of being your prisoner than mine, anyway."

"What are you talking about?"

"She's become quite enchanted with the whole hostage thing," Dirk explained, turning his back on the horizon and crossing his arms, as if he were suddenly chilled. "And I think she's more than a little disappointed I'm not living up to my reputation as the Butcher of Elcast. Caterina has four sisters at home who are—she assures me—going to be green with envy she got to have such a grand adventure and they missed out. But I'm afraid that other than helping the cook cut up a few onions, her adventure's not turning out to be quite as thrilling as she'd hoped." He shook his head with despair. "She's driving me insane, actually."

Dirk's obvious discomfort gave Kirsh a degree of malicious satisfaction. "You brought her on board, Dirk. Don't look to me for sympathy."

"I don't expect sympathy from you, Kirsh," Dirk said, looking at him with those inscrutable metal-gray eyes. "What I look to you for is that sense of nobility you like to think you're so famous for."

"What's that supposed to mean?"

"The Baenlands, Kirsh. Tomorrow, when we reach Mil, before you order scores of innocent women and children put to the sword just because you're pissed off about your brother being kidnapped, remember *you're* the one who likes to think he has honor."

Dirk didn't wait for his reply. He pushed off the rail and headed back toward the stern, leaving Kirsh staring after him, wondering how, with a few well-chosen words and not a drop of blood spilled yet, Dirk Provin could make *him* feel like the butcher.

Chapter 23

The *Makuan* had already left Mil the day before, but the *Orlando* was still taking on evacuees when the word came from the lookouts in the Straits that the Lion of Senet's fleet was heaved to at the entrance to the delta. The news hit Eryk with almost physical pain. There was no doubt in anyone's mind any longer: Dirk Provin had betrayed them and was leading their enemies into the Baenlands.

There were several hurried meetings when the news arrived, then Dal Falstov climbed onto the foredeck to address the people crowded onto the *Orlando*'s deck. He explained to them there was no chance of slipping past the Senetian ships now, and they would all have to disembark and head for the caves surrounding Mil, where he hoped they could hide until the attack was over. It had taken nearly all day to load the passengers. It took the best part of the night to disembark them.

Exhausted and close to collapse, Eryk sought his bunk in the single-men's bunkhouse just on second sunrise. He hoped to get a few hours' sleep before the attack began, but he had to suffer the accusing stares of the other sailors, who sat around the bunks in small groups, talking quietly among themselves, as he made his way to his bed. Eryk lay down with his face to the wall and tried not to listen to the conversations going on around him. It was impossible. Every third word he heard seemed to be "Dirk Provin," and most of the words in between were curses.

"Provin's not so smart," one of the sailors scoffed, loud enough (perhaps deliberately) for Eryk to hear. "It's not much of a surprise attack when you heave to under the very noses of our lookouts."

"Aye," another man agreed. "If he was half as smart as he thinks he is, he'd have sailed straight through the delta, instead of giving us a whole night's warning they were coming."

"You gonna stay and fight?" a third sailor asked.

"Maybe," the first man replied. "Cap'n Falstov seems to think we'd be better off fleeing to the caves, but I don't like the idea of running away. Bring 'em on, I say!"

"Well, I'm going to the caves," the second man announced. "My sister and her two little girls will be hiding up there and, with my brother-in-law on the *Makuan,* I ain't leaving 'em to be butchered by the Senetians."

The first man chuckled. "I kinda like the idea of the Senetians coming all this way and finding nothing to kill."

"I tell you one thing, though," the third man said. "If I see that Provin prick anywhere about and can get a clean shot at him, I'll take it. Even if it means dying afterward . . ."

Eryk covered his ears with his hands and tried helplessly to shut out the sailors' voices. Sleep was a long time coming.

The attack, when it finally came, happened close to midday. The Senetian ships had negotiated the delta flawlessly, but they'd been very careful as they made their way upriver, which had given the Baenlanders more than enough time to flee the settlement. There were less than a hundred men left when the *Tsarina* heaved to in the bay, and every one of them was a volunteer, their mission simply to harass the Senetians long enough to give the last of the villagers time to make it to the caves.

Eryk had volunteered along with most of the crew of the *Orlando.* If Dirk was truly part of the invasion fleet, he had a much better chance of finding him if he stayed near the water, rather than hiding up in the caves above the settlement. From his place of concealment behind a cluster of rocks near the beach, he watched the Senetian crews hauling down the sails, trying to spot Dirk, but he could not see him anywhere. Eryk's heart thumped loudly in his chest as he watched the other ships sail into the bay behind the *Tsarina*. He had never been in a battle before.

While they were still lowering the longboats, archers on the deck of the *Tsarina* fired burning arrows into the furled sails of the *Orlando*. There was nobody on board, but the sight of their ship in flames infuriated the sailors around Eryk. They were surprisingly well disciplined, however. They had orders not to attack until the Senetians made landfall, and no man broke ranks, despite the unhappy muttering that ran through them. As the first wave of soldiers reached the beach, more ships appeared through the delta. There seemed to be no end to them. Eryk watched them fill the small bay with a growing sense of dread.

Eryk wasn't sure who gave the order to attack, but it seemed that one moment they were hiding behind the rocks, the next moment the Baenlanders were running down the beach, screaming at the top of their lungs, charging the invaders. Fear of what would happen if he were left behind—as much as a desire to join the fight—spurred Eryk into following them. Arrows whistled overhead as the pirates' hidden archers picked off individual targets, but they were only moderately successful. The Senetians carried shields and used them to protect each other, so most of the arrows finished up harmlessly embedded in the black sand as they bounced off metal shields.

Despite the fact that he was brandishing a sword and yelling like a berserker, Eryk was largely ignored by the soldiers of both sides. He must have appeared too insignificant to bother with. Several Senetians pushed him out of the way in their haste to engage a more worthy foe. Infuriated, Eryk turned on the next man who brushed him aside, but he could not bring himself to strike the man's exposed back as he dueled with a Baenlander. A few moments of vicious sparring and the pirate ran the Senetian through. Still clutching his unblooded sword, Eryk stared at the man as he fell.

"Thanks for nothing, half-wit!" the Baenlander snarled as he pushed Eryk out of the way on his quest to seek out another opponent.

Eryk stumbled and fell onto the sand. He picked himself up and looked around, lost, frightened and alone in a sea of destruction and death. Smoke from the burning *Orlando* drifted over the beach. His eyes watered. The war cries, the yelling, the clash of metal on metal, the death and the overwhelming smell of blood smothered his senses until he was almost paralyzed by it.

Although Eryk didn't really notice, for a time the Baenlanders seemed to prevail. Their unexpectedly bloody response to the first wave of Senetians had driven the enemy back almost to the waterline. But the enemy was too numerous for their minor victory to be anything but a temporary respite.

Eryk jumped with fright when he heard Captain Falstov shouting to the sailors to regroup. The next wave of invaders was almost at the beach, and the Baenlanders were beginning to tire. Another flight of arrows darkened the sky overhead as Eryk turned to watch the boats nearing the shore. Somebody shoved him from behind, and he stumbled to the black sand once more, his eyes fixed on the second sortie. These were not Senetians. They wore the royal blue-and-silver livery of Dhevyn and, standing in the prow of the lead boat, was a figure Eryk knew very well.

"Prince *Kirsh*?" he cried, not realizing he spoke aloud.

Kirshov stood proud and tall, as if impervious to the arrows of the Baenlanders skittering off the shields of the Guardsmen. Then the longboats reached the beach and the Queen's Guard, with Kirsh in the lead, splashed through the shallows to join the fray.

Eryk barely noticed the battle intensify around him. Prince Kirsh was here, the man who had helped Dirk save him from the butcher's son on Elcast. Kirsh had always been good to Eryk, he recalled. He had always treated him like a sort of lovable stray puppy—not too bright, but not to be treated unkindly. Warm memories of Avacas, most of them filtered through the veil of Eryk's fear and loneliness, endowed Kirshov Latanya with an aura of shining hope. Here was someone who could help him. Here was someone he trusted, Lord Dirk's best friend.

He stumbled forward, tripping over a body he discovered was Grigor Orneo, the first mate of the *Orlando*. The mate's belly was slashed open, his guts spilling out on the black sand like a fresh string of sausages. Blinded by the smoke, and by tears of terror and desperation, Eryk moved through the battle, jostled aside by the combatants, pushed and shoved as he made his way toward the only familiar face in the crowd.

"Prince Kirsh!"

Kirshov was in the thick of the fighting near the shore, and was battling his way forward, cutting through his foes with devastating effectiveness. The Guardsmen beside him were no less efficient as they cut a swathe through what was left of the Baenlander resistance.

"Prince Kirsh!" Eryk yelled. He tripped again and hauled himself up, his mission to reach Kirsh the only thing he cared about.

Hearing his name called, Kirsh looked around, but did not notice Eryk in the melee. The prince turned his attention back to another sailor from the *Orlando,* deflecting the man's blow almost instinctively before slashing him across his bare chest on the return swing.

"Prince Kirsh!" Eryk sobbed, thinking he would never reach him. Kirshov Latanya had become a beacon of hope for Eryk, the only thing he was certain of in a world suddenly gone mad. In his mind, Kirsh was his salvation; his only chance of deliverance from this nightmare.

"Prince Kirsh!" he cried desperately, as another Baenlander fell. The body landed on top of him, hurling him to the ground. The dead man's staring eyes looked out from a shocked and lifeless face. It belonged to Holen Baker, the boy who always won at stingball.

"Eryk?"

He looked up to find Kirshov Latanya, blood splattered and panting heavily, standing over him.

"Goddess, boy! What are you doing here?"

Eryk burst into tears. Kirsh dragged Holen Baker's body off him and pulled Eryk to his feet.

"Can I thurrender now, Printh Kirsh? *Pleath*..." he begged.

"I think you'd better, Eryk," Kirsh agreed with a hint of a smile. "Are you hurt?"

"I don't think so."

Kirsh glanced back toward the longboats. "Go and wait for me by the boats."

Eryk nodded willingly and moved to obey, but he found his way blocked. While Kirsh had been talking to him, a few of the remaining Baenlanders had been able to work their way between Kirsh and his Dhevynian Guardsmen.

Eryk's fleeting moment of relief withered as he looked around. More than a dozen Baenlanders surrounded them, with only one thing on their minds: the murder of Kirshov Latanya and anybody foolish enough to be standing by his side.

Chapter 24

Kirsh realized the danger even sooner than Eryk. He glanced back over his shoulder, but in his surprise at finding Eryk in the midst of this carnage, he had lost touch with the rest of his men.

It was a stupid and fatal mistake.

The Baenlanders hesitated once they had him surrounded, perhaps a little stunned by the importance of their quarry. Behind him, Alexin and the rest of the Guardsmen were busy with their own battles, and the rest of the Senetians were fighting with Sergey farther along the beach. There was another wave of longboats heading for the shore, but they had orders to make for the village, and were headed away from where Kirsh stood, trapped and surrounded.

It took him only a few seconds to take all of this in. He turned and faced the pirates defiantly.

"Who's going to try to take me on first, then?" he yelled, brandishing his sword. It was a gamble, but Kirsh knew there was no way he would survive a concerted attack. His only chance lay in challenging these men to single combat. He could take them one at a time. Of that, he was certain.

"Think we're idiots, do you, Latanya?" one of the men replied. He was a small man in his midforties, but much better dressed than Kirsh expected of a pirate. "There's no chance for honor here, your highness. Still, we're not unreasonable men. You've got about five seconds to say a prayer to your imaginary Goddess before we send you to meet her. Actually, we'll be sending you off to find out she doesn't exist, now that I think about it. There's a happy thought."

"Cap'n Falstov..." Eryk begged, wiping away his tears as he stepped forward. "Please don't hurt him..."

The pirate looked at Eryk for a moment and shook his head. "You're as bad as that treacherous bastard who brought you here," he spat. "You've chosen who you stand with, boy. Now you can die with your Senetian friend."

"Leave the boy out of this," Kirsh warned.

"If he's big enough to hold a sword, he's big enough to wield it," the pirate replied, "Take 'em, lads. And don't leave any pieces bigger than my fist."

They charged all at once. Kirsh's only defense was to swing his sword in a wide arc, hoping his swiftly moving blade would be enough to discourage them from coming any closer. Eryk hampered his ability to move, waving his sword around wildly. But his unpredictability made him dangerous and the sailors gave him a wide berth. Kirsh beat back one attacker only to find him replaced by another, then another. He stepped back and crashed into Eryk, both of them tumbling to the ground. As he fell, he noticed the Queen's Guard were closer. He cried out, hoping to catch their attention.

Alexin looked up at the cry, took in the situation with a glance...and hesitated.

It was the last thing Kirsh saw before the pirates closed in on him. He stabbed at them wildly, but there were too many of them and Eryk lay beneath him squirming and screaming.

He saw the blade that would end his life coming for him as

if the world had suddenly slowed down. Every little detail burned into his brain: the blood-splattered sword, the rotten-toothed grin of the man who wielded it, the hate-filled faces looming over him, even the position of the second sun, which burned bright and uncaring in a sky almost too blue to be real...

And then the man collapsed on top of him with a dagger protruding from his throat, and the screams of bloodthirsty triumph turned to screams of despair, as Alexin and the Guardsmen cut their way through to him and Kirsh realized he wasn't going to die today after all.

Eventually, they wore down the pirates by the sheer weight of numbers. As each ship in Kirsh's fleet disgorged its fighting men, the pirates were beaten back a little more. The battle was all over within an hour. Corpses littered the beach. Those left living were stripped of their weapons and placed under guard near the remains of the burning village.

"There's barely a woman or child among them," Sergey pointed out, as Kirsh inspected the prisoners. "The village was empty."

"Where have they gone?"

Sergey shrugged. "More to the point would be *when,* your highness. If they left before we reached the Bandera Straits, they could be anywhere on Ranadon by now."

"You agree with Dirk, then?" Kirsh asked with a scowl. "You think they were tipped off by someone in Senet?"

"It wouldn't be the first time we've had to weed out Dhevynian sympathizers in Senet, your highness. A vocal minority at home believe Senet shouldn't involve itself in the affairs of other nations. The rebels often find fertile ground for their propaganda among them."

"I want them found, Sergey, and dealt with."

Sergey nodded and then added, a little hesitantly, "There *is* another possibility you may not have considered, your highness."

"What's that?"

"You have fifty-odd Queen's Guardsmen who knew about this. Perhaps one of them betrayed us?"

"Are you speculating on the possibility or accusing someone, Sergey?"

The captain glanced over to where Alexin and his men were guarding the prisoners. "Your guard captain is Reithan Seranov's cousin, your highness. And you know what they say about blood being thicker than water..."

"He's one of Alenor's most trusted captains," Kirshov pointed out, shaking his head. "Besides, I served with him for two years in the guard. I think I'd know if he was a rebel sympathizer." Kirsh did not add there was a time when that's exactly what he had thought. But any lingering suspicions he might have had about the captain's loyalty were banished when Alexin came to his rescue. If he was in league with the Baenlanders, he could have rid Dhevyn of her regent and struck a body blow to Senet, simply by not lifting a finger to aid him.

"Well, you know him better than I, sire."

"But you don't like Alexin, do you, Sergey?"

"I think he's a pompous fool," Sergey agreed pleasantly. "But he's useful in a fight, I'll give him that much." The captain glanced at the prisoners again with a frown. "Who did you want to start with?"

Kirsh studied the sullen, defiant faces of the prisoners. They were hard men, all of them. It was going to be a long and laborious process breaking them one by one. And even then, Kirsh would have no way of establishing the veracity of their information.

"We'll start with Eryk," he announced.

Sergey frowned. "That half-wit who almost got you killed? What useful information would he have?"

"Not much, probably, but what little he knows will be the truth, and he'll tell me willingly. That's worth a dozen confessions of dubious value gained by torture."

Sergey shook his head with a sigh. "You've been spending too much time around Dirk Provin, Kirsh. You're starting to think like him."

"Perhaps you should spend more time with Alexin and

the Queen's Guard, Captain," Kirsh retorted coldly. "You might learn something about the correct way to address your prince."

The captain bowed apologetically. "I beg your pardon, sire. I'll bring the boy to you."

"Not here," Kirsh said. "I don't want him intimidated by the prisoners. Bring him up to the house. And then I want you to search it and report to me when you're done."

Without waiting for Sergey to acknowledge the order, Kirsh walked away and headed for what had once been the home of the notorious heretic Johan Thorn.

Kirsh waited for Eryk, sitting on the wooden steps leading up to the house. A cursory search had proved the house empty, but Kirsh wanted to speak to Eryk before he proceeded any further.

Still looking shaken and confused, Eryk was delivered by a Guardsman to the foot of the stairs. Kirsh dismissed the guard and indicated Eryk should come and sit beside him. The boy complied willingly, taking a seat beside Kirsh on the steps with a weary sigh.

"Well, you've certainly had your share of adventures since I saw you last, haven't you, young Eryk?"

"I didn't mean to," the boy assured him apologetically. "It just all seemed to... you know... just happen."

"Dirk's on board my ship, did you know that?"

Eryk's face lit up. "Is he? Can I see him, Prince Kirsh? Is he all right? They say he did such awful things around here, but if you're still his friend, then he's not a bad person, is he?"

"Dirk's not a bad person," Kirsh promised the poor boy, thinking the lie justifiable. "He's been helping us because Misha was kidnapped."

"Prince Misha looked pretty sick when they brought him on board the *Orlando*," Eryk confirmed. "But Tia looked after him. He looked much better before he left Mil."

"Do you know where he went?"

Eryk shook his head. "Nobody does. One day they were just gone."

"Who is 'they'?"

"Prince Misha, and Tia and Reithan and Mellie. And Master Helgin."

"Helgin? The old physician from Elcast?"

The boy nodded. "I think he was looking after Prince Misha."

It was something of a relief to realize the Baenlanders had sent a physician along to care for his brother. On the other hand, it indicated they had long-term plans for him, which wasn't good at all.

"Where are the rest of the villagers, Eryk?"

"Some of them left on the *Makuan,*" he said with a shrug. "The others...well, I don't really know for certain. Nobody tells me anything, especially not since I tried to kiss Mellie. They all hate me here."

Kirsh smiled, thinking Eryk's world was still defined by his own limited experiences. He had no concept of the broader picture. He judged the Baenlanders not by their rhetoric or the value of their cause, but by the fact that he had obviously gotten in trouble for kissing some girl. "Well, you need fear them no longer, Eryk. I'll have you sent back to the ship, and you can see Dirk again and then when we get back to Avacas, we can decide what to do with you."

"Do you think I could be Dirk's servant again, Prince Kirsh? I used to be really good at that."

"We'll see."

Eryk smiled tentatively and climbed to his feet. "I'm glad you came, Prince Kirsh."

Kirsh couldn't help but smile. "You'd have to be the *only* one in the Baenlands who thinks that, Eryk."

Chapter 25

Taking a chance on the fact that the ordinary sailors on the *Tsarina* would not know of Kirsh's orders to remain on the ship, Dirk ordered a dinghy lowered once the battle was fully under way. He guessed it unlikely he would be missed for a while. As he rowed across the bay, smoke drifted across the water from the burning pirate ship, hanging in silent drifts like a fog. He did not head to the settlement where the fighting was going on, but to the small beach leading up to Neris's cave.

Dirk beached the boat and then scrambled up the goat track to the rocky plateau. Once he had climbed above the smoke, he could see the whole bay below him, and the destruction Kirsh was wreaking on it, laid out before him like a board game.

Neris was waiting for him when he arrived, perched on the precipice above the ledge where he had so often threatened suicide in the past.

"Hello, Neris," Dirk said, shading his eyes against the second sun as he looked up.

"You've really gone and done it this time, haven't you?" Neris remarked. "Impressive entrance, by the way."

"Well, I thought you might appreciate the show."

Neris chuckled insanely, and then suddenly his grin vanished. "I'm no longer the Deathbringer. That title is yours now."

"Come down from there, Neris."

The madman shook his head. "No. I don't think so. I think this time I'm really going to have to jump."

"Don't be crazy..."

Neris laughed. "Crazy? Don't be *crazy*? I'm already *crazy*, Dirk! I'm mad, remember! Mad as a cut cat!"

"Neris! Come down before you hurt yourself."

He shook his head sadly. "People are dying down there, Dirk.

And it's as much my fault as yours. I've hurt so many people in this lifetime. And you're going to hurt many more before you undo the damage I did. Why should you or I be spared the pain? Shouldn't we be allowed to share in what we've done? Isn't that the point of any endeavor? To share the triumph and agony of our victories...and our defeats?" He stopped suddenly and looked off into the distance. "I'm not sure there's a difference anymore..."

"So stop fooling around!" Dirk ordered impatiently. "I need your help."

Neris shook his head. "No, you don't. You're doing just fine without me. Better, probably, because you, at least, have some idea of what you're up against. I was too blinded by love and poppy-dust to realize what I'd unleashed, until it was far too late. It would have been better for everyone if I'd died years ago. I should have taken my own life before Tia was born..."

"They already think you're dead, Neris," he assured him. "Now, you need to get out of here."

"I told Tia I wasn't leaving."

"Is she here?" Dirk had not let himself wonder about that until now. He hoped she was safe. He thought it more than likely she was down on the other side of the bay with her bow, giving Kirsh's soldiers something to remember her by.

"She's gone," Neris told him. "They all leave eventually, you know. In the end, you're alone. Always alone..." He looked down at Dirk with a frown. "Do you think it's high enough up here to kill me, or will it just break a few bones when I jump?"

"I think you'll probably just break a few bones."

"Then you'll need to finish the job for me."

Dirk shook his head determinedly. "Don't even ask."

"You killed Johan when he asked you to. What made him so special?"

Dirk couldn't believe he was having such a conversation. "Who told you that?"

"Nobody *told* me," he declared. "I am the smartest man on Ranadon. I worked it out for myself. And don't try to change the subject. Why won't you kill me if I ask you to? Aren't I good enough for the blade of the Butcher of Elcast? Now that you're the Lord of the Shadows, you're too good for the rest of us? Too high and mighty now, are we, to do an old friend a favor?"

"What is it with you Baenlanders?" Dirk snapped. "Why do I keep getting asked to do things like this? Why didn't you ask Tia to put you out of your misery if you wanted to die so badly?"

"I did ask her." Neris shrugged. "She wouldn't do it. Talk about the young having no respect for their parents..."

"For the Goddess's sake, Neris, come down from there."

Neris shook his head and pointed to the harbor. "You're going to have to get back soon. You'll be missed."

"That's my problem. Now get down here this instant," he ordered, like a parent talking to a particularly intransigent toddler, "or I'll go back and tell them you're up here."

Neris thought about it for a while, looked down at the ledge and then shrugged. "You're right. I'd probably just break a few bones. I'd need something much higher to actually kill myself."

Dirk let out a sigh of relief as Neris turned from the edge and headed down the well-worn path to the lower ledge, where he was standing. While he waited, he turned and looked back at the battle still in progress on the other side of the bay. The *Orlando* was well and truly alight now, and there was some hand-to-hand fighting going on near the beach, but, from what he could see, it was a token resistance force. Most of the people in Mil were gone.

"It's like the end of an era," Neris remarked, as he came to stand beside Dirk to watch Mil reduced to ashes. "It felt a bit like this when the Age of Shadows ended."

"Speaking of the Age of Shadows, you lied to me, you old charlatan. There was nothing useful in that damned cavern. You destroyed it before you sealed the tunnel."

"But the Eye is very pretty, don't you think?" Neris asked cheerfully. "And, you have to admit, it must have been a fairly impressive building in its heyday. I never did figure out what it was for, though. Maybe it was a museum. It might have been a temple, but I'm not convinced it was. I've a feeling any civilization smart enough to work out something as complex as the orbit of a binary star didn't waste a lot of time worshipping gods."

"I spent months up in those ruins. And it was all for nothing."

"No, it wasn't," Neris disagreed. "You got to see northern Senet."

"There's a lifelong ambition fulfilled."

"Don't be such a child! I gave you the key to untold wealth by sending you to Omaxin."

"Untold wealth? Is that what you call it?"

"Don't be so dense!" Neris scolded. "Didn't you see that place? Didn't you have your eyes open at all? Omaxin was built by our ancestors, Dirk. They were like gods compared to us. But what happened to them? What happened to the wondrous world they created? Find that out, and you'll truly bring enlightenment to Ranadon. That's the real challenge, my boy."

Dirk scowled at him, but didn't reply.

"Anyway, if nothing else, you got to sleep with my daughter, didn't you?" he added with a sly grin.

"Did Tia tell you that?"

"She didn't have to. Of course, it was only a matter of time, I suppose. She's always had a thing for you. Probably because you look so much like Johan. Although you have your mother's eyes . . ."

"Can we talk about something else?"

Neris frowned at him. "No, we can't. I'm having a rare paternal moment here and I'm not going to be denied. What you did was very cruel, Dirk—"

"Just mind your own business, you old fool."

"You knew you'd have to betray her eventually."

Dirk shook his head, knowing his actions were probably indefensible but somehow still needing to find a way to defend them. "I didn't plan on it happening, Neris. And if I could do it over again, I'd go to Omaxin alone. Or take someone else. And if I ever get the chance, I'll apologize to her."

Neris suddenly giggled. "That's unlikely. She's going to kill you the next time she sees you."

"I know," he sighed.

With one of his lightning mood changes, the problem suddenly no longer seemed to bother him. "Well, that's a challenge for another day. Tia said you told them about the eclipse. You don't believe in doing things by halves, do you, boy?"

"This is worse," he replied, waving his arm to encompass the destruction of Mil as he stood by and did nothing to prevent it.

Neris placed a comforting hand on his shoulder. "You might not be as smart as me, lad, but I wish I had even a fraction of your balls. I'd have had the courage to kill myself as soon as Belagren got that gleam in her eye when she realized what she could do with the information about the return of the second sun, if I did."

"Having a gift for sophistry doesn't make me a hero, Neris."

"No, but being willing to act on it does. It's a pity nobody but you or I will ever know the truth." They stood together in silence for a time, watching the battle below. "Tell Tia, someday, if you ever get the chance."

Dirk smiled ruefully. "I doubt that will ever happen."

"It might. If you succeed."

"If I succeed, she'll hate me even more than she does now, for not taking her into my confidence. She won't be too thrilled with you, either, I suspect."

Neris didn't answer, apparently absorbed in the battle below. Dirk glanced at the madman for a moment, wondering what he was thinking.

"You know, I told Belagren that her followers were pathetic. I wonder what I'll think of them if they follow me."

"They'll still be pathetic," Neris predicted. "Most people are. It's why we have gods and goddesses. The human race is so insecure and afraid, we must invent a protector or cower in the shadows, hiding from a universe full of things bigger, uglier and more powerful than we are. People want a parent figure to alleviate their pain, Dirk. To make their crops grow, to shield them from the realities of life. If we can't find a real god, then we have to make one up. Do you think that makes us a higher species or a lesser one? Every other species seems to cope just fine without the need to imagine there's a divine being out there somewhere masterminding the whole show."

"You really are a cynic, aren't you?"

"The greatest of them all," Neris agreed. "It's one of the little-known side effects of faking insanity."

"I wish there were another way."

"They've all been tried, Dirk, and they've all failed. Spectacularly."

"But this . . . I'm really no better than Belagren."

"It's not about who's better or worse, or even who's good or evil. It's about the road we take. One path leads to barbarism, the other leads to enlightenment."

"Are you sure what I'm doing will lead to enlightenment?"

"No. But I *am* sure of where the other path leads."

Down below, Dirk spied another boat rowing across the bay. The longboat was crewed by half a dozen sailors, and had several armed men on board. Dirk turned to look at Neris. "They're coming for me."

"And me."

"We probably won't meet again after this."

"Probably not," Neris agreed.

They were silent for a while.

Suddenly, Neris smiled. "Shall we go down to meet them?"

"Are you sure, Neris?"

The madman nodded. "It's time."

With a nod of understanding, Dirk led the way to the narrow beach and waited with Neris by his side as the longboat drew nearer. Even before the boat reached the shore, the soldiers jumped out and splashed through the shallows toward them with swords drawn. Neris's eyes were alight with anticipation, which Dirk was fairly certain was genuine, not inspired by poppy-dust.

The madman turned to Dirk again with a broad grin.

"Don't let me down, Dirk," he said.

And then he charged at the soldiers with a blood-curdling yell.

The first sword thrust took him in the chest. Dirk didn't see the rest of it. He turned his head away, unable to watch the soldiers cutting Neris Veran down.

The Senetians were efficient and made little fuss as they brushed Neris out of their way with a few sword strokes. Then strong hands latched on to Dirk's arms and he was forcibly marched down toward the boat.

"You weren't supposed to leave the ship, my lord," one of the men reminded him gruffly. Dirk glanced down at the body as they pushed him past it. Neris was covered in blood, but his eyes were closed and his face was not pain-stricken. It was serene.

"Who was that?" the other guard asked as he stepped over the body.

"Just a stray villager," Dirk told him tonelessly. "I saw him over here and thought there might be more of them."

"Noble sentiments, my lord, but Prince Kirshov's orders were very specific."

"I know," Dirk said, shaking free of his captors once they reached the longboat. "I'll go back quietly. There's no need to treat me like a runaway debtor slave."

The sergeant waved the others back as Dirk climbed into the longboat. The two guards who had restrained him ran the boat out into the water and then clambered aboard. As they drew away from the beach, Dirk turned back again to look at Neris's body lying on the black sand as the smoke drifted over the water.

The madman had finally found the courage he'd been searching for. For the first time in decades, Neris Veran was at peace.

Chapter 26

Dirk was not taken back to the *Tsarina,* but across the bay to what was left of the village of Mil. The soldiers climbed out of the boat when it hit the sand and beckoned Dirk to follow. The beach was littered with bodies, most of them Baenlanders. There were a few familiar faces among the dead, but he was given no chance to stop and examine them. The soldiers escorted him across the beach and onto the steep path leading up to Johan's stilted house that looked out over the bay.

Kirsh was waiting for him in Johan's study, sitting behind the desk going through a pile of papers. He glanced up when Dirk entered. He was splattered with blood, but none of it seemed to be his.

"You disobeyed my orders."

"I was bored," Dirk shrugged, looking around the room. It was untouched by the battle. "Did you find Misha?"

"The best we've been able to extract out of anybody is that he was here and then he wasn't. Nobody seems to know where he is now." Kirsh looked up at him with a frown. "There's no sign of your girlfriend, either."

"You mean Tia? That's not likely to be a coincidence."

"Where would she have taken him?"

"I have no idea," Dirk answered honestly.

"One of the prisoners mentioned something about caves."

"The caves above the settlement?" He shrugged. "You could check them, I suppose, but it's unlikely. I've been through those caves. There's barely enough room in them to hide a couple of children and a milk goat. And they're far too accessible from the settlement to be safe, not to mention dangerously unstable."

"I think I'll have them checked, anyway."

"If you think you can spare the time," Dirk agreed.

"I've got plenty of time, Dirk."

"Have you?" Dirk wandered over to the open doors leading out onto the veranda. Mil was a smoking ruin below him. His nonchalant tone was at complete odds with his inner turmoil. Even the longhouse was nothing more than a charred shell. Dirk felt physically ill. "If Tia Veran managed to slip out of the Baenlands with Misha," he added, "you've got very little time to find them before she goes to ground again."

Kirsh was not so easily put off the idea of searching the caves. "But I don't know she *has* slipped out of the Baenlands with Misha."

"Of course she has," he scoffed. "Look around you, Kirsh. Those bodies on the beach don't belong to the villagers. They're mostly sailors from the *Orlando*. Tia Veran, your brother and most of the population of Mil are long gone. I warned you they'd probably been tipped off. You'd be far more gainfully employed finding out who did that, than wasting time here on a lost cause, giving the pirates—incidentally—all the time in the world to stash Misha somewhere you'll never find him."

Dirk sounded so reasonable that Kirsh had little choice but to agree. While he was determined to raze Mil, he was even more determined to find Misha. The thought that he might lose his brother completely if he lingered too long here in the Baenlands was an easy fear to encourage.

But it was time to change the subject. Dirk had been responsible for enough death for one day. He didn't want Kirsh dwelling on the idea of searching the caves. "What have you got there?" he asked, indicating the papers Kirsh had been examining when he walked in.

"These are Johan Thorn's journals."

"They would make some interesting reading," Dirk remarked.

"They are the ravings of a heretic," Kirsh replied. "I'm going to burn them along with the rest of this place."

"They're an important historical record, Kirsh," Dirk told him, aghast at the idea. "You can't just destroy them out of hand."

"Care to wager on that?"

A knock at the door prevented Dirk from being able to argue his case. Alexin Seranov and the captain of Kirsh's Senetian Guard came in. Between them, they held two prisoners, both of them women. One of them was Finidice, the old servant who had tended Johan and his family since they had fled to Mil. The other woman, Dirk realized with a sinking heart, was Lexie Thorn.

"We found these two hiding in the pantry," Sergey announced, shoving Finidice forward. The old woman turned and hissed at them. She was unable to say anything more. Belagren had cut out her tongue during the Age of Shadows.

Kirsh studied the women for a moment and then looked at Dirk. "Who are they?"

"The old woman is called Finidice," Dirk told him in a disinterested voice. "She was the cook here. The other woman is... Alexandra...somebody or other. I never did learn her full name. She was a seamstress, I think. I saw her around the village now and then while I was here. Neither of them is important."

Lexie met his eye, but she was too smart to let her surprise show. He hoped she understood what he was trying to do and that, under these awkward circumstances, it was all he *could* do for her.

Kirsh stared at the women for a moment and then shrugged. "Kill them, Sergey."

"I've got a better idea," Dirk suggested, before Sergey could act on the order.

Kirsh looked at him in surprise. "What better idea? I've got enough prisoners to find out what I need to know without these two, and you just said they weren't important."

"Have Alexin do it."

Sergey appeared disappointed. Lexie was stunned. Finidice hissed at him. Alexin Seranov stared at him with eyes burning with fury and hatred. Even if he hadn't been secretly allied with the Baenlanders, Lexie was his aunt, and what Dirk was asking of him was unconscionable.

"Why?" Kirsh asked.

"Because the whole purpose of bringing the Queen's Guard

on this little excursion was to make it patently clear to the world they are allied with you, and through your regency, with Senet. You let Sergey do all the killing in Tolace. Right now, all the blood is on Senetian hands. Share it around a bit, Kirsh. Have the Queen's Guard put a few innocent women and children to the sword. Then they'll be feared as much as your father's soldiers, and they won't be able to take the high moral ground the next time you order them to do something they find unpalatable."

Kirsh stared at Dirk, obviously surprised at his harsh and uncompromising reasoning.

"You have a point," he conceded after a moment of heavy silence, then turned to Alexin and nodded. "Do it."

Alexin threw Dirk a look that promised savage vengeance for forcing him into such a dreadful corner. He drew his sword reluctantly.

"Not here!" Dirk snapped. "For the Goddess's sake, Captain, we don't need to watch. Take them outside, at least. His highness wants you to kill them, and while I'm sure he appreciates the sentiment, there's no need to prove your loyalty quite so enthusiastically by doing it here. We don't need to suffer through the pitiful death throes of a couple of serving women."

At last, comprehension dawned on Alexin. "I'm sorry, my lord," he muttered, and then he pointed the sword at Lexie, who also had the presence of mind to understand that Dirk was desperately trying to save them. "Out!"

Sergey stood back to let them pass. "Need a hand?"

"I can take care of a couple of serving women without any Senetian help," Alexin told him coldly.

The Senetian smiled and said nothing further. As soon as Alexin and the women had left, he turned to Kirsh. "Did you want me to follow him and make sure he does it, your highness?"

Kirsh shook his head. "That man just saved my life, Captain."

"It doesn't automatically follow he'll kill in cold blood for you, sire."

As if in answer to Sergey's doubts, a scream echoed through the house, and was abruptly cut off.

Kirsh glanced at Sergey and shrugged. "Does that answer your question, Sergey?"

"He really did it," the captain laughed. "I'm astonished."

"Well, when you're finished being astonished, Captain," Dirk remarked frostily, "do you think you could arrange to have some men sent in here to pack up these papers?"

Kirsh glared at him. "I told you, Dirk. I'm burning them."

"I can't let you do that, Kirsh," Dirk told him. "These aren't just the ravings of a heretic. They are the personal journals of the man who very nearly brought the Church of the Suns down. How he did it cannot be destroyed just because you're feeling a little miffed. As Lord of the Shadows, and the right hand of the High Priestess, I am claiming these records on behalf of the Church."

Kirsh glanced at Sergey uncertainly. "Can he do that?"

"I'm no expert on Church law, your highness, but I suspect he can."

Kirsh turned his attention back to Dirk. "Are you sure that's the only reason you want them?"

"What other reason would there be, Kirsh?"

"Take the damn journals, then," he snapped impatiently, rising to his feet. "I've got more important things to worry about. Sergey! Get some men in here to pack these up and then burn this damned house to the ground."

"I'll do it," Dirk offered.

Kirsh didn't seem to care. "Whatever, Dirk. Just see that it's done."

Sometime later, Dirk took a last walk through Johan's house as the soldiers packed up the dead king's papers, ready for removal to the *Tsarina*. The house reeked of oil. It had been splashed around quite liberally to accelerate the flames once Johan's journals had been removed. Memories Dirk didn't feel strong enough to deal with crowded his mind, demanding his attention. He forced them away. He couldn't afford the luxury of nostalgia.

The last room he checked was Tia's bedroom. There was little of her presence left. Most of her possessions were gone. Dirk wondered where she had taken Misha, thinking she must have found a safe haven in Dhevyn somewhere.

Then Dirk noticed a dagger embedded in the wall near the bed. He walked across to examine it, his stomach lurching when he discovered why. Pinned to the wall was the silver bow and arrow necklace he'd given Tia in Bollow. The blade had been driven right through the silver wire, almost cutting it in half. Dirk reached up to pull the dagger free. It took him a little time to work the blade out of the wall. The anger and the pain behind the thrust that had driven the knife into the wood must have been considerable, and he did not doubt for a moment that it was all directed at him.

He slipped the dagger into the side of his boot and stared at the delicate silver chain for a moment, wondering if it had been a random act of fury on Tia's part or if she had left it here as a message to him.

"Dirk."

He jumped with fright, and spun around to find Lexie and Finidice emerging from the wardrobe where they'd been hiding.

"Get out of here!" he hissed. "We're about to torch the place!"

Lexie nodded. "I know. As soon as the flames take hold, we'll slip down the back stairs. Thank you for what you did."

"It was little enough in light of what else I've done recently," he said, glancing nervously down the hall. If they were discovered with him now, it wouldn't just be Alexin who'd be facing Kirsh's wrath.

"Our people in the caves?" Lexie asked, uncertainly.

"Are safe for now. I think I've talked Kirsh out of searching them."

"And it was you who stopped the fleet in the Straits, too, I'll wager, to give us time to get them clear?"

"I'm just trying to survive, Lexie..."

"I think you've a much grander plan in mind than that, Dirk." She smiled at him and then crossed the room and kissed his cheek. "I've no idea what it is, but I wish you well."

Dirk couldn't meet her eye. "Lexie..."

"It's all right," she assured him. "You don't need to explain. Did you want me to give Tia a message for you?"

"Tell her...tell her you didn't see me, Lexie."

"Are you sure?" she asked, searching his face.

"Yes."

She nodded and stepped back. "Good luck, Dirk."

Footsteps sounded along the hall. Dirk hurriedly pushed Lexie back out of sight and walked to the door.

"We're ready, my lord," one of Sergey's soldiers informed him. "The papers have all been taken down to the beach."

"Then let's burn this place," Dirk ordered. The soldier saluted and headed back toward the front of the house.

Dirk glanced back at Tia's room. Lexie was helping old Finidice climb through the window onto the veranda. She turned and smiled wanly at Dirk as she lifted her skirts to climb through after her faithful maid.

"I think Johan would be proud of you, Dirk," she said, and then she was gone.

Filled with unease, Dirk hurried back through the house to Johan's study, snatched the torch from the trooper who was preparing to set the house alight and ordered everyone out of the building. Then he walked back through the house methodically and deliberately setting fire to each room.

He came to Tia's room last, and hesitated for a moment before he tossed the torch onto the oil-soaked bed. Uncaring of the flames searing his face and scorching his clothes, Dirk walked back though the burning house and out onto the veranda. The smoke made his eyes water—at least he told himself it was the smoke. When he emerged, he glanced back at the hill behind the house and noticed two figures scrambling up the slope to safety.

As the flames intensified behind him, Dirk walked down the steps to the path and headed back to the beach without looking back.

PART TWO

LORD
OF THE
SHADOWS,
LORD
OF THE
SUNS

Chapter 27

Prince Oscon of Damita lived in Garwenfield, a tiny hamlet some four hundred miles north of Tanchen, the capital of Damita, where his son now governed the country Oscon had once ruled absolutely. Garwenfield had been in the Damitian royal family for generations, kept as a retreat for those seeking solitude and an escape from the pressures of court life. It was inaccessible by road, its small lagoon protected by a wide reef.

Since the Age of Shadows, the name Garwenfield no longer conjured up images of pristine white beaches, of tall palms curved by the weight of their foliage waving gently in the warm breeze, of long, languid days and peaceful tropical nights. The name Garwenfield had become synonymous with disgrace and defeat.

To Tia, raised on the black sands of Mil, in the shadow of a volcano, it seemed unnatural, like a painting done by an artist who had drawn a place imagined, rather than seen. Tall palms shaded the path to the house, which was a sprawling, thatched building not far from the beach. The few other scattered houses she could see through the trees, Tia guessed, must belong to the staff who cared for the aging prince.

Tia and Mellie helped Reithan secure the *Wanderer,* and then waded ashore. There was a thin, pockmarked man waiting for them on the beach, staring at them suspiciously, as they approached.

"This is a private estate," the man informed them, his hand on his hips. "We do not welcome visitors here."

"I'm Reithan Seranov."

Apparently, Reithan's name was enough to gain them entry. The pockmarked man studied him for a moment and then nodded and looked at the two girls.

"Who are they?"

"This is Tia and Mellie."

"And the men on the boat?"

"I'd rather speak to Prince Oscon about them."

"He doesn't like to be disturbed," the man warned.

"I think he'll make an exception for us," Reithan predicted.

The man shrugged. "Be it on your own head then. I'm Franco, the caretaker. Follow me."

With Franco in the lead, they walked along the sandy path toward the main house. It was a large building with a deep veranda surrounding it, similar in construction to Johan's house in Mil, although it wasn't stilted and the walls were constructed of stone rather than wood. Tia looked around curiously as they entered the cool dimness of the main hall. The house was quite untidy, cluttered with books and scrolls and artifacts from all over Ranadon. It must have taken Oscon a lifetime to collect them all. Franco disappeared into another part of the house, returning a few minutes later with a large, white-haired man with a thin beard and a thunderous look on his face.

"Which one of you is Seranov?" he demanded as he blustered into the room. He squinted at the three of them shortsightedly, then fixed his eyes on Reithan. "Well, as you're the only fellow, I suppose it must be you."

Reithan bowed to the prince. "That's a reasonable assumption, your highness."

"Bah! Don't call me that! We don't waste breath on titles around here. I suppose it's too much to hope Lexie sent these two lovelies to keep me entertained?"

"Far too much," Reithan agreed. "This is Tia Veran, and this is Lexie's daughter, Melliandra."

"And the two on the boat? Who are they?"

"Misha Latanya and Master Helgin, his physician."

"What do you call this, then?" Oscon scowled. "The next generation of trouble?"

"We need your help, Oscon. Antonov has learned the route through the delta. Mil will be invaded any day now."

"Then I can understand why Lexie sent Mellie here," Oscon said with a frown. "But what are you doing with the Crippled Prince in your company?"

"It seems the Crippled Prince isn't as crippled as everyone

thinks, your...sir," Tia told him. "He's a poppy-dust addict. Ella Geon has been trying to destroy him the same way she destroyed my father."

Oscon turned his attention to Tia and she received a nasty shock. His eyes were steel-gray, the same shade as Dirk's. She had forgotten Oscon of Damita was Dirk's maternal grandfather. She wondered what his reaction would be when he learned what his grandson had been up to.

Oscon's eyes were much easier to read than Dirk's. They blazed with fury at her words. "Then why bring him here? Why don't you *let* her destroy him, foolish girl? That's one less Latanya to deal with."

"We've done a deal with Misha to free Dhevyn once he inherits his father's throne," Reithan explained. "But he's no good to us dead or addicted to poppy-dust. Lexie was hoping you'd shelter him here while he recovers."

"Was she? Well, you're here now," he grumbled, "so you might as well stay. But I don't want to hear you. Or see you. Or have you get in my way. I'm far too busy with my work to be running after you. Franco will see you settled and maybe, if I'm feeling generous, I'll see you at dinner."

And with that, Prince Oscon of Damita stormed out of the room and left them staring after him, a little bemused by his brusque and ungracious welcome.

"The prince is writing a history of Ranadon," Franco explained later as he showed them to their rooms. "He's been working on it for years now. Not that it will ever get published while that worm Baston sits on his father's throne."

"Why not?" Mellie asked curiously.

"Prince Oscon's history differs somewhat from the official line, I imagine," Misha suggested, leaning heavily on his crutch. The walk up the sandy path to the house had exhausted him. He was pale and sweating heavily.

Franco snorted with bitter amusement. "Differs *somewhat*? It's outright treason, what he's writing! But he doesn't care. His study is at the end of the hall on the other side of the house, so if you're quiet, you shouldn't disturb him too much. The girls can share this room. The three of you will have to bunk in together across the hall. Can't do better than that, I'm afraid. This isn't an inn, you know."

"It'll be fine," Reithan assured him. "Anyway, I'm not staying. I have to get back to Mil."

Tia hadn't known that. "You're just going to leave us here?"

"You'll be safe enough." He turned to Franco, without giving her a chance to argue about it. "We've no wish to put you out, Franco, or disturb Oscon if we can help it. Mellie and Tia will be more than happy to help you if you need it, and I'm sure Master Helgin will be able to ease the prince's ailments if he's required."

"Then the first thing they can do is make the beds up," Franco said. "I'll go find some linen and tell the cook she'd better put some more water in the stew to make it go around." He glanced at the old physician and shrugged. "I'm sure you're greatly skilled, Master Helgin, but what ails Oscon of Damita can't be fixed by herbs and poultices. He's lost his country, his crown and both his daughters to the Lion of Senet, and his only son is a treacherous swine who'd sell his own soul for the price of a loaf of bread. Unless you have some magic potion in your bag to fix a broken heart, there is nothing you can do for him."

Tia walked down the beach with Reithan just before first sunrise to see him off. He carried a wicker cage full of plump gray pigeons that Franco had given him. The birds were the only way Lexie or Reithan would be able to get a message to them and let them know when it was safe to leave.

"Don't let Mellie annoy Oscon too much," he instructed as they walked toward the water.

"I won't."

"And keep an eye on Misha. I'm sure he means what he says now, but he might have a change of heart once he starts going through withdrawal."

"I will."

"And try to relax a little."

She glared at him. "Was that a joke? You're abandoning me here with a child, a cripple and an old man, Reithan. How am I supposed to relax?"

"Try anyway, Tia."

"I wish I was going with you."

"Be thankful you're not. I just hope I get back to Mil in time."

"Don't get yourself killed or anything stupid like that, will you?"

He smiled and tossed the cage up onto the *Wanderer*'s deck. "I'll try not to."

Impulsively, Tia hugged him. "Be careful. You're the closest thing I have to a big brother, Reithan. I'll never speak to you again if you die on me."

Reithan kissed the top of her head, and then waded into the warm shallows to push the *Wanderer* out into the deeper water of the lagoon. Tia splashed after him and helped him shove the boat free of the sand. As soon as she felt the water pick up the keel she stepped back. Reithan clambered aboard and began to haul in the anchor. He turned and waved as the *Wanderer* bobbed in the gentle swell, each one taking the small yacht farther from the shore.

She waited until the *Wanderer* was nothing more than a speck on the red horizon before returning to the house.

Tia found Mellie and Misha in the kitchen with Master Helgin when she returned. They were discussing the best way to tackle weaning Misha from the poppy-dust. He was impatient to get started and resented every grain of dust he was forced to consume in the interim.

"I've been thinking about how to do this," the physician told Misha, as he took the seat beside Mellie at the scrubbed wooden table. "It's going to involve a lot of work. For all of us."

"What do you mean?"

"You need to build up your strength, Misha, not just to fight the poppy-dust, but to reduce the pain and weakness you suffer. Once you start on this road, you'll not be able to turn to poppy-dust to relieve your pain again, not ever."

"I understand."

"You understand my words, perhaps. But I'm not sure you appreciate what they mean," Helgin warned.

"What does he have to do?" Mellie asked.

"Exercise is the first thing. Can you swim, Misha?"

"No."

"Then you must learn. You must swim every day. The water will support you and allow you to work your muscles without having to bear weight at the same time. And we must massage your muscles daily, particularly the left side, to improve circulation. It will also aid in ridding your body of the toxins that poison it." Helgin turned to Tia. "I will need your help, Tia. I'm neither competent nor strong enough to teach Misha to swim, and my hands are not what they once were. I will need to show you how to give a massage properly."

Tia nodded. "I can learn that, I suppose."

"We shall maintain your dose of poppy-dust at its current level for another week or so," he added to Misha, "and then we'll begin to taper it in extremely small quantities. After that, it's really just a matter of repeating the procedure. Reduce the dose, let your body adjust to it and then reduce it some more."

"How long will it take, do you think?" Misha asked. "Before I'm free of it?"

"Several months at least," Helgin told him. "And that's assuming you suffer no adverse effects once we reduce the dose. This is not something we can rush."

"I *will* be free of it, Master Helgin."

The old man nodded. "If your head is as strong as your heart, Misha, I've no doubt you will."

Chapter 28

As Avacas nervously awaited news of the Lord of the Suns, Alenor D'Orlon grew more and more desperate to return home to Kalarada.

The atmosphere in the Avacas palace was unbearable. Paige Halyn was perched on the brink of death, Marqel was now the High Priestess of the Shadowdancers, Misha was a prisoner of the Baenlanders, Kirsh and Dirk were leading an invasion force to Mil, and her lover, Alexin, was fighting by their side against the people he was secretly allied with.

The sheer complexity and danger of it all kept her awake at nights, tossing and turning, second-guessing what would happen next. She was exhausted from trying to find a way to predict the future. Exhausted by trying to think of a way she could protect her nation and herself from the inevitable fallout when the whole thing collapsed in on itself, as she was quite certain it would.

The only bright note in the past weeks had been the arrival of a ship from Kalarada. On it were Alenor's cousin, Jacinta D'Orlon, whom Alenor had sent for to replace Lady Dorra as her lady-in-waiting, a contingent of her guard captained by Tael Gordonov, and, quite unexpectedly, her mother.

Alenor threw herself into Rainan's arms when Lord Ezry announced the former queen into Antonov's presence. The Lion of Senet was obviously displeased by her arrival, but there was little he could do about it, now that she was here.

"Your visit to Avacas is an unexpected pleasure, your highness," Antonov remarked, in a tone implying quite the opposite.

Rainan hugged Alenor tightly for a moment and then looked across the room at Antonov. "I am here for my daughter, Anton, and for no other reason. I *should* have been summoned the moment she fell ill."

"Alenor has had the best care available," Antonov informed her, a little put out by Rainan's implied criticism. "Everything she needed has been made available to her."

"She *needed* her mother."

Alenor turned to look at Antonov with a wan smile. "You've been so wonderful to me, your highness. And I can't thank you enough for sending for my mother. It must have been difficult for you to do such a selfless thing."

Alenor was quite certain Antonov had done no such thing. But she knew him well enough to know that he went to great pains to portray himself as a considerate and generous man. If he thought Alenor believed he had sent for her mother, he was unlikely to do anything to disabuse her of the notion, which meant he would not send Rainan straight home, or do anything other than treat the deposed queen as an honored guest.

Antonov hesitated for a moment and then smiled. "I was thinking only of you, my dear."

Alenor smiled at him gratefully and then beckoned her cousin forward. "Your highness, this is the Lady Jacinta D'Orlon, the daughter of my late father's brother, Lord Ivan, and the Lady Sofia. She's to be my lady-in-waiting."

Jacinta curtsied a little nervously. Although she was a member of the extended Dhevynian royal family by marriage, that wasn't quite the same as being introduced to the Lion of Senet.

"I shall have to issue a proclamation ordering the lords in my court to restrain themselves," Antonov said gallantly. "Such beauty should not be allowed to roam the halls of my palace un-protected."

"Stop flattering my lady-in-waiting!" Alenor scolded with a laugh. "You'll turn her head, your highness, and I'll never get any work out of her!"

Antonov smiled at Alenor. "It's good to see you smiling and laughing again, Alenor. If your cousin has achieved that re-markable feat simply by arriving in Avacas, then she is already firmly in my favor."

"She's probably exhausted, too," Alenor declared. "May we be excused, your highness, so I can arrange for my mother and my lady to get settled in?"

"Of course you may. Shall we see you at dinner tonight?"

"I'll see how I feel," Alenor promised. "All this excitement has drained me, I fear, but if I'm feeling up to it, we'll be there."

Alenor curtsied and turned to leave, her mother and her new lady-in-waiting following meekly behind her.

As soon as they were alone in Alenor's room, she turned to Jacinta. "What did you think of the Lion of Senet?"

"I think I was very fortunate to have been raised away from court," she replied with a frown. "Is he always so overpowering?"

"No," Alenor assured her with a smile. "Sometimes, he's worse."

"You should see him when he's angry," Rainan added as she checked the doors to the bedroom and the bathroom to ensure they were alone. "Alenor, what is going on?"

Alenor sank down on to the settee with a sigh. "I hardly know where to begin."

"Let's start with that treacherous little bastard, Dirk Provin."

"Funny," Alenor remarked, a little hurt. "I thought your first question might be how I was feeling, Mother."

"I'm sorry, darling," Rainan said, instantly remorseful. "It was thoughtless of me not to ask. How are you doing? You look very pale."

"I've barely left the palace since...it happened."

"And are you fully recovered?" Jacinta asked with concern, taking the seat opposite.

"I'm not sure if *recovered* is the right word. I'm feeling stronger and the bleeding has finally stopped. But I feel like a part of me is...missing...somehow." She shrugged helplessly. "I don't know how to explain it."

Jacinta leaned forward, took Alenor's hands in hers and gave them a reassuring squeeze. "There'll be other babies for us to spoil rotten."

She nodded, forcing a smile. "I suppose."

"This is obviously upsetting you, Alenor. Perhaps we

should discuss Dirk Provin, after all. It might be a little less harrowing for you."

For once, Alenor agreed with her mother. She discovered she really didn't want to talk about the miscarriage. "I'm not sure what to tell you, Mother. He's joined the Shadowdancers, is now the right hand of the High Priestess—which is another saga—and is called Lord of the Shadows. He's with Kirsh at the moment, invading the Baenlands."

"I'd like to meet this Dirk Provin of yours."

"Are you so anxious to involve yourself in the treachery and politics of Avacas, Jacinta?" Rainan asked with a frown.

"Dirk asked me to trust him, Mother," Alenor said. "I don't believe he's doing this to hurt us."

"And, like a fool, you believe him. Stay away from Dirk Provin, Alenor. He will bring us nothing but trouble."

"What do you mean he asked you to trust him?" Jacinta asked, ignoring the queen's disapproval.

Alenor glanced at her mother and realized that to tell Jacinta anything further, she would have to admit to meeting the Baenlanders in Nova.

"Nothing really..." she said, lowering her eyes.

"Tell us about the Lord of the Suns, then," Jacinta asked, taking the hint. "Is it true he's dying?"

"He's clinging to life rather tenaciously at the moment," Alenor told her. "He took a bolt in the neck from a crossbow meant for Dirk. He was recovering nicely for a while, but the wound became infected, and now Master Daranski is desperately worried about him."

"Paige Halyn dying is not such a bad thing," Rainan remarked, taking a seat next to Alenor. "We might get lucky and find ourselves with a Lord of the Suns who is actually strong enough to control the Shadowdancers."

"Don't hold your breath, Mother. There's a rumor in the palace he's already named his successor, and it's Madalan Tirov."

"Belagren's old partner in crime?" Rainan sighed unhappily. "Things just seem to be going from bad to worse, don't they?"

"And this new High Priestess we've heard of?" Jacinta asked. "What do you know about her?"

"It's Marqel."

Rainan looked her, clearly shocked. "The Shadowdancer that Kirsh..."

"The one and the same."

"How did *that* come about?" Jacinta asked, just as surprised as Rainan.

Alenor looked at her mother closely before answering Jacinta's question. "Do you really want me to tell her, Mother? It involves admitting to a few distasteful truths you've managed to ignore up until now."

Rainan did not answer her.

"Well, *I'd* like to know," Jacinta said. "Unpalatable truths or no."

"Dirk arranged it," Alenor explained to her cousin. "After Misha was kidnapped, he told her the way though the delta to the Baenlands. Armed with that information, Marqel told Antonov she'd had a visit from the Goddess. Much the same as Neris told—"

"Alenor! That's enough!" Rainan gasped. "You could be burned at the stake for even thinking such heresy, let alone voicing it aloud in the palace of the Lion of Senet!"

"Even if it's the truth?"

"*Especially* if it's the truth," Rainan snapped. "Dear Goddess, did I teach you nothing? You can't listen to such things! You certainly can't repeat them!"

"And therein lies the root of all Dhevyn's ills," Alenor said to Jacinta. "We can't speak the truth, we can't even think it. This is the fear that fills our streets with Senetian troops and taxes our economy into oblivion to support them."

"We could use this," Jacinta suggested. "If Dirk Provin is providing the High Priestess with information she is claiming comes from the Goddess, why can't we have him suggest to her the Goddess wants Senet to withdraw from Dhevyn?"

"You'll do no such thing!" Rainan cried in horror.

Alenor ignored her mother's outburst. "To be honest, Jacinta, I don't know Dirk would do it even if I asked it of him.

He's got his own plans, and I wish I could say I knew what he was up to, but I don't."

"He's looking after Dirk Provin," Rainan snapped. "That's what he's up to."

"What are we going to do, then?" Jacinta asked Alenor. Like her cousin, she was not nearly so timid as Rainan about offending Senet.

"I want to go home."

"Will Antonov allow it?"

"He's been very reluctant to even discuss the matter," Alenor said.

Jacinta smiled. "I wonder if he's suffering any guilt over the fact that his new lover once belonged to his son?"

"Jacinta!" Rainan gasped. "You mustn't listen to such dreadful gossip. And you shouldn't be upsetting Alenor with it."

"Kirsh's affair with Marqel is no secret, your highness. And I think you'll find Alenor is not nearly as blind to the truth as you imagine."

"She's right, Mother," Alenor said. "I know about Kirsh and Marqel. As for Antonov taking the High Priestess as his lover, that hasn't happened . . . yet. Marqel was taken back to the Hall of Shadows, and we haven't seen her for weeks. Antonov's getting a little peeved about it, but with everything else going on, I don't think it's the most important thing on his mind right now."

Jacinta smiled. "I don't imagine Marqel's too pleased about being trapped in the Hall of Shadows, High Priestess or not."

"I don't really care, Jacinta," Alenor shrugged.

"Perhaps I should pay my good friend Marqel a visit," Jacinta suggested.

"To what purpose, Jacinta?" Rainan snapped. "You just can't help interfering in things that are no concern of yours, can you? I knew it was a bad idea to let you come to Avacas."

"It was a wonderful idea, Mother," Alenor corrected, with a smile at her cousin. "I feel better already."

Chapter 29

When Dirk returned to his cabin on the *Tsarina*, he received a shock, for sitting on the bunk, talking to Caterina, was Eryk. The boy flew off the bed and threw himself at Dirk the moment he entered the cabin, blubbering and stammering as he tried to explain everything that had happened to him in the last few months, all in the same breath.

Dirk hugged him for a moment, letting Eryk prattle on, and then looked over his head at Caterina.

"One of Prince Kirshov's men delivered him a few hours ago," she explained. "They ordered me to wait here with him until you got back."

That was typical of Kirsh's Senetian Guard. Eryk was an unimportant half-wit. They would think nothing of leaving him in the care of someone who was essentially a prisoner herself. He disentangled Eryk's arms from around his waist and smiled down at the boy.

"All right, Eryk, that's enough," he said gently. "Everything's going to be fine now. You can tell me all about it in a little while. Have you eaten?"

Sniffing loudly, Eryk shook his head.

"Can you fetch him something?" Dirk asked Caterina.

She slipped off the bunk, squeezing past them to the door.

"Fetch something for yourself, too," he suggested. "It might be a while before I get back."

Caterina nodded and let herself out of the cabin.

"You're not going away again, are you, Lord Dirk?" Eryk asked with a panicked edge to his voice.

"I've got a meeting with Kirsh and Captain Clegg, that's all."

"I like Caterina," he said, sniffing again. "She's nice."

"I'm sure she is."

"Is she your girlfriend?"

Dirk smiled. "No."

"She said she's your prisoner. She says you kidnapped her because you were overcome by her beauty."

"She also has a rather vivid imagination, Eryk. The first part is true enough, though. She is my prisoner."

"Are you going to do something terrible to her?"

Dirk looked at him oddly. "Why would you think that?"

Eryk looked away. "Tia said...well, she said some pretty horrible things about you when she got back. I tried to make her take them back, but she wouldn't listen to me..."

"It's all right, Eryk. There is nothing you could have said or done to make her take it back. Tia's got good reason to hate me."

"They said you betrayed everyone in the Baenlands."

"I did, Eryk. I led the Senetians to them."

"But *why?*" he cried.

"Do you trust me, Eryk?"

The boy nodded dumbly, sniffing back a fresh round of tears.

"Then don't ask any more questions. There *is* a reason for this; I just can't explain it to you. I couldn't even explain it to Tia, which is why she's so angry with me. But one day you'll understand. I promise."

"I didn't tell Prince Kirsh anything," Eryk assured him. "He asked me all sorts of questions about where everybody was hiding but I didn't tell him. Did I do the right thing, Lord Dirk, or should I go back and tell him about the caves?"

"You did the right thing, Eryk," Dirk assured him, almost faint with relief. It had never occurred to him Kirsh might think of interrogating Eryk. He was expecting him to line up a few hapless sailors and beat the truth out of them, but Dirk was confident most of the Baenlanders would die, even under torture, rather than betray their people. Eryk, however, was liable to blurt out anything. "Look, I really have to go. Kirsh is waiting for me. Will you be all right here with Caterina until I get back?"

Eryk nodded, wiping his eyes. "Yes."

Dirk turned for the door, and then he looked back at Eryk

curiously. "Do you know where Tia went, Eryk? Where she took Misha?"

The boy shook his head. "One day they were just gone. Even Eleska didn't know where Mellie went."

"Tia took Mellie with her?"

"You don't think Tia would hurt her, do you, Lord Dirk?" Eryk asked, rather alarmed by Dirk's tone.

Dirk smiled and shook his head. "No, Eryk, I think Tia did the smartest thing in the world taking Mellie from Mil. She won't hurt her. She probably saved her life."

"You're late," Kirsh said, looking up from the chart table as Dirk let himself in to Captain Clegg's stateroom.

"Why didn't you tell me you'd found Eryk?"

"You didn't ask," Kirsh replied, turning his attention back to the map.

And that was all Kirsh was going to say on the subject, Dirk realized. But he had sent the boy to Dirk's cabin, not thrown him in with the other prisoners, which was probably Kirsh's way of helping Eryk without actually having to admit doing it.

"Have you decided what our next move is?" Dirk asked, thinking any further attempt to talk about Eryk's future would be wasted.

"We were just discussing it," Captain Clegg informed him. "Did you have any suggestions?"

"Actually, I do," Dirk told him, walking to the table where a map was spread out. "We've got nine ships. When we leave here, we should fan them out. Send one to each of the main Dhevynian islands, but don't waste time searching the cities. Have them sail around the islands. Have them stop in the smaller ports, where they wouldn't normally be seen. The Baenlanders will be in Dhevyn somewhere."

"What about Senet?" Kirsh asked. "If they have sympathizers there, it would be a good place to hide."

"Sympathizing with the Baenlanders is a long way from being willing to risk your life harboring them, or helping to keep the crown prince captive. Besides, you might be able to conceal one or two foreigners, but not scores of them. I wouldn't bother with Damita for the same reason. The only place the Baenlanders can reasonably hope for shelter is Dhevyn."

Clegg nodded his agreement. "Dirk's right, your highness. Besides, your father's ground forces already stationed on the mainland can search Senet far more effectively. The same applies to Prince Baston's forces in Damita. We should concentrate our strength on Dhevyn."

Kirsh thought about it for a moment and nodded. "That's what we'll do, then. The rest of the fleet can begin searching the Dhevynian islands. The *Tsarina* will return to Avacas."

"You'll not be leading the search yourself, your highness?" Clegg asked, a little surprised by the announcement.

Dirk wasn't surprised. The news he had delivered regarding Marqel was eating Kirsh up. The Senetian prince had a gift for turning a blind eye to things he didn't want to know about, but that did not mean he was unaware of them. Kirsh knew his father and Belagren had been lovers, just as he knew much of his father's desire for her was *because* she was the High Priestess, not in spite of it. The chances that Marqel would now be called upon to fill her predecessor's role as the Lion of Senet's consort were extremely high. Kirsh had beaten Dirk savagely for sleeping with Marqel once. The idea that his own father might take Marqel as his mistress was intolerable.

Kirsh wasn't going to stay away from Avacas for one moment longer than he had to now that a quick resolution to this whole affair with Misha seemed unlikely.

"Searching the islands will take weeks, maybe even months," Dirk told Clegg, as Kirsh seemed unable to come up with a plausible excuse. "His highness has other duties he can't afford to neglect for that long."

Kirsh glanced at him with a look caught somewhere between annoyance and gratitude.

"Of course," Clegg agreed. "When did you want to set sail, your highness?"

"As soon as the second sun rises tomorrow," Kirsh ordered.

Clegg gave a short bow in acknowledgment of the order and let himself out of the cabin.

Kirsh straightened up from the chart table and indicated the decanter sitting on the shelf near the porthole. "Join me?"

Dirk nodded and waited in silence as Kirsh poured wine for them both. He accepted the glass from Kirsh and waited for him to say something. Kirsh drank down his first glass in one swallow and then poured himself another drink.

"When he learned about Marqel," Kirsh said finally, "what was my father's reaction?"

"Skepticism," Dirk told him. "He thought she was lying."

"*Is* she lying?"

Dirk shook his head. "The Goddess has spoken to her, Kirsh. Even the Lord of the Suns confirmed it. I think the only thing preventing your father from believing her now is this expedition. Until he's sure we got through the delta, I don't think he'll fully accept her elevation."

Kirsh laughed bitterly and downed his second glass of wine. "Then I've sealed my own fate."

"What do you mean?"

"When we cleared the delta this morning, Dirk, I dispatched a bird to my father, letting him know the instructions we had were accurate. I've just handed her to him on a plate."

"You don't know that for certain, Kirsh. Marqel might refuse him."

Kirsh smiled skeptically. "Nobody refuses my father, Dirk. You, of all people, should know that."

"Perhaps your father won't see her in the same light as he saw Belagren," Dirk suggested, wondering why he didn't just come right out and tell Kirsh to grow up. He should accept the cold hard reality that Marqel was lost to him. "She's much younger than he is."

"It wouldn't be the first time my father has bedded a woman even younger than me."

Dirk thought it interesting Kirsh was laying the entire blame for this at his father's door. He seemed to think Marqel was the innocent party.

You poor, deluded fool, Kirsh. But he didn't say it aloud.

Kirsh wanted to be reassured, not forced to face the truth. "I think you do your father an injustice. Whatever her role is now, Antonov knows how you feel about Marqel and how much she loves you. It would be cruel beyond comprehension for him to expect her to put you aside for him."

"And do you honestly think my father is not capable of doing something cruel beyond comprehension?"

"That's not the point, Kirsh. Your father won't take Marqel against her will. She is the Voice of the Goddess and such a violation would be unthinkable to him. The question you should be asking yourself is whether Marqel is capable of such a thing."

Kirsh frowned, obviously disturbed by the question.

"Marqel loves me," he insisted stubbornly.

"Then you have nothing to worry about, do you?"

Kirsh shrugged and studied his empty wineglass for a moment.

"Alenor missed you when you left Avacas," he said.

Dirk smiled. "I'll bet *you* didn't. You were too busy fulfilling your lifelong ambition in the Queen's Guard."

"My lifelong ambitions," Kirsh snorted. "None of them have even come close to being realized, Dirk. I spent two years in the guard being ostracized because of who I am. I'm regent of a country that would prefer it if I was dead, and married to a woman who hates me. She won't even let me into her bed. Did you know that? Your precious, innocent little queen got herself knocked up by a lover, not by me."

He was more than a little drunk, Dirk realized. Although Kirsh had only had two glasses of wine with Dirk, there was no telling how much he'd consumed before Dirk arrived.

"Kirsh..."

"And now the one thing in my life I thought I could count on, the one person I thought was truly on my side, is going to be taken from me..."

"Oh, for pity's sake, Kirsh!" Dirk snapped. "Stop feeling so damned sorry for yourself! If you think Marqel is going to put you aside so she can take up with your father, then she's not nearly as in love with you as you'd like to think, is she? And don't you *ever* repeat that nonsense about Alenor to anyone!

You'd be killing her just as effectively as if you wielded the blade yourself."

Kirsh glared at him. "You *knew,* didn't you? She told you."

"I would never betray Alenor. Or you, for that matter."

"Really? That's why you made me let Tia Veran go? So she could kidnap my brother? If you don't call that betrayal, Dirk, what *do* you call it?"

"I called in the favor you owed me, Kirsh, that's all. What happened afterward was none of my doing."

Kirsh was silent for a moment. Dirk couldn't tell what he was thinking, but in his present state, it wasn't likely to be very coherent.

"I was going to save Misha," he said eventually. "I was going to prove I was more than just a second son; more than a spare heir whose only use is standing at stud for his father's dynastic ambitions. I was going to wipe out the Baenlands and return to Avacas a hero."

"Is that what's got you wallowing in self pity? You're afraid you won't be hailed as a hero?"

Kirsh shook his head. "This was my chance to prove myself to Antonov, Dirk. To prove that I really am the son he likes to think I am. But I've screwed it up. There's no sign of Misha, and the Baenlanders got away from us. All I have is a smoking village and a few prisoners who say they know little more than their own names."

"That's hardly your fault, Kirsh."

"Antonov will think it is. Yet again, I fail the test."

"What test?"

"The test he applies to everything I do, Dirk. The one where my father measures my every decision, my every action, against his benchmark of what constitutes a son he can be proud of."

"What are you talking about?"

"*You,* Dirk. I'm talking about *you.*"

"That's absurd!"

"You're everything he could have hoped for in a son, don't you see? Goddess, even after you burned the *Calliope* it was obvious he secretly admired your daring. Look at you! You're the ultimate survivor. And—bastard or not—you have the added advantage of being the son of a *real* king. My grandfather was a commoner, who rose through the ranks and seized control of Senet, Dirk. You think my father doesn't remember that? But you're the last in a line of kings reaching back into antiquity. Why do you think he's never just overthrown Dhevyn and appointed himself her king? It's because he knows that a couple of generations of power don't make you royal. Goddess, he's let you get away with murder—literally! How can I compete with you?"

"I never tried to compete with you, Kirsh," Dirk said.

"And that's what really pisses me off," Kirsh replied. "You are everything my father wanted his own sons to be and you don't even care."

Chapter 30

By the second month of her reign, Marqel realized that Madalan Tirov was deliberately preventing her from retuning to the Lion of Senet's palace, or having anything else to do with him. The reason was clear, even to Marqel. Until the fleet returned, and Dirk's reliability was either proved or disproved, Madalan didn't want Marqel to have a chance to get close to Antonov Latanya. If word came back that the fleet had been destroyed, Marqel would be the one to wear the blame, and Madalan didn't want Antonov flinching from passing her death sentence because he had grown attached to her.

Marqel was at a loss as to how to fight Madalan. She had never had any friends among the other Shadowdancers, viewing them as competition rather than potential allies, so there was nobody she could even trust to run a message for her without it finding its way into Madalan's hands. Her elevation to High Priestess was unpopular; she had still been an acolyte and she wasn't even Senetian. Marqel was alone in a gilded cage, trapped amid undreamed-of wealth as she waited to find out if she would live or die, her fate in the hands of a man who openly despised her.

Madalan kept her busy. Marqel spent almost every waking moment buried in boring administrative matters that she was certain Belagren had never had to deal with. She said as much to Madalan once, who smiled nastily, and pointed out that much of the work was the responsibility of the right hand of the High Priestess, but since the Lord of the Shadows was currently otherwise engaged, Marqel would just have to deal with it herself.

Marqel was tempted to test the limits of her power by simply removing Dirk in his absence and reassigning Madalan to the job, which would force the old sow to take on the work herself, but she thought better of it. That would be handing the bitch far too much power, and she was afraid to think of what Dirk's reaction might be if he returned to Avacas to find himself deposed. Besides, if things went bad in the Baenlands, the last thing Marqel needed was Madalan Tirov at her right hand, close enough to wield the knife that stabbed her in the back.

The Lion of Senet questioned her absence from the palace. Madalan made no attempt to hide his messages and invitations from Marqel. But she replied to each one with an apologetic missive on Marqel's behalf, claiming the new High Priestess was under a great deal of pressure and had far too much to deal with in her new role to take time out to socialize, even with someone as important as the Lion of Senet.

Just when Marqel began to grow truly desperate about her predicament, she received a ray of hope from the most unlikely source. Jacinta D'Orlon, lady-in-waiting to the Queen of Dhevyn, requested a private audience with the High Priestess, and there was not a damn thing Madalan Tirov could do to prevent it.

"You do me a great honor, my lady," Jacinta said graciously, looking around the opulent, almost tasteless wealth decorating the High Priestess's private suite. The whole room, from the small side tables to the large inlaid murals on the walls, was touched with gilt. Even the vase in the corner of the room, filled with freshly cut flowers, was solid gold (Marqel had checked on that personally the day she moved in). Marqel enjoyed the look of surprise on Jacinta's face. She could remember thinking, the first time she had entered this place, that one day all this would belong to her. And now it did.

Then Jacinta turned to face Marqel with a friendly smile. "You've come a long way since I saw you last."

Although she would not go so far as to call Jacinta a friend, Alenor's lady-in-waiting had always treated her with respect, and Marqel was delighted to see someone who wasn't a damned Shadowdancer.

"The Goddess spoke to me. I'm the High Priestess now."

"So I hear," Jacinta agreed. "That's why I was so surprised to find you buried here in the Hall of Shadows and not at the palace. I thought the High Priestess had duties there as well."

Marqel was instantly suspicious. "What do you mean?"

The Dhevynian woman smiled. "Why don't we sit down?"

Marqel nodded her agreement and took the seat opposite Jacinta, as the lady-in-waiting fastidiously straightened her skirts.

"What duties?" she asked again.

"Well, it's just I thought the High Priestess and the Lion of Senet..."

"I've been busy," Marqel shrugged uncomfortably. "I haven't had time to get back to the palace."

"That's such a pity. Antonov has been asking for you, I understand."

"He has?" she asked, a little too eagerly.

Jacinta looked at her with great concern. "Marqel, may I ask you something personal?"

"Like what?"

"Well, it seems to me your elevation to the position of High Priestess might be unpopular among the Shadowdancers. You're Dhevynian, for one thing, and new to their ranks. They're not *deliberately* keeping you from Antonov, are they?"

Marqel's natural distrust of anything or anybody connected with Alenor began to wane a little in the face of Jacinta's obvious sincerity. "I think they might be," she confided in a low voice.

"But that's terrible," Jacinta cried. "Can't you order them to let you out of here?"

"If I could, do you think I'd be sitting here?"

"Oh, Marqel! How dreadful for you. Is there anything I can do to help?"

"What can you do? I'm the High Priestess of the Shadow-dancers. You're just the Queen of Dhevyn's maid."

Jacinta smiled conspiratorially. "I may just be the Queen of Dhevyn's maid, Marqel, but I think I *might* be able to help you."

"How? How can you get me into the palace? More to the point, why would you want to?"

"The *how* is easy enough. I'll simply have Alenor insist you return."

"Antonov's already sent several messages asking about me. Madalan just fobs him off with one excuse after another."

"Alenor won't just ask after you, Marqel, she will insist on your spiritual guidance. If she begs your company of Antonov, instead of simply asking after you, he will *insist* to Madalan that you attend the palace. She can ignore an invitation, but not a direct order."

"Why would you do something like this for me?"

Jacinta sighed heavily. "Because Alenor wants to go home, Marqel."

"So?"

"Well, I was thinking...in exchange for getting you out of here, perhaps you could return the favor by insisting Antonov sends her back to Kalarada."

Marqel smiled. She was always more comfortable when she knew what someone wanted of her. And Jacinta obviously wanted her help. Better yet, she obviously *needed* it. "But why would he listen to me?"

"Because you are the Voice of the Goddess."

Marqel's smile faded. She didn't like the sound of this. She certainly did not want to give Jacinta anything she could hold over her at some stage in the future. "You're asking me to lie to him."

Lady Jacinta met her eye and smiled knowingly. "If lying to Antonov bothered you, Marqel, you'd not be the High Priestess. It's part and parcel of the job, I understand."

The comment worried her. As far as Marqel knew, Jacinta was supposed to be a faithful follower of the Goddess. Antonov would never have allowed her to remain in the queen's service if she wasn't. Jacinta should not even be questioning the truth of her visions. But then, the little queen of Dhevyn was uncomfortably close to Dirk Provin, Marqel recalled. The Goddess knew what *he'd* told her about all this and what she'd told her lady-in-waiting.

For a moment, Marqel wavered with indecision. But when all was said and done, whatever Jacinta believed, she was offering her a way out of the Hall of Shadows and, in truth, Marqel would be glad to see the back of the pallid little queen. And if it came to a showdown, it would be the word of a Dhevynian lady-in-waiting against the Voice of the Goddess.

"Very well, I'll help you. *If* you help me."

Jacinta rose to her feet. "Then I will look forward to seeing you at the palace sometime soon, Marqel."

The lady-in-waiting headed for the door without waiting to be excused. She had almost reached it when Marqel thought of something else. Jacinta must be truly desperate if her only recourse was to turn to Marqel for help.

"I have a condition."

Jacinta turned and looked at her curiously. "And what is that?"

"Getting me into the palace isn't enough. Get me into Antonov's bed."

"I'm not your pimp, Marqel," she responded with a frown.

"Oh yes, you are, Lady Jacinta," Marqel told her, feeling a lot more confident about her ability to bargain. "If Alenor wants out of Avacas, then get me into Antonov's bed. That's the deal or we have no deal at all." She smiled and opened her arms to encompass the luxurious suite she occupied. "As prisons go, this isn't so bad, you know. I can stay a little longer if I have to."

Jacinta thought about it for a moment and then shrugged. "I'll see what I can do."

"You do that, my lady, because I won't be having *any* visions about your queen going home to Kalarada until the morning *after*."

Chapter 31

Mellie Thorn was a strong swimmer, so she volunteered to teach Misha. It was a little embarrassing for Misha to admit he couldn't swim. He was a grown man who had spent his whole life near the sea. But Mellie seemed glad she was able to do something to help. Misha suspected she was bored. After the initial excitement of their flight from Mil and arrival in Damita had worn off, with no friends her own age nearby, Mellie found herself with little else to do but work her way through Oscon's extensive library, or go for long, solitary walks. On the rare occasions she *had* disappeared for a walk, Tia had been so angry at her for wandering off that Mellie soon discounted it as a viable way to pass the time.

Misha promised he would go walking with Mellie when he was strong enough, to which Tia responded contemptuously: "Over my dead body!"

Misha smiled. He suspected that Tia didn't doubt he would eventually be strong enough to walk unaided. It was the idea she would let either Mellie or Misha roam the countryside around Garwenfield unescorted that prompted her comment.

They were sitting on the beach, letting the warm second sun dry their skin. The ocean lapped the white sand with hypnotic regularity. The screeching of gulls searching the shoreline for scraps was the only thing preventing them from being caught in its spell. Misha was tired, but not unbearably so. Mellie was a surprisingly patient teacher, and Tia always remained close by, to make sure he didn't drown when they paddled out into the deeper water. He could not swim yet, but he could tread water for longer and longer periods each day. His right arm and leg felt as strong as they ever had, although the weakness in his left side was an endless source of frustration.

"I fear our jailer plans to let neither of us out of her sight, Mellie," Misha predicted with a smile.

"I'll give you *jailer*," Tia snapped. "If I catch either of you even *thinking* about wandering off without me, I'll lock you both in a dungeon and you can survive on bread and water and whatever food I can slip under the door."

"There are no dungeons here, Tia," Mellie laughed. "She's such a grouch, isn't she?" she added to Misha.

"I know," he agreed with a grin. "What do you think we should do about it?"

"We could throw her back into the water," Mellie suggested.

"You and Misha?" Tia scoffed. "That'll be the day."

"She's right, Mellie. But give me time to get stronger and then we'll catch her unawares one day and toss her into the sea."

"It's a bargain!" Mellie laughed, climbing to her feet. "Do you want to try again?"

Misha shook his head. "I've had enough for one day, I think. But don't let me stop you if you want to keep swimming."

Mellie ran down the sand toward the water and splashed into the small waves. Misha watched her for a while, and then turned to look at Tia, who was staring out over the water with a pensive expression.

"I envy Mellie Thorn."

"Why?" she asked, turning to look at him.

"Because she's so unaffected. I wish I was as innocent of the dangers of being an heir."

"Mellie's not the heir to anything."

"Don't kid yourself, Tia. While Alenor D'Orlon remains childless, there is no other logical heir to Dhevyn unless you want to see Dirk Provin on the Eagle Throne."

As usual, her expression darkened at the mention of Dirk's name. "Are you suggesting that Dirk would kill Alenor, and then try to remove Mellie as well?"

He shook his head. "I know your opinion of Dirk, Tia, but

the more I think about it, the more I don't believe the Eagle Throne of Dhevyn is what he's after."

"What is he after then?"

"I think he's trying to destroy the Church."

Tia snorted skeptically. "He *joined* the damned Church, Misha!"

"It's sometimes easier to pull a thing down from the inside," he said, "than to stand outside throwing rocks at it."

"You're as bad as Lexie," she complained. "You just can't help trying to find a reason to convince yourself he hasn't betrayed us, can you? I hope you haven't been telling Mellie your bizarre theories. I warned you about that."

"She's not mentioned him to me since Mil."

"Good. The less time she spends dwelling on her bastard half-brother, the better."

"You didn't know him before he came to Avacas, did you?" he asked. "The Dirk Provin you describe is different from the boy I once played chess with."

"You knew the *boy,* Misha. It's the *man* you should worry about."

If Tia thought her anger masked the pain behind her words, then she was mistaken. Misha thought Master Helgin was right when he speculated that Tia and Dirk had been more than friends. It would account for why her rage seemed to have no limit.

"Did you love him very much, Tia?"

She glared at him for a moment, and then scrambled angrily to her feet and stalked off toward the house without answering his question.

Misha only began to fully appreciate how much he had angered Tia later that day when it came time for the daily massage Helgin had prescribed.

Over the past weeks, Tia had been a conscientious student, as she learned under Helgin's careful guidance how to mix the oils, how to warm the muscles gently before working them, and how to ease the knots and twists that half a lifetime of being bedridden had wrought on his body.

He had been reluctant at first. Master Helgin had stood over

Tia, instructing her in the correct techniques, while he lay on the table like an undressed side of beef. He was self-conscious about his lopsided body, and while he didn't have a problem with Master Helgin's professional gaze, there was something extremely unsettling about Tia Veran's touch. She had been very businesslike about the whole thing, however, and three days before, Master Helgin had declared her sufficiently competent to continue without his supervision.

But there was nothing gentle or considerate about her touch today. She was brutal. Her strong hands, which he usually found so soothing, were not easing his muscles, they were pulverizing them. Her fingers felt like iron bars, and she seemed to be seeking out every sore spot on his back and making it her mission to bruise it even more.

"Ouch!" he yelped, as she found one of the pressure points at the base of his spine and applied far more pressure than was necessary.

"Don't be such a baby."

Misha was lying on his stomach so he couldn't see her expression. He turned his head to look at her. "Do you mind? You'll break something if you keep on like that."

"Stop complaining. This is good for you."

Misha snatched at her arm with his good hand to prevent her doing him serious damage. "Don't take your anger at Dirk out on me, Tia."

"Let me go," she ordered coldly.

Misha kept hold of her arm and twisted himself around into a sitting position. The mere fact he could manage such a thing was a testament to how much he had improved, but he didn't have time, just then, to savor his achievement.

"Tia, I don't know what happened between you and Dirk—"

She snatched her arm free of his grasp. "That's right, Misha, you *don't* know. So just mind your own damn business!"

"Tia, if you hate him as much as you claim, why are you letting him get you like this? He's not here. He's not even on the same continent. Despise him for what he's done, if you must, but don't let him ruin your life by turning you into a bitter old woman. That's giving Dirk far more than he deserves."

Tia's eyes blazed angrily for a moment, and then she sighed, as if her rage had exhausted her and she no longer had the will to sustain it.

"I just can't help myself, Misha," she said, leaning on the table beside him. "Just the mention of his name makes me want to kill something."

"I noticed," Misha said with a thin smile.

"I'm sorry. Did I hurt you?"

"The bruises will fade eventually."

She was silent for a moment and then looked at him with a smile. "I hope Master Helgin doesn't come in and catch us like this."

"Like what?"

Tia bent down and picked up the towel that had fallen to the floor when Misha had pulled himself up. He felt his face warming with embarrassment as he snatched it from her hand and hurriedly threw it across his lap.

"You're blushing!" Tia laughed.

"Don't be ridiculous."

"You are too! There's no need to be embarrassed, Misha. It's not as if I haven't seen plenty of naked men before."

"Really?" he asked with a raised brow.

She rolled her eyes. "I didn't mean that the way it sounded..."

Misha smiled. "Now who's blushing?"

"Just lie down and shut up, Misha, so we can get this finished."

"I'll bet you didn't say *that* to all the naked men you've seen before."

Tia scowled at him, shoving him none too gently in the chest to force him to lie down. He fell backward, banging his head painfully on the table.

"Ow!" he yelled, although he did have the presence of mind to keep the towel in place.

"You're such a girl," Tia told him unsympathetically.

"What is going on in here?" Master Helgin demanded,

opening the door with a disapproving frown. "I can hear you yelling all the way down the hall."

Misha turned his head to look at Helgin. "There's no problem, Master Helgin. Tia just seems to think a slight concussion might speed my recovery."

Helgin stared at both of them with a puzzled frown, and then turned away, muttering to himself as he closed the door behind him.

Misha looked back at Tia, who was silent for a moment, and then, like guilty children caught doing something naughty, they both burst out laughing.

After that, Tia's mood was much improved. Misha was not sure if he'd been responsible or not. Perhaps it was pointing out that Dirk still had power over her while she was angry with him. Or it might have been that she had seen him—all of him—and was still laughing about *that*.

Whatever the reason, even Oscon remarked on the change in her.

Tia Veran fascinated Misha. She would laugh wholeheartedly if she thought something was funny, but could explode into fury at the slightest provocation. She could argue politics better than Lord Palinov and play chess better than anyone he knew (not counting Dirk). She was tougher than a drill sergeant when he was exercising, but when Master Helgin began to taper the dose of poppy-dust and Misha became so skittish he couldn't sleep, she would stay up all night talking to him so that he did not have to suffer alone.

He had never met anyone so blunt, so honest or so open. She was equally passionate about those she loved and those she hated. Raised at court, and surrounded all his life by people who played political games to advance themselves in his father's favor, he found her frankness enchanting.

Misha knew he was more than a little bit in love with Tia Veran, although he made no attempt to act on it. For one thing, she was still aching over Dirk, and he was certain the last thing she was interested in was another man.

The second reason was simple pride. If he ever declared

himself to Tia, he could not bear her accepting his love out of pity.

So Misha settled for silence, and turned his mind to fighting the poppy-dust that seemed determined not to relinquish its grip on him. As the doses he took were reduced, some of his earlier symptoms reappeared. He was trembling and quite often nauseous, but he had not suffered any fits and was stronger than he had been in years, so it was easier to deal with the symptoms than it had been in the past.

The long, languid days in Garwenfield blurred into one another. He lost track of time; did not know if he had been here for weeks or months. Each day was more difficult than the day before as the drug reluctantly loosened its hold on him, but each day he survived made him stronger and more determined. Helgin often warned him the worst was yet to come, but Misha found the prospect less daunting than it had been in the past.

For the first time in many years, he had *hope,* and he discovered that was almost as powerful a narcotic as poppy-dust. In spite of his illness and his unrequited love, Misha was the happiest he could ever remember being.

And then a bird arrived sent by Lexie from Mil. Oscon came down to the main hall to inform them the Baenlands had been invaded and it was Dirk Provin who had led the Senetian forces.

Chapter 32

She had no idea how Jacinta managed it, but less than a week after the lady-in-waiting's visit, Madalan informed Marqel she was to attend a banquet at the palace in honor of the Dhevynian queen. Not only that, but she was also to stay the night at the palace, returning the following morning to the Hall of Shadows. Marqel made a point of appearing less than pleased with the interruption to her work—so effectively that Madalan actually scolded her for her lack of enthusiasm.

She took great pains with her appearance, brushing her fair hair to a shine, and wearing only those pieces of jewelry she could not recall seeing Belagren wear in Antonov's presence. There was no guarantee Antonov would not recognize some of them, but she shied away from the more familiar pieces, hoping to give the impression she was frugal as well as pious and divine.

The dinner itself proved tedious beyond belief. The food was excellent, naturally, but the discussion around the table centered almost entirely on Dhevyn's economic woes, in which Marqel had no interest. She was seated at the foot of the long table opposite Antonov, and could barely even catch his eye through the forest of silverware, crystal and bowls of flowers covering the table.

After dinner, things improved a little when they retired to the terrace to enjoy a nightcap and to watch the heat lightning streaking the red sky over the Tresna Sea. Marqel managed to extricate herself from an awkward conversation with the Galinan ambassador, and made her way to where Alenor was talking to Antonov. The queen saw her approach and smiled at her warmly.

"My lady! Please, won't you join us?"

"I've no wish to interrupt a private conversation, your majesty."

"Nonsense! We were just admiring the lightning, weren't we, your highness? Do you think the Goddess means anything by it, my lady, or is she just showing off?"

The question caught Marqel unawares. She was here to seduce the Lion of Senet, not get into a theological discussion.

"I . . . er . . . I think she's reminding us she controls the weather," Marqel suggested warily.

Antonov raised his glass in her direction. "You've gone right to the heart of the matter, my lady. I feel more and more easy with the Goddess's choice each time I see you."

Marqel smiled coyly. This was better.

"Then I'm glad someone does," she replied. "Every time I

see another pile of dispatches, I fear the Goddess is punishing me for something, not rewarding me, your highness."

Antonov smiled. "Belagren often said the same thing."

I know she did, Marqel replied silently. *That's why I said it.*

"I trust the troops I sent to Omaxin to sort out the Sidorians were sufficient."

For a moment, Marqel had no idea what he was talking about. Then she remembered the letter Madalan had drafted in her name her very first day on the job. "They were most appreciated, your highness."

"Well, I've left orders they should stay up there for a while, just in case the Sidorians haven't gotten the message yet."

Alenor saved her from having to come up with something that sounded like an intelligent answer.

"Would you excuse me, your highness?" the queen asked. "I'm still not feeling all that strong. I'd like to retire. I'm sure the High Priestess will be happy to keep you entertained."

"Of course you may go, my dear. Retire as soon as you wish. Nobody will be offended."

"Thank you, sire," she said with a small curtsy, and then she walked back toward the dining room, leaving Marqel alone with Antonov.

"So, my lady, you've been let out for the evening," Antonov remarked, turning to face her.

"Your highness?" she asked with alarm. Did everyone in Avacas think she was a prisoner?

"I was referring to Lady Madalan's numerous refusals to my previous requests for your presence in the palace."

Marqel sighed. "Dear, dear Madalan. She's very protective of me. Please don't be angry with her. She's just trying to make things easier for me. She's been such a tower of strength. I don't know what I'd do without her."

"She was a great help to Belagren, too," Antonov agreed.

She nodded sagely. "I believe the Goddess never burdens us with more than we can bear, your highness. And when she does, she puts people like Madalan in our path to help us carry it."

"Wisely spoken, my lady. You appear to have undergone a remarkable change since we first met."

"I would hope so, your highness. I was but a foolish girl back then."

"You were also a thief, as I recall."

Marqel smiled. She had known this would come up eventually and had spent quite some time perfecting her answer. "I know you thought I was lying, your highness, but the truth is, I never stole Rees Provin's dagger. The girl I shared my wagon with was the thief, but I was too afraid to say so."

"Afraid of me?"

"Afraid of Mistress Kalleen. Had I betrayed a member of the troupe, your worst punishment would have seemed merciful by comparison. But when I look back now, I see the Goddess at work, even then. Without my arrest, without you deciding to hand me over to Lady Belagren, I would never have joined the Shadowdancers. I believe the Goddess arranged the whole thing."

"Perhaps she did," Antonov agreed, although she could not tell if he accepted her explanation. "I supposes she arranged for you and Kirsh to become...friends...as well."

"No, your highness, that was Lady Belagren."

Antonov stared at her in shock. "Are you saying the High Priestess arranged for you to become my son's mistress?"

"You can ask Madalan if you doubt it, your highness. At the time, I was quite horrified by the suggestion, but I believe I now know the reason."

"And I'll bet it's a good one," Antonov remarked, clearly skeptical of her revelation.

"I've had the opportunity to examine some of her personal journals, your highness," Marqel explained. She got the idea from Dirk. He'd made Madalan believe this whole High Priestess thing was Belagren's idea. There was no reason why she couldn't do the same. "I believe the Goddess spoke about me to the Lady Belagren, indicating I was to become the consort of the 'Son of Senet.' At least that's what she wrote in her journal. The High Priestess assumed I was destined to be consort to one of your sons, and as Misha was so ill, it left only Kirshov. I don't think it ever occurred to her the Goddess thinks of *you* as her son, not your heirs."

Antonov said nothing for a moment, and then he glanced around the terrace. Most of the dinner guests were still there, standing in small groups discussing whatever it was nobles stood around discussing at dinner parties. Alenor and her party were gone, but the rest of them were waiting on the Lion of Senet to retire before they could leave without giving offense.

"I have a number of matters I must discuss with the High Priestess in private," he announced. "Please, stay as long as you like, but forgive my rudeness." He turned to Marqel and offered her his arm. "My lady?"

Doing her best to hide her triumphant smile, Marqel accepted his arm and walked from the terrace with the Lion of Senet at her side.

Somewhat to Marqel's disappointment, Antonov didn't take her upstairs to his suite, but escorted her along the hall to his study. She looked around, thinking the rug by the unlit fireplace was probably good enough to get the job done, and then she turned and looked at him, wondering when he would make the first move. But Antonov wasn't staring at her lustfully. He was pouring himself a glass of wine from the sideboard.

"Could I have one of those?"

Antonov handed her the glass and turned to pour another for himself, and then he leaned against the sideboard, sipping his wine, and studied her curiously.

"You know, somebody told me once he never ceased to be amazed by my gullibility, and I must admit my first reaction to the news the Goddess had spoken to you was that you're a devious little minx who had somehow found a way to make the whole world believe she's something she's not."

"Surely you suffered the same doubts when Belagren first came to you?"

"Belagren wasn't a thief picked up off the streets of Elcast, my lady."

"Nor is the Goddess only a Goddess of the highborn, your highness," she responded.

He nodded. "And when I remembered that, I realized the Goddess was simply testing my faith. It's frightening how close I came to denying her. It's fortunate I received a message today from Kirshov."

Marqel held her breath. Her very life depended on the contents of that message.

"Your instructions were correct. They got through the delta without incident. So it seems the Goddess *has* chosen you."

Marqel could have cried with relief. "You should have had more faith, your highness," she advised with a smile.

"I will when you stop lying to me."

"But they got through the delta," she protested. "I spoke the truth!"

"I wasn't referring to that. I was referring to your rather fanciful story out on the terrace. I knew Belagren longer than you've been alive, Marqel. She never kept a journal."

Marqel realized her error immediately, but she knew instinctively it wasn't so much the lie she had told him. She was pretending to be somebody she wasn't and Antonov Latanya was far too sharp to fall for anything so transparent. She was going about this all wrong. What did Dirk keep telling her? *Make his faith work for you. It's Antonov's one great strength and his one great weakness. He'll do anything you want, believe anything you want, if he believes it is the will of the Goddess.*

"The Goddess sometimes needs a helping hand, your highness."

"I don't believe she expects you to lie to me, Marqel. I'd not like to begin our time together with lies."

Our time together. Marqel smiled. "Perhaps I did get a bit carried away. But you're an honorable and devout man, your highness. You're old enough to be my father. You have sons older than me, one of whom I've been sleeping with. I feared I would not be able to fulfill my role as High Priestess if you thought..." She let her voice trail off. She hoped she had said enough. It was time for him to make the next move. *And he'd better do it soon.* She only had tonight. If she couldn't get into

Antonov's bed before second sunrise tomorrow, it would be back to the Hall of Shadows and Madalan Bloody Tirov.

Marqel swallowed her wine, walked across the rug and placed the empty glass on the sideboard. Antonov made no attempt to move out of her way, nor did she make any pretext of trying to avoid touching him. She stood only inches from him and looked up into his eyes.

"I would not ask anything of you that you would not willingly give, my lady."

"I am the Voice of the Goddess, your highness," she said softly. "It is my duty. *And* my pleasure."

Marqel stood on her toes and kissed Antonov with every ounce of skill she owned. He hesitated for only a second or two before he responded.

"I can see why Kirsh finds you so irresistible," he breathed huskily after a moment. If there was one thing Marqel had learned about men, it was that once they were aroused, common sense and reason were usually forgotten.

"Shhh..." she said, placing a finger against his lips. "It is the will of the Goddess."

He was breathing hard, and that wasn't the only part of him reacting to her expert touch. Marqel pressed her body against his, letting her hands and her lips do the work.

But he wasn't an easy conquest. Perhaps some residual discomfort about her role as Kirsh's lover remained. Or perhaps that stupid story about Belagren's journals was still bothering him. He resisted her efforts longer than she thought he would... or could.

"Have faith," she commanded in a breathy whisper. "I am the Voice *and the body* of the Goddess."

Marqel didn't know if it was her words or the hand she had slid down the front of Antonov's trousers, but she knew the moment he put aside reason and gave in to desire. In some ways, he was like the men Kalleen had sold her to. He was living out his sexual fantasies. Antonov's fantasy, however, was not the sordid desire to bed a prepubescent girl. It was the ultimate expression of his faith. It was the notion that through the body of the High

Priestess, he was somehow making love to his Goddess. It was his reward, his payment for the sacrifices he had made.

Lost to the notion the Goddess was with him, Antonov lifted Marqel into his arms as she wrapped her legs around him. He carried her to the desk, brushing aside the scattered documents, the inkwell and everything else in his way with a sweep of his arm. She landed heavily on her back, but was too busy fumbling with his trousers to notice. He lifted her long red robe and took her there on the desk, quickly and urgently and with little care for Marqel's pleasure or discomfort.

She didn't care.

Marqel the Magnificent, the Dhevynian Landfall bastard who didn't even have a last name, had just become the mistress of the Lion of Senet. And that was all that really mattered.

It wasn't until she woke the next morning in Antonov's bed, curled in his arms, sore, exhausted and filled with a deep sense of accomplishment, that she remembered her promise to Jacinta, and turned to Antonov with the suggestion the Goddess would look kindly on him if he sent the Queen of Dhevyn home.

Chapter 33

The *Tsarina* returned to Avacas quietly. The pomp and ceremony Kirsh had imagined would accompany their triumphant return was nowhere in evidence. He and Dirk left the ship as soon as it docked and headed for the palace to report to his father.

Antonov had already received word Kirsh was back by the time they arrived at the palace. He was waiting for them in his study with Lord Palinov and the new High Priestess. Marqel stood behind his father's chair, her hand resting lightly on his shoulder. The casual ease of her touch, and the careless familiarity in the way she was standing, told Kirsh all he needed to know before anyone uttered a word. It wasn't unexpected, but his last vestige of hope vanished as Antonov rose to greet them.

Kirsh let Dirk do the talking, preferring to brood as Dirk delivered his report. His cousin was far better at explanations than he was, and had a gift for making everything sound perfectly reasonable. Dirk did not attempt to lie, but he managed to present the facts in a way that made Kirsh sound a much better commander than he felt he deserved.

"There was no sign of Prince Misha at all?" Lord Palinov asked when Dirk finished speaking.

"We know he was there," Kirsh confirmed, tearing his eyes from Marqel long enough to answer the question. "But it seems that even the pirates don't trust their own. The best we can establish is that Misha, Tia Veran, Master Helgin, the old physician from Elcast, and some girl called Mellie disappeared with Reithan Seranov on the *Wanderer* sometime before we arrived. We've got our people looking out for the boat, but he's been giving us the slip for years, so I don't hold much hope we'll find them anytime soon."

"Why would Helgin go with them, Dirk?" Antonov asked.

"Misha's a sick man, your highness. I told you they wouldn't kill him. By the sound of it, they're going to some pains to keep him alive."

"You never mentioned Helgin was in Mil."

"You never asked me about him, sire."

"And the others in Mil? There was no sign of the ringleaders?"

"The only prisoner of importance we had was the captain of the *Orlando,* Dal Falstov," Dirk informed him. "But he was wounded in the fighting and died before we could question him. It wasn't a complete disaster, your highness. Mil no longer exists. We fired the poppy fields, so they'll have nothing to fund the rebuilding of the settlement, and now we know the way through the delta, they're going to have to find some other place to work any mischief against you."

Antonov was silent for a moment, and then he turned to Palinov. "Have a message sent to Kalarada. Inform the queen we suspect the Baenlanders are using the Dhevynian islands to hide the fugitives from Mil. You can tell her we expect her full cooperation in our search to uncover them."

"Alenor's not here?" Kirsh asked in surprise.

"I let her return to Kalarada. She left about a week ago. I'm sorry, son. I should have realized you'd want her here to greet you when you got home, but she was pining away with you gone and, as the High Priestess so wisely pointed out, she would recover much more quickly in more familiar surroundings."

Marqel smiled at him serenely. Kirsh stared at his father for a moment, wondering if he was being sarcastic, but he wasn't. Antonov genuinely believed Kirsh and Alenor were happily married. It occurred to Kirsh that Antonov's belief in that lie was his undoing. It was one of the reasons Marqel now stood at his father's side. The Lion of Senet truly believed his son loved Alenor, and that Marqel had merely been a distraction. If he had known the truth, he might not have been so quick to take her from him.

On the other hand, *had* he known the truth, Marqel might not have lived long enough to become High Priestess.

There was not a damn thing he could do about it, Kirsh realized, except smile and be polite and accept the fact that the woman he loved was now his father's mistress and probably lost to him forever.

It was much later that night before Kirsh got a chance to speak to Marqel alone. She was occupying the suite previously reserved for Belagren, right next to his father's rooms. Marqel opened the door and admitted him with some reluctance. Kirsh looked around as he entered, thinking she had barely changed a thing. The rooms looked as if Belagren still lived here, not her successor. He glanced across at the door connecting the suite to his father's bedroom.

"He's downstairs with Dirk and Lord Palinov," Marqel said, when she noticed the direction of his gaze.

"What's he talking to Dirk about?"

"I don't know," she shrugged. "Did you want some wine? I only get the good stuff in here."

She seemed so...chirpy.

"Are you all right?"

"Why wouldn't I be?" she asked. "I'm the High Priestess now."

"And you've assumed *all* of her duties?" he asked pointedly.

Marqel sighed. "Oh, Kirsh, what was I supposed to do? I'm the Voice of the Goddess now. I didn't have a choice."

He stepped closer to her, but she backed away from him. "I can't bear this, Marqel. I can't stand seeing you with him. The thought of him and you...it's killing me."

"It's just one of those things, Kirsh," she shrugged. "You'll get used to it in time."

"I don't want to get used to it," he cried. He tried to take her in his arms. "Maybe we could still find somewhere..."

"Are you out of your mind?" she gasped, pushing him away. "He'd kill us both!"

"I won't stay here and watch him look at you like that."

"Then go back to your wife, Kirsh," she said harshly.

Kirsh could not believe the change in her. He *refused* to believe it. "Why are you acting like this? What has he done to you, Marqel?"

"He's acknowledged me as the High Priestess of the Shadowdancers," she retorted. "He's made me his mistress, and he doesn't care who knows it. I'm *somebody* now, Kirsh. I don't have to sneak around, or hide away and fear I'm going to be discovered. I don't have to serve anybody and I don't have to pretend I'm something I'm not. Come and see me again when you can offer me the same. In the meantime, go back to your little wife and rule her little country for her. I've got more important things to worry about than the jealous son of a man who holds me above all others except the Goddess!"

Kirsh stared at her speechlessly for a moment, stunned by her callousness.

And then without another word, he turned and left the room, slamming the door behind him.

The following morning Kirshov Latanya announced to his father he wished to supervise the search of the Dhevynian islands personally. Antonov granted his permission gladly, and by first sunrise, he was back on the *Tsarina* sailing for Kalarada, leaving Avacas, Marqel and all the splinters of his broken heart behind him.

Chapter 34

Marqel managed to avoid Dirk for several days after he and Kirsh returned from Mil. Now that Antonov was willing to have her at his side, the business of statecraft was enough to keep her occupied. She saw him frequently, but it was always with Antonov or someone else present, which saved her from having to deal with him.

She discovered Eryk in the palace a few days after they returned. Her first impulse was to brush the little toad aside. She had no need to pretend friendship with him now. But then it occurred to her that nobody was closer to Dirk Provin, and now that he was back in the palace, the half-wit would be an excellent source of intelligence about what the Lord of the Shadows was up to. She had learned that much while a prisoner in the Hall of Shadows. It paid to have people on your side, and Eryk, thanks to their last encounter, was firmly convinced Marqel was a good and trusted friend.

Waiting until she was sure Dirk was downstairs with Antonov, Marqel knocked on Dirk's door and was rather surprised when a chubby blond girl, rather than Eryk opened the door.

"Who are you?"

"Who are *you*?" the girl responded tartly.

"I am the High Priestess of the Shadowdancers," Marqel declared haughtily. The girl visibly crumpled before her.

"Marqel!"

Eryk's delighted greeting prevented her from fully savoring the reaction of the blonde. She changed her scowl to a smile, and pushed past the hapless girl to embrace Eryk warmly.

"Oh, Eryk! I'm so glad to see you safe."

"Me too!" he told her happily, as he wriggled out of her embrace uncomfortably, and turned to point at the blonde. "This is Caterina. She's Dirk's prisoner."

"His prisoner, eh?" she asked, eyeing the girl critically. "A bit hefty for Dirk's tastes, aren't you? He prefers them taller, too, I thought."

The girl was too stunned by the importance of their guest to be offended.

"She's not *that* sort of prisoner," Eryk explained, rolling his eyes.

"What other sort is there?"

"I'm his hostage, my lady," Caterina told her, dropping into a deep and rather ungainly curtsy.

On hearing that news, Marqel lost interest in the girl. If she was Dirk's hostage, for whatever reason, then he would not allow her to come to any harm, and he certainly wouldn't get attached to her, which meant she was of no use whatsoever to Marqel.

"Leave us!" Marqel ordered. "I wish to visit with my good friend Eryk."

"Where shall I go, my lady?" Caterina asked.

"Out!" she snapped. "After that I don't really care."

"She's not allowed to leave, Marqel," Eryk told her. His face creased with concern, and she realized Dirk might not be attached to his hostage, but Eryk certainly was. She immediately changed her tack and smiled at Caterina.

"Then far be it from me to get you into trouble, Caterina. Why don't you join us?"

"Are you sure, my lady?"

"Of course I'm sure." Marqel glanced at Eryk and noticed his frown had turned back into a beaming smile.

"Didn't I tell you she was really nice?" he said to Caterina.

The girl nodded as she perched nervously on the edge of the settee. Marqel took the seat opposite and patted the space beside her for Eryk. "Come now, I want to hear all about your adventures, Eryk. What are you doing back here in the palace? Weren't you a pirate or something?"

"Sort of. But I surrendered to Prince Kirsh and he said it wasn't my fault I got caught up with such bad company and he let me go back to serving Lord Dirk."

"You're very fortunate it was Kirsh who found you." She treated him to a conspiratorial smile. "He probably remembers it was you who told me Dirk was safe the last time we met in Nova. He never forgets a favor."

Eryk nodded in agreement, her explanation fitting perfectly with his innocent view of the world. That Kirsh had no idea Marqel had seen Eryk in Nova was something Eryk didn't need to know, and now with Kirsh returned to Kalarada, he wasn't ever likely to find out about it, either.

"Are you really the High Priestess now, Marqel?"

"I certainly am," she assured him. She held out her arm to display a stunning bracelet inlaid with row upon row of diamonds. "Look. The Lion of Senet gave me this himself."

"You're still a whore, Marqel. It's just the price that's gone up."

She jumped with fright when she realized Dirk was standing behind her. She hadn't even heard him come in.

"Eryk," he said, before she had time to respond, "why don't you take Caterina down to the kitchens and find some lunch? Tell the guards on the door I said it was all right. The High Priestess and I have some things we need to discuss."

As usual, the boy obeyed Dirk without question. Caterina seemed just as thrilled to escape her presence. The two of them hurried from the room, leaving Dirk alone with Marqel. She rose to her feet and glared at him.

"How dare you speak to me like that in front of others!"

"How foolish of me," he agreed. "We wouldn't want word

to get around the place I despise you, now, would we? What are you doing in my room? Surely you're not bored with Antonov already, and turning your attention to poor Eryk."

"Eryk thinks I'm his friend."

"Which just proves he's not very bright. What did you say to Kirsh that made him take off for Kalarada so abruptly?"

She shrugged uncomfortably. "I told him I didn't need him anymore now that I have his father."

He shook his head in amazement. "You really have a gift for letting people down gently, don't you?"

"Don't you lecture me about being nice to him! *You're* the one who suggested I should dump him so I could be Antonov's mistress."

"And *you're* the one who grabbed at the suggestion with both hands," he reminded her. "Still, it's probably not a bad thing that he's gone. Kirsh moping about the palace getting all hot and bothered about what's going on in his father's bedroom is a complication we're well rid of. Have you seen Paige Halyn in the last few days?"

Marqel shook her head. She had trouble keeping up with Dirk's lightning-fast questions at times. "Master Daranski won't let anyone near him since the wound got infected. I hear he's almost dead."

"He can't die," Dirk said. "Not for another three days."

"He can die anytime he wants for all I care," she shrugged. "Once he's dead, Madalan will go to Bollow and I'll finally be rid of her. Speaking of that miserable old sow, can you do something about her? She's driving me insane with all this stuff she keeps sending me. I'm the High Priestess. I shouldn't have to deal with that sort of thing. That's what I have minions like you for."

Dirk smiled, which was a rare thing for him to do in her presence. "I'll take care of it. You won't be bothered by paperwork anymore."

That was easy, she thought contentedly. The power of being Antonov's mistress was enough to cow even the mighty Dirk Provin, it seemed.

"And you have to tell her I'm staying here in the palace. Antonov needs me."

"That didn't take you long."

"I'm very good at what I do, Dirk," she reminded him smugly. "As you should know."

"Just don't forget you're the High Priestess first, and his plaything second. Even Antonov will get suspicious if you don't make some attempt to pretend you're actually doing something other than screwing him."

"You leave Antonov to me and go take care of the rest of it, Dirk. Can I go now?" She regretted the question as soon as she asked it. She didn't need his permission to come and go in the palace. Not anymore.

"You can go. Just stay away from Eryk. He's got enough trouble without having you for a friend."

"Like having *you* for a friend, for instance?"

"Get out."

Satisfied at least one of her barbs had hit its mark, she walked to the door and opened it, unable to resist one last taunt. "You know, I hope the Lord of the Suns doesn't die. I hope the old bastard lingers on for years, because then you'll have to put up with Madalan Bloody Tirov looking over *your* shoulder, all day, every day, and she might leave me alone."

Marqel slammed the door before Dirk could respond, feeling rather pleased with herself.

The feeling did not last long, however.

Paige Halyn lingered for barely another four days before Antonov was woken in the early hours of the morning by a messenger from Master Daranski. Marqel wandered out of the bedroom, rubbing her eyes sleepily, in time to hear the messenger inform the Lion of Senet that the Lord of the Suns was dead.

Chapter 35

Paige Halyn's will was delivered from the Tabernacle at the Temple in Bollow to the Hall of Shadows nearly two weeks after he died. By then his funeral was over, but there was a feeling of anticipation in Avacas as the city held its breath, waiting to hear who the next Lord or Lady of the Suns would be.

Although the rise of Belagren and the Shadowdancers had seriously undermined Paige Halyn's authority, Belagren had been far too clever to cut herself off completely from the established religion of Senet. That was why she had suffered the indignity of being nominally subordinate to the Lord of the Suns all through her reign. Antonov was a devout man and would never have followed a breakaway religion, but a cult that—on the surface at least—enjoyed the tacit approval of his church was far easier to accept.

They gathered in the main temple of the Hall of Shadows for the reading, the ceremony restricted to Shadowdancers and the sizable contingent of Sundancers who had arrived from Bollow. Even Antonov was not permitted to attend. This was church business and out of his control. A messenger was standing by to deliver the news as soon as the new leader was acclaimed, but until then, the Lion of Senet was no more than another anxious parishioner, awaiting word of the decision like everyone else.

The atmosphere in the Hall of Shadows was one of contained excitement. Somehow, the rumor had spread that Madalan was to be the new Lady of the Suns, and there was an air of gleeful expectancy among the Shadowdancers as they waited for one of their own to finally occupy the ultimate position of power in their church.

Dirk had greeted the delegation from Bollow personally. He did not trust Marqel with anything so delicate. The senior Sundancer who led the delegation was a man named Claudio

Varell. He was almost as withered and old as Paige Halyn had been, but he had bright, alert eyes and had been the Lord of the Suns' closest aide for longer than Dirk had been alive.

Dirk greeted him on the steps of the hall with a respectful bow. "Welcome to the Hall of Shadows, my lord. You and your Sundancers are welcome here."

"That would have to be a first," the old man replied testily. "Who are you?"

"I am Dirk Provin, the right hand of the High Priestess."

"You don't wear the robes of a Shadowdancer," he said, looking over Dirk's somber outfit with a frown.

"But I am one, nonetheless, my lord," Dirk assured him. "My duties are varied, and the High Priestess understands our robes of office sometimes prevent truly harmonious dealings with outsiders when they are constantly being reminded of our closeness to the Goddess."

"You've a slick tongue, too," Lord Varell remarked with a scowl.

"Eloquence is not a skill restricted to the elderly, my lord," Dirk replied with a faint smile. "Shall we proceed? The High Priestess and the rest of the Shadowdancers are waiting for you in the temple. Do you have the will?"

Claudio pointed to a heavily bound wooden chest carried by two Sundancers, who, despite their yellow robes, looked burly enough to be hired guards. Dirk nodded and turned to lead the way through the Hall of Shadows with Lord Varell, the locked chest containing the will, and the fifty or more Sundancers he had brought with him following in his wake. Their number surprised Dirk a little. He didn't think there were that many Sundancers left.

They walked in silence past the exquisite tapestries, past the gilded vases filled with fresh flowers, past all the blatant evidence of the Shadowdancers' wealth. The mood of the Sundancers in his wake grew increasingly morose as they neared the temple. They all knew the Sundancers had been impoverished to keep the Shadowdancers in such a manner. Dirk stopped when they reached the doors leading into the temple and turned to Lord Varell before he opened them.

"Whatever happens today, my lord," he said, "I want to assure you I will do everything in my power to see the Lord of the Suns' last wishes are carried out."

"This ceremony shouldn't even be happening here in Avacas," Varell complained. "The traditional place for the reading of the Lord of the Suns' will is the temple in Bollow."

"But I'm sure you'll agree that with the death of the High Priestess and the unfortunate circumstances of Lord Halyn's death, expedience is more important than tradition."

When Varell did not reply, Dirk turned to open the door.

"Lord Provin."

He glanced back at the old man. "Yes?"

"If things…if things should go against us in there… would you see to it my people get out? Alive."

Dirk looked at him curiously for a moment and then nodded. He decided he liked Claudio Varell. The old man was a realist.

"I don't think it will come to that, my lord. In fact, you may find the Goddess is watching over your people far better than you imagine."

Claudio shrugged, his expression resigned. Obviously, he thought Madalan's first order as Lady of the Suns would be the destruction of what remained of the Sundancers. He also seemed to be of the opinion his Sundancers would (quite understandably) object, and the result would be a bloodbath. There was no way to assure him he was wrong. No way to tell Varell that the Lord of the Suns' successor was a lot more sympathetic to the Sundancers' cause than he imagined.

Like everybody else gathered in the temple to hear the will read, Lord Varell would just have to wait and see.

The first part of Paige Halyn's will dealt with the personal bequests he wished to make to friends and family. He freed the debtor slaves who had been in his service and bestowed modest endowments on a number of other faithful retainers. He bequeathed his personal belongings to his niece, and his journals to the Sundancers' archives in Bollow. The list was long and comprehensive, and it bored everyone to tears.

When Claudio Varell came to the next part, however, the entire temple suddenly seemed to be holding its breath. The hall was packed with every Shadowdancer who had been within traveling distance of Avacas, as well as a number of Sundancers additional to those Varell had brought from Bollow. The numbers were not as uneven as Dirk thought they might be. The Sundancers were a dying breed, he thought, but they were a long way from being extinct.

"As to my successor," Lord Varell read in a voice noticeably shaking, "this is a matter to which I have given a great deal of thought. In my time as Lord of the Suns, I have witnessed many changes. I have seen the Age of Shadows come and go. I have watched the rise of the Shadowdancers and the perversion of our beliefs, and have been powerless to stop them..."

A murmur of uneasiness rippled through the hall, mostly from the Shadowdancers.

"I cannot, however, alter the winds of change," Lord Varell continued reading. "If I believe everything happens as the Goddess wills it, then I must believe the changes that have come upon us since the second sun returned are also her doing. I must therefore bow to the inevitable, and appoint a successor who can guide both the Sundancers and the Shadowdancers through the turbulent times ahead."

Lord Varell hesitated for a moment. Dirk didn't think he was doing it for dramatic effect. He had probably read on a little further and was disturbed by what he saw. Madalan was smiling, unable to contain her glee. Marqel looked resplendent in her red robes and what Dirk was sure must have been every piece of jewelry Belagren had owned, but she had a bored look on her face. This was a show where she was not the main attraction, so she wasn't terribly interested in it. The only pleasure she took from the proceedings was probably the thought that very soon she would no longer have to put up with Madalan Tirov dictating her every move.

"I name my successor as the one who stands at the right hand of the High Priestess of the Shadowdancers," Varell read.

"Let the man or woman who occupies this position at the time of my death become the Lord or Lady of the Suns. Let this person do his or her utmost to do what I have failed to do and restore Ranadon to the Goddess."

The Hall erupted as Madalan stepped forward. She had composed her expression into one of humble acceptance. The Shadowdancers were cheering. The Sundancers were muttering among themselves unhappily.

Varell looked up from the document as Madalan approached.

"My lady?" he asked, sounding a little puzzled. "Do you wish to challenge the will?"

"Of course not, my lord. I am honored to accept the position."

"Accept it? But the will doesn't name you, my lady. It names the right hand of the High Priestess . . ."

As the truth dawned on her, Madalan's pious smile turned to a snarl of helpless fury as she looked across the podium to where the High Priestess stood with Dirk and a number of other senior Shadowdancers.

Dirk smiled at her serenely and stepped forward.

"That would be me," he said.

Dirk had a bad habit of running scenarios through his mind in advance, trying to imagine what people would do and say, trying to think up ways to counter them, even before they knew themselves what they would do. As he turned to face the Shadowdancers and the Sundancers gathered to witness the appointment of the next Lord of the Suns, he promised himself he would stop doing it.

Nothing was ever the way he imagined it, and it just complicated things hoping they would be.

"The will is invalid!" somebody called, probably a Sundancer. "The Lord of the Suns was assassinated!"

"There must be an election!" somebody else shouted angrily.

The gathering seemed in total agreement in their disapproval.

Probably for the first time in history, the two sects of the Church of the Suns were united.

"The will is legal," Lord Varell responded unhappily. "The Lord of the Suns died sixty-one days after being wounded. By law, he died of an infection. There is nothing we can do."

Dirk let the hubbub wash over him, wishing there had been a way to do this without having to address several hundred angry members of the Church, who at that moment were probably imagining how much better he would look with his throat slit.

"I will not accept this honor," he shouted over the ruckus, which brought the entire hall to a standstill. If his shout had gotten their attention, his words stunned them into silence, when he added, in a much more reasonable tone, "Unless you agree to my terms."

He waited, but nobody said a word.

"I will not preside over a divided Church," he announced. "Nor will I tolerate those who would elevate one arm of the Church over the other." He cast his eyes over the crowd, unaware of how indomitable his gaze appeared. "I will be Lord of the Suns only if you believe me when I say I will not abide dishonesty. I will not stand for *any* behavior that might bring the Goddess or her Church into disrepute. If I accept this role, I will expel any member of the Church, Sundancer or Shadowdancer, who thinks they are here for any other reason than to bring the truth to the people of Ranadon!" He hesitated for a moment, letting his words sink in. "Is there anybody here who objects to my terms? Is there anyone among you who takes issue with the Sundancers and Shadowdancers being free of corruption?"

As Dirk was expecting, nobody uttered a word in protest. There was not a man or woman in the hall prepared to stand up and declare themselves opposed to being ethical or just.

"Then I accept the position of Lord of the Suns," he declared into the shocked silence. "And I will begin my reign with an announcement of great importance!"

Dirk turned and held out his hand, beckoning Marqel forward. She complied hesitantly, looking confused. It would take a little time before the full implications of Dirk's new position truly sank in to her rather self-absorbed consciousness.

"Out of respect for my predecessor, the High Priestess begged me not to mention this today, but last night, the Goddess spoke to her again."

Another murmur rippled through the crowd, but this one was more curious than angry. Dirk noticed the slight shift in the mood of the gathering and knew he had judged their reaction well. They would get over their shock soon enough. He was going to give them something else to worry about, more important even than the appointment of a new Lord of the Suns whose nickname was the Butcher of Elcast.

"The Goddess told the High Priestess of a miraculous event! There will be an eclipse. The Goddess is sending us a moment of darkness all the world will witness!"

Marqel stared at him in bewilderment. He had said nothing to her about the eclipse since he returned from the Baenlands.

"It is a sign!" he yelled over the panicked murmuring of the crowd. "A sign of both her bounty and her wrath! The High Priestess has assured me the Goddess will speak to all of us! I charge you now to go forth and bring this wondrous news to your people. Let everyone from the Sidorian wastes to the Galina islands witness the power of the Goddess and remove once and for all any doubt that the High Priestess of the Shadowdancers is the Voice of the Goddess!"

In the chaos that followed his announcement, Dirk turned to face the others standing on the podium. Madalan looked set to murder him. Claudio Varell wore a look of quiet horror. Marqel appeared to be rather put out that she'd been upstaged.

"We need to talk," he said to them.

And so began the reign of the new Lord of the Suns.

Chapter 36

Dirk was the last to enter the anteroom off the main temple where they gathered to object to his sudden and unexpected ascension to the position of Lord of the Suns. Marqel still appeared a little bemused by the whole thing, but neither Claudio nor Madalan were under any illusions about what it meant.

What none of them could figure out was how he had managed it.

"You can't possibly mean to do this," Madalan cried as soon as he closed the door behind him.

"Why not?"

"Paige Halyn never meant for you to be his successor. He named me! He told me he did!"

"I believe, when you spoke to him, my lady, you were the right hand of the High Priestess. It was the holder of that position he nominated, not you. It was reasonable to assume it was you who would succeed him, but I don't believe he ever said he named you specifically."

She glared at him suspiciously. "How did you know what was in his will?"

"I didn't know. Lord Varell can confirm that. Nobody knew for certain but Paige Halyn."

Claudio nodded unhappily. "The will was sealed in my presence, Lady Madalan. Dirk Provin could not possibly have known its contents."

"Then you must refuse the position," she insisted. "You must go out there and announce you've changed your mind."

"I don't think so."

Madalan turned to Claudio for support. "Are you going to let him get away with this?"

"Of course he's going to let me get away with it," Dirk told her with quiet confidence. "The alternative is to let you have the job, Madalan, and he would rather disband the Sundancers himself than see that happen."

Claudio stared at them for a moment, and then looked across at Marqel, who had sat herself down on the small settee and was staring at the three of them with cautious eyes. Marqel might not be the smartest person in the room, but she had a natural sort of animal cunning that served her well when she was faced with uncertainty.

"The High Priestess is remarkably silent on the affair."

"That's because she has nothing to do with this," Madalan snapped. "You cannot allow this to happen, Claudio!"

"Why should I object? The lad is right. If he refuses the position, then you'll find a way to take it for yourself, or we go to an election. The only way you can win an election is if my Sundancers start meeting with unfortunate accidents. Either way, the Sundancers are doomed. You have a Shadowdancer as Lord of the Suns, my lady. Be thankful for it!" He turned to Dirk then, but his anger was just as firmly directed at him. "As for you, young man. Have you any notion of what you've unleashed by announcing that eclipse?"

"I know exactly what I've unleashed," Dirk assured him.

"I seriously doubt that! You have signed the death warrant for the Sundancers. Another episode as dramatic and miraculous as the return of the second sun will see the end of the only shred of decency left in the Church. There will be no more Sundancers. There will be nothing but the barbaric practices of a wicked, self-serving cult founded on drugs and lies."

"I have a responsibility to the Shadowdancers, too, my lord. I just announced how I intend to rule—without fear or favor. I'm sorry you don't like it, but I won't pretend the Goddess didn't speak to the High Priestess just to keep your Sundancers happy."

"The Goddess never spoke to anyone," he scoffed. "Who is it, Madalan? What poor fool with more brains than sense have you found to browbeat into submission this time? Or did you find Neris Veran in the Baenlands and torture the information out of him?"

"Neris Veran is dead," Dirk told him.

"But his legacy of lies lives on," Claudio snorted. "And

what is to become of my people? You have made them redundant."

"Oh, I don't know." Dirk shrugged. "Perhaps we can find something else for them to do."

"What are you talking about?"

"Have you considered education?"

"What?"

"Schools, my lord. I understand it was Paige Halyn's fondest wish to establish schools in every village in Senet. I intend to honor that wish and establish a legacy in his name. We'll make them free, which should encourage attendance. And it'll give your Sundancers something to do. As you say, once the eclipse has happened, there won't be much of a role for your lot in the pastoral side of things."

"It's a stupid idea," Madalan snapped at him. "Even if the Sundancers could afford it, aren't you aware of the dangers of educating people above their station? That path leads to social collapse."

"It's ignorance that leads to people standing around cheering a man being burned alive, Madalan," Claudio retorted. He was clearly surprised and wary of Dirk's suggestion, but seemed cautiously willing to go along with it. For that matter, he would have been cautiously willing to go along with anything that did not involve the disbanding of the Sundancers entirely.

"But Madalan has a point. How will we fund such a massive project?" Claudio asked. "The reason Paige Halyn was never able to do anything about setting up schools was the lack of resources. All our funds were drained by the establishment of the Shadowdancers."

"Then it's about time the Shadowdancers returned the favor." Dirk walked across the room to where Marqel was reclining on the couch, watching him warily. He reached down to the diamond choker she wore, snatched it from her throat and tossed it to Claudio.

"Hey! That's mine!"

"That should cover the first year's expenses," he said, as Claudio fumbled to catch it. "I'll arrange to have an inventory taken in the Hall of Shadows. There's a vase in the High Priestess's suite that should pay for the second year. You will have the resources, my lord, I assure you of that."

"I won't let you bankrupt the Shadowdancers to keep a bunch of whining old men and women happy," Marqel declared, jumping to her feet. She might not care about the morality of Dirk's plans, but she was damn sure who the Shadowdancers' wealth belonged to. "You can't touch the Hall of Shadows or anything in it."

"Actually, I can. It's in the charter of the Shadowdancers. Clause three hundred and twenty-something. I checked."

"That was remarkably foresighted of you, my lord," Claudio observed. He was still angry, but he was enjoying seeing Marqel even angrier than he was at this unexpected turn of events.

"I'm a remarkably foresighted person," Dirk told him. "It would pay to remember that, my lord."

"This is intolerable!"

Dirk turned on Madalan impatiently. "Shut up, Madalan. I just handed your Shadowdancers a chance to consolidate their power for an eternity. After the eclipse, there won't be a soul on Ranadon who doubts the High Priestess speaks for the Goddess. You'll be able to burn whole villages down at Landfall if that's what you want. If I choose to throw a bone to the Sundancers to keep them happy, then that's my concern, not yours. Be grateful for what I've given you, or when I finish going through those notes from Omaxin and I work out when the next Age of Shadows is due, the first person I tell about it will be a *Sun*dancer."

"It was *you?*" Claudio gasped, as he realized what Dirk was implying. "*You're* the one who worked out when the eclipse was due?"

"One of my many talents, my lord," Dirk agreed.

"*But why tell them?*" he asked indicating Madalan and Marqel. "If you'd only come to us ..."

"You would have ignored my advice, the same way Paige Halyn ignored Neris when he told him what Belagren was up to during the Age of Shadows until it was too late."

"So rather than expose the truth, you'd perpetrate the lies?" he concluded bitterly. "You'll actively aid this conspiracy of evil?"

"Gladly," Dirk told him, without a hint of remorse. He turned back to Madalan. "If it's any consolation, my lady, you can have your old job back. You are once again the right hand of the High Priestess. I suggest you keep it firmly around her throat."

"You can't do that," Marqel objected. "If you're leaving, I want to pick my own right hand."

"You'll do exactly what you're told, Marqel," he ordered. "Or would you prefer it if I went to Antonov and told him about some of your other...misdemeanors?"

Marqel took the hint and crossed her arms sulkily. She wasn't going to endanger her newfound power by letting Dirk tell Antonov about what she'd done to Alenor.

Madalan looked at the two of them with a suspicious frown. "What was all that about? What have you got on her?"

"Nothing you need concern yourself with, Madalan. You are her right hand, which means you are effectively running the Shadowdancers. Leave her at the palace to amuse Antonov, and do what you're best at. Trust me, Marqel is doing what *she's* best at."

"You're up to something, Dirk Provin," Madalan said.

"Of course I'm *up* to something," Dirk laughed disparagingly. "I was born with a gift only one other man on Ranadon has ever been afflicted with, and I saw what happened to him. I'm protecting myself, Madalan, on a scale you can't even comprehend."

"So what will you do now?" Claudio asked.

"The first thing I'm going to do is pay Antonov a visit and break the news to him. Then I'm going to Bollow to get ready for the eclipse."

"You're not going anywhere until I know every detail about this damned eclipse," Madalan declared. "I want to know down to the last minute. I want to know when, I want to know where and I want to know how long it will last. Give me that, and I'll play along with you. Deny me and I'll destroy you, Dirk

Provin, even if it means destroying the Shadowdancers along with you."

He shrugged. "The announcement's been made now, so there's no harm in sharing the details. Did you want to know them, too, Lord Varell?"

He glared at Dirk and then shook his head. "I want no part of this abomination."

"You can't really avoid it, my lord," Dirk warned. "Because this time, it won't just be a sacrifice held overlooking a battlefield marking the Goddess's miracle. It'll be the biggest celebration ever witnessed on Ranadon. It's a long time until the next eclipse, so we're going to make the most of it."

"I'm not sure what's worse—your gift for deception or your cynicism."

"You haven't even seen close to my worst, Lord Varell," Dirk assured him. "And now, if you don't mind, I wish to be left in peace for a while. I still have to face Antonov today, and I'd like some time to prepare for it."

"This isn't over," Madalan warned. "You've been named as Paige Halyn's successor, Dirk, but that's a world away from being confirmed in the position. I'll find a way to prevent you ever being sworn in."

"Then you'd better get to it, my lady, because the swearing-in will take place just as soon as I can arrange it."

When they were gone, he locked the door behind them and sank down to the floor with his back against the door, his legs trembling so hard they could no longer hold him. He hadn't won yet, but their arguments were stalled for the time being.

Dirk put his head between his knees to stop the dizziness, and forced himself to breathe deeply and evenly. Then he leaned his head back and closed his eyes.

This is never going to work! he told himself unhappily. *They'll slip a knife in my ribs the minute I step out of this door, or the Brotherhood will get me on the way back to the palace, or Antonov will slit my throat when he hears the news . . .*

The list of his enemies was growing in direct proportion to the number of friends he had lost. And things could only get worse.

"Why did I ever *listen* to you?" Dirk asked aloud.

Not unexpectedly, there was no answer. He smiled faintly, thinking if he had heard a voice answering his question, he would be as crazy as the maniac who had suggested this.

Chapter 37

Still smarting over Dirk's high-handed manner, Marqel sulked all the way back to the palace, trying to decide what Dirk's elevation to Lord of the Suns meant to her. The job itself had no interest for her and at best, all it meant was Dirk would soon be out of her way. Hadn't Paige Halyn hidden up in Bollow for years doing nothing? She was a little relieved, in fact, to realize he'd had his eye on the position of Lord of the Suns all along. It had always worried her that Dirk seemed content to be the right hand of the High Priestess. For someone with his ambition, the role was far too menial to please him for long. She understood now. He'd obviously been working toward this right from the beginning. Somehow he had known what was in Paige Halyn's will. That's why he had been content to let Marqel become the High Priestess. He'd had his eye on bigger and better things.

But why had he given Madalan her old job back? If Marqel had her way, that interfering old bitch would be put out to pasture like the broken-down nag she was. Perhaps, once Dirk left Avacas, she could do something about that...

Then again, it might be better to leave her in the job. With Madalan taking care of all the finicky little details back at the Hall of Shadows, Marqel could stay at the palace with Antonov, which was much more to her liking. Antonov was no great lover, but for Marqel, it wasn't about that. Sex was something she did to get what she wanted. She cared little for it in reality. With the possible exception of Kirshov, no man had ever tried to make it pleasurable for her. She allowed Antonov the use of her body because in return she got wealth, power and respect. If all it took was to smile and moan and look like she was enjoying it, then it was a small price to pay. It was better than doing it for a few silver dorns, or worse, pledging your life and your body to some idiot just to keep a roof over your head and food in your belly, which was Marqel's definition of marriage.

Dirk rode in the carriage with her but she might as well have been back at the Hall of Shadows for all the notice he paid her. He stared thoughtfully out of the window at the city as the carriage clattered over the cobblestones toward the palace.

I wonder what sort of lover Dirk Provin is when he's not out of his mind with the Milk of the Goddess? She tried to imagine those cold eyes inflamed with passion, but it was beyond her. *He should be grateful I gave him that stuff,* she decided. *It was probably the only time he's ever been laid . . .*

Dirk continued to stare out of the carriage, oblivious to Marqel or the direction of her thoughts.

"What's Antonov going to say?" she asked.

"Hmmm?" Dirk replied, as if he hadn't heard the question.

"I asked you what Antonov's going to think about you becoming the Lord of the Suns. Do you think he'll be angry?"

"I hope not."

"You must have some idea."

"I'm guessing he'll be delighted."

Marqel frowned. "Why? Doesn't he want you to be King of Dhevyn or something?"

"He wants me to help him bring Dhevyn to the Goddess," Dirk corrected. "It's a small but important distinction."

"I thought he just wanted to conquer it?"

"But that's *why* he wants to conquer Dhevyn, Marqel," Dirk explained. "He believes the only way to ensure the whole world pays the Goddess the respect she's due is for him to rule it."

"I still don't see how you being the Lord of the Suns helps."

"It helps because with the *whole* Church supporting him, not just the Shadowdancers, he has a much better chance of forcing the will of the Goddess on Dhevyn."

That made sense. "You'd better tell me about this eclipse before we get back," she reminded him. "That's the first thing Antonov is going to ask *me*."

"The ninth hour on the ninth day of Ezenor in the year ten thousand, two hundred and forty-one."

"That date sounds familiar."

"It's the twentieth anniversary of the day Antonov sacrificed his son, so don't get it wrong."

"That's a bit odd, isn't it?"

"What do you mean?"

"I mean it happening exactly twenty years later."

"The Goddess likes symmetry," Dirk replied unhelpfully.

"The ninth hour on the ninth day of Ezenor in the year ten thousand, two hundred and forty-one," she repeated, to make certain she remembered it. "Do I need to tell him anything else?"

"Tell him the occasion needs to be marked by great pomp and ceremony. Tell him he must gather every leader of note in Bollow for the eclipse."

"Why Bollow? Why not Avacas?"

"Bollow is much higher above sea level than Avacas. You'll be able to see the eclipse better there."

She smiled. "It's going to be quite a memorable party, isn't it?"

Dirk glanced at her and returned her smile briefly. "You have no idea *how* memorable, Marqel."

There was something in his smile that chilled her. "Does that mean you're leaving Avacas?"

He nodded. "As soon as I can get away."

That news pleased Marqel so much she didn't think to ask what Dirk meant by memorable.

Antonov waited for them on the terrace outside his study, the place he always preferred to meet with Dirk. As soon as they stepped onto the flagstones she could tell he'd already heard the news. His expression was expectant, even a little awestruck, Marqel thought.

"So," he said as Dirk and Marqel halted before him, "the Goddess begins to reveal her true design. Congratulations, Dirk."

"Your congratulations may be a little premature, your highness," Dirk replied humbly. "Being named and being sworn in as Lord of the Suns are two different things. The decision is not a popular one. Someone is bound to challenge me."

"Then I will see they don't," Antonov promised. "It is clear to me now your return, Lord Halyn's death—everything that has happened recently—has been for no other purpose than to place you in a position to bring your countrymen back to the Goddess. I always assumed the only way to do that was to put you on your father's throne. I should have known better than to try and second-guess the Goddess."

"I didn't ask for this honor, your highness."

Marqel frowned, thinking that an outright lie. The way he'd been throwing his weight around in the Hall of Shadows, you'd think he'd been planning it for months.

"That in itself is encouraging," Antonov agreed. Then he turned to Marqel. "And you, my lady? Were you planning to keep the Goddess's latest revelation to yourself?"

Marqel smiled and crossed the terrace to him. "No, your highness. I merely wanted the Lord of the Suns to be remembered properly."

"The message I received mentioned a sign?"

"The Goddess is sending us an eclipse, your highness," Dirk answered before Marqel could. "She told the High Priestess she would give Ranadon a moment of darkness to remind the world what the Age of Shadows was like. Once the world has witnessed her power, there should be little resistance to accepting her will, even from the most intransigent heretic."

Antonov nodded in agreement. "Do you remember, Dirk, the day Johan Thorn was washed up on Elcast? I recall watching the ash clouds stain the sky that day, thinking the Goddess had something momentous planned. That eruption in the Bandera Straits led us to this moment. Johan Thorn was captured, which led me to Elcast, where I found both you and the new High Priestess. And now, as the High Priestess Belagren always promised me, the Goddess has revealed her plans to bring the whole of Ranadon to her bosom."

Marqel smiled, rather relieved he was able to interpret everything that had happened so conveniently. She wondered for a moment if it was just a good guess, or if Dirk had *really* known what Antonov's reaction would be. If the Lion of Senet had reacted any other way, both Dirk and Marqel would be heading for the garrison and Barin Welacin's torture racks by now.

"And when is this sign from the Goddess due, Marqel?"

"The ninth hour on the ninth day of Ezenor in the year ten thousand, two hundred and forty-one," she told him solemnly.

Antonov was silent for a long time.

"The Goddess likes symmetry," she added, not sure what the words meant, but they had sounded profound when Dirk said them in the carriage.

The Lion of Senet nodded slowly. "Then she will require a sacrifice."

Marqel glanced at Dirk worriedly. He hadn't said anything about a sacrifice.

"She will, your highness," Dirk agreed.

"Did she say who?"

Marqel didn't know how to answer him. She looked over her shoulder at Dirk again, but if he kept on answering for her, the whole charade would fall apart. He said nothing, did nothing, to help her out.

"The Goddess...she said she would reveal who should be sacrificed...when the time is right," Marqel stammered uncertainly.

Antonov seemed content with that. "Then let us pray that

her sacrifice this time is not as difficult as the last sacrifice she asked for."

Marqel thought he must be talking about his baby son. Even now, the child's death still pained him. What would he do if he ever realized Belagren had made the whole thing up?

Probably the same thing he'd do to me if he ever realized I'm making the whole thing up, too...

Chapter 38

The news that Dirk Provin was now the Lord of the Suns upset Tia less than she thought it might—partly because she was so busy with Misha, and partly because she had reached the point where nothing Dirk did surprised her anymore. She felt numb when she heard the news, although Misha was quite intrigued by it. That Dirk had somehow managed to get himself appointed Lord of the Suns only strengthened Misha's belief that Dirk's ultimate aim was the destruction of the Church of the Suns.

Tia believed quite the opposite. He wasn't trying to destroy it; he was trying to take it over and was doing it at a speed that defied belief—it was less than a year since Dirk had handed her over to Belagren in return for a place in the Shadowdancers.

Misha's condition varied from day to day, and some days were better than others. He was down to about two-thirds of the dose of poppy-dust he'd been taking when they arrived, but the withdrawal was ravaging his body. He kept fighting it, though, even when Tia felt like simply giving in and offering him more poppy-dust to relieve his pain.

He would often pace the house at night, limping endlessly up and down the hall as he did his best to get through the night without giving in. Other nights she could hear him across the hall, thrashing about restlessly in his bed, unable to sleep or even to rest while every cell in his body cried out for the one thing he refused it.

Tia had grown accustomed to listening for him during the night. Although he shared his room with Master Helgin, Tia would wake when she heard him stir and often sat with him on the wide veranda, listening to the noises of the red night and the soothing lap of the sea, talking about anything and everything to distract him from the pain and the unbearable cravings he was suffering.

Hearing the familiar snick of the door opposite followed by the sound of uneven footsteps in the hall, Tia threw back the covers and tiptoed to the door, careful not to wake Mellie. She walked through the silent house and found Misha sitting on the steps of the veranda, gazing out over the blood-washed sea.

"I didn't wake you, did I?" he asked without turning around.

Tia sat beside him on the step, shaking her head. "I wasn't asleep."

"Still thinking about Dirk?"

"No."

"I was."

"It's getting harder and harder to justify what he's doing, isn't it?" she asked. It sounded better than just saying: *I told you so.*

"Justifying what he's done isn't the problem," Misha replied thoughtfully. "It's trying to imagine *how* he's done it that gives me a headache. And it's not just his political machinations that leave me gasping. He's only nineteen years old, Tia. Most boys his age are only interested in girls. Are you sure he didn't discover some magical talisman up there in Omaxin he's using to bend the world to his will? It doesn't seem possible he's doing it without some sort of supernatural intervention."

"Dirk is working so fast because he's no longer burdened by all the things that slow decent people down, like morals or conscience, Misha. There's no magic involved."

"Perhaps..." He shrugged, not entirely convinced. "One

thing is certain. When all this is over, I'd very much like to have a talk with that young man."

"You'll have to get in line, I'm afraid," she warned. "And there wouldn't be much point because the first few dozen ahead of you will probably kill him."

"Your assassin has had no luck then?"

Tia shook her head. She couldn't understand that either. "We'll know more when Reithan gets here, I suppose."

When Misha didn't answer her, she glanced at him in concern.

"Are you all right?"

He held out his hands. He was visibly trembling.

"It's going to be another long night, I fear," he said, trying to mask the pain with a smile.

"Can I get you something?"

"The only thing I want is the last thing I need, Tia. Dear Goddess, this gets harder and harder."

"Master Helgin says you're doing very well."

"He also uses that delightfully tempting phrase: *manageable addiction*. On nights like this, I start to think about that. A lot."

"You've come so far, Misha. Don't give in now."

He forced a smile. "How easy it is for you to sit there and be sympathetic. Not that I don't appreciate it, mind you. It's just..." He stopped to take a deep breath. "It's just that it doesn't really help much to be told how well I'm doing by someone who's fit and whole and has no concept of what this feels like."

"I can go if you want to be alone," she offered, a little hurt.

"No, don't go. I'd like you to stay." He closed his eyes and took another few deep breaths to try to control the shivering. "I *need* you to stay. Talk to me."

"About what?"

"Anything. Just give me something else to think about."

"Well...Oscon is teaching Mellie to ride," she told him, a little worried. Sweat beaded his forehead and he had wrapped his arms around his body as if he was suddenly chilled.

"I'll bet...she's enjoying that."

"So is Oscon. He blusters around a lot and pretends to be a grumpy old man, but I think it's mostly for show. Either that, or Mellie's worn him down. He's really quite fond of her."

"It's those big brown eyes," Misha said, forcing a laugh. "They're irresistible."

"I never really noticed."

"Trust me, Tia. Melliandra Thorn is destined to break quite a few hearts before she's done."

Tia didn't like the sound of that. "Misha, I hope you're not thinking that perhaps you and Mellie?..."

He was rocking back and forth concentrating on anything but the pain. "Me and Mellie? Goddess! What a...terrifying thought!"

"Why is it terrifying? She's a princess. You're a prince..."

"I'm also...twelve years her senior and a crippled...drug addict, Tia. I wouldn't inflict myself...on her, even if she wanted me, which she doesn't." He hesitated for a moment, almost doubled over with the pain. Then he forced a weak smile. "Besides, fond...of her as I am, she's not...my type."

"And what exactly *is* your type?" Tia asked, starting to wonder if she should fetch Master Helgin. She'd not seen him this bad before.

"I find myself growing quite attached to...Oh Goddess!" he suddenly cried out.

"What's wrong?"

"My leg..." he gasped. The muscles contracted violently and his left leg jerked involuntarily. It was as if some invisible hand was testing his reflexes with a sledgehammer. Tia jumped from the step and knelt on the sand in front of him. She pushed up the loose cotton trouser leg and began to massage his calf, trying to stretch the muscles out, which brought another howl of pain from him.

"Your cures are worse...than what you're trying to cure," he rasped. "Are you...sure you can't do it any harder? There must...be...at least one spot you...missed turning into...a bruise."

"You're doing fine if you can still complain about it,

Misha." She kept massaging until she was certain the jerking was under control and then knelt back on her heels in the sand and looked up at him with a frown. "I think I should fetch Master Helgin."

Misha shook his head. "There's nothing he can do for me you're not already...doing. Unless you'd rather not stay."

"I don't mind staying."

Misha smiled at her weakly. "I'd have given in long ago if not for you."

"I haven't done anything special. All this has been your doing, Misha."

"You believe in me. Even when I don't believe in myself. Dirk's an idiot."

"What's Dirk Provin got to do with it?" she asked with a scowl.

"He's an idiot for not realizing what he had in you, Tia. And he's a damned fool for throwing it away."

Tia didn't know how to answer him.

"I'm sorry," he said, suddenly contrite. "I shouldn't have brought Dirk up. I know how much it hurts you."

She shook her head. "No, you don't."

"Perhaps I don't," he conceded, shivering as if caught in a blizzard. "But I do think you're getting over him."

"I got over him about two seconds after he handed me over to Belagren, Misha."

"Really?" he asked with a raised brow.

"Really," she repeated, with a surprising amount of confidence. When he still looked skeptical, she shrugged. "The rest of it was mostly anger at myself for being so stupid. I've been thinking about what you said, you know—about becoming a bitter old woman. You're right. He shouldn't be allowed to do that to me. I refuse to let him."

"So you're not in love with him anymore?"

"I don't know if I ever was, Misha," she admitted, surprised at how much better it made her feel to finally share it with someone. "I think I was in love with the *idea* of Dirk Provin, not who he really is. He's Johan's son. Even after everything I saw him do, I still wanted to believe there was something of Johan in him."

"And there isn't?"

"If there is anything of his father in him, it's all the bad bits I never saw Johan display. And then we spent all that time alone together, and he seemed so anxious to find out when the next Age of Shadows was due . . . well, he was anxious, I suppose, but not for the reasons I imagined."

Misha was silent for a time as he fought off another wave of pain. "Can I ask you something?" he said, when he was recovered enough to speak.

"If you must."

"Suppose someday you find out Dirk really didn't betray you, Tia? Suppose you discovered he was really just doing all these terrible things to destroy the Church. What would you do then?"

"That's your delusion, Misha, not mine."

"Humor me. Suppose my delusion isn't a delusion? What would you do?"

"Drop dead from the shock," she replied with a thin smile.

"Would you go back to him?"

"The last time I saw Dirk Provin, I put an arrow in him, Misha. Even if your wild hypothesis were true—which it isn't, I hasten to add—I don't think there's much of a chance Dirk and I will ever be friends again, let alone anything else."

Oddly enough, her answer seemed to please him. "Well, in a way, I'm glad. I'd probably be dead by now if I hadn't met you at the Hospice in Tolace."

"Keep bringing the subject of Dirk Provin up and you will be," she warned, smiling to take the sting from her words.

"Are you afraid of nothing?"

"Nobody's afraid of nothing unless they're a complete fool."

"Tell me what you're afraid of, then."

"Why?"

"Because right now I'm afraid I won't make it through the night. I need to know I'm not alone."

"I'm scared of the dark," she admitted with a shrug, not sure how such an admission would help him.

"I can't imagine that."

"And yet you can imagine Dirk is doing something noble. What a strange imagination you have."

He smiled, but Tia could tell it took an effort. "You wouldn't believe...some of the strange things...I daydream about."

"Are you sure you don't want me to fetch Helgin?" she asked with concern.

He shook his head and held out his trembling hands to her. "Stay with me."

"I will, Misha," she promised, humbled by his quiet courage. She took his hands and squeezed them encouragingly. "Always."

Chapter 39

Jacinta delivered the news that the *Tsarina* was heading into port while Alenor was still having breakfast in her room. The little queen sat propped up in bed with a tray on her lap that almost groaned under the weight of food. Alenor ate doggedly, obviously unenthusiastic about the task. Sitting beside her on the bed was a plump gray cat, eyeing the contents of her plate with a hopeful expression.

"Do you think it's Kirsh?" she asked through a mouthful of toast, looking rather alarmed by the prospect.

Alenor had been home just for long enough to start taking control of things. Her seal remained lost, so she was able to delay signing the alarming number of laws and proclamations that Kirsh's Senetian advisers had drawn up in her absence. The stalling tactic had proved very effective but it would mean nothing if the regent had returned. He had his own seal and until Alenor came of age, it far outweighed her authority.

"I've a bad feeling it might be," Jacinta said, walking to the window. She looked down over the sea crashing against the cliffs far below them, but the harbor wasn't visible from the palace.

"But that means his guard will be with him. Alexin is coming home."

"Yes," Jacinta sighed. "Alexin will be coming home. And if you've any sense at all, Allie, you'll post him to the other side of Dhevyn for a while. Kirsh will still be on the lookout. You can't risk so much as a sideways glance at him."

Alenor nodded in reluctant agreement. "What are we going to do?"

"Well, the first thing we're going to do is not panic," Jacinta declared, turning back to Alenor. "The second thing you're going to do is finish your breakfast. And the third thing you're going to do is get up and get dressed and greet your husband as if you're actually glad to see him."

"He won't believe that," the queen scoffed.

"No, but it's important his advisers do."

"You know, Jacinta," Alenor noted with a slight frown, "I think you actually enjoy all this dastardly intrigue and court politics."

"Well, it's more interesting than fending off unwanted husbands," she replied with a smile. "Eat the sausage, too, Allie. Red meat is good for you."

"*I* should find you a husband," Alenor threatened. "Someone old and ugly and warty with a lecherous drool and scabby skin and a really foul body odor."

"None of which would bother me in the slightest if he had half a brain," Jacinta announced airily, sitting on the bed beside her. "Now finish your breakfast or I'll have you force fed. And don't let me catch you feeding that damned cat, either. You spoil her shamelessly."

"You're worse than Dorra," the queen accused through a mouthful of eggs. "If I keep eating like this I'll get fat."

"You could do with some fat on you," Jacinta told her. "You're nothing but skin and bones. I don't know what Alexin sees in you."

"*Jacinta!*" Alenor hissed. "Don't say such things."

"We're alone, Allie. Nobody can hear us."

"That's not the point. If you keep making comments like that, one day somebody *will* hear you, and then where will you be?"

"I'll be fine," she shrugged. "It's your scrawny little neck on the line, my queen, not mine."

"You are truly the most terrible person I know, Jacinta D'Orlon," she said with a grin. "No wonder nobody wants to marry you."

Jacinta smiled at her cousin, glad to see she had eaten most of the eggs.

"That's just the way I like it, too," she agreed. "Finish your toast."

"You're a bossy old cow," Alenor grumbled as she took a bite.

"And don't you forget it," Jacinta warned as she rose to her feet to answer a knock at the door. She opened it to find Dimitri Bayel standing outside.

"The queen really isn't ready to receive visitors, my lord."

"This can't wait, my lady."

She stood back to let him enter, knowing the Seneschal would never intrude upon Alenor in her rooms so early if it wasn't important.

"We've already had word about the *Tsarina* docking this morning," she informed him as she closed the door.

"A minor inconvenience in light of the news I bring, my lady. Good morning, your majesty."

"Good morning, Dimitri," Alenor replied. "You haven't come to bully me about how much I eat, have you?"

"I wish that was the only concern I have, your majesty. I would undertake the task gladly. The news I bring is much graver. I've just received a bird from Avacas. They have appointed the new Lord of the Suns."

"*Lord* of the Suns?" Jacinta asked. "I thought we were expecting a Lady of the Suns?"

"We were, my lady. The new Lord of the Suns is Dirk Provin."

"That's ridiculous," Alenor laughed. "Who sent you that message, Dimitri? They are pulling your leg, I'm certain."

"No, your majesty, I fear the message is genuine."

"How did *that* happen?" Jacinta asked with a frown.

"Paige Halyn's will named the man or woman holding the position of right hand to the High Priestess of the Shadow-dancers as his successor. Dirk Provin is, or was, the holder of that position at the time of Lord Halyn's death."

"But the Lord of the Suns was assassinated. Surely the appointment of the new prelate should have been done by election?"

Dimitri seemed surprised Jacinta had known that. "He died more than sixty days after he was wounded, my lady."

Jacinta looked at Alenor, who had gone very quiet. "He's quite a piece of work, this cousin of yours, Allie."

"What do you mean?" Alenor asked in a small voice.

"I *mean* we have a Dhevynian ruling the Church of the Suns for the first time in history," she explained.

"Dirk Provin's nationality does not seem to have influenced his actions thus far," Dimitri pointed out. "I don't see he has much concern for our needs."

"This can't be an accident," she concluded. "The coincidences *that* would imply defy logic."

"Which makes his appointment all the more disturbing, my lady."

"What should we do?" Alenor asked. The news seemed to have rocked her to the core.

"You'll have to send an envoy, Allie. To officially extend your congratulations and assure the new Lord of the Suns of your undying loyalty to the Church."

"The Lady Jacinta is right, your majesty," Dimitri agreed. "You must send someone. And the sooner the better."

"Who?"

"I'll go," Jacinta volunteered.

"But I need you here."

"You need to find out what Dirk Provin is up to more than you need me standing over you to make sure you eat breakfast, Alenor."

"Once again, the Lady Jacinta speaks the truth, your majesty. And I'm inclined to support her suggestion she represent you. She is your cousin, and as such has sufficient rank to do so without insult, and she, at least, can be trusted not to be corrupted by the taint that surrounds Dirk Provin."

"Why, thank you, Lord Bayel," Jacinta said graciously. "That was very kind of you to say. Not to mention very dramatic. *The taint that surrounds him?* I do believe adversity brings out the poet in you."

Dimitri smiled sourly. "In truth, my lady, I fear it usually brings out my gout. But I do think you are the best person for this job. From what little I know of Johan Thorn's bastard, he's neither easily fooled nor easily thwarted, but in you, I think, he may meet his match."

Jacinta wasn't sure if that was a compliment or not.

"I wish you wouldn't call him that, Dimitri," Alenor said. "You make him sound so . . . evil."

"Perhaps he is, your majesty. I suggest we won't know until the Lady Jacinta has seen him at work."

"Please let me go, Allie," Jacinta begged. "I want to do this for you."

"You want to run out on me just when I need you the most," Alenor objected. "Kirsh is sailing into Kalarada Harbor as we speak."

"You can handle Kirshov Latanya," she assured the queen. "Besides, you've been ill. You can get away with swooning and fainting for months if you have to, whenever you don't want to deal with him."

Alenor thought about it for a moment and then shrugged. "All right, you can go, I suppose. I think we'd better find out what Dirk is up to and there's no way I can go myself. I was away far too long the last time and I refuse to leave Kirsh in Kalarada on his own. But I have one condition."

"What's that?"

"That you find me another lady-in-waiting before you leave." The queen smiled and added, "One that isn't a bully like you."

Jacinta was relieved it was the only thing Alenor asked for. "I'll see what I can do," she promised.

Jacinta saw Dimitri to the door, stepping outside with him when she noticed the expression on his face.

"There's something else I didn't mention," he told her in a low voice. "The High Priestess announced the Goddess has spoken to her again."

"What did the *Goddess* have to say this time?"

"There's to be an eclipse. It's supposed to be a sign."

"A sign of what?" Jacinta asked skeptically.

"I don't know, my lady, but if it's true, even the most cynical nonbeliever will start to wonder at the power of the Shadowdancers."

"What's he up to, do you think?"

"Dirk Provin?" Dimitri asked. "I have no idea, my lady, but I'll tell you this much. Whatever it is, it doesn't look good for Dhevyn."

"Alenor clings to the hope he's on our side."

Dimitri frowned. "She also clings to the hope that somehow she and Alexin Seranov will one day find happiness." When he saw Jacinta's shocked expression, he smiled sadly. "Oh yes, I know all about it. And have no fear, I would never betray my queen, but she is hoping for a miracle when there are none to be had. She has your heart, but not your head, I'm afraid. You must let her down gently when you break it to her that her hopes and dreams lack substance."

"You say when, not *if*," Jacinta pointed out. "Don't you allow for even the remote possibility some good may come of this?"

He shook his head, a weary and disillusioned old man. "Nothing good ever comes of dealing with Senet and the Church of the Suns, my lady, and it can only get worse if it involves Dirk Provin. You mark my words."

Chapter 40

After several more nights of cramps and shivering, of sweats and chills, Misha was looking particularly haggard. Tia was worried about him, although Master Helgin seemed quite pleased with his progress. He also seemed a little surprised Misha had come this far and not given in to the call of the poppy-dust.

Tia found the old physician in the kitchen carefully measuring out Misha's next dose. It had been another long night and neither she nor Misha had slept much. Rubbing her eyes, she sat down, and then folded her arms on the table, put her head down and closed her eyes.

"You should have woken me," Helgin scolded.

"Why?" she mumbled. "It's not like you could have done anything. Misha just needs someone to hold his hand to help him get through the night. We just talk most of the time."

"Well, your hand is far more pleasant to hold than mine," he remarked with a smile in his voice.

"What's that supposed to mean?" she asked, looking up at him.

"Just that if I had a choice between sitting up all night with a crusty old physician or a beautiful young woman, I'd know which one I'd choose."

"It's not like that."

"I wasn't implying it was *like* anything, Tia. In fact, I'm very glad you're here. I don't have your stamina anymore. I can't get by on two hours' sleep at my age."

"I'm not too thrilled about it at my age, either," she said, stifling a yawn.

"It was never my intention to force you to share my suffering, Tia."

She looked to the door as Misha limped into the kitchen. Despite the ravages of withdrawal, he could walk without the crutch now and if you looked at him when he was dressed and standing still, you couldn't even tell he was crippled. It was only when he walked and his limp betrayed him, or he tried to lift anything with his left arm, you noticed there was something wrong.

"You're not forcing me," she assured him with a wan smile. "I get a kick out of seeing how long I can go without sleep."

Misha sat down heavily on the bench opposite Tia and looked up at Helgin.

"How much longer, Master Helgin?"

"It will be ready soon," Helgin said, stirring the dust carefully into the cup.

"I meant before I'm free of the poppy-dust."

"Another few months at least."

Misha shook his head. "I can't do this for another few months."

"You can't quit now!" Tia urged. "You're almost there!"

"But that's exactly what I intend to do, Tia. Quit. Completely. Master Helgin, what will happen if I simply stop taking the poppy-dust?"

"I wouldn't recommend—"

"I didn't ask for your recommendation, Helgin, I asked what would happen to me."

"Well, you're down to considerably less of the drug than you were taking when you first came to Mil. But the symptoms you suffer now would become much worse. You may even start to have fits again. And the cravings will be unbearable."

"How long will it last?"

"If you survive them, the acute symptoms may go on for two or three days. But only, I stress—*if* you survive them. Simply stopping the dust could kill you, Misha."

"I can't keep this up for months, Helgin. I'm exhausted and so is everyone else. I can't put myself through it and I won't put Tia through it with me."

"Misha, I was only joking about not getting any sleep," Tia hurried to assure him, thinking she was responsible for his sudden decision to do this dangerous thing.

"I know you were, Tia, and in truth, concern for your sleeping habits is not my only reason for this."

"I would think you'd need an excellent reason for attempting such a foolish and dangerous course of action," Master Helgin said.

"This has got something to do with Dirk, hasn't it?" Tia asked.

He nodded. "I know you think I'm imagining things, Tia, but I can't believe Dirk Provin is now Lord of the Suns by some strange set of circumstances that placed him in the right place at the right time. And with this eclipse the Goddess—or rather, if I am to believe your version of events, Dirk Provin—has predicted, then the logical assumption is that he's planning something to coincide with it. As he already appears to have removed Belagren, I can only conclude my father is his next target. Either way, I need to be there, either to protect my father or to step up and take his place if Dirk succeeds."

"You want *us* to help *you* protect the Lion of Senet?" Tia snorted. "You're asking a bit much, don't you think?"

"My offer still stands, Tia," he promised. "I will withdraw the Senetians from Dhevyn as soon as I have the power to do so. Saving my father from Dirk Provin will give me that power almost as certainly as assuming the throne myself."

"If you survive," Helgin warned.

"I'm not going to go on like this for the rest of my life. And I'll not listen to your logical arguments about a manageable addiction. I'll either be free of this or I will die trying and I have neither the time nor the will to take the safe road in doing it."

"What if you die?" Tia asked bluntly. "Have you thought about that?"

"If I don't survive it, Tia, it will make little difference to anyone. My father probably thinks I'm already dead. He may even be hoping I am."

"It would make a difference to me," she objected. "I haven't sat by you for all these weeks just so you can throw it away on a noble gesture, Misha."

"I wish it was noble, Tia," he sighed. "But I fear I'm driven by cowardice more than courage. I've had enough. I can't even bear the thought of this going on for another week, let alone months. I would rather suffer a few days of unbearable agony and be done with it, one way or another."

Master Helgin held out the cup to Misha with a sympathetic smile. "Take this, your highness. Once you've stabilized, you'll be able to think about it more clearly."

Misha held out his trembling hands for them to see. "Look at me, Helgin. I'm a wreck. I would *rather* risk death than keep on like this."

"Then we'll start tomorrow," Helgin suggested, offering him the poppy-dust again.

Misha slapped the cup from his hand, spilling the precious drug on the floor. "No! We do it now. While I still have the strength to deny it. Don't offer it to me again, Helgin. Get rid of what you have stashed away. I'm done with it, even if it kills me."

Without waiting for their response, Misha pushed himself to his feet and limped from the kitchen. Tia watched him leave, torn between admiration for what he was attempting and fear for what it would do to him.

Helgin turned to Tia, desperately worried. "Talk to him, Tia. Tell him how foolish this is."

She shook her head slowly. "I think he's right, Helgin."

"You can't be serious!"

"He can't take much more of this. Maybe it's better this way."

"He'll die! Do you want that?"

"Of course I don't want him to die," she said. "But he has a point. Would you want to go on living as he is?"

"The point is would I want to go on *living,*" the old man retorted. "Why not just give him a blade and let him slit his wrists? It would be kinder than what he's proposing."

Tia climbed wearily to her feet. "Maybe it will come to that, Helgin, but in the end, it's Misha's choice, not ours."

Later that day, she found Misha sitting on the beach, staring out over the water. He looked up with a frown as she approached.

"Save your breath, Tia. I am determined to do this and lecturing me won't help."

"I didn't come to lecture you," she said as she sat down beside him. "I think you may be doing the right thing."

He laughed bitterly. "Will you still think that tomorrow when I'm foaming at the mouth?"

"My father was an addict, Misha. I've seen the worst poppy-dust can do to a man. That doesn't frighten me."

"It frightens me."

"Then you'll just have to find a way to deal with it. If this works, in a few days, you'll be a free man."

"And if it doesn't, I'll be dead, and that will be a release in itself."

Tia said nothing for a time, just sat with him on the warm white sand, listening to the soothing wash of the ocean.

"Will you promise me something?" he asked.

"Of course."

"No matter how bad it gets. No matter how much I beg, cajole or threaten you, don't give in to me. Don't let me take any more; not out of pity. If it kills me, that's the price I'm willing to pay. If I'm alive, then you must assume I can bear the pain, even if *you* can't bear watching it."

"If you want."

"Swear it, Tia," he insisted. "I've barely got the strength to do this once. If you give in to me out of pity or compassion or even anger, then I'll never have the courage to try again. Swear to me you'll let me die rather than give me more poppy-dust to relieve my suffering."

"Are you certain?"

"Yes."

"Then I swear it," she promised. "But I have a bad feeling you're going to hate me for that oath before this is over."

He smiled at her and placed his trembling hand over hers. "Not as much as I'd hate you if I awoke to discover I was still an addict because you pitied me."

"I don't pity you, Misha."

He looked at her closely. He had to force his eyes to focus on her. It wouldn't be much longer now, she guessed, before he began to wish he'd not refused the poppy-dust Helgin had offered him.

"I'm not sure I've done anything to deserve much else."

"Pity is something you give to helpless creatures with no control over their fate." His hand was still resting on hers. The palm was sweating and she could feel him shaking.

"And you think I have control...over my fate?"

"You've made the choice to live or die the way you choose, Misha. That's not the action of a helpless creature."

"No, it's the action of a desperate one." He forced a thin smile, but his forehead glistened with sweat and the trembling was getting worse. He was long overdue for his next dose of poppy-dust.

She smiled, hoping the conversation was distracting him. "Well, just don't tell anybody how desperate you are, and nobody will ever know."

"I read about an ancient cult once that believed one kept coming back after each life to pay for the previous one." He smiled shakily. Tia wondered if he was trying to drag up any old memory he could find to keep the present at bay. "Ella had a fit when she found me reading the book and confiscated it before my eternal soul could be endangered. But it was an interesting idea. And if it's true, then I must have done something very good in a previous life to deserve a friend like you in this one."

"I'm more interested in what you're planning to do in *this* life, Misha."

"Ah!" he said. "That's what this...is all about, isn't it? You don't care...about me at all. You're only interested in freeing... Dhevyn."

"And taking down Dirk Provin," she added with a grin. "You forgot that bit."

"How silly of me. I think I should—" He doubled over suddenly, clutching his stomach, unable to speak.

"Misha!"

"Get me...back to the...house..." he gasped.

Tia hauled him to his feet and forced him to walk with her back along the sand, although he was shivering so hard she could barely hold him upright. But she could no longer carry him. He had gained a considerable amount of muscle since she'd freed him from the Hospice in Tolace. Mellie was emerging from the house as they approached. When she saw them, she ran down to see what was wrong.

"Fetch Helgin," Tia ordered.

"What's the matter with Misha?" she asked worriedly.

"He's in withdrawal."

Misha groaned in her arms. Franco heard the ruckus and emerged on to the veranda. He took one look at them and hurried to take some of Misha's weight from Tia. Between them, they managed to get him up the steps.

Mellie stared at them with concern. "But he's been in withdrawal for weeks, and he's never been—"

"Just get Helgin, Mellie!" she shouted. "Now!"

"What shall I tell him?"

"Tell him it's begun," she said, as Misha cried out weakly and collapsed against her. "Just tell him it's begun."

Chapter 41

By the time Jacinta arrived in Avacas, the Lord of the Suns had already left for Bollow. She had traveled to Senet in unexpected luxury in the Lion of Senet's own cabin on the *Tsarina*, which was headed back to Avacas after delivering Kirsh to Kalarada. Kirsh offered her passage on the ship. Jacinta suspected Alenor's husband was so delighted by the idea she would not be around to irritate him, he had offered her a berth to ensure she really did leave. They had never really gotten along, Jacinta and Kirshov. The prince considered her a bad influence on Alenor and often accused her of interfering with things that were none of her concern.

Her new position as the envoy of the Queen of Dhevyn gave Jacinta an unexpected amount of freedom. Her mother would never have countenanced her traveling alone to Senet, even with the escort of Queen's Guardsmen Alenor sent along with her. But as Alenor's envoy, she was—for the time being, at least—free from her mother's protective and smothering domination. With luck, Lady Sofia might even give up on the idea of marrying her off for a while. *There's probably more chance of the Age of Shadows returning tomorrow,* Jacinta thought with a sigh as the carriage rattled along Avacas's cobbled streets, *but one can hope . . .*

All she had to do now was prove herself worthy of the trust Alenor had placed in her by discovering what Dirk Provin was up to.

Jacinta didn't like her chances. Alenor's cousin had managed to keep everyone in the dark and she doubted he would confide in a stranger when he'd pointedly refused to tell Alenor what was going on. But the challenge intrigued her.

And so did Dirk Provin.

She had a mental image of him in her mind. He would have the same overpowering aura as Antonov Latanya, she imagined. The same hypnotic charisma. Jacinta couldn't imagine him being able to achieve the rank of Lord of the Suns at the tender age of nineteen any other way. Dirk Provin was the wrong age, the wrong nationality, even the wrong parentage, to logically be thought of as Paige Halyn's successor. Maybe it was that which fascinated her most. If the bastard son of Johan Thorn and Morna Provin could achieve the rank of Lord of the Suns, then nothing was impossible. If he could do that, then maybe the only daughter of an important Dhevynian duke could avoid a future filled with a husband she didn't want, babies she didn't need and a mindless existence filled with nothing more meaningful than tomorrow night's banquet menu.

When Jacinta presented herself at the Hall of Shadows she was served tea and politely but firmly told that if she wished to meet with the Lord of the Suns she would have to find her way to Bollow on her own. More than a little put out, Jacinta then made her way to Avacas palace with the intention of seeking an audience with the High Priestess.

To her relief, Marqel agreed to see her without delay, and she was led to a small, tastelessly—to her eye—furnished chamber on the ground floor of the palace. The Lion of Senet was not in. He had gone to the horse auctions in Arkona for the day, Lord Ezry, the Palace Seneschal, informed her, and wasn't expected back until later that evening. Jacinta was rather glad of the news. Antonov Latanya scared her a little, and if she could avoid dealing with him, she would. Anyway, she wasn't here to see the Lion of Senet. She was here to find out what Dirk Provin was up to.

Marqel breezed into the room a few moments later, dripping with gold bracelets and diamond rings, as if trying to remind everyone of her newfound wealth by wearing it all at once. Jacinta rose and curtsied politely to her, guessing Marqel would like the gesture. Commoners elevated to high office always delighted in seeing those born to rank paying them homage. The Mayor of Oakridge, the town where the bulk of her family's estates were located on the island of Bryton, was just as easily impressed. He'd been a bookbinder before being raised to the exalted position of mayor and he almost slobbered with glee whenever Jacinta had acknowledged him in public.

"Lady Jacinta! What a pleasant surprise!"

"The pleasure is all mine, my lady," Jacinta assured her. "I must say, the role of High Priestess seems to suit you. You're looking very well."

"It's an honor I do my best to be worthy of," Marqel replied, with entirely false modesty. "But please, be seated and tell me to what I owe this unexpected pleasure."

Jacinta resumed her seat as Marqel took the chair opposite, forcing herself not to smile at Marqel's wordy turn of phrase. "I come to Avacas as the envoy of the Queen of Dhevyn, my lady. I was hoping to meet with the Lord of the Suns."

A fleeting frown flickered over Marqel's face, which Jacinta thought rather interesting. "He's not here. He's gone to Bollow."

"So I understand. I'm rather put out by the news, actually. I didn't come prepared to traipse halfway across Senet to meet with him."

"I can arrange for you to get to Bollow, if that's what you want," Marqel offered, probably delighting in the thought she was in a position to do Jacinta a favor. It wasn't inspired out of friendship, Jacinta was certain. More likely she was doing it to prove she had the power to make things happen at will.

"I'd be most grateful if you could, my lady," Jacinta replied. "I don't know Senet at all, and I'm afraid I'm easy prey for unscrupulous merchants. I have a small escort with me, but even with their help, left to my own devices, I'd probably end up paying a fortune for a coach."

"Oh, you don't have to pay for a coach!" Marqel declared. "Dirk's— I mean the Lord of the Suns' servants are leaving tomorrow with the rest of his gear. You and your escort can travel with them."

Jacinta smiled and realized the trap she'd walked into. She'd accepted the offer and it was too late to go back on it, but Marqel wasn't offering her a coach and four. She was to travel in the Lord of the Suns' baggage wagon.

"I can't thank you enough, my lady."

"Don't mention it," Marqel assured her. "Believe me, it's nothing."

The transport to Bollow turned out considerably better than Jacinta expected. The carriage that arrived to collect her the following morning was battered and poorly sprung, but it was a carriage, although it was perilously loaded with a number of trunks tied to the roof. Sitting inside was a young couple who looked both nervous and uncomfortable to learn they must share their journey with the Queen of Dhevyn's envoy.

Jacinta decided not to watch the coachman abusing her trunks, so she climbed into the carriage and smiled at the young man and woman as the driver cursed and muttered to himself while he tied her luggage down. Tael Gordonov and the half dozen men of her escort took up position around the coach while the passersby in the street wondered at the strange sight of a baggage wagon surrounded by a detail of Dhevynian Guardsmen.

"I'm Lady Jacinta D'Orlon," she told her fellow passengers, taking her seat with a friendly smile. "And you are?"

"I'm Caterina Farlo," the young woman replied uncertainly. "This is Eryk."

Jacinta turned to the young man with a delighted smile. "Eryk? Why Alenor has told me so much about you. I'm so glad to meet you at last."

The boy looked at her in astonishment. "You *know* Printheth Alenor?"

"But of course I do. She and I are cousins."

"So *you* say," Caterina replied skeptically.

"Not that I'm required to explain myself to you, but I'm here on her behalf to meet with the Lord of the Suns." She pointed to the mounted escort. "See. I have an escort of Guardsmen with me. Is that not sufficient credentials for you?"

Eryk treated Jacinta to a beaming smile. "Alenor ith the nitheth... I mean... the *nicest* princess in the whole world."

"She certainly is, Eryk," Jacinta agreed. "And she says you are the most loyal and faithful *servant* in the whole world. Your master is very lucky to have you."

"I'm glad you're coming with us then, Lady Jacinta. Isn't this good, Caterina?"

The young woman wasn't quite so easily won over as Dirk Provin's dull-witted servant. "I suppose."

The coach jerked as it moved off, hitting every bump and pothole in the road as they traveled. It was going to be a very long journey, Jacinta thought with a silent groan.

"So tell me, Caterina, what is your role in Lord Provin's entourage?" She was genuinely curious about the girl's answer. Alenor had mentioned nothing about an attractive blonde in Dirk's service.

"I'm his hostage, my lady," Caterina explained.

"Oh, you poor thing," she sighed, hoping she'd covered her surprise well. "What did you do to find yourself in such an unfortunate position?"

"She didn't do anything," Eryk volunteered. "Caterina's

papa is in the Brotherhood and she's staying with us so they won't kill Lord Dirk."

"Eryk!" Caterina scolded. "Mind your tongue!"

Jacinta smiled at the girl. "Please, don't be angry at him. I'll keep your confidence. But I'm surprised to hear there is a Brotherhood assassin after someone as important as Lord Provin."

Eryk's face crumpled into a frown. "It was the Baenlanders, my lady. They're the ones that put a contract out on him. Tia told them all this mean stuff about him and now they don't like him anymore."

Hardly surprising. What *was* surprising was that Dirk Provin had the wits to find a way to prevent the contract from being carried out. A Brotherhood assassin on your tail was nothing to be blasé about.

"Well, I just hope you haven't been mistreated, Caterina," she said. "Or I would feel compelled to raise the matter with Lord Provin myself."

"Oh no, my lady," Caterina hurried to assure her. "He's been a real gentleman. I mean, even when we were on the ship on the way to the Baenlands, he didn't ravage me or anything like that, and he didn't let any of the crew hurt me, either."

"A true gentleman," Jacinta agreed, fighting the urge to smile. "Still, these things are usually temporary arrangements. Perhaps he'll let you return home soon."

"I don't think so, my lady," Caterina told her confidently. "I mean everybody knows when the Brotherhood accepts a contract, they never stop until it's been carried out. I may have to stay Lord Provin's hostage for ever and ever . . ."

And you're not the least bit disturbed by the prospect, are you? Jacinta thought, slightly amused. Was Dirk Provin aware of the fact that this girl was besotted by him? Did the thought amuse him? Had he taken advantage of it? Or was he too blind to notice?

"Will you be staying with us in Bollow, my lady?" Eryk asked. She had obviously won him over, heart and soul. Her credentials as Alenor's cousin put her firmly in the young man's good graces.

"No, I'll find an inn when we get there. I wouldn't dream of imposing myself on Lord Provin's hospitality at such a time." *Or putting myself in his power,* she added silently.

"You'll like him," Eryk predicted confidently. "He's really nice."

Jacinta smiled, thinking of all the descriptions she heard of Dirk Provin, "really nice" was not among them.

"I'm sure he is, Eryk," she agreed. "Alenor told me all about him and she says *exactly* the same thing."

Eryk nodded happily as the carriage and her escort continued to wend their way through the crowded streets of Avacas. Jacinta didn't even notice the rough ride any longer, too enchanted by the idea that for the next few days she would have nothing better to do than grill Dirk Provin's loyal servant and his love-struck hostage.

Marqel had unwittingly done her a huge favor by packing her off to Bollow in Dirk's baggage wagon. By the time they got to the northern city, she would probably know what color his underwear was.

And that, Jacinta expected, was going to give her the edge she needed to deal with the enigmatic and dangerous Dirk Provin.

Chapter 42

Tia woke to a room filled with dull light and the soft pattering of rain on the thatched roof. It took her a moment to remember where she was, then she frowned as she realized she'd been sleeping. Lifting her head from her folded arms resting on the edge of the bed, she blinked sleepily. Her neck was stiff from dozing in such an uncomfortable position, perched on a chair beside the bed. Misha lay amid a tangle of sheets, but his breathing was deep and even. He was asleep, she realized, not unconscious, his face peaceful and serene.

"He's over the worst of it, I think," Master Helgin said softly behind her.

She sat up, rubbing her eyes. "Why did you let me doze off?"

"One invalid is all I can cope with at the moment," he told her. "You needed the rest."

"Is he going to be all right?"

Helgin nodded slowly. "Yes, I think he's going to be just fine."

The relief Tia felt was indescribable. The horror of the past few days was something she never wanted to live through again. There had been so many times when she almost broke her vow and gave into Misha's cries for relief. So many times when she was sure he must die, because it didn't seem possible his body could take much more punishment.

"So it's all over now?" she asked.

Helgin nodded. "The physical symptoms should diminish the longer he's free of the drug, although he may have the odd relapse. The worst is over but he's not out of the woods yet. And the mental cravings may never leave him. He's going to have to be very strong to resist them."

"He's strong enough," she assured the old man. Stronger than any person she had ever met. "Not physically, perhaps, but he's a lot tougher than he looks, Master Helgin."

Helgin smiled. "You've no need to convince me of that, lass. I've only seen one or two people survive sudden withdrawal. Few men have the courage to even try it. He's quite a remarkable young man." He placed his hand on her shoulder. "Why don't you go and get some sleep. I'll stay with him."

"No," she said, shaking her head. "I want to be here when he wakes up."

"Your room is just across the hall," Helgin reminded her. "I promise I'll call you the moment he opens his eyes."

Tia thought about it for a moment and then nodded, rising stiffly to her feet. Misha might sleep for hours yet and she was exhausted, in mind and body. She had no idea what day it was, whether it was morning or evening. The last few days were just a blur.

"You will call me, won't you?" she insisted.

"I promise."

Tia closed the door to Misha's room behind her gently and all but staggered across the hall to her own bed. She collapsed onto it fully clothed, asleep before she'd had time to notice she was lying down. She slept dreamlessly and deeply until she was woken by a gentle hand on her shoulder, shaking her awake.

"Is it Misha?" she asked, a little surprised to find Franco standing over her.

"No, he's still sleeping as far as I know, lass. Reithan's here," the caretaker advised her. "And he has the Lady Lexie with him."

"Lexie!"

They were gathered in the kitchen: Lexie, Reithan, Mellie and Prince Oscon. Tia threw herself into Lexie's arms, relieved to see her alive and well. Reithan stood near the stove, sipping a steaming mug of tea and talking to Oscon, who was tolerating this intrusion into his peaceful domain with a remarkable degree of equanimity.

"Is everyone all right? When we heard about Mil we were so worried about you all."

"The bulk of our people got away," Lexie assured her. "A few of them stayed to fight. Dal Falstov and most of his crew were killed during the battle, but Porl got the *Makuan* clear before the attack. And we were able to get the rest of the people up to the caves before the Senetians arrived, thanks to Dirk."

Tia scowled at Lexie. "Thanks to *Dirk*? Thanks to Dirk they *invaded* the Baenlands, Lexie!"

"I think you'd better hear Lexie out, Tia," Reithan suggested.

"What do you mean?"

Lexie took a seat at the table, her expression grave. "Dirk

arranged for the invasion fleet to heave to at the entrance to the delta for almost a full day before they attacked," she explained. "We had plenty of time to evacuate Mil."

"Then Dirk never really betrayed us at all," Mellie announced. "I *knew* he wouldn't do it. That proves it!"

"That doesn't prove anything, Mellie, other than the fact that he's an idiot."

"Which we all know is not the case," Lexie reminded her. "But that's not all, Tia. I was captured by the Senetian Guard. I am only alive today because Dirk intervened. He lied about who I was to Prince Kirshov. He stopped the Senetians from searching the caves above the settlement."

"So he's got some small shred of conscience left," Tia shrugged. "It's hardly evidence he's doing anything noble."

"But if Dirk has joined the Shadowdancers to destroy them," Mellie pointed out, determined to believe the best about her half-brother, "if he is still on our side, then he would have no choice but to pretend he wants to destroy us."

"You haven't heard, then," Tia concluded as she listened to Lexie and Mellie trying to justify everything Dirk had done as having some noble purpose. "Dirk's not a Shadowdancer any longer, Lexie. He's moved up in the world. He's the Lord of the Suns now."

Lexie was clearly shocked by the news.

"I got word from Tanchen a few days ago," Oscon added. "He was named as Paige Halyn's heir a couple of weeks after the old man died."

"And you still think he simply left us to hide away in Avacas in comfort?" Lexie asked Tia with a raised brow.

"I don't know what to think, Lexie. Misha believes he's trying to bring down the Church."

"And who better than the Lord of the Suns to do that?" Oscon remarked. "I'm inclined to think Misha may have the right of it. This reeks of a well thought out plan, my lady, not a chance set of coincidences."

"You're clutching at sunbeams," Tia accused. "All of you. If Dirk had some grand plan to bring down the Shadowdancers, why keep it a secret from us? Why not tell us what he was doing? Why not trust us? We could have helped!"

"Perhaps he trusted us as much as we trusted him, Tia," Lexie suggested. "What would you have done if Dirk came to you and told you he wanted to return to Avacas to join the Shadowdancers so he could become the Lord of the Suns and destroy the Church?"

"I wouldn't have believed it then, any more than I do now," she replied.

"Which is precisely my point, dearest," Lexie said. "He had no reason to believe we would have supported his plan."

"His *plan*, Lexie, is to gain as much power for himself as he possibly can, and he doesn't care who he steps on along the way to gain it. He's even told the new High Priestess about this eclipse that's coming. That's the same High Priestess he slept with, by the way."

"What eclipse?" Reithan asked.

"Don't you remember, Reithan? The eclipse he bought his way into the Shadowdancers with," Tia reminded him. "And when I told Neris about it, all he did was laugh." She sighed, wondering what it would take to make her people see Dirk for what he really was. "How is Neris, by the way? I suppose he thought the sight of the Senetian fleet sailing into Mil a grand old show."

Lexie leaned forward and took her by the hand. "I'm sorry, darling. Neris is...he was killed in the fighting..."

Tia stared at her for a moment, numbed by the news. On top of everything else that had happened lately, it felt as if she had nothing left with which to grieve for her father.

"He wasn't captured, then?" she asked tonelessly.

"Small consolation that it is," Lexie assured her. "They didn't take him alive."

Tia couldn't help her feeling of despair. "So Mil is destroyed, our people are scattered and the only person left alive who might be able to predict the next Age of Shadows is Dirk Provin."

"Tia..." Lexie said, reaching out to her.

She shook off Lexie's proffered sympathy and rose wearily to her feet. "I think I'll go sit with Misha for a while."

"How is he?" Reithan asked.

"He's doing just fine," she said. "He's finally free of the poppy-dust and itching to get back to Avacas."

"It's been worth it, then?" Lexie asked.

"I hope so, Lexie, because the way things are going for our people lately, I've a bad feeling the son of our worst enemy is our only hope."

Tia shooed Master Helgin out of Misha's room and sent him down to the kitchen to greet Reithan and Lexie. She took the chair beside the bed and studied Misha's sleeping form for a while, wondering what he would make of the news Lexie had brought about Dirk's strange behavior in Mil. He'd no doubt think it simply strengthened his argument that Dirk was planning to destroy the Church.

Maybe he was right. Maybe she simply refused to accept the evidence everyone else seemed determined to believe. On the other hand, they'd fallen into this trap before with Dirk Provin and she was the only one who had insisted he couldn't be trusted. *But I fell under his spell, too, just like the rest of them,* she reminded herself. For a moment she tried to recall that time in Omaxin, wondering what it was that had made her let her guard down. Was it the isolation? Or was it the desperate hope that in Johan Thorn's son lay the future his father had refused to consider?

"Tia?"

All thoughts of Dirk fled as she realized Misha was awake.

"Is it...over?"

"It's over."

He reached out his hand for hers with a wan smile. "I feel like I've been run over by a herd of stampeding horses."

"You'll start to feel better soon," she assured him, giving his hand an encouraging squeeze.

He smiled and raised her hand to his lips, kissing it gently. "Thank you."

"I didn't do anything, Misha," she said, strangely moved by the simple gesture.

"You stayed with me. And you kept your promise."

"Only just," she told him. "I came awfully close to giving in."

"But you didn't. I wish there was some way I could repay you for your kindness."

"Free Dhevyn," she reminded him with a smile. "That'll do for a start."

He laughed softly. "You're never going to let me forget that promise, are you?"

"Never."

He studied her for a moment and then frowned. "You look exhausted."

"I'm all right. I've had a few hours' sleep."

"You should rest."

"You sound like Helgin."

"I mean it, Tia. I'll be all right. Go and get some of the rest you've denied yourself on my account. It'll make you feel much better." And then he added with a smile, "And it will ease my conscience, too."

She *was* exhausted, she knew, and numb over the news about her father. Perhaps Misha was right. He was awake now and it would feel good to rest without worrying about him.

"Are you sure? I can stay if you like."

"Go!" he commanded with a smile.

Tia rose to her feet. She leaned over to place a sisterly kiss on his forehead, but for some reason she couldn't explain, in the last instant she changed her mind and lowered her mouth over his.

Misha seemed a little shocked at first, then put his arm around her and pulled her closer. A world of promise suddenly opened to her as the kiss deepened into something far beyond simple friendship.

Tia pulled away from him, mortified. "I'm sorry..."

"Please," he said with a smile. "Don't apologize."

She turned to leave but he grabbed her hand and pulled her back.

"Tia, don't ever be sorry..."

"I have to go," she muttered, shaking free of his grasp.

He let her hand go and searched her face. "Will you be back?"

"I don't know," she said, and then she fled the room, trying to outrun the sudden confusion kissing Misha had evoked.

Chapter 43

Word that the new Lord of the Suns was in residence in Bollow spread quickly throughout the city and precipitated a sudden rush of people who had urgent business with him. Dirk didn't have the time or the inclination to deal with any of them. He was on a tight schedule, its urgency dictated by his certainty that the longer he gave his enemies to plot his downfall, the greater the chance they had of succeeding. Forty-one days now before the eclipse. In that time, he had to get everything in place, because the day of the eclipse was going to be the most momentous since Antonov sacrificed his youngest son to bring back the second sun.

When he arrived in the Lord of the Suns' private study, Claudio Varell presented him with the long list of people seeking an audience. Dirk glanced over it, and then looked up at Lord Varell with despair.

"They *all* want to see me?"

"Every one of them, my lord," Claudio confirmed. "And they all claim it's a matter of life or death."

"I've never even heard of half these people. Who is Master Galen?"

"He represents the Bollow Chamber of Commerce, my lord."

"What's his problem?"

"There is some concern among his members you might prefer to deal with foreign suppliers... given your nationality."

Dirk looked at him with a shake of his head. "So he's demanding a meeting to make sure the Church doesn't start ordering vegetables from Dhevyn?"

"I think that is his major concern, my lord."

"Then get rid of him. Who's Lord Parqette?"

"Ah, Lord Parqette owns most of the vineyards around Bollow."

"Tell him I don't drink. Who's next on the list?"

"That would be Lady Ortain. She is the widow of Lord Gavan Ortain, who owes the Church rather a large sum of money. No doubt she wishes to meet with you to discuss the debt."

"How did her late husband come to owe the Church money?"

"His estate borders the Lord of the— your estate, my lord. He purchased a tract of land from the Church to expand his crops, planted it, harvested it and then failed to make good with the payment. I believe he had a gambling problem."

"Tell her the debt is absolved," Dirk ordered. "We'll simply take the land back. Is there anybody on that list I *have* to see?"

"It would probably be impolitic to refuse the Lady Jacinta an audience."

"Who?"

"The Queen of Dhevyn's envoy, my lord."

Dirk inwardly groaned. "Jacinta *D'Orlon?*"

Claudio looked at him oddly. "Are you acquainted with the lady, my lord?"

"I'm acquainted with the gossip about her," he answered. "Is she here?"

"Waiting in the anteroom, my lord."

Dirk wasn't sure he was ready for this. Jacinta D'Orlon had convinced Alenor to go to Avacas when she discovered she was pregnant, a decision that almost cost the young queen her life. She was undoubtedly the one who covered for Alenor and allowed her to conduct her dangerous affair with Alexin Seranov in the first place. And she had seriously offended Lord Birkoff from Tolace by the manner in which she'd refused his offer of marriage. To Dirk's mind, she was an irresponsible troublemaker. Alenor might have even sent her here to get her out of Kalarada before she could do any *real* damage.

"I suppose you'd better send her in," he sighed. Best to get this over and done with, and then he could get rid of her.

Claudio bowed and left to follow Dirk's orders. A few moments later, a knock sounded on the door and he called permission to enter. But it was not Jacinta D'Orlon who walked in. It was Eryk and Caterina.

"What are you two doing here?"

"We've been shopping in the markets," Caterina explained.

"Caterina's really good at haggling, Lord Dirk."

"I'm sure she is," Dirk agreed with a scowl. "I don't recall giving you two permission to go wandering through the Bollow markets."

Caterina smiled brightly. "It's all right. I didn't try to escape or anything."

"Why not?"

"Because I'm your hostage," she replied, as if that explained everything.

He smiled. "One would think that would be the *reason* you tried to escape, Caterina."

"But where would I go?" she asked, looking genuinely puzzled.

"Home to Tolace, perhaps?" he suggested. "The Brotherhood would help you if you asked them, surely?"

"I suppose," she shrugged, "but what would be the point? Why would I want to go home to sharing a room with four sisters and making baskets all day, when I can live in a palace and be the hostage of the Lord of the Suns?"

Dirk hadn't really thought about it like that. "You're not homesick?"

"I'm having the time of my life." She frowned suddenly. "You're not thinking of sending me back, are you, Lord Dirk?"

Caterina had picked up the annoying habit of calling him Lord Dirk from Eryk.

"You can't!" she cried in alarm when Dirk didn't reply. Caterina grabbed his hand with both of hers, fell to her knees before him and stared up at Dirk imploringly. "Don't make me go home!"

"Your parents must be worried sick about you, Caterina. They don't know what's happened to you."

"Yes, they do. I've written them several times. I told Mama where I was and how well you were treating me. And how nice you've been."

"You wrote to your mother and told her I was being nice?" Dirk asked with a shake of his head. "When did this happen?"

"Ages ago," Caterina shrugged.

Dear Goddess, what have I unleashed? She's writing to the Brotherhood and telling them I'm nice.

When Dirk didn't answer immediately, Caterina became quite panic-stricken. "You can't send me away, Lord Dirk. I mean...suppose the Brotherhood contract is still out on you? I *have* to stay. Your life depends on it!"

Somebody else knocked on the door. Dirk absently called permission to enter as he stared down her. "Caterina..."

"You must let me stay with you," she begged. "Please don't send me away."

"I can come back later if I'm interrupting something...*personal,*" a rather amused voice announced.

Dirk's head jerked up. Jacinta D'Orlon was standing at the open door, studying the scene before her with a raised brow. For a moment, he was rendered speechless by the sight of her. He had heard the daughter of the Duke of Bryton described as "pretty," but confronted with her in person, the word seemed woefully inadequate.

When he realized he was staring, Dirk hurriedly shook himself free of Caterina, wondering what it must look like, with the girl on her knees before him, begging to stay.

"Lady Jacinta?"

"Lord Provin?"

"Er...this is Caterina Farlo," he said, as the girl climbed to her feet. "She's my hostage," he added, by way of explanation.

"Obviously," Jacinta remarked wryly. Then she turned to Eryk with a warm smile. "Hello, Eryk."

Dirk looked at the boy in surprise. "You know the Lady Jacinta?"

"She was in our carriage on the way from Avacas, Lord Dirk. She said Princess Alenor told her all about you."

Dirk turned to Jacinta. "She did?"

Jacinta didn't answer him. "You must come and visit us in Kalarada someday, Eryk. If your lord will permit it, of course."

She closed the door and stepped farther into the room. Jacinta was taller than her cousin Alenor, with rich dark hair. She walked with the natural grace that only came with impeccably good breeding. As she neared him, Dirk noticed her eyes but he couldn't decide what color they were. It seemed every time she moved they were a different hue.

No wonder Birkoff had been willing to spend half his fortune trying to win her hand...

Dirk forced his attention to the matter at hand and frowned at Jacinta. "Did you come all this way just to extend an invitation to visit Kalarada to my servant, my lady?"

"Not at all. I came all this way to find out what you're up to, my lord."

"Would you like us to leave, Lord Dirk?" Caterina asked.

"No," Dirk told her, for some reason not wanting to be alone with this unsettling young woman. "The Lady Jacinta won't be staying long."

Jacinta's eyes narrowed a fraction. "You and I need to talk, my lord. And soon."

"And we shall, my lady. After the swearing-in."

"Then if you survive the ceremony tomorrow, I will expect to be given a private hearing as soon as you can arrange it."

"If I *survive*?"

"You're not out of the woods yet, Dirk Provin, if you think this ceremony is merely a formality. You can be challenged right up until you take the oath."

"By whom?"

"By any one of the several thousand people who would

rather see another Age of Shadows than allow a Dhevynian to be appointed Lord of the Suns," she suggested. "Particularly the bastard son of the Heretic King of Dhevyn."

Dirk found himself rapidly reassessing his opinion of Jacinta D'Orlon. She was neither the vapid girl he assumed, nor would she be so easily dismissed as he had hoped.

"Did Alenor send you with a message?"

"She said to wish you luck."

"Really?"

"No," Jacinta admitted. "I made that up. Mostly she wants to know why she should trust you in light of everything you've done lately."

"Because I asked her to," Dirk replied, in no mood to explain himself to a complete stranger.

"You ask a lot."

"That's between Alenor and me."

"I'm curious as to how you manage to keep her trust."

He met those disconcerting color-changing eyes evenly. "What would it take to win *your* trust, I wonder?"

Jacinta thought about her answer for a moment. "You could arrange for the Senetians currently searching Dhevyn for refugees from Mil not to go anywhere near my family's orchards near Oakridge. That would probably do it."

Dirk stared at her in shock. Was her question a trap, or was the cousin of the queen and the daughter of one of the most distinguished and wealthy families in Dhevyn actually harboring fugitives?

"Eryk. Caterina. Out!"

His tone startled them enough that they both hurried from the room without so much as a whimper of protest. Jacinta said nothing as they slammed the door behind them, turning to study Dirk curiously.

"You implicate yourself in treason, my lady."

"Only if you're a blind follower of the Lion of Senet, my lord. If you're the loyal Dhevynian Alenor believes you to be, then I'm in no danger at all."

"You've a pretty risky method of testing your theory."

"But an effective one," she pointed out, and then she

shrugged airily. "Besides, I'm just a silly girl, didn't you know? Accuse me of anything and I'll deny I ever spoke of any refugees in Oakridge and if you find them there, I will simply swoon with shock at the news and it'll be your word against mine."

"You seem to forget, I have witnesses," he reminded her, indicating the door where Caterina and Eryk had just gone.

"Your common-born hostage who is obviously besotted with you and your half-witted servant?" she asked. "I think not."

Dirk shook his head, not at all certain what this woman wanted of him. "Even if I wanted to help the refugees from Mil, I have no say over what Kirsh's forces in Dhevyn are up to. That's something you should have taken up with the queen before you left Kalarada."

"And implicate *her* in treason?"

"You're ready enough to implicate yourself, my lady."

"It's a risk I'm prepared to take. One I almost have to take. I don't see how else I can establish whose side you're on, Dirk Provin. Actions speak louder than words." Jacinta met his eyes with a blatant challenge. "Will you do it? Will you call off the search?"

"I don't know if I can."

"Think about it, my lord," Jacinta suggested. "I'm staying at the Widow's Rest in the city if you wish to see me again."

Jacinta turned and left the room without another word. Dirk watched her leave, quite speechless. Caterina and Eryk were back so soon after she left that Dirk figured they'd been waiting outside. Caterina closed the door behind her and leaned on it with a knowing smile. "You like her, don't you?"

"What?"

"Lady Jacinta. You like her."

"I only just met her, Caterina," he shrugged, wondering how she could have come to that conclusion from a meeting lasting barely five minutes. "I've hardly had time to form an opinion about her."

"You formed your opinion the moment you laid eyes on

her, my lord. I could tell. And it didn't have anything to do with her diplomatic status, either."

Dirk glared at the young woman in annoyance. "Haven't you got something better to do than stand around here inventing things that don't exist?"

"No." She shrugged. "Right now, I've nothing better to do at all."

"Then find something," he snapped, turning back to the list he had been going through before Eryk and Caterina arrived.

"I'm right, you know," Caterina told Eryk sagely. "He *really* likes her."

"I like her, too," Eryk agreed. "She's very pretty."

"Out!" Dirk ordered impatiently. "Both of you!"

"Come on, Eryk," Caterina said. "Let's go find some lunch. Lord Dirk has a lot on his mind, I think."

He heard the door closing and glanced up, relieved to find them gone. Dirk sank down in his chair and leaned back. He closed his eyes wearily, thinking perhaps he should send Caterina home. She was starting to get a little too comfortable, although Caterina and Eryk had become such fast friends he was a little worried what sending her away might do to the boy.

Dirk sighed. There was always another complication. Always something he hadn't anticipated...

And right now, at the top of the list of things he hadn't anticipated was Jacinta D'Orlon.

Chapter 44

Jacinta allowed Tael to help her up into her carriage and was being driven back toward Bollow before she let herself think about her meeting with the Lord of the Suns. She loosened the high collar of her light jacket, wondering why she felt so uncomfortable. It couldn't have been her meeting with

Dirk Provin, she concluded. He was just a boy, really, no older than she was.

He was nothing like she imagined. Alenor had told her a lot about Dirk but it was colored by her affection for him as a friend. Her cousin spoke of his sense of humor, of his intelligence, of his loyalty (although that was stretching it a bit, perhaps). She'd never mentioned those impossibly cold gray eyes, or the very presence of him. It wasn't like the overwhelming presence of the Lion of Senet, who dominated the room, drawing every eye to him. It was far more subtle than that. Dirk hadn't raised his voice or even said anything terribly profound, but she realized she'd been hanging off his every word. If he had that effect on everyone he met, it was no wonder he had come so far, so quickly. Just the way he spoke, the way you kept searching those unreadable eyes for some hint of what he was thinking, kept you wanting to listen to him.

Jacinta had known Dirk Provin would be dangerous. He couldn't have achieved what he had so far and be anything else. But she was only just beginning to realize *how* dangerous. She might have signed her own death warrant by telling him about the refugees in Oakridge. She would know soon enough. There might even be a detail waiting to arrest her when she returned to the inn.

But if there wasn't? If Alenor was right and he was on their side, then he was doing all this to help Dhevyn. Exactly what his plan was remained a mystery, but anyone with the skill to get himself appointed Lord of the Suns probably had a few things up his sleeve even she couldn't guess.

When Jacinta returned to the Widow's Rest, she was quite relieved to find nobody waiting to arrest her. Either she had judged Dirk Provin correctly, or he was waiting for a more opportune time to expose her. She preferred to think—and fervently hoped—the former was the case.

As she walked through the entrance of the inn, she discovered the lobby filled with people waiting to be shown to their rooms. With the swearing-in tomorrow of the Lord of the Suns, travelers had come to Bollow from all over Senet and Dhevyn to witness it. Those who had arrived so close to the ceremony were finding it difficult to get a room. There was barely an empty bed in the whole city.

"Lady Jacinta!"

She turned to the man who hailed her and smiled politely. "Lord Seranov. I didn't expect to see you here in Bollow."

"Can't miss something as important as the swearing-in of a new Lord of the Suns, my lady," he declared, brushing the hair from his face, as always. Jacinta often wished she had a pair of scissors handy when she was in Saban Seranov's company. She found his habit irritating beyond belief.

"No, I suppose you can't," she agreed. "Are your sons not with you?"

"Alexin is still in Kalarada with the Queen's Guard, my lady," he reminded her. "But if I'd known you were going to be here, I would have insisted Raban accompany me."

Jacinta smiled. Raban Seranov had as much chance of winning her hand as Lord Birkoff. "Isn't Raban recently a father, my lord? I hear some Shadowdancer in Nova just delivered a healthy boy that bears a remarkable resemblance to your eldest son."

The Duke of Grannon Rock shrugged. "You know how it is with young people, my lady. They need to run a bit wild before they settle down."

"Indeed," she agreed wryly.

The duke's eyes narrowed, sensing her disapproval. "You shouldn't be too hard on him, my lady. I understand you have been testing the limits yourself, lately."

"I beg your pardon?" she asked, quite offended.

"I speak of your application to enroll at the university in Nova, Lady Jacinta, under an assumed name. And a boy's name at that."

"A deception that would not have been necessary, my lord, if your narrow-minded academics were willing to acknowledge a woman is just as capable of higher learning as a man."

"Even if that were the case, my lady, a young woman of

your station in life should not even be thinking of such a future. You have a duty to your class to bear the next generation."

"And breeding cows don't need an education."

Saban Seranov smiled. "A crude but effective way of putting it, my lady."

"You know, someday, my lord, you may find yourself having to reassess your position on that matter."

Saban shrugged. "I live for the day the only thing I have to occupy my time is debating the advisability of allowing women access to my university, Lady Jacinta. It would mean a great many of the ills that plague our world are no longer an issue."

She studied him closely for a moment, wondering if she was reading his meaning correctly. "Perhaps with the unexpected elevation of one of our own countrymen to the position of the Lord of the Suns, we might begin to hope a little, my lord."

"Do *you* believe that's the case?" he asked cautiously.

"I'm really not in a position to say."

"You've met with the Lord of the Suns, I understand, Lady Jacinta, which is more than anybody else has been able to manage. What is your opinion of him?"

"I think he's very..." She hesitated for a moment. The first word that leapt to mind was *dangerous,* but she didn't think that was what Saban Seranov wanted to hear. "He's very interesting, my lord. And very intelligent. Don't make the mistake of underestimating him."

"One rather hopes it will be the Senetians who make that mistake, my lady," he suggested with the faintest hint of a smile.

Jacinta was reluctant to be drawn into commenting. She knew Saban's youngest son, Alexin, was loyal to the cause. Even if Alenor hadn't been his lover, he had quite a history with the Baenlanders. She was reasonably confident about his eldest son, Raban, too, despite his rather inappropriate taste in bed partners. But nobody, not even his sons, was really certain where Saban Seranov's loyalties lay.

"I'm not sure I understand your meaning, my lord."

Saban flicked the hair out of his eyes and smiled. "And you...clever enough to gain entrance to the university." He bowed, and added more loudly for the benefit of those around them wondering what the Queen of Dhevyn's envoy and the Duke of Grannon Rock were discussing, "May I offer you the use of my carriage tomorrow, Lady Jacinta? I'd be more than happy to escort you to the temple for the ceremony."

"Thank you, my lord, but I have hired my own carriage."

"Then I'll see you at the ceremony tomorrow, perhaps?"

"Undoubtedly."

Saban bowed elegantly and turned and walked away from her, leaving Jacinta to climb the polished staircase to her rooms, wondering what the Duke of Grannon Rock had really been after.

The ceremony to formally appoint the Lord of the Suns was scheduled to take place at first sunrise the following day.

Jacinta was delivered to the massive onion-domed temple in plenty of time to make her way inside and find a good vantage from which to watch the confirmation of Dirk Provin as the Lord of the Suns. The Lion of Senet had already arrived and was standing just below the altar with the High Priestess at his side. Marqel was enjoying her role as his mistress and clung to his arm, looking up at him adoringly whenever he spoke. Jacinta wasn't sure what annoyed her the most—Marqel's obvious coquetry or the fact that Antonov Latanya was lapping it up. *Is he really fooled by her, or is he simply taking advantage of the fact that a stunning young woman less than half his age is willing to share his bed?* And what must Kirshov Latanya be feeling, now that his precious Shadowdancer had become his father's mistress?

Jacinta was still puzzling over it when the trumpets blew and announced the start of the ceremony. From an anteroom to the right of the altar a door opened and a number of Sundancers filed out, followed by Lord Varell and lastly Dirk Provin. He was wearing the yellow robes of a Sundancer, something she realized he hadn't been wearing when she met him yesterday.

The color didn't suit him, making his complexion look sallow. In fact, he hardly looked a daunting figure at all, which made him even more dangerous, because to look at him, there was nothing about Dirk Provin that gave any warning about the intelligence lurking behind those unreadable eyes. He looked young, uncomfortable and even a little uncertain.

As the fanfare ended Dirk turned to face the crowd. The temple was packed to overflowing with Sundancers, Shadowdancers and members of both the Senetian and Dhevynian nobility.

"We gather here today to hear the oath of the Lord of the Suns," Dirk announced.

There was the faintest hint of a quiver in his voice, so slight Jacinta wondered if she imagined it. It was the only sign of Dirk's nervousness.

"I am the successor appointed by the Lord Halyn," he continued. "Named in his will, which has been proved to be a true and legal statement of his final wishes. If any person present can show cause why Lord Halyn's successor should not be appointed, let them speak now, or accept this as the will of the Goddess."

There was silence for a moment, and then Claudio Varell stepped forward and coughed nervously.

"You have an objection, my lord?" Dirk asked, a little surprised. Jacinta doubted anybody else in the room was. There was no way Dirk Provin was going to take this oath without a fight.

Claudio didn't answer Dirk, but turned to the gathering and addressed the congregation instead. "This boy is a murderer, a rapist and an arsonist! I charge that even if it was Paige Halyn's will, he is not fit to assume the post of Lord of the Suns!"

A shocked murmur rippled through the temple. Nobody was surprised by the accusation—Dirk Provin's nickname was the Butcher of Elcast, after all—what shocked them was that the Sundancers would openly admit such a thing.

"I have never been charged with any crime, my lord," Dirk

pointed out. Jacinta was impressed by how calm he sounded for
a man on the brink of losing everything.

"The issue does need to be put to rest, though," Antonov
agreed, staring at Dirk with an odd look. "Are you willing to
answer your accusers, Dirk?"

"Bring them on, your highness," he declared gamely.

Claudio turned on Dirk. "Then I accuse you of the murder
of Johan Thorn, and I ask the Lion of Senet to stand as witness
to your guilt."

A gasp rippled through the hall, mostly from the Dhevynians present. Alenor had told Jacinta what happened that night
in Avacas. With a terrible feeling of impending doom, she suspected Dirk's only defense would destroy any shred of trust the
large number of Dhevynians in the temple might have had in
him.

"You've no need to call Prince Antonov as a witness, my
lord," Dirk replied. "I willingly admit I killed the Heretic King
and would do it again tomorrow, if the Goddess asked it of me.
I would kill every heretic on Ranadon if I could. Isn't that the
role of the Lord of the Suns? To stamp out heresy?"

Claudio glared at him. "You committed murder!"

"Be careful how you define murder, my lord," he warned.
"If killing heretics is murder, then the Shadowdancers—conse-
crated members of your Church—have more to answer for
than I do."

Claudio must have realized he was stepping onto dangerous ground so he backtracked hurriedly. "You destroyed the
Calliope."

"Reithan Seranov burned the *Calliope,* my lord, a fact that
any number of the Lion of Senet's men can attest to. They were
pursuing me across Elcast Common at the time the ship caught
fire."

Antonov nodded in agreement. "Did you have anything to
do with it at all, Dirk?"

"I asked Reithan Seranov to create a diversion, your highness. He took me literally."

The Lion of Senet smiled briefly, and Jacinta realized Dirk
had a powerful ally. Antonov was still on his side. No doubt he

liked the idea of Johan Thorn's bastard being the Lord of the Suns. It suited his ambition much better this way.

"And how do you intend to wriggle out of the charge of rape?" Claudio asked, paying his trump card with an edge of desperation.

"There is no charge, my lord."

Dirk's eyes sought out Marqel standing beside Antonov. She was staring at him thoughtfully. *Now what's she got to do with it?* Jacinta wondered curiously.

Claudio also turned to look at Marqel. "My lady?"

Marqel hesitated for a very long time before she answered. "The Lord of the Suns is right, my lord. There is no charge."

Jacinta almost fainted with relief. Marqel must be enjoying her role as Antonov's mistress too much to endanger her position by helping Claudio Varell unseat the man who had put her there.

At that point, Claudio realized he'd lost the fight, but Jacinta knew the battle was far from over. That he had voiced his doubts publicly was enough to disturb even the staunchest supporters of the Church. There was a tense moment of silence and then a slight disturbance to Jacinta's left.

A red-robed Shadowdancer stepped forward.

"I can also show cause," the woman announced.

"Lady Madalan Tirov," Claudio replied, vastly relieved. "You are the right hand of the High Priestess. You will be heard!"

"I bid you show cause or step back and be silent," Antonov suggested with an edge of impatience.

"Dirk Provin cannot be appointed Lord of the Suns," Madalan announced. "He's not come of age yet. This *boy* is just that—a boy. He is only nineteen years old. Under Senetian law he cannot be considered an adult until he reaches the age of twenty. He doesn't come of age until after Landfall. Regardless of the will of the late Lord Halyn, we cannot legally appoint him Lord of the Suns."

"The Lady Madalan speaks truly," Claudio agreed so quickly Jacinta suspected it was rehearsed. She glanced up at Dirk but his expression still betrayed nothing. *He must be shocked,* she thought. *Had he overlooked such a minor but important detail?* Like everyone else in the temple, she held her breath, waiting for somebody to explain what happened now.

Finally the Lion of Senet stepped forward. Although this was Church business, and strictly speaking he had no power here, nobody chose to challenge him when he took charge.

"I believe this needs to be cleared up before the ceremony proceeds," he declared. "I suggest an adjournment of one hour. We will reconvene then and continue...one way or the other."

Jacinta didn't wait around to find out what would happen next. She pushed and shoved her way back through the crowd until she reached the doors and then ran outside. She hailed the driver she'd hired for the day as she ran down the steps and ordered him to bring her carriage up, catching her escort off guard. As soon as it arrived, she climbed in and ordered the driver to move off.

Tael Gordonov countermanded the order and jerked the carriage door open.

"Lady Jacinta? Is something wrong?"

"Nothing at all, Captain. Please close the door."

"Back to the Widow's Rest, my lady?" the driver asked.

"No," she told him. "I don't want to go back to the inn. Take me to the library."

Tael looked at her in alarm. "The *library,* my lady?"

"They do have a library in Bollow, don't they?"

"Yes, of course, my lady! It's just..."

"Just what?"

"Well, it's not the sort of place one expects to find a lady..."

Jacinta muttered a very unladylike curse under her breath. "Just get me there!"

Tael shook his head and closed the carriage door as she commanded. "As you wish, my lady."

Chapter 45

The difference in himself being free of the poppy-dust astounded Misha at first. Having lived most of his life in the cycle of high awareness followed by the savage letdown of the drug, to awaken each morning and know by the end of the day he would not be trembling and nauseous filled him with a sense of elation he found hard to describe. There were times when he could feel his body calling for the drug, but for now, at least, it was easy to refuse. He was too enamored of the unusual feeling of well-being to give in to it.

Lexie's arrival with Reithan did much to distract him, and the news she brought about what had happened in Mil did nothing but strengthen his suspicion Dirk was playing his own dangerous game, a game in which only he seemed to understand the rules. Tia was adamant he was simply a traitor. Misha was privately of the opinion it didn't matter what Dirk did, she would always think that of him.

Although it was wearing at times, Misha didn't mind Tia's prejudice. That she and Dirk had been lovers for a short time was no longer a secret between them. What Misha wanted to be sure of, what he hoped for beyond reason, was that she was over him; that the unreasonable hatred she had for Dirk Provin was not simply her way of covering up her true feelings. The expectation she had awoken in Misha that day she kissed him was more powerful than a dose of poppy-dust. Every time he closed his eyes, he could feel her lips on his. Unfortunately, every time he opened them again, he recalled the look of shock and despair she had worn afterward.

With Reithan and Lexie here in Garwenfield, there was little chance to speak to Tia alone. Lexie had been unaware of what was happening in Senet while in transit with Reithan on the *Wanderer,* so once everyone had been brought up to date, much of their discussion centered on what their next move should be. Tia wanted to go straight back to Bollow and put an arrow though Dirk's forehead herself. Reithan counseled caution, suggesting they wait until the eclipse before taking any action. Lexie wanted to keep Mellie hidden and Misha wanted to return to Avacas to see his father and do something about removing Ella Geon from her position of trust in the palace. They talked around and around, but the decision was not an easy one and a week after Lexie and Reithan had sailed into Garwenfield, they still hadn't decided what to do.

Tia avoided his eye as they sat around the kitchen table, and found any number of excuses not to be alone with him. Mellie seemed never to leave her side, or she was with Reithan, or Lexie. He knew Tia was avoiding him. He also suspected Tia *knew* he knew it. But he could do nothing to force the situation. To push Tia now might be to lose her forever, and that was something he didn't even want to contemplate. So he waited, took long walks on the beach in the soft sand near the tree line to strengthen his legs and hoped given enough time, Tia would come to him of her own accord.

The second sun was almost set as Misha limped along the sand, brooding on what might have been—on what might yet be. They'd spent the day talking over what action to take next and Misha had a bad feeling Tia was winning the argument. For all her passion and unreasonable hatred of Dirk Provin, she could put forward a rational and convincing argument when she wanted to. She had modified her original suggestion that she simply kill Dirk to one where she and Reithan returned to Senet to find out what was happening, before allowing either Misha or Mellie to leave Garwenfield. It was probably the best idea anyone had put forward so far, and Misha thought they would agree to it, sooner rather than later.

Within a few days, Tia might be gone. The chances were good he might never see her again. The prospect was almost unbearable.

Reaching the end of the beach, Misha turned back toward the house as the first sun bled into the sky, lost in his morose thoughts. He could make it all the way to the rocks and back without the crutch now. Although Master Helgin had warned him his left side would always be weaker than his right, he was walking unaided and had never felt stronger. He was looking forward to walking back into Avacas palace.

Let them sneer at the Crippled Prince now.

He looked up and noticed a figure walking along the beach toward him and stopped dead when he realized it was Tia. She was alone.

Misha waited for her, partly because he was too surprised to continue, and partly because he was still a little self-conscious about his limping gait. Tia walked toward him slowly, almost reluctantly. When he saw the look on her face as she neared him, his heart sank.

"Hello, Tia."

"You've come a long way," she remarked. "I remember when we first brought you here. It almost killed you just walking from the *Wanderer* to the house."

"A lot's happened since that day," he reminded her.

"Hasn't it," she agreed with a noncommittal shrug. She said nothing for a time and Misha was too afraid to break the silence, certain whatever he said, it would be the wrong thing.

"I'm leaving tomorrow with Reithan," she told him eventually. "We're going to Senet to see if we can figure out what Dirk's up to. And maybe put a stop to it."

"I thought you might."

"Once we know it's safe, Reithan will come back for you and Lexie and Mellie."

"Lexie's staying?"

Tia nodded. "She doesn't want to leave Mellie again."

"That's understandable, I suppose."

They said nothing more for a time. Misha found the silence unbearable.

"Tia..."

He had no idea what to say. And there was so much he wanted to say. He wanted to thank her. He wanted to hold her. He wanted to kiss her again the way she'd kissed him the day he woke free of the poppy-dust...

But for some reason, he couldn't find the words. Or the courage.

"You will be careful, won't you?" he warned, cursing his own cowardice. "There's a price on your head, remember."

"I'll be careful."

"I'll miss you."

"I'll miss you, too."

He wondered if she meant it, or if she was just saying that to be polite. "I would have thought you'd be relieved to see the back of me."

"No. I think I really will miss you," she said, and then she smiled. "I probably won't know what to do with myself if I start getting a full night's sleep."

He smiled uncertainly. They fell back into an awkward silence for a while.

"So this is good-bye, then."

Tia looked away. "I suppose."

"Well, good luck." *Goddess ... I sound like a damned fool.*

She glanced back at him and nodded uncertainly. "You, too."

They stared at each other for a moment, and then she turned abruptly and headed back toward the house.

Misha watched her leave with a feeling akin to having his heart sliced out of his chest with a rusty blade. He had ruined his only chance, he realized. Once she left Garwenfield he would lose her forever.

"Tia!"

She stopped and turned to look at him, waiting for him to add something. But his courage deserted him again and he was suddenly lost for words. He took a hesitant step toward her.

"Don't go."

She hesitated for a moment longer, and then it felt as if the whole world shifted beneath Misha's feet. Perhaps she read his mind. Whatever the reason, Tia covered the short distance between them at a run. Before he had time to realize she had come to him, she was in his arms.

He kissed her urgently and she kissed him back with all the passion and ardor he'd wished for. He pulled her to him with all his newfound strength, afraid he was dreaming; afraid this was just an illusion and at any moment he would wake up and find himself lying in bed, weak and trembling in the grip of a drug-addled fantasy.

"I love you, Tia," he managed to stammer between kisses.

She broke away suddenly. Misha was terrified he had ruined everything with his foolish declaration.

"Don't say that unless you mean it," she warned, searching his face for some hint that he was merely toying with her.

"I mean it, Tia. More than you could ever know."

She frowned at him. "Do you really love me, Misha? Or are you just confusing what you're feeling with friendship and gratitude?"

"I love you, Tia," he repeated, never more certain of anything in his life. "I'm grateful to you, I'm indebted to you and I'm overwhelmed by you. But I know what I'm feeling and it's none of those things. I'm in love with you. I have been for a long time." He smiled. "Actually, I think I fell for you that day you came into my room to change the sheets in the palace in Avacas and you told me how to play chess."

Tia returned his smile hesitantly. "I think I fell for you the day you told me to get over Dirk or I'd turn into a bitter old woman."

Her words elated him, but there was a hint of caution in them. There was still one thing he needed to know. Still one thing Misha had to be certain of.

"*Are* you over Dirk, Tia?" he asked. He wanted her to love him, not use him as a distraction or a way to get back at Dirk.

Tia thought about her answer for a moment and then she nodded. With a smile that set Misha's heart racing, she slid her arms around his neck and kissed him again, leaving no doubt about her feelings.

"Dirk who?" she asked.

Chapter 46

Dirk had listened to Madalan Tirov's declaration that he was too young to assume the mantle of the Lord of the Suns with a feeling of stunned disbelief. He had thought this through so carefully. He had covered every eventuality—so he thought.

But this...to be thwarted by something so simple...

He couldn't believe it. Couldn't believe everything was lost. The events he had set in motion would all be for nothing if he wasn't standing beside Marqel on the day of the eclipse as Lord of the Suns. If he failed in his bid to be appointed to the ultimate position of power in the Church, he was nothing more than Dirk Provin, bastard son of Johan Thorn and his paramour, Morna Provin. He would no longer enjoy the protection of the Church and could not return to the Shadowdancers. Madalan would not give up her role as right hand of the High Priestess a second time.

If he failed, Dirk would be at Antonov's mercy, instead of the other way around. The only people on Ranadon whom Antonov believed capable of interpreting the will of the Goddess were the High Priestess of the Shadowdancers and the Lord of the Suns. Dirk *had* to be there for the eclipse. Everything he had done since he slipped away from Tia to meet Paige Halyn on their way to Omaxin—for that matter, even the suggestion they *go* to Omaxin—had been toward that end.

What had Neris said? *You don't need to kill anyone; you need to kill an idea. That is a much harder thing to do.*

But he could only kill the idea by proving the unprovable. By being there in a position of power on the day of the eclipse, when the Goddess showed her will to the world. If he wasn't standing in the wings, ready to step up and take charge, then everything he had done, everything he still needed to do, everyone he had betrayed, everyone who had died because of him...all of it would have been in vain.

Antonov paced the anteroom impatiently while they waited for Claudio to return. The Lion of Senet was furious with the challenge to Dirk's appointment, but far more accepting of the possibility that it might not happen than Dirk was. *That's because he has a backup plan,* Dirk knew. If Antonov couldn't bring Dhevyn to the Goddess by appointing her true king's bastard Lord of the Suns, then he'd make the bastard Dhevyn's next king. Dirk didn't have that luxury. His was an all-or-nothing gamble with no safety net, no fallback position. He either succeeded or he failed.

But despite the number of choices Antonov had, he wasn't happy. He wanted proof of Madalan's claim and had sent Claudio to fetch it.

Dirk truly had no idea what Lord Varell would return with. Was there some charter he knew nothing of that stipulated the Lord of the Suns must be of age under Senetian law? Was there a chapter in the *Book of Ranadon*—written before Belagren came along and started adding her own chapters to it—that laid down the rules?

He knew the Lord of the Suns was appointed by the previous incumbent. He knew the rules that applied to his will and the consequences of tampering with it. But Dirk had never even questioned the issue of age, because it was never supposed to have been a problem. His original timetable was much longer than the one he'd been forced to work to. In Dirk's original plan, Belagren was still alive. Paige Halyn was supposed to have lived for years yet, giving Dirk plenty of time to consolidate his power and his credibility. He'd not counted on Misha being kidnapped, either.

The scope of his design was vast and it should have taken years—not months—to come to fruition. *Was that why Paige Halyn agreed so readily?* Had he known he would soon be dead and Dirk was too young to succeed him? Surely not. Dirk was in this mess because of Marqel's murderous nature, a stray assassin's bolt and a birthday inconveniently several months away.

Although outwardly unperturbed, Dirk couldn't avoid the feeling it was all about to come crashing down around him.

And there was the Lion of Senet, lurking in the wings, like a spider eyeing an unsuspecting bug, waiting for his chance to get Dirk back into his power. And Dirk would have little choice but to follow him. There was no refuge for him among the rebels any longer. He'd burned those bridges behind him well and truly. Anyway, Antonov's patience would not suffer Dirk defying him a second time. If he failed to be appointed the Lord of the Suns, Dirk would follow Antonov or die.

And Antonov expected Dirk to follow him all the way to the throne of Dhevyn.

Dirk tried to recall the day he'd met Paige Halyn in Bollow, in this very room, and told him what he wanted to do. It had taken quite a while to convince Paige he was genuine, even longer to enlist his cooperation. The old Lord of the Suns had extracted two promises from Dirk in return for naming him his heir. The first was that he would restore the Sundancers to the rightful place as the true representatives of the Goddess. The second was that he would kill nobody in his quest.

He wasn't doing very well on either count. The Sundancers were in more danger of being destroyed than they had ever been, and the body count was nearing three figures, when one included the Baenlanders who had died during the invasion of Mil. He suddenly remembered something Tia had said to him on their way to Mil the first time he fled Avacas: *That's the problem with people like you and my father. You never mean to do any harm, but you think you're so damn clever, all you end up doing is causing trouble.*

She was right about that much. Dirk had caused enough trouble in the last few months to last a lifetime.

The door opened and Claudio returned with Madalan and another Sundancer Dirk didn't know. Claudio introduced the newcomer as Marco Morgenov, the Chief Archivist. He looked even older than Claudio. *That's half the problem with the Sundancers,* Dirk realized. *All the young blood went to the Shadowdancers.*

"Well, do you have a solution to this dilemma?" Antonov asked as soon as Claudio had finished the introductions.

"Perhaps not a solution, your highness," Marco replied. "But I can offer you plenty of historical evidence—"

"Historical evidence is not law," Dirk cut in, feeling vastly relieved. If they couldn't produce a document flatly stating he must be of age, then there was a chance he might still survive this.

Marco turned to him impatiently. "My lord, you didn't let me finish. I was going to say the historical evidence supports the Lady Madalan's contention, but in order to clarify the issue, it will take more than an hour's browsing through the archives." Marco turned to Antonov. "Your highness, I would like to ask for more time. This question is too important to be settled hastily."

"I agree," Antonov said. "How much more time do you need?"

"The records of the Sundancers go back more than ten thousand years, your highness. If such a decree was ever made, it would have been issued a long time ago. The search may take months."

So that was their plan. *If they can't stop me, they can stall me, indefinitely if need be.*

"Months!" Antonov snapped impatiently. "Surely you have some record of your laws that can be consulted more quickly than that?"

"Might I suggest, your highness, they want months to check this because no such law exists?"

"You can suggest it, Lord Provin," Marco retorted, "but that still won't make your appointment legal until the issue is resolved."

Antonov glanced across the room to Marqel, who had wisely said nothing so far.

"Does the Goddess have anything to say on this, my lady?" Antonov asked.

Marqel looked around the room before she answered. Other than Antonov, there was not a soul in the room who believed she actually spoke to the Goddess. Marqel knew that. She also knew that at the moment, Dirk's authority was looking decidedly shaky.

"The Goddess has not spoken to me on this matter, your

highness," she replied carefully. "But I believe she would counsel prudence over hasty action."

You treacherous little bitch, Dirk thought.

Antonov nodded in agreement. "I'm afraid I'm inclined to agree. It would be unwise to swear in the Lord of the Suns until this matter is clarified."

"And if it *can't* be clarified?" Dirk asked, hoping he didn't sound as desperate as he felt.

"Then we will hold an election," Claudio said.

"That will take months," Dirk pointed out. "By then I *will* be of age under Senetian law, my lord."

"Then that is the solution to our problem," Antonov announced. "You have until Dirk's twentieth birthday to find your answer, my lords. If you can't come up with one by then, I suggest the will stands and Dirk is sworn in, as Paige Halyn intended."

The Sundancers glanced at each other uncertainly and then nodded. It wasn't the resolution they were hoping for—which was to remove Dirk from contention completely—but it stalled his appointment by several months.

It wasn't the answer Dirk wanted either. He needed to be Lord of the Suns. Now. Before the eclipse.

"Sire..."

Antonov ignored him. "Then I suggest we go back out there and announce the swearing-in ceremony has been postponed and that Lord Varell will assume temporary leadership of the Church until the matter has been resolved."

"An excellent suggestion," Claudio agreed. Being appointed acting leader was probably more than he'd hoped for. Even Madalan seemed satisfied Dirk's rise to power was slowed down.

They filed out of the room one by one, heading back into the main temple. Marqel spared Dirk a smug little smile as she took Antonov's arm. As usual, she had acted on a selfish impulse, with no real understanding of what she had done.

Dirk was the last one to emerge from the anteroom. Claudio stepped up to the altar and turned to face the crowded temple.

An expectant hush fell over the hall as he raised his hands for silence.

"My lords and ladies! The issue of the age of the new Lord of the Suns cannot be resolved in the space of a mere hour! It is the consensus of the Church, the swearing-in of the new Lord of the Suns must be delayed..."

Dirk didn't hear the rest of it. It was over. There was no chance he would be confirmed as Lord of the Suns now. Either an assassin would find him or Claudio and Madalan would see to it the wheels of bureaucracy ground his ambitions into the dust. The eclipse would come and go and the Shadowdancers would rule supreme. His interference had not helped Dhevyn's cause. He had just strengthened his enemy's position so much the Shadowdancers would be unassailable.

And then out of nowhere, rescue appeared in the unlikely shape of Lady Jacinta D'Orlon.

Chapter 47

"Surely in light of the existing precedent, a delay is unnecessary, my lord," Jacinta suggested loudly, pushing through the gathered dignitaries who were watching the proceedings with intense interest. She looked flushed and a little breathless.

Madalan turned to look at the young woman, shocked by the interruption. "I think you would be better minding your own business, Lady Jacinta. I believe you are also not of age according to Senetian law."

Jacinta smiled serenely, unperturbed by Madalan's derisive tone. "That may be the case, my lady, but I *am* of age under Dhevynian law and I am here as the representative of the Queen of Dhevyn. I believe my diplomatic status takes precedence over my youth in this case."

"Let her speak," Antonov ordered.

Madalan bowed in reluctant acquiescence. Nobody defied the Lion of Senet, even on Church ground.

"There are a number of precedents for the Lord or Lady of the Suns to be underage, your highness," Jacinta explained, addressing her remarks to Antonov. "Monique Karyov, who was later known as the Mother of the Light, was merely fourteen when she became Lady of the Suns. Lord Astin of Versage was only sixteen. I believe he was the first Lord of the Suns to earn the title of Guardian of the Light. In fact, not only have there been more than a dozen cases of the new Lord or Lady of the Suns being appointed before they reached their majority, most of them went on to long and distinguished careers." Then she smiled ingenuously at Madalan. "Of course, I realize that you probably know the *Book of Ranadon* better than I do, my lady, but I'm quite sure I'm correct."

Dirk stared at Jacinta D'Orlon in amazement, wondering how she knew such things. Where had she gotten hold of a copy of the *Book of Ranadon*? And more important, why was she defending him? Madalan looked shocked. Claudio hung his head in bitter disappointment, as he realized their one chance to remove Dirk was rapidly slipping away from them.

"The instances you quote are not precedents, my lady, they are anomalies," Marco Morgenov pointed out. "Besides, every one of them was Senetian."

"And where is it written, my lord, that the Lord or Lady of the Suns must be born in Senet?" Jacinta countered. "Even the Goddess has chosen a Dhevynian as her voice. Are you suggesting *she* is wrong?"

Dirk mentally winced at Jacinta's question. She was daring a great deal to challenge the Church so publicly, particularly on the issue of the new High Priestess. But Jacinta seemed unfazed—in fact, she seemed to be enjoying herself. Her strange, color-shifting eyes were bright and her whole stance was proud and confident. How much of it was genuine bravado and how much was simply the result of a few hundred generations of noble breeding, Dirk couldn't guess.

Then something else occurred to Dirk. Jacinta was either a blindly faithful follower of the Goddess, or when Eryk claimed Alenor had told her everything, he wasn't exaggerating. As the former was unlikely in light of her connection with the Baenlanders, that meant she must know who was responsible for Marqel's elevation to Voice of the Goddess. And yet she was standing up for him; doing her utmost to see him confirmed as Lord of the Suns. Dirk wasn't sure if he should be grateful or extremely worried.

"Of course I'm not suggesting the Goddess is wrong," Marco retorted impatiently. "What I'm suggesting, my lady, is that you are a Dhevynian noblewoman with no formal education and in no position to set yourself up as an authority on the *Book of Ranadon*."

"Excuse me, my lord," Saban Seranov interjected, surprising everyone with his interruption. "While I've no wish to comment on the theology of this discussion, I must challenge the assertion that the Lady Jacinta is uneducated. She was accepted into the University of Nova based on nothing but merit. You should be grateful if even one of your Senetian women were half as well educated." He brushed the hair from his face and winked at Jacinta.

There was more going on here than simply a discussion about whether or not Dirk Provin was old enough to be Lord of the Shadows. There were allies here he hadn't expected. Whether they were supporting him because they believed him capable or simply hoped to use him to their own ends was yet to be determined. Dirk recalled the suspicion with which the Baenlanders had always viewed Saban Seranov, the man who had denounced his brother to assume his title. Both his sons were actively involved with the pirates. Perhaps he wasn't as blind to his sons' rebellious activities as everyone imagined.

"I'm sure Lord Marco meant no offense to the Lady Jacinta," Madalan apologized. "I do, however, stand by my assertion this appointment is neither legal nor the intention of the late Paige Halyn."

"What say you on this matter, Lord Varell?" Antonov asked Claudio.

"The Lady Jacinta speaks truly, your highness," he replied unhappily. "Perhaps, now I think of it, there is a precedent which allows the Lord of the Suns to assume the position before reaching his majority."

"And does the *Book of Ranadon* specify that your leader must be Senetian by birth?"

"The Goddess knows no boundaries," Jacinta pointed out piously. "We are all her people under the suns."

Dirk caught Jacinta D'Orlon's eye. She winked at him and then stepped back, her role in this now done.

Of all the games going on around him, Jacinta's worried him the most. Dirk could usually anticipate Madalan's clumsy intrigues. He knew Antonov well enough to counter him at almost every turn, but Alenor's envoy was an unknown quantity. He didn't know her. He couldn't tell what she was up to, or even guess her motives. On one hand, she was here representing the queen, yet she had asked him to help the refugee Baenlanders. Whose side was she on? What game was Jacinta playing? She seemed to have a gift for surprising him, and the one thing Dirk couldn't afford in this dangerous enterprise was surprises. He'd certainly had enough of them for one day.

"Well spoken, Lady Jacinta. And to my mind, that settles the issue. My lady?" Antonov asked Madalan. "Do you have any further accusations to bring against the Lord of the Suns?"

Madalan turned her hate-filled glare to Dirk. "No, your highness."

Her retreat didn't shock Dirk as much as it did the rest of the gathering. Publicly she had been defeated, but she was clever enough not to resign in protest. Madalan Tirov understood power was much more easily wielded when you actually had it in your grasp.

"Then let's get on with the ceremony, shall we?"

Claudio nodded reluctantly and stepped forward. He looked up at Dirk with eyes filled with resignation.

"Would you repeat the oath after me, my lord?"

Dirk nodded and in a clear voice, swore by a Goddess he didn't believe in to uphold the laws of her faith and bring her truth to every soul on Ranadon.

Even Madalan seemed surprised to realize that, for the last part of the oath at least, Dirk sounded as if he really meant it.

Chapter 48

When Kirshov Latanya returned to Kalarada to resume his role as Regent of Dhevyn, Alenor was astonished by the change in him. The cheerful boy she had adored as a child was a distant memory. Kirsh was morose and untalkative and surprisingly dedicated to his work. He no longer found excuses to avoid meeting with his advisers; he no longer put off making decisions. He dealt with everything he was asked to rule on without prevarication. His decisions were surprisingly sound, always fair and totally lacking in compassion.

But Kirsh did what was required of him and nothing else. He ate in his rooms and rarely joined Alenor for dinner, even when there were important guests to be entertained. He drank a great deal and usually alone, but it seemed to have little effect on him. The only company he kept was the small Senetian Guard he had brought with him, captained by a tall dark-haired Senetian named Sergey, who always gave Alenor the uneasy feeling he was watching her wherever she went.

Alenor knew the reason for the change in Kirshov and a part of her ached for the pain he must be in. Another part of her, however, viewed his current state of mind without sympathy. Kirsh had brought this on himself. If he had been too blind to realize Marqel was simply using him as a stepping stone, then he had nobody to blame but himself.

Alenor discovered a strength she hadn't known she possessed when it came to dealing with Kirsh. She missed Jacinta, but found she was more than capable of handling her husband's moods. Things were tense between them, but it wasn't as bad as it had been when they were first married and Kirsh's anger had been directed at her. Now it was different. It was as if they had both unconsciously accepted the truth about each other. Alenor didn't inquire after Marqel and Kirshov showed no interest in discovering the identity of her lover. They worked side by side, like two strangers whose personal lives did not intrude on the job they had to do.

One unexpected benefit of Kirsh's return was his impatience with the number of Senetians his father and the late High Priestess had placed in Alenor's court. Within a week of his return, he had sent nearly half of them home to Avacas. Kirsh was angry at his father as much as Marqel, she guessed, and wanted as little as possible to do with those people who had been placed in Kalarada for the sole purpose of reporting back to the Lion of Senet.

With a court reduced by half, and Kirsh actually taking an interest in what was going on, Alenor's load was considerably lessened. She still refused to reveal the location of her seal, assuming an innocent look whenever Kirsh questioned her about it. He suspected Jacinta of hiding it, but the palace had been searched twice and no sign of it had been found. For the time being, everything that came out of the palace bore the seal of Dhevyn's regent, but not her queen. The laws were probably legal, but if anyone challenged them, chances were they would not stand up to close scrutiny. Alenor knew she couldn't stop Kirsh issuing any law he chose, but without her seal, on the day she came of age and became queen in her own right, she could declare every law he had issued null and void.

Assuming she was still queen by then...

Alenor opened the door to Kirsh's summons, wondering what his reaction would be on that day when she overturned all the work of his regency. Kirsh looked up when she entered and tossed an envelope across the desk to her without even bothering to say good morning.

"We've been invited to Bollow," he told her, as she picked up the envelope bearing the seal of the Lord of the Suns.

"Why?"

"For the eclipse. It's due to take place on the twentieth anniversary of my father's sacrifice."

"Do we have to go?"

"Yes."

She studied him for a moment, but he wasn't looking at her. He was concentrating on another document and seemed disinterested in discussing the matter further.

"Kirsh..."

"What?" he asked impatiently.

"Did you want to take a contingent of the guard with you?"

"With *us,* Alenor," he corrected. "We're both going to Bollow. And don't give me any nonsense about not being well enough to travel. You'll be there if I have to carry your corpse."

"I wasn't going to try to get out of it, Kirsh. In fact, I think I'd rather like to see Dirk again. And Marqel."

Kirsh glared at her. "Then perhaps when we get to Bollow, you can ask your damn cousin what she did with the royal seal."

"I don't know why you keep insisting Jacinta had anything to do with its disappearance, Kirsh."

"You left it in her care and now it's gone. That makes her responsible. If I could prove she's deliberately misplaced it, I'd burn her at the next Landfall Feast."

"I can't understand why you dislike her so much."

"I can't understand why you *like* her so much. She's disrespectful, snide and interferes in things that are none of her concern. Sending her to Bollow as your envoy was a stupid idea."

"Then why did you let her go?"

"Because while she's in Bollow she's bothering Dirk and not me. Did you want anything else? I have work to do."

"I'll start making arrangements for the trip to Senet when I get back," she told him.

"Are you going somewhere?"

"Just for a ride. Circael wasn't ridden nearly enough while I was away. She needs the exercise as much as I do."

"Enjoy your ride," he said without looking up. He was dismissing her, not wishing her well.

"I intend to," she said and then she left the room, slamming the door ever so slightly behind her.

Alexin escorted Alenor on her ride, with a small guard that kept a discreet distance to allow them some privacy. Their consideration concerned Alenor a little. Her affair was not nearly as secret as she would like. But as far as the Queen's Guard was concerned, Kirshov Latanya was a foreigner and an interloper. They would far rather have their queen in the arms of one of their own and went out of their way to make certain she could be whenever she wanted.

But the more people who knew about Alexin, the greater the danger. Sooner or later, Kirsh would learn who had fathered her lost child. Perhaps Jacinta was right. Perhaps she should have sent him away. But every time she made up her mind to issue the orders posting Alexin out of Kalarada, she began to imagine how unbearable life would be without him. It was only a small step from there to find another excuse for him to stay.

She dismounted as they reached the top of the bridle path and walked a little way with Alexin to stand near the edge of the cliff. The sea crashed against the rocks below, the sound muted by distance, and the cool wind whipped the hair across her face.

"You're shivering," Alexin remarked, putting her arm around her. She leaned into the solid warmth of him and closed her eyes for a moment, pretending this was the way it really was. For a few precious heartbeats she allowed herself to be happy.

"We're going to Bollow for the eclipse," she told him after a time.

"Take me with you."

"Jacinta would say that was stupid and dangerous, my love."

He kissed the top of her head. "So is standing here with the Queen of Dhevyn in my arms less than a mile from the palace, Alenor."

She smiled up at him. "Admit it! You like living dangerously."

"I'm getting used to it," he conceded. "It would be nice to think it isn't always going to be like this."

"I know," she sighed. "But I can do nothing until I come of age. Once that happens, I can divorce Kirsh..."

"Do you really think the Lion of Senet will allow you to divorce his son?"

"I don't care whether he allows it or not."

"You misunderstand my meaning, Alenor. It's not just a case of you asking for a divorce. You're a ruling monarch and your marriage was sealed by more than just a grandiose ceremony. There are agreements and treaties signed that day that can't be overturned quite so easily."

Alenor realized he was right, but didn't want this rare moment spoiled by being reminded of it. "Well, it may prove to be a moot point. The way Kirsh is going, he'll drink himself to death long before I'm in a position to divorce him."

Alexin didn't answer her, simply content to hold her in his arms.

"I saved him, you know," he said after a time. "When we were in Mil."

She looked up at him in concern. "Alexin, you don't need to explain..."

"I almost didn't," he admitted, determined to unburden his guilt. "Kirsh got himself cut off from the rest of us on the beach. He was surrounded. All I had to do was wait and he would have been dead."

"But you didn't wait."

"I thought about it," he told her. "Believe me, you've no *idea* how tempted I was. But I could never kill a man—or allow him to be killed—just because I was in love with his wife."

Hadn't Dirk warned her about that? She felt incredibly guilty for placing Alexin in such a predicament. And a little relieved he'd not acted on his first impulse to let Kirsh die. Alenor wasn't sure she could be happy if it came at the expense of Kirsh's life. She didn't hate him that much.

"So we are doomed to unhappiness because of your honor."

Alexin bent his head down and kissed her. She closed her eyes, lost in the sheer bliss of an embrace that—for a moment at least—banished all her other woes.

Finally he broke off the kiss and smiled at her sadly. "If I had any honor, Alenor, I'd not be here with you now."

"I'm inclined to agree with you, Captain."

Alenor jerked free of Alexin's embrace to find Kirsh standing behind them on the bridle path, leading his horse and Circael. Behind him were the remainder of her guard that had been watching the path, and behind them stood Kirsh's Senetian Guardsmen with drawn swords.

"You look surprised, my dear," Kirsh remarked. "Did you think I'd forgotten about your little indiscretion?" He turned to his own captain and beckoned him forward. "Arrest Captain Seranov and his accomplices. I'll see to it the queen gets back to the palace safely."

Sergey saluted and stepped toward Alexin.

"Kirsh! Please! You can't do this!" she cried as her happiness disintegrated into her worst nightmare.

"Oh, yes I can, Alenor," he reminded her. "The penalty for adultery with the queen is death. Did you know that?"

"And what's the penalty for the regent's whore?" she cried.

"Show some restraint, Alenor, you're embarrassing yourself."

Alexin didn't resist when Sergey arrested him. Nor did the rest of the Queen's Guard. Every one of them knew Kirsh had the law, if not right, on his side, and they were too well disciplined to do anything but accept their fate stoically. Alenor wanted them to fight. She wanted them to protect their captain and defy Kirsh, but their honor and their oath prevented it. *Damn all men and their stupid honor!*

"Kirsh! *Please!*"

"Stop making a fool of yourself, Alenor," he told her, and then he turned to Sergey. "Take them down to the garrison. And don't let the Queen's Guard get their hands on them, particularly Captain Seranov."

"What are you going to do to him?" Alenor begged, unable to hide the edge of panic in her voice.

He turned back to look at her. "I'm not going to do anything, Alenor. He's coming to Bollow with us, where I intend to hand Alexin Seranov over to the Lion of Senet and then you and your lover can explain to my father whose child you were carrying."

Kirsh's punishment went beyond simple vengeance. Antonov wouldn't just kill Alexin. He'd more than likely kill her as well. And Kirsh knew it.

Her vision was blinded by tears as they led Alexin and the escort away. Kirsh watched them leave, and then turned back to Alenor. "Tidy yourself up, Alenor. You look a wreck."

"Don't do this, Kirsh. Please...don't do this..."

"Why not?" he asked bitterly. "What makes you think you can be happy when I..." He didn't finish the sentence, but Alenor could guess what he had been going to say.

"You're doing this because of Marqel, aren't you?" she asked. "If you can't be happy then nobody can! You're not a man, Kirsh; you're a selfish, spiteful little boy!"

"I'm your husband, Alenor, and I just caught you in the arms of another man. Perhaps you should be more worried about that than insulting me."

"You won't get away with this, Kirsh. When I explain to your father why I took a lover—"

"He won't do a damned thing," Kirsh predicted. "Marqel is the Voice of the Goddess, now. She's beyond any harm you can do her."

It was a bitter realization for Alenor. The reason Kirsh had kept her secret—to protect Marqel—no longer existed. *Oh, what a fool I've been!* What a fool for thinking Kirsh no longer cared she had come to Avacas carrying another man's child. What a fool for not listening to Jacinta and sending Alexin away as soon as he returned to Kalarada. And now her own stupidity and selfishness were going to cost Alexin his life.

That it might also cost Alenor her life didn't seem important right now.

She searched Kirsh's face for some hope of understanding or compassion, some remnant of the boy she had loved as a child.

"Do you hate me so much you'd condemn me to death, Kirsh?"

He didn't answer her. He just turned away and gathered up his reins before swinging into the saddle.

It was then that Alenor realized that Kirsh didn't hate her at all.

He hated himself.

PART THREE

A

MOMENT

OF

DARKNESS

Chapter 49

Tia's most lasting memory of Bollow was sitting in a tavern with Dirk Provin on their way to Omaxin, berating him over his foolish gambling habits after he'd won all that money playing Rithma. When she and Reithan reached the spired city a week before the eclipse was due, the memory rushed back, but her thoughts didn't disturb her as much as she expected they would. They were just memories, she realized, of a time when she was younger and more foolish. They couldn't hurt her. They didn't even bother her that much.

Tia couldn't explain why she felt older, why she felt more accepting of her own mistakes. Perhaps that was the difference between love and infatuation. She could admit to herself now that she'd been infatuated by Dirk, but she loved Misha. When she needed strength to deal with her own troubles, all she had to do was recall what he had endured these past few months. It made her angst seemed trite and insignificant. If Misha had freed himself of a poppy-dust addiction, Tia could deal with a few unfortunate reminders of an old boyfriend.

The lakeside city was crowded to overflowing. Dirk's decision to hold a massive ceremony honoring the Goddess's eclipse on the twentieth anniversary of Antonov's sacrifice of his youngest son worried Tia a great deal. She was certain now that Neris must have told him about the eclipse, but couldn't remember her father ever hinting at such a momentous event. She was angry at Neris for that. If there was something as important as an eclipse due, why had he entrusted the information to Dirk Provin, rather than his own daughter? She felt betrayed. Knowing about the eclipse would have been almost as useful as knowing when the next Age of Shadows was due. They could have broadcast the information across Senet and Dhevyn months ago and there would have been nothing divine attached to the event at all. It would have simply been a natural phenomenon nobody could make any political or religious mileage out of.

But Neris had only confided in Dirk and now things were as bad as they had ever been. There was a sacrifice planned, she'd heard when they passed through Avacas, but who was to be killed had not yet been announced. Everybody of note in both nations had been summoned to Bollow to attend. Almost every Sundancer and Shadowdancer had been recalled.

All to attend a ceremony Dirk Provin had masterminded to further his own political ambition.

Tia still refused to believe he was doing this for any other reason.

Because the city was bursting at the seams, a tent city had sprung up outside its walls to cater for the overflow. It wasn't just those who could not afford an inn who were accommodated there. Quite a few noblemen had brought entire entourages with them and had set up luxurious camps in between the more humble dwellings of their neighbors. A rather large contingent of Senetian soldiers patrolled the city and the tents surrounding it to keep the peace. Their job was relatively easy. Other than the large number of pickpockets and other petty criminals that such a large gathering usually attracted, the air in Bollow was more festive than tense. The Goddess was sending a sign. Nothing like it had been seen since the end of the Age of Shadows. There was a whole generation who had never seen the Goddess at work so visibly and everybody was determined to make the most of the occasion.

The markets had been moved outside the city walls as well, to clear the plaza in front of the temple for the massive crowd expected for the ceremony. Reithan and Tia found a place to sleep in a large tent run by an enterprising merchant who had turned her tent, which was usually home to a dozen or more seamstresses, into temporary accommodation. She had sent her workers home and would probably make more in the coming week than she'd made in the previous year, renting out floor space to travelers who couldn't find a bed in the city. Once Reithan had handed over the outrageous fee the woman was asking, they headed into the city proper to find out what was going on.

They pushed and jostled their way through the gates into a city that had a carnival atmosphere about it. The flow of people through the streets was severely hampered by the numerous performers who had flocked to Bollow to take advantage of the large crowds. There were enterprising hawkers selling relics, too. One was offering a lock of the late High Priestess Belagren's hair. By the look of the sack he carried, filled with tiny jars containing a small snippet of badly dyed auburn hair, he was expecting to do quite a brisk trade. Tia smiled as she declined his offer of a lock of Belagren's hair for the amazingly low price of ten copper dorns and wondered if she should tell the man the High Priestess Belagren had been a blonde, not a redhead.

"Do you think we should head for the temple first?" Reithan asked, looking around with a shake of his head. He'd never been to Bollow before. Tia wasn't sure what impressed him most, the city's elegant (if declining) architecture, or the madhouse atmosphere of the streets.

"It's likely to be where all the action is," she agreed, grunting as she was pushed aside by a hurrying passerby. "Maybe it's a little less crowded near the temple, too."

They shoved their way forward toward the center of the city, walking on the road. The sidewalks were too crowded. Several times they were almost flattened against the pillars shading the footpaths by carriages forcing their way through the throng, the coachmen yelling and cursing the pedestrians as they passed.

The crowd thinned hardly at all until they reached the broad plaza in front of the temple where the ceremony was to be held in a few days' time. The streets leading to the plaza had been cordoned off and workmen were busy erecting shaded tiered seating for the hundreds of distinguished guests planning to attend. Two massive wicker suns had been erected on either side of the vast temple doors, their pyres already stacked and waiting for the victims who would be sacrificed to the Goddess.

As they neared the barricade blocking the end of the street where a few curious spectators had gathered to watch the preparations, Tia saw Dirk emerging from the temple, talking

to a yellow-robed Sundancer. The man with Dirk was old and
bent and seemed to carry the weight of the world on his shoulders.

Despite his new position, Dirk was not dressed as a Sundancer. He wore a plain shirt, dark trousers and high Senetian
boots, and if she hadn't known it was the Lord of the Suns
standing there talking to the old man, she might easily have
mistaken him for a scribe or an engineer. Tia thought it a little
odd. *You'd think he'd be anxious to remind everybody of who he
was, particularly after all the trouble he's gone to, to get himself
there.*

"There's Dirk," Reithan pointed out, spying him at the
temple entrance a moment after Tia caught sight of him.

"Can he see us from up there?" she asked, not sure what
Dirk would do if he realized she and Reithan were so close.

"He's got other things on his mind," Reithan concluded,
looking around at the frantic workmen. "He's planning to
make it quite a show by the look of things."

"And you still think he's doing this for any other reason
than his own glorification?"

Reithan shook his head as he watched Dirk, and then he
sighed. "I don't know what to think anymore, Tia. I keep hoping for the best. But in light of all this," he added, pointing to
the preparations under way, "it's getting harder and harder to
think any good can come of it."

Tia nodded in agreement, unconsciously measuring the
distance between her and Dirk. "You know, if I had my
bow..."

Reithan smiled. "Even the Brotherhood hasn't been able to
take him out, Tia. What makes you think you'd have any more
luck?"

"That brings up an interesting question, actually."

"What question?"

"Why *hasn't* the Brotherhood been able to kill him? Are
they even trying? Look at him, Reithan! He's standing up there
on the top step of the Bollow temple—a perfect target for anyone with a mind to put an arrow through him—and he's not
even concerned! He must know by now there's a contract out

on him. Where's the wall of bodyguards protecting him? Why aren't they sweeping the streets for assassins?"

"Maybe he's starting to believe his own propaganda," Reithan suggested. "Maybe he truly thinks he's divinely blessed and the Goddess will protect him."

"You don't believe that any more than he does," she scoffed. "Do you think he found a way to call off the Brotherhood?"

"I don't see how he could have."

"Dirk's proving to have quite a talent for performing the impossible," she reminded him. "Getting the Brotherhood to renege on their contract probably didn't even cause him to raise a sweat."

"It might be worth asking around," Reithan mused. "Somebody in the Brotherhood in Bollow might know the reason."

"Just be careful," she warned. "We don't know how far the Brotherhood in Senet can be trusted."

Reithan smiled thinly. "About as far as the Brotherhood can be trusted anywhere else on Ranadon, Tia—not one damn bit."

While they were talking, a slender blond Shadowdancer emerged from the temple and stopped beside Dirk. She wore so much gold the radiance of the second sun actually glinted off her, casting refracted light from her throat and wrists, making her appear somehow more than a mere mortal. Dirk said something to her and then finished his discussion with the old Sundancer. Together they turned to walk down the steps to a waiting closed-in carriage.

"That must be the new High Priestess."

"That's Marqel," Tia muttered, realizing the young woman was the same Shadowdancer who had pretended to be so solicitous of her comfort when she was a captive of Prince Kirshov after Dirk betrayed her in Omaxin. "She claimed Dirk raped her. She said she hated him."

"He's made her High Priestess. I'm betting she's forgiven him by now."

Tia shook her head in amazement. Was there no end to the lies and deception surrounding Dirk Provin?

On his way down to the carriage, Dirk stopped to speak to a young man and woman who were sitting on the steps, apparently waiting for him.

"That's Eryk!" she hissed, as the pair climbed to their feet and followed Dirk and the High Priestess to the carriage. "I thought you said he was killed in Mil?" The chubby blonde sitting beside him was familiar, too, but Tia couldn't remember where she'd seen her before.

"I thought he was," Reithan said with a frown. "I wonder how he wound up here?"

"Here and back as Dirk's servant by the look of things," she pointed out with a scowl. "I know that other girl, too, but I can't for the life of me recall where I've seen her before."

The carriage moved off, turning down between the seating still under construction.

"Worry about it later," Reithan suggested. "They're heading this way!"

Tia turned and pushed her way back with Reithan by her side. Several soldiers posted around the perimeter of the plaza hurried to the barricade to move it aside and allow the Lord of the Suns' carriage through. There was nowhere to hide and with so many people pressing close, no way they could flee. In the end they simply pressed themselves flat against the wall, with their eyes downcast, hoping they hadn't been noticed or recognized by anybody in the carriage.

The carriage clattered past without stopping. Letting out a sigh of relief, Tia turned to watch it moving down the street. It was then she realized that Eryk was leaning out of the carriage, staring, open-mouthed.

Tia's heart began to race as she realized Dirk's half-witted servant had recognized her.

Chapter 50

In the weeks leading up to the eclipse, Jacinta D'Orlon had the time of her life. As the envoy of the Queen of Dhevyn, she was wined and dined and feted by almost everyone in Bollow who thought she was a person whose friendship they needed to cultivate. Despite her rather outspoken performance at the swearing-in ceremony, almost without exception, they assumed her nothing but a vapid young woman who had gained her position because she was the queen's cousin. That she was beautiful, unmarried and the daughter of the richest duke in Dhevyn merely added to her charms.

Jacinta delighted in watching them trying to win her over. She could barely move in her cluttered suite at the Widow's Rest for the gifts she'd been sent. Her rooms were filled with flowers sent by numerous admirers. She'd been given bolts of silk from Galina, jewelry ranging from the exquisite to the absolutely tasteless, a fantastic statue of a lion cut from a single piece of Sidorian crystal, and countless boxes of sweetmeats (which she gave away to the maids at the inn), and she had refused at least four offers of marriage.

But of all the gifts she had received, the most unexpected had come from Dirk Provin. The day after the swearing-in ceremony, Eryk had arrived at her door bearing a small parcel. In it was a book, a rare copy of *A Brief History of Dhevyn,* a text banned by the High Priestess years ago because it chronicled Dhevyn's rise before the Age of Shadows without any reference to the Goddess.

Inside was a note that simply said: "Thank you. Dirk Provin." He gave Eryk no other message to pass on, and asked for none in return.

Jacinta worried about the gift a great deal. She had thought the book no longer existed. The mere possession of it was enough to have her charged with heresy. Her first thought—that the gift was an astonishingly thoughtful gesture—quickly turned to fear. If Dirk was planning to set her up to be arrested, it was the perfect way to do it.

How had he known she would never throw away something so rare and valuable? And if she did keep it, how long before she answered her door to a troop of Senetian soldiers wanting to search her room because she was suspected of being a heretic? Was that why Dirk had done nothing after she asked him to keep the Senetians away from Oakridge? Had he merely found a more subtle way of removing her? He must know that as far as witnesses to her treachery went, both Eryk and Caterina were unreliable. The word of a commoner and a half-wit would never stand up against the word of a noblewoman and even the Lord of the Suns couldn't accuse the cousin of Dhevyn's queen without proof. If she was found with such a book in her possession, he wouldn't have to accuse her of anything.

A dozen times in the past weeks she'd taken the book from its hiding place in the bottom of her trunk and flicked through the fragile pages in awe. A dozen times she had promised herself to get rid of it. A dozen times she hadn't. The book remained hidden while Jacinta tried to work out the meaning of the gift. It told her much about Dirk Provin, she knew. The problem was, she couldn't decide if it told her he was a thoughtful and insightful young man, or a fiendishly clever despot.

Jacinta fervently hoped the latter was not the case. She had gone out of her way to help him gain the position of Lord of the Suns. If she was wrong about him, then she may have single-handedly done more damage to Dhevyn's hopes for freedom than any other event since the Age of Shadows. She clung to the hope she'd done the right thing. She clung to the belief that Dirk Provin was not the Butcher of Elcast, but the thoughtful, intelligent young man Eryk and Caterina had described to her on the journey from Avacas. For her own peace of mind, she had no choice but to believe Alenor's faith in Dirk was grounded in reality and not wishful thinking. Dirk Provin had asked Alenor to trust him. No matter what. As the queen's envoy, Jacinta was compelled to share that trust. Share it, but not actively aid him in whatever he was up to. Had she taken Alenor's trust too literally? There were nights when Jacinta couldn't sleep, wondering what she had done.

But a few days before the eclipse, her fear she may have hastened Dhevyn's ruin, suddenly didn't seem important anymore. The threat of being arrested as a heretic paled in light of a new calamity that faced her. The thought of being burned alive seemed almost pleasant when faced with the alternative. She would have welcomed the prospect of torture at the hands of Barin Welacin.

It was the single most disastrous thing that could have happened, as far as Jacinta was concerned. When she heard the news, she *wanted* them to find that damn book, to drag her away in chains, never to see the light of day again...

Because Jacinta's mother, the Lady Sofia D'Orlon, Duchess of Bryton, arrived in Bollow for the eclipse.

"Oh, Ja*cin*ta!" her mother cried in horror as she swept into her rooms at the Widow's Rest without even saying hello. "How can you bear living in such *appalling* squalor?"

It always amazed Jacinta how her mother could turn a simple, three-syllable word into such a production. And how she always managed to emphasize the middle syllable as if there was some special meaning attached to it. When Lady Sofia spoke her name, Jacinta always imagined it spelled "Ja-*sin*-ta."

"This is the best inn in Bollow, Mother,"

"But it's an *inn*!" she objected. "Why aren't you staying at the Lord of the Suns' palace? Was this Alenor's idea? What was she thinking, sending you here as her envoy and then making you bunk down in some flea-ridden hovel?"

"The Widow's Rest isn't a hovel, Mother, nor is it flea-ridden. It's a perfectly respectable establishment. The Duke of Grannon Rock is staying here. So are Lord and Lady—"

"It's intolerable!" Sofia cut in. "I will see the new Lord of the Suns at once, and arrange to have you moved to more suitable accommodation."

"That may be rather difficult, Mother," Jacinta pointed out calmly. "For one thing, he probably won't see you. For another, the Lion of Senet and the High Priestess are already staying at the palace. Prince Baston of Damita is on his way and Alenor will be staying there, too, when she arrives. I probably *would* be bunking down in the stables if I tried to move to the palace."

"Then you must come with me. Your father and I are staying with Lord Parqette. I will not leave you here in this... this... fleapit. How many servants have you got with you? I suppose we'll have to find room for them, too."

"I didn't bring any with me. The inn has more than enough to cater for my needs."

Lady Sofia was mortified. "Jacinta! You don't mean to tell me you traveled all this way on your *own*? Dear Goddess, where did I go wrong with you? What did I ever do to be punished like this?"

"Oh, Mother, do be quiet," Jacinta groaned. "I sailed from Kalarada on the Lion of Senet's ship and traveled to Bollow in the Lord of the Suns' own carriage with an escort of Queen's Guardsmen. You make it sound as if I stood by the side of the road and hoisted my skirts up to get a ride from the first wagon driver who happened by."

"A thing I'd not put past you, young lady. You have no sense of decorum, no sense at all, now that I think of it. I should *never* have let you go to court on your own."

"You wanted me to go, as I recall."

"Only because I thought being at court would civilize you. I should have known better than to imagine you'd learn anything in such a licentious place."

"Licentious?" Jacinta asked with a smile. That was overdoing it, even for her mother.

"What else do you call a court where the regent openly flaunts his mistress and the queen gets caught with a lover?"

Jacinta's heart skipped a beat. "What are you talking about?"

"Oh, you probably haven't heard," Sofia shrugged, taking a seat by the window as she pulled off her gloves, after running her finger along the window sill to check if it had been dusted. "Alexin Seranov—you know him, don't you? Saban's second boy—was caught in a rather compromising position with the queen. Prince Kirshov arrested him along with a half-dozen other Guardsmen who were hiding the affair. He's bringing the young man here, I understand, so Antonov can deal with the pair of them. It was bound to happen. I mean, Alenor is far too young for the responsibilities of a queen and marrying her to someone as dissolute as Kirshov Latanya was a disaster simply waiting to happen. Of course, now there's all sorts of questions being asked. People are even starting to wonder about that baby she lost. Or if she lost it accidentally..."

"Mother!"

"What, dear?

"When did this happen?"

"Oh, a few weeks ago now, I suppose. Just after that awful business at Oakridge."

Jacinta's chest constricted even further. "What awful business at Oakridge?"

"Well, you know how the Senetians have been turning Dhevyn upside down looking for the people who escaped Mil...well, some fool started a rumor we were hiding them in the fruit-pickers' cottage near Oakridge. I mean, as if anybody would believe such ridiculous gossip."

"Inconceivable," Jacinta agreed tonelessly, wondering how many more things could go wrong.

"Anyway, when your father heard about it, he was furious, of course, so he sent a message to Prince Kirshov in Kalarada protesting the idea we would have anything to do with those criminals from Mil..."

"Naturally..."

"And then that damned Sundancer turned up..."

"What Sundancer?"

"Brahm Halyn. He used to be on Elcast until Lady Morna was...well, after she died he returned to Bollow, apparently. Anyway, Brahm Halyn arrives in Oakridge with a decree from the Lord of the Suns and announces the temple there—which is little more than a ruin, mind you, since it was struck by lightning a few years ago—is a site of great historical and religious importance. And now we're not even allowed on our own lands. The whole place has been declared off-limits to everyone but the Sundancers. Your father will be taking that up with Lord Provin, I can tell you. He can't just arbitrarily acquire Dhevynian land just because the Goddess is supposed to have smote the temple...or whatever it is he's claiming happened. I don't know what the world is coming to. Paige Halyn never threw his weight around in such a manner."

Jacinta stared at her mother in shock. "So what happened to the Senetian forces that were planning to search Oakridge?"

"They've had no more luck getting near the place than we have. And the harvest is coming up soon. We'll lose a fortune if that fruit is allowed to rot on the trees."

The implications of her mother's news made Jacinta's head reel. She rose to her feet and crossed to the chair where her shawl was hanging.

"I have to go."

"Go? Go where?"

"I have to see somebody," she explained, throwing the shawl over her shoulders. "Perhaps I can drive out to Lord Parqette's estate later to see you and father."

"Jacinta! Don't you dare just walk out on me!"

"I'm sorry, Mother, but this is very important." She hurried back to the settee by the window, kissed her mother's cheek hastily and then fled the room before Lady Sofia could object.

When she reached the lobby, Jacinta strode through it without acknowledging any of the greetings directed her way. There were several carriages for hire waiting outside. She climbed into the nearest one and gave the driver orders to take her to the palace of the Lord of the Suns.

Chapter 51

Had he known in advance how beautiful the Lord of the Suns' residence was on the shores of Lake Ruska, Dirk might have found himself wanting to attain the post simply to lay claim to the estate. Set apart from the city, the palace had been constructed of alternating blocks of dark granite and creamy ignimbrite, its elegant design untouched by time, earthquakes or the Age of Shadows. The carefully tended gardens reached all the way down to the lake, where long-necked swans glided across the surface and the raucous calls of the ducks roosting in the rushes at the water's edge echoed over the water.

Dirk had taken to disappearing from the palace whenever the pressure began to reach boiling point; taking a walk along the shore gave him time to sort out his thoughts. It was peaceful by the lake and he'd just about convinced the servants not to reveal his whereabouts whenever he fled the chaos around him for a few moments of blessed peace.

"Lord Dirk! Lord Dirk!"

Almost all the servants, he thought as Eryk hailed him.

He turned to see what the boy wanted and realized with despair that Jacinta D'Orlon was with him. He suddenly became very conscious of the fact he had been caught skipping stones like a ten-year-old boy. Cursing under his breath, he tossed away the pebbles he had been skimming over the surface of the lake, brushed his hands clean on his trousers and strode across the lawn to meet them.

"See! I told you I knew where he was," Eryk declared happily as Dirk reached them.

Jacinta smiled at the boy. "Yes, you did, Eryk, although by the look of him, I'm not sure your master wanted to be found."

"He doesn't mind seeing *you,* my lady," Eryk told her. "It's just everyone else he's hiding from." ·

Jacinta looked at him curiously. Dirk wanted to cringe with embarrassment.

"Go find something to do, Eryk," he ordered.

"Like what, Lord Dirk?"

"Like fetching Lady Jacinta something cool to drink, perhaps?"

"That would be lovely, Eryk," Jacinta agreed.

The boy nodded eagerly and ran back toward the house. Jacinta watched him leave and then turned back to Dirk with an apologetic smile. "I'm sorry, my lord. I truly didn't mean to disturb you."

"It's all right," he shrugged. "He's right, actually. I was hiding from everyone."

"Are we not enjoying being the Lord of the Suns?" she asked with a slightly raised brow.

"Actually, we're not," he admitted, a little surprised to find himself confiding in her.

"I have noticed you seem rather reluctant to assume the robes of your office."

He glanced down at his shirt and trousers with a wan smile. "I just can't bring myself to walk around in a long yellow dress."

Jacinta laughed. "I'm sure the rest of your order would be quite offended to hear you refer to their traditional robes in such a manner."

"You're probably right. Still, there's no way I can get out of wearing them for ceremonial occasions. But I'm damned if I'm going to wear them any other time."

"Well, I for one applaud your stance, Lord Provin. I think you're right. You'd look ridiculous in a long yellow dress. Shall we walk?"

Jacinta fell in beside Dirk and they began to walk along the shore. Within a few steps the trees obscured the palace and they were effectively alone.

"It's quite beautiful here," Jacinta remarked, looking around with interest.

"It is, isn't it?" he agreed, and then he looked at her curiously. "But that's not why you're here."

"No, it's not. I came to thank you."

"For what?"

"For helping the refugees in Oakridge."

"What makes you think I had anything to do with that?"

"You had *everything* to do with it, my lord. Alenor was right about you, wasn't she? You are still on our side."

"I'm going to rather a lot of trouble to prove that I'm *not*, my lady."

"And you've succeeded admirably," she assured him. "The Dhevynians who believe you shouldn't be hung, drawn and quartered are a very small minority."

"Well, there's a comfort."

She was silent for a moment, as if working up the courage to speak. He wondered if she was planning another test to prove where his loyalties lay.

"I need to ask you another favor, my lord," she said eventually.

Apparently she was. "What sort of favor?"

"Alexin Seranov has been arrested."

"What for?"

"Adultery with the queen."

Dirk stopped and stared at her. "Please tell me this is your idea of a joke."

"I wish it were."

He closed his eyes for a moment. *Poor Alenor.* "What happened?"

She shrugged. "I don't know the full story. All I know is he was caught with Alenor, and Kirshov is bringing him here to face the Lion of Senet."

"Then he's as good as dead, my lady." Dirk's mind was reeling. *Why this? Why now?*

"And so is Alenor unless you intervene."

"How can I help?" he asked, a little impatiently.

"You're the Lord of the Suns, Dirk Provin. You are the only person on Ranadon who can pull rank on the Lion of Senet and get away with it. You control the High Priestess of the Shadowdancers. You're probably the single most powerful man in the world right now. If you can't save Alenor and Alexin, no-body can."

Dirk stared at her, wondering how much she knew. Or what she had guessed. Jacinta scared him a little. That such a sharp mind lurked behind such as disarming face was extremely disturbing. For a fleeting, inexplicable moment he was tempted to confide in her, to tell her everything. He resisted the temptation. He'd come this far alone. He would see it through to the bitter end.

"Do you trust me?"

"That's an odd question."

"But an important one. Do you trust me?"

She thought about her answer for a moment and then nodded. "Yes, I think I do."

"Do you believe I would never do anything to hurt Alenor?"

"She certainly believes it."

"But do *you*?"

Once again, she considered her response carefully before she answered. "Yes."

"Then if I'm to save them, I'll need your help."

"What do you want me to do?"

"I want you to denounce Alexin."

"What?"

"When Kirsh and Alenor arrive in Bollow, I want you to stand up and declare you know for certain Alexin is in league with the Baenlanders and he seduced Alenor with the sole intention of turning her from the Goddess."

"That will brand him a heretic."

"I know."

Suddenly Jacinta smiled. "And if he's a heretic, it becomes a matter for the Church and the Lord of the Suns can take a hand in his fate. You're smarter than you look, Dirk Provin."

She was very quick, this girl. He would never have gotten away with half the things he'd done lately if there was anybody else around him with even half her wit.

"You'll have to be convincing," he warned. "And Alenor will be furious with you until you can explain it to her."

"I can be convincing, but will my word be enough?"

"Probably not," he agreed. "But in that, we may have had a stroke of luck. I have it from a *very* reliable source that Tia Veran is currently in Bollow. Her presence would lend such a theory a great deal of credence if I can find her before Alenor and Kirsh get here."

"*Will* you find her?"

"If I don't, it won't be from lack of trying. I've got every soldier and city guard in Bollow looking for her."

"And with Tia Veran in custody, what then? She won't acknowledge Alexin is a member of the rebel underground willingly."

"That won't matter provided I don't let Antonov question her directly. All I really need to do is have her arrested and then assure him that she has verified your story. He'll believe me. And after the eclipse . . . well, it won't matter so much then."

She stared at him suspiciously. "You just thought this up now, didn't you? You're making this up as you go along."

"That doesn't mean it won't work, my lady. I'll speak to Marqel. She'll back me up when I demand Alexin is handed over to me. With the Lord of the Suns and the Voice of the Goddess demanding justice, you implicating Alexin as a heretic and the greatest heretic of all's daughter confirming your accusation, Antonov won't be able to deny me."

"Do you trust the High Priestess to do such a thing?"

"I don't trust her at all," he told her. "But I have ways of making her toe the line."

She searched his face curiously for a moment. "What *are* you up to, Dirk Provin?" When he didn't answer, she smiled suddenly, and let the question go unanswered. Jacinta was obviously dying to press him on the subject, but she had the sense not to insist he elaborate. "Do you know when Kirsh and Alenor are due to arrive?"

"The day after tomorrow, I believe," Dirk told her.

"I'll need to be here when they arrive. Kirsh won't wait on this."

"Perhaps you should think about moving up to the palace,

then?" he suggested. "Alenor will need you close by and we have plenty of room."

Unaccountably, Jacinta burst out laughing.

"My lady?"

"I'm sorry," she chuckled. "I'm not laughing at you or your kind offer. I was just thinking about . . . you see, my mother . . . Oh, it's just too hard to explain . . ."

Dirk smiled. "You'll stay then? I can have someone sent into town to collect your things."

Forcing her laughter under control, Jacinta's smile faded. "I'd best go with them. And be careful who you send to aid me, my lord," she cautioned. "There's a certain book in my possession that could get me into an awful lot of trouble if it were discovered among my things."

He smiled knowingly. "I'll send Caterina and Eryk with you. They could come across you burning effigies of the Goddess in the middle of the Bollow Temple and I'm sure they'd swear you were doing nothing wrong."

"Are you angry with them?"

"Jealous, actually."

She eyed him skeptically. "You've nothing to be jealous of, my lord. I'd be delighted to engender even a fraction of the devotion Eryk and Caterina have for you in my servants."

"The people who'd like to see me dead outnumber my loyal followers rather dramatically, my lady."

"Which doesn't seem to bother you at all," she remarked, studying him with those strange, color-shifting eyes. "Are you sure you know what you're doing?"

He smiled. "No."

"Well, that's a relief. You'd be rather scary if you weren't even a little bit uncertain." They walked on in silence for a way. "I can't thank you enough for helping Alenor and Alexin."

"I haven't done anything yet." He was uncomfortable with her gratitude. Jacinta was placing a great deal of trust in him he wasn't sure he deserved. His plan sounded clever, but Antonov's fury on learning Alenor had taken a lover and fallen pregnant with a child that wasn't Kirsh's might be much stronger than his belief in church law. Despite his stated approval of Dirk's new role, Dirk had not challenged Antonov openly since becoming Lord of the Suns. He wasn't sure what would happen when he did.

"But you will," she said confidently. "And now, if you will excuse me, I'll leave you in peace to continue ... hiding. Would you be offended if I wasn't in attendance for dinner this evening? I need to visit my parents."

"I'll see there's a carriage made available to you."

"You're being very generous."

"Actually, since you're the queen's envoy, I probably should have invited you to stay at the palace when you first arrived in Bollow."

She stared at him suspiciously. "You haven't been talking to my mother, have you?"

"No. Why?"

"Nothing," she shrugged, and then smiled. "Just an idle thought. I'll see you later then?"

"Undoubtedly."

She turned to leave but had only gone a few steps before she turned back to him with a slight frown. "There was one other thing I wanted to ask."

"Name it."

"Who are you planning to sacrifice at the ceremony?"

Dirk had been dreading that question. And avoiding it. Not even Antonov had been able to get an answer out of him.

"I haven't decided yet," he told her honestly.

"Did you have anybody particular in mind?"

"There are a few people I'd *like* to see burn," he admitted, wondering what it was about Jacinta D'Orlon that made him so garrulous.

"Is that why you're searching the city so anxiously for Tia Veran?"

Dirk shook his head, amused by the idea. Jacinta had no idea of his past history with Tia. She wouldn't appreciate the irony. But if Eryk was right, if he really had spied Tia in the crowd near the temple the other day, and Dirk was able to find her before the eclipse...

First I killed the man you loved like a father in cold blood right in front of you, then I betrayed you to the High Priestess, and now I'm going to burn you alive, Tia...

Come to think of it, Tia probably wouldn't appreciate the irony, either.

"My lord?"

Dirk dragged his attention back to Jacinta's question. "Sorry. I was just thinking...if I have to burn someone, our new High Priestess would do for a start."

"I'm surprised to hear you say that, my lord," Jacinta remarked. "I gathered she was one of your staunchest supporters. She certainly seemed that way at the swearing-in ceremony."

"In public, perhaps," he agreed. "But make no mistake about it, my lady, Marqel is dangerous, self-centered, untrustworthy and completely amoral. She'd destroy me in a heartbeat if she thought she could get away with it."

"Then why do you deal with her?"

"Because at this point, I have no choice."

"You choose odd allies, Dirk Provin."

"So do you," he pointed out, still uncertain why she had supported him. Or what she hoped to gain from it.

As if she knew he wanted to ask her why she'd gone to such pains to see him confirmed as Lord of the Suns, she laughed airily and changed the subject.

"You know, I always thought Barin Welacin would make a rather attractive sacrifice. Perhaps you could arrange for him to be the main feature of the eclipse ceremony."

"That's a very tempting suggestion, my lady."

"Well, if you are in need of any further ideas, I'd be more than happy to provide the names of a few potential suitors I wouldn't mind seeing turned to ashes."

"Including Lord Birkoff?" he asked.

"Especially Lord Birkoff," Jacinta replied with feeling. Then she curtsied politely. "My lord."

"My lady."

Jacinta picked up her skirts and turned back toward the house, leaving him alone by the lake. Dirk watched her leave with the strange feeling that of all the people he was dealing with in this dangerous enterprise, Jacinta D'Orlon might prove the most perilous of all.

Chapter 52

Eryk hurried back to the house, delighted he'd been able to find Lord Dirk so Lady Jacinta could see him. He really liked Jacinta, and, as Caterina had pointed out, she was just perfect for Lord Dirk. The two of them had secretly agreed to facilitate their meeting at every opportunity. Caterina was like that. She treated Eryk like a fellow conspirator, never as if he was stupid or dull. And Eryk was her willing accomplice. He knew why Caterina wanted to stay with Lord Dirk. Going home to her overbearing mother and her four bossy sisters sounded like no fun at all. This was her only chance at a better life. Caterina speculated if the Lady Jacinta married Lord Dirk, then maybe she'd be allowed to stay at the palace as a servant, once Lord Dirk no longer felt the need to keep her hostage.

That seemed like an eminently reasonable plan to Eryk. He didn't have many friends and was anxious to retain the few he did have. Lady Jacinta was very nice and very pretty and she was the right age and everything, and—according to Caterina—Lord Dirk was smitten with her. Eryk wasn't actually sure what *smitten* meant, but it sounded good, so he happily went along with Caterina's scheme.

Of course, there were a few hurdles to overcome. Getting Lady Jacinta and Lord Dirk alone was only the first thing. Simply getting them to refer to each other by name might prove insurmountable, Caterina worried. All this noble-born nonsense about courtesy was severely limiting. All those polite "my lords" and "my ladys" were quite a hindrance to getting to know somebody. And Dirk being the Lord of the Suns probably didn't help, either. Suppose he had to take a vow of chastity?

Caterina explained a "vow of chastity" meant he couldn't kiss anyone, but Eryk wasn't that stupid. He knew it meant Lord Dirk couldn't do any of the things Marqel had shown him that time he'd met her in Nova, which might not be a bad thing because he couldn't imagine anyone as well bred as Lady Jacinta doing that sort of thing anyway.

He was still wondering about it when he reached the terrace overlooking the lake. He climbed the steps thoughtfully, wondering if there was anything else he could do to help things along between Lord Dirk and Lady Jacinta.

"Why the troubled look, Eryk?"

Startled to hear his name, he looked up to find Marqel sitting on one of the wrought-iron recliners laid out for the palace residents to enjoy the view of the lake.

"I wasn't troubled." He shrugged. "Just thinking."

"And very deep thoughts, I'd wager." Marqel smiled. "I've not seen much of you since I got to Bollow, Eryk. You're not avoiding me, are you?"

"Oh no! Marqel, you're my friend."

"Good. Because you're my friend, too, and we've had hardly any time to chat since you came back from Mil."

"I will chat with you, Marqel," he promised. "But right now I have to fetch something cool for Lady Jacinta."

Marqel's eyes narrowed. "What's she doing here?"

"She came to see Lord Dirk."

"Why?"

"I don't know. Maybe she just wanted to talk to him?"

"The highborn never do anything unless they're plotting something, Eryk. Especially Lord Dirk."

"What do you mean?" he asked, a little concerned by her tone.

But Marqel smiled brightly and laughed at her own foolishness. "Nothing, Eryk. You'd better run along and fetch Lady Jacinta her drink." Marqel looked at him in concern as his face crumbled into a worried frown. "What's the matter?"

"I forgot to ask her what she wanted. Lord Dirk just said something about a cool drink."

"Perhaps you'd better go ask her."

"She'll think I'm stupid."

"Who? Jacinta? Of course she won't think you're stupid, Eryk. She's very nice. Why, I remember her from the palace when I was in Kalarada. She was always very nice to me."

"I suppose. Caterina really likes her."

"And who could ask for a more glowing character reference than that?"

"I hope she's right about Lady Jacinta and Lord Dirk."

The High Priestess smiled warmly and swung her legs around so she was sitting on the edge of the chaise. She beckoned him forward and patted the space beside her.

"What do you mean, you hope she's right about them?"

Eryk sat beside her and took a deep breath. It was good to talk about these things to another friend besides Caterina. And Marqel was really good at this sort of thing. She'd known *exactly* what Eryk needed to do about Mellie.

"Can I ask you something, Marqel?"

"I'm your friend, Eryk," she assured him. "You can ask me anything."

"Well, Caterina thinks Lord Dirk and Lady Jacinta... well, that they like each other."

"Really?" Marqel asked with interest. "How do you know? Or, more to the point, how does Caterina know?"

"She just does. She says it's her women's intrusion."

"Women's intuition?" Marqel corrected with a soft laugh. "I suppose it must be. Unless she's seen something?"

"I don't think so," Eryk said. "That's the problem, you see. I mean we know they like each other, but we don't know how to make *them* see it."

"So you and Caterina are worried that Dirk hasn't got the... wherewithal to get things moving, eh?"

"Maybe he doesn't know what to say to her."

"Yes, well, I can see how being romantic might prove a bit of a challenge for him," Marqel agreed. "Dirk's not the most open sort of fellow, is he?"

"Could you help, Marqel?"

His comment sent Marqel into a fit of choking coughs.

"Are you all right?" he asked in alarm.

She nodded, wiping streaming eyes. It took her a moment or two to get her breathing back under control. "You want *me* to help Dirk seduce Jacinta D'Orlon?"

"Well, you know all the right things to say. And what to do. Don't you remember what you showed me in Nova?"

Marqel looked around nervously. "I remember, Eryk. But that's our little secret. You promised not to mention it again."

"I'm sorry. I haven't told anyone else about it, I promise. But I was just thinking that if you could do the same for Lord Dirk...then he'd know what to do, and Caterina could stay here..."

"Ah, so that's what all this is about. You don't want Caterina to leave. But I thought you were in love with Mellie?"

"Well, I was...am," he agreed, suddenly confused. "But Caterina...well, she's here, and Mellie's gone..."

Marqel put her arm around his shoulder and gave it an affectionate squeeze. "It's all right, Eryk. I understand. It doesn't make you a bad person. Most boys can't be faithful if there's another girl close by to distract them. It's just the way men are made."

"Will you help Lord Dirk, then?"

She smiled broadly. "Of course I will. In fact, I think I'll follow them right now and see how things are going between Lady Jacinta and Lord Dirk, just so I can figure out the best way to deal with the situation."

Eryk sighed contentedly at the suggestion, thinking there were few friends as selfless or generous as Marqel. In fact, he was probably the luckiest person in the whole world to have friends like Lord Dirk and Caterina and Marqel.

"You're just the best friend, Marqel."

"Don't mention it, Eryk. Believe me when I say *nothing* will give me more pleasure than finding out there is something going on between Dirk Provin and Jacinta D'Orlon. And doing something about it."

Chapter 53

Marqel cut across the lawns when she couldn't see Dirk or Jacinta, guessing they had walked down past the trees, so she angled off the left to take a shortcut through the woodland, cursing her foolishness for not paying more attention.

How could something like an affair between Dirk and Jacinta D'Orlon be going on without her noticing anything? She allowed herself a small smile over Eryk's request that she show Dirk what he needed to do to win Jacinta over.

I've already shown your precious Lord Dirk things you wouldn't even dream of, you loathsome little creep.

What would Eryk think of Dirk if he knew that? Marqel would never confide such a thing to the boy, of course. Regardless of what he might think of Dirk, the news would tarnish her saintly image in Eryk's eyes and that was far too valuable a commodity to throw away for the fleeting pleasure of seeing the half-wit's crestfallen expression.

Marqel stilled suddenly as voices reached her. She crept forward, unable to see Dirk or Jacinta, but their voices carried clearly through the thick foliage.

"There was one other thing I wanted to ask," Jacinta was saying.

"Name it," Dirk replied.

"Who are you planning to sacrifice at the ceremony?"

Marqel halted, wondering at the answer. She still couldn't believe Dirk was going to burn anybody at the ceremony. He seemed to despise Landfall too much for that.

"I haven't decided yet," Marqel heard him say.

"Did you have anybody particular in mind?"

"There's a few people I'd *like* to see burn."

"Is that why you're searching the city so anxiously for Tia Veran?"

Tia Veran? The name set alarm bells ringing in Marqel's

head. If Tia Veran was a candidate for an eclipse sacrifice, did that mean she was here in Bollow? Did Dirk know where she was? Is that why he was looking for her? Or was Jacinta simply taking a stab in the dark, thinking that Tia Veran would make an excellent sacrifice because of who she was, even though she wasn't actually anywhere near Bollow?

"My lord?"

Marqel held her breath, waiting for Dirk's answer.

"Sorry. I was just thinking…if I have to burn someone, our new High Priestess would do for a start."

Marqel gasped, furious to hear Dirk say such a thing about her. And to Jacinta D'Orlon, of all people.

"I'm surprised to hear you say that, my lord," Jacinta's disembodied voice remarked, echoing Marqel's feelings. She couldn't believe it either. Then she heard Jacinta add: "I gathered she was one of your staunchest supporters. She certainly seemed that way at the swearing-in ceremony."

"In public, perhaps," Dirk agreed. "But make no mistake about it, my lady, Marqel is dangerous, self-centered, untrustworthy and completely amoral. She'd destroy me in a heartbeat if she thought she could get away with it."

Marqel was too angry to take notice of the rest of their conversation. The idea Dirk could even contemplate burning her alive made her furious beyond reason. That he would voice his desire aloud to that superior, stuck-up little bitch, Jacinta D'Orlon, made it a thousand times worse.

Will I ever learn not to trust that double-dealing little prick?

She leaned against the rough trunk of the nearest tree, digging her nails into the soft bark to stop herself from screaming out her fury and betraying her presence. For a moment, she had forgotten why she had come here. The prospect of Dirk Provin and Jacinta D'Orlon having an affair seemed laughable now. They were not involved. She should have known better than to listen to Eryk and believe they might be. Jacinta D'Orlon was just a spoiled, airheaded noblewoman, inhibited and confined by her upbringing. Dirk, on the other hand, was all ambition and anger and nothing would be allowed to get in his way, particularly not a woman. He'd betrayed Tia Veran without so much as blinking. He'd killed his own father. He'd led the invasion into Mil against the people who thought he was their friend.

There was no room in Dirk Provin for anything other than an insatiable thirst for power.

Yet there was a level of intimacy in his conversation with Jacinta that was worrying. Dirk went to great pains to portray himself a certain way to everyone he met, and admitting the opposite to someone who should be little more than a stranger was not like him at all.

Did he know Jacinta? Had they been childhood friends? That would account for the familiarity of their conversation, the ease with which he spoke to her. It was possible, of course. The nobility all moved in the same circles and both Dirk and Jacinta were the children of ruling houses. Maybe that's all there was to it. Perhaps Jacinta was someone he'd known all his life and Caterina's "women's intuition" was just the mistaken belief that their childhood friendship was something more than it really was.

Whatever the case, Dirk had proved one thing beyond doubt with his careless words. He couldn't be trusted and he had to be dealt with, sooner rather than later.

Marqel knew she couldn't safely remove Dirk until after the eclipse. But she needed some leverage, some way of making him toe the line—her line—in the interim. What form that leverage should take was another matter entirely.

She could do nothing to Jacinta that would make a difference. Besides, the Queen of Dhevyn's envoy was too obvious a target and there were too many people who could—and would—vouch for her innocence, should she try to accuse Jacinta of anything. The only other sure way to get at Dirk that Marqel knew of was through Alenor, but she wasn't here yet and it was hard to say what would happen when she did arrive. Would Kirsh support his wife against Marqel out of spite for being rejected?

It was impossible to say. Since the news arrived from Kalarada that Kirsh had caught Alenor in the arms of Alexin

Seranov—a minor detail she had quite deliberately not shared
with Dirk—the question over whose child she'd been carrying had loomed large in Antonov's mind. When he thought
the baby was his grandchild, he would have strangled Marqel
with his bare hands had he discovered it was she who had in-
duced Alenor's abortion. In light of Alenor's affair, however,
Antonov wouldn't be angry with her. He'd probably be grateful.

She sighed heavily. The problem was giving Marqel a
headache. There must be some way. Some chink in Dirk's ar-
mor that would allow her to protect herself against his machinations.

And then it came to her.

Tia Veran.

If Tia was in the city, Dirk must be looking for her.
Whether he wanted her for fair deeds or foul was not the issue.
The fact is, he *would* want her and if Marqel found her first,
then she would have the leverage she wanted, the safety net she
so desperately needed.

Marqel waited a while longer until she was certain that
Jacinta was gone and Dirk was no longer in the vicinity of the
trees before she turned and hurried back toward the palace.

The day was still young, and with luck she could be in the
city in less than an hour. That gave her quite a long time to look.
Plenty of time to rally the City Guard and, more important,
Antonov's own guard, in the search for Tia Veran.

Once she found her—and Marqel allowed for no other
possibility—she would confront Dirk with her prize...

And then she could start to lay down a few terms of her
own.

One way or another, she decided, Dirk would finally learn
she was not a force to be trifled with. In Marqel's opinion, it was
a lesson long overdue.

Chapter 54

Tia and Reithan learned the reason Dirk Provin no longer feared assassination several days after they had seen him at the temple, from a woman named Bethany who ran one of Bollow's discreet brothels for the Brotherhood. The reason, she told them, was widely known among her associates. Dirk Provin had taken Caterina Farlo hostage and had left orders she would be tortured and killed if anything happened to him.

"So the Brotherhood called off our contract to save a basket maker's daughter?" Tia spat in disgust.

"Not just a basket maker's daughter," Bethany told them. "Her mother is Gilda Farlo."

"So?"

"Gilda Farlo's name before she married the basket maker was Gilda Lukanov."

"She's related to Videon Lukanov in Kalarada?" Reithan asked in surprise.

"His sister," Bethany said. "Dirk Provin picked his hostage well, Reithan. He picked the niece of the man who runs the Brotherhood in Dhevyn."

"But this is Senet."

Bethany smiled, revealing a row of unnaturally perfect teeth. "There are no borders in the Brotherhood, Reithan. You should know that."

"Why haven't you just taken her back?" Tia asked. "I saw her the other day. She's not even guarded."

"I can't say for certain," Bethany shrugged. "He's an intriguing boy, this Dirk Provin of yours. He betrayed every person he'd met in the Brotherhood while he was with your people in Mil, yet he was able to get a list of the names to Boris Farlo in Tolace before a single one of them was arrested. He's involved in a fascinating game. I think the Brotherhood is willing to see it play out before they decide what to do about him one way or the other."

"I'd rather the Brotherhood just did what we paid them to do," Tia complained.

"Look at it from our point of view. For the first time in history we have a Lord of the Suns willing to deal with the Brotherhood," Bethany pointed out. "Paige Halyn didn't even know we existed. Fulfilling a contract with your people in Mil—who even you must admit are now powerless and scattered—against the chance to have a Lord of the Suns we can negotiate with? What would you do in our place?"

"Honor the contract," Tia replied without hesitating.

Bethany smiled. "You say that because from where you sit, it seems the honorable thing to do. But don't fool yourself, Tia. There is no honor here. This is business. I suppose I might be able to arrange for you to get your money back if the Brotherhood decides not to proceed with the assassination."

"We should get our money back anyway," she said. "You're playing your own game with Dirk Provin and it's got nothing to do with us. Why should we pay for something you're probably going to do anyway? As you said, this is the first Lord of the Suns who even knows the Brotherhood exists. What are you going to do if you can't get him to cooperate? Send him a thank-you note?"

Her words seemed to have little impact on the woman.

"I'll see what I can do about the money, Tia," Bethany repeated. "I can't promise more than that."

After they left the brothel, Tia and Reithan shoved their way back through the crowds toward the tent city. It had begun to rain lightly while they were inside, but the crowd had thinned only a little. Tia cursed and snapped at anybody foolish enough to get in her way, her anger at the Brotherhood's double-dealing finding an outlet in the bustling streets of the Senetian city. They had spent a fortune on that contract. Money that could have been spent helping the scattered refugees who fled the Baenlands.

Reithan seemed rather more philosophical about the news. Tia suspected it was because, like Misha, Reithan still harbored a faint hope Dirk was actually doing something useful. Small chance of that. Still, her bow was hidden among the gear they had left at the dressmaker's tent, and on the day of the eclipse she knew exactly where Dirk would be—standing on the steps of the Bollow temple, a perfect target ...

"Wouldn't go that way if I were you," a man muttered impatiently as he pushed past Tia.

"Why not?"

"The damn guard's checking everyone going in or out the city gate."

"Are they looking for anyone in particular?" Reithan asked, glancing at Tia.

"Didn't hang around to find out," the man shrugged, shoving his way past them.

Tia turned to Reithan. "I wonder what's going on?"

"Do we want to risk the gate to find out?"

Tia glanced up at the overcast sky. It was raining lightly, but the sky was darker in the west as another storm rolled in. "It's going to start bucketing down soon."

Reithan smiled briefly. "I'd rather get wet than arrested."

"Me, too," she agreed, "but I'd like to know what's going on. Maybe if we get a bit closer, we can find out."

"Or we could go back to Bethany's," he suggested.

Tia scowled at his hopeful expression. "See something at Bethany's that caught your fancy, did you?"

"Saw quite a few things there that caught my fancy, actually."

She rolled her eyes impatiently. "Don't you men ever think of anything else?"

"Not if we can help it."

"We're going to the gate, Reithan," she announced firmly.

"Yes, *mistress*."

Tia let out a snarl of frustration and began pushing her way forward again. The crowd was even denser as they neared the gate, the large number of soldiers checking everyone with a thoroughness that disturbed her. She recalled the look on Eryk's face as the Lord of the Suns' carriage trundled past the other day. Had he said something to Dirk? Was that the reason they were checking everyone's identity?

Suddenly fearful, she turned to Reithan. "I think maybe we shouldn't try getting through the gate right now."

"I think you're right. Back to Bethany's?"

The crowd carried them forward as they tried to decide the best course of action.

"I guess that's the safest place."

"What do you suppose prompted them to start checking people?"

Tia was afraid she knew, but if she told Reithan, he would be furious she'd not mentioned it before now. And it wasn't as if she knew for certain that was the reason . . .

"I don't know. Let's just get out of here."

The crowd behind them had grown so dense that there was no way they could go back the way they had come. Tia glanced around and noticed the throng seemed a little thinner on the street to the left, so she shoved her way across with Reithan close on her heels. When they reached the end of the side street, Tia stumbled as she suddenly stepped out into an open space and the reason the area was less crowded became apparent.

The wider street at the other end was lined with soldiers and less than ten feet away was a carriage with the Lion of Senet's crest on the door. Inside the carriage sat a young woman robed in red.

Reithan stumbled into Tia as he broke through. "Watch it!" Tia snapped as she regained her balance.

The young woman in the carriage turned her head at the sound of the commotion.

Marqel recognized Tia in the same instant that Tia recognized her.

"There she is!" Marqel screeched. "That's her! Quickly!"

Tia had no time to react. The soldiers were on her before she had time to cry out a warning to Reithan. She heard the sound of a blade unsheathing behind her as her legs were kicked out from beneath her and she was shoved facedown onto the wet cobbles. Her hands were jerked savagely behind her. A knee pressed into her lower back. The sound of metal against metal filled her ears. The taste of the rain-slick street filled her mouth and nose. She heard shouts. Heard Reithan cry out. Tia tried to move her head, but she could see nothing but the booted feet of her captors and the little rivulets of water than ran between the cobbles.

And then the sound of fighting suddenly stopped and the pressure on her back was eased. She was hauled to her feet.

Tia looked around urgently for Reithan. She couldn't see him at first. Then she spied him, lying on his back on the ground near the street entrance. His sword lay discarded, a few inches from his open hand. His vest was open, his shirt covered by a slowly spreading bloodstain. The rain pattered down on him. His eyes were half open, staring blindly into the distance, but he didn't seem to notice the water dripping into them. The water trickling away from him toward the gutters was tinted red. One of the soldiers walked over to him and poked him with his boot. Reithan's eyes didn't blink. He didn't move.

"No!" Tia sobbed in a strangled whisper.

The soldier turned to the High Priestess. "He's dead."

"No!" Tia cried, as if by denying the truth, then it couldn't be real. Reithan wasn't dead. He mustn't be dead. She would not *allow* him to be dead.

The High Priestess shrugged. "He doesn't really matter. She's the important one."

Numb with shock and grief, Tia turned to look up at Marqel, sitting in the carriage with a smug, malicious smile on her face.

"Hello, Tia," she said. "Fancy meeting you here."

Chapter 55

Marqel waited until she was headed back to the Lord of the Suns' palace outside the city before she let her delight show. Alone in Antonov's luxurious carriage, she laughed until tears streamed down her face. The look on Tia Veran's face when she realized she was cornered was priceless.

I'm High Priestess now. Mistress of the Lion of Senet.

It was about time Dirk Provin remembered that. He might have arranged for her to get there, but that didn't mean he could treat her as if she no longer meant anything. As for that superior little bitch Jacinta D'Orlon, well, sooner or later, Marqel would find a way to cut her down to size, too.

Stupid prick! Did Dirk Provin really think he could say those things about me and get away with it?

Marqel couldn't wait to return to the palace. She couldn't wait to see the look on Dirk's face when she told him she'd found Tia Veran and had her arrested. Or that the fellow with her—Reithan somebody-or-other—was dead. Marqel didn't really know who the man was, but she was betting Dirk knew. And even if he didn't know him, Dirk was squeamish when it came to people dying.

It was nice to feel as if she had the upper hand for a change. Despite her newfound wealth and position, things weren't going quite as she would have liked. Antonov welcomed her into his bed each night, but seemed to have little interest in conversing with her. He certainly didn't ask her advice on matters of state as often as she imagined he would. Or should. He sometimes asked what the Goddess thought of things, but he wasn't interested in Marqel's opinion. And Madalan rarely consulted her about the running of the Shadowdancers since resuming her role as the High Priestess's right hand, a circumstance that had pleased Marqel enormously, until she realized the old hag was deliberately keeping her in the dark.

She would have to do something about that eventually, too.

But neither Madalan nor Antonov was really a problem at the moment. One was keeping her free from the mundane tasks of administration; the other was keeping her in the manner to which she had very quickly become accustomed.

Her immediate problem was Dirk. His attitude toward her had grown increasingly impatient since he'd been appointed Lord of the Suns, a fact that had been driven home to her forcefully when she overheard him talking to Lady Jacinta. He had little time for Marqel and when he did deign to notice her, it was usually to demand she hand over more and more of the Shadowdancers' wealth to appease that senile idiot Claudio Varell. In fact, other than provide her with a carefully choreographed set of instructions for the eclipse ceremony, Dirk had barely even acknowledged her existence since she arrived in Bollow.

Well, he was about to learn the folly of treating her like she was insignificant. The Goddess was about to speak again, and Dirk Provin wouldn't know a thing about it until Marqel announced that at least one of the sacrifices to be burned at the eclipse would be the daughter of the heretic, Tia Veran.

Dirk would be livid. She knew that, but no longer cared. He might be the Lord of the Suns now, but the balance of power had shifted subtly in her direction. She had given Antonov the route through the delta; she had announced the eclipse—strictly speaking Dirk had announced it, but everyone thought it came from her—and she was about to sacrifice the heretic's daughter to the Goddess. Her position grew more secure every day, and after the eclipse, nothing could threaten her. Not even Dirk Provin.

Antonov wasn't at the palace when she arrived. Despite the rain, he'd gone hunting with Lord Parqette, Lord D'Orlon, Prince Baston of Damita and the Duke of Elcast, Dirk's brother, Rees, who had arrived yesterday and was also staying at the palace.

Dirk was in the Lord of the Suns' study with Claudio Varell. Marqel entered the room without knocking and took the empty chair opposite the desk without waiting for either of them to offer her a seat.

Dirk glanced up at her with a frown. "I thought you went into the city."

"I did."

He said nothing, simply waited for some sort of explanation for this unwelcome interruption.

"Ask me what I did in the city," she suggested brightly.

"We're busy, Marqel. I don't have time for your games."

"Well, if you don't want to know who I arrested..." she said, rising to her feet.

Claudio's eyes narrowed suspiciously. "You had somebody arrested?"

"Who?" Dirk asked.

"An old friend of yours, actually."

"Who, Marqel?"

"Tia Veran." Marqel watched Dirk closely, but as usual, he gave away nothing. *What does it take to surprise him?* What would she have to do to get a reaction from him?

"You've arrested Neris Veran's daughter?" Claudio gasped. "How did you even know she was in Bollow?"

"The Goddess told me," she replied smugly, her eyes fixed on Dirk.

For a moment, she thought she saw a flicker of anger deep in those cold gray eyes. Then he turned to Claudio. "Would you mind excusing us for a short time, my lord? The High Priestess and I need to talk."

Obviously annoyed he was to be excluded, Claudio rose to his feet and bowed stiffly.

"As you wish, my lord."

As soon as the door closed behind Claudio, Marqel turned to Dirk with a smirk. "I don't think he likes you very much."

"What did you do with her?"

"Tia? The City Guard is holding her in the garrison in town until I tell them what to do with her."

"It's not up to you to decide her fate."

"She's my prisoner and once I tell Antonov about her, she'll be *his* prisoner."

"If you arrested her, Marqel, then she's the Church's prisoner," Dirk corrected. "I'll take it from here."

"You'll do nothing of the kind. She's my prisoner and I'll decide what to do with her."

"I outrank you, Marqel, in case it slipped your notice. There's not a man, woman or child in the whole of Senet who wouldn't do my bidding before they did yours. And I include the Lion of Senet, his guard and the Bollow City Guard in that. Think about it."

Suddenly, Marqel wasn't quite so sure of herself. Dirk seemed very confident he could take over, and she knew next to nothing about the law, except that as High Priestess she was effectively above it. Perhaps he was right. Perhaps by placing Tia Veran in the custody of the City Guard, Marqel had inadvertently lost control of her.

"I won't let you have her."

"You don't have any choice in the matter."

"What are you going to do?"

"That's no longer any of your concern."

"What are you going to tell Antonov?"

"That is also none of your concern."

Marqel began to get angry. This was supposed to give her an edge over Dirk. She had no intention of simply handing Tia over.

"I'll speak to Antonov. I'll tell him the Goddess told me Tia Veran was to remain my prisoner."

"Try that and I'll have her killed before you can get anywhere near Antonov to tell him your news. Then you can have the pleasure of telling him how the Goddess wanted you to keep Tia as your prisoner, but she died. Only wait till I get back from the city before you say anything. I want to be there when you try to explain it."

"You wouldn't kill Tia Veran."

"Try me."

Marqel stared at him, wishing there was some way to tell what he was thinking. It was useless and she wasn't sure enough of herself to call his bluff. But if she'd lost this round, she still had one other piece of news that might yet rattle him.

"Then I suppose you'll want the corpse as well."

"What corpse?"

"The man who was with Tia Veran when we caught her. He resisted arrest. The City Guard had to kill him. His name was Reithan something."

For the first time, Marqel saw a hint of genuine emotion in Dirk's eyes, but it was impossible to tell what it was. Shock, maybe? Or grief? Did Dirk know the dead man? If he was a Baenlander like the Veran girl then it was more than likely he did.

"Did you know him?"

"Never heard of him."

Marqel looked at him curiously. It was the first time she could remember catching Dirk Provin in a lie.

"You don't look too happy about it," she smirked. "I thought you'd be thrilled to learn our escaped prisoner has been recaptured. Antonov is certainly going to be pleased."

She waited, expecting Dirk to order her to be quiet, but as usual, he did the last thing she expected. He shrugged. "I imagine he will be."

"Don't you *care* I'm going to tell him about her?"

"Should I?"

"I thought she was a friend of yours."

"She put an arrow in my back, Marqel."

"I know, but..."

"Was that all you wanted to tell me?"

"What are you going to do?"

"As I said, that's none of your concern."

"If Tia Veran escapes, I'll tell Antonov it was you who let her go," she warned.

Dirk seemed genuinely amused. "Don't threaten me, Marqel. If I chose to let Tia Veran go, or set free every prisoner in the Bollow Garrison, for that matter, I'd do it in such a way I could *never* be blamed for it. I might even find a way to implicate you, just to remind you who's got the most power."

"After the eclipse, I'll be the one with all the power," she retorted. "Antonov will believe anything I tell him."

"I was under the impression he believes anything you tell

him now," Dirk remarked. "Does this mean he still doubts you? How unfortunate."

"You know what I mean!"

"Just stick to what you know best, Marqel," Dirk suggested. "Leave the politics to those of us who understand it. Have you been practicing for the ceremony?"

"Of course I have," she replied with a scowl. "Although it seems a bit melodramatic, if you ask me."

"I didn't ask you."

"I suppose you need momentous acts to mark momentous occasions."

"What?"

"It's something Belagren said to Madalan once. That you need momentous acts to mark momentous occasions."

"Belagren had a very good understanding of human nature," Dirk agreed. "You could learn a lot from her. Oh, but that's right—she's dead, isn't she? You killed her."

Marqel glared at him. "I don't see it interrupting *your* climb to the top."

"You don't see anything past your own nose, Marqel. And now, if that was all you had to tell me, I'm busy."

"You're not going to see her?"

"See who?"

"Tia *Veran*!"

Dirk turned his attention back to the document he'd been discussing with Claudio when she came in. "I'll see you later, Marqel."

She glared at him, furious he seemed so unconcerned, so untouched; furious that she had so quickly lost the one chance she had to get something over him and nothing she did seemed to crack his facade.

"You won't be able to treat me like this for much longer, Dirk Provin."

He glanced up at her with a faint smile. "Don't be too sure of that, Marqel," he said, and then he went back to reading the document as if she were no longer in the room.

Chapter 56

Tia's cell was in the back of the Senetian garrison near the southern wall of the city. It was bare, but for a smelly straw mattress, a bucket and a disturbingly long tally scratched on the stone wall by a previous tenant.

The City Guard threw her into the cell with little care and left her there to wonder about her fate. She had seen nothing more of Marqel and there was no sign of the Lion of Senet. She had no doubt he would be here soon. No doubt her own death would follow shortly after, probably preceded by unimaginable torment at the hands of Barin Welacin. But her own fate didn't concern her much. She paced the cell restlessly, filled with bitter grief that was almost swamped by an overwhelming guilt.

Tia couldn't rid herself of the realization that she was responsible for Reithan's death. Replaying those last few fatal moments over and over in her mind, she imagined a thousand things she could have done differently, any one of which might have saved him. If only they'd gone back to Bethany's when Reithan first suggested it. If only they hadn't gone down to the gate to find out what was happening. If only they hadn't turned down that street. If only she'd warned Reithan she thought Eryk had recognized her the other day.

Barely aware of the tears streaming down her cheeks, she was still tormenting herself with the possibilities when the lock rattled and the door to her cell opened. Tia sniffed back her tears hurriedly and spun around to face the guards, but only one man stepped into the cell. The door closed and the lock rattled again.

She took a step backward, even though there was nowhere to run, nowhere to hide.

"You shouldn't have come to Bollow, Tia."

Dirk thrust his hands into his pockets. He looked older. More careworn than he had in Omaxin. And he seemed uncomfortable, even a little nervous to be face-to-face with her again. Yet he wasn't afraid. He'd kept no guards to hold her back and he wasn't armed that she could see. But then, he had little to fear other than her anger. If she attacked him, one shout was all it would take to bring the guards back.

Tia glared at Dirk with all the contempt she could muster. "Did I mess up your meteoric rise to the top of the slime heap? Good!"

"You risked your life for no good purpose," he said. "And Reithan's."

"Don't you stand there and talk to me about Reithan. It's your fault he's dead."

If she was hoping to shift the burden of her guilt, the accusation seemed to have the opposite effect. He shed the last of his uncertainty and stood a little straighter. "How do you figure that? Nobody asked you to come here. If you'd stayed away, Reithan would still be alive."

"You're very good at shrugging off the blame, aren't you? How's the shoulder, by the way?"

A brief smile flickered over his lips, so quickly Tia wondered if she imagined it. "It's a little stiff at times. Did you miss my heart on purpose?"

"You don't have a heart, Dirk Provin," she retorted. "There was nothing to aim at."

Dirk was silent for a time, his eyes as unfathomable as ever. She watched him cautiously, wondering what she had ever seen in him; wondering how she could ever have imagined she loved him or even wanted him to touch her. Tia suddenly wanted Misha so badly the ache was almost physical. She needed his strength, his courage.

"I don't suppose there's much point in asking you to trust me." It sounded as if he was thinking out loud rather than actually asking her a question.

"I let you betray me once, Dirk. That was your fault. If I gave you the opportunity to do it again, then I really would be as stupid as you think."

He sighed, unsurprised by her rage. "For what it's worth, I'm sorry, Tia. I never set out to hurt you."

"Of course not. You're just doing what's best for Dirk Provin. And you don't give a damn about who you have to step on along the way to achieve it."

"I'm sorry you feel that way, I truly am, and if I had the time, I would explain things to you, but I don't. What I need to know is if Misha is still alive."

His question surprised her. "I don't know what you're talking about."

"Tia, please don't make this any harder than it has to be. I mean him no harm. I mean *you* no harm. But I need to know if he lives."

"Why?"

"I can't explain."

"You won't explain," she snapped angrily. "That's how you work. *Trust me, believe in me. Just stand there while I screw you over, because I know what's best!* You can go to hell, Dirk Provin. I won't tell you a damned thing, about Misha or anybody else. You can torture me. You can kill me. I won't say a thing."

"I admire your bravado, Tia, but you have no idea what you're talking about. Do you have any idea what Barin Welacin will do to you?"

She held up her maimed left hand in front of his face. "I think I've got a fairly good idea."

He shook his head. "You have *no* idea. All he did the last time was cut off half your finger with a pair of horseshoe pliers. Just wait until he introduces you to ergot poisoning."

"You don't scare me, Dirk. I'm not afraid of you. Or your sadistic little Prefect."

"I'm trying to help you, Tia," he said, sounding a little exasperated.

"Oh? So now you're my friend? Pity you didn't remember that before you handed me over to the High Priestess."

"I remembered it when I asked Kirsh to let you go."

Tia stared at him. "I don't believe you. Why would he let me go if you asked him?"

"He owed me a favor."

"Well, bully for you! I hope you sleep better at night, dreaming about what a big hero you are."

"Tia, please listen to me!" he pleaded. "I know you hate me and I know you have good cause, but don't let it blind you to reason. Marqel had you arrested, so right now you're a prisoner of the Church, but the moment Antonov hears about you being here, he'll demand I hand you over to him."

"Then you won't have to deal with me. What a relief for you."

"Don't you understand what I'm saying? You're the only person who knows the whereabouts of his son. He isn't going to rest until he knows Misha is safe."

"He's safe," she snapped, conceding with some reluctance that Dirk spoke the truth. "Is that good enough for you?"

"Is he well?"

"Never better."

"Where is he?"

Tia laughed. "You can't be serious?"

"Tell me this much, then. Are you able to get a message to him?"

"I won't tell you that, either."

He threw his hands up. "Is there *anything* I can do to make you believe I'm trying to help you?"

"Throw yourself on your sword. That'll do for starters."

Her intransigence was really starting to irritate him. "You're signing your own death warrant, Tia."

"Well, that will save you from having to take responsibility, won't it?"

"You can't see past your hatred, can you?"

"I can see past it just fine, Dirk," she told him. "The trouble is, what I see behind it is you and the might of the Church of the Suns and your good pal, the Lion of Senet. And for your information, I don't hate you. I don't care enough about you to waste the effort. I despise you for being a craven bastard and I pity you for having so little humanity you're willing to trample over everyone you ever counted as a friend to save your own precious neck. I might die at the hands of

Barin Welacin in unbelievable pain, but it won't be anything compared to the pain you'll suffer for the rest of your long and miserable life—a lonely old fool with every material possession a man could desire and not a friend in the world to share it with."

Tia was surprised at her own passion. And the truth in her words. She really didn't care enough to hate him. She met his eye defiantly, this boy who looked so much like Johan Thorn, except for those metal-gray eyes. Lexie used to say a person's eyes were the windows to his soul. If that was true, then Dirk's soul was as cold and inflexible as steel. Except steel probably had more compassion.

But if her words had any impact on him, she couldn't tell. He knocked on the door without answering her. The key rattled in the lock and the door opened.

"I'm sorry, Tia."

"Not half as sorry as you will be."

He shook his head, but didn't reply. Dirk stepped through without further comment. With a disturbingly final clang the door was closed behind him, followed by the rattling lock once more.

Tia stared at the door for a time and then turned to stare at the small patch of overcast sky visible from the high window on the southern wall of the cell. Somewhere, under that same sky, far away in Garwenfield, Misha was waiting for her to return.

Only she wouldn't return. Not now.

Her guilt returned to haunt her as she realized the pain of that thought was worse than the prospect of torture.

Worse even than the realization that Reithan was dead.

Chapter 57

Jacinta sat on the window seat with her knees tucked under her in the Lord of the Suns' palace, watching the rain patter on the graveled drive. The glass was cool against her forehead, the steady beat of the rain almost hypnotizing. She'd been sitting here for a long time, lost in thought.

Jacinta had watched Dirk ride out at a gallop several hours ago, but he hadn't returned yet, and nobody, not even Eryk or Caterina, had any idea why he'd left in such a hurry. Marqel was back from her little jaunt into the city, but Jacinta didn't want to ask her if she knew the reason for Dirk's hasty departure. Dirk's warning about Marqel remained in her mind.

The last of her things had been transferred from the Widow's Rest to the palace with the aid of Eryk and Caterina and she had been given a well-appointed room next door to the suite put aside for Kirsh and Alenor when they arrived. The room on her left was given to Dirk's brother, Rees, and his heavily pregnant wife, Faralan. Across the hall, another suite had been allocated to that boorish prig Prince Baston of Damita.

Jacinta had exchanged little more than casual pleasantries with Lady Faralan when she and her husband, the Duke of Elcast, arrived yesterday. The poor girl was so close to giving birth; she seemed bowed under by the weight of the child she carried. *Such is the fate of all noblewomen,* Jacinta lamented, watching Rees help his wife climb the stairs to their rooms. He'd left her alone and gone hunting today.

Perhaps I should pay Faralan a visit. Sit with her for a while.

It was the third time in the last hour Jacinta had thought that. She still hadn't moved. Faralan seemed a nice enough girl, but Jacinta was reluctant to spend time in her company. Faralan's condition was too blatant a reminder of her own eventual fate. *That will be me, someday. Fat, awkward and pregnant, doomed to do nothing more momentous than bring the next generation into the world, while my husband is off having a good time with his friends.*

And what friends they were. Rees Provin seemed as anxious to be counted a good friend of Senet as his uncle, Prince Baston of Damita. Jacinta couldn't stand the Damitian prince, and not only because of his fondness for Senet. The man was insufferable. He looked at Jacinta speculatively when they were introduced, eyeing her up and down as if she were the prime attraction at a cattle sale. Her mother had broached the subject of marriage with Baston after Lord Birkoff had been turned away, even though Jacinta was just as vehemently opposed to the idea of a union with Baston of Damita as she was to marrying the Baron of Tolace. That didn't bother Lady Sofia much. Jacinta was almost twenty and still unmarried. The shame of that was all that seemed to concern the Duchess of Bryton. Her daughter's wishes came a poor second.

Still, nothing had been agreed, and Jacinta planned to go out of her way to discourage Baston's attentions. That didn't mean he wouldn't make an offer for her, of course, but she was legally of age under Dhevynian law, and her mother couldn't actually *force* her to marry anyone against her will. She could—and would—simply make her life a living hell until she agreed. The chance to go to court as Alenor's lady-in-waiting had saved Jacinta from the worst of her mother's wrath after she had insulted Birkoff, but the situation was only a temporary reprieve.

There was no telling what would happen when Alenor and Kirsh arrived in Bollow, and if Dirk couldn't find a way to save Alenor and Alexin, then her position in the Kalarada court would very quickly become obsolete. Worse, she might be implicated in the affair herself. Jacinta was the one, after all, who covered for them. She was the one who kept Dorra away to allow the lovers a little solitude. She wasn't sorry she had. Alenor was only truly happy when she was with Alexin. If they were all going to die for those few stolen moments of happiness, then so be it.

Wasn't it better to live a short life, with at least a few bliss-ful moments, than a long and unhappy one, doing the expected thing?

Jacinta couldn't bring herself to believe the end was nigh—not for Alenor or Alexin or herself. Dirk would find a way to save them.

Where her faith in him came from, she had no idea. Per-haps it was learning he'd helped the refugees in Oakridge. Per-haps it was that book he'd sent her. Or perhaps it was the sight of a boy, caught in an unguarded moment, skipping stones across the lake. That image seemed branded in her mind. The Lord of the Suns, the most powerful man on Ranadon, doing something so ordinary, so mundane, so...childlike. That one unexpected act encapsulated the contradiction that was Dirk Provin.

Jacinta's thoughts were interrupted by movement near the gates—Antonov, Rees Provin and Prince Baston returning from the hunt. It didn't look like they'd caught much. Perhaps the rain had gotten the better of them and they'd spent the day at Lord Parqette's drinking around the fire, telling each other what great hunters they would have been if the weather hadn't let them down.

If they'd spent the day at Lord Parqette's estate, then the chances were also good her mother had managed to get Baston aside and raise the topic of marriage again. She wondered if Antonov would approve the union. He might not like the idea of strengthening the ties between Dhevyn and Damita. With luck, he had his own bride for Baston in mind; some nice, well-bred Senetian virgin who could be trusted to know her place, have lots of healthy babies and not interfere in the politics of her husband's court.

While there's life, there's hope, Jacinta told herself wist-fully.

The rain continued to fall steadily. Antonov, Rees and Baston vanished from view, heading for the stables. She looked up at the gray, leaden clouds and wondered if it would still be raining to-morrow. It would ruin the effect of the eclipse if it remained over-cast. Then she smiled. Somehow, if Dirk had managed everything else so competently, she had a feeling even the weather would be too afraid to defy him.

What would happen tomorrow was still a mystery to Jacinta, although she had a suspicion. The trouble was, the idea was so wild, so totally unbelievable, so potentially dangerous, she couldn't bring herself to believe that anybody would deliberately plan such a thing.

Yet the alternative would do nothing but strengthen the Shadowdancers, make Marqel unassailable and convince Antonov so thoroughly he was right about everything he believed that Dhevyn would never have a chance to be free.

Jacinta wished she had the courage to come straight out and ask Dirk what he was doing. He'd hedged around the topic the other day, and for an instant, Jacinta had thought he meant to tell her. But it was a fleeting moment that passed before he had a chance to act on it. Dirk Provin was too used to keeping his own counsel; too used to trusting nobody but himself to suddenly start sharing his plans with somebody he barely knew. He hadn't even told Alenor what he was up to, and by all accounts, he was closer to her than any other living soul.

All he'd said to Alenor was: trust me. No matter what I do, no matter how bad it seems. Trust me.

It was quite a promise to ask of someone, but now she'd met him, Jacinta could understand why Alenor had so readily given it to him. There was something about Dirk—an intensity that made you *want* to believe him. Jacinta was quite certain he could deliver the most outrageous falsehood with such convincing sincerity, you couldn't help but take his word for it, even if you knew for certain what he was telling you was absolutely untrue. It was as if he could embrace a lie so wholeheartedly that it *became* the truth.

A lone figure in the distance on horseback caught her attention. She recognized him immediately. Dirk returning from Bollow. Where had he been? Had he gone to see someone? Was there a girl in the city he had hurried off to meet? Jacinta hadn't heard so much as a whisper of any romance involving the Lord of the Suns, which in itself was quite amazing. There was nothing more avidly discussed at court than the love affairs of powerful men. She had thought he and Marqel might have been involved, but the Shadowdancer was firmly settled into the role of Antonov's mistress and after Dirk's comments the other day, any lingering doubts she had about Marqel were soundly dismissed. It made the enigma of Dirk Provin even more puzzling.

How did one get to be so single-minded at his age?

She watched Dirk canter along the drive to the stables, alone and unguarded and seemingly unconcerned about the inclement weather. Was he so sure of himself he no longer feared assassination? Or was he deliberately courting danger? Daring his enemies to take a shot at him? Did he want to die? Or did he simply not care?

Dirk disappeared from view while she was still wondering about it. Jacinta glanced down at the book in her lap. She should hide it, she knew, but for some reason, the mere temptation of holding it was almost too much to resist. She still had no idea why Dirk had given it to her, and he'd pointedly ignored the opportunity she offered him the other day to explain his gift.

Jacinta looked up again a few moments later as another pair of horsemen entered the estate. Her stomach clenched when she saw they were dressed in the familiar blue and silver of the Dhevynian Queen's Guard. Squinting through the rain, Jacinta could just make out more horses following in their wake surrounding a carriage drawn by six white horses.

With a sigh, Jacinta rose to her feet and turned from the window. It was time to put the book away. Time to get ready. Time to face Antonov. Time to denounce a man she counted as a friend and hurt a young woman who trusted her implicitly.

This is what Dirk must feel like, she thought.

Kirsh and Alenor had arrived.

Chapter 58

Alenor rode alone in the carriage as they entered the grounds of the Lord of the Suns' palace. Kirsh was riding in the van with Sergey and the significantly increased Senetian Guard he'd collected in Avacas. Her own guard had been reduced to riding in her wake, a clear insult to them. Kirsh's message was quite blunt and insulting. The Queen's Guard had harbored Alexin Seranov and many of them had known of his affair with the queen. They could no longer be trusted to protect her.

The closer they came to Bollow, the more frightened for Alexin she had become. Alenor did not fear for her own life. She had made her own decisions and was willing to bear the consequences, but Alexin should not be made to suffer. She was the one who had made the first move. Alexin would never have kissed her if she hadn't invited it and he would certainly never have made love to her without her making it quite clear she wanted him to. He was far too aware of his position in the guard to do anything so foolish.

It was her fault. She was the queen. It was her responsibility.

Kirsh had not physically mistreated Alexin. He didn't have to. The humiliation of riding in chains, surrounded by Senetians, as they rode first through Kalarada and then Senet was more than enough pain for him to bear. His shame was reflected in the eyes of every Guardsman, his dishonor a stain that would leave an indelible mark on them forever.

Assuming there was a forever. Antonov might well order the guard disbanded. Kirsh certainly wanted to be rid of them. His childhood dreams of honor and glory among the Queen's Guard were well and truly shattered. Alenor suspected his anger was as much about his broken dreams as it was about a captain in the guard having an affair with his wife. Had she taken a civilian lover, Kirsh might not have been nearly so angry. She almost felt sorry for him. Kirsh had been betrayed by so many people. First by Marqel, then by Alenor and now the Queen's Guard. He could do nothing about Marqel and was limited to what he could do to Alenor because of her rank. But he could, and would, vent his wrath for all the ills that had befallen him on the Dhevynian Queen's Guard.

The carriage drew to a halt outside the front entrance to the palace. The door opened and an unfamiliar hand reached in to help her down. Alenor felt exhausted by the journey from Avacas, although she suspected it was because she had worn herself out worrying, rather than the strain of the trip. As she stepped down onto the gravel, the palace doors opened and a servant hurried out with a cape to protect her from the rain. She was climbing the steps, her head bowed against the downpour, when Dirk appeared beside her. He was soaked to the skin, his dark hair plastered against his forehead, and his boots were spattered with mud, as if he'd been riding.

"Hello, Alenor."

The sight of him made her want to cry. She wanted to throw herself into his arms and beg him to make the world right again. But she had no idea what Dirk would do. No idea if he would even try to help her. As Lord of the Suns, it was his duty to condemn her adultery. But there was no hint of censure in his eyes, not trace of anger in his smile.

"Let's get you inside out of this rain," he suggested.

They hurried through the door, followed by Kirsh, who shook a shower of raindrops from his cape as they stepped into the foyer.

"Where's my father?" Kirsh asked, not even bothering to greet Dirk.

"I'm not sure," Dirk told him. "He went hunting this morning and I've only just gotten back from the city myself. I don't even know if he's here."

"Where is the Lion of Senet?" Kirsh demanded of the nearest servant.

"In his room, I believe, your highness," the man answered with a low bow. "He only just—"

"Fetch him. We'll be in there." Kirsh pointed to the open doors of the morning room, where a rare fire had been lit against the cooler weather.

"Perhaps Alenor would like to get changed first," Dirk suggested.

"Alenor is just fine as she is." He turned to the servant impatiently. "Are you deaf, man? Fetch my father!"

"Kirsh..."

Dirk's appeal had no effect. Kirsh pulled off his riding gloves as he strode across the black-and-white tiles toward the morning room.

"Where's Alexin?" Dirk asked her in a low voice, watching Kirsh with a frown.

"With Kirsh's men. We left him in the garrison in Bollow on the way here."

Dirk frowned. "I must have just missed you."

"Dirk," she hissed urgently. "What's going to happen?"

"Alenor!"

She bit back the rest of her question and hurried to answer Kirsh's summons. She was afraid to do anything that might anger him further at the moment. Dirk hurried up the stairs, taking them two at a time. Perhaps he would be able to delay the servant sent to fetch Antonov. *Perhaps...* Alenor's life had far too many uncertainties in it at present for her to be sure of anything.

Kirsh stood in front of the fire and waited, his hands clasped behind his back, deliberately not looking at her. Alenor perched on the edge of the settee, wishing a servant would come and offer them wine. She could do with a drink. She wanted to get drunk.

"Alenor!"

She almost sobbed with relief when Jacinta hurried into the room. Jumping to her feet she embraced her cousin, hoping to absorb some of Jacinta's strength for the coming ordeal.

"Look at you, Allie, you're all wet. Come on! Let's go get you changed into something dry."

"Alenor is not going anywhere, my lady," Kirsh informed her.

Jacinta turned to Kirsh impatiently. "Don't be ridiculous. There is nothing so important it can't wait until you're both clean and dry. You'll catch your death, too, if you don't get out of those wet clothes."

"I'm touched by your concern, my lady."

Before Jacinta could answer, Dirk came back. His hair was still damp but he had changed into dry clothes. A servant followed him carrying a tray of glasses and began to offer them around. Alenor snatched at the wine and downed most of it in a single gulp.

"Your father's on his way down," he told Kirsh, waving away the servant who offered him a drink. "And the Lady Jacinta does have a point, Kirsh. Are you sure you and Alenor don't want to change first?"

"I'm sure."

"As you wish," he shrugged. "Did you have a good trip?"

"Good enough."

"The weather's been awful," Jacinta added.

"Hasn't it," Alenor agreed, tonelessly. *I'm about to hear my lover condemned to die and we're talking about the weather.*

"I hope it clears up by tomorrow," Jacinta added. "It'll be such a pity if we miss the eclipse because of the clouds."

"I'm sure if the Goddess has gone to the trouble of arranging an eclipse," Antonov remarked as he strode into the room, "she'll make sure we are able to view her handiwork."

They all turned to face the Lion of Senet. Alenor's worst fears were realized when she saw the look on Antonov's face. Kirsh had sent word on ahead of their arrival in Senet, and the reason they brought Alexin with them as a prisoner, so at least she would be spared having to listen to Kirsh deliver the news. But Antonov was furious.

"Father."

"Kirsh."

Antonov turned his leonine head toward Alenor and stared down at her. She had grown up terrified of the look he now wore, praying it would never be directed at her.

"I'm very disappointed in you, Alenor," he said.

"I..." she began helplessly. She didn't know how to answer him. Her eyes fixed on Dirk, begging him silently for help, but he said nothing.

"It's not her fault," Jacinta declared in the uncomfortable silence.

Antonov looked at her curiously. "Are you claiming a captain of the Queen's Guard forced himself on his queen?"

"No, your highness," Jacinta replied. "I'm suggesting Alenor is very young and easily led. She was a ripe target for subversion by the people who oppose you."

"What are you talking about?" Kirsh scoffed.

"I'm talking about Alexin Seranov, your highness. The cousin of Reithan Seranov. Alexin is a heretic, just as his cousin is. The seduction of Alenor D'Orlon was a deliberate and calculated attempt to turn her from the Goddess."

"No!" Alenor cried in despair. "That's not true!"

"Be quiet!" Antonov ordered. "Your very words condemn you, Alenor."

"I don't care! It wasn't like that!"

"How do you know Alexin is a heretic, my lady?" Antonov asked Jacinta.

Jacinta glanced at Alenor apologetically and then hung her head in shame. "Because I helped them, your highness. I was the one who arranged for them to be alone."

"Then you are as culpable as Alenor is," he told her angrily.

"I admit that, your highness," Jacinta replied meekly. "But when I confessed my part in the affair to the Lord of the Suns, he said the Goddess would forgive me if I openly admitted my guilt."

"The Goddess may forgive you, but I'll be damned if I will," Kirsh growled. Then he turned to Alenor. "No wonder you were so keen to keep your cousin close to you. Who else was involved in this sordid little cover-up?"

Alenor barely heard Kirsh. She stared at Jacinta in despair and then turned to look at Dirk. *What is she doing?*

"Leave us!" Antonov ordered Jacinta. "I'll decide what to do with you later."

Jacinta curtsied and fled the room, refusing to look at Alenor.

How could you? Alenor cried silently after her. *How could you say such things about Alexin? How could you betray me like that?*

"So Jacinta D'Orlon is a Baenlander sympathizer," Antonov remarked when she was gone.

"I don't think so, sire," Dirk said, sounding rather amused by the idea. "A bit impetuous maybe, but I doubt she has any deep sympathies for their cause."

"If I believe her confession, she arranged for one of them to seduce Alenor," Antonov pointed out.

"That's probably because she's an incurable romantic, your highness. You must know of her reputation. Jacinta would have gotten involved just for the thrill of covering up the queen's affair."

"Even if you overlook the charge of adultery, she actively aided a heretic in his attempt to subvert the Queen of Dhevyn," Kirsh reminded him. "That's high treason."

"I doubt that occurred to Lady Jacinta at the time."

Why are you defending her? Alenor cried silently. *Why are you letting her turn on me?*

"You never told me Jacinta D'Orlon knew of the affair," Antonov said to Dirk. "For that matter, you never said you knew about it, either."

"I'd be a poor Lord of the Suns if I repeated things told to me in confidence as the Goddess's representative, your highness."

"He's known about it since Alenor lost the baby," Kirsh told his father with an angry glance in Dirk's direction.

"Is that true?"

"Yes."

"And you said nothing?"

"My first loyalty is to the Goddess, your highness. Not to Senet. And not to Dhevyn."

"If you're so damned loyal to the Goddess, why didn't

you do something to put an end to the affair?" Kirsh demanded.

"I prayed to her, Kirsh," Dirk replied calmly. "And then you discovered them together, and my prayers were answered."

Alenor wanted to cry. How could Dirk stand there and lie so sincerely about praying to a Goddess she knew he didn't believe in? How could he be so cruel, so ruthless? Had he fallen so far under the spell of his new position he could turn on her without a second thought?

Then Alenor looked at Antonov and thought she understood why Dirk had said such a thing. Antonov was nodding unconsciously in agreement. He often prayed to the Goddess and considered his prayers answered when things worked out the way he wanted. He could believe no less of the Lord of the Suns. Whatever his reasons for not helping her, Dirk knew exactly what to say to keep Antonov on his side.

"Where is Seranov now?" Antonov asked Kirsh.

"I left him at the garrison in town."

"Then after the eclipse, we'll hang him," Antonov announced.

"I'd rather you didn't," Dirk said.

"Did you have something else in mind?"

"He's a heretic, your highness. Alexin's crimes against the Goddess are far more heinous than simply seducing the Queen of Dhevyn."

"And what would you do with him?" Kirsh asked skeptically.

"I'll burn him, Kirsh. At the eclipse ceremony, tomorrow. That should satisfy even your lust for vengeance."

"No!" Alenor cried in horror.

Even Kirsh looked surprised by Dirk's suggestion, but Antonov didn't hesitate before assenting.

"I can't imagine a more fitting fate," he agreed. "Along with the daughter of the heretic, the Goddess should be well pleased with our offering."

"The daughter of the heretic?"

"Tia Veran," Antonov explained. "The High Priestess told me about how the Goddess led her to finding her in the city. And the reason."

"What reason?" Kirsh asked.

"To be sacrificed, of course. To appease the Goddess for the sins of her father."

"If you burn Tia Veran you may never learn where Misha is," Dirk reminded him. He seemed truly shaken by the news. Had Marqel ordered Tia Veran burned without consulting Dirk? It served him right. If he was going to turn on his true friends then he deserved to be burdened with a treacherous fiend like Marqel.

"Misha is dead, Dirk," Antonov said, his voice laden with regret. "He was dying when they took him and if the Shadowdancers couldn't help him, I don't see how the Baenlanders could do any better. We've not heard from them. We've not even had a ransom demand. It's been months. If he was alive, we would have heard something by now."

Dirk was silent for a moment and then to Alenor's dismay, he nodded in agreement. "As you wish, your highness."

"It's what the Goddess wishes," Antonov replied piously. He returned his attention to Alenor. "As for you, young lady, I *should* burn you next to your heretic lover."

"Why don't you?" she snapped. She had nothing left to lose, no reason to pretend anymore. Even Dirk and Jacinta had abandoned her.

"Were it not for the fortuitous arrest of Tia Veran, you *would* burn beside him tomorrow," Antonov told her harshly. "In the meantime, you will be exiled from Dhevyn and Kirsh will rule in your stead until I decide you've repented sufficiently."

"I will not!"

"You will, or you will be tried and executed for adultery."

"You wouldn't dare!"

"He would dare, Alenor," Dirk warned. "And he'd be quite within his rights to do so. You should be grateful for the mercy his highness is showing you."

"*Mercy!* Nobody cares Kirsh openly kept a mistress and you expect me to be grateful that all he wants to do is banish me and take my kingdom?"

"That will be quite enough, Alenor," Antonov ordered. "At least have the sense to accept your fate with a modicum of decorum."

Alenor turned on Antonov furiously. "You've seen all the decorum out of me you're ever likely to see, Antonov Latanya. I hate you! I have *always* hated you. I despised every moment I was forced to spend in your company, every minute I lived under your roof. I hate your Goddess, I hate your sick religion and I hate that little slut you call a High Priestess. I hate all of you and I wish I *was* going to die because I'd rather be burned alive than spend another minute breathing the same air as you."

Without waiting for anybody to respond, Alenor fled the room and ran out through the foyer to the main door and out into the rain.

She stopped on the top step and looked about, realizing she had nowhere she could go. So she stood there, sobbing with despair and drenched to the skin, unable to distinguish her tears from the raindrops.

A short time later the guards arrived and she was escorted politely but firmly back into the palace.

Chapter 59

The ninth day of Ezenor in the year 10,241 dawned bright in a cloudless sky, the previous days of overcast and rain a distant memory. From the top step of the Bollow temple Dirk watched the second sun rising with an odd feeling of displacement. The world was just coming awake, the red fading from the sky, yet somehow, he had no part in it. He felt as if he was standing slightly out of kilter with reality, as if the rest of the world was something to observe, not something he was actively a part of.

Shaking off the strange feeling, he turned at the sound of footsteps behind him. Claudio Varell and a dozen other Sundancers had gathered behind him waiting for their instructions. Dirk glanced over the men and women with a frown. He could feel their resentment emanating from them like heat from a campfire.

"I need to tell you what's going to happen at the ceremony," he announced. His voice was calm and steady. That surprised him. The enormity of what he was about to set in motion should have left him a jibbering wreck.

"We know what's going to happen, my lord," one of the Sundancers said. She looked to be in her fifties, a tall, stern-looking woman who wore the yellow robes Dirk so despised with pride and dignity. "The Sundancers will be destroyed."

"You should have more faith in the Goddess, my lady. She won't turn her back on you." Before the woman could argue with him about it, he turned to Claudio. "Do you trust these people?"

"Implicitly," Claudio said. The old man was filled with barely contained excitement. His eyes were glittering. He was more animated than Dirk had ever seen him. Claudio been like that ever since the early hours of the morning when Dirk had roused the old man from his bed and told him what would happen today. He'd debated telling Claudio sooner, but looking at him now, with his sprightly step and his excited eyes, Dirk knew he'd been right to keep him in the dark until the last minute.

Dirk turned at the sound of horses behind him. A large contingent of Senetian foot soldiers were heading across the plaza toward the temple, led by two mounted captains.

"I'll meet you all in the anteroom in about ten minutes," he told the Sundancers. Then he turned and walked down a few steps and waited for the soldiers.

The troop halted a little back from the temple steps as the captains rode up to meet Dirk. He didn't know the man in charge of the troop, but the other captain who rode with him was Kirsh's old friend Sergey.

"My lord," the captain said, with a smart salute.

"Are your men armed, Captain?"

"Of course."

"Then disarm them."

"My lord, you can't expect the men to be able to control the crowd——" Sergey began, but Dirk cut him off.

"That's *exactly* what I expect, Sergey. We are here to witness the glory of the Goddess. I will not allow you to spill innocent blood on a day like this."

"Then how do you expect us to keep control, my lord?"

"By using a little bit of tact and courtesy, Captain. This is a day of celebration. Cutting down women and children with swords tends to put a damper on things, don't you think?"

"But, my lord——"

"You have your orders, Captain. Prince Antonov placed you and your men under the command of the Church today. You will do as I demand, or I will have you arrested as a heretic."

The captain saluted reluctantly and turned his horse around. He trotted back to the troop and began to order them to shed their weapons.

"That was a foolish order, my lord," Sergey suggested once the other captain was out of earshot.

"I don't remember asking your opinion on the matter, Sergey. Where are the prisoners?"

"Still at the garrison."

"Bring them here now. Before the crowd starts to get too unwieldy."

Sergey nodded, but made no attempt to leave.

"Was there something else?"

"Are you going to disarm the Dhevynian Guardsmen as well?"

"No, Captain," Dirk replied. "I thought I'd leave them armed so that when we burn one of their captains alive, they can cut him free and then carve their way through stands filled with every nobleman of note in the whole damned world and a few thousand unarmed innocent Senetian civilians, without anybody getting in their way."

"I'm sorry, my lord, I didn't mean to question your orders."

"If you don't mean to question my orders, then I suggest you stop doing it."

"Yes, my lord," the Senetian said, gathering up his reins.

"And Sergey . . ."

"Yes, my lord."

"I don't want them drugged."

"Sire?"

"I don't want either Tia Veran or Alexin Seranov given any poppy-dust before they're burned. I want them to know what's going on."

A slow, cruel smile spread over Sergey's face. "Of course, my lord."

The Senetian saluted and cantered his horse back across the plaza. *Sadistic bastard,* Dirk thought, as he watched him leave. He took the remaining steps down to the plaza two at a time. The stands built to accommodate the important guests smelled of freshly sawn timber, which reminded Dirk of something else. He beckoned the other captain forward.

"Have your weapons stored in the temple for now," he ordered. "You can collect them after the ceremony."

"Yes, my lord."

"And there are some urns just inside the temple. I want you to soak the wood with the oil inside them. Those pyres have been rained on for days. The wood is damp. They'll never burn without help."

"I'll see to it, my lord."

Dirk glanced around the plaza and nodded with satisfaction. Already people were starting to arrive, although it was several hours until the eclipse. Most of the nobility would probably not arrive for some time yet. He glanced up at the sky, as if expecting to see it darken, but the second sun was fully risen now. There was no hint in that flawless blue that anything important would happen soon.

More horses arrived and Dirk looked across the plaza with a feeling of intense relief as he realized Jacinta had arrived early

as he asked, with Tael Gordonov and two other Guardsmen as
her escort. They rode toward him, Jacinta sitting her mount
like a woman born to the saddle. He stepped forward to greet
them, almost wilting under the hatred in the Dhevynian captain's glare.

Tael dismounted and then turned to help Jacinta out of her
saddle.

"Good morning, my lord."

"Lady Jacinta."

"It's a beautiful day. The Goddess truly does smile on you."

"It will get better yet," he promised. "Could I have a word
with your captain, my lady?"

Tael stared at him with open hostility. "You might have the
Senetian troops under your command, Lord Provin, but the
Queen's Guard are not subject to your orders."

"I wasn't planning to give you any orders, Captain. I
merely want a private word with you."

"Go on, Tael," Jacinta said.

With some reluctance Tael accompanied Dirk a little way
from the Senetians and Jacinta. He watched the soldiers shed-
ding their arms and piling them on the ground, while another
two men carried the weapons into the temple.

"You've disarmed the Senetians?" Tael asked in surprise.

"I don't want your men *visibly* armed today, either."

Tael looked at him suspiciously. "Not *visibly* armed? Are
you expecting trouble, my lord?"

"Let's just say that when the Goddess reveals her will today, I want to know if I can count on you to protect your
queen."

"It's an insult you even ask such a thing."

"Perhaps. Will you do what's required of you?"

Tael was furious Dirk dared question his loyalty. "Every
man I have with me would die to protect the queen."

"I sincerely hope it doesn't come to that, Captain."

"Then why ask it of me?"

"Because at some point today, you're going to have to make
a decision, and you'll only have a split second to decide whose
orders to follow. I just want you to remember you are here to

protect Alenor, not Alexin, nor anybody else in the world. Just your queen."

Obviously unsettled by Dirk's words, Tael stood a little straighter and glared at him. "You need have no fear of that, my lord. If it came to it, I'd kill you in order to protect my queen."

Dirk smiled. "I sincerely hope it doesn't come to that, either."

"My lord!"

He turned to see who had hailed him. Another carriage had arrived in the plaza while he was talking to Tael. Marqel was here—late, of course—but he had no more time to explain things.

"Good luck, Captain," he said, and then he left him standing there with a puzzled and rather unhappy expression on his face.

Dirk could feel Tael's eyes on his back as he walked away. He'd done what he could to warn the Queen's Guard. Done what he could to help Alenor and Alexin. Done what he could for Tia, although he doubted she would appreciate the gesture when they tied her to the stake. *Poor Tia*. It seemed every time their paths crossed, he did something even worse to her. But today would see an end to it. After this, she would no longer be in a position to condemn him. Whether or not she would live long enough to forgive him was a question he couldn't answer.

He climbed the steps to the temple slowly, wondering if he should have tried to explain what he was doing to Tia to Alenor. They all believed he had turned on them now. Dirk glanced up at the sky again. It would be over soon. The only thing left to do now was speak to the Sundancers Claudio had so carefully chosen and then watch Marqel conduct the ceremony.

After that, all their fates were in the hands of the Goddess.

Chapter 60

Tia learned she was to be sacrificed at the eclipse ceremony from one of the guards when he delivered her meal. The news shocked her. She was certain Dirk intended to hand her over to the Lion of Senet so Barin Welacin would have his chance at her. She'd been preparing herself mentally to face whatever torment he had in mind. But to learn in passing she was to die in a few hours, burned alive with half the world watching, felt like a physical blow. Tia wasn't ready to die. She had far too much to live for. She cried when she heard the news, but they were tears of anger, not grief.

They came for the prisoners just after second sunrise. She was escorted out into the hall and received another shock. The man who was to burn alongside her was Alexin Seranov. Surrounded by guards, he stood outside a cell farther up the hall, his expression haunted. They were not permitted to speak to each other as they were escorted through to the main reception hall of the cell block. Another guard was waiting for them there, holding two cups, into which had been poured a carefully measured dose of poppy-dust. Tia almost sagged with relief when she saw it. The sound of Morna Provin's screams still tormented her at times. She was sure she didn't have the strength to bear her execution stoically. But they were to be given some respite, probably because of the number of important people who'd come to watch. It wouldn't do to upset all those well-bred ladies with the sound of agonized screams as the sacrifices crisped and blackened before them. This was supposed to be entertaining.

The guard offered the cups to the prisoners. Neither of them was stupid enough to refuse. It was awkward, trying to raise the cup to her mouth with her hands chained. The poppy-dust was only a few inches from her lips when another officer entered the room.

"No!" he ordered. "They're not to be drugged!"

The cup was snatched from her hand before she could swallow it. Alexin's was taken from him just as quickly.

The Dhevynian captain glared at the newcomer. "You always did like to watch people suffer, didn't you, Sergey?"

The Senetian shrugged. "These are not my orders, Alexin. They come from the Lord of the Suns."

"Dirk ordered it?" Tia gasped. *How much does he hate us? Is he so far gone he not only wants to kill us, but wants to watch us suffer as well?*

"He was quite specific," Sergey confirmed. "Said he wanted you both to know what was going on." Then the captain smiled. "You both thought him a friend once, didn't you? I'll bet you're regretting that now."

"You seem to be enjoying it, though," Alexin remarked.

"What can I say, Alexin? I love my work." He turned to the guards who were holding them. "Take them to the temple. Lord Provin will tell you what he wants done with them once you get there."

They were jostled out of the cells and into a closed and barred wagon. As soon as the door slammed shut, the wagon jolted forward. Alexin caught Tia awkwardly as she fell forward and helped her unsteadily to her feet.

"What did you do to get here?" she asked him, clutching at the bars for balance.

"Adultery with the queen," he replied in a voice devoid of emotion.

"With Alenor?" she asked in surprise. "Who would have thought it?"

"And your crime?"

"I was born to the wrong parents."

"Then we're both victims of fate."

She shook her head. "We're both victims of Dirk Provin's ambition, Alexin. There's nothing predestined about it."

"I find it hard to believe Dirk ordered we were not to be offered any relief."

"I don't. What I find hard to believe is I'm going to be dead in a few hours. I'm not even scared. Just furious."

Alexin smiled wanly. "I know what you mean. Do you suppose there's any chance—?"

"That we'll be rescued?" She laughed harshly. "By whom, Alexin? We're in the middle of Senet about to be murdered by one of our own, for the entertainment of people who have traveled from all over the world to witness the power of the Goddess. How can you possibly imagine we're going to survive this?"

"Dirk asked Alenor to trust him, you know, no matter how bad things got."

"Then she's a fool. And so are you if you think there is any hope we're going to be alive at the end of the day."

The wagon jolted to a halt. The door was unlocked and thrown open. They were taken from the wagon up the steps of the temple. The pyres loomed large on either side of the massive bronze doors. Any doubts Alexin had he was really going to burn today vanished at the site of several guards laying fresh kindling over the damp wood and pouring liquid from several large earthenware urns around the base of the posts. They were halted on the broad top step while somebody went inside to fetch the Lord of the Suns.

Dirk emerged a few moments later. He was dressed in the ceremonial robes of his office, which extinguished the last flicker of hope Tia might have harbored that Dirk was doing this for any other reason than his own advancement. He glanced at the prisoners disinterestedly and then turned to the guard.

"Tie them to the pyres," he said tonelessly. "I don't want the ceremony interrupted once we get started."

He turned to leave. Even now, Alexin couldn't believe he would just walk away like that.

"Dirk!"

He stopped and glanced back at him. "This is necessary, Captain. When the Goddess reveals herself, you'll both understand." Then he disappeared into the temple without waiting for either of them to reply.

Tia was manhandled roughly across to the pyre on the left. It was larger than the one on the right. *I'm to be the second sun.*

How ironic. She struggled against the guards as they forced her up the pyre and shoved her roughly against the post. Her resistance was futile. Within moments she was chained securely and then left alone looking down over the plaza rapidly filling with people. The pyre reeked. It stank not of oil, but of something else Tia vaguely recalled, but couldn't quite place. Perhaps it was the stuff they were pouring on the wood to make it burn the right color.

The fumes were making her eyes water. Blinking back her angry tears, Tia turned to look at Alexin. He was dealing with this much better than she was. He stood proud and erect, as if he was to be burned alive by choice, not by the decree of the Lord of the Suns for the crime of loving his queen far more than duty demanded of him.

The stands in front of the temple were quickly filling with people. The eclipse was scheduled for the ninth hour of the day, but Tia had no idea what time it was. She guessed she had a little time yet. The ceremony hadn't started and people were still pouring into the plaza hoping for a good vantage from which to watch the proceedings. Not to mention the chance to witness the queen's lover and the heretic's daughter burn.

Tia closed her eyes and tried to forget about the gawking crowd. She thought of Misha instead, wishing she'd been able to get a message to him. What would he do when he learned her fate? Would he feel the same wrenching torment she felt at the thought of never seeing him again? Would the same grief for a lost opportunity haunt his soul? She remembered what Lexie had said about not understanding true love until you'd experienced it for yourself. Finally, Tia understood what Lexie was talking about. It was a pity she had to wait until she was standing here, counting down the minutes until they lit her pyre, before the realization came to her.

Opening her eyes, Tia discovered the stands were almost full. The last dignitary to arrive was the Lion of Senet, dressed in white as usual, accompanied by Prince Baston of Damita, Kirshov and Alenor. The little queen took her seat reluctantly in the front row. She looked beaten down, almost shriveled by what was about happen. Tia had that much to be grateful for. Alenor would be forced to watch Alexin burn. Misha, at least, would be spared the torment of witnessing the excruciating death of the one he loved.

The doors to the temple on Tia's left began to open ponderously. The High Priestess stepped out of the temple, followed by the Lord of the Suns and a dozen or more Shadowdancers who spread out along the steps. Two of them carried burning torches. They took up their positions in front of the pyres and turned to face the crowd. So Dirk wasn't planning to set her alight himself. He was probably too gutless. Even Antonov had accused him of that once. The night he had killed Johan. Tia found herself a little disappointed. She was hoping to look him in the eye. Hoping she had enough left in her to spit in it as well.

And then Marqel stepped forward and opened her arms wide. A hush fell over the thousands gathered in the plaza. The silence was broken by the slow tolling of the town bells, marking out the ninth hour.

"I call on the Goddess!" Marqel cried in a surprisingly strong voice. "Hear us, my lady, and accept this sacrifice!"

At Marqel's command, the two Shadowdancers with the torches turned to the pyres and plunged the burning brands deep into the oil-soaked kindling at the base.

The eclipse ceremony had begun.

Chapter 61

One...
Marqel jumped a little as the bells started tolling. She hadn't realized it was so close to the ninth hour. Although she had been in Bollow for some time now, she had never noticed before how loud the city bells were. But now, when the whole

world stood holding its breath, they seemed unnaturally loud and ominous.

Dirk stood on the temple steps behind her in those unflattering yellow robes, letting the High Priestess have center stage. She looked out over the sea of people and smiled. This was probably the greatest audience anyone had ever played to. The greatest performance since Belagren convinced Antonov to sacrifice his own son in order to restore the world to the Age of Light.

Two...

"I call on the Goddess!" Marqel cried again as the bells tolled.

The crowd was silenced by her words. The power she had over them was dizzying. For this she had been born. The stage was set, the props were perfect. This would be a show nobody would ever forget.

The plaza was crammed full of people, both highborn and common. Along the edges of the crowd was the large contingent of Senetian Guardsmen. The Dhevynian Guardsmen, less than a hundred in all, were ranked along the front of the temple steps with another line of Senetians. They were an impressive sight in those smart blue-and-silver uniforms lined up alongside the white and gold of Antonov's guard. Behind her she could feel the heat building from the pyres as they burned. They were massive, built on a scale suitable to the occasion, so the flames would take a little while to reach the victims. Marqel just hoped they didn't start screaming until she was finished. She didn't want them distracting her audience.

"The Goddess spoke to our beloved mother Belagren and showed us the way back into the light!"

Her voice was strong and clear and rang out over the plaza. She was a born performer. Everything she had ever been taught about how to hold an audience in her grasp seemed to make sense now. It wasn't even an act. This was who she was.

Three...

"The sacrifice of the Shadow Slayer during the Age of

Shadows proved to the Goddess that we had seen the error of our ways! We have sought her truth ever since, but some of you have been wavering! So the Goddess took our beloved mother, Belagren, to her breast, to comfort her for an eternity, and spoke to me of the same fears she had when Ranadon last turned from her teachings!"

Marqel hesitated, looking down over the crowd that was caught in her thrall. Even the two prisoners chained to the pyres seemed entranced by her mesmerizing performance. But then, the flames hadn't reached them yet.

"'I will give you a sign,' the Goddess said to me!" Marqel cried. "'I will show the people of Ranadon, once and for all, that they are my people. I will show them who speaks with my voice! I will show them the truth...'"

Four...

The bells rang out again. Marqel glanced upward, but there was as yet no sign of the promised eclipse. Would the people panic when the darkness came, or would they be too stunned by the darkness to do anything more than stare at it in wonder? Was her power sufficient to quell their fears?

"When the Goddess speaks, all of Ranadon will know her power!" Marqel declared. "Those who doubt her will be silenced. Those who believe in her true faith will be rewarded! Those who follow her teachings will be honored! Those who have strayed from her path will be exposed!

"I speak as the Voice of the Goddess! I, to whom she has entrusted the care of this world, order you now to bow your heads in prayer. Speak to the Goddess with your hearts. Let her see what is in them. Open yourselves to her judgment!"

Five...

Every head in the crowd lowered in silent prayer. Marqel opened one eye and risked a look at the others standing on the steps around her. The massive building behind her cast a shadow over the steps and the first few rows of the tiered seating. Dirk's head was bowed respectfully. Claudio Varell was looking around nervously. The other Shadowdancers behind her were still. *Where are all the Sundancers?* she wondered.

Except for Dirk and Claudio, there's barely a yellow robe in sight. It was probably a good thing. This ceremony marked the ultimate proof of the power of the Shadowdancers. Who needed that lot of senile old men and women around? The flames of the pyres were well alight by now. It wouldn't be long before Tia Veran and Alexin Seranov began to sizzle. Tia tugged against her bonds, a wild, panicked look in her eye, as the flames lapped closer and closer. Alexin did not move, did not even blink.

Six...

Marqel held her arms wide. "Come to us, my lady!" she called. "You find us here, gathered at your request, to witness the full might of your awesome power! Show us the truth! Bring forth the moment of darkness you promised, so the disbelievers may be humbled. Let us be reminded of the Age of Shadows. Let the darkness come! We welcome it because the truth in our hearts will return us to the light!"

Seven...

The second sun blazed bright and uninterrupted. There was no hint of the promised darkness. Marqel glanced at Dirk again nervously. *Had he gotten the time wrong? The day, perhaps?*

"Show us, my lady! Show us your might! Assure us our sacrifices have not been in vain!"

Dirk had composed her rather dramatic speech. The words were far too eloquent for an uneducated Landfall bastard. But he'd promised the eclipse would begin while she was beseeching the Goddess.

Like a lot of other people, she surreptitiously glanced up at the sky, expecting to see something, *anything,* but still there was no hint of encroaching darkness. Marqel was starting to feel more than a little uncertain.

Eight...

Truly concerned now, she glanced over her shoulder at Dirk again. The Lord of the Suns met her eye evenly but remained unmoved. This was her show. The High Priestess was the one who spoke to the Goddess, not the Lord of the Suns. He was merely lending her support. Marqel glanced over to where Antonov sat with Kirsh and Alenor. She couldn't see the queen's expression, but she could see the Lion of Senet and his son. Antonov's face was set in a rapturous gaze of absolute faith. Kirsh simply stared, transfixed by the sight of her.

"I call on the Goddess!" Marqel cried again, her voice almost desperate now. An uneasy restlessness began to infect the people in the plaza. They had come to witness a show. Surely, by now, something should have happened...

Nine...

Marqel bit her bottom lip to stifle her outrage as it slowly dawned on her what was really going on..

Dirk Provin had used her. She'd been set up.

In the most spectacular way imaginable.

He had elevated her to High Priestess, just so he could knock her down. The exquisite subtlety of his vengeance was lost on Marqel. All she understood was the glittering world she had come to know was suddenly in danger.

The sound of the ninth bell faded slowly, taking with it Marqel's only chance to publicly prove she was the Voice of the Goddess.

Silence filled the plaza. A hush of anticipation. Then a gasp of awe. Marqel looked over her shoulder at the pyres behind her. Instead of the flames taking hold of the sacrifices, they sputtered and hissed and smouldered and suddenly died.

The Goddess had refused the sacrifice of the High Priestess.

As the last bell tolled over the city, Marqel began to understand she had been betrayed.

The Goddess had spoken to the people of Ranadon.

She had—unequivocally—demonstrated to the world she no longer favored the Shadowdancers. Her position, the respect, the wealth and the fear she engendered—all of it slipped from Marqel's grasp in those few fatal seconds. Worse than that, she had been publicly exposed as a fraud. She risked a glance at Antonov. His expression was dumbstruck, shattered. Antonov understood the implications even better than Marqel did.

Because when the bells rang out the ninth hour of the ninth day of Ezenor in the year 10,241, absolutely nothing happened.

PART FOUR

AFTERMATH

Chapter 62

The seconds after the eclipse failed to materialize were the most critical. Dirk held his breath as the truth settled on the gathered crowd, desperately hoping he had judged things correctly. What was it Marqel said that day in the carriage on the way to inform the Lion of Senet that Dirk was now the Lord of the Suns?

You need momentous acts to mark momentous occasions.

And this was a momentous occasion. This was the beginning of the end of the Shadowdancers. They had risen to power so quickly because Antonov supported them. Dirk was counting on their demise being just as rapid once that support was withdrawn. But he couldn't even begin to tackle the rest of the Shadowdancers or the hundreds of thousands of people who believed in them until Antonov's faith was fractured.

Dirk knew there was no quick fix, no one clean, sweeping deed he could perform to break the power of the people's belief in the Shadowdancers, but he *could* rattle that belief. Shake it so profoundly that it would take only a little more persuasion to bring the whole thing down. Like a building damaged in a quake, it would take very little to make it collapse on top of itself once the foundations were weakened. Antonov and the High Priestess were the foundations and before he could bring this building down, he needed to discredit the High Priestess and shatter Antonov's faith.

That he had discredited the High Priestess was a given. What really worried Dirk was Antonov's reaction. He looked down at the Lion of Senet. He was clutching at Kirsh's arm, his expression frozen in shock, and for the first time in his life . . . doubt.

Dirk felt a sudden wave of relief mingled with satisfaction. For that look of doubt Dirk had let Tia and the Baenlanders think he had turned on them. He had joined the Church of the Suns; clawed his way to the ultimate position of authority. For this moment of clarity in Antonov he had burned Mil and betrayed every friend he owned. For this one, crucial instant when Antonov Latanya was confronted with the possibility that he was wrong, Dirk had made Marqel the Magnificent High Priestess of the Shadowdancers.

One hint of suspicion and he would never had gotten this far. Jacinta D'Orlon might have guessed what he was up to. Given much longer to think about it, she probably *would* have worked it out. But the only person who had known for certain what would happen this morning was Claudio Varell, and Dirk had taken him into his confidence only a few hours ago.

Everything he had done had been for these few precious moments of stunned immobility as Antonov was confronted with the truth.

It's all about faith. Give them something tangible to believe in, and nobody suspects the truth. Even when the truth makes more sense. He'd learned that from Belagren.

Dirk gave Antonov a few seconds for the full impact of what he had witnessed to sink in, and then he stepped forward.

"The Goddess has spoken!" he declared into the nervous silence. "See how she spurns the sacrifices of the Shadowdancers! It is a sign. She has declared the visions of the Shadowdancers false!"

Dirk's eyes were fixed on Antonov as he spoke. To watch the truth sink in; to see him visibly crumble made everything Dirk had done suddenly seem worthwhile. It made the treachery, the lies—all of it—seem justified.

You have to kill the idea, Neris had told him.

But not just in the minds of the people, Neris, he told the old man silently. *The idea has to be killed at the source. In the heart of the man who sanctioned the Shadowdancers and gave their cult credence. You have to kill the idea in the heart of the man whose faith sustained and supported the lies. The man the rest of the world followed.*

As he watched him, Antonov sagged against his son. Visibly broken.

Now it was time. Now was the moment he had been waiting for. Dirk raised his arms to the heavens.

"The Goddess has shown us the way," the Lord of the Suns shouted, his words meant for Antonov. "She has turned her back on the High Priestess and exposed her as a fraud. She has spurned the darkness and offered us light. Now you must do the same!"

And then something happened that Dirk hadn't anticipated.

The crowd erupted, but rather than an outpouring of renewed faith in the Sundancers he was hoping for, they began howling for Shadowdancer blood. Dirk had anticipated a certain degree of anger at his words—he'd disarmed the Senetian soldiers for that reason—but he didn't expect the mob to interpret his advice quite so literally. Before his words had reached the far corners of the plaza a chant was taken up by the crowd: *"Give us the light! Give us the light!"*

Betrayed and angry, within moments the crowd had disintegrated into a mindless mob, turning on anybody wearing red, anybody who even *looked* like he might be a Shadowdancer. Claudio begged for order, but it was doubtful anybody heard him over the din. Over the chanting, screams tore through the air—of mothers frightened for their children, of those who, after two decades of smug superiority, suddenly found themselves the target of the people's wrath. The Senetian soldiers moved in to restore order, but without weapons they could do little to quell the anger of the raging mob.

Dirk glanced back at the temple entrance. The Sundancers he had addressed before the ceremony hurried out. He had not told them exactly what was going to happen, just that they would be needed when the time came. The woman who had questioned him earlier had asked how they would know when the time was right.

Dirk had smiled at her and said, "You'll know."

He didn't bother to check if they were doing as he'd ordered. He pushed forward down the steps against the press of angry people trying to rush the temple until he reached Tael Gordonov. Some people were trying to get to Marqel, others wanted a piece of the pyres the Goddess had so dramatically extinguished, or maybe a chance to vent their anger on the sacrifices the Goddess had deemed unworthy. Many of them wanted nothing but to be free of the mob, but were carried along by the weight of the crowd.

"Get Alenor," he ordered, shouting to be heard over the ruckus. "And Antonov. Get them into the temple." The stands full of dignitaries were surrounded by a sea of raging commoners, the stand to the left in danger of being toppled.

The Dhevynian captain stared at him, making the decision Dirk had warned him about earlier, in less than a heartbeat.

"We'll need more weapons than the knives we carry," he warned.

"In the temple, Captain," Dirk shouted back. "Ready and waiting for you."

Tael grinned suddenly and then nodded and called his men to him. They were forcing their way through to Alenor as Dirk raced back up the steps two at a time. Marqel was gone. Forcibly removed back into the temple by Claudio's Sundancers, if they had followed his orders. Alexin had been freed by another Sundancer and was rubbing his wrists as he fled inside. Dirk heard Kirsh's voice over the ruckus, calling the Senetian soldiers to him. The man assigned to freeing Tia was still fumbling with the chains that held her. The outraged mob pressed closer. They would have their vengeance for being duped, and the sacrifices offered by the High Priestess and spurned by the Goddess were their obvious target. Dirk clambered up the pyre and pushed the man out of the way.

"Get inside," he ordered. "We'll be torn apart if they can't hold the crowd back."

The old man nodded and gladly climbed down backward as Dirk turned to the chains. Tia was staring at him, dumbstruck.

He cursed as he tried to free her. The old Sundancer had

fumbled when he tried to open the chains and the key was jammed crookedly in the lock.

"There was never any eclipse, was there?" Tia said shakily, finally finding her voice. "It was all a trick . . ."

"Not now, Tia."

"You faked it . . . all of it . . ."

Dirk cursed loudly again as the key finally turned. He pulled Tia free of the chains. Pushing her off the pyre, he jumped down after her as the Queen's Guardsmen thrust through with Alenor and Antonov between them. Dirk looked around but could see no sign of Kirsh and had no time to worry about him. He shoved Tia through the big bronze doors a step behind the Guardsmen and then ordered the doors closed.

They boomed shut a moment ahead of the mob.

His heart pounding, Dirk sagged against the doors and looked around. Antonov was ashen, held up by a Dhevynian Guardsman. Alenor was sobbing, her arms around a visibly shaking Alexin, uncaring of who might be witnessing her infidelity. Tael was over by the pile of weapons Dirk had collected from the Senetian soldiers and distributing them among his men. The Sundancers were looking at him expectantly. Tia was staring at him, her shock almost equal to her anger.

But there was one person missing.

"Where's Marqel?" he said.

Chapter 63

As Kirsh watched the world disintegrate around him when the fires fizzled out, one thing was foremost in his mind. Marqel was in danger, and somehow, Dirk was responsible for it. His father clutched at his arm for support but he couldn't tear his eyes away from Marqel. She looked terrified and alone, a slight, red-robed figure stranded in a sea of hostility.

As the crowd rapidly fractured into a raging, mindless mob, Kirsh caught sight of Tael Gordonov and his men pushing through the melee toward them. Without question, Kirsh thrust Antonov at one of the Guardsmen and then grabbed Alenor by the arm and all but threw her at Tael. The captain swept the tiny queen up into his arms and headed for the temple, his men cutting a path through the horde like a blue-and-silver wedge. Kirsh didn't know who'd given the captain his orders and didn't really care. His father and Alenor would be safe in the temple. His duty done, Kirsh was free to help Marqel.

He called to her as she backed away from the surging rabble, and somehow she heard him through the bedlam.

"Kirsh!" she screamed in terror.

He pushed his way forward until he reached the line of Senetian soldiers trying to hold back the mob. They had let the Dhevynians through and closed ranks behind them. Kirsh spied Sergey in the line and screamed at him to help the High Priestess. The captain might not have heard his words, but he must have guessed his meaning. Sergey surged up the steps and grabbed Marqel, pulling her clear as the mob broke through near the doors. Once he was satisfied Marqel was safe, Kirsh turned his attention back to the temple entrance. He caught sight of Dirk shoving Tia Veran through into the safety of the temple as the doors boomed shut a hairbreadth ahead of the rioters.

Kirsh watched the crowd bang on the temple doors, but was fairly certain they were solid enough to withstand an angry mob. Even if they did manage to break through, there were nearly a hundred Dhevynian Queen's Guard inside. Putting the problem of the temple out of his mind, he called the Senetian soldiers to him and they bludgeoned their way back through the plaza. A few others followed his lead, including, he noted with surprise, Dirk's brother, Rees Provin. The soldiers he gathered to him were unarmed, which was inconvenient, but it probably meant there would be more broken heads than corpses before this was brought under control.

"What you need is horses!" Rees shouted as he shoved

his way to Kirsh's side. "People prepared to face down an armed man will flee from the hooves of a determined cavalry charge."

Kirsh nodded his agreement and looked back toward the entrance to the plaza. "We have to get back to the garrison. Or hope somebody in the City Guard has the sense to get some mounted troops in here before these rioters destroy the city."

More and more of the soldiers had managed to push their way through to him and he now had a sizable force with which to cut his way through the bedlam. They pushed back where they could, but it was more like a barroom brawl than a coordinated effort. The stands where the dignitaries had been watching had emptied. Many of the spectators were sheltering underneath. Kirsh made no effort to rescue them, although he did wonder for a moment what had happened to Rees's pregnant wife. The only way to fix this was to quell the riot. Trying to save a few people here and there was useless.

"Look!" someone shouted behind him. "It's the City Guard!"

Kirsh turned in the direction the soldier pointed, relieved to discover that the small and largely ceremonial City Guard had the wit to send in reinforcements. And they were mounted. He forced his way toward the troop, which numbered less than fifty men, but more important, fifty horses. It seemed to take forever to reach them, but they didn't have to fight much. Most of the crowd fled before the wedge of soldiers pushing through the throng.

"Give me your horse!" Kirsh shouted as soon as he reached the captain of the City Guard.

A little nervous about plowing into a crowd of his own people, the young man willingly dismounted and handed the reins to Kirsh. He swung into the saddle, relieved to have a better view of the melee from horseback.

"Get back to the garrison," Kirsh ordered Rees. "Get every man you can mounted, and then get them back here as fast as you can."

He didn't wait for the Duke of Elcast to acknowledge the

order. With a savage yell, Kirsh kicked his borrowed horse into a canter and drove straight back into the mob.

By the middle of the day the riot was broken. The plaza in front of the temple was littered with the remnants of the disturbance and several dead bodies. Some had been trampled in the crush; others had been deliberately targeted by the mob. There were more than a few Shadowdancers among the dead. Most of the nobility present appeared to have escaped unscathed, except for Prince Baston of Damita. They found his body near the temple steps, beaten so savagely Kirsh only recognized him by the red clothes he wore.

Once Kirsh had mounted troops to aid him, the rioters lost much of their enthusiasm for the fight. Most of them had fled back to their homes, or out to the tent city. By midafternoon, Kirsh declared a curfew, which left them free to clean up the last of the troublemakers. There were a number of fires lit throughout the city, which Kirsh assigned Bollow's City Guard to bring under control. They had rarely been called on to do more than break up the odd street fight before today, and they didn't have the heart for the ruthless task of rounding up the last of the agitators.

It was late afternoon before he made it to the garrison. He issued orders to keep hunting the last of the rioters and finally got a chance to see Marqel.

Sergey had installed Marqel in a small anteroom off the main barracks dining room and stayed with her to ensure she was safe. Marqel flew into Kirsh's arms when she saw him, sobbing inconsolably and babbling something about Dirk. He held her for a moment, forgetting all that had happened between them. She was back in his arms and in trouble and right now, not even his father could help her.

"Shh," he said soothingly as he held her. "It's all over now."

"It's not my fault," she sobbed. "You must believe me! Dirk

told me to say it. He told me to do it, Kirsh. I didn't want to lie, but he made me..."

Kirsh disentangled her arms from around his neck so he could see her face. "*Dirk* put you up to this?"

She nodded miserably. "He told me to say the Goddess had spoken to me. He told me to lie to Antonov. That's why he killed Belagren. He wanted me to take her place. He *made* me do it. I'm so sorry, Kirsh..."

"Hang on... are you saying Dirk *killed* Belagren?"

"I was afraid he'd kill me," she cried. "That's why I went along with him. Oh, Kirsh, I was so afraid. I wanted to tell you, but I thought he'd kill you, too, if I said anything. He hates you all so much. That's why he did it. He wanted to destroy your father. He wants to destroy Senet."

"Can you prove Dirk killed Belagren?"

Marqel seemed a little taken aback by the question. But Kirsh wasn't entirely blinded by love. To accuse the Lord of the Suns of murder would require more than the word of the High Priestess who had just been so spectacularly brought down. Kirsh had learned another hard lesson recently. One didn't accuse Dirk Provin of a crime unless one had incontrovertible proof. Dirk could weasel out of anything. He'd gotten away with Johan Thorn's murder. He'd gotten away with raping Marqel. He'd spent two years with the Baenlanders, actively working against his father. He'd even burned the *Calliope* and managed to avoid Antonov's wrath. If Kirsh could prove he had murdered Belagren, he could destroy Dirk. If he couldn't prove it, there was no point in even trying.

"Don't you believe me, Kirsh?" Marqel asked in a small voice.

"Of course I believe you. But I can't accuse Dirk of Belagren's murder unless I can prove it."

"So he'll get away with that, too..." she sighed. "Nobody will believe my word against his after today."

And that was precisely what Dirk had been counting on, Kirsh realized.

"We'll make them believe you," he promised her.

"How?"

"I don't know yet. But we'll find a way. The first thing we need to do is get back to the temple. I need to speak to my father."

Marqel began to cry again. He gathered her into his arms and held her close.

"I'm so sorry I said those terrible things to you in Avacas, Kirsh," she sobbed into his chest. "Dirk told me to get rid of you. He made me say those things. He forced me to say I didn't love you." She leaned back in his arms and stared at him with shame-filled eyes. "I only ever wanted you, Kirsh. I only slept with your father because Dirk said I had to. I never wanted to..."

He pulled her close again, unable to bear the pain in her eyes. His hatred of Dirk at that moment seemed to know no bounds. To Kirsh's mind, Dirk had not set out to destroy his father, or the Shadowdancers. All he could see was that Dirk Provin had deliberately and ruthlessly set out to destroy a helpless young girl whose only crime was that she had rejected him.

Chapter 64

By first sunrise the city was just about under control. Tia prowled the temple restlessly, her mind so overwhelmed by all that had happened in the last day, she was barely able to form a coherent thought. Her close brush with death, the realization Dirk had faked everything, even back as far as Omaxin, simply to bring down the Shadowdancers, was too much for her to cope with. The scope of his plan defied reason. How much more he planned before he was done was too terrifying to imagine. The danger involved, to himself and everyone around him, was insane.

That he appeared to have succeeded so far was unbelievable.

The Lion of Senet was still on his knees near the altar, praying silently to his Goddess. He'd been there all day and nobody had been able to get a word of sense out of him. To have his beliefs so cruelly exposed had shattered the once powerful man. *Antonov Latanya must be torn apart inside,* she thought. The realization the Goddess had turned from him; that his beloved deity had denied the High Priestess ... it made a mockery of his whole life. Antonov turned to the Goddess he believed in so ardently for an explanation.

Tia thought he'd be a long time waiting for one.

The sounds of the riot in the city had died down some time ago. Kirshov Latanya was still out there, she knew, along with Dirk's brother, Rees, and a few other noblemen who had rallied to Kirsh's call. It was Kirshov Latanya who was forcing order on the people. There had been reports coming in to the temple all day about the number of killed and wounded. Among them was Prince Baston of Damita, torn apart by the rampaging mob that took his elegantly cut red clothes to mean he was a Shadowdancer.

"My lady?"

Tia turned to the Guardsman who had hailed her. She wasn't used to being addressed in such a manner.

"Are you talking to me?"

"The Lord of the Suns wishes to see you."

Tia allowed him to lead her to the small anteroom off the main hall where Dirk had been closeted for most of the day. He was alone when she entered, staring out of the window into the red night, his expression pensive. There were several fires burning in the distance, set by looters and other miscreants taking advantage of the trouble to work a little mischief of their own. Dirk had shed the yellow robes of his office and was dressed once again in a simple shirt and plain dark trousers.

"They said you wanted to see me."

Dirk turned to look at her. "Are you all right?"

"Why wouldn't I be?"

He smiled wearily. "I'm sorry about letting you think I was

going to burn you alive, Tia. I'm sorry about most of what I've done to you, actually."

"*Most* of it?"

"There were some things that didn't seem so bad at the time."

She met his eye without flinching. "Go to hell, Dirk Provin."

"Tia...I just wanted you to know I didn't...I wasn't..." His voice trailed off as if he couldn't find the words he needed to explain himself.

"Was that what you wanted to tell me?" she asked. "That you're sorry you screwed me and then betrayed me, and then almost had me killed? Fine. Can I go now?"

"I didn't mean for things to turn out the way they did, Tia."

"Really? Then why did you want me in Omaxin with you, Dirk? Why drag me all across Senet with you? You were always planning to betray us. I realize that now. What was I there for? The pleasure of my company? Or did you just like the idea of having an audience to play to?"

"I needed somebody to bear witness to what happened. Someone who would be certain to broadcast the news of my defection. It was the only way to be certain news got back to Mil fast enough."

"Why me?"

"I meant what I said when I first asked you to go with me, Tia. You knew everything Neris ever said about the Labyrinth. For all I knew, you had the answer without even realizing it." He shrugged, and smiled a little sheepishly. "Besides, you hated me anyway. I figured there wasn't much I could do to make your opinion of me any worse than it already was."

"Well, you got that wrong."

Dirk shook his head, wounded by the anger in her tone. "I had to make it look good, Tia, or Belagren would never have believed me."

"Oh, you made it look good," she assured him coldly.

He seemed desperate to make her understand. "You were never in any real danger. I knew I could make Kirsh let you go.

I insisted Belagren bring him along, just so I *could* make certain you got away."

"And was sleeping with me part of your grand plan, too?"

"Of course not," he said, looking away. "That just ... happened."

"It just *happened*? You've got a nerve, Dirk Provin, thinking I will ever forgive you for what you did to me."

"It wasn't all my fault," he pointed out. "*You* made the first move, as I recall." Dirk seemed quite hurt that she wouldn't see reason. Stung that she clung to her pain and anger and refused to accept his coldly rational explanation for why he had treated her so cruelly.

"You knew what was going to happen. You could have said no."

His eyes narrowed impatiently. "Of course. I can see it now. What I obviously should have said when you came to my tent was 'Sorry, Tia, we can't do this right now because in a couple of weeks I'm going to hand you over to the High Priestess.' Maybe then you wouldn't have felt the need to shoot me."

"You deserved it."

"You're still very angry, aren't you?"

"After everything you've done, I have a right to be angry. Why didn't you tell me about all this in Mil? Why didn't you tell us what you were doing? We could have helped you."

"That's exactly why I didn't tell you, Tia," he explained. "The best way you could help me was to believe that I'd betrayed you."

"Was this your idea?" she asked suspiciously. "Or Neris's?"

"I'm not sure, really," he shrugged. "We used to talk about how to bring down Belagren and Antonov quite a bit. It just sort of evolved from that."

She rolled her eyes. "What? So the two of you sat around his cave playing chess one day and decided: *Hey! Let's destroy a goddess?*"

Dirk smiled. "That's surprisingly close to how it happened."

"You're incredible! I mean Neris was crazy, so I suppose I can forgive him. What's your excuse?"

"Well, there was a precedent, you know. The whole Shadowdancer cult started much the same way."

She shook her head, staggered at the thought of what Dirk had undertaken on such a flimsy foundation. "Did Paige Halyn know what you were planning?"

"He knew what I was trying to do, but not the details."

"Yet he trusted you enough to name you his heir. How did you manage that?"

"The same way I get most people to do what I want, Tia. I offered him something he wanted. I promised to destroy the Shadowdancers and restore the Goddess to what she had been before Belagren came along. I promised I'd build the schools he always wanted. Everybody has their price, you know. Even the Lord of the Suns."

"Why promise him that? You know there isn't a Goddess."

"Actually, I don't," he disagreed. "I'm certain there's no Goddess making the second sun disappear at whim, and I promise you, those fires died today not because the Goddess willed it, but because I'd soaked the wood in sinkbore before the pyres were lit. But I have no idea if there is a deity out there somewhere, looking down over Ranadon."

"Sinkbore? The stuff they use to clean mold?"

"Magical stuff. Wood just won't burn if you splash enough of it around. Neris told me about it."

That's what she had smelled when they tied her to the stake. That's what they'd been pouring out of those urns. Not oil. Just ordinary, everyday, blessedly flame-retardant Sidorian sinkbore. Tia stared at him in wonder. "Then you never intended to burn me alive?"

"Of course not! What do you take me for?" He smiled suddenly. "On second thought, perhaps you shouldn't answer that."

"You're almost as bad as Belagren," she accused. "You're going to allow the world to believe a lie, just to suit your own purposes."

"You can't destroy everyone's belief and just hope they'll move on, Tia. People need something to believe in. If Paige Halyn's benign version of the Goddess is what it takes to rid the world of Belagren's version, then I'm quite happy to let people worship that. It's easier than trying to convince them they're fools for worshipping anything at all."

"And you were willing to throw everything away for it?"

He shrugged philosophically. "Every*one* has his price, Tia. And so does every*thing*. Sometimes you have to weigh up the cost and decide if it's worth it. That's what Johan did."

"He thought the cost was too high."

"He had other people to worry about. The only thing I had to lose was me. That's why I never told you what I was doing. You or anybody else."

"You're unbelievable."

"And no matter how spectacularly I succeed in bringing down the Shadowdancers, you'll never forgive me for it, will you? Just as you've never forgiven me for killing Johan."

"Is that what you want from me, Dirk? Forgiveness?"

"I don't think I know myself." He shrugged as if he was tired of arguing with her. He squared his shoulders and looked at her, the Lord of the Suns again. "In the meantime, I need you to do something for me."

"What?" she asked suspiciously.

"I want you to bring Misha back to Avacas."

"I don't know where he is."

"Don't lie to me, Tia. You know exactly where he is. I need him."

"Why? Have you an even grander plan in mind?"

"I need him as insurance. I don't want Kirsh ruling Senet."

"That would imply Antonov was no longer around to rule it. Are you going to kill him, too?"

Dirk shook his head. "Of course not. Believe it or not, Tia, I don't want anybody to die if I can avoid it. But he's a broken man. I don't want Kirsh stepping into the void."

"I thought he was a friend of yours."

"That doesn't mean I think him capable of ruling Senet at a time like this."

"And what makes you think Misha will be any more cooperative than his brother?"

"Misha's got a better head on his shoulders, for one thing. And he's not in love with the High Priestess of the Shadowdancers, either, which might prove very awkward if Kirsh decides to step into his father's shoes."

They were interrupted by the door opening. Alenor entered the anteroom, followed by Alexin. The queen had not let the captain out of her sight since they'd taken refuge in the temple.

"Tael said you wanted to see Alexin," Alenor said, glancing curiously at Tia before fixing her attention on Dirk.

"I'm sending him away."

"I won't let you," the queen declared.

"I'm not asking for your permission, Alenor. If you want Alexin to live, then we have to get him out of Senet. Tonight. I told you once before to send him away and you didn't listen to me. This time I'm not giving you a choice."

"Where are you sending him?"

"He's going with Tia Veran to bring Misha back."

"I haven't agreed to do anything of the kind," Tia objected.

"Then go back to Misha and tell him what's happened," Dirk suggested. "Let him decide."

Tia frowned, thinking Dirk knew Misha better than she suspected. There was no way she would be able to keep Misha from coming home once he learned what had happened here today.

"I'm sending you back through Avacas with an escort of Sundancers," he told Alexin, as if the matter was already decided. "I'll see you have travel warrants and enough money to get you safely out of Senet. After that, Tia will have to tell you where you're going. Don't stop for anything. Or anyone."

"Why Sundancers?" Tia asked.

"Today is merely the start of a long and laborious process, Tia. There is doubt now, where once there was blind faith, but it's only the beginning. I'm sending the Sundancers to Avacas. I want Madalan Tirov confined, and possession of the Hall of Shadows."

"You've still got big ambitions, haven't you?" she accused. "Even when you're supposedly doing it for the right reasons."

"I've got an idea to kill, Tia, and that takes more than one grand gesture." He turned to Alexin. "Once you're out of Senet, I suggest you stay out. But don't go back to Kalarada. There's a place in Oakridge on Bryton where you should be safe until this is sorted out. One way or another."

"Dirk, please..." Alenor begged.

"Dirk's right, Alenor," Alexin told her. "Today has given us a stay of execution, not solved the problem. You're still married to Kirsh and I will still be executed for treason once Kirsh has had time to think about it."

"Then I want to go with you," she announced petulantly.

"You can't, Allie," Dirk told her in a slightly more sympathetic tone. "If you go with Alexin, Kirsh will have no choice but to follow you. Alexin's only hope is to leave. Now. We haven't got much time before Kirsh has the city back under control."

"It just seems so unfair..."

"It is unfair," Dirk agreed. "It's also the only intelligent thing to do."

And that, Tia thought, was the whole reason Dirk was standing here now, the Lord of the Suns, with Bollow rioting and the Shadowdancers facing ruin. Because it was the intelligent thing to do. Not the noble thing; not even the right thing. Just the *intelligent* thing.

For the first time, Tia wondered if she was starting to understand what drove Dirk Provin. She glanced at Alexin, resigned to the inevitability of Dirk's suggestion she bring Misha back to Senet. "Are you sure you want to do this? We've a long way to go."

"I'm sure."

Dirk nodded with satisfaction. "Then I wish you both luck."

"You're the one who needs the luck, Dirk," Tia pointed out. "We're just going to fetch Misha. You're trying to save the world."

Chapter 65

Once Tia, Alenor and Alexin had left, Dirk allowed himself a few moments to let the exhaustion he felt wash over him. It had been a long day and it was far from over. The idea of sleep seemed so far distant he doubted he'd remember what a bed looked like by the time he found a chance to rest. There was so much to do.

The riot in Bollow had not been part of Dirk's plan. He knew there would be trouble, but he hadn't counted on succeeding quite so spectacularly. The people of Bollow weren't just angry. The notion that the Goddess had turned her back on the High Priestess and the Shadowdancers—the whole foundation of their beliefs since the end of the Age of Shadows—was more than they could deal with.

Dirk was not sorry he'd disarmed the Senetian Guard. There were more than a dozen dead and hundreds more wounded, but the toll would have been much higher if the soldiers had tried to bring the mob under control wielding swords. He wished he knew where Marqel was, though. The thought of her dying didn't disturb him nearly as much as the thought of creating a martyr. He needed her alive for the same reason he hadn't wanted Belagren killed. He needed to prove the High Priestess was human. That was going to be difficult if she was dead.

The door opened again. Dirk sighed, wondering what new calamity he would be required to deal with, but to his vast relief, it was Jacinta D'Orlon who stepped into the anteroom. She looked rather disheveled, but her eyes were bright and she was smiling. The mere sight of her washed away some of his tiredness.

"Well, haven't you been busy, my lord?" she remarked cheerfully. "Nice touch with the fires, by the way. How *did* you manage that?"

He smiled wearily. "Sinkbore. It's a cleaning solution they use to get mold off stone. I think I used up every drop in Bollow to make sure those flames never reached their intended victims."

"Zinc borate, you mean," she corrected absently.

"Is that its proper name? Neris never said."

"Well, it explains why you were gone for so long yesterday." She smiled conspiratorially. "But I'd not spread it around if I were you, that your miracle was nothing more than cleaning fluid. That rather fortuitous sign from the Goddess has every Sundancer in the city ready to throw their life away for you. It would be a pity to disillusion them."

He looked her over carefully. "You didn't get hurt in the riot, did you?"

Jacinta shook her head. "I was sitting near your brother and Duke Saban of Grannon Rock. He has a very useful streak of cowardice in him that saved us from the mob. Rees went charging off to be a hero while Faralan and I cowered under the stands with Saban during the worst of it, and then we managed to find shelter in a rather seedy tavern for the rest of the time. All in all, it's been a very interesting day." Her smile faded a little and she studied him with concern. "You look exhausted."

"I'll be fine."

"Why don't men ever admit they're tired?" she asked. "Or that they're hurt?"

"I wasn't denying I'm tired. I just need to keep telling myself I can cope with it. We're not out of the shadows yet."

"Well, the city's a lot quieter now. Kirsh imposed a curfew."

"Have you seen him?"

"He got here just after I did," she told him. "He's out in the temple now with Rees and Marqel, talking to his father... *Dirk?*"

He didn't hear the rest of what she said. Dirk ran from the anteroom, filled with the sick certainty that everything he'd achieved today would be unraveled if Marqel had a chance to speak to Antonov before he did.

The Lion of Senet was still on his knees near the altar when Dirk arrived. Kirsh was squatting next to him, trying to coax an answer out of his father, but he received no more response from Antonov than anybody else had been able to get all day. Marqel stood beside Kirsh, surrounded by a guard of Senetian soldiers.

"Kirsh."

The prince looked up as Dirk approached. He rose slowly to his feet and, with a final worried glance at his father, strode purposefully across the hall. Dirk realized a moment too late what Kirsh intended. He wasn't quick enough to dodge the blow. Kirsh hit him squarely on the jaw, sending Dirk flying backward.

With alarming speed, the Dhevynian Guards closed in to protect Dirk, facing Kirsh with drawn swords. The Senetians responded to the threat to their prince with equal alacrity. Stunned and disoriented, Dirk shook his head and tried to focus his eyes. The pain from Kirsh's anger-driven fist hadn't hit him yet. It was still numb.

"Stand down!" he cried, blinking away the white spots dancing before his eyes as the numbness began to be replaced by unbelievable pain. Somebody rushed to help him up. He was a little surprised to discover it was Jacinta.

"You really do inspire extremes in people, don't you, my lord?" she remarked in a wry voice meant only for him as he staggered to his feet.

He glared at her balefully for a moment then looked back at Kirsh. The prince stood in front of the Dhevynians, spoiling for a fight, his own men arrayed behind him. They were glaring at each other like alley cats over a fish bone. It would take very little to set them off.

"Stand down!" he snapped, impatiently. "And that goes for your men, too, Kirsh. This is a temple. Have some respect for the Goddess, at least."

Kirsh hesitated defiantly for a moment, and then conceded the wisdom of Dirk's words. With a wave of his arm, the Senetians sheathed their weapons, followed a few nervous seconds later by the Queen's Guardsmen.

Dirk made his way unsteadily back to Kirsh, stopping out of range of his fist this time.

"You did this," Kirsh accused before Dirk could say anything. "You set Marqel up, just so you could destroy her."

"Did *she* tell you that or did you work it out all on your own, Kirsh?"

Dirk glanced across at Marqel. She spared him a spiteful little smile that quickly faded to a solemn frown when Kirsh looked back at her, too.

"You're not going to get away with this," Kirsh warned. "When my father learns the truth—"

"He's seen the truth, Kirsh," Dirk cut in. "That's why he's kneeling over there by the altar, muttering like a madman. He doesn't like the look of the truth any more than you do."

"You staged this whole thing just to hurt Marqel," Kirsh exploded.

"Are you *crazy*?" Dirk cried. "You think I organized a miracle just to upset your girlfriend?"

Everyone in the temple had stopped to watch the altercation. Alenor stood beside Jacinta, clutching her cousin's hand for support. Rees stood next to Faralan, who looked pale and wan. The Sundancers watched them curiously, amazed by the sight of the Lord of the Suns and the Regent of Dhevyn shouting at each other like a couple of roughs in a tavern brawl. The soldiers stood by cautiously, hands resting on the hilts of their swords.

Nobody attempted to intervene, however. Nobody in the temple was that brave. Or that foolish.

"She told me everything," Kirsh shouted angrily. "You were the one who told her what to say."

"Marqel tells you exactly what you *want* to hear, Kirsh," he retorted. *Goddess, I don't have time for this...* "Right now, you should be more worried about what's going to happen when word spreads about what happened here today, than whether or not that spiteful little whore you're so enchanted with is telling you the truth."

"Don't you dare speak about the High Priestess in such a manner!"

"Your precious High Priestess has admitted to you the Goddess didn't really speak to her. She's claiming I told her what to say. So either she's not the Voice of the Goddess and therefore has no right to be called High Priestess, or she really did speak with the Goddess and she's lying to you now to cover up the fact that the Goddess abandoned her. Which is it, Kirsh? Is she lying or is she lying?"

Dirk could never hope to defeat Kirsh in a physical encounter, but when it came to a battle of wits, the Senetian prince was woefully outmatched. He had no answer to Dirk's question. He was shaking with rage and frustration.

"I'll destroy you for this, Dirk Provin."

"Then you'd better hurry, Kirsh, because if you're fool enough to listen to her, Marqel will destroy you long before you get the chance to destroy me."

Dirk quite deliberately turned his back on Kirsh and began to walk away. His face was on fire and he was certain he'd cracked his spine when he landed so heavily on his back on the polished granite floor.

"Arrest him!" he heard Kirsh order.

Dirk turned to look at him. To his intense relief, not even Kirsh's own men had moved to obey the order.

"You've got to be joking, Kirsh."

"I'm arresting you for the murder of the High Priestess Belagren," Kirsh told him coldly.

You cunning little bitch, Dirk thought, looking over at Marqel. She smiled at him nastily.

"You've no proof she was even murdered, Kirsh, let alone that I was the one who killed her."

"I have the word of the High Priestess," he retorted.

"And I'm quite sure in these uncertain times there will be any number of Shadowdancers willing to swear she speaks the truth."

This was Marqel's game, Dirk realized. Kirsh would never think of anything so devious. But he spoke the truth. If it meant saving the Shadowdancers, every one of them, from Madalan down, would perjure themselves to be rid of the Lord of the Suns who had exposed them. And that included the palace physician, Yuri Daranski, who could testify—quite honestly—that in his opinion, Belagren had been poisoned. He could also testify Dirk had asked him to cover up the crime.

He was trapped by his own deeds. Caught out by Marqel once again doing the unexpected. Her ability to undermine his plans with her selfish manipulation was staggering.

"Arrest him!" Kirsh repeated. This time, the Senetians moved to do as their prince bid.

"Kirsh, you can't do this," Alenor protested, suddenly finding her voice.

"I'd hold my tongue, if I were you, Alenor," Kirsh warned in an icy tone. "Your fate is no more assured than Dirk's at the moment."

"But surely, your highness," Jacinta suggested reasonably, "if you would just allow the Lord of the Suns a chance to defend himself…"

"Take him!" Kirsh cried impatiently. "And when you've arrested him, get rid of *her*!" he added, pointing to Jacinta. "I want the Lady Jacinta D'Orlon out of Senet. And she can take her damned queen with her."

The soldiers closed in on Dirk as Kirsh strode from the temple, leaving a smirking and intensely satisfied Marqel standing there, gloating over how easily she had turned her defeat into a resounding victory.

Chapter 66

Early the following morning, Kirsh received a summons to attend the Lion of Senet. He was greatly relieved by the news. His father's catatonic state of the day before had worried everyone, Kirsh most of all. It was one thing for a prince to die; it was quite another for him to be rendered ineffective, but still go on living. Kirsh wanted his father either alive and well and capable of making a decision, or . . .

The alternative was almost unthinkable, but even Kirsh recognized they would all be better off if he was dead rather than insane. Selfishly, Kirsh prayed for his father to make a complete recovery. Although he had always harbored the secret desire to make a name for himself, he'd planned to do it as a military hero, not a bureaucrat. He had no desire to rule Senet, particularly in light of the events of the last few days.

Kirsh hurried along the hall to his father's room, ready to argue his case. He had a lot to defend. Arresting Dirk would not endear him to his father, nor would he win points for accusing his cousin of murder. The suggestion that Dirk had staged the whole eclipse fiasco simply to disgrace Marqel was not going to make him very popular, either. But Kirsh was certain he had done the right thing and was prepared to fight even his father to prove it.

There were other consequences of yesterday's riot to deal with, too. The Prince of Damita was dead and as far as Kirsh knew, his only living heirs were his nephews, the sons of Baston's two older sisters, Analee and Morna. If one accepted the likelihood Misha was dead, that made Kirsh or Rees Provin the new Prince of Damita. Even worse, Dirk Provin could claim the throne if Rees didn't want it. Kirsh certainly had no desire to rule Damita. He loathed being Regent of Dhevyn and was desperate to see his father up and about and back in control for fear he might be called on to govern Senet.

Reaching the door to his father's room in the Lord of the Suns' palace, Kirsh wondered what had happened to his boyhood dreams of being a soldier. His naive hopes for glorious battles and heroic deeds... He was doomed now. Alenor was to be banished, so there was no way he could avoid his responsibilities in Dhevyn, and the chances were good his father would insist Kirsh claim Baston's seat in Damita as well. And one day, when Antonov died, with both Kirsh's brothers dead, he would become the Lion of Senet. It seemed so unfair. He hadn't even wanted to be a regent and he was going to end up being responsible for half the damn world.

"Kirshov!" Antonov greeted him with a beaming smile.

"Father," he replied miserably, still lamenting the cruel hand of fate he'd been dealt.

"You look tired, son," the Lion of Senet remarked. "I hope you didn't stay out too late celebrating last night."

"Celebrating?"

"It was a great day for the Goddess yesterday, Kirsh." He smiled indulgently. "I know what you're like. You just don't know when you've had too much of a good thing. Still, after such a momentous day, one can't blame the young for wanting to spread the joy around a little bit."

"There was a riot yesterday, father," Kirsh reminded him, a little worried by Antonov's cheery demeanor. "Don't you remember?"

"No, no...it was a great day! She was testing our faith. And we passed the test."

"What?"

"The Goddess, Kirsh," he said. "That's what yesterday was all about. She was testing our faith. *My* faith."

"Father, nobody was testing anything," he ventured cautiously. "Dirk staged the whole thing to destroy Marqel and the Shadowdancers."

"It's not up to us to question the Goddess's methods," Antonov scolded.

Kirsh stared at his father, noticing for the first time the fanatical gleam in his eyes.

"Did you hear me? It wasn't the Goddess's work. It was Dirk Provin's."

"Yes, yes, I heard you," Antonov said. "But we mustn't question her, you see. If Dirk staged it then he did it because the Goddess wanted him to do it. She was testing me. Testing my faith. She promised me a sign and she gave me one. Only it wasn't the sign we were all expecting, you see. It was a *different* sign. She rattled us a bit, Kirsh, to remind us we must have faith."

The realization Antonov was no longer completely sane took some time to sink in. His eyes glittered brightly and he paced the room as if something agitated him.

"I prayed to her, you see," Antonov explained, talking to himself as much as Kirsh. "I told her everything I'd done for her. I reminded her of the sacrifices I've made for her. I gave her one of my sons, you know. Two of them, if you count Misha. And Analee. She took her own life, but I know—I *know*—it was the Goddess who made her do it. She probably wanted Analee to stay with Gunta. He was only a baby, when I gave him to the Goddess... you'd be too young to remember, I suppose... but he was such a beautiful child... and then Analee was gone... But I still had Belagren..."

Antonov continued to rant, pacing up and down the room. Kirsh watched him with a growing feeling of dread. The Lion of Senet was completely divorced from reality, consumed by the need to convince himself yesterday's calamitous events were simply a reaffirmation of his faith, not the total destruction of its foundation.

"I've arrested Dirk, Father," he said.

Antonov didn't even notice he'd spoken. "Bela was the Goddess's voice, you know. She knew what to do. She always knew what to do. She spoke to the Goddess... that was how I knew I was right. But since she died... I was so shocked by that... I started to doubt her. It was my fault, you see. In my grief I doubted the Goddess. I questioned her. So the Goddess sent me a test. She offered me proof she didn't really exist and dared me to accept it. But I prayed to her. I spoke to her. And I saw what she was doing. I realized it was a test. And I passed it, Kirsh. I passed it..."

"I'm going to paint all the houses in Avacas pink and hang dead babies over the gates of the palace."

"I passed the test, Kirsh. Don't you see? I had to have my faith challenged before I could be humbled. I'd grown arrogant. The Goddess knew that. She sees everything..."

"I'm going to hang Dirk Provin."

Antonov suddenly seemed to notice Kirsh had spoken. "Hang Dirk? What for?"

"He murdered Belagren."

"Did he?"

"You don't seem surprised."

"Well, of course I'm not surprised," Antonov scoffed, as if Kirsh was just a little bit dim for expecting such a reaction. "He's the Goddess's instrument."

"The what?"

"Her instrument. Don't you see? The Goddess put Dirk Provin in my path to tempt me. She gave me Johan Thorn's bastard and taunted me with him. I thought I knew what she wanted. I thought she wanted me to make him a king, but she knew better—the Goddess always knows better, Kirsh, remember that—she knew Dirk wasn't put on Ranadon to be a king. Belagren told me the same thing, but I was too arrogant to heed her advice. So the Goddess took a hand in his fate. She made him Lord of the Suns. That was what she always intended for him, but I was too blind to see it. I see it now, though... oh, yes, I see the truth now..."

"Father..."

"We have to go to Omaxin," Antonov announced abruptly. "To the cavern where Belagren first spoke to the Goddess. It all seems so clear now. That's why she sent Dirk there... to open the cavern so we could hear her voice clearly again..."

There was no reasoning with him. "You want to go to Omaxin?"

"We must go, Kirsh. All of us. You and Marqel and Dirk, too. Dirk *must* come. He can read the Goddess's writings, did you know that? That alone should have told me I was wrong trying to make him King of Dhevyn. Yes, yes…that's what we'll do. We'll go to Omaxin. Today."

"We can't leave today. Baston of Damita is dead. Everything is going wrong…Senet is falling apart around us, Father."

"Don't be ridiculous, Kirsh. Now do as I say! We're going to Omaxin."

Kirsh nodded slowly, realizing the futility of arguing with him. "I'll make the arrangements. Although I have a few things to take care of. I may have to follow you in a few days."

"That's fine," Antonov said, nodding eagerly. "Marqel and I will leave today and you and Dirk can follow us in a day or so. He'll not be able to just drop everything either, now that he's Lord of the Suns."

"No, I suppose he won't."

Antonov stared at him suddenly, as if only just noticing Kirsh was standing there. "You're my heir now that Misha is dead."

"We don't know for certain—"

"It's a good thing, Kirsh. Misha was deformed. He was never going to be any good as a prince. It might have been easier if he'd been born into a lesser family. I think he might have made a reasonable bookkeeper, given half a chance. But he wasn't of the same mettle as you. The Goddess knew he wasn't strong enough to rule Senet. That's why she took him." His maudlin frown unexpectedly changed to a bright smile. "We'll build a monument to him when we get back from Omaxin. A statue of him, perhaps—not a lifelike one, of course, we don't want him remembered as the Crippled Prince. But we'll honor his memory. He'd like that, don't you think?"

"I'm sure he would," Kirsh replied tonelessly.

"Good, good…well, you should go now. You've got a lot to do, you said."

"Yes, sir."

"And make sure you release Dirk immediately. I want to

hear no more of this nonsense between you two. He is the Goddess's instrument."

"Yes, sir."

Antonov resumed his pacing as if Kirsh was no longer in the room, muttering to himself about passing the test the Goddess had set for him. With his heart breaking to see this great man reduced to such a state, Kirsh let himself out without disturbing his father's ranting.

Kirsh closed the door softly and leaned against it. He had thought yesterday Dirk Provin had done the worst he could do, but what his "sign from the Goddess" had done to Antonov made it a worse crime than murder. It would have been better, kinder, to have killed Antonov Latanya, than reduce him to a gibbering madman.

And Dirk was going to get away with it, yet again, because Antonov wanted him in Omaxin. Even worse, Kirsh realized he was going to have to be complicit in Dirk's escape.

The Goddess's instrument, Antonov called him. *What a crock.*

But the harsh reality was that Kirsh was now effectively responsible for governing Senet. A task he didn't kid himself for a moment he was capable of undertaking without help. Kirsh was caught in an intolerable bind. He could only countermand his father's orders—only rule Senet, for that matter, at a time she was badly in need of a leader—if he announced to the world the Lion of Senet was insane.

He closed his eyes in a futile attempt to shut out the world for a moment. The irony was exquisite. Only Dirk, the "Goddess's instrument," probably fully appreciated the depth of the calamity facing Senet.

Finally, Kirsh opened his eyes and pushed off against the door. If he couldn't execute Dirk Provin then it left him only one other course of action. The man who had orchestrated this disaster, and brought Senet to the brink of ruin in the first place, could damn well help him put the pieces back together again.

One way or another, Kirsh promised himself, *Dirk has to pay.*

Chapter 67

Dirk spent only one night in prison before Kirsh sent for him. The order for his release surprised Dirk a little. He had spent a long sleepless night trying to work out how he was going to get himself out of this particular mess and had come up with absolutely nothing.

Dirk had finally run out of answers.

The problem all stemmed from dealing with someone like Marqel, he'd concluded in the early hours of the morning. Dirk had a gift for anticipating the behavior of his adversaries, in part because he understood how they thought. He could put himself in his opponents' boots and instinctively extrapolate their most likely course of action. But to do that, he had to be able to think like they did. Dirk's weakness—his failure in dealing with Marqel—was that he could barely conceive of a mind so amoral, self-absorbed, so willing to do whatever it took to protect her own position without any thought for the consequences.

It was almost midday when he returned by carriage to the Lord of the Suns' palace, unshaven, dirty and hungry, his jaw swollen and bruised where Kirsh had hit him. The prince was waiting for him in the study that had, until yesterday, been Dirk's. He was sitting behind the desk, a glass of wine in his hand, an almost empty decanter on the desk beside him.

Kirsh looked up when Dirk entered, scowling. "I'd offer you some wine, but I intend to drink every last drop of this myself."

"Be my guest," Dirk offered. It was his wine, after all.

"Enjoy your night in the cells?"

"Not particularly."

Kirsh swallowed the remains of his glass and poured himself another. "I was going to hang you this morning."

"Without a trial?" Dirk asked, taking the seat opposite the carved desk.

"Without so much as a fanfare."

"What changed your mind?"

"The fact my father seems to have lost his," Kirsh snapped.

"I'm sorry..."

"No, you're not!" he spat in disgust. "It's what you intended all along. You set out to destroy him, Dirk. Marqel has that much right. Well, you'll be delighted to know you succeeded. He's a broken man. His mind is completely gone."

Enough of Dirk's plans had gone awry in the past day that the news did not surprise him. And from what he'd seen of the Lion of Senet yesterday, it wasn't hard to guess what had happened. But he was disappointed in Antonov. He thought the shock and the madness would be temporary. Was counting on it, in fact. Just a short time of dazed insanity before Antonov realized the truth. And then, with Antonov enraged and determined to seek vengeance for the needless killing of his youngest son to return the Age of Light, Dirk would barely have had to lift a finger. With the depth of the deceit played on Antonov exposed, Dirk wouldn't need to bring the Shadowdancers down.

Antonov would have—*should* have—done it for him.

"He'll get over it, surely?"

"He's upstairs explaining to himself how the Goddess set you up as her instrument to test his faith, Dirk. He's not going to get over it. He won't allow himself to. That's asking him to face a truth he isn't able to deal with."

"And what about you, Kirsh? Are you ready to deal with the truth?"

"I don't know what the truth is, Dirk, but I'm damn sure it's nothing you're mixed up in."

"So why delay my execution? If you believe I deliberately set out to destroy your father, I would think you couldn't kill me quick enough."

"*He* wants you alive. He's actually *calling* you the 'Goddess's instrument,' now." Kirsh laughed harshly at the irony. "Personally, I think you're evil incarnate, but as my only alternative is to execute the Lord of the Suns for murder and announce to the world the Lion of Senet is a babbling lunatic, I have no choice but to play along with him for the time being."

"For the time being?" Dirk asked. "I'm not interested in a temporary stay of execution while you get your mess sorted out, Kirsh, just to have you turn on me again as soon as I'm no longer required. Either I'm free and reinstated, or you can execute me today and to hell with the consequences."

Kirsh glared at him. "I wish I knew if you were bluffing."

"Try me and find out."

He downed the wine in a single swallow and poured the dregs of the decanter into his glass. "Is Misha alive, Dirk?"

The question caught Dirk off guard. "As far as I know... yes, he is."

Dirk was astonished by the obvious relief in Kirsh's eyes at the news.

"What will it cost to get him back?"

"I have no idea."

"But you can find out, can't you?" There was an edge of desperation in Kirsh's voice. And he was more than a little drunk, despite the early hour. "I don't care what you've been pretending these last few months, you *know* the Baenlanders, Dirk. They'll treat with you, won't they?"

"I can talk to them," he said cautiously, not willing to share the news he had already sent Tia to fetch Misha. Until he knew what Kirsh was up to, he didn't want to reveal something so valuable. "I can't promise anything."

Kirsh nodded thoughtfully. "Here's the deal, then. You're free and you're reinstated. You can be Lord of the Shadows, Lord of the Suns, Lord of the whole freaking universe for all I care. In return, you'll help me keep a lid on things until Misha gets home."

"And then what?"

"And then it's Misha's problem."

Kirsh was truly desperate, Dirk realized. And out of that

desperation, Dirk might yet have a chance to redeem things. He nodded cautiously. "I'll agree on two conditions."

"You're in no position to demand anything, Dirk Provin. I could send you straight back to that cell I just hauled you out of and leave you there to rot. Antonov's mad, remember. Push me too far and I'll lock you up, throw the key into Lake Ruska and just explain your continuing absence to my father by telling him you're busy."

"I don't want anything unreasonable, Kirsh."

"What *do* you want?"

"I want your word you'll not interfere in anything I do as Lord of the Suns."

Kirsh thought about that for a moment and then shrugged. "If it doesn't endanger Senet, you can do whatever you damned well please. What was the other condition?"

"Divorce Alenor."

Kirsh didn't answer him.

"You might as well, Kirsh. The only reason you married her was to keep Antonov happy. And you don't have to be married to her to be Regent of Dhevyn." When Kirsh still didn't reply, he added: "If you won't do it for Alenor, do it for Marqel."

"She's the High Priestess, Dirk. I couldn't marry her, even if I wanted to."

"No, but I'm sure she'd appreciate the gesture."

"You're a cynical little bastard, aren't you?"

"*I'm* cynical? You want me to help you cover up Antonov's insanity while you wait for your invalid brother to get back so he can pick up the pieces, saving you from having to deal with the responsibilities of being a prince, Kirsh. Don't lecture me on being cynical."

"I want you to take responsibility for what you've done, Dirk. Antonov's lost his mind because of something *you* did. You created this mess. Now you can damn well help me fix it."

"And what about Marqel?"

"What about her?"

"She's been exposed as a fraud. Do you think you can just

ignore that? If I remain Lord of the Suns, she can't remain High Priestess."

"Why not?"

"Because the first thing I intend to do is disband the Shadowdancers and outlaw them as heretics."

"I told you I won't permit you to do anything to endanger Senet."

"Getting rid of the Shadowdancers is the biggest favor I can do Senet, Kirsh."

The prince was silent for a time, and then he looked at Dirk with a puzzled expression. "Is that why you did this, Dirk? Is that why you destroyed my father? Why you murdered Belagren? Why you're so determined to ruin Marqel? What did the Shadowdancers ever do to you to warrant such hatred?"

"They stole my life from me, Kirsh," he replied flatly. He didn't deny the charge of murdering Belagren. There didn't seem much point. "Your father and Belagren destroyed everything I loved. They took away the man I thought was my father. They made me kill my real father. They burned my mother alive... How much more do you think I was going to take before I decided I'd had enough?"

"I thought you were my friend," he accused, as if that alone should be enough to cancel out all the wrongs that had been done to him.

"I am your friend, Kirsh, which is the only reason I'm willing to help you now. But I was never your father's friend. Or Belagren's. They both had plans for me about which I was neither consulted nor concerned."

"You'll help me then?"

"Yes."

"How do I trust you to keep your word?"

"By keeping yours."

Kirsh seemed to accept that. He nodded. "Then we'll compromise," he said. "I can't remove Marqel from her position of High Priestess, even if I thought she should be denounced, which I *don't*. My father still believes in her, just as he still believes in you, more fool him. But he's decided he needs to go to

Omaxin to speak to the Goddess. I'll make sure she goes with him. That will keep her out of sight until the furor over the eclipse dies down, at least."

"That's only a temporary solution."

"That's all I care about, right now."

"And Alenor?"

"She can have her divorce," he shrugged, picking up the empty decanter with a frown. "All we ever did was make each other miserable." Kirsh looked up at Dirk, suddenly suspicious. "Which reminds me, what did you do with Alexin and Tia Veran?"

"They're gone."

"They were condemned to die. Alexin committed treason."

"He committed the crime of falling in love with the wrong woman, Kirsh. That's a crime you're just as guilty of. I'd be careful about setting a precedent, if I were you."

Kirsh scowled at the reminder. "Just make sure I never see him again, Dirk. Or that troublemaking little bitch Tia Veran."

Dirk smiled faintly. "I don't think you need worry about Tia or Alexin. I can't imagine either of them wants to see you again."

Kirsh leaned back in his chair, spinning his empty wine-glass back and forth by the stem, staring at it as if he could find all the answers he needed in the play of light reflected off the cut crystal surface. "So what happens now?"

"Get Antonov out of Bollow. If he wants to go to Omaxin, then there's no better place for him. Up there he'll be out of the sight of prying eyes. Keep him there as long as you can. Let him pray to the Goddess as much as he wants. You and I need to get back to Avacas. We can't rule Senet from Bollow."

"I don't want to rule Senet at all, Dirk."

"I know," Dirk agreed, thinking Kirsh's lack of political ambition was half the reason he got mixed up with Marqel. He thought like a soldier, not a statesman. "But you may not have a choice."

"What do you mean?"

"Misha was at death's door when he was taken. If he's no

better when he gets back, or worse, if he dies, you'll be right back where you are now."

"Baston of Damita is dead, too," Kirsh reminded him, miserably. "Who's going to rule Damita?"

"Recall Oscon from exile."

Kirsh scoffed at the suggestion. "You want me to reinstate the man who fought against my father with Johan Thorn during the Age of Shadows? You'll want me to restore Rainan next."

"If the alternative is that you have to worry about Damita, then yes, you should reinstate Prince Oscon."

"He's your maternal grandfather. Is that why you want him back in power?"

"He's your maternal grandfather, too, Kirsh. Besides, like you, I'm a second son. Rees has a much better claim to Damita than I do. Misha has the best claim of all. He's the eldest son of Oscon's eldest daughter. Whether or not you want to add to his burden once he returns to Avacas by asking him to take on Damita's throne as well, is another matter entirely."

"But the Church declared Oscon a heretic."

Dirk smiled. "I *am* the Church, Kirsh. As of now, he's forgiven."

Kirsh shook his head in bewilderment. "Is nothing sacred to you?"

"Political decisions imposed by the Church to suit the ambitions of a prince they're trying to placate aren't sacred, Kirsh. They not only deserve to be overturned, they *must* be, if you intend Senet to survive this and prosper."

"And that's the difference between you and me, Dirk," Kirsh replied heavily. "You're a born politician. You're already thinking about ten years from now. I just want to keep Senet intact until Misha gets home."

Chapter 68

Marqel exploded with fury when she learned Kirsh had not only released Dirk Provin, but reinstated him. Eryk told her about it. He was bubbling with the news Prince Kirsh had reconsidered his rash decision of the previous day and had rightfully released Lord Dirk and restored him to his position as Lord of the Suns.

The stupidity of the decision left her gasping. And it worried her. If Kirsh loved her as much as he claimed, he should have killed Dirk with his bare hands. He should have destroyed him without hesitation. Instead, he had caved in like a tunnel built of sand and allowed Dirk to take charge the way he took charge with everything.

She found Kirsh in the morning room, talking with Rees Provin. Storming into the room, she didn't even wait for them to acknowledge her presence before she let loose with her tirade.

"You let him *go*!"

Kirsh looked up at her, wincing at her tone.

"What were you *thinking*? Do you realize what you've *done*?"

"Would you excuse us, Rees?" he said to the duke.

Rees Provin bowed silently and left without a word, deliberately avoiding meeting Marqel's eye. He thoughtfully closed the doors behind him when he left.

"You freed him," she spat angrily. "You let him just walk away."

"I didn't have a choice, Marqel."

"Of course you had a choice. Your choice was not to let Dirk Provin get away with murder."

"I need him."

"For what? To remind you what an idiot you are?"

"Antonov's sick," he tried to explain. "I need Dirk's help…"

"What's wrong with doing it on your own?"

"If these were normal times, there'd be nothing wrong with it," he said, wounded by her lack of sympathy. "But in case it slipped your notice, yesterday the Goddess very publicly turned her back on the Shadowdancers, Marqel, and made a mockery out of your whole religion. Without the Lord of the Suns very publicly supporting me, I haven't got a hope in hell of controlling anything. Strange as it may seem, threatening to execute him for murder isn't really the way to secure his cooperation."

"So he gets away with it. Like he gets away with everything else he's done."

"Unfortunately."

"Why can't you just kill him and appoint a new Lord of the Suns?"

"Because the appointment would take months. Months I don't have. Dirk is Lord of the Suns and I'm stuck with it."

Marqel was livid. "And what happens to me? Did you spare *that* a thought while you were forgiving your old chum for everything else?"

"You're still High Priestess," he assured her.

"High Priestess of *what*?" she snarled. "Leave Dirk Provin in charge of the Church and within a month there won't be anything for me to be High Priestess *of*!"

"And if I execute the Lord of the Suns after the Goddess so loudly declared her support for the Sundancers, it will rip Senet apart. I don't mind fighting a war, Marqel, but I'm damned if I'll start one among my own people."

"So I'm to be sacrificed to save Senet from a civil war?" she concluded bitterly. "If you really loved me, you'd fight a dozen wars for me, Kirsh."

He tried to take her in his arms, but she pushed him away impatiently.

"Marqel, please try to understand. I *am* doing this for you. I won't let Dirk denounce you. I won't let him remove you and I won't let him destroy the Shadowdancers. But you saw what happened in Bollow after the eclipse didn't eventuate and those fires didn't burn. That will happen again, all over Senet, if I don't do something to nip it in the bud."

Marqel realized anger wasn't getting her anywhere, so she decided to try a different tack. "But he's dangerous, Kirsh," she said, leaning into his arms. "I'm afraid for you more than I'm afraid for myself."

"I'll be fine, Marqel," he promised, pulling her close. "And you'll be safe in Omaxin for the time being. Once this is—"

"Omaxin?" she cut in.

"My father wants to go to Omaxin to speak to the Goddess. You'll have nothing to worry about. Nobody will be able to harm you up there. I'll send plenty of troops with you. You'll be well protected."

She looked up at him, her eyes suddenly filled with crystal tears. "You're sending me away?"

"It's for your own safety, Marqel."

She pushed him away impatiently. "And did you want me to sleep with your father while I'm there? Is that all I am to you? Someone you can pass around the family? Thank the Goddess Misha's gone, or I suppose you'd have me servicing the Crippled Prince as well."

Her accusation cut him to the core—which was precisely what she intended.

"I'm trying to keep you safe, Marqel," he said, begging for her understanding.

"No, you're not," she accused. "You're trying to save your own precious neck. My fate runs a poor second to that."

"Then what do you *want* me to do?" he cried in frustration.

"Kill Dirk Provin."

He shook his head helplessly. "Don't you think I have as much reason to want him destroyed as you do? But I can't, Marqel. He's got me by the balls."

"That would account for why you don't seem to have them anymore."

"Marqel . . ."

"Don't even bother, Kirsh," she told him coldly. "If you need Dirk Provin to hold your hand while you try to sort out the mess he created in the first place, you're not the man I thought you were."

She turned on her heel, heading for the door. Dirk was right. *Why settle for the boy when you can have the man?* Antonov would never have let himself be manipulated like this.

"I'm divorcing Alenor."

She stopped and turned to stare at him.

"You're *what*?"

"I'm divorcing Alenor," he repeated. "When all this is straightened out, we can be together, Marqel. No more hiding. No more sneaking around. Just like you wanted."

"Does Alenor know?"

"Not yet. But she won't object."

"What about your father?"

"My father's dead, Marqel. The man who inhabits the shell of his body is not the Lion of Senet. You'll realize that as soon as you see him."

Marqel stared at him in wonder. "So you're the Lion of Senet now?"

"In practice, if not in reality."

A world of possibility suddenly opened up to Marqel. Her eyes filled with compassion, she hurried back to Kirsh and threw her arms around him. "Oh, Kirsh! That's awful!"

"Nobody must know he's mad, Marqel."

"They'll not learn it from me," she promised. She searched his face for a moment and then let the light of comprehension dawn in her wide, ingenuous eyes. "That's why you want me to go to Omaxin with him, isn't it? To look after him. To keep his terrible secret. Oh, my love, I'm so sorry. You should have explained. I didn't mean those awful things I said just now. Of course I'll go to Omaxin. And I'll stay with your father for as long as you need me to."

"You have to cover for him, Marqel. If anybody learned the Lion of Senet was no longer capable of ruling...even if they smell a hint of weakness..."

"It's all right, Kirsh," she said soothingly. "I understand. I won't let anyone near him. As far as the rest of the world is concerned, he will be simply deep in his devotions to the Goddess."

He kissed her and then held her close. Marqel bore his embrace patiently, although she was itching to get away from him now. This was an unbelievable opportunity and she wanted time alone to savor its full potential.

"I wish I didn't have to send you away."

"We'll be together soon," she promised. "Just be careful while I'm gone. Don't let Dirk get the better of you. And don't trust him."

"I can handle Dirk," he assured her.

Don't kid yourself, Kirsh, she replied silently. *He'll play you like a balalaika. But you're too dense to realize it.*

"I know you can, my love. Just promise me you'll be careful."

"I promise."

She sighed heavily. "I suppose you want us to leave as soon as possible."

"Sergey's getting things organized now."

"Then I should go and pack," she said, disentangling herself from his arms.

He let her go reluctantly. Marqel stood on her toes and kissed him lightly and then she fled the morning room, afraid if she stayed any longer Kirsh would see the excitement in her eyes.

Chapter 69

The Queen of Dhevyn had spent her entire life living in a palace, so the experience of staying at an inn, even a good one, was something she found rather novel. It was Jacinta's idea, of course. Although there was no question Alenor would be welcomed at the palace in Avacas, Jacinta thought it prudent not to risk placing themselves within the power of the Lion of Senet any more than was absolutely necessary.

It would take just one small carrier pigeon from Bollow to change their status from guests to prisoners, and she didn't intend to let that happen to her queen.

The inn they found was located in the better part of Avacas, a little too close to the palace for comfort, but Jacinta reasoned their anonymity demanded it. The better inns were discreet and solicitous of their guests' privacy. Putting the Queen of Dhevyn up in a dockside tavern, even under an assumed name, would be as good as hiring a town crier to broadcast their presence to the whole city.

Tael and his men had shed their uniforms at her insistence, although she wondered why she had bothered suggesting it. The Guardsmen rode like Guardsmen, they walked like Guardsmen, they even ate like Guardsmen. If they had been standing stark naked in a field *full* of naked men, she could have picked them out, just by the way they carried themselves.

"You're looking very pensive," Alenor remarked.

Jacinta was sitting by the window, looking out over the busy Avacas street, lost in thought. They had been at the inn for six days now and the queen was feeling trapped.

"I was thinking about a field full of naked men, actually."

"Jacinta!"

She turned to her cousin with smile. "One has to do something to pass the time. It beats wearing a hole in the carpet."

Alenor self-consciously stopped her pacing. "Tael's been gone a long time."

"He's hardly been gone any time at all, Allie. Stop fretting."

"Do you think he'll be able to find us a ship?"

"Avacas is the busiest port in the world. I'm sure he'll manage something."

"I hate this sneaking around. I was never any good at it."

"We're not 'sneaking around,' Alenor," Jacinta corrected. "We're keeping a low profile. There is a subtle but distinct difference."

"Well, I'm glad you can see it. Do you think Alexin got away safely?"

"I'm sure Avacas would be abuzz with the news if he hadn't."

"Where do you suppose he went?"

Jacinta sighed. "Alenor, if I knew the answer to that, I would have told you. On one of the several thousand occasions you've asked me the same question in the past few days."

"I'm sorry. I just can't help but worry about him."

"Worry if you have to, Allie, but at least think up a new question every now and then."

"You're mad at me, aren't you?"

"Of course I'm not mad at you," she exclaimed in surprise. "Whatever gave you that idea?"

"You've been really snappy ever since we left Bollow."

"That's probably because I've never been thrown out of a whole country before." Jacinta smiled. "I've been thrown out of a university. And a tavern—don't ever tell my mother that—but not a whole country. I'm not sure if it means I'm moving up in the world, or down in it."

"Why don't you ever take anything seriously?"

"I do so take things seriously."

"Not the really important things," Alenor observed. "The more serious a thing is, the more you joke about it."

"Have I made any tasteless jokes about Alexin?"

"No," Alenor conceded. "And you haven't said a word about Dirk, either."

"What's to say?" Jacinta shrugged. "By now I imagine the Lord of the Suns is swinging in the breeze by a very long rope, feeding the ravens through his eye sockets. Unless Kirsh burned him, in which case they might use him for fertilizer."

"There!" Alenor exclaimed. "That's exactly what I mean. You're joking about it."

Jacinta looked back over the street, not willing to meet the young queen's alarmingly perceptive gaze. "It doesn't mean anything, Allie."

"It means you're worried about him. Seriously worried."

"Aren't you?"

"Of course I am, but then he's my cousin and my friend. I didn't realize he meant so much to you."

"Don't be absurd!" she snapped. "I spoke to Dirk Provin only a handful of times the whole time I was in Bollow."

"You like him, though, don't you?"

"It's really rather a moot point what I thought about him," she shrugged. "He's probably dead by now, swinging in the aforementioned breeze."

"There! You're doing it again!"

"Oh, do stop this nonsense, Alenor," she grumbled. "Making snide and rather tasteless remarks about Dirk Provin's execution does not imply that I feel anything for him."

"I never said you felt anything for him. Is there something you're not telling me?"

Jacinta was rescued from this decidedly bizarre and uncomfortable conversation by Tael's return from the docks. She called permission to enter before he'd even finished knocking on the door.

"Did you find a ship that will take us back to Kalarada?" she asked as soon as the captain stepped into the room.

"Yes and no, my lady," he replied. "I can get you and the queen a berth and perhaps a third of the men, but we'll have to find another ship to get the rest of the guard and the horses back to Dhevyn."

"When does this ship sail?"

"Just after first sunrise," Tael told her. "It's a Dhevynian trader. Not the grandest ship afloat, but I thought speed was more important than comfort."

"That's all right," Jacinta assured him. "We don't mind roughing it a bit, do we, your majesty?"

She shook her head, but she wasn't really listening to the question. "Did you hear any other news, Captain?"

"If you mean about Captain Seranov, your majesty, then no, there's not a whisper about him. There's news aplenty about what happened in Bollow, though."

"I can imagine," Jacinta agreed. "Is it anything new, or just the same rumors we've been hearing for days?"

"Mostly the same. The word on the streets is that nothing

much will happen until Prince Kirshov and the Lord of the Suns return to Avacas tomorrow."

"Kirsh didn't waste any time finding a replacement for Dirk, did he?" Alenor said bitterly.

Jacinta stared at her in wonder. "But he can't."

"Can't what?"

"He can't replace the Lord of the Suns. That's Church business and not even the Lion of Senet can interfere in it. If Dirk was executed, that means he didn't die by natural causes and *that* means he can only be replaced by an election."

"The fastest election in the history of the Church by the sound of it," Tael remarked.

"No, you don't understand," she said. "We're not talking about a show of hands by anybody who happens to be in the room, Captain. We're talking every Sundancer and Shadowdancer in Senet. And Dhevyn. And Damita. Even as far away as Galina, if there are any of them there. It's something that takes months to arrange."

"What are you saying, Jacinta?" Alenor asked with a puzzled frown. "That Kirsh has defied Church law?"

"That or he's changed his mind about executing the current Lord of the Suns."

Hope suddenly flared in Alenor's eyes. "Then Dirk is alive?"

"I don't know," Jacinta shrugged. "I guess we won't know until they get here tomorrow."

"Oh, Jacinta! That's wonderful news! But what made Kirsh change his mind?"

"We don't know that he has, Allie," she warned. Jacinta wasn't quite as ready to believe the unbelievable. It was far too dangerous to allow that sort of hope to grow, only to have it dashed again when they learned the truth. "All we have is a rumor we can't substantiate until tomorrow."

"And your ship sails tonight, your majesty," Tael reminded her.

"But we can't leave now," Alenor cried. "Not if Dirk is still alive."

"Whether he's alive or dead, you must get back to

Kalarada, Alenor," Jacinta advised. "Senet is a tinderbox waiting to explode and we are sitting far too close to the kindling. There is no question of you staying in Avacas."

"But..."

"The Lady Jacinta speaks the truth, your majesty," Tael added.

"Then *you* must stay, Jacinta," the queen decreed.

"Kirsh ordered me out of Senet, Alenor. He'll not be too pleased to discover I didn't leave."

"You're not afraid of Kirsh," she scoffed. "Anyway, two-thirds of the guard will still be here until they can find another ship. You can always claim you sent me on ahead because you couldn't find a berth. And if Dirk is alive, I'm certain he won't let you come to any harm."

Jacinta shook her head doubtfully. "I don't know, Allie..."

"I'm not asking your advice, my lady," Alenor told her regally. "I am ordering you, as your queen, to stay here in Avacas and find out if the rumors are true. If they're not, then you can come straight home to Kalarada on the next available ship."

"And if your cousin lives?"

"Then ask Dirk what he needs of us."

"Your majesty..." Tael ventured uncertainly.

"Yes, Captain?"

"There may be another explanation. One a little less palatable, but a tad more believable than the notion Prince Kirshov suddenly changed his mind about the High Priestess Belagren being murdered and simply let the Lord of the Suns go."

"What do you mean?"

"Have you considered the possibility that if Dirk Provin lives, it's because he may have bought his freedom?"

"With what?" Alenor demanded.

"With anything he could use as currency, your majesty," Tael suggested grimly. "Up to and including Dhevyn."

Chapter 70

Dirk gave Kirsh little time to rethink his decision to release him, even though he thought Kirsh optimistic in the extreme to think he could conceal Antonov's current state of mind for long. Already, rumors circulated in Avacas about his behavior after the ceremony and the fact that he hadn't been seen publicly since then merely lent credence to the rumors.

But Kirsh wasn't interested in the long-term consequences of his attempts to preserve his father's reputation. He simply wanted to hold Senet together until Misha could be returned and then leave his brother to deal with the problem. So Dirk stepped in to relieve the prince of as much of the tedious detail involved in managing the crisis as he was able to, with little complaint from Kirshov.

Dirk found plenty of things to keep Kirsh busy. The riot in Bollow had proved one thing Dirk had always suspected: Kirsh was a cool head in a crisis. But when bogged down in the mundane day-to-day tasks of government, he grew morose, moody and difficult. So Dirk set Kirsh to tasks that used his talents best, which left Dirk free to deal with the rest of it.

Trouble flared up frequently in the days following the ceremony. There was trouble in both Tolace and Paislee and another riot in Talenburg—albeit on a much smaller scale than the Bollow riot—in which the Shadowdancers' temple was attacked. Most of the damage, however, came from looters taking advantage of the disturbance. Kirsh had no sooner arrived in Avacas than he was forced to turn around and head back to Talenburg with a sizable force, leaving Dirk to deal with Lord Palinov.

Antonov's chancellor was less than pleased to find himself taking orders from Dirk Provin, even if he was now Lord of the

Suns. Palinov was an oily creature, whom Dirk had never liked much. He did everything he could to undermine Dirk's authority, even though Kirsh had made it patently clear before he left for Talenburg that Dirk spoke with the full authority of the Lion of Senet.

The morning after Kirsh left, Dirk let himself into Antonov's study to meet with the chancellor for another conference that would no doubt turn into a subtle battle of wits between them. He understood Palinov's irritation. Although snide and condescending, the man was a capable bureaucrat and was used to being given a free hand during Antonov's frequent absences from Avacas. In that, Dirk had no quarrel with him. He was only interested in keeping Senet from falling into anarchy. This was the most powerful nation on Ranadon and if it fell, the rest of the world would tumble down behind it like a house of cards. To protect Dhevyn, Dirk had to protect Senet. But right now, he had no more interest in the size of next year's corn harvest than Kirsh did.

He stopped just inside the door for a moment. The second sun was shining brightly, illuminating Antonov's desk and bathing his empty chair in light. It was strange to think he was about to sit in that chair.

"You'll be wanting to read all of these, won't you, my lord?" Lord Palinov announced, pushing through the door behind Dirk. He was followed by two scribes carrying a mountain of documents and several large ledgers. The scribes dumped their load on the desk, sketched a hasty bow and fled the office, leaving Palinov standing there with a faint sneer on his lips.

"What's all this?" Dirk asked.

"Everything requiring the Lion of Senet's attention, my lord," Palinov explained. "He has been away from Avacas for several weeks now, and if, as Prince Kirshov claims, you are authorized to act in his highness's absence, these matters must be dealt with immediately."

"And what have *you* been doing while the Lion of Senet was in Bollow, my lord?" Dirk asked, walking around the desk to stand behind the chair. He couldn't bring himself to sit in it. Not yet.

"I don't understand what you mean, my lord," Palinov replied with a wounded look.

"I mean, Palinov, if this is everything that required the Lion of Senet's attention in the past few weeks, what is it doing here?"

"Waiting for him to return, of course."

Dirk smiled. "You should get out more, Palinov. We have a road between Avacas and Bollow now. And they've discovered it's possible to train pigeons to carry messages."

"My lord is trying to be witty, I think."

"Actually, I'm trying to understand how you've kept your job as long as you have, if this is your idea of efficiency."

Palinov scowled at him. "And your extensive experience makes you an expert in these things, I suppose, my lord?"

"I may not be an expert, Palinov, but I'm pretty good at smelling a rat. I suggest you get your little minions back in here to clear this desk and then come back when you've sorted out what really needs my attention from the rubbish you've dumped here to keep me busy while you do what you please."

Palinov bristled angrily. "I will not be spoken to in such a manner! My position as Chancellor of the Exchequer demands respect."

"Your position might, but you've got a way to go before *you* get any respect from me."

"I cannot believe Prince Antonov agreed to let you act for him in his absence," Palinov snorted. "Even if you are now the Lord of the Suns. I intend to write to him in Omaxin immediately and protest this outrage."

"You do that. In the meantime, get rid of this," he ordered, indicating the mountain of parchment covering the desk.

Palinov stormed out of the room, muttering to himself. Dirk winced as the door slammed behind him. It was probably not a good idea to aggravate the man; he was an influential member of Antonov's court and had it in his power to make life quite difficult for Dirk. But there were some things that had always irritated Dirk about Avacas, and Lord Palinov was one of them.

Dirk looked down at Antonov's chair again, wondering what it would feel like to sit in it. He would find out eventually, he supposed. He couldn't do his job standing behind it until Kirsh got back from Talenburg. But it didn't seem right. He had set out to bring down a religion; to destroy an idea. He had never imagined he'd find himself back in Avacas, effectively ruling Senet.

Neris would have seen the irony, but everyone else would think this was just another part of his evil plan to rule the world. Then he smiled wryly, remembering something Wallin Provin had said to him once: something about reluctant rulers making the best kings, because they put duty before ambition. Dirk's only ambition, if he had one anymore, was simply to survive this time of upheaval so he could finish what he'd started. That was the promise he'd made Neris Veran.

"My lord?"

He looked up as the door opened at the servant who had spoken. He was so lost in thought he hadn't even heard him knock.

"Yes?"

"The Queen of Dhevyn's envoy is demanding an audience, my lord."

"Her envoy?"

"The Lady Jacinta D'Orlon, my lord," the servant explained. "I told her you were busy, but she insists on seeing you immediately. She claims it's a matter of life and death."

"Then you'd better show her in," Dirk ordered, suddenly fearful for Alenor. Had she not been able to get out of Senet? Was that the reason Jacinta was still here after being exiled?

The servant bowed and hurried away, returning a few moments later with Jacinta in his wake. She swept into the room and ordered the man gone before Dirk could utter a word. Then she glanced around the office, taking in the richly gilded furniture and the elegantly carved desk that was almost collapsing under the weight of Palinov's latest attempt to confound him, before turning to him with a curious look.

"Does anybody really believe you are the Lord of the Suns, Dirk Provin?"

The question took him completely by surprise. "Why wouldn't they?"

"Well, for one thing, you don't dress the part. I'm sure you'd have much more success with people like Palinov if you didn't keep rubbing his nose in the fact he's old enough to be your great-grandfather."

"Did Palinov say something to you?"

"He didn't have to," she remarked. "I could hear him cursing you from the other end of the hall. Not that I blame him for being a little peeved. Your fortunes change faster than the tides, my lord. First you're Lord of the Suns, then you're a condemned man, and now here you are, about to take Antonov Latanya's throne."

Dirk self-consciously took his hands from the back of the large gilded chair. "I thought Kirsh banished you, my lady."

"Did he?" she asked ingenuously. "Oh, that's right, in the same breath he accused you of murder and had you arrested, wasn't it?"

"You said it was a matter of life and death."

"I made that up," she said with a shrug, taking the seat opposite the desk.

"Then what are you doing here?"

"Why don't I tell you what I'm doing here right after you tell me what *you're* doing here?"

Too uncomfortable with the idea of sitting in Antonov's seat, Dirk walked around the desk and leaned on the edge of it, crossing his arms.

"There's nothing terribly sinister in it," he explained. "You saw Antonov after the riot. Kirsh released me when it dawned on him he was going to have to take charge until his father recovers." He was relieved he no longer had to keep his own counsel. There was little point in being secretive anymore, and he was confident he didn't need to explain the ramifications of

Antonov's incapacity to Jacinta. She was sharp enough to work it out on her own.

"Will Antonov recover?"

"I have no idea."

She raised an elegant, if somewhat skeptical brow at him. "So Kirsh just forgave you everything and let you go?"

"He let me go, but I don't think forgiveness had anything to do with it. Kirsh is of the opinion it's all my fault, therefore I can take responsibility for cleaning up the mess."

"He thinks it's *your* fault? How perceptive of him."

He smiled. "Why are you really here, my lady?"

"Alenor was worried about you," she told him. "We were expecting to hear the news of your execution. Instead we heard you were riding into Avacas at Kirshov Latanya's side. I'm not sure which she found more disturbing."

"Did she get away safely?"

Jacinta nodded. "A few days ago. She clings to the hope you're still trying to help her."

"What do you think?"

"Does it matter what I think?"

It mattered to Dirk a great deal what Jacinta D'Orlon thought, but he had no idea how to tell her without sounding like a complete idiot.

"If you're going to stay here as Alenor's envoy, then it does," he said, a little uncomfortably.

"Well, seeing as how you put it like that, I suppose I'd better give you the benefit of the doubt," she declared in a businesslike manner, rising to her feet. "You will see to it that I'm not arrested and shipped off to Galina as a body slave when Kirsh learns I'm still in Senet, won't you?"

"Pardon?"

"You just invited me to stay on as Alenor's envoy, didn't you? I can hardly do that if I'm still under order of exile."

"I'll take care of it," he promised.

"In that case, I'll have my things sent to the palace. I am correct in assuming that as the Queen of Dhevyn's envoy, I'm welcome here?"

"Yes," he agreed, a little bemused. "You're welcome here."

"Then I'll see you at dinner?"

"Probably."

Suddenly she smiled at him. "I am glad Kirsh didn't kill you."

"So am I," he agreed feelingly.

She turned for the door, but stopped and looked over her shoulder at him before she opened it. "And Dirk, get another chair for that desk. You'd look just as uncomfortable in Antonov's seat as you did wearing those ridiculous yellow robes."

She was gone before he could answer her, leaving Dirk with the uncomfortable feeling that Jacinta D'Orlon could read his mind.

Chapter 71

By the time Kirsh forced Talenburg under control, the suspicion Antonov Latanya was no longer in command of Senet had taken a firm hold and there was nothing Dirk could do to quell the rumor. His mere presence in Avacas fueled it. There were many Senetians who believed only a madman would have appointed a boy not yet come of age—and a Dhevynian at that—to act for him in his absence.

Kirsh couldn't get back fast enough for Dirk. While he didn't mind dealing with Palinov, the fact that he was dealing with him at all was half the problem. If Kirsh had been here, issuing orders in his father's name, then nobody would have thought anything of it. But the Lord of the Suns was in control and even if Paige Halyn had still held the post, there was a great deal of unrest at the thought Antonov had abdicated too much of his power to the Church.

Only a madman would do that, too.

But there was an even more pressing reason Dirk wanted Kirsh back in Avacas. The news he had just received from Bollow left him with a cold feeling in the pit of his stomach and he read the dispatch from the garrison commander again, wondering if he was missing something. He wasn't. The letter was clear and unequivocal.

Antonov had ordered all of the troops stationed in Bollow to Omaxin. With the troops already there, the escort Kirsh had sent with his father and the soldiers withdrawn from the northern city, Antonov had a force of almost two thousand men. What he wanted with an army that size in the ruins of Omaxin remained a mystery.

Even Palinov was worried by the news and for once had not even hesitated before bringing the letter to Dirk's attention.

"What do you think we should do?" Palinov asked with a frown.

"You're asking *my* advice?" Dirk replied with a raised brow.

"My lord, there are some things above even politics. The Lion of Senet gathering a sizable fighting force in the middle of nowhere for no apparent reason is something we all should be concerned about."

Dirk looked at him curiously. "You believe the rumors he's lost his mind, don't you?"

"I didn't need to hear any rumors to believe that, my lord. The mere fact you are sitting in that chair, apparently with his full support, while he takes a holiday in the wilderness, is living proof the Lion of Senet is no longer in complete control of his faculties."

"He went to Omaxin to speak to the Goddess."

"And apparently the Goddess is now telling him to raise an army."

Dirk had a bad feeling he knew how that happened. He should never have agreed to Marqel going to Omaxin with Antonov. That he couldn't have stopped Kirsh sending her there did little to ease his mind.

"And having raised his army," he mused, "what do you suppose he's planning to do with it?"

"One hopes he's planning to invade Sidoria."

It was an idle hope, Dirk thought. Antonov had no interest

in Sidoria. He could have invaded his northern neighbor at any time he pleased in the last two decades.

"And if he isn't?"

"Then I have a problem, my lord."

"*You* have a problem?"

"I must then decide whose side I'm on. If my prince is raising an army to use against his own people, then I rather think I'd be better off having you arrested."

"And how would that help?"

"If Prince Antonov has decided to take issue with Prince Kirshov's handling of this crisis, then a prudent man would see to it that when his prince returned, he had done everything he could to restore power to the man who rightfully owns it."

"But..." Dirk prompted, guessing Palinov had a few other options in mind.

"But one can't help but wonder about the advisability of siding with a man who turns on his own people at the behest of a Dhevynian whore."

Dirk was stunned by Palinov's words. "Then you don't think Marqel is the Voice of the Goddess?"

"No more than Belagren was." Palinov shrugged. "But I respected Belagren. She rarely interfered in things that didn't concern her. The new High Priestess, however, seems much less...restrained."

Dirk was flabbergasted. "You *knew* Belagren lied about speaking to the Goddess?"

"Lies are the fuel that feed the fires of power, my lord. That's a lesson I would have thought you well versed in."

Dirk was silent for a moment, not sure he believed what he was hearing.

"Are you saying if it came to a choice you'd turn on Antonov?"

"What I'm saying, my lord, is we have come to the end of an era. If I am to continue to serve Senet, the chances seem good it will be in a court ruled by Kirshov Latanya, not his father. I am a pragmatist. Faced with a choice between the man who seems determined to bring order out of chaos and the man who seems determined to start a civil war, I find myself leaning toward the son, rather than the father." Then he frowned and added disapprovingly, "Despite his rather disturbing tendency to rely on you for counsel."

Dirk shook his head with reservation. "You'd support Kirsh over Antonov?"

"I would support sanity over madness. There's a difference."

"Such a position might be misconstrued, my lord."

"Only if the madness wins."

Dirk stared at the chancellor suspiciously. The chance Palinov spoke the truth was about equal with the chance he was deliberately trying to draw Dirk into doing something that could be labeled treason. Dirk's mandate from Kirsh was to hold things together. Palinov was tempting him with something far beyond simple caretaking.

"I gather you have a plan then," he asked carefully, "about how to deal with this situation?"

"No plan, my lord, merely a suggestion."

"Which is?"

"That you recall the troops currently engaged in searching the Dhevynian islands for the Baenlanders who fled Mil. If things…get awkward, we'll need those men here in Senet."

"And how would I explain such an order?"

Palinov smiled. "Don't explain anything; just expect your orders to be obeyed. It's the first rule of kingship."

"I'm not Senet's king, my lord."

"That doesn't seem to have bothered you until now."

Dirk thought about it for a while before cautiously nodding his agreement. "I'll order the troops back," he decided. "But they won't set one foot out of Avacas until Kirsh gets back from Talenburg. I'm not going to start a war with the Lion of Senet when we don't even know what he has in mind. For all I know the Sidorian raiders are getting out of hand in Omaxin and he simply called on the nearest troops to deal with them."

"Are you sure that's the reason?" Palinov asked slyly. "Or

are you just too squeamish to take on Antonov? It is a task that would require a great deal of . . . courage."

Palinov was a fool if he thought he could goad Dirk into doing something rash, simply by casting doubt on his manhood. That sort of tactic might work on Kirsh, but Dirk wasn't trying to be a hero.

"I'm not too squeamish, Palinov, I'm too smart," Dirk informed him flatly. "I didn't come to Avacas to start that sort of trouble. Or be provoked into starting it, either."

"Then why did you come, Dirk Provin? You've done nothing *but* cause trouble from the first day you set foot on the mainland."

"I'm here because I'm the Lord of the Suns and Senet is facing a crisis that requires the full cooperation of both church and state to bring it under control. Above and beyond that, I won't be forced into anything that you can use against me the next time you decide to shift your allegiance."

Palinov didn't look offended. He looked at Dirk with begrudging respect. "You will withdraw the troops from Dhevyn though, won't you?"

"Yes," he agreed. "But I'm placing them under the command of Kirshov Latanya."

"But Prince Kirshov is not here."

"By the time the order reaches Dhevyn and the fleet gets back to Avacas, Kirsh will be back, my lord. And then he can decide if his father's activities warrant punitive action. That's a decision neither you nor I have the right to make."

Palinov nodded in agreement. Dirk couldn't tell if he was surprised or disappointed Dirk refused to be drawn into his plans.

"Then I'll have the orders drawn up and you can sign them, my lord."

"I'll write them," Dirk told him, certain if he left the task in Palinov's hands he would word the order in such a way its meaning could easily be misinterpreted.

Dirk had enough problems. He didn't need to add a charge of treason to them.

Chapter 72

Several days later, Kirsh sent word he would be back in Avacas by the end of the week. Dirk read the message with a vast feeling of relief. He felt balanced on a knife's edge. As the rumors grew about Antonov's insanity, and word spread about the troops he was gathering in the north, the tension in Avacas became unbearable.

Palinov wasn't the only one weighing his options. Every face in the palace seemed to wear a considering look, as if the court were trying to decide where the safest option lay. Was Antonov insane? And if he was, would Kirshov be strong enough to wrest control of Senet from his father? More important, would he even try? Kirsh had a reputation for being a competent military leader, and his actions since the eclipse had done nothing but enhance that reputation. But many doubted he lacked the will to challenge his father. Others doubted he had the support. Ruling Dhevyn as her regent was one thing. Being strong enough to take on the Lion of Senet on Senetian soil, even if he was no longer sane, was a different matter entirely.

And suppose Antonov wasn't insane? Suppose he had good reason to gather an army in Omaxin?

Suppose there was nothing amiss at all?

Antonov's willingness to forgive Dirk Provin the most outrageous sins was well known at court, and it was no secret Kirshov was his favorite son. Everything might be just as it seemed: the Lion of Senet was in Omaxin to seek spiritual guidance from the Goddess and had sent his favorite son and his beloved nephew to Avacas to mind the store in his absence.

But if all was well, why had the troops been recalled from Dhevyn?

The only thing that didn't seem to be the subject of rumor and speculation was the news that Misha was on his way home.

Kirsh and Dirk had privately agreed to say nothing until Misha returned for fear of adding even more grist to the rumor mill. Dirk had heard nothing from Tia and had no idea if she even intended to do as he asked. Nor did he know what state Misha would be in when he got here.

And when he did return? What then? The Crippled Prince had only his position as Antonov's eldest son to back his authority. If the people of Senet were forced to choose between the brothers, Kirsh was by far the more popular prince. That he didn't want the responsibility wasn't the issue.

Dirk could only hope that when Misha arrived he was well enough to cope with the massive load Kirsh intended to dump on him the moment his brother stepped foot in Avacas. And that he had the strength to deal with it. If Antonov really *was* planning something in Omaxin, Dirk wasn't sure Misha would be any more willing to go up against his father than Kirsh was.

Palinov had said nothing further to Dirk about Antonov, seemingly content for now that Dirk had recalled the troops from Dhevyn. With Kirsh due back soon, perhaps that was the end of it.

Dirk doubted it, but then, one could always hope.

Jacinta had asked for another audience, although she didn't claim it was a matter of life and death this time. He had seen her only in passing since their last meeting, despite the fact that she was a guest in the palace. She was always polite, if a little cool, toward him, a fact that he appreciated greatly. After issuing an order to withdraw the Senetian troops from Dhevyn, it would have been unwise to give the impression he and the Queen of Dhevyn's envoy were overly friendly with each other. Not that they *were,* he mused. In fact, he wasn't sure what they were. Not quite conspirators, not quite friends, but more than acquaintances. Dirk sometimes wished Jacinta had gone back to Kalarada with Alenor. Not only would it have been safer for her, but then Dirk would not have to deal with the uncertainty of having her around.

She was waiting for him in Antonov's study when he arrived, standing by the window looking out over the terrace. She was wearing an elegantly cut green silk robe and when she turned to look at him, her eyes seemed to reflect the shade of her dress.

"Good morning, my lord," she said pleasantly. "I hope you don't think me rude for being so early."

"Not at all."

She smiled. "I wanted to speak with you before Palinov got you in his clutches and you're unavailable for the rest of the day."

"He won't be here for a while yet," he assured her, crossing to the window where she stood. "What did you want to see me about?"

"I've had word from Alenor. She says you've ordered the Senetians to call off the search for the Baenlanders." She seemed amused. "It seems Alenor's faith in you was justified. The tone of her letter was rather . . . smug, actually."

"I'd have ordered *every* Senetian in Dhevyn home if I could have," he assured her. "But there are limits to what I can do."

"Not many," she observed wryly. "Alenor asked me to give you something else, too."

"What was that?"

"I believe her exact words were, 'Please tell Dirk I love him and give him a great big kiss for me.'" Jacinta rolled her eyes. "I really need to speak to that girl about the appropriate way to word official correspondence. I can't imagine what historians will think a few years from now if I allow *that* little gem to wind up in the royal archives."

Dirk smiled. "I imagine they'll wonder if you did it."

She eyed him warily. "You don't really expect me to, do you?"

"More to the point: does Alenor expect it of you?" he suggested, moving a little closer. "She is your queen, you know. I'm sure it would be treason if you defied her."

"I've delivered Alenor's message," Jacinta pointed out rather stiffly, "and I'm quite certain you appreciate her sentiments without me having to provide a physical demonstration of her gratitude."

Dirk sighed. "Then please convey my regards to your queen," he said formally, disappointed to discover Jacinta did not intend to carry out Alenor's instructions. "And tell her I'm doing what I can to help Dhevyn."

"She knows that."

Jacinta was far too close for comfort, particularly with all this talk of gratitude and kisses. He could smell the faint scent of the jasmine-perfumed soap she used to wash her hair. She was so close he could see his own reflection in those strange, color-shifting eyes. He took a step backward, afraid that if he didn't, he would do something fatally stupid.

She smiled knowingly, as if she knew what he was thinking. Or worse, what he was feeling.

"Of course, now that I've expressed Alenor's appreciation, I suppose I should add my personal gratitude to you for ridding Dhevyn of a couple of thousand Senetian troops."

Dirk stared at her in surprise, wondering if he had misread her meaning. Hope suddenly warred with despair inside him. One false move and this could quickly change from one of the most pivotal moments in his life to one of the most embarrassing.

Jacinta sensed his uncertainty and seemed amused by it. She moved a little closer, leaving Dirk in no doubt about her intentions.

"Palinov's due any moment..."

"He'll knock," Jacinta said with a smile and then she kissed him lightly, barely brushed his lips with hers.

That was her idea of gratitude? Dirk thought he would die from the torment. The look in her eyes didn't speak of chaste and grateful kisses. Her eyes spoke of wild abandon, of shredded clothes and sweaty bodies and damning the consequences. Dirk wanted to pull her into his arms and kiss her hard. He wanted to forget for a time he was the Lord of the Suns and she was the Queen of Dhevyn's envoy and that they were standing in the Lion of Senet's study, likely to be disturbed at any moment by the Chancellor of the Exchequer.

Jacinta stepped away from him, as if she had read his thoughts.

"That's more than enough...*gratitude*...for one day," she said.

"I'm sorry."

"For what, exactly?" she asked, daring him to confess his thoughts.

Dirk felt his face warming and was certain he was blushing like a fool. He couldn't think of anything to say that wouldn't make matters worse.

"I think I should leave now."

"That's probably a good idea," he agreed raggedly. His position was far too fragile to endanger it by risking a liaison with any woman, let alone the Queen of Dhevyn's envoy. And he suspected Jacinta's life wouldn't be worth living if her mother caught so much as a whiff of scandal. *But I'm willing to take the risk,* he wanted to say to her. *If you are.* The words remained unspoken. He'd come too far to endanger everything for something so foolish and self-indulgent. To put some distance between them he stepped away from her and sat in Antonov's chair behind the desk.

"Perhaps you should go before Lord Palinov gets here."

She nodded, a little sadly. "I should, I suppose..." There was a wealth of unspoken feeling in her words.

"I'm sorry, my lady."

"What have you done this time, Dirk?"

They both turned and stared at the man who had spoken. Dirk blinked in shock as a tall, dark-haired man limped into the room with Tia Veran at his side.

It took both of them a moment or two to realize it was Misha Latanya.

PART FIVE

THE CRIPPLED PRINCE

Chapter 73

Misha had spent a lot of time trying to imagine what his return to Avacas would be like. Months in Garwenfield, particularly after Tia left, gave him more time than he cared for to dwell on the possibilities. Mostly, his conjecture involved confronting his father and seeing the look of stunned surprise on the Lion of Senet's face when his son returned, hearty and whole. He had imagined the look of awe on Antonov's face. Imagined—or rather hoped—his father would be...what? Pleased? Relieved? Misha had never been able to decide about that.

But one thing was certain. He had not expected to find Dirk Provin sitting in his father's chair.

"Misha!"

"You sound surprised, Dirk. Tia said you were expecting me."

Is he really glad I'm back? Or is he faking it? Misha wondered, studying Dirk closely. He looked a little too comfortable in Antonov's chair for Misha's liking. Unfortunately, he was no better at reading Dirk than anybody else. Misha knew Dirk had released Tia with the specific intention of bringing him back to Senet, but was it because he genuinely wanted Misha home? Or did he have some other devious plan in mind, as Tia suspected?

"I'm delighted to see you...but...I expected some warning. Goddess! Look at you! You're so..."

"What? Upright? Coherent?"

"What...*what* happened to you?"

"It's a long story."

Before he could elaborate, the door opened again and Lord Palinov bustled into the study. He glanced at Misha and Tia, pushed past them without a second glance and stopped before Dirk impatiently. "My lord, we have a lot to do this morning. Perhaps you could socialize with Lady Jacinta and her friends at a more appropriate time?"

Dirk glanced over at Misha before he replied. "I'm not sure there is a more appropriate time, Palinov."

"There is a great deal to be done before the prince returns, my lord."

"The prince *has* returned, my lord, although not the one you were hoping for, I suspect."

"My lord?" Palinov asked in confusion.

Dirk said nothing. Neither did Misha. He waited until Palinov thought to glance over his shoulder again.

Misha was delighted to see the old man suddenly go pale.

"Goddess! Prince *Misha*? Your highness! But...but this can't be! You're...well, you're dead!"

"I realize it's probably something of a disappointment to you, Palinov, but as you can see, I am clearly *not* dead." He turned to Dirk and added without rancor, "Get out of that chair, Dirk. You don't belong there any longer."

The Lord of the Suns didn't even hesitate before vacating Antonov's chair and surrendering it to him. "I never belonged in it, Misha."

Tia snorted skeptically, but Misha smiled with relief. In those few words Dirk had told him all he wanted to know about how far his cousin could be trusted.

Misha limped across the study and took the seat, glad of the chance to sit down. He was trembling, but it was excitement rather than pain making him shake. Tia had apprised him of what she knew about the situation in Senet on the journey back from Damita, but there was a great deal more to be learned, and until he knew what was going on, he could do little but look commanding and sound confident.

"Palinov."

"Er...yes, your highness?"

"This is the Lady Tia Veran."

"The heretic's daughter?"

"My *friend*," he corrected sternly. "You will see to it she is treated as an honored guest. If she has any complaints, I will hold you personally responsible."

"Of...of course, your highness."

Misha turned to the girl Dirk had been apologizing to when he came in. She was a slender, stunning girl with thick dark hair and eyes that seemed to be a different color every time he looked at her. "My sudden appearance seems to have robbed everybody of their manners, my lady. You are?"

"This is Jacinta D'Orlon, your highness," Palinov hastily answered for her. "The Queen of Dhevyn's envoy."

"Alenor's cousin?" he asked curiously. He'd heard about her.

"That's correct, your highness," she confirmed with a regal curtsy. "My father is the Duke of Bryton."

"Aren't you the one who caused Birkoff so much grief?"

She smiled faintly. "I refused his offer of marriage, sire. I'm not sure he grieved over the insult so much as the loss of my dowry."

Misha took an instant liking to the young woman. He was curious about why Dirk was apologizing to her, though. He had a feeling it wasn't over a matter of state.

"Might I impose upon you to aid Lady Tia in getting settled into the palace, my lady?"

"It would be my honor, your highness."

"Palinov, please see that Lady Tia is given a suite on the fourth floor. And then report back to me in an hour. I want to know exactly what's going on, and I expect you to have all the answers when I see you next."

Palinov was too stunned to object. He bowed and backed out of the room, followed by Tia and Jacinta. Tia spared a faint smile for Misha and a suspicious glare for Dirk before she followed them out into the hall.

"*Lady* Tia?" Dirk asked with a slightly raised brow.

"She's as much right to the title as anyone. Her mother was highborn."

Dirk nodded and said nothing further on the subject. Misha wondered if he was going to have a long talk to Dirk about Tia at some point. One of those "hands off, she's mine" type discussions. But now was not the time.

"Lock the door," Misha ordered Dirk. "I want a few

moments of peace before the news gets out the Crippled Prince is back."

Dirk did as he asked and then came back to the desk, taking the seat opposite him. He shook his head in wonder. "You don't look much like the Crippled Prince I remember, Misha. I haven't seen you looking so well since the first time we met on Elcast. What happened to you?"

"I discovered life without poppy-dust."

"Poppy-dust?"

"Apparently it was the main ingredient in Ella Geon's tonic. You were planning to be a physician once, Dirk. Look it up sometime. I had all the symptoms. But nobody expects the Lion of Senet's son to be an addict, do they? So who would know?"

Dirk was flabbergasted. "She was *drugging* you? Why?"

"She was killing me. As to the reason, Tia speculates it was all part of some grand plan of Belagren's to place Kirsh on the throne when my father died. Where is Ella, by the way?"

"She's back at the Hall of Shadows. I sent all the Shadow-dancers back there under house arrest until I can formally disband them."

"Then I am making an official request of you as Lord of the Suns to have her handed over to me for trial. I want that pitiful excuse for a physician, Yuri Daranski, and Madalan Tirov, too. They had to be in on it."

"Consider it done."

It wasn't until that moment it dawned on Misha how much he could achieve with Dirk as Lord of the Suns. Paige Halyn had been afraid of his own shadow. Dirk was *Lord* of the Shadows and, more important, Lord of the Suns. He had proved himself afraid of nothing. Misha was glad his instincts about Dirk were correct, even if Tia still nursed a core of distrust she would probably never be able to totally let go.

"Where's Kirsh?"

"In Talenburg. We're expecting him back tomorrow. *He's* going to be very glad to see you alive and well."

"He left you in charge?" Misha smiled. "That must be driving Palinov to distraction. And my father?"

"He's in Omaxin. With the High Priestess." Dirk hesitated for a moment and then added, "And an army."

"What does he need an army for?"

"That's the question we've all been asking ourselves, Misha."

"Tia says he was...rather disturbed...after your dramatic denunciation of the High Priestess."

"That's putting it mildly."

Misha was silent, waiting for Dirk to elaborate.

"He appears to have completely lost his mind," Dirk admitted uncomfortably.

"You've been a busy lad while I was away, haven't you?" Misha remarked with a frown. "And don't think I don't appreciate the fact that you've brought down the people who were trying to kill me. But I don't suppose you could have found a way to put an end to the Shadowdancers without destroying my father in the process?"

"The two are inextricably linked, Misha. The Shadowdancers drew their strength from Antonov. If the Lion of Senet had not embraced their cult, Belagren would never have been more than a Sundancer with good family connections. I couldn't destroy one without affecting the other."

Dirk spoke the truth, although it was an unpleasant fact to acknowledge. "Did you kill Belagren?"

He shook his head. "Marqel did."

"Someday, when we have the time, I'd really like you to explain to me what possessed you to involve that devious little bitch in all this. Do you know she even tried it on with me, once?"

"Really? What did you do?"

"Fortunately, I was too sick to do anything. But she really does like to keep her options open, doesn't she?"

"Trust me," Dirk replied heavily. "If I regret anything I've done, it was giving Marqel a taste of power."

"And she's with my father now, you say?"

"Kirsh sent her to Omaxin with him," he confirmed. "I think he was afraid I was going to do something to her. With the Shadowdancers currently the target of a great deal of rage, he figured it was the safest place for her."

Misha rolled his eyes. "He's not *still* infatuated with her, is he?"

"As much as he ever was."

"But if she was High Priestess," he said thoughtfully, "doesn't that mean she and my father..."

Dirk shrugged. "Kirsh is apparently willing to forgive Marqel anything. Including that."

"I will never understand my brother," he sighed, shaking his head. "From the moment he first laid eyes on that thief on Elcast, he's been a complete fool about her."

"That foolishness may end up causing you a civil war, Misha. If Marqel is in Antonov's ear—and it's pretty much a given that she is—then I've a good idea why he's gathering an army in Omaxin."

"He'll want to set things to rights," Misha concluded. "He'd probably feel the need to do that even if he wasn't insane."

"Kirsh says Antonov told him the eclipse never happened as some sort of test of his faith."

"That's understandable," Misha conceded. "My father believes he is a pious man. He thinks killing my baby brother, Gunta, brought back the Age of Light. To admit he was wrong would make him a murderer and a fool. Which brings me to another question. I can guess how you managed most of this, but how the hell did you stop those pyres from burning?"

"Didn't Tia tell you?"

"She said something about some cleaning fluid."

"Sinkbore," Dirk confirmed. "It's a natural flame retardant. Just between you and me, I wasn't really sure it would work."

"You risked Tia's life on a guess?"

"It worked."

"Lucky for Tia it did," he warned with a scowl.

"I'm not sure your father, or Baston of Damita, thinks

much of what happened that day was lucky, though. Did Tia tell you about Baston being killed?"

"I was there when Oscon got the news he'd been reinstated."

Dirk was genuinely surprised. "You were in Garwenfield with Oscon? No wonder they couldn't find you."

"Fortunate for me they didn't. I owe my life to Tia. And to Master Helgin and Mellie, too."

"How is Mellie?"

"You can ask her yourself later."

Dirk's eyes clouded with concern. "You brought Mellie to Avacas? Was that wise?"

"Probably not, but given the urgency of our departure from Garwenfield, there wasn't time for a detour to drop her off somewhere safer."

"Goddess, that means Alexin is with you, too, doesn't it? You'd better keep him out of Kirsh's sight."

"Don't worry," Misha assured him. "I intend to put them both on a ship for Kalarada on the next tide. They'll be gone before Kirsh gets back."

"And then what are you going to do?"

"I'd rather know what *you're* planning to do, Dirk," he replied. "You've orchestrated this rather grandiose symphony of disasters up until now. Is there anything else on your program I should know about? Another eclipse? A volcano? A devastating earthquake, perhaps? The next Age of Shadows isn't going to appear tomorrow, is it?"

Dirk smiled. "No. I can pretty much guarantee you don't have to worry about that."

Misha glanced around his father's study for a moment and then frowned. "You know, I used to lie awake at night in Oscon's house, imagining what it would be like to come home. I've been here less than an hour, and already nothing is as I envisaged it."

"Well, I can't speak for anyone else, but *I'm* glad you're back, Misha. And relieved beyond words you're well. And I know Kirsh has been counting the minutes until you returned." Dirk sounded sincere, but this was the man who had convinced the world there was an eclipse coming. It was impossible to tell if he was genuine or if he was lying through his teeth.

"Then that makes three of us who are pleased to see the Crippled Prince," he said, deciding to accept for the moment Dirk meant what he said. "When the count gets into double figures, let me know. Then I might start to feel like I'm welcome."

Chapter 74

Marqel took it upon herself to care for the Lion of Senet with a level of dedication that astonished everyone. She would let nobody near him. She would let nobody speak to him. By the time they reached Omaxin, she had everyone in his entourage so accustomed to going through her to communicate with him that she could have ordered them to all stand on their heads and they would have believed the order came from Antonov.

In private, Antonov drove her to distraction. He was obsessed with the notion that the nonexistent eclipse and the refusal of her sacrifice were all staged by the Goddess to test his faith. He refused to allow the idea he might have been mistaken to take root in his mind. He questioned her about it constantly, seeking the Goddess's reassurance, more determined than ever to believe Marqel was her spokeswoman. He wanted to be certain he'd read the Goddess's intentions correctly.

For Marqel, Antonov's insanity was fertile ground, into which she was able to plant the seeds of her own ambitions. She was the Voice of the Goddess, and Antonov's only alternative to believing every word she uttered was to contemplate the possibility he had lived his entire life believing in a lie. He had sacrificed his son to the Goddess and believed he had done the right thing. To even suspect his sacrifice had been needless was something he would not allow.

The ruined city came into view some three weeks after

they left Bollow. The trip had been torturously slow, mostly because Antonov insisted they stop each sunrise to offer thanks to the Goddess. Marqel didn't mind. The longer they took to get there, the longer she had to poison his mind, to feed his fears and doubts. Marqel had learned a great deal from watching Dirk Provin at work. If he could bring the Shadowdancers to their knees, then she could go one better.

If she was clever about it, she could remove the irritation of Dirk Provin. Permanently.

When they arrived at the ruins, she was surprised by the number of people already there. Marqel had forgotten about the troops Antonov had sent to Omaxin to deal with the Sidorian raiders. Between them and the large escort Kirsh had sent with them, she had the beginnings of a small army, which gave Marqel an even grander idea than simply convincing Antonov she was invincible.

Antonov couldn't wait to get into the cavern. It was almost as if he expected to hear the voice of the Goddess for himself. The massive chamber was lit with countless torches when they arrived, glittering off the creamy ignimbrite walls. The Shadowdancers who were studiously copying down the inscriptions and diagrams on the walls all jumped to their feet when the Lion of Senet entered the chamber.

Antonov stopped just inside the entrance, awestruck by the size and magnificence of the hall. She had forgotten Antonov had never seen it before. The look on his face was almost comical, he was so enthralled. Marqel couldn't see the point in getting worked up over a big empty hall. It was just another building, really, even if it was rather impressive.

"Your highness!" Rudi Kalenkov gasped when he realized who his visitor was. Then he glanced at Marqel and frowned. "My lady."

"His highness would like to be alone with the Goddess," Marqel announced. She didn't want Rudi explaining anything to Antonov. Didn't want anyone speaking to him if she could avoid it. Particularly not another Shadowdancer and certainly not one who could claim to be an expert on the Omaxin ruins.

"Of course," Rudi said, snapping his fingers at his people to hasten their departure. "I'd be more than happy to stay and show—"

"That won't be necessary," Marqel cut in.

Rudi scowled at her and then bowed in acquiescence. He knew she was now the High Priestess, but Marqel didn't know how much he had learned about what had happened in Bollow. She wouldn't have trusted him in any case. Rudi was one of Belagren's old cronies, a scholar, not a priest. He probably knew as well as Dirk Provin that what he and his workers were so assiduously copying down was not the words of the Goddess but the writings of some ancient civilization long ago destroyed by Mount Probeus.

"As you wish, my lady."

Once they were alone, Marqel took Antonov by the hand and led him to the center of the hall. The thick golden Eye glittered malignantly in the torchlight, as if the Goddess herself was staring at them.

"I can feel her," Antonov whispered in awe.

Marqel couldn't feel the Goddess. Mostly, Marqel felt cold, and even a little oppressed by the idea there was half a mountain hanging over their heads.

"So can I," she agreed piously.

Antonov walked closer to one of the walls to study the strange inscriptions. He stared at them in silence.

"I hope Dirk gets here soon," he said after a time.

Marqel scowled at his back. "Why?"

"Because only he can read the Goddess's writings."

The hell he can! she sneered silently. *He was just pretending he could to shut Kirsh up when he . . .*

She didn't even finish the thought before stepping forward and tracing her finger over a line of incomprehensible squiggles. "Listen to me. Gather all those who believe in me and celebrate my . . . gifts."

Antonov looked at her in amazement. "You can *understand* this . . . Why didn't you tell me this sooner?"

"I was never allowed in here before long enough to see the writing," she lied.

"Not even Belagren was able to tell what was written here."

"Perhaps the Goddess had other plans for the Lady Belagren, your highness. She gives us only those tools we need to serve her."

"Of course..." Antonov agreed absently, still staring at the walls in wonder.

"So I can tell you whatever you want to know," she pointed out, a little impatiently. "You don't need Dirk."

"Is there anything here about what happened in Bollow?" he asked anxiously. "About her test?"

Goddess! Doesn't he think of anything else? "I won't know what the inscriptions say until I've had time to study them further, your highness." She smiled at him with touching concern. "Why don't you go back to your tent for tonight and then tomorrow we can have a good look around?"

"No. I want to stay awhile. I want to pray."

Oh, for pity's sake! Don't you ever get sick of praying?

"Of course. Did you want me to stay with you?"

"Don't *you* need to pray?" he asked, a little concerned.

Idiot, Marqel scolded herself. *You're supposed to believe this shit even more than he does.* "The Goddess is with me wherever I go, your highness," she replied, hoping that was enough to cover her error.

"Of course," he agreed, as if he should have known such a thing without asking her. "Will you see I'm not disturbed?"

"Take as long as you like," she said understandingly, while silently cursing him under her breath.

Antonov walked back to the middle of the hall, falling to his knees in the very center of the golden eye etched into the floor. He bowed his head and began to mutter under his breath, begging the Goddess to forgive his doubts.

Marqel watched him for a while and then quietly left the cavern, issuing orders to the guards outside on the way out that the Lion of Senet was not to be disturbed. She walked back out through the torchlit tunnel into the red sunlight, looked around the busy camp as she emerged and smiled with a deep sense of satisfaction.

It wouldn't take much, she knew, to convince Antonov the Goddess expected him to right the wrongs of this world. And now he believed she could read the writing in the cavern; how hard could it be to think up some dire prophecy foretelling the failure of the eclipse and those damned fires going out? If she thought about this, she could even work in the death of Belagren and Paige Halyn. Something along the lines of the "Mother and Father of the Suns being taken and replaced by the true daughter and the false son ..."

That would be the best part. The part where her false prophecy declared Dirk Provin an evil tyrant, bent on distorting Antonov's faith and destroying all his beloved Belagren's hard work. If she put her mind to it, there was no end to the prophecies she could supposedly translate. Since meeting Eryk in Nova more than a year ago, she'd known about a young girl in Mil named Mellie Thorn, too; a small, hugely valuable fact she'd kept to herself against the day the information might be useful. She could reveal it now and nobody could prove she'd gotten the information from any other source than the Goddess. Dirk's demise was all but guaranteed. She would make up something that foretold the Shadow Slayer rising up to rid the world of him ...

And then, when Antonov had served his purpose, she could dispose of him. Kirsh would become the Lion of Senet and now that he was divorcing Alenor, he would be free to marry Marqel.

The future looked brighter than the second sun.

She sighed with satisfaction and decided to get something to eat before she went back to her tent. It was going to be a long night and she had a lot of work to do before the second sunrise.

Chapter 75

Kirsh arrived back in Avacas, stiff, weary, dirty and fed up with civil disturbances. There was no honor to be found facing a mob. No glory in beating back a rampaging crowd bent on destroying something that had, until very recently, been sacred to them. Kirsh didn't waste much time wondering why they were rioting. If he thought about it at all, he reasoned it was because since the end of the Age of Shadows, the people of Senet had lived according to the edicts of the Shadowdancers. That included the Landfall Festival and everything that went along with it. But when the foundation for their beliefs had been proved doubtful, the pious self-righteousness with which they had participated turned to shame, and that shame very quickly turned to anger. Kirsh despised what Dirk had done, while at the same time he begrudgingly admired the skill with which he'd done it.

Had Kirsh been in Dirk's place, with his ambitions, he would have raised an army and tackled the problem head on. Just as Johan Thorn had done. And probably have been just as unsuccessful, he realized. That didn't justify what Dirk had set in motion, but he thought he understood why.

What he couldn't understand is how anybody could conceive of such a plan and then have the balls to carry it through.

He was met at the palace entrance by the usual bevy of servants come to attend his every need. He shook them off impatiently, tired from the long ride from Talenburg and in no mood for any of them. "Where is Lord Provin?"

"In your father's private sitting room, I believe, your highness. He's with Prince Misha."

"*Misha's* here?"

He didn't even wait for the man to answer. Kirsh ran down the hall, skidding to a halt on the polished tiles, before bursting

into the room. He stopped dead when he saw his brother. Dirk
was seated in a chair by the unlit fireplace. Misha stood beside it,
leaning on the mantel, nursing a half-empty wineglass.

He was *standing*.

"Ah! Our hero returns from the battlefield!" Misha exclaimed.

Kirsh crossed the room in three paces and crushed his
brother in a bruising hug before holding him at arm's length
and studying him closely.

"You're alive!"

Misha smiled. "So everybody keeps reminding me."

"Goddess! I can't believe it! You look so...so *well*! And
you're walking again! When you were kidnapped, we feared
the worst."

"I wasn't kidnapped, Kirsh."

He let his brother go, and stared at him in confusion. All
his earlier doubts about Misha and the news that he was a
poppy-dust addict, all those unpleasant details he'd learned in
Tolace—that he'd killed people to conceal—suddenly rushed
back to haunt him.

"What do you mean, you *weren't* kidnapped?"

"You'd better sit down, Kirsh," Dirk suggested. "Misha's
got quite a tale to tell and I don't think you're going to like it
very much."

"You knew where he was all along, didn't you," he accused.

"Tia knew. I sent her to fetch him the day of the eclipse."

"When I get my hands on that bitch—" Kirsh sputtered
angrily.

"You will thank her profusely, Kirsh," Misha cut in sternly.
"I wouldn't be alive if it wasn't for Tia Veran. She deserves your
gratitude, not your anger."

"Sit down, Kirsh," Dirk repeated. "You need to hear the
whole sorry saga before you start lopping heads off."

"I need a drink," he growled.

"I'll get it," Dirk offered. "You sit down and listen to
Misha."

Kirsh took the seat opposite Dirk and looked up at his

brother. He was still stunned by the change in him. It was almost as if he were a different person; as if Tia Veran had stolen away his brother and replaced him with a newer, better version of the same man.

"I met up with Tia in the Hospice in Tolace," Misha explained.

"I know. She was hiding there after she escaped from us on the way back from Omaxin."

"Escaped?" Misha asked curiously. "Dirk says he asked you to let her go."

Kirsh glared at Dirk. "How many other people have you told?"

"Only Misha. I told Tia, but she didn't believe me." He handed Kirsh a glass of wine, along with the decanter, to save him asking for a refill.

"Dirk and I have talked a great deal in the last day. We have few secrets left, Kirsh. We can't afford them anymore."

Kirsh downed the wine in a swallow and looked back at Misha. "I heard some disturbing things about you in Tolace."

"That I was a poppy-dust addict?" Misha asked, unsurprised. "Well, if you were shocked, brother, imagine how I felt when I learned the truth."

"They said you asked for it. Why would you do that if you didn't know you were an addict?"

"You need to listen to the whole story, Kirsh."

By the time Misha had finished relating his tale of his meeting with Tia, of learning he was an addict and asking her for help, of his trip to Mil and his subsequent flight to Damita, where he was finally able to get free of the drug, Kirsh had finished the decanter.

The implications of Misha's tale were horrific. If he believed his brother—and he could think of no reason why Misha would lie—then the Shadowdancers had systematically poisoned him, hoping to kill Misha and clear the way for Kirsh to inherit his father's seat.

Whether Antonov had known what was going on was something not even Misha was willing to speculate on. What *was* certain was Misha's support of the terrible thing Dirk had done to bring the Shadowdancers down. Kirsh had reluctantly released Dirk because he needed his help. Misha obviously thought him a hero.

"With all this talk of plots and intrigue, you sound like a heretic, Misha," Kirsh accused when his brother was done. "All those months among the Baenlanders have turned you from the Goddess."

"Several months of agonizing withdrawal from poppy-dust turned me from the Goddess, Kirsh. And I didn't suffer through that just to come back here and thank the Shadow-dancers for all they've done for me. I came back to expose them. Dirk beat me to it."

"And what about Antonov?" he asked. "Dirk's little game has all but destroyed him."

"Do you think if I'd walked into Avacas like this and told him about the plot to poison me that he wouldn't have had his faith shaken just as savagely?"

Kirsh wasn't able to answer that. He turned on Dirk, who said nothing the whole time Misha was speaking. "Did you know about this?"

"None of it," Dirk replied. "Although I wasn't as shocked as you are. I knew what the Shadowdancers were capable of."

"And now I suppose you're determined to put an end to them, too?"

"More determined than Dirk, probably."

"We have to tell Antonov. Insane or not, none of us is the Lion of Senet. If he wants to destroy the Shadowdancers for what they did to you, Misha, then it has to be his decision."

"It's a decision he's not capable of making, Kirsh," Dirk warned.

"Nevertheless, he's the one who must make it."

"I fear the decision is already made in our father's mind," Misha said. "He's gathering an army in Omaxin. If the High Priestess has his ear, you can bet he's not doing it to disband the Shadowdancers."

"What army?" Kirsh scoffed.

"He's called all the troops in Bollow north to Omaxin," Dirk explained. "He's got nearly two thousand men up there."

"And has anybody thought to ask him why? Or is it just easier to sit here and place your own interpretation on events? One that suits what you believe?"

"We've sent countless messages to Omaxin," Dirk assured him. "He's replied to none of them."

"And does he know yet that you're back, Misha?"

His brother shook his head. "I've only been back a day. We thought to wait until you came home before deciding how to break the news to him."

"It's not the sort of thing you scribble down in a message," Dirk added. "And we have no way of making certain the news actually reaches him. It could easily be intercepted by . . . some-one else."

Kirsh scowled at him. "Intercepted by Marqel is what you really mean."

"That's your conclusion, Kirsh, not mine."

"We're not going to start arguing about it, either," Misha ordered impatiently. "I think the only way to handle this is for one of us to go to Omaxin and speak with Antonov in person. There is no possible way to make him believe this any other way."

"I'll go," Dirk volunteered. "Now that you're back, Misha, I'm probably better off out of Avacas anyway. Antonov will be-lieve me."

"Just as he'll believe you when you demand Marqel be held accountable for the actions of her predecessors?" Kirsh asked bitterly.

"I'd be happy if Marqel was called to account for what *she's* done recently," Dirk retorted. "Never mind what her predeces-sors got up to."

"Enough!" Misha snapped at them. "The three of us are all that stands between Senet and anarchy at the moment. I've nei-ther the time nor the patience for your bickering."

"I'll go to Omaxin," Kirsh said, a little surprised at Misha's commanding tone. "I'll tell Antonov what's happened. And I'll find out what he plans to do with his army."

Misha glanced at Dirk, who shook his head. "I don't think that's a good idea."

"Why not?" Kirsh asked. "Do you think I can't explain what's happened as well as you or Misha?"

"I'm more concerned about your...bias on the matter, Kirsh," Dirk replied.

"You think *I'm* biased? As opposed to what, Dirk? *Your* patently objective stance? This from the man who thinks the Shadowdancers ruined his life? Yes, I can see how *your* bias would be so much less than mine."

"At least I won't confuse the facts with what I feel for Marqel."

"I beg to differ, Dirk. Your whole sick little scheme is influenced by what you feel for Marqel. The difference is that I don't hate her."

"No, you think you're in love with her, which is likely to be far more damaging. It's blinded you to—"

"Enough!" Misha commanded again, halting the argument with a word. "If Kirsh wants to go, then he can. Anyway, Dirk, I need you here."

"But Misha..."

"That is my decision, Dirk. Kirsh will go north to Omaxin."

"And the minute Marqel opens her mouth—or her legs—Kirsh is going to start rationalizing away the whole thing and before you know it, he'll start believing the reason the Shadowdancers poisoned you was for the good of mankind, and how dare we do anything to question the will of the Goddess."

"You smart-mouthed little bastard..." Kirsh began, lunging out of his chair at Dirk. Misha hurriedly stepped between them and shoved his brother backward into his seat. Kirsh fell back and stayed there. He looked stunned. Never, in all his life, had Misha attempted to best him physically. And won.

"For the Goddess's sake, stop acting like children!" Misha

ordered. "Both of you! I don't care if Dirk's insulted your precious Shadowdancers, Kirsh. He has a point. You're going to have to be on your guard."

"Marqel was not responsible for poisoning you, Misha. That was Belagren and Ella."

"Even so, she's not going to appreciate you telling Antonov the truth."

"Then why let him go?" Dirk asked.

"Because you've done enough, Dirk!" Misha said, turning to look at him. "You've brought Senet to the brink of ruin and you're working to your own agenda. It's no longer up to you. This is a family matter now and it's up to Kirsh and me to see it through. Besides, you're the Lord of the Suns. There's way too much to be cleaned up here in Avacas for me to let you go north and get embroiled in that particular fiasco." Without giving Dirk a chance to argue, he turned back to his brother. "You must leave first thing in the morning. We can't risk the news finding its way to Omaxin before you've had a chance to explain it to Antonov. Once you've found out what's happening up there, we can decide how to proceed next."

"None of this is Marqel's fault, Misha."

"I never said it was."

"Just so long as you understand that," he said. "I'm not defending what's been done to you, or suggesting it was motivated by anything other than greed. But you can't destroy innocents in your quest for vengeance."

"Pity you didn't take such a noble stance in Tolace," Dirk remarked sourly.

Kirsh turned on Dirk angrily. "I've spent just about every waking moment since your eclipse never happened beating back unarmed innocents with swords and cavalry charges, Dirk! Don't you dare sit there looking blameless and talk to me about hurting innocents."

"There *are* no innocents, Kirsh. Those people you've been riding down in the streets of Bollow and Talenburg are the same people who merrily fronted up to Landfall every year. The same ones who cheered and shouted while someone burned alive. The same people who willingly took the Milk of the Goddess so they could do things at the Landfall orgy that any other day of the year they would be ashamed to admit they were capable of."

"You keep telling yourself that, Dirk," Kirsh sneered. "I suppose that way you can live with what *you've* done."

"I can live just fine with what I've done, Kirsh," Dirk told him. "Because what I *did* was do something about putting an end to it."

Chapter 76

Eryk was at something of a loose end once Dirk left in such a hurry for Avacas, and in the weeks that followed he fretted constantly, fearful something might happen to change Kirsh's mind again. Caterina told him not to worry about it, but Eryk couldn't help himself. He had little in the way of duties with Dirk gone, and that left him plenty of time to imagine all sorts of dreadful things that might happen to his master. He didn't understand what was going on, but then hardly anybody seemed to know. The uncertainty of the people around him did little to ease his concern.

The Lord of the Suns' palace was still full of strangers. Lord Rees hadn't left yet, because Lady Faralan was so close to having her baby he feared the journey home to Elcast might precipitate the birth. Eryk had always liked Faralan, but she was obviously unhappy. He thought it must be because she was so uncomfortable, but he'd overheard her arguing with Lord Rees on several occasions. He didn't know what the fights were about, although Dirk's name had been mentioned once. All Eryk knew was their raised voices had been filled with anger and bitterness. It never used to be like that. Back on Elcast, when Faralan came to visit each year, she had been a happy, gentle soul and Lord Rees had really cared for her. Now they were separated by a gulf of hostility. Maybe things would get better once the baby was born. Until then, Eryk resolved to stay out of Rees's way.

Claudio Varell eventually got fed up with Eryk moping around the palace and sent him to work in the kennels. Eryk liked the dogs and the handlers treated him with a degree of deference he was unused to. In the palace of the Lord of the Suns, Dirk Provin wasn't despised the way he had been in Mil after he left the pirates and went back to Avacas. Here in Bollow, among the Sundancers at least, Dirk was revered as the man who had exposed the Shadowdancers (although exactly *what* he'd exposed was beyond Eryk's comprehension) and they treated his loyal servant accordingly.

Nikolai, the kennel master, let him help care for an orphaned litter of puppies being hand-raised in the kennels. Eryk got to feed them and pet them and talk to them. But he was still lonely and feeling more than a little bit lost. He was in a strange country, surrounded by foreigners and not certain from one day to the next how his future would unfold. Eryk was never good at dealing with uncertainty so he spent a lot of time sitting on the floor of the kennels amid the pungent smell of the dogs, talking through his troubles with the puppies, who listened to him without complaint and nudged him affectionately whenever he seemed to need reassurance.

Caterina found him there, several weeks after Dirk left Bollow, explaining to a small speckled puppy about how things were always going wrong, ever since the mess he'd made of things with Mellie.

"Who's Mellie?" Caterina asked curiously, leaning on the fence with a quizzical expression. Eryk jumped with fright and then reddened with embarrassment, wondering how long she had been standing there listening to him. "Is she your girlfriend?"

"Not really. I wanted her to be, but she didn't..." He shrugged uncomfortably. "I made a mess of it."

"Have you ever had a girlfriend, Eryk?"

He shook his head self-consciously. "Girls don't like halfwits. Not the nice girls, anyway."

"I like you and I'm a nice girl."

"But you're my friend. I'm talking about other girls. They think I'm dumb."

"You shouldn't think that," she scolded. "You're not so stupid. In fact, you have a great deal to recommend you."

"Like what?" he asked skeptically.

"Well...for one thing, you're not cruel, Eryk. I had a friend in Tolace who married the best-looking boy in town and every time she did something he didn't like, he punched her in the face. I know which one I'd pick if had a choice between a handsome husband who liked giving me a black eye and someone who wasn't so pretty but cared for me. And you have a very good position—you're the Lord of the Suns' personal servant. Lots of girls would find that attractive."

"Maybe," he said doubtfully. "But I don't think it will make much difference to Mellie. She's a princess."

"Then it's probably not her fault she doesn't love you, Eryk," Caterina told him sympathetically. "The highborn aren't like *real* people. They get married to do deals and seal treaties and stuff. They don't even talk to each other properly. Look at Lord Dirk and Lady Jacinta! If they were like you and me, they'd be rollicking around in the hayshed by now. But they're highborn so they dance around each other all the time, being all polite and cagy. They never say what they really think, or what they really want. I feel sorry for them, actually."

"I suppose," Eryk agreed, not entirely convinced. "I just wish..."

"You're a good boy, Eryk. If I can see it, so will some other nice girl, someday."

"But you wouldn't be my girlfriend, would you?"

Caterina smiled. "Are you asking me to be your girlfriend or just inquiring about the possibility?"

"What do you mean?"

"Nothing really," she shrugged. "Come on. Brush that hay off your bum and tidy yourself up a bit. I came to fetch you back to the house. Prince Kirshov just arrived from Avacas and he wants to see you."

Kirsh was in the morning room talking to Lord Rees when Caterina led him back into the house. The summons to meet Prince Kirsh worried Eryk a little. He knew things were tense between the prince and Lord Dirk and he was afraid Kirsh had come to deliver the news he'd changed his mind and had Dirk arrested again.

But Kirsh smiled when he saw Eryk. Caterina closed the door on her way out.

"Well, you seem none the worse for wear," Rees remarked as he looked him up and down. "Still hanging off Dirk's every word and deed, I suppose?"

Eryk looked at Rees worriedly, not sure what he meant. His tone was anything but friendly. "Lord Rees?"

"Never mind."

"Is something wrong, Prince Kirsh?" he asked, turning to the prince.

"Not that you need concern yourself with," Kirsh assured him. "Dirk just asked me to check on you on my way through to Omaxin. He was afraid you'd think he's abandoned you."

"Are you still mad at him?"

"A little bit."

"You're not going to arrest him again, are you?"

Kirsh smiled but he didn't seem happy. Just...resigned. "Probably not. Things have changed a bit since we left Bollow. Misha's back."

The news cheered Eryk considerably. "I like Prince Misha. He used to get really annoyed 'cause Dirk beat him at chess all the time, but he knew some really good stories and he didn't mind explaining things to me."

"That sounds like Misha."

"Are you going to stay for a while, Prince Kirsh?" he asked hopefully. "I could be your servant if you do. I haven't got much else to do with Lord Dirk away."

"Only tonight, I'm afraid, Eryk. We just stopped in here to get fresh horses. I'm on my way to Omaxin to see my father and Marqel."

"I miss Marqel," he admitted. "She's one of my best friends."

Kirsh seemed amused. "She's very fond of you, too, I'm sure."

"Are you sure you don't need me to help, Prince Kirsh?" he asked eagerly. "I could, you know. I could even go with you."

"To Omaxin?"

"Why not? There's nothing here for me to do. And if Lord Rees is going with you then I could be his servant, too, until you get back to Avacas."

"I don't think so, Eryk," Kirsh said doubtfully.

"*Please,* Prince Kirsh? Please, can I come with you? I'll be really good. I promise."

Kirsh glanced at Rees. "What do you think, Rees?"

"I think he's Dirk's servant and he shouldn't abandon his post here without Dirk's permission," the young duke replied.

"But he wouldn't mind, Lord Rees," Eryk assured him. "Not if it was for you and Prince Kirsh. And it's not as if Lord Dirk needs me at the moment. Not while he's in Avacas doing...stuff."

Kirsh smiled thinly. "Doing *stuff*? And what sort of *stuff* do you think Lord Dirk is doing?"

"I dunno." He shrugged. "But it must be good."

"Why must it be good?" Rees asked.

"'Cause Lord Dirk wouldn't do anything bad, would he, Prince Kirsh? I mean, I know what Tia said about him and all, but she was just mad at him for going back to Avacas."

The prince looked at him with an odd expression and then glanced at Lord Rees. "Maybe I will let him come."

"Why, for pity's sake?"

"At the very least, I'd be interested in hearing what Tia Veran and the Baenlanders had to say about Dirk after he left them."

"Leave him here, Kirsh," Rees advised. "You don't need the added burden."

"I don't think Eryk will be a burden. He may even be useful."

"Do you mean it?" Eryk asked excitedly. "I can go with you?"

"Sure," Kirsh said. "Why not? I'm sure Dirk wouldn't

mind. In fact, if you prove yourself too good a manservant, young man, Lord Dirk may have to fight me to get you back, once we return to Avacas."

Eryk frowned. "I hate it when you and Lord Dirk fight over stuff, Prince Kirsh."

Kirsh's smiled faded. "Sometimes it can't be helped, Eryk."

"But he's your friend."

"Even friends don't agree on everything."

"But they should forgive each other," Eryk told him sagely. "Lady Morna used to say friends were like brothers and they should always forgive each other because like brothers, when you lose a friend, he's not so easily replaced. Isn't that right, Lord Rees?" Eryk was proud of himself for remembering that little pearl of wisdom. He'd heard Lady Morna give that lecture to two of the grooms she caught in a fistfight. The boys had slunk away feeling very chastened by the time she was through with them.

Kirsh didn't seem impressed, though. "Did she also say friends shouldn't lie to each other?"

"No...but Lady Lexie said something." Eryk smiled. He was rather warming to the idea he had a quote for every occasion. "She said it takes two people for a lie to work. One to tell it and one to believe it."

Now Kirsh looked confused. "Who is Lady Lexie?"

"Mellie's mama."

"And who is Mellie?"

"Mellie Thorn. She lived in Mil."

Kirsh stared at him for a moment, clearly shocked. "Mellie *Thorn*? Johan Thorn had a daughter?"

"I suppose. Her papa was dead, so I never met him. But Lady Lexie was her mother. She was really nice. I don't know what happened to her after Mil was destroyed, though. I hope she's all right. I think Mellie must be safe, though, 'cause she left with Tia and Prince Misha before you got to Mil...Is something wrong, Prince Kirsh?"

The prince shook his head. "No. Nothing's the matter, Eryk. I'm just surprised, that's all."

Rees looked at Kirsh with concern. "Dirk never mentioned Johan had another child?"

Kirsh shook his head. "Misha never mentioned it, either."

"Can I really come to Omaxin with you, Prince Kirsh?"

Kirsh nodded distractedly. "Why don't you run along, Eryk, and get your gear packed. We're leaving before second sunrise tomorrow."

"You won't be sorry you let me come, Prince Kirsh," Eryk promised.

"I'm sure I won't be," Kirsh agreed.

Eryk sketched a hasty bow and fled the room excitedly. He couldn't wait to tell Caterina he was going to Omaxin with Prince Kirsh and Lord Rees; he couldn't wait to see Marqel again.

Chapter 77

Kirsh's arrival in Omaxin, without Dirk Provin, was more than Marqel could have hoped for. She had spent a great deal of time and effort since her arrival in the ruins composing ever more elaborate prophecies she supposedly read from the walls of the cavern at the end of the labyrinth. It would have all been wasted if Dirk turned up and exposed her.

Antonov believed Dirk Provin could read the cavern walls as well as she could so he wouldn't even have to call her a liar to expose her fraud. All he had to do was disagree with her, even on a minor point, to throw her whole plan into disarray. As it was, Rudi Kalenkov was extremely suspicious. He kept trying to pin her down on what part of the wall she had read particular passages from, but Marqel refused to be drawn. She fobbed him off with a few barely adequate excuses. Antonov believed her and that was all that really mattered.

The Lion of Senet was feverish with anticipation when he learned Kirsh was on his way. The army he had gathered in the ruins was also delighted, and more than a little relieved by the news. The troops brought north were bored with nothing to do and nobody to fight. No one had seen so much as a glimpse of a Sidorian raider for months. Their idleness was turning to discontent. They had no idea why they were here. There was no enemy to face and they had been taken from a city perched on the brink of chaos where their presence had actually been of some use. Marqel couldn't risk Antonov addressing the troops to reassure them. His ranting would alarm them and she would have no hope of controlling them if they realized he was insane.

Kirsh was her salvation. The army would follow him without question. And Antonov would probably cede command of it to his favorite son without resistance, provided he believed that was what the Goddess wanted.

Of course, she had to convince Kirsh yet that his duty lay in taking Senet back for the Goddess. That might have proved an insurmountable hurdle if Dirk Provin had been around to counter her arguments, but Kirsh had left him back in Avacas.

Sometimes, things really did go according to plan.

Marqel was in the cavern with Antonov—who was praying *again*—when she got word the prince had arrived, just after first sunrise. She hurried out to meet him before Antonov realized Kirsh was here. It was too risky to let him speak to his son before she had a chance to prepare him.

Kirsh smiled wearily when he spied her.

"You're safe," he said by way of greeting.

"Of course I'm safe," she replied. "That's why you sent me here, isn't it?"

Kirsh nodded, aware everyone was looking at them and every word they said to each other would be the subject of rumor and speculation.

"You look tired, your highness. Come. I'll show you to the tent set aside for you. Dismiss your escort. I'm sure they deserve a rest."

Turning to Sergey, Kirsh gave the order, and then turned to follow Marqel. It was then that Marqel realized that among the escort was Dirk's brother, Rees Provin.

"My lord," she said, with a small bow. "What brings you to Omaxin?"

Rees dismounted, handing his reins to Sergey. "Boredom, mostly, my lady. A trip north to see the legendary ruins of Omaxin seemed far more interesting than waiting around in Bollow for Faralan to give birth."

Typical male, she thought. *Get your woman knocked up and then abandon her to deal with the agony of childbirth alone, while you go off sightseeing.* Rees Provin's presence in Omaxin simply reinforced Marquel's belief pregnancy and childbirth were a curse.

"I'm sure you'll find them fascinating, my lord," she replied with a noncommittal shrug. In truth, she cared little about Rees Provin. He could do whatever he wanted, provided he didn't get in her way.

"What about me, Prince Kirsh?"

They looked back at Eryk, who stood alone and rather forlorn, a little aside from the rest of Kirsh's escort.

What is that pathetic little moron doing here?

"Eryk!" she cried with a beaming smile. "Goodness, what are you doing here?"

"I'm Prince Kirsh and Lord Rees's servant until we get back to Avacas," he explained.

"Well, then we'll have to find you a special tent of your own." *Because there is no way in hell you're going to sleep on a pallet in Kirsh's tent and get in my way, you disgusting little creep.* She turned to one of Rudi's Shadowdancers who was standing around watching the arrival of the prince. "You there! See to it young Eryk is given his own tent. And make sure he gets fed, too. He's a very good friend of mine. Be sure you look after him."

Eryk smiled with relief, delighted Marqel was so obviously concerned for his welfare. "Thank you, my lady."

"You take your rest, Eryk," she ordered. "I'm sure you must be exhausted after such a long ride. I'll take care of Prince Kirshov tonight."

Eryk trotted off happily in the wake of the Shadowdancer.

Marqel led Kirsh through the camp to the tent set up next to hers and led him inside.

As soon as they were out of sight of the rest of the camp, she threw herself at him. Kirsh kissed her with fervor.

"Marqel..."

"Shh..." she said, slipping the robe from her shoulders. "We can talk later. Afterward."

She knew Kirsh so very, very well. He did as she bid and said nothing for a long time after that, other than to whisper her name as if it were a cry of ecstasy.

Antonov was pacing his tent anxiously when Marqel finally led Kirsh into his presence the following morning. Kirsh was obviously concerned when he saw him. Antonov's determination to spend almost every waking moment in prayer meant he wasn't eating, and he had lost weight since coming to Omaxin. His once powerful frame was wasted and thin and his clothes hung on him as if made for a much larger man.

"Kirsh!" he cried. "You're here at last! Why isn't Dirk with you?"

Marqel bit back a private little smile at the pain Antonov's question caused Kirsh.

"He had some things to take care of in Avacas."

"He knows I want him here, doesn't he?"

"Yes, sir, but—"

"He's not defying me again, is he?"

"I'm not sure I understand what you mean."

"My meaning's clear enough, Kirsh. I've heard some disturbing things since I've been in Omaxin. News of riots and temples being burned. The prophecies speak of a false redeemer, you know."

"What prophecies?" Kirsh asked.

Antonov kept pacing as if Kirsh hadn't spoken. "The more I hear of them, the more I fear they mean Dirk. Since I learned Marqel is able to read the Goddess's writings, things have become very confused. Very confused, indeed. The prophecies speak of a time of great trouble if the false redeemer is allowed to prevail. But I'm taking precautions. If he proves himself false, I'll deal with it. *We'll* deal with it."

"Father..."

"I want your oath, Kirsh."

"My oath on what?"

"That you will always follow the Goddess. That you will defend her to the death."

"You know I would."

"Your oath!" Antonov insisted. "You're my only heir, Kirsh."

"Well, actually, that's not—"

Antonov wasn't listening to him. "When I die, the task will fall to you. Swear to me now you will see this through. That you will make certain no false redeemer is allowed to turn Senet from the teachings of the High Priestess."

"Father, there's something I need to talk to you about."

"Are you refusing to swear it, Kirsh?"

"No, of course not."

"Then I want your oath."

Marqel nodded encouragingly. "Go on, Kirsh." Dirk's advice about Antonov had never proved so useful. *Make his faith work for you. It's Antonov's one great strength and his one great weakness. He'll do anything you want, believe anything you want, if he believes it is the will of the Goddess.*

Kirsh sighed heavily. "You have my oath."

Antonov smiled with relief. "Then I can die content."

"You're not dying, Father."

"No. But my days are numbered," he informed Kirsh, seemingly undisturbed by the thought. "The prophecies say I shall not live to see this through. That's why it's so important I have your oath. I can go to the Goddess with a clear conscience, knowing I have done all I could to defend her."

Kirsh looked to Marqel for help. She shrugged. It had taken her quite a while to convince Antonov he was about to die, even longer to get him to accept it. She wasn't about to say a word that might throw doubt on his beliefs now.

"There are other things that have happened since you've been here in Omaxin, Father," Kirsh began, a little hesitantly. "Things that might alter your assessment of the situation."

Marqel looked at Kirsh in alarm. What was he talking about? He hadn't warned her he was going to say anything like this.

"Then perhaps you can tell your father about them after his morning prayers," Marqel hurriedly suggested, desperate to put an end to this conversation until she found out what Kirsh was talking about.

"I should pray," Antonov agreed. "I must tell the Goddess I have your oath, Kirsh. That even if she takes me before the next sunrise, her truth will be protected."

Marqel glanced at Antonov for a moment, thinking that sounded like a fine idea. She was sick of his ranting, sick of his prayers and his desperation to prove himself innocent. Now Kirsh was here and had sworn to carry on his father's cause, she didn't really need him anyway.

"Then we will leave you to pray," Marqel assured him. "Prince Kirshov and I will return later and he can tell you the rest of his news."

Antonov was already on his knees, his head bowed, by the time they left the tent.

Kirsh was not happy about it, though.

"Marqel, I have to speak to him," he insisted, stopping just outside the tent. "You don't know what's happened..."

"It wouldn't matter to him if the next Age of Shadows had just started, Kirsh," she warned. "He's only interested in saving Ranadon from the false redeemer."

"Do you believe it's Dirk?"

"It's easier to believe he's a false redeemer than the Goddess's instrument."

The prince nodded unhappily. "I must speak with him, Marqel."

"What's so urgent that it can't wait a few more minutes?"

"Misha is back."

"Back?"

"In Avacas."

Marqel stilled warily. "Is he all right? Who rescued him?"

"Nobody," Kirsh shrugged. "He came back on his own. Sort of. But it's not as simple as whether or not he's none the worse for the experience, Marqel. He's well. Better than he's ever been. Barely even limping."

"You mean the Baenlanders cured him?" she asked in astonishment.

"They helped him shake off a poppy-dust addiction," Kirsh told her heavily. "He claims Belagren was deliberately poisoning him."

Marqel was so shocked that Belagren's scheme had been exposed that she didn't have to fake her reaction at all. "Goddess! You can't be serious, Kirsh? That's...that's dreadful!"

"So you can see why it's so important that I speak to my father. Goddess knows what his reaction is going to be."

"Of course," she agreed, relieved beyond words that she'd not allowed Kirsh to say anything to Antonov about this. This news would undermine everything she had been working toward. Everything she had achieved would be thrown into doubt.

She would not allow that to happen. Not while she still had some hope of redeeming the situation.

"You must tell him about this immediately, Kirsh. But it would be best to wait until after he's said his prayers," she advised. "You won't get any sense out of him until then, anyway."

"I suppose."

"Go and get some breakfast," Marqel suggested considerately. "I'll call you as soon as he's finished praying."

Kirsh reluctantly did as she recommended and headed off toward the cook tent. Marqel bit her bottom lip, torn with indecision. It took her too long to get Antonov to believe her way of thinking to risk everything now. There was really only one thing she could do. But she didn't want to risk implicating herself...

Then across the camp she spied Eryk making his way toward her, smiling with eagerness.

"Good morning, Eryk," she said cheerily, as he approached. "Did you sleep well?"

"Really good, Marqel. Have you seen Prince Kirsh? I went to his tent but he wasn't there."

"He's having breakfast, I think."

"I should go find him and see what he wants me to do."

"Would you do me a favor first, Eryk?"

"Of course," he agreed willingly.

"Prince Antonov is praying at the moment, but he sometimes forgets himself. If I make some tea, would you take it to him for me?"

He nodded gladly. "I could get him some from the cook tent, if you like," Eryk offered. "To save you the trouble of making it."

"It's all right, Eryk, I don't mind," she assured him with a selfless smile. "Besides, his highness needs a bit of a boost. I thought he'd like some peppermint tea."

Chapter 78

Misha planned to convene a formal tribunal to try Ella Geon, Yuri Daranski and Madalan Tirov for attempted murder. Tia was all for summarily executing the three of them, but Misha knew the value of a public trial and Dirk supported his decision. The more public outcry about the Shadowdancers and what they had done to the Crown Prince of Senet, the better chance their cult would eventually be eliminated. The Shadowdancers' credibility was severely shaken after Bollow, but with the High Priestess still at the Lion of Senet's side, Misha's options were limited. While Marqel remained at large, Dirk couldn't really disband the Shadowdancers. He could issue all the decrees to that effect he wanted, but they would have no meaning unless the Lion of Senet withdrew his support.

So Misha decided on a public trial and as he was the

key witness, he appointed the Lord of the Suns to preside over the case, which was the main reason he hadn't wanted Dirk to go to Omaxin. As he realized the very first day he returned to Avacas, having Dirk Provin in such a position of power was proving rather useful, and he intended to make the most of it.

Tia remained skeptical. Despite the fact Dirk had given Misha his unstinting support since his return, Tia still harbored a great deal of mistrust for Dirk Provin. She was afraid he would do something to sabotage the trial. Or worse, rule in favor of the defendants.

"There is nothing to worry about, Tia," Misha assured Tia for the hundredth time since he'd told her of his decision to try Ella and her cohorts publicly. "Dirk will see that justice is done."

"Whose idea of justice?" she asked, as they walked along the graveled path away from the palace. Even now, Tia insisted he take a long walk each day to keep up his strength. Misha enjoyed the break and the chance to be alone with her, even if only for an hour or so. "Yours or Dirk's?"

"He won't let Ella get away with what she's done, my love. He promised me."

"He promises you anything you want to hear, Misha."

"I don't know why you still think he can't be trusted. He's done nothing but help me since I got back."

"Only because it's helping him."

Misha shook his head, at a loss as to how he could convince her. Then something else occurred to him that might account for her anger. "Tia, Dirk hasn't said or done anything...I mean he doesn't still think that you and he?..."

"No, Misha," she sighed. "Dirk hasn't said anything. Or done anything, either. He acts like we're little more than strangers, actually. In a way, that almost hurts more. You'd think he'd have some shred of guilt. Some glimmer of feeling in him."

"Is that what's causing you so much grief then?" he asked, carefully. "That he seems to be so...unaffected by your presence?"

Tia looked at him for a moment, thoughtful rather than angry at his suggestion. "I don't know. Dirk made a rather half-hearted attempt to apologize in Bollow, but I'd just escaped being burned at the stake by him, so I wasn't really in the mood to listen to excuses. I never thought of it like that, though." Then she shrugged, slipping her hand into his. "Nobody on Ranadon can tell what's going on inside that head of his, so for all I know, he's dying from unrequited love. I doubt it, mind you. That would imply he was capable of normal human emotions. But anything's possible."

"I can speak to him if you want," he offered.

"And tell him what, Misha?"

"To leave you alone, perhaps? Or ask him to apologize?"

"And let him think he meant something to me once? Don't you dare!"

"I'd like to do something to resolve the situation," Misha said, concerned by her obvious pain. "Like it or not, I'll be Lion of Senet someday. There is no way I can rule effectively without the support of the Lord of the Suns, particularly after what happened in Bollow. Dirk is going to be in our lives for a long time yet, my love, and I'd hate to think his presence causes you distress."

"In *your* life, Misha," she corrected. "I have no idea what the future holds for me."

He stopped walking and stared at her in surprise. "What are you talking about?"

"The future, Misha," she said. "I can't just hang around the palace looking decorative forever, can I? Certainly not once your father and brother get back. And you'll have to get married someday and produce an heir and there'll be no place for me unless I want to be your mistress, and I don't think I could bear that. I suppose I could go to Kalarada with Mellie. I haven't really given it much thought."

"But I thought..."

She smiled. "Thought what? That I would be there for you to lean on forever? You don't need me, Misha. Not anymore. You've beaten the poppy-dust. You're strong enough to take on the whole world without any help from me. You've proved that time and again since you got back. Even Palinov is afraid of you now."

"But I love you."

"And I love you," she assured him. "But that's not enough. You know it as well as I do. You're the Lion of Senet's heir and I'm the heretic's daughter." She laughed suddenly, but it was tinged with bitterness. "It's not like you're planning to marry me, is it?"

Misha was dumbfounded.

She smiled understandingly. "It's all right, Misha, truly. And I know it's not your fault. You can't help being who you are, any more than I can."

"No," he objected. "You don't understand. I thought... well, I suppose I just assumed you wanted to marry me. Goddess, what a fool I am. I never even thought to ask."

Tia was obviously unconvinced. "You don't have to say that to make me feel better."

"Damn it, Tia! I'm saying it because I mean it. What do you want me to do? Get down on my knees and *beg* for your hand?"

She searched his face for a moment and then frowned. "You're serious?"

"Of course, I'm serious."

"But I'm the heretic's daughter."

"And I'm the Crippled Prince. We'll make a fine pair, don't you think?" He pulled her to him and kissed her, just to make certain she knew he meant what he said, and then he smiled. "Besides, the Lord of the Suns is a friend of mine. I don't think Neris Veran's heresy is an issue anymore."

"Are you sure this is what you want?" she asked uncertainly. "Aren't you supposed to marry some well-bred virgin with all the right credentials?"

"Like who?"

"I don't know. Someone like... Jacinta D'Orlon, maybe?"

"Let me tell you something about the immaculately credentialed Lady Jacinta D'Orlon, my love. She has her sights set on someone far more unattainable than the Lion of Senet's heir. Anyway, I don't love anyone else. I love you."

"You're a prince, Misha," she reminded him. "You don't have that luxury. In fact, you're an idiot for even considering the idea. Nobody will accept me. There's a price on my head, remember? And I don't know the first thing about being the consort of a prince."

"I can get rid of the price on your head with the stroke of a pen, Tia, and you can learn to be a princess, if you really want to. Anybody would think you didn't want to marry me."

"I do, Misha, but that's not the point."

"Then we'll do it right now," he declared. "We'll get Dirk to perform the ceremony."

"The hell we will," she snorted. "The last person I want at my wedding is Dirk Provin."

"Just so long as you want *me* there."

She was silent for an agonizingly long time.

"Don't torture me, Tia. Will you marry me?"

After a long time, she shrugged. "I suppose."

He kissed her again, wishing he could bottle this moment for the future. Then a polite cough interrupted them and he looked up to find Dirk standing on the path behind them.

"Do you mind?" Misha said with a smile. "I just got betrothed."

"And I wish you and Tia all the happiness in the world, Misha," Dirk replied heavily. "But right now, you've got another problem."

"What problem?" Tia asked with a scowl, no doubt thinking Dirk had deliberately invaded their brief moment of happiness out of spite.

"Antonov is dead," Dirk told them. "You're the Lion of Senet now, Misha."

"Oh, Goddess..." Misha gasped, clutching Tia for support.

"It gets worse," Dirk added grimly. "Kirsh has declared war on us."

They met in Antonov's private study a short time later: Dirk, Tia, Lord Palinov and Misha. The letter from Omaxin was waiting for him on Antonov's desk. It was written in clear and concise words and left no doubt about Kirsh's intentions.

Misha read it through and then looked up at Dirk. "He can't mean this."

"He means it," Dirk replied. "He says he swore an oath to Antonov that he would see Ranadon is true to the teachings of the Goddess as set down by the High Priestess of the Shadowdancers. He knows you and I intend to get rid of them. What other interpretation can you put on it?"

"But war? How did it come to that?"

"You sent him up to Omaxin alone," Dirk pointed out. "I warned you it wasn't a good idea to let Marqel at him."

"I knew Kirsh was besotted by Marqel, but I don't believe he'd plunge Senet into a civil war, just to keep her in power."

"But he *would* honor an oath, Misha," Dirk warned. "Particularly an oath he made to your father."

"I'm inclined to concur with the Lord of the Suns, your highness," Palinov agreed. "Your brother takes his honor very seriously."

"When I want your opinion, I'll ask for it," Misha snapped, in no mood for Palinov right now. He turned to Dirk with a look of despair. "I can't fight Kirsh. He's my brother."

"He'll be counting on that," Tia suggested.

"Tia's right," Dirk said. "And I'm guessing Kirsh doesn't want to fight you, any more than you want to fight him. But unless you're willing to give in to his demands, then you have no other choice."

"He demands you," Misha pointed out. "The burden of heresy has shifted somewhat, it seems."

"That's Marqel talking, not Kirsh."

"If Kirsh wants Dirk, then maybe that's exactly what you should give him," Tia mused.

They all looked at her for an explanation.

"And I don't mean that the way it sounds," she added, impatiently. "This isn't about you and your brother, Misha; it's about the Lord of the Suns and the High Priestess of the Shadowdancers. You and Kirsh just happen to support different sides and unfortunately, you're the ones with the armies."

"What are you suggesting, Tia?" Dirk asked. "That *I* lead Misha's forces into battle against Kirsh?"

"That's exactly what I'm suggesting."

"I'm not a general," Dirk objected. "And what army in Senet would follow me?"

"Any army I ordered to follow you," Misha pointed out thoughtfully.

Dirk stared at him. "Don't send me to war against Kirsh, Misha. Not that."

"The way I see it, I have two choices," Misha concluded. "I can send the Lord of the Suns to Omaxin to put down a minor uprising led by the disgraced High Priestess of the Shadow-dancers, or I can lead an army against my own brother. One choice will cause a fuss that will more than likely blow over in a few months. The other will tear Senet apart and plunge us into civil war."

"This isn't my fight, Misha."

"That's where you're wrong, Dirk," Tia told him. "You made this your fight the moment you asked Paige Halyn to name you his heir. Now you're going to have to see it through to the bitter end."

Misha nodded slowly. "Tia's got a point, Dirk."

"But I don't know anything about fighting a war."

"That's a real pity, Dirk," Tia said unsympathetically. "Because from what I hear, Kirshov Latanya is pretty good at it."

Chapter 79

The news of the sudden death of the Lion of Senet somehow seemed less important in the face of impending war. Jacinta heard from Lord Palinov that Dirk Provin was to lead Misha's army against the High Priestess. It was interesting, she thought, that everyone was going to great pains to point out this altercation was between the Lord of the Suns and the High Priestess. The fact that Senet's army had been split between Misha and Kirshov Latanya—which constituted the very essence of a civil war in Jacinta's opinion—seemed to be very deliberately downplayed.

Her concern was not for Senet, though. The mainland could tear itself to shreds for all Jacinta cared. Her concern was for Alenor and what such a thing would cost her people. Somebody had to pay for Senet's war and she was damned if it was going to be Dhevyn.

Jacinta demanded to see Misha as soon as she heard the news, and somewhat to her surprise he granted her an audience almost as soon as she asked for it. He was alone when she arrived, sitting in the large gilded chair Dirk had been keeping warm for him. It was his by right now. Misha didn't seem nearly as uncomfortable in it as Dirk had.

"Lady Jacinta."

"It was good of you to see me on such short notice, your highness," she said with a graceful curtsy. "I realize what a trying time this must be for you."

"More trying than you imagine," he agreed. "Please. Sit down."

Jacinta took the seat he offered her and folded her hands in her lap. "I was sorry to hear about your father."

"Were you?" he asked with a raised brow. "I thought every Dhevynian alive would be rejoicing at the news."

"I said *I* was sorry, your highness. I can't speak for the rest of my countrymen."

"I thought that was why you were here in Avacas, my lady. To speak for your countrymen."

"I'm here representing my queen, your highness."

"And what does your queen want with the new Lion of Senet?"

Jacinta took a deep breath before answering. "Well, you could start by overturning the order your father issued, banishing Alenor from Kalarada. And you could revoke the sentence of treason hanging over Alexin Seranov. And I suppose it would be rather nice if you removed your brother from his position as Regent of Dhevyn."

Misha smiled faintly. "You don't want much, do you?"

"I want what's best for Dhevyn, sire."

"And believe it or not, I don't happen to think Dhevyn abruptly going it alone is the best thing for your nation, my lady," he said. "You're economically dependent on Senet, for one thing. You will find it very difficult to manage without us. Autonomy may not sit very well with the merchants who have gotten rich supplying our garrisons over the past two decades."

"They will just have to get by some other way. And we're not seeking autonomy, your highness. We're seeking independence. Dhevyn was a sovereign nation before your father came along."

"You'd risk economic ruin for the intangible notion of freedom?"

"Even if it is an intangible notion, surely that's Dhevyn's decision, not Senet's."

"Very well then," he shrugged. "You may have it."

"What?"

"You may have Dhevyn, my lady. I will issue the orders today, withdrawing all Senetian governors from Dhevyn. I'm sure you'll appreciate that the logistics involved prevent me from simply ridding Dhevyn of every Senetian citizen overnight, but I'll get them out as fast as I can. And as Senet no longer has any interest in who governs Dhevyn, your queen can rule in her own right if she wishes. The regency is also dissolved."

"Just like that?" she gasped in shock.

Misha smiled. "I should be a gentleman and let you think it was your remarkable diplomatic skills that persuaded me, shouldn't I?"

"What has persuaded you, if not my remarkable diplomatic skills?"

"I'm simply keeping a promise I made some time ago, my lady, to someone who means a great deal to me."

Jacinta was flabbergasted. "Then you really mean to do it?"

"You have my word."

"I . . . I don't know what to say."

"Thank you would seem appropriate."

"Of course! I mean . . . of course I thank you. I'm just . . . overwhelmed."

"You're welcome," he said. "Although to be honest, I need the men currently stationed throughout Dhevyn to deal with my own troubles, so my decision is not quite as altruistic as it appears on the surface."

For a moment she forgot her own joy. "It's true then? You mean to fight Kirshov?"

"The Lord of the Suns is going to Omaxin with the support of the Lion of Senet to put down an uprising instigated by the disgraced High Priestess of the Shadowdancers," he corrected. "That's not the same thing, my lady."

"It's a very fine distinction, your highness."

"But it's enough of a distinction for my purposes, my lady."

Jacinta smiled appreciatively. "You'll make a fine Lion of Senet, your highness."

"History will be the judge of that, I suppose."

"Well, you have my vote."

"What a pity this isn't a democracy."

Jacinta rose to her feet. "I shall inform my queen of your decision immediately."

"Thank you. And congratulations, by the way."

"For what?" she asked with a smile. "I thought we'd already established it wasn't my remarkable diplomatic skills that prompted your decision?"

"I was referring to your upcoming marriage to Raban Seranov."

"My *what*?"

He looked at her in surprise. "You haven't heard?"

"No, I haven't heard. But *you* apparently have."

"I'm sorry, my lady. I would never have mentioned it if I didn't realize you hadn't been informed. I gathered it was a done deal. I received a letter from Lady Sofia several days ago, informing me you would be leaving my court soon to prepare for the wedding."

"My mother arranged this."

"That is usually the way these things are done, Lady Jacinta."

"She never even consulted me."

He smiled. "Given your previous responses to her arrangements, I can't say I blame her."

Jacinta glared at him. "Are you making fun of me?"

"Not at all, my lady, and I sympathize with your plight, truly I do. But I don't see how you can escape it. And Raban is Dhevynian, after all. That's got to be better than Lord Birkoff. And you must concede that uniting the D'Orlon and Seranov houses is a smart political move in light of Dhevyn's uncertain future."

"You *are* making fun of me," she accused.

Misha smiled sympathetically. "You're the only daughter of one of the richest and most influential dukes in Dhevyn, my lady, and a cousin of the queen. You're a fool if you imagined you could avoid a marriage like this for much longer. Even with the protection of your position as the Queen of Dhevyn's envoy."

"Raban Seranov is not my idea of a husband, your highness. I don't care how good his pedigree is. He's a dissolute fool. He's already fathered one bastard I know of."

"And will probably father a dozen more," Misha agreed. "But I can't see how you're going to avoid this, my lady. I suspect you're on the brink of being disinherited if you refuse another husband."

"That doesn't seem such a bad fate, right now."

"I wish I could help," he said regretfully. "But unless you

find yourself another husband between now and when your mother gets here, your fate is sealed, I fear."

Jacinta eyed him quizzically. "Have *you* got anything planned for this afternoon?"

Misha laughed. "I can't help you, I'm afraid. I'm already spoken for."

"All the decent ones are," Jacinta lamented. "Or they're just plain unavailable."

"Do you speak of someone in particular?" he asked with a canny look.

"No," she replied with a resigned shrug. "I'm just making an observation. I really should go. I have letters to write and you've already spared me more time than you have. Thank you, your highness. For what you're doing for Dhevyn and the warning about my impending doom."

"I wish I could do more."

"So do I," she agreed.

Jacinta fled up the stairs to her room, torn between delight at the notion that Dhevyn was suddenly and unexpectedly free of Senet, and despair that her mother had betrothed her to Raban Seranov behind her back. How could she do such a thing? Without so much as a word of warning?

She stopped at the door to her room, and then on impulse, she walked up the hall and knocked on Dirk's door. He opened it himself. Dirk looked surprised to see her.

"Can I come in?"

He stood back to let her enter then closed the door behind her. "Are you sure it's wise for you to come to the Lord of the Suns' rooms unescorted?"

She walked into the room, looked around for a moment and then turned back to face him. "I'm to be married. To Raban Seranov."

"Congratulations."

"I don't suppose you're interested in making mad, unbridled, passionate love to me just once, so I don't have to go to my marriage bed a virgin?"

Dirk visibly blanched at her question, too stunned to answer.

"No, I suppose not," she shrugged. "And you're right. I shouldn't have come here. It was just a foolish impulse."

Jacinta headed back to the door where Dirk still stood. He hadn't moved a muscle.

"I really should go."

"Yes, you should," he agreed in a strangled voice.

She reached out for the doorknob, which was a stupid thing to do, because Dirk still had hold of it. Touching him was her undoing. She was in his arms and he was kissing her before she realized what she was doing. Before either of them realized what they were doing. The moment of insanity lasted just long enough for Jacinta to wonder what would happen if Dirk took her up on her rather outrageous suggestion.

Dirk pulled away first, more mindful of the danger they were courting than she. He looked at her for a moment and for once she could read his eyes clearly. They were filled with yearning. And remorse.

"If I thought for a moment you were even half serious..." he said.

"I think if you kiss me like that again, I would be."

"Don't, Jacinta..."

"I'm sorry. Not about...I'm sorry you're the Lord of the Suns, mostly."

"I think you'd better go."

"Yes," she agreed. "I should."

He opened the door for her. She stopped on the threshold and looked at him.

"You want to know something funny?" she said with a hint of bitter irony. "You were on my mother's list of suitable husbands once. If none of this had happened, it might have been you I was made to marry."

Jacinta hurried down the hall from Dirk's room before he could answer, locking the door to her own suite as soon as she was inside. She was shaking, from shock as much as from embarrassment.

She hadn't expected Dirk to kiss her like that. Hadn't expected him to kiss her at all. Or had she? Jacinta couldn't even explain why she'd gone to his room. Was she looking for sympathy? Help?

Whatever the reason, Dirk wasn't supposed to have reacted like that. He was supposed to be the one who was always in control. The man with the cold eyes and the even colder heart. And he was the Lord of the Suns. There was absolutely no point entertaining ideas about a future with him. For one thing, the Lord of the Suns usually didn't marry; on the rare occasion the head of the Church had taken a wife in the past, she was always a Sundancer. For the only daughter of the Duke of Bryton, Dirk could not have been more out of reach if he was living on the other side of the second sun.

Which just makes you a damn fool, Jacinta told herself crossly, taking a deep breath to calm her racing heart. *Don't dwell on it. Don't even think about it. He doesn't love you, and even if he did, he can't do anything about it. So just get over it, girl. It was simply one stupid, thoughtless kiss and it didn't mean anything. To him or to you.*

But despite the stern lecture she gave herself, it was quite some time before Jacinta felt composed enough to put pen to paper to inform her queen the Lion of Senet had agreed to free Dhevyn.

Chapter 80

Despite Misha's assurances Dirk would see justice done, Tia was still worried about Ella Geon's fate being left in the Lord of the Suns' untrustworthy hands. Tia didn't want the blind eyes of justice delivering a fair sentence for Ella's crimes. She wanted vengeance: for what had been done to Neris, for what had been done to Misha and for what the burden of knowing Ella Geon was her mother had done to her.

The death of Antonov and Kirsh's stance in Omaxin seemed to take some of the urgency out of the problem about what to do regarding the Shadowdancers. Dirk had told Misha he planned to offer most of them a choice, which was to embrace the teachings of the Sundancers or leave the Church completely. That decision worried her. There was nothing ruthless about it. It almost seemed as if he was faltering on the brink of triumph and taking the easy way out. They'd ended up having quite a heated argument about it, with Tia demanding he have some balls and make the hard decision to be rid of them once and for all, and Dirk trying to explain something about it being hypocritical to execute people in the name of a Goddess who preached forgiveness. She couldn't stand it when Dirk used theological arguments. He no more believed in the Goddess than she did, yet he seemed determined to perpetrate the lies.

The trouble was, Misha agreed with him. Later that evening, when she'd calmed down a little, he tried to explain to her that every Shadowdancer had family, a mother or father, or children of his own, who would grow up full of resentment if the Shadowdancers were executed out of hand. They had to be disbanded and discredited, he insisted, so they became nothing more than a forgotten paragraph in history. Nobody wanted to give them a cause to fight for. When she'd tried to argue with him, too, he had simply pointed out if she wanted an example of what happened when people were dispossessed, or killed out of hand, all she need do is remember why she grew up in the Baenlands.

Misha had no intention of ruling a nation plagued by an underground rebel movement, he said, when he had only just gotten rid of the last one.

But even if Tia conceded Misha and Dirk had a point about the rank and file of the Shadowdancers, there was no way she was going to allow the ringleaders to get away with what they'd done.

Tia tried to tackle Dirk on the subject, but the need to gather the troops for Omaxin meant he had neither the time not the inclination to deal with her. There was now talk of postponing the trial until Dirk got back from Omaxin. That could mean a delay of months. Misha wanted vengeance, but he wanted vengeance that was just and seen to be fair. Tia was concerned only with removing several people from Ranadon who were polluting the air simply by breathing it.

The feeling of unfinished business with her mother left Tia edgy and unsettled. There *had* to be a trial. Soon. She wanted to hear what Ella had to say for herself. It was untenable living with the knowledge she was born of a woman capable of anything so heinous. For her own peace of mind, Tia wanted to be told there was a reason, a *good* reason, why Ella had done what she did. Until Tia knew the reason, she could never be at peace.

When there seemed no hope of an early resolution, Tia decided to confront Ella herself. Certain Misha would object, she was careful to let nobody in on her plan, but it took her longer than she imagined it would to get up the courage to visit her mother.

The prisoners were confined in the city garrison, which was now under the command of a new Prefect. He was a jovial young man named Lanon Rill, the youngest son of Elcast's former governor, Tovin Rill, who had been studying law at the university in Avacas when Misha plucked him from obscurity and made him one of the most powerful men in Senet.

Tia had thought the appointment rather strange until she learned he was a childhood friend of Dirk's from Elcast. His justification for recommending him was that despite his inexperience, Lanon Rill was a decent human being, a quality sadly lacking in Barin Welacin. While Tia couldn't argue on that point, she still didn't like the idea of Dirk surrounding Misha with his old cronies. And she wanted to slap Misha when he agreed to Dirk's suggestion with barely any objections. She understood that for Misha to rule Senet effectively, he needed his own people around him and his illness meant he had few close childhood friends he could trust to appoint. For that reason alone Palinov still held his post. But surely there was a better way than appointing people Dirk Provin recommended?

In spite of her misgivings, Lanon Rill had proved a good choice so far. He was conscientious, fair and appeared to be totally loyal to Misha. But Tia worried about him a little. He smiled too much for her liking.

Lanon met her when she reached the garrison and escorted her personally down to the cells where Ella, Madalan and the physician Yuri Daranski were held. He gave her a running commentary as they passed the various rooms of torture along their route, in such graphic and vibrant detail Tia eventually had to ask him to stop.

"I'm sorry, my lady," he said hastily, when he realized he was upsetting her. "I didn't mean to...well, I thought you should know..."

"I know what they used to do in this place, Prefect Rill," she reminded him, holding up her left hand with its missing finger. "I am personally acquainted with your predecessor's horseshoe pliers."

"His highness charged me with investigating the full scope of Barin Welacin's activities, my lady. I thought perhaps you wanted to be certain his orders were being carried out." He looked so earnest she was almost sorry she'd scolded him.

"I appreciate your enthusiasm, Prefect, but spare me the details, if you don't mind."

"Of course, my lady. This is the cell."

"The cell for what?"

"Ella Geon's cell, my lady. The prisoner you came to see."

"Of course." Tia was suddenly afraid to go on.

"Did you want me to come with you?" Lanon offered, sensing her nervousness.

She shook her head. "No. I can deal with this."

Lanon snapped his fingers and the guard who accompanied them hurried to unlock the door. "Just knock when you're done. The guard will let you out."

Tia smiled thinly. "I know the routine, Prefect Rill. I've been a prisoner a few times, myself."

Lanon smiled. "I'll be right out here if you need me."

The offer surprised her, mostly because it seemed to be made out of genuine concern for her. Perhaps Dirk and Misha were right. Perhaps this young man's greatest asset was his basic decency.

"Thank you," she said, and she stepped into the cell.

Ella looked up as Tia entered and rose to her feet from the pallet where she was sitting. The cell was small and despite the change in the jail's administration, it was neither comfortable nor clean.

"Yes?" Ella inquired of her curiously.

She doesn't know who I am. Admittedly, Tia looked nothing like the girl who had knelt on Antonov's balcony and had her finger chopped off. She was dressed in a beautifully tailored silk dress, her short hair neatly trimmed and fashionably arranged, her hands manicured and clean. Jacinta had been responsible for that. Alenor's cousin had taken Misha's request to help Tia get settled into the palace quite literally and had saved her from any number of awkward gaffes since she'd arrived in Avacas. The Dhevynian queen's envoy had also taken it upon herself to ensure the Lion of Senet's fiancée was clothed and catered for in a manner befitting her new status. In some ways, Jacinta D'Orlon reminded Tia of Lexie. Jacinta was one of those people for whom nobility was second nature. She radiated such a powerful sense of her own worth Tia wondered if she'd ever suffered a moment's doubt about her place in the world.

Perhaps that's why Ella didn't recognize Tia now. Maybe some of Jacinta's subconscious sophistication had rubbed off on her pupil.

"I'm not sure if I should be relieved or disappointed you don't recognize your own daughter," Tia said in the tone she imagined Jacinta would use in the same situation.

"Tia?"

"And you only had to be given one clue. How instinctively maternal of you, Mother."

"Haven't you come up in the world since I saw you last?"

Ella remarked coolly, looking her up and down with a critical eye.

"Haven't you come down?" Tia retorted.

"Is that why you're here? To gloat over my misfortune?"

"There's nothing unfortunate about the reason you're here, my lady. You're here as a direct result of your actions. The misfortune, in your mind at least, seems to be that you got caught."

Ella smiled wanly. "Surely you don't believe the ridiculous charge I was trying to kill poor Misha? I treated the boy like a son."

"If you treated your son the same way you treated your daughter, I don't wonder you're sitting here waiting to die."

"I never mistreated you, Tia. I never had the chance. Johan stole you away when you were still a baby. Any hatred you have for me is because your father and Johan poisoned your mind against me, not because of anything I did to you."

"You destroyed Neris," she accused.

"He destroyed himself. I merely supplied what he wanted to do the job a little faster."

Her total lack of remorse left Tia breathless. "And what's your excuse for what you did to Misha? He was only a child when you started dosing him with poppy-dust. How could you hurt an innocent child like that?"

"I never knew anything about poppy-dust in his tonic," she shrugged. "The news came as a dreadful shock to me. I would never have allowed him to take it, had I known. I adore Misha. How can you think such a thing of me?"

"Why shouldn't I believe you capable of it? You stood there and watched Barin Welacin cut my finger off and you never even blinked!"

"And Dirk Provin drove a knife into Johan Thorn's throat, Tia. Who is it you call your friend now, my dear? The mother who couldn't have saved you, even if she tried, or the young man who committed cold-blooded murder right in front of you?"

The accusation hit her hard. Ella smiled coldly. "So perhaps you really are my daughter after all, if you're so willing to put aside your conscience for the sake of a taste of power."

"I'm nothing like you," Tia spat in disgust.

"Don't be too sure of that, Tia. You stand there now in your fine gown and your high dudgeon and look down on me, but you are truly no better than I am. I followed Belagren because she offered me power. I hear you're planning to marry our new Lion of Senet. Even I never aspired to such high ambitions as that."

"Misha loves me."

"Well, of course he believes he's in love with you, dear. That's all part of the game, isn't it? Your father loved me, too, pathetic fool that he was."

Tia stared at her, wondering what she had hoped to achieve by coming here. Had she hoped for some glimmer of maternal concern? Some hope that facing death, Ella would see the error of her ways? That she might be sorry for the lives she had ruined?

"I despise you. I despise what you are and I despise what you did."

Ella seemed unaffected by her declaration. "Hate me all you want, Tia. It means nothing to me."

Tia banged on the door, fighting back tears of despair. She should never have come here. Never had tried to look for something she had known in her heart did not exist.

"I hope they burn you alive," she spat as Lanon's guard opened the door for her.

"You're as wretched as your father, Tia," Ella remarked. "You don't even have his intelligence to redeem you. Enjoy your new life, my dear. Because it won't last. He'll tire of your Baenlander coarseness in time and then, when you're back on the street, ruined and broken, spare you mother a thought and remind yourself, that in the end, you were really no better than she was."

Chapter 81

Helgin had warned Misha that his withdrawal was not yet complete, and with no sign of his symptoms appearing again, Misha was starting to believe the old physician may have been mistaken. But the night before Dirk was due to leave for Omaxin, while going over the supply details with Dirk and two of his captains, he noticed he was trembling. Misha had raised his hand to point out something on the map spread out on the desk, but when he saw how shaky it was, he lowered it and simply looked at the map instead.

"Are you all right, your highness?" Dirk asked, his formality for the benefit of the other two men.

Misha nodded, but he was cold. So cold he was starting to shiver. He knew what would come next. The stomach cramps. The muscle spasms. Maybe, if it got bad enough, he would start a fit. He couldn't afford this now. And he certainly couldn't afford to show weakness in front of his captains.

He was saved by the fortuitous arrival of Jacinta D'Orlon. She curtsied politely, apologized for the interruption and then turned to Misha with concern.

"Your highness, I know how busy you are, but there's a personal matter I need to bring to your attention urgently."

Puzzled by her obvious anxiety, Misha looked up at his captains. "Would you excuse us, gentlemen?"

The men saluted and left the study without a word. Dirk rose to his feet, and bowed coolly to the Queen of Dhevyn's envoy. "I'll leave you to your business, then, my lady."

"There's no need, Dirk," Jacinta said, dropping the formality she had also assumed for the sake of Misha's captains. "In fact, you might be able to help."

"Help with what?" Misha asked, sinking down in his chair with relief. He wasn't sure how much longer he would have been able to fake well-being for the sake of his men. But in

Dirk's company, he didn't feel the need to try. As for Jacinta...
well, he would just have to trust that the Queen of Dhevyn's envoy didn't gossip.

"Tia is in her room, your highness, sobbing inconsolably. I
don't know what's wrong with her, but she's distraught. She's
talking about leaving."

Misha looked at Dirk with suspicion. "Did you say something to her?"

Dirk shook his head. "I haven't even spoken to her today."

"Did she say why she's so upset?"

Jacinta shrugged. "I have no idea, your highness. All I
know is she went into the city earlier and when she came back
she was very distressed."

"It must have been something that happened in the city,
then," Dirk concluded, rather obviously, Misha thought. "Do
you know where she went?"

"No. And she won't tell me, either."

"I'll go to her," Misha said, rising to his feet. "Can you carry
on here, Dirk? We need to get this finished before you leave tomorrow."

"Of course. Are you sure you're all right?"

He nodded shakily. "It's nothing to be concerned about. A
leftover from the poppy-dust withdrawal, that's all. Master Helgin warned me the symptoms could reoccur without warning. I
should have known it would happen at the most inconvenient
time possible."

"I'll come with you, if you like," Jacinta volunteered.

He shook his head. "Thank you, my lady, but I'll be fine.
There's nothing you can do to help."

"You don't have to go through this alone, Misha."

"There is no other way to go through this, Dirk. Trust me,
what I have suffered is the very essence of loneliness." Then he
smiled wanly. "I've been through worse. Don't worry about me.
It'll pass."

Without waiting for them to reply, Misha limped from the
study, leaving Dirk and Jacinta staring after him with concern.

Misha had to threaten to have the door broken down before Tia would let him in. When she finally did consent to unlock it she simply turned the key and left him to open it himself. She was dressed in her old trousers and worn linen shirt, and obviously packing.

"What are you doing?"

"I'm leaving." She was stuffing her gear into the small canvas bag she had taken with her from Mil to Garwenfield. Her eyes were swollen and red, but she was no longer crying.

"Why?"

"Because it's never going to work, Misha."

"You're not giving it much of a chance."

She stopped packing and looked at him. "It hasn't got a chance, Misha. I'm not cut out for a life prancing around in fine dresses and being diplomatic. It's better if I just leave now."

"Where will you go?"

"I haven't decided."

"Might I inquire as to the reason for this sudden change of heart?"

She sighed, but refused to tell him why she'd suddenly decided to pack her bags and walk out on him. "Don't be mad at me, Misha."

"Then tell me why this morning you were prepared to spend the rest of your life with me, and this afternoon you're ready to abandon me?"

She sank down on the settee, wiping away a fresh round of tears. "I spoke to my mother."

Misha took a deep breath to calm his trembling. "And she advised you to leave?"

"No. She just pointed out the similarities in our situations."

"What similarities?" he asked with a forced smile. "Goddess! You're not poisoning me, too, are you?"

Tia glared at him. "This is no joking matter, Misha."

"It is if you're ready to up and leave at the behest of that murderous bitch."

"But don't you see," she pleaded. "She's my mother. How can you love someone who was begotten by such evil?"

"Much the same way you can love the son of Antonov Latanya, I suppose," he pointed out.

Tia wiped her eyes again. "It's not the same thing."

He limped toward her and held out his arms. "It's exactly the same thing, my love. And if you can love me, even with the stain of being Antonov's son on my character, there is no reason at all why I can't love the daughter of the woman who tried to kill me."

She came to him almost reluctantly, but as soon as he had her in his arms, he knew everything would be all right.

"I'm so sorry, Misha. I shouldn't have gone to see her. It's just...you're shivering!"

"It's nothing to worry about. Just a little reminder that I'm not as cured as I'd like to think."

Tia leaned back in his arms and studied his face. "You don't have to lie to me, Misha."

"I'm not lying," he assured her, keeping his body still by sheer force of will. "I'm simply putting a brave face on a rather inconvenient relapse. I'll be fine in a little while. Promise me you won't leave."

"Are you sure, Misha? Really sure?"

"I'm sure."

"Then I promise."

"I love you, Tia," he whispered soothingly as she laid her head on his shoulder. "And I don't want you worrying about Ella. I'll take care of it. She won't bother you ever again, my love. I give you my word."

Misha made it to his room before he collapsed, but he wasn't able to take his rest yet. He needed to keep his promise to Tia first. Staggering to the settee, he rang for a servant, his shivering almost uncontrollable.

"Your highness?" the servant asked as he entered the room, looking at Misha with alarm.

"Fetch Lord Provin. Bring him here. Now."

The man fled the room and Misha sank down on to the couch, pulling a rug over himself to ward off the chill, even though the room was quite warm. He didn't need this. Not now. Not when it was so vital he keep his wits about him.

Dirk answered his summons with little delay. He took one look at Misha and dismissed the servant who accompanied him, and then he crossed the room and knelt beside the prince. "Is there anything I can do?"

Misha liked that about Dirk. He didn't waste time on useless platitudes.

"Not about this," he said, holding up a trembling hand for Dirk to see. "I need you to do something else for me. A favor. A big favor."

"Name it."

"I want you to take care of Ella Geon."

"I promised I would. As soon as I get back, we can convene the trial and—"

"No. I don't mean that. I mean I want you to take care of her. Now. Permanently."

Dirk was silent for a moment, and when he did finally speak there was no emotion in his voice, no censure. "You want me to kill her."

"I shouldn't ask it of you," Misha admitted, leaning back against the coach with his eyes closed. "But don't you see what will happen? She'll stand up in court and do nothing but dredge up a world of pain, which will do nothing but hurt the people I love."

"You mean Tia, I suppose."

He opened his eyes and stared up at the ceiling, wishing the pain would go away. Not just the pain of withdrawal. The pain of betrayal by the people he trusted. The pain of seeing the woman he loved suffering. "How ironic I fell for her. I never did have much of a choice, did I? Not with my . . . disabilities."

"I don't think Tia cares about that."

"Ella probably did me a favor, you know," he said, aware he was rambling, finding it hard to concentrate. "She gave me a chance to forget for a while. I don't think I was really aware of how much more my father loved Kirsh than me. How much he despised my weakness. My imperfections. Perhaps I should be grateful I spent most of my time coddled in poppy-dust. The reality of my position might have been a lot more painful if I'd known what was really going on around me."

"You don't mean that."

"Don't kid yourself, Dirk," he laughed sourly. "I sometimes think I'm just as deluded now as I was when I was an addict. Do you think Tia really loves me? Maybe she's using me, because I can give her the life Johan Thorn stole from her when he took her from the Hall of Shadows. And how long can I keep hold of my father's throne, anyway? Against Kirsh? If he doesn't take it from me, then all the able-bodied nobleman in Senet who resent being governed by a cripple certainly will."

"It's not like you to wallow in self-pity, Misha."

"It's not like me to ask another man to kill for me, either. It's the pain, I think. It's making me foolish. I never...I never..."

"Killed anyone before? Your father told me once it gets easier."

"Does it?"

"Not that I've noticed."

"Do you think I'm a monster? For a man who swore to rule by the law, I'm making an impressive start, aren't I? At the first test of my character, I choose vengeance over justice."

"Deal with it, Misha," Dirk said unsympathetically. "You're the Lion of Senet. If this is the worst thing you ever order, you'll still be streets ahead of your father."

He forced his eyes to focus on the Lord of the Suns. "You'll do it, then?"

"Wouldn't you rather wait until you're feeling better? You might have a change of heart—"

"Which is exactly the reason I don't want to wait, Dirk," he cut in. "I don't *want* to have a change of heart. I don't want to decide this rationally and coolly. I want the bitch who poisoned me and hurt the woman I love to be gone from our lives forever."

Dirk thought about it for a long time, and then he shrugged. "I'll take care of it. I think I owe Tia that much."

"You hurt her, Dirk."

"I know."

Misha stared at him, trying to read what was behind that flat admission of guilt. There was nothing in Dirk's expression that provided Misha with a satisfactory answer. "How will you—"

"Don't ask for details, Misha."

He nodded, glad Dirk had placed that condition on him. In truth, he didn't want to know the details. He just wanted it over.

"I'm sorry, my friend. I should have the courage to do this myself. It's not even for me really. It's just that Tia . . ."

"It doesn't take courage to kill someone. Sometimes it takes more courage to let them live."

"Then I am twice damned," Misha sighed. "I've neither the courage to let Ella Geon live, nor the strength to kill her myself. I will be in your debt forever, Dirk."

The young man stared at him for a long moment with those unreadable, metal-gray eyes and then he nodded.

"Yes, Misha," he agreed heavily. "You will."

PART SIX

A

QUESTION

OF

HONOR

Chapter 82

It was Marqel's idea to hold Antonov's funeral in the cavern at the end of the labyrinth. He had come all this way to speak to the Goddess, after all. It seemed only fitting the Lion of Senet should go to meet his Goddess in the place where everyone believed her voice could be most clearly heard.

Kirsh nodded silently when she suggested it, too stunned by the realization that his father was dead to care about his funeral arrangements. Marqel had kissed his forehead, smiled sympathetically and promised to take care of everything for him. Kirsh, grief-stricken and dismayed by Antonov's sudden demise, accepted her offer without a whimper of protest.

Marqel had arranged for Kirsh to find his father, sending him in to deliver the news about Misha about an hour after Eryk delivered the tea. The nightshade-laced peppermint had done its work long before Kirsh arrived. Antonov was lying on the floor of his tent, his tongue lolling out of the side of his mouth. He had—rather thoughtfully—placed the cup back on the saucer on the side table before collapsing. Marqel was able to remove the incriminating evidence before anyone even noticed it was there.

She announced that Antonov had been taken by the Goddess, just as the prophecies had foretold, but her announcement was met with a great deal of suspicion by the rank and file of both Antonov's army and the Shadowdancers stationed in Omaxin. Antonov was a healthy man in the prime of life. It didn't seem possible he could be struck down so easily without foul play being involved.

Marqel still had one trick to play, however. One more bit of information that would remove all doubt in the minds of the disbelievers; one ace to play that would lend her prophecies credence and banish forever any question that she could read the writings in the cavern and hear the voice of the Goddess.

Her way was not entirely without obstacles, though. Rudi Kalenkov demanded to see her when he learned what she had planned. Marqel had been avoiding the old Shadowdancer because he kept trying to pin her down on what part of the cavern wall she had read the prophecy about the false redeemer. Unfortunately, she would need all the Shadowdancers at the funeral, so she couldn't really deny him the audience he sought.

When she finally relented and allowed Rudi a few moments of her valuable time, she thought it was to nag her about the prophecy again. Picking a section at random, she pointed to it with a shrug and turned to leave. But Rudi didn't seem to care about the wall. He'd demanded an audience just so he could object strenuously to the idea of lighting a pyre in the cavern, claiming the ventilation was too poor and she was likely to suffocate them all if they were foolish enough to hold the funeral indoors. Marqel brushed aside the Shadowdancer's concerns until Rudi pointed out that as High Priestess, she would be standing closest to the pyre and would be the first overcome by the smoke. With that in mind, Marqel modified the ceremony so that only the lighting of the pyre would take place with an audience. She only needed a few minutes, anyway. Just enough time for the Goddess to make an appearance and for Marqel to make her announcement and all would be well.

After that, they would retreat from the cavern and let Antonov burn in peace, consumed by the flames that would carry his soul to his beloved—albeit nonexistent—Goddess.

With everyone in the habit of following her orders anyway, it was little trouble to get what she needed. The young Shadowdancer in charge of the medical supplies didn't question her when she claimed she had a toothache and needed access to his medicine chest. He simply stood back and watched as she rifled through the chest, taking the vial of oil and the whole jar of sulfur.

"You'll need to mix the oil and sulfur with vinegar for a toothache," the young man advised.

"I know that."

"You only need a little bit," he reminded her, looking worriedly at the large jar she had commandeered from the medicine chest.

"Are you questioning me?" she snapped, having learned most people responded to the threat of authority by backing down if they were challenged.

"Of course not, my lady," he hurried to assure her.

"I should think not!" she declared, flouncing out of the tent in high dudgeon, guaranteeing the young Shadowdancer would not query her need for all that sulfur.

Marqel waited until the day of the funeral before revealing her trump card. She waited until Antonov had been laid on his pyre, his arms crossed peacefully, clutching his diamond-bladed sword, the sulfur strategically placed for maximum effect when it caught fire. The irony amused her. Dirk had almost destroyed her by somehow preventing the sacrificial fires in Bollow from burning. Marqel intended to destroy him with exactly the opposite tactic.

When the Goddess was called on for a sign, this time (with a little bit of help from Marqel), the old bitch would oblige.

The pyre was smaller than Antonov deserved, given his rank and importance, but they couldn't light too big a fire in the hall, so Marqel made up for it in magnificence. If Marqel had learned anything in her life, it was the value of putting on a good show.

She had extinguished all other light in the cavern. Antonov was draped with white and gold cloth (the interior drapes of Antonov's tent, but she didn't think anyone would notice), with torches standing at the four cardinal points, casting flickering shadows over his inanimate features. The effect was very dramatic, she thought, even poignant. The silence in the huge cavern, the echoing loneliness of the place, simply added to the atmosphere.

She led Kirsh into the cavern the night before the funeral, determined he should appreciate the full, heartrending impact of Antonov lying in state. Kirsh planned to keep a vigil over his father, a common practice following the death of a king. Privately, Marqel couldn't see the point. The man was dead and watching over him all night wouldn't bring him back.

Sliding her hand comfortingly into Kirsh's, she led him to the pyre. He stared at his father for a long time, not saying a word.

"You are his heir," she told him softly.

Kirsh shook his head. "That's Misha. I'm just a second son."

"No," she corrected. "It's you, Kirsh. You are the one he trusted. You are the one who swore an oath to see the Goddess's will is done."

"But he didn't know Misha was back. He never got the chance to—"

"And do you think Antonov would have asked Misha for the oath he asked of you, even had he come here to Omaxin?" she cut in, before Kirsh could get too maudlin about his brother. "Misha, the poppy-dust addict? Misha, the *cripple*? Misha, the man who wants to destroy the Shadowdancers? No, Kirsh. Your father asked that oath of you because you are the only one on Ranadon capable of seeing justice prevail."

"What do I tell Misha?"

"The truth. That you have sworn an oath to see Antonov's wishes fulfilled, and you intend to do it, whether he likes it or not." She smiled and squeezed his hand. "What are you afraid of, Kirsh? It's not like he's going to declare war on you for wanting to keep your oath."

"Of course he wouldn't declare war on me," Kirsh agreed. "It's just... with Dirk in his ear... I don't know. He may not be as sympathetic as we'd like. And he has good reason, Marqel. Belagren and Ella were poisoning him."

"And will you deny the Goddess her due because of the actions of a couple of grasping, evil old women?"

"I'll write to him," Kirsh announced after a long tense moment of silence. "I'll tell him what happened. I'll explain the oath I made to our father and what I have to do, and then we'll just wait and see."

"It will be all right, Kirsh," she promised. "The Goddess is on our side."

When they gathered in the cavern the following day, Kirsh was bleary-eyed from lack of sleep but seemed to have dealt with much of his grief. *Perhaps that was why people thought all-night vigils were useful,* Marqel decided. *Maybe they were more about the living than the dead.*

Almost everyone in Omaxin gathered in the cavern at first sunrise, to bid farewell to the Lion of Senet. Kirsh delivered the eulogy in a surprisingly steady voice, detailing his father's remarkable life with a sense of genuine admiration and a remarkable economy of words. He read his speech from notes Marqel thought Rees must have prepared. Kirsh wasn't the type to think about what he said before he said it. But Rees Provin was. Perhaps, while Kirsh kept his vigil, Rees Provin was composing the eulogy Kirsh would deliver.

Marqel looked around the cavern as Kirsh spoke, amazed that even with more than two thousand people in here, the hall barely looked crowded. Some of them would have to leave soon, which was a pity, because the more people who witnessed her moment of glory, the better. But Rudi was right. Once the flames took hold the smoke would become deadly, and there wasn't much point in having a triumphant moment if everyone who saw it wound up dead.

Kirsh finished his speech and hung his head in a moment of silent prayer. When he was done, he glanced across at Sergey and nodded, the signal for those not permitted to watch the burning to depart. Briefed before the ceremony by their captains, at Sergey's signal, the troops in the cavern stood to attention, raised their swords in salute and then turned and marched from the hall, followed by those members of Rudi's staff that he felt were surplus to requirements. It took awhile, but before long there were less than twenty people in the cavern. It was a small audience, but an important one.

As the footsteps faded in the Labyrinth from the last of the mourners, Sergey stepped forward with a torch. Kirsh took it from him, holding it high for a moment, its uneven light reflecting off the edge of the golden eye he stood upon.

Then, carefully, and with a great deal of reverence, his eyes glistening with tears, Kirsh lowered the torch to the pyre.

Marqel hung her head, mostly because she was overcome by a sudden urge to smile, which would have ruined everything.

The tent hangings caught quickly and soon burned away, exposing the pyre underneath. The flames burned high, the oil-soaked wood billowing thick scented smoke toward the cavern's roof. Marqel glanced at the fire and then up at the smoke with concern. She hoped it wouldn't take too long before the sulfur caught. Although the cavern was enormous, Rudi had made a very valid point about the smoke and the ventilation in here.

The flames licked upward, reaching Antonov's clothes, which began to smoulder. Marqel unconsciously held her breath in anticipation. *Any minute now ...*

"The Goddess speaks!"

Everyone turned to stare at the High Priestess as she cried out, falling to her knees, her eyes suddenly filled with tears. At that moment the flames reached the sulfur she had liberated from the medicine chest and without warning, the pyre flared so brightly for an instant that everyone was forced to shield his eyes.

"The Goddess speaks!" she cried once more, for good measure.

"Marqel!" Kirsh cried in alarm. He tried to come to her but Rees held him back.

"What does the Goddess have to say, my lady?" Rudi asked in a voice that sounded skeptical rather than awestruck.

Marqel looked up at Kirsh, her eyes streaming silent, crystal tears. "She speaks of your father," she told him in a strangled whisper. "She is joy. She is sadness."

"Does she say anything useful?" Rudi insisted.

He's going to pay for using that tone with me.

"She speaks of your father's faith," she said to Kirsh, ignoring Rudi and everyone else in the cavern. "And of ... betrayal."

Kirsh looked shocked. "The Goddess thinks my father betrayed her?"

"Not your father. Someone else." Marqel shook her head and looked at Rees. "She speaks of a brother. And a sister."

"A sister?" Rees asked in confusion. "I have no sister."

"Your brother's sister?" she ventured, as if she was just as confused. "She speaks of the false redeemer. And the girl-child he intends to use to usurp her power."

"And does this girl-child have a name?" Rudi asked, sounding even more incredulous.

Before Marqel could answer, Rees glanced at Kirsh, who nodded grimly.

"Melliandra Thorn."

Marqel looked at Kirsh in surprise. "You know of whom the Goddess speaks?"

She didn't think he knew about Mellie Thorn. In fact, her whole plan was based on the assumption that he didn't. Marqel was supposed to reveal it to him... another vital piece of information she could only have learned from the Goddess; the proof that the Goddess confided in her. Then she realized this was even better. If Kirsh knew about Mellie Thorn and thought that Marqel didn't... well, it just made her story that much more plausible.

"Dirk's half-sister by Johan Thorn and Lexie Seranov," Rees explained to the others in the cavern. "Eryk let it slip while we were in Bollow."

"I wish I could interpret her words more... clearly, my lord, but she speaks of great danger. She fears for her people. She fears that some will be easily led into false beliefs." Marqel turned her attention back to Kirsh. "I'm sorry, Kirsh. She speaks of Misha as if he has already turned from her path..." She wiped her eyes again, and realized that it wasn't her brilliant acting that was bringing on the tears, it was the thickening smoke from the pyre.

"What do you expect?" Rudi asked with concern. "What... with the false redeemer advising him?"

Kirsh was too disturbed to notice the insolence in the questions of the elder Shadowdancer. He nodded in agreement, taking Rudi's word at face value. And then coughed and looked up. The smoke seemed trapped above the pyre and was billowing downward at an alarming rate. Rudi looked up, too, and then smiled faintly at the young prince.

"Perhaps, if the High Priestess is willing," Rudi suggested, "she might finish her discussion with the Goddess outside? It would be a pity if we are all asphyxiated before she can tell us what the Goddess wants of us, wouldn't it?"

Chapter 83

In the days following the announcement of Antonov's death, Jacinta D'Orlon found herself growing quite fond of the new Lion of Senet, particularly when Misha called her to his study about a week after Dirk left for Omaxin for a private meeting. His pretext was clearing up some minor details over the withdrawal of the Senetians from Dhevyn. In the course of the discussion, he quite deliberately let it slip that her mother was due the following day to escort her home. Misha then suggested, with a perfectly innocent expression, that as the Queen of Dhevyn's envoy, Jacinta might be interested in carrying some urgent dispatches north to Omaxin on his behalf, and that once in the north, she might wish to stay for a time. The High Priestess was a Dhevynian citizen, after all, and it was only fair Senet allow the sovereign nation of Dhevyn an observer to ensure her citizens were treated according to the rules of war.

Jacinta could have kissed him.

It was only a temporary respite, she knew. That her mother had gone to such pains to keep the betrothal to Raban Seranov from Jacinta spoke much of Lady Sofia's determination to finally see her wayward daughter wed. And it was a torment beyond words to send her north for the protection of the only man she actually wanted, who was also—rather inconveniently— the only man on Ranadon she probably couldn't have. But Jacinta was desperate, and as the sailors claimed, any port in a storm was a welcome one.

Jacinta squared her shoulders determinedly as they neared Omaxin. The army was larger than she expected, spread out between the low foothills surrounding the ruins in a manner that looked rather haphazard to her inexperienced eye. Although Jacinta had never been in a war camp before, she wondered, for a moment, if Dirk had any idea what he was doing. He wasn't a soldier and looking around, she thought his lack of expertise seemed painfully obvious.

Quailing a little under the speculative gazes of the soldiers she rode past, they entered the camp just south of Omaxin. Did they think her a camp follower? Some floozy looking for a quick profit? The Queen of Dhevyn's envoy unconsciously lifted her chin, as if her regal demeanor was enough to herald her intentions as honorable and that she rode into camp as a diplomat, not a courtesan.

Misha had sent her with only a small escort, understanding speed was more important than comfort. They had ridden hard from Avacas. It was over a month now since Dirk had headed north with the army sent to force Kirsh to surrender.

One of Misha's captains came out to greet them as they rode into the center of the camp. He looked surprised to find a woman in the party, even more so to find a Dhevynian of noble birth.

"My lady?"

"Where is the Lord of the Suns?"

"He's not here, my lady."

"Where is he?"

"Er . . . I believe he's gone for a walk."

He's probably hiding, she thought, tempted to ask the man if they'd checked down by the lake. Perhaps he was skipping stones again.

"Which direction did he go?"

"That way, my lady," the captain replied, pointing north.

"Then I shall find him myself," she declared, kicking her horse forward before anybody could stop her.

She found Dirk not far from the camp, standing on a rise that gave him a good view of the ruins. She dismounted and tied the reins of her mount to a straggling tree branch and climbed up the small hillock toward him.

He heard her footsteps and turned to see who was disturbing him. If he was surprised to see her, she couldn't tell. It must mean he was worried, she thought. She'd noticed that about Dirk. The tougher things got, the more he shut down, as if by not letting anything out, nothing that hurt could get in.

Jacinta stopped for a moment. "Everybody's looking for you."

He wordlessly offered her his hand and pulled her up the last few steps. She stopped when she reached the small plateau and looked out over the ruined city. It was the first time she'd seen the ruins and they left her speechless. She had no idea they would cover such a large area. No idea that up here a city of hundreds of thousands of people must have once thrived. The small rise was high enough to afford a grand view of Omaxin, which brought another, rather more urgent thought to mind.

"Is it wise, standing up here silhouetted against the sun, such an obvious target?"

"For me to be a target, Kirsh's forces would also have to be in range," he pointed out with a shrug. "It's safe enough."

"It must have been a truly impressive city once."

"Neris Veran claimed this place was the most valuable thing on Ranadon."

"He's probably right. Perhaps..."

"Perhaps what?"

"I was just thinking...perhaps, when all this is done, you could come back here and study it. *Really* study it, I mean. There must be so much down in those ruins we could learn."

Dirk shrugged. "I'd like that. But I don't think it's possible. I'm not sure if the Lord of the Suns can take time off to indulge his curiosity."

"Then do it officially. Belagren had people up here for years, didn't she?"

"They were simply trying to break through the Labyrinth."

"But you have a precedent, my lord. That's half the battle, right there."

He studied her face in the ruby light of the second sun. Feeling his gaze on her, she turned to look at him. "You're worried about what's going to happen, aren't you?"

"Is it that obvious?"

"Not to others, I think. You've a knack for keeping your thoughts secret."

"Not from you, apparently."

"Ah, but then I'm not like everyone else."

Dirk didn't answer her for a moment. "Kirsh is far better at warfare than I am. I'm not a general, Jacinta."

"You are today."

He looked at her curiously. "You think I can win this?"

"I don't think you have a choice, Dirk. If Marqel is allowed to gather people to the banner of the High Priestess, then all you've done, all you've worked for, will have been for nothing. You need to put an end to her and you must do it quickly, while the world is still reeling from the revelation her visions were a sham. The longer it takes, the more time people will have to fall back into their old beliefs. And you need to stop Kirshov, too. Senet will be torn apart if brother is pitted against brother in a religious civil war."

He laughed sourly.

"Did I say something funny?"

"Brother against brother."

She looked at him curiously.

"Rees is down there with Kirsh," he explained. "I'm here leading Misha's army against his brother, and my brother is down there with Kirsh, ready to fight me."

Jacinta knew Rees Provin had gone north with Kirsh. Faralan had told her when she stopped overnight in Bollow on her way here. But until now, the full implication of his presence in Omaxin hadn't really dawned on her.

"Speaking of your brother," she said. "Did you know you're an uncle? Faralan had a boy. She named him Wallin."

Dirk smiled briefly, but it was a perfunctory smile, one of politeness rather than genuine pleasure. "That would have pleased my father."

"Your...oh, you mean Duke Wallin."

"I still think of him as my father, you know...I mean, I know Johan Thorn sired me, but he's little more than...I hardly knew him."

"I think I understand."

"I'm glad somebody does. I'm not sure I do."

She smiled. "I think you're too hard on yourself, my lord. You've done a lot of good since you decided to take a hand in the fate of the world. The Shadowdancers are in ruins. Dhevyn is free. There will be no more Landfall sacrifices..."

Dirk glanced at her, his expression grim. "You only say that because you don't know half the things I've done."

"I know what you've done for Alenor. That makes you more hero than monster in my opinion."

"Then I treasure your opinion, my lady."

Jacinta looked away, a little uncomfortable with his scrutiny.

As if he understood her awkwardness, Dirk suddenly smiled. "I keep asking myself how I ever wound up trying to prevent Senet being torn apart. I can't recall that being part of the plan."

"We all do things we never imagined we'd do." She returned his smile, a little shyly. "I can't recall ever imagining I'd follow the Lord of the Suns to war."

"Which raises a rather interesting question—what *are* you doing here, my lady?"

"I'm here to observe your conduct of this conflict," she replied simply.

"Whose idea was that?"

"Misha's, actually."

"I see. I thought you were getting married?"

"Am I?" she asked. "That's news to me. My mother hasn't told me anything about it. I wonder if that means she was disappointed when she arrived in Avacas and discovered I'd already left for Omaxin."

Dirk seemed amused. "You've run away, haven't you?"

"Don't be ridiculous! I am merely bringing you dispatches and staying to ensure that you treat Marqel with the courtesy due any Dhevynian citizen."

"Then what are you going to do when I strangle her with my bare hands?"

"I'm a well-bred lady, my lord. I'd probably have to swoon and look away and swear afterward I never saw a thing."

Dirk looked back at the ruins where Kirsh's forces were

gathered, preparing for the battle. Their campfires spread like pinpoints of danger in the red light.

"He'll kick my arse, you know," Dirk warned. "Kirsh is a professional soldier. He spent his whole life preparing for this moment. And Rees is no slouch, either, when it comes to a fight."

"Then why fight them at all? Why not meet with Kirsh? Ask him to surrender?"

"I don't think the word *surrender* is in Kirsh's vocabulary."

"Maybe not," she conceded. "And I know Kirsh can be an idiot, but he must realize that the only end to this is the complete devastation of Senet. If you can't appeal to his reason, maybe you could appeal to his honor."

"Kirsh's honor is half the reason we're in this mess. Do you really think he'd agree to a meeting to discuss surrender?"

"You won't know unless you ask."

Dirk thought about it for a moment and then he nodded. "Maybe we can sort this out without any more bloodshed."

"I'm sure you will," she told him.

Dirk smiled. "I wish the rest of the world had your faith in me."

"Misha does. Tia's not particularly fond of you though, is she?"

"We were close once," he admitted carefully.

"How close?"

"That's none of your business."

"Oh," she said with a knowing little smile. "*That* close, eh?"

Dirk looked at her. "Does that bother you?"

"Should it?"

"You keep answering my questions with more questions."

"I must have picked up that irritating habit from you. Did you know Misha intends to marry her?"

"Yes."

"It's going to cause quite a stir, the Lion of Senet marrying the heretic's daughter. Still, Misha doesn't seem afraid to make unpopular decisions. He's withdrawn all the Senetians from Dhevyn, too."

"That was none of my doing. It was Tia who made him promise to do that as soon as he had it in his power." He sighed and looked down over the ruins again. "Sometimes I think I should have just left well enough alone."

"What to do you mean?"

"Misha was being poisoned by the Shadowdancers. Even if I hadn't lifted a finger that might have eventually been discovered. Antonov's faith would have been just as rattled to learn of it. The Shadowdancers might have been destroyed anyway. And I wouldn't be standing here trying to figure out how I'm suppose to win a battle against my own brother and a man I once counted as my best friend."

"You don't know that," she sad, trying to reassure him. "Besides, there's no point dwelling on what might have been."

"Not much point at all," he agreed.

His voice was filled with regret. Jacinta was certain he wasn't talking about bringing down the Shadowdancers, either.

"We should get back to the camp."

He shrugged. "There's no point hiding now, I suppose. If you found me, it won't take the others long."

"I was half expecting to find you down by the lake, actually. Skipping stones."

He smiled. It was the first genuine smile she'd seen from him in quite a while. "I thought about it."

"I wonder what the army would have thought about that, if they'd caught you at it?"

"I suspect it would have merely reinforced their opinion I'm a boy trying to do a job better left in the hands of a real man."

"You're man enough for this job, Dirk."

"Let's hope you still think that after the battle call is sounded," he said.

Chapter 84

The army Dirk had gathered outside the ruins of Omaxin surprised Kirsh. He was alarmed by the size of it and stunned that Misha had reacted to his letter by sending an army to confront him. He'd gone to great pains to explain the oath he'd given their father. He was hurt and more than a little angry with Misha's unsympathetic response.

Didn't his brother understand the bind Kirsh was in? Didn't Misha realize he had no choice? That his oath, once given, was irrevocable?

It would have been much simpler if Dirk had come alone, not with Misha's army at his back. If only he could have convinced Dirk he must support Marqel; that he must forget any ambitions he might have for his half-sister and support the Shadowdancers and their High Priestess, because that was what Antonov wanted. It was his dying wish. And that was what Kirsh had sworn to Antonov he would do.

"How many men do you estimate they have?" he asked Rees. They had climbed to the top of a ruined building near the edge of the old city to view the forces sent against them. But it was hard to calculate how many were out there. Most of the army was concealed by the fold of the hills.

"Easily as many as we have," the Duke of Elcast estimated. "Two thousand or so. There could be a lot more. It's hard to tell with the way they've set up the camp."

"Misha's pulled some of the troops out of Dhevyn, then," Kirsh remarked, thinking that was the only way his brother could have raised an army so large in such a short time.

"He's pulled *most* of them out, I'd wager," Rees suggested. "To send this many men against you."

"Do you think they really intend to fight, or is Misha bluffing?"

"He's your brother, Kirsh. You can answer that question more easily than I."

There was little chance of it reaching a negotiated settlement, Kirsh thought. Misha wanted the Shadowdancers destroyed as much as Dirk did. And even if Dirk had been inclined to compromise, Misha was in no mood to be generous after what had been done to him.

"It's your brother in command down there, Rees. What do you think he'll do?"

Rees shrugged. "I've never been able to read Dirk well. Even when we were children. He was always so... different."

"You don't have to stay," Kirsh offered. "It's bad enough that I'm at odds with Misha. You don't have to take sides against your brother, too. If you want to leave..."

"My *brother*," Rees said, his voice heavy with bitterness. Kirsh looked at him curiously. "He was always her favorite, you know."

Kirsh didn't offer a reply. He supposed Rees was talking about Morna.

"I never really understood why," Rees continued, "until your father told me Dirk was Johan Thorn's bastard. It all made sense after that. Why she always doted on him. Why she was so protective of him. Even after he left, she still wouldn't tolerate a bad word said about him. She poisoned Faralan with her attitude, too. Or maybe it was Dirk. I don't know. I found them together, you know. The day before Dirk left Elcast. They were talking about me. At least, I think they were. The truth is, I don't know what he said to her—Faralan would never tell me—but she was different after that. It's wrong for a woman to keep secrets from her husband, don't you think? Anyway, whatever he said to her, Faralan was almost as bad as Morna after that. Disagreeable. Snide. Always making comments about the Landfall Festival being barbaric. Questioning her beliefs. Doubting things... Goddess, she even helped Dirk get away the night Morna was..." Rees's voice trailed off unhappily. "Dirk has a talent for ruining other people's lives."

Rees's rambling soliloquy surprised Kirsh. He had thought himself to be the only one suffering because of Dirk. It never occurred to him Rees might harbor such bitterness. Or that he would have such good cause.

"Why do you suppose Misha sent Dirk to lead the army?"

"Because he's the Lord of the Suns. That makes it a religious war now, not a civil war."

"It's brother against brother, Rees. That's a civil war in my book."

"What do the prophecies say?"

"They say we'll win."

"Against a force so large? I wonder what the Goddess knows that she's not telling us?"

"Don't you believe the High Priestess?"

"I admit to being a tad doubtful at the outset," Rees admitted. "But when she told us about the Thorn girl... well, how could she have known about that if the Goddess hadn't told her?"

"Perhaps if you speak to Dirk?"

"I doubt it would make a difference," Rees warned. "Besides, what would I say to him, Kirsh? I'm taking your side because my brother is the false redeemer? I don't think that tactic would work too well."

Kirsh shrugged. "Still, we have one more advantage. Dirk doesn't know the first thing about fighting a battle."

"But the men advising him will know," Rees warned. "And Dirk is smart enough to heed good advice when he hears it. I'd not count on his inexperience to aid us."

"Why do you think he asked for a meeting?"

"He probably doesn't want to fight. Dirk hasn't the heart for it. Knowing my brother, he'd rather talk his way out of it. He's good at that."

Very good at it, Kirsh agreed silently, thinking of how often Dirk's quick tongue saved him in the past. "Do you think there's a chance he'll back down?"

Rees shook his head. "He's probably trying to give *you* a chance to back down."

"I won't," Kirsh said.

"Then let's meet with the Lord of the Suns, your highness, and find out if he's bluffing."

When Kirsh returned to the camp, Marqel was nowhere to be
seen, but Rudi Kalenkov was waiting for him. He'd been trying
to get Kirsh alone ever since Antonov's funeral, but Kirsh was
in no mood to be bothered with him. He had too many other
things to deal with to bother listening to the Shadowdancer's
complaints about the interruption a battle might cause to their
work.

"Your highness! I must speak to you," the Shadowdancer said, clutching Kirsh's bridle as they rode back in to the
camp.

"Not now, Rudi, I'm busy." Kirsh dismounted, jerked the
bridle from the Shadowdancer's grasp and handed the reins
of his mount to Sergey, who led both horses away toward the
corrals.

"But I really *must* speak with you, sire."

"I don't have the time," he snapped. "In case you haven't
noticed, we're about to go to war."

"This is very important, your highness."

"We have a different definition of important, Rudi."

He turned his back on the Shadowdancer and strode
toward his tent.

"It's about the prophecies, sire," Rudi called after him.

Kirsh stopped and looked back at him. "What about
them."

"Come to the cavern with me. I have something to show
you."

Kirsh had spent very little time in the cavern since he'd been in
Omaxin. The huge hall oppressed him and the golden eye in the
center of the floor seemed to follow him wherever he went.
Their footsteps echoed through the chamber as Rudi led him
across the torchlit hall to a section of wall where several other
Shadowdancers were working, assiduously copying down
every sign and sigil on the walls.

"This is where the High Priestess claims she read the
prophecy regarding the false redeemer," Rudi told him, point-

ing to a panel that looked no different to Kirsh than any other part of the wall.

"So?"

"Well, it doesn't make sense."

"That's why *she's* the High Priestess and you're not," Kirsh pointed out frostily. "Only Marqel can read the Goddess's writings."

"That's not what I mean, sire." Rudi took a sheet of parchment from one of his workers and held it up for Kirsh to see. "You see, we have the translation the High Priestess provided. And now we know where she read it from, we should be able to use her translation to aid us in working out the rest of it."

"I see," Kirsh agreed, a little doubtfully. He really had no idea what Rudi was driving at.

"Certain words reoccur frequently in any written language," Rudi explained in a rather lecturing tone. "Even simple words like *and* or *the* can be enough to provide us with the key to translation. Just as we always write those words the same way, the symbols for those words in another language should be consistent. We should see them repeated over and over. And there *are* many symbols that are repeated on these walls, which implies this writing forms a language which has its own, not unfamiliar, rules of structure and grammar, if only we could understand them."

"Then what's the problem?"

"They're not there, your highness. The words of the prophecies as told to us by the High Priestess cannot be reconciled with the writing she claims to have translated it from."

Kirsh glared at him in the flickering torchlight. "Are you suggesting the High Priestess is wrong?"

"I'm suggesting you might want to allow for the possibility she is mistaken," Rudi said carefully. "Particularly before you embark upon a battle against a significantly larger force than our own, with only the words of the High Priestess's prophecy to assure you of victory."

Kirsh began to feel as if the whole world was against him. First Misha sent an army against him and now Marqel's own

Shadowdancers were beginning to doubt her. "What you are suggesting is heresy, my lord."

"Only if I'm wrong, sire," Rudi retorted.

"Have you told anybody else of your theory?"

"No, your highness. I thought you should be first to know."

"Then you are to repeat your heretical nonsense to no one. In fact I want your people out of this cavern altogether. We're about to go to war, Rudi. I'll need your Shadowdancers to help the wounded. I don't have time for them to sit in here, poring over something they don't understand, trying to prove the High Priestess is a liar."

"That wasn't my intention, your highness," Rudi objected. "I was merely trying to point out that—"

Kirsh glared at him. "Get your people out of the cavern. I don't want anyone in here without my permission from now on."

"As you wish, your highness," Rudi reluctantly agreed, but there was a gleam of malicious satisfaction in his eyes.

Or maybe it was the torchlight that made Kirsh wonder if Rudi was deliberately trying to destroy his belief that Marqel spoke the truth.

Chapter 85

Dirk met Kirsh and Rees in the no-man's-land between the ruins and the vast camp of Misha's army. Although accompanied by their captains, they rode out alone to talk on the open ground between them, out of earshot of their escorts. The second sun beat down mercilessly, glittering off Lake Ruska in the distance, making it almost too bright to look upon.

Dirk reined in first and waited for Kirsh and his brother to reach him. He hadn't seen Rees since the day of the eclipse ceremony, and by the scowl his brother wore, he guessed there was little hope of reason from that quarter. Kirsh looked tired and careworn as he trotted across the broken ground, as if the strain of the past months had aged him far beyond his years.

"So now you're a general," Rees remarked icily as he and the prince reined in to confront Dirk.

"Not by choice."

"You say that a lot, you know," Kirsh remarked. "*I didn't mean it. I didn't plan for it to work out this way.* It's always somebody else's fault."

Dirk shrugged, prepared to acknowledge a certain amount of truth in Kirsh's accusation. "I'm quite willing to accept the blame, Kirsh. But my mistake was making Marqel High Priestess and I'll probably regret that deed as long as I live."

"So now it's *her* fault?"

Dirk shook his head. "We're equally to blame, Kirsh. We both put ideas in her head that she could be more than she should have been."

"All I ever did was love her, Dirk."

"And you think that wasn't a dream beyond imagining for a Landfall bastard picked up out of a traveling show? I'll admit I should never have set her up as the Voice of the Goddess, but be honest enough to admit your own contribution."

"What do you mean, *you* set her up as the Voice of the Goddess?" Rees demanded, obviously confused.

"I told her what to say," Dirk informed him, "just as Neris Veran told Belagren what to say when he discovered when the Age of Shadows was due to end."

"You took advantage of her," Kirsh accused, angrily. "You manipulated something that should have been sacred and used it to your own ends."

"She never spoke to the Goddess, Kirsh. *I* told Marqel how to get through the delta. It took me weeks to get her to memorize the instructions. Nobody has *ever* spoken to the Goddess. Not Belagren, and certainly not Marqel."

"You're lying."

"I've no need to lie. I have an army at my back three times the size of yours and don't think for a moment I'm going to try to lead it myself. I have no interest in seeking glory in battle."

"With your limited experience, there won't be much glory to speak of," Rees suggested with a contemptuous sneer.

"My experience or lack of it isn't the issue, Rees. I've got plenty of experienced campaigners among my staff. I'm more than happy to let them decide the best way to annihilate your forces in the most efficient way possible."

Rees glared at him. "Then why did you ask for this meeting? If that's what you think, go back to your staff of experienced campaigners, little brother, and sound the attack."

"I was hoping you'd both see reason."

"This is not a question of reason," Kirsh announced flatly. "I swore an oath to my father."

"You swore an oath to a madman who was being manipulated by a murderous little slut with no thought for anything but her own ambition. She murdered Belagren. She almost killed Alenor out of jealousy and spite, and I have my suspicions about a few others who got in her way, too."

"You're lying," Kirsh insisted, growing angrier with every word Dirk uttered. "I've seen her speak to the Goddess. I have proof."

"How did Antonov die, Kirsh?"

"The Goddess took him."

Dirk snorted skeptically. "And who decided the cause of death? *Marqel?*"

"It makes no difference, Dirk. You're clutching at sunbeams. He wasn't murdered, and I wouldn't try to cover for his killer if he was. I'd burn the man myself before I let anybody get away with killing my father. Antonov was alone when he died. There is no question of foul play."

"Doesn't it strike you as being just a tad convenient he died right after you swore an oath to see Marqel restored? He wasn't drinking peppermint tea, was he?"

"You think *Marqel* killed him?" Kirsh scoffed. "Don't be absurd! Anyway, she was with me when he died. The last person who saw Antonov alive was Eryk. Perhaps you think it was he that killed my father?"

Dirk was genuinely shocked by that news. "What is Eryk doing here?"

"Serving the Goddess," Rees snapped.

"Send him back," Dirk urged. "He'll be safer with me."

"Only if we lose, Dirk."

"There's no chance you can win, Rees."

"The prophecies say we can."

Dirk looked at him askance. "What prophecies?"

Kirsh smiled. "You didn't know about them, did you? Perhaps if you'd stayed longer in Omaxin you might have read them for yourself. Marqel has told me what they say and the Goddess has confirmed it. They foretold my father's death. They call you the false redeemer."

"*Marqel* read your prophecies for you and foretold Antonov's demise?" Dirk laughed. "She can barely make out her own name, Kirsh. And I should know. I taught her how to read."

"Are you jealous you're not the only one who can read the writings in the cavern?" Rees asked.

"I might be if I *could* read them," he shrugged. "I really have no idea what they say, and neither does anybody else on Ranadon. Especially not an illiterate like Marqel."

"But you claimed you *could* translate them," Kirsh reminded him. "I was there when you read them to me."

"I also said there'd be an eclipse, Kirsh. Do you remember that?"

Kirsh fell silent, his expression dark and brooding.

"Let it go, Kirsh," Dirk urged. "Come back to Avacas with me and let's sort this out sensibly. There is nothing to be gained by going to war."

"And if he did go back with you?" Rees asked. "What then? Has Misha had a change of heart? Have you? Have you decided to let the Shadowdancers remain? Will you support their High Priestess?"

"Even if I didn't intend to destroy the Shadowdancers, Rees, Misha won't stand for them. And Marqel cannot be allowed to remain High Priestess. She murdered Belagren and probably Antonov the moment he was of no further use to her. If you insist on supporting her, she'll be the death of you, too."

"You offer nothing but lies, Dirk," Kirsh said heavily.

"Everything you've done is a lie. You hold the rank of Lord of the Suns under false pretenses. You have no faith in the Goddess. You accuse Marqel of being evil for doing exactly what you have done. You claim she's lying about the prophecies, yet I stood there and watched you read them to me. You claim Marqel killed Belagren, yet you willingly admit you set her up to replace Belagren. And now you want us to believe the High Priestess he believed in so ardently killed my father. *You* drove him to insanity, Dirk, and what's more, I suspect you're proud of it."

"You know why I lied, Kirsh. I've explained it to you a dozen times since Bollow."

"And what about the things you haven't told me?"

"What things?"

"Like the existence of Johan Thorn's wife and daughter?" he asked. "What was the point of keeping them a secret, Dirk? Goddess, when I think about you standing there in Johan's house in Mil, claiming you didn't know who those women were... You didn't even blink when you saw them. I suppose there's no chance Alexin really killed them, is there? You were secretly allied with my father's enemies all along, weren't you? Does Misha know of your talent for playing both sides against the middle? How long does he have before you turn on him, too?"

"Kirsh..."

"You always claimed you didn't want to be a king, and now I realize why. You don't need to be a king. You're much happier manipulating things from behind the throne. Misha's playing right into your hands, isn't he? How lucky for you he came back to Avacas a changed man. And what could be better for you than a little sister sitting on the Eagle Throne who'll do anything you tell her?"

"If you choose to believe such an idiotic scenario, Kirsh, then you're as mad as Antonov was."

"I *have* no choice, if my choice is to pick one liar over another."

"It's a question of motives, Kirsh."

"And your motives are so much purer than ours, is that it?" Rees said.

Dirk stared at Rees, unsure what he'd done to engender such bitterness in his brother. "I did what I did because it was the right thing to do, Rees."

"You did what you did because you wanted vengeance," Kirsh corrected. "The fact that it had global consequences was just a convenient peg for you to hang your morals on. There is nothing noble in what you've done. You simply set out to get even with Belagren and my father and decided to bring the whole world along for the ride."

"I exposed a lie, Kirsh. A lie that was driving the whole of Ranadon along a path to total barbarism."

"And the end justifies the means? Who the hell set you up as the moral guardian of Ranadon? You don't believe in the Goddess, so where does your authority come from, Dirk? What gives you the right to decide the path the whole world should take?"

The question surprised Dirk, particularly when he realized he couldn't think of a satisfactory reply.

"Don't have an answer for that one? Funny, I thought you had an answer for everything."

"Kirsh, this is getting us nowhere. Stand your troops down and come back to Avacas with me," he pleaded. "Talk to Misha. However much you despise what I've done, you have no quarrel with him."

"I *didn't* have a quarrel with him," Kirsh pointed out coldly. "Until he sent an army against me with you at its head."

"The people you're so determined to protect tried to kill him, Kirsh. Do you *blame* him for being upset?"

"I blame him for reacting like a prince, not like a brother."

"He's the Lion of Senet now. Your father would have reacted in exactly the same way if he was in Misha's position."

"But we'll never know that for certain, will we, Dirk? My father is dead."

Dirk sighed, realizing they had done nothing but talk around in circles. He gathered up the reins of his mount and sat a little straighter in the saddle.

"You've got until second sunrise tomorrow, Kirsh. After that, the matter is out of my hands. There will be no quarter given."

"And no quarter asked," Kirsh replied.

Dirk stared at him, thinking that if anybody had suggested that he might one day face Kirsh over a battlefield, he would have laughed at him and called him mad. But then war was a particular type of madness. Especially one as unnecessary as this one.

"Kirsh..."

Kirsh didn't answer him. He turned his horse and cantered toward his escort. Rees watched him leave and then turned back to glare at Dirk.

"Mother would be proud of you." It wasn't meant as a compliment. Rees's voice was bitter, almost petulant.

"I wonder what she'd think of *you*," Dirk retorted, surprised at how angry Rees's taunt had made him. "Tell me, did you stay and watch your own mother burn or did you simply walk away once you'd issued the order to have her killed?"

"Morna deserved to die, Dirk. She was a traitor and a harlot."

"She was our mother, Rees."

"She was *your* mother, Dirk. She was never mine. Morna abandoned me. For you she gave up everything. Don't you dare sit there and try to make me feel guilty for seeing justice was done."

"There was nothing just about burning your own mother alive, Rees."

"And where is the justice in abandoning your husband and child to run off with a lover?" Rees asked resentfully. "You might hold Morna up as a paragon of virtue, Dirk, but to me she was nothing more than a treacherous whore who tried to raise her lover's bastard as another man's son."

"You couldn't possibly remember her leaving Elcast, Rees. You were barely old enough to walk when she left you to join Johan."

"I remember when she came back, though," Rees said. "I

remember when you were born. And I remember spending the rest of my childhood being pushed aside for you."

"That's nonsense."

"You were always her favorite. She used to brag about how special you were. I wonder what she'd think of you now? Lord of the Suns! You've made a mockery of her whole pitiful cause, haven't you? You haven't just turned your back on her, you're actively aiding her enemies. You should be grateful I killed her. At least she can't see you like this."

Dirk had not felt the urge to hit anyone so badly since the morning Belagren died and he'd slapped Marqel. He knew what Rees was doing. He was trying to provoke him. Trying to justify his own role in this fiasco.

"Dhevyn is free, Rees," he pointed out, keeping his temper by sheer force of will. "You're the one siding with her enemies. Kirsh is backing the wrong horse, and you know it."

"Kirsh is fighting *you*, Dirk. That makes his cause as right as it can be in my eyes."

There was no reasoning with him. But Dirk couldn't walk away from this without trying. He owed Wallin Provin that much.

"You have a wife and child, Rees. Have you thought about them?"

"You poisoned Faralan against me."

"I didn't need to, Brother. You did that yourself, the first time you took part in the Landfall Festival. Don't try to blame me for the fact that Faralan has a better sense of what's right and wrong than you. Still, if you want to stay here and get yourself killed, then so be it. Perhaps your son will make a better duke than you."

"With you there to guide him, I suppose?" Rees asked scornfully. "Well, if I do get myself killed, at least you'll finally have a chance at Elcast."

"What?"

"You're a second son, Dirk. The spare heir. You were never going to amount to anything unless I died. And now, here's your chance, except...oh, that's right, you're not Wallin's son. You're Johan Thorn's bastard, aren't you? So you can't claim

Elcast. Is that why you did this? Is that why you became Lord of the Suns? Because you could never have rank or prestige any other way?"

"I was never jealous of you, Rees. And I never minded being a second son."

"So you say. But I've seen what it's done to others. Kirsh is willing to go to war with his brother. Look at Alexin Seranov. He couldn't inherit Grannon Rock, so he seduced the queen. You're all as bad as each other. All of you, just sitting like vultures, waiting for your elder brothers to die. Just waiting in the wings for your chance at glory. And if it doesn't happen quick enough for you, then you'll just make it happen some other way."

Dirk shook his head, unable to believe his brother's bitterness. Had Rees always thought that way, or was this anger something new? Something Antonov had fostered in him after Wallin died? There was no way of knowing and no time to waste finding out. Rees had taken sides, not against the Lion of Senet, not even against Dhevyn. He had taken sides against his brother.

"I'm sorry you feel that way, Rees," he said, unaware of how cold and unaffected he seemed to his older brother. "But if you insist on joining Kirsh in this venture, then I can offer you no more quarter than I offered him."

"I expect none," Rees retorted, just as coldly.

Dirk was hardly expecting any other response, but Rees's answer disappointed him. He nodded wordlessly in reply, wondering how Rees could look so much like Wallin, and yet have so little of his father's compassion. Or even good judgment.

"Good-bye, Rees."

His brother did not return his farewell. He simply turned and rode back to where Kirsh and their officers were waiting without looking back.

Chapter 86

Eryk was waiting for Kirsh when he got back to the camp, all but jumping out of his skin to know what had happened when Kirsh met with Dirk. The boy fetched him wine when he entered the tent, without being asked, and then waited expectantly while Kirsh drank it down.

"Did you speak to him, Prince Kirsh?" Eryk burst out when the silence got too much for him. "Did you speak to Lord Dirk?"

"I spoke to him."

"Is he all right?"

"He's just fine, Eryk. Doing very nicely for himself, your Lord Dirk."

The boy frowned at Kirsh's tone. "Are you still mad at him, Prince Kirsh?"

Kirsh sighed and gave his cup to Eryk for a refill. "I don't know, Eryk. I don't know what to feel anymore. I don't even know who to be angry at."

"You can be angry at me if you want," Eryk offered manfully. "Then you don't have to be mad at anyone else."

Kirsh smiled at the offer. "Dirk wants you to go back to his camp. You can if you want."

"Don't you need me here?"

"There may not *be* a 'here' by tomorrow if the prophecies prove untrue."

"But Marqel is always right," Eryk assured him. "At least all the advice she's given me has been good. Well, some of it I never really got to put to the test, but she was right about everything else in Nova."

Kirsh sank down heavily onto the stool as Eryk chattered away behind him, tidying up the tent as he talked, which to Kirsh's mind, had been tidied more than enough for one day. There had been too much said in his meeting with Dirk, too many things to digest, to worry about Eryk's feeble attempts to reassure him. But he didn't stop the boy from working. Eryk needed something to keep him occupied.

Kirsh wished he could find something to distract him so easily. The weight of the future before him was almost unbearable. *How did it ever come to war?* he wondered. *How did I end up here, facing the man I once counted as my best friend leading my brother's army against me?*

What irritated Kirsh most were the doubts that plagued him. Suppose Dirk was right? Suppose there was no Voice of the Goddess? It was obvious Misha believed the Baenlanders' heresy now. Was that because the Shadowdancers had poisoned him? Or was he simply prepared to believe anything about them that fitted with his notion of their perfidy? Maybe he'd been manipulated by the Baenlanders while captive among them? It wasn't an uncommon thing, a hostage growing to sympathize with his captors. Perhaps that's what happened to him...

Or perhaps his father's whole life had been based on a lie. Perhaps there was no Goddess at all. Perhaps Belagren had lied to his father and Marqel was perpetrating the lie for her own purposes. Rudi Kalenkov obviously thought she was lying. He'd said as much yesterday in the cavern when he'd tried to explain the problems they were having with the translations. Was he right? Had Marqel merely taken a leaf out of Dirk's book and pretended to read the inscriptions, safe in the knowledge there was nobody who could refute her?

He couldn't believe she would do that to him. He was angry at himself for even allowing the doubt to fester. He loved Marqel. He believed in her. Kirsh told himself that over and over, but found it little comfort. He wished he had even a fraction of his father's unwavering faith. His total lack of doubt. For Antonov there had been no decision to make, no question he was on the right path. He had done what he had to. He had killed his own son and slept easily, content he had done the right thing.

So why is it so hard for me to believe I'm doing the right thing, too? Perhaps Antonov never had to deal with anyone like Dirk

Provin. All he'd had to contend with was a couple of discontented kings and a madman...

Kirsh tried hard to find the same inalienable belief in the righteousness of his cause within himself. It was impossible. He was assailed on every side by doubt. Rudi thought Marqel was lying. Dirk was certain she was. Even Rees Provin was here for his own reason, not because he believed in Marqel or her divine mandate.

I wanted to make a name for myself, Kirsh thought sourly. *And so I will. But will I go down in history as the greatest defender of the faith that ever lived, or simply the most gullible fool that ever walked Ranadon?*

"Anyway, after Nova, I tried to tell Mellie what Marqel told me to say but I never got the chance, 'cause they wouldn't let me near the house or anything, and besides, we spent most of our time in the Straits doing pirate stuff..."

"What are you rattling on about, Eryk?" he asked absently. Eryk's constant chatter was making it hard to concentrate.

"About Nova," Eryk answered, as if he expected Kirsh to remember. "After she showed me the right way to touch Mellie."

"Who?" Kirsh asked in confusion.

"Marqel."

That got Kirsh's attention. "She did *what*?"

"Don't you remember, Prince Kirsh? It was just after you got beaten up. I met Marqel in the marketplace and she said she'd give you the message that Lord Dirk and me was safe, and then I told her about Mellie and she was real understanding and she showed me what to do... which was really nice of her, cause I didn't know anything but she was really patient about it and—"

"Whoa!" Kirsh cried in alarm. "Slow down a bit, Eryk. Are you telling me you met Marqel in Nova? That she...and you..." Kirsh couldn't bring himself to say it. The mere thought was too dreadful to comprehend.

Eryk nodded gravely. "There's not many friends would do something like that for you, Prince Kirsh."

Kirsh was staggered. Dirk might lie to him, even Misha's word could no longer be trusted. But not Eryk. He had no political agenda. He wouldn't make something like that up. He didn't have a deceitful bone in his body. Kirsh dropped his head into his hands to gather his thoughts for a moment, and then looked up at the boy.

"Tell me what happened when my father died, Eryk."

"He was praying when I took him his tea," Eryk answered, a little puzzled about Kirsh's abrupt change of subject. "I left it for him, and then I came back here to clean your boots."

"Did he ask for the tea?"

"Of course he did," he nodded. "That's why I took it to him. Marqel said—"

"Marqel gave it to you?"

"She said Prince Antonov wanted peppermint tea. She was really good to him, Prince Kirsh. I don't think I know anybody nicer than Marqel. Except maybe Caterina."

Kirsh stared at the boy for a long time before he rose to his feet. "Eryk."

"Yes, Prince Kirsh?"

"I want you to go back to Dirk."

"Don't you want me here any longer?" he asked, looking a little hurt.

"I need you to take him a message for me."

Eryk brightened a little. There was a world of difference between being sent away and being a royal messenger.

"Did you want me to bring back his answer?"

Kirsh smiled grimly. "I don't think there'll be any need for that, Eryk. I know what his answer will be."

Chapter 87

Dirk met Misha's generals after his fruitless parley with Kirsh and Rees to inform them there was little hope of a peaceful solution. They took the news stoically, torn as they were between the prospect of a good fight and the thought of going to war against one of their own. After giving the men orders to meet again later that day with their battle plans, Dirk dismissed them and went for a walk down by the lake. Jacinta found him there about an hour later, sitting on the shore, staring out over the sun-kissed water, deep in thought.

"Hiding again?" she asked as she came up behind him.

Dirk glanced up at her and nodded. "I'd be running away if I thought it would do any good."

Jacinta walked forward and studied the lake for a moment before sitting on the ground beside him with a sympathetic smile. "The meeting didn't go well, then?"

"Not particularly."

"What happened?"

Dirk turned his attention back to the lake. "Kirsh wants to fight."

"And your brother?"

"He's not in it for the Goddess. He just wants to fight *me*."

"It's not your fault, Dirk," she said.

He looked at her and laughed bitterly. "Then whose fault is it?"

"This situation is not something you can lay the blame for at any one door, my lord." She always referred to him as "my lord" when she thought she was right, he noticed. "Antonov, Belagren, Misha, Kirshov and even Paige Halyn have all contributed to getting us here."

He shrugged. Perhaps she was right. It didn't make him feel any better, though. "You know what really irks me?"

"The lack of decent sanitation in this place?" she suggested.

Dirk smiled briefly at her attempt to cheer him. "What irks me is that I seem to be able to do anything I want if I lie about it. The first time I try telling the truth, I end up going to war."

"Then perhaps you should have thought up a plausible lie."

"You may be right," he agreed. "I think Kirsh would have found it easier to deal with a plausible lie than the truth."

"Are you so sure he doesn't believe you?"

"He's going to fight, my lady."

"Yes, but that might be his male pride talking, as much as anything else." Jacinta was silent for a moment, considering her words carefully. "Kirshov Latanya doesn't have his father's unshakable faith in the Goddess, Dirk. He believes in himself. You may find he acknowledges a lot more of the truth than he's willing to admit."

"That doesn't help us much if he's still prepared to fight over it. In fact, that just makes it worse. I can understand—even admire—a man fighting for something he believes in, but to fight for something that he doesn't? Where's the logic in that?"

"Well, there is none," she shrugged. "But that's my whole point. He's not like you. Kirsh is ruled by his heart, not by his head. He's doing what he believes, in his heart, to be honorable, even if his head is telling him the complete opposite."

"And when did you become such an authority on the inner workings of Kirshov Latanya's mind?"

"You forget I served in Alenor's court. I know him well enough to guess what he's thinking now. I'm guessing that he's wishing for a way out of this that doesn't involve going to war against his own brother."

Dirk shook his head. "Kirsh wants to fight. And he'll keep on fighting until the Shadowdancers are restored or Marqel is dead."

"Then why don't you sneak a team of assassins into his camp and remove her?" Jacinta suggested.

Dirk stared at her in surprise. She didn't seem to be joking. "Are you serious?"

"Quite. If the solution to this problem is Marqel's death, then why not do something to facilitate it?"

"You expect me to order Marqel killed in cold blood?"

"How many more will die if you go to war?" she asked pointedly.

"I can't," he said with a shake of his head. "And not because I don't have the will to order Marqel's death. I'd strangle her myself if I had the chance. But even if I killed her now, Kirsh would still fight. He'd be after vengeance. And I don't need a martyr. I need the Shadowdancers discredited, not sanctified. I want Marqel led through the streets of Avacas in chains, not carried through them on her funeral pyre."

"And that's the difference between you and Kirshov," Jacinta noted. "In your heart you want to murder her, but your head is telling you different. And you listen to it. Have you ever done anything impulsive?"

"Lots of times," he replied, not sure he liked what her question implied.

"I doubt it," she chuckled. "I don't think you've ever done a thing without considering the consequences."

"I left Elcast and came to Senet," he reminded her. "Trust me, I had no idea of the consequences of *that* particularly impulsive act."

"And how different a world we would live in now if you had stayed at home," she mused. "Is that why you blame yourself? Do you trace all the tangled threads of this mess back to that one decision?"

"It's difficult not to."

"You're too hard on yourself. You said the other day this might have happened even without your interference. Misha was being poisoned by the Shadowdancers long before you came on the scene."

"But Marqel wouldn't be High Priestess."

"You don't know that for certain," she said. "Alenor told me Kirsh met Marqel on Elcast. It was he who asked Belagren to take her into the Shadowdancers. She might not have gotten to the top so fast without your aid, but you've no way of knowing if it might have happened anyway, even without your help."

"Did Misha really send you here to deliver dispatches?" he asked, curiously. "Or to keep my spirits up?"

She smiled. "The truth? He was just being nice, I think.

He liked the idea of saving me from a fate worse than death, even if only temporarily."

"You mean marrying Raban Seranov?"

"Do you know him?"

"Not well. I've met him."

"He's not a bad person, I suppose. His loyalties are certainly in the right place. He's just...*dissolute,* I think is the best word to describe him."

"If you really don't want to marry him, why don't you refuse?"

"I'll take it from that optimistic suggestion you've not had much to do with my mother," she replied with a groan. "Anyway, life's not that simple. Not for someone in my position. I have a duty. To my family. And to Dhevyn. We're finally independent of Senet, but it will take a long time before we're able to call ourselves free. Now, more than ever, the ancient noble families of Dhevyn must show unity, and what better way than the union of the D'Orlon and Seranov houses?"

"So you'll do your duty," he concluded, "despite what you feel."

"You're a great one to talk about doing your duty despite what you feel."

He frowned, uncomfortable with the truth in her words. "At least your duty won't result in people dying."

"I don't know," she said with a grimace. "After one too many nights with Raban Seranov across the dinner table, while he talks with his mouth half full about nothing but his hounds and his hawks, I may not be able to restrain my impulse to run a carving knife through him."

Dirk smiled. "It won't really be that bad, will it?"

"I hope not."

They sat in companionable silence for a while, watching the play of the second sun on the water. Dirk wished he knew what to say to Jacinta. He couldn't think of a way to help her avoid her fate, any more than he could find a way to avoid going to war with Kirsh. She was right when she said life wasn't so simple for someone in her position. The reality of being highborn was a lot less romantic than those not born to the responsibility realized.

"I wish I could do something..."

"It's not your place to rescue me, Dirk," she sighed. "Anyway, what could you do? You can't change who I am. You can't change what you are. And you can't change the political reality..." She laughed. "Well, maybe *you* can change political reality. But not fast enough to save me, I'm afraid."

"I could make some sort of religious declaration," he offered. "I could declare your union with Raban to be against the Goddess's wishes."

"No, you wouldn't," she told him confidently. "For one thing, the Lord of the Suns no longer holds any real sway over Dhevyn, now that Misha has cut Senet's ties with us, so the decree would be meaningless. And for another, you would never do anything so politically foolish, not even if it meant watching me being dragged off in chains."

"Do you think so little of me?" he asked, a little hurt she thought him so calculating.

"No. But I do have my pride. Besides, I'd be furious if you endangered everything that's been achieved so far, just to save one whining noblewoman from an awkward marriage." Jacinta smiled suddenly. "Of course, if you *really* wanted to help, you could have taken me up on the offer I made in Avacas..."

Dirk looked away, unable to meet her eye. "I wish you'd stop joking about that."

"I thought you'd forgotten about it. Or were you just being a gentleman by not mentioning it again?"

He hadn't forgotten what Jacinta asked of him. Or stopped wishing he'd taken her up on the offer. One night of mad, unbridled, passionate love. *Could anything be more tempting? Or more fraught with danger?*

"I thought you'd rather not be reminded of it."

"Why are you so certain I was joking?" she teased.

The silence between them, so companionable a few moments ago, was suddenly filled with tension. Before Dirk could think of an answer to Jacinta's question, he was hailed by a soldier hurrying down the slope behind them.

"My lord!"

Dirk scrambled to his feet, glad of the interruption. "What's wrong?"

The officer saluted hurriedly, sketched a hasty bow in Jacinta's direction and then turned back to Dirk. "Prince Kirshov sent a messenger, my lord. He has a letter, and he's refusing to hand it over to anyone but you. We tried to take it from him, but the boy is adamant." The man smiled. "I believe he was chosen as a courier for his determination, not his intelligence."

"You said a boy. What's his name?"

"I believe he said it was Eryk. I don't think he gave a last name."

"Eryk is *here*?" Jacinta asked in surprise. She held out her hand to Dirk and he pulled her to her feet.

"Do you know him, my lord?"

"He's my servant. Or at least he was. I'd better speak with him."

"Can I come, too?" Jacinta asked.

No, Dirk desperately wanted to say. *I want you to leave. I want you to go back to Dhevyn and marry Raban. I want you to stop asking the impossible of me.* But he didn't say it. He simply nodded his permission as if her request was a mere trifle, her presence of no consequence at all.

Eryk was taking his role as a royal messenger very seriously. He bowed gravely when Dirk and Jacinta entered the command tent and handed over the letter to Dirk without hesitation.

"Prince Kirsh told me to give you this, Lord Dirk."

"Are you all right, Eryk?" Jacinta asked with concern.

The boy nodded. "I've been helping Prince Kirsh, my lady. He made me his servant while Lord Dirk was away."

"You must be very good to have your services in such high demand."

Dirk broke the seal and read it while Jacinta talked to Eryk.

Dirk, the letter said in Kirsh's untidy scrawl. *I'm sending this with Eryk, because I trust him not to let it fall into the*

*wrong hands. I trust you to destroy it after you've read it. If
our friendship meant anything to you once, then you'll not
show it to anybody, not even my brother.*

*I wish there was a simple way out of this, but too much
has happened for me to simply lay down my sword and admit
you and Misha were right. However, being willing to admit
that to you is a world away from being willing to give you or
my brother the opportunity to gloat over it. The Lion of
Senet is dead and the world believes he died a great man. I
will not allow Antonov's memory to be sullied by the sordid
truth. I will not allow you to try Marqel for murder and
publicly expose the fraud my father believed. I can't do that
to Antonov's memory and I won't do it to the woman I love.
If you and Misha want to bring down the Shadowdancers,
you must do it without my help.*

*Don't go looking for vengeance or justice. I will take
care of it. When this is over, go back to Avacas and do what
you can for Misha. He's going to need all the help he can get.*

No quarter asked or given. Remember that.

Kirsh.

Dirk read the letter through twice before folding it carefully.

"What does it say?" Jacinta asked.

"It says we're going to war," Dirk replied.

Without any further explanation, he walked out of the
tent, past the officers waiting outside to hear what was in
the letter, and across the camp to the cook fires. He tossed the
folded letter on the nearest fire and watched as the parchment
blackened and curled in the flames. He didn't turn away until
Kirsh's note was nothing but a dusting of white ash amid the
glowing coals.

Then Dirk turned and in a flat, unemotional voice, he ordered his waiting generals to prepare for an attack.

Chapter 88

Kirsh sent for Marqel after he had gotten rid of Eryk and spoken to Sergey and Rees Provin. He was calm and surprisingly clearheaded. He wasn't even drunk. The last wine he'd had was before Eryk left. He didn't need alcohol. For the first time since he was a boy, boasting about the great deeds he would do as a soldier, Kirsh felt he knew what he was destined for. The feeling was headier than wine.

She came to him after first sunrise, when the sky had turned bloody. Kirsh kissed her before she could say anything, made love to her without uttering a word. Marqel seemed surprised but more than willing.

But then, Marqel was always more than willing.

It was only afterward, when she was lying cradled in his arms that he finally spoke to her.

"Dirk gave me until second sunrise tomorrow to surrender."

"You told him what he could do with his offer, I hope," she said, snuggling closer to him. She sounded confident, excited even, at the prospect of war.

"Never fear, my love," he promised. "I'll go to war for you. Even against my own brother."

"It's not your brother out there, Kirsh. It's Dirk Provin."

"Did you really sleep with Eryk in Nova?"

Marqel went still in his arms and then she pushed herself up onto her elbow and looked at him in total bewilderment. "*What* did you say?"

"Why?" he asked, genuinely curious about her answer. "Why Eryk?"

"Did *he* tell you that?" she laughed, covering her concern well. He almost believed her. The Goddess knows, he *wanted* to believe her. But he saw the momentary panic before she laughed. It was fleeting, but it was unmistakably there. "Honestly Kirsh, you can't believe anything that half-wit says. He doesn't even know what day it is."

"Eryk doesn't know how to lie, Marqel."

"He's dreaming then," she scoffed. "He's made something up in his own mind because he fancies me. I'm hurt you could even spare such a ridiculous notion a second thought."

"I can understand why you slept with my father," he mused, as if she hadn't spoken. "I think I even know why you slept with Dirk. But Eryk? That's just... bizarre."

"Dirk raped me, Kirsh," she reminded him, starting to get annoyed. She was a very good actress. He'd never realized how good, until now.

"No, I don't think he did, my love. I think you drugged him and then lay with him, quite deliberately, because there was something in it for you. The same reason you slept with every other man you've been with. Including me."

Marqel was horrified. "Kirsh! Why are you saying such terrible things?"

"Do you even enjoy it?" he asked curiously. "Or is it just something you do to get what you want?"

"What did Dirk say to you out there today?" she demanded, truly angry now. Her eyes filled with crystalline tears, as they always did when she was losing the argument. It was almost as if she could call on them at will. "He's put these ideas in your head, hasn't he?" she sobbed. "How can you even listen to a word that bastard says? You know how much he hates me."

He smiled at her and kissed away her angry tears. "I've been such a fool, haven't I?"

She sniffed and pouted at him. "Yes, you have."

"Well, it'll all be over soon."

Marqel snuggled back down into his arms. "Yes, it will. And then we can be together forever, and nobody will be able to get in our way."

"I promise we will, my love," Kirsh said.

Marqel closed her eyes with a sigh of satisfaction. He was glad she did. He didn't want to frighten her. He reached down beside the pallet. The knife he concealed there before Marqel arrived felt strangely light, as if some hand other than his was guiding it.

Kirsh didn't want her to suffer. With a short, sharp upward stroke, he punctured her heart from just under the base of the sternum, the surest way he knew to cause instant death from this angle. He would have preferred to take her in the left shoulder, driving the blade down into the aorta, but that meant coming at her from behind. He couldn't do that.

Marqel's eyes flew open in shock. She stared up at him in that instant before the light fled from her eyes, a moment of uncomprehending terror, a fleeting look of wounded betrayal as she understood what he had done. Her body jerked in the throes of death, but he held her tightly as her blood gushed over his hands and chest and pooled on the bed beneath them. It was probably only a minute or two but it seemed like an agonizing lifetime before she relaxed in his arms and was still.

And then, in the distance, he heard trumpets sounding, and knew Eryk had delivered his message to Dirk.

Kirsh gently kissed Marqel's forehead and laid her back against the pillows. He rose from the bed feeling strangely light-headed and dressed himself carefully, although he made no attempt to clean the blood from his hands. He pulled the diamond-bladed dagger from her body and sheathed it in his belt before crossing her hands on her breast and covering her with the blood-soaked sheet. He wished Marqel looked more peaceful in death, but she seemed to be accusing him. Turning away, Kirsh picked up his sword and left the tent.

Sergey and Rees were waiting for him. If they noticed the blood on his hands, they gave no sign. But their expressions were grim.

"You remember what I ordered?"

"Yes," Sergey replied, clearly unhappy.

"As *soon* as it's over, Sergey," he reminded him. "There's no point in carrying on the fight once I'm dead."

"This is suicide, Kirsh," Rees pointed out angrily. Kirsh wondered who the Duke of Elcast was concerned for most, his prince or himself?

"Yes," Kirsh agreed calmly. "I suppose it is."

"I'm coming with you," the Duke of Elcast suddenly declared.

Kirsh didn't blame him. It was going to be awkward for Rees after this. He'd chosen the wrong side in this fight and would be at the mercy of both the Lion of Senet and the Lord of the Suns—the brother he had so foolishly spurned this morning—and more than likely the Queen of Dhevyn, once the battlefield was cleared.

"It's your choice, Rees," he said as he swung into the saddle of the mount Sergey had waiting for him.

"That's right," he agreed. "It is. And I choose the same path my father chose."

"Your father followed the Lion of Senet to war," Kirsh reminded him. "That's Misha, not me."

"My father followed the man who believed in the Goddess," Rees corrected. "I intend to do the same."

There was no arguing with him, and no point. If Rees wanted to throw his life away, that was his choice. Kirsh was not in a position to pass judgment on him.

"As you wish," he shrugged. The calm was still on him, the feeling of being somehow detached from the world around him. He turned to the rest of the troop waiting for him and gave the order to move out.

Kirsh rode out of the ruins with only a small force. Enough to look like a serious attack, but not enough that any more lives would be needlessly wasted. Kirsh wondered if Dirk would be waiting for him on the battlefield. Perhaps not. Dirk wasn't a soldier and didn't pretend to be. He'd do the smart thing, as he always did, and leave the battle to the men who knew what they were doing.

Rees caught up with him as he neared the edge of the ruins. Kirsh smiled when he saw the forces arrayed against them. Dirk hadn't let him down. He drew his sword and raised it high, letting out a yell as he kicked his horse into a gallop. He spared Marqel a fleeting thought as they thundered toward the line archers blocking the road, wondering if she would ever forgive him.

He hadn't wanted to kill her, but it was the only thing to do. She couldn't be captured now, couldn't be tortured or humiliated or be made to publicly reveal how she had played both him and Antonov for a fool. Played the whole world for a fool. Kirsh could live with her killing Belagren. He may have even forgiven her someday for sleeping with his father and Dirk and Eryk and the Goddess knows how many others...

But there was one thing he could not forgive. She had killed the Lion of Senet.

In her own way, Marqel might have even done it for him. But that simply made him complicit in the crime. Kirshov Latanya couldn't kill his own father, even indirectly, and live with the knowledge.

He wasn't Dirk Provin.

It was the last thought he had before the archers let fly. Miraculously, every one of the arrows missed, as if the Goddess were shielding him from harm. He let out a wordless yell and spurred his horse on.

Another flight of arrows. Another escape. Rees Provin rode at his side, his face a mask of mindless rage. Kirsh had time to wonder why Rees was so angry before the cavalry rode out to meet the charge.

He slashed his way through them, fighting as if there was no tomorrow. It seemed appropriate. For Kirshov Latanya, there was no tomorrow. Only now. Only one glorious moment to be a hero. One instant in time where he was more than a younger brother of a king, the second son of a legend.

Out of the corner of his eye, he saw Rees fall. It distracted him. He turned back too late to counter the strike of the man who had ridden up on his blind side.

Kirsh didn't even know the face of the man who cut him down.

Chapter 89

Dirk strode through the battle debris, stepping over bodies of the defeated guard, past fallen statuary and the ruined buildings, trying to recall Omaxin as he had seen it the last time he walked these ruins.

This was necessary, he reminded himself. *Unavoidable.* It was small comfort.

"My lord!"

Dirk stopped and turned to the officer who hailed him. "We found the High Priestess, my lord," the soldier informed him.

"Is she alive?"

"No, my lord."

"I gave orders for the High Priestess to be taken alive."

"It wasn't us, my lord. You'd best see for yourself..."

Dirk followed the officer back through the ruins for some way to the larger tents belonging to nobility who had been camped here in Omaxin. The officer led him to the largest tent, pushed back the tent flap.

"It's a bit...strange," he warned.

Dirk hesitated on the threshold. For no apparent reason, his comment reminded Dirk of something else that needed to be taken care of, even before he confronted whatever waited for him in the tent.

"I want a guard posted on the entrance to the cavern. And separate the Shadowdancers from the rest of the prisoners."

"What did you want to do with the troops who surrendered, my lord?"

"I'll speak to them," he said.

"Just speak to them, my lord?" the man asked warily.

"There's no point in seeking retribution. They were following the Lion of Senet's orders and the orders of his son. You can't condemn them for that."

The Senetian officer bowed, his relief obvious.

Dirk smiled thinly. "What did you think I was going to do, Captain? Order you to put them to the sword?"

"They did support Prince Kirshov against Prince Misha, my lord."

"They supported the High Priestess against the Lord of the Suns," Dirk corrected. "The former is treason; the latter is simply a matter of poor theological judgment. So that will be the end of it. Anyway, most of them are here out of a simple geographic accident. If you'd been stationed in Bollow when Antonov ordered the troops north, *you'd* be surrendering today, Captain."

The captain nodded and smiled cautiously. "Your mercy is appreciated, my lord."

And rather unexpected from the Butcher of Elcast, I'll wager. That's what the man really thought. Dirk understood the captain's fears. Had Antonov been here to put down a rebellion, it was unlikely any man who dared take up arms against him would have seen the next sunrise.

But Antonov wasn't the Lion of Senet now. Misha was.

"See to it, Captain. And then find Rudi Kalenkov for me."

"Sir!" the man replied smartly and hurried off to carry out his orders.

Dirk looked about him, trying to delay the moment when he must step into the tent and confront the consequences of his actions. And he *was* to blame. He was the one who had set Marqel on this path. Kirsh was right. *What gave me the right to decide the path the whole world should take?*

He hesitated again, and then remembered something his foster father had often said.

Never run from anything, Wallin Provin had taught him. *Always face up to your fears; that way they can't sneak up on you from behind.*

He braced himself and stepped into the tent. The scene that greeted him was better than he expected. The interior seemed untouched by the battle. The pavilion was large, its walls paneled with hand-painted red-and-gold silk. The High Priestess lay on the bed, her naked body covered by a blood-soaked sheet, laid out as if the morticians had already prepared her for the funeral pyre. *Had Kirsh done that?* Probably.

The scene depressed Dirk, as if some residual trace of Kirsh's pain and anger still lingered in the tent like mist. *What had it cost him?* Dirk wondered. What had finally convinced him Marqel must die? Whatever it was, even Kirsh had not been able to deny the truth in the end.

The tent flap billowed out in an errant gust of wind. Marqel was not beautiful in death. Not as she had been in life. And she had been beautiful. So beautiful that she had split Senet and almost brought the nation to its knees.

Not so superior and self-righteous now, are we? he asked her silently, the same words Marqel had taunted him with that night so long ago in Avacas when she'd spiked his wine with the Milk of the Goddess and then accused him of rape.

With a shake of his head, Dirk looked away, a little disturbed that Marqel's death relieved him so much. And it wasn't even his doing. It was Kirsh who had destroyed Marqel in the end. And then he'd destroyed himself.

Dirk hadn't tried to lead the battle, if you could call the short, brutal engagement a battle. Rather, like a good general, he watched helplessly from a rise overlooking the field of engagement as Kirsh threw his life away.

He hadn't even tried to defend himself. Kirsh *wanted* to die in battle. He always had. Rees's reasons for joining Kirsh on his suicidal charge were more complicated, Dirk knew. But Kirsh had known he was riding to his death. Rees probably believed Kirsh would win.

Dirk managed to keep his grief at bay, but he couldn't help feeling responsible. He knew Kirsh well enough to know once he accepted the truth there was nothing left to him. Is that how Kirsh defined honor? Was it better to die gloriously in battle defending something, no matter how fallacious, than admit you were wrong? Kirsh's honor—that strange, indefinable sense Dirk had always found so irritating—apparently allowed no other course of action.

Was there something else he could have said to Kirsh or Rees that could have ended this differently? If he'd been less impatient, less defensive of his own actions? Kirsh's words haunted Dirk. *Who set you up as the moral guardian of Ranadon?*

"Has anything been touched?"

The officer who stood on guard just inside the pavilion entrance shook his head. "We thought you should see it first, my lord. It's a pity really."

"Why?"

"Would've been better for everyone if she'd been hanged, my lord. Would've put an end to things much quicker."

"Perhaps," Dirk conceded. "But there'll be no civil war now, Captain. No further resistance. That's what we came here for."

And the end justifies the means, he heard Kirsh say.

And then another thought occurred to him. Perhaps Kirsh had not killed Marqel to spare her the hangman's noose.

Perhaps he had killed her because he knew he was going to die and even in the afterlife, he could not bear to be without her.

It was sometime later that Dirk entered the tunnel, walking through the torchlit darkness to the cavern beyond. It was empty when he arrived and for a fleeting moment, that same feeling of awe that had overwhelmed Dirk the first time he stepped into the hall came back to him. But there was no lingering darkness here now. No shadows concealing the truth. The cavern was brightly lit, the eye reflecting the torchlight with an accusing, unblinking stare.

"Come to read the prophecies, my lord?"

Dirk turned to find Rudi Kalenkov entering the cavern behind him.

"I wish I *could* read them."

Rudi stopped a few paces from him and eyed him quizzically. "You *can't* read them, my lord?"

"You know damn well I can't, Rudi. No more than Belagren heard the voice of the Goddess in here. No more than Marqel could translate these walls."

"Prince Antonov and Prince Kirshov believed she could," he pointed out cautiously.

"One was mad, the other was in love. Neither of them was thinking clearly."

"And what about you, my lord? What is your position? Is this place to be sealed again, to hide the truth?"

Dirk shook his head. "Far from it. I want to know everything this place can tell us. And not just this cavern. There must be other buildings here in Omaxin that can shed some light on who these people were. And this time we'll do it properly. Systematically. We'll bring people in from the universities in Avacas and Nova to study the ruins."

Rudi was shocked. "You'd open the ruins to scholars, my lord?"

"What's a lion, Rudi?" Dirk asked, instead of answering his question.

"It's a cat," the Shadowdancer replied, rather puzzled by the odd question. "A very large cat. It's the emblem of the Latanya house."

"Have you ever seen one?"

"Of course not. It's a mythical creature, like a dragon or a fairy."

"How do you know that?"

Rudi shrugged. "It's...just one of those things everyone knows, my lord."

"That's what I said to Neris when he asked me the same question."

Rudi stared at him doubtfully. "For a man sworn to guide the people of Ranadon to the Goddess, you have a strange attitude, Dirk Provin. You talk like a scholar, not a cleric."

"I want to *know*, Rudi. Better yet, I want *everyone* to know the truth, not just a few people who can use the truth to manipulate the ignorant."

"Are you accusing *me* of something, my lord?" he asked, sounding a little worried.

"I probably should have you burned at the stake, actually," Dirk scolded. "I'm sure if I thought about it, I could come up with something plausible."

"I've done nothing wrong!"

"You were here when Neris first learned the truth. You

knew what Belagren was up to. And you did nothing to stop her. Nothing to stop Marqel, either."

"I tried," Rudi assured him. "Not at first, I'll admit. But I tried to throw doubt on Marqel's prophecies. Before then... well, I was much younger and much less cynical when Belagren first started us on this path."

"You're fortunate you know these ruins better than anyone else on Ranadon," Dirk informed him. "That makes you more use to me alive than dead."

The Shadowdancer seemed genuinely surprised. "And I appreciate the sentiment, my lord, more than you can imagine. But to turn these ruins from a holy place into an archaeological dig would be heresy."

"I'm the Lord of the Suns, Rudi. My definition of heresy is the only one that matters, and I say we have an obligation to find out everything we can about the people who once lived here." He studied the Shadowdancer curiously for a moment. "Of course, if you intend to remain here in charge of the excavations, then you'd better have a moment of divine clarity pretty damn quick and decide you'd rather be a Sundancer again. The Shadowdancers are to be disbanded and anybody who insists on perpetrating their lies *will* be declared a heretic."

Rudi smiled. "I feel the presence of the Goddess calling me to my new vocation even as we speak, my lord."

"I thought you might," Dirk agreed wryly.

Rudi studied him thoughtfully for a moment in the torchlight. "You know, when I came back to Omaxin with Belagren to find you'd opened the Labyrinth, I had a feeling then, you'd end up changing everything."

"I've only just begun," Dirk warned. And then explicably, he decided to fix something else that had always grated on his nerves. "And will you stop calling it a labyrinth, Rudi? It's a damned tunnel, that's all. The sooner we start demystifying this place, the better."

"And so we step out of the Age of Light and into the Age of Enlightenment," Rudi remarked.

Dirk hadn't thought about it like that. It sounded rather grand.

Almost as if it was worth the lives it had cost to achieve it.

Chapter 90

They burned Kirsh's body on Lake Ruska, the pyre floating out across the blood-stained water in the dim red light of the first sun. Marqel lay beside her lover, a gesture Jacinta thought both touching and foolish. Dirk should have tossed her into a shallow unmarked grave. The world needed to forget Marqel almost as badly as it needed to forget Belagren.

He stood by the water's edge for a long while, watching the pyre float on the lake, still clutching the torch he had used to set it alight. Jacinta ached for him. Dirk may seem a tower of implacable strength to everyone else, but she knew he was hurting. She knew he blamed himself for Kirsh's death, knew he was grieving for his brother. But there was nothing she could do to console him. Nor was it her place to try.

Dirk had already emptied Omaxin of many of the troops Antonov had gathered, along with those he had brought with him to confront Kirsh. There were only a few dozen of them left now. Jacinta suspected Dirk had deliberately delayed the funeral until most of them were gone. Watching Kirsh's pyre burn was heartbreaking, even for Jacinta, who had never really liked him much. For the men who would have willingly followed Kirshov Latanya to war, the specter was just too disturbing to risk letting them witness it.

There were quite a few Shadowdancers still in Omaxin, but not a red robe in sight. Dirk had given them a clear choice. Change their allegiance to the Sundancers and stay here to continue studying the ruins, or go back to Avacas in chains as condemned heretics. Not one of them had opted for the latter. They had shed their robes and gone back to doing exactly what they were doing before Dirk arrived: trying to puzzle out the writings in the cavern at the end of the Labyrinth...or rather the *tunnel,* she corrected absently. Dirk got quite annoyed if anybody called it the Labyrinth.

The smoke from the pyre hung over the water in the still air. The evening was clear, the red sky vast and bloody; a fitting backdrop for the death of a prince. Behind Jacinta stood a small guard wearing the black and green livery of Bryton and the reason she was dressed in her riding habit rather than mourning clothes. Her father had sent an armed guard to escort her home.

Her father's men had arrived a few days after the surrender bearing a very abrupt and annoyed note from her parents and a rather more sympathetic letter from Alenor. Both letters reminded her of the same thing. She had a duty she had managed to avoid until now. The time for prevaricating was over. Dhevyn was free and needed all the stability the union of the Seranov and D'Orlon houses would bring. Raban Seranov was waiting for her. The wedding was arranged and set for just over two months from now. She dreaded the future before her, but knew her duty to Dhevyn. She could argue with her mother, but not her queen.

Jacinta would leave as soon as the funeral was over.

She had learned something recently that made her feel older for owning the wisdom. *The greater good sometimes came at a high personal cost.* She needed only to look at Dirk to remind her of that.

After a few more moments of hushed reverence, Dirk turned and headed back toward her. The gathered troops began to disperse, although Jacinta did not move. She wanted to say good-bye.

Dirk handed the torch to one of his captains and walked up the slope a little farther before he bowed politely to her.

"My lady."

"My lord."

"You're all set to leave then?"

She nodded. "I think it's best."

"You'll give my regards to your parents? And my apologies

for asking you to undertake the duties that kept you away from them for so long?"

"Of course."

He was saying that for the benefit of her escort. *Always the politician, aren't you, Dirk?* She was grateful, but a little hurt.

"Will I see you in Avacas before I sail for Dhevyn, my lord?"

"Probably not," he told her. "There's a great deal more to do here before I leave. And I have to escort Rees's body back to Elcast. Faralan is going to need some help sorting out his affairs. Besides, I think Misha might appreciate not having me around for a while. Tia certainly will."

"Shall I give the queen a message from you?"

"Give her my love," Dirk said. "And tell her I said thank you."

"For what?"

"For trusting me."

Jacinta nodded. "I'll make certain she knows how much you appreciate her support."

"And you can tell her Alexin is no longer considered a heretic by the Church. As to whether or not her relationship with him still constitutes treason, that will be up to her to decide since now she's a queen in her own right."

"I can't imagine her decision will be anything less than favorable for Alexin."

He nodded in agreement. "Your new father-in-law will be pleased by that news."

"I'm sure he will be," she agreed. "He's very fond of both his sons."

An uncomfortable silence fell between them.

"I would ask another favor of you, my lady."

"I'm yours to command, my lord," she announced formally, shattered by the cold formality of their parting.

"I would ask you take care of Lady Lexie and her daughter, Mellie."

"I give you my word they will both be accorded the full respect and privilege their rank deserves," she assured him.

"And give Mellie my love, too," he asked. "Tell her I'll try to get to Kalarada to see her as soon as I can."

"I'm sure she'll anxiously await your arrival, my lord."

"You'll like Mellie," he added, as if he was looking for a reason to drag out their conversation. "And she'll need friends at court."

"Then I will be certain she has them," Jacinta promised. "Although I will be in Nova for much of the time, I fear. But she and Alenor are not so far apart in age. I'm sure they'll become firm friends."

Dirk smiled. "Perhaps, once you're the Duchess of Grannon Rock, they'll finally let you into the university."

"I'm not sure what my husband will have to say about that."

"I'm quite certain you could persuade Raban to agree to anything, my lady."

"You vastly overestimate my powers of persuasion, I fear." *If they were any good at all, I wouldn't be leaving.*

He hesitated for a moment and then bowed politely. "I wish you well, my lady. I hope you'll be content."

Content, he said, not *happy*. At least he hadn't been so cruel as to suggest that.

"I'm sure I'll come to terms with my fate in time," she agreed. "As you seem to have done."

"Good-bye, Jacinta."

She couldn't bear to return his farewell. Jacinta curtsied as elegantly as she could manage on the loose slope. He stood there watching as she turned and walked up toward her waiting horse and the rest of the escort of Senetian troops Dirk had provided for her journey back to Avacas.

No sooner had she mounted than he turned and strode back toward the ruins. She couldn't tell if it was because he couldn't bear to watch her go, or if he was just too busy to care.

Chapter 91

Alenor waited for Jacinta when she returned from Senet in the throne room of Kalarada Palace, the first time she'd ever felt the need to meet with her cousin in formal surroundings. But with Lady Sofia waiting in Jacinta's rooms, her own mother starting to develop grandiose ideas about taking back her throne and everything else that had happened since the day of the eclipse, she clung to whatever symbols of her position she could claim.

The Queen of Dhevyn was feeling the need for a little protocol.

Jacinta seemed a little surprised by the formality when she was escorted into the queen's presence by Dimitri Bayel. Alenor sat on the Eagle Throne, the heavy crown giving her a headache, her expression determinedly neutral. It was a form of protection. She hoped the weight of her crown would force down the other emotions that she was afraid might undo her perfect imitation of a reasonable and controlled monarch.

"Welcome home, Lady Jacinta," she said when her cousin stopped before the throne and curtsied politely. "I trust your journey from Avacas was not too rough?"

"No, your majesty," Jacinta replied, looking a little puzzled by Alenor's stiff tone. "The seas were quite smooth for this time of year."

"You bring us news, I take it?"

Jacinta glanced around at the courtiers surrounding the queen. There were no Senetians left in Alenor's court, but Rainan was standing just behind the throne on Alenor's left and several other underlings were hovering about the bright, sun-warmed chamber, listening to every word.

"Perhaps you'd prefer to hear my news in private, your majesty," Jacinta suggested.

"I already know of the death of Prince Kirshov," Alenor said, a little amazed that she was able to say it and sound so calm. Although she didn't know the details, the news had rocked her to the core. Grief mixed with relief and a rather uncomfortable dose of guilt warred for dominance in her heart. In truth, if anybody had asked her what she was feeling, she really couldn't have given him an answer.

"The Lion of Senet sent a messenger to inform us of the outcome of the...*troubles*...in Omaxin," Rainan informed Jacinta before Alenor could. "I hear the High Priestess is dead, too."

"Yes, your highness," Jacinta confirmed warily. "She is."

"Did Dirk Provin kill her?"

Jacinta glanced at the others in the hall pointedly before replying. "No, your highness. Dirk didn't kill her. Kirsh did."

Alenor felt the blood drain from her face and realized what a fool she was for thinking this could be dealt with in an open forum. She should never have tried to impress anybody, least of all her cousin and closest friend, by trying to act like a queen. Or give her mother a chance to act like she was back at the helm.

"Leave us!" she announced, rising to her feet.

"Alenor," her mother began. "Perhaps you should..."

"I said leave us!" Alenor repeated forcefully.

Rainan stared at her, obviously put out by Alenor's abrupt dismissal of the court, but she nodded silently and turned on her heel, followed by Dimitri and the rest of Alenor's attendants. Jacinta watched them leave curiously, turning to Alenor when the last of them closed the door behind them.

"What was all that about?"

Alenor sighed heavily and stepped down from the podium. "It was a mistake. Ever since we got word about the Senetians pulling out of Dhevyn, my mother has been making noises about resuming the throne." Alenor sat herself down on the steps leading up to the dais and rested her chin in her hands. "Am I a bad person, Jacinta, for not wanting to let her have her old job back?"

"Not if you think you're doing a better job."

Alenor lifted the heavy crown from her head and placed it on the step beside her. "What really happened in Omaxin?"

Her cousin sat next to her on the step, silent for a moment, choosing her words carefully. "There was a battle. A very short, sharp and brutal one. I don't think Kirsh expected to come out of it alive. Or wanted to. Rees Provin died in the same charge. It wasn't until later they found Marqel. Dirk thinks Kirsh killed her just before he attacked. He was fairly certain Marqel murdered Antonov, too, although Kirsh wouldn't believe it when Dirk tried to negotiate with him."

Alenor was silent, wondering what strange set of circumstances would make Kirsh kill the woman he loved. And he had loved her. Blindly and foolishly, perhaps, but he had loved Marqel the way Alenor always wanted to be loved by him. Maybe, in hindsight, she'd gotten the better end of the bargain. She lost Kirsh to Marqel, but at least she was still alive to remark the fact.

"I suppose we'll never really know why," Jacinta added, watching Alenor closely.

She smiled wanly. "It's all right, Jacinta. I'm fine. I'm not hypocrite enough to pretend I'm a grieving widow, but I never wished Kirsh harm. The news that Rees Provin is dead is going to cause problems, though. Who is going to rule Elcast? I can hardly let Dirk have it. I mean, even if he wasn't Lord of the Suns, it's fairly old news by now that he wasn't actually Wallin's son." She rubbed her temples, wondering if being a queen ever got any easier. "I guess Rees's baby son is the logical choice, but he's only a few weeks old...still, I can worry about it later, I suppose. Right now I have a lot more urgent things to worry about."

"Like what?" Jacinta asked.

"Well, for one thing, I have your mother here demanding I release you from my service immediately so you can go home and marry Raban Seranov. I suddenly have a new cousin I didn't know about called Melliandra Thorn and Johan's widow to contend with. I have an entire country reeling from the shock of the sudden withdrawal of Senet. For every man out there cheering for freedom, there's another accusing me of ruining them with my shortsightedness. I'm afraid to let Alexin out of my sight for fear the Church will demand he be returned to Senet for execution as a heretic..."

"Well, that's one worry you don't have any longer," Jacinta assured her. "Dirk's wiped the slate clean of charges against Alexin. As far as the Church is concerned, he is an innocent man."

Alenor's smile widened. "You know, sometimes it's rather handy having one of your best friends as Lord of the Suns."

Jacinta smiled, but there was an oddness about it. A hint of regret or bitterness, perhaps, that Alenor couldn't quite define.

"He said to give you his thanks, too, Allie. For trusting him. And he asked you to treat Mellie and Lady Lexie in a manner befitting their station."

"Is he coming to Kalarada?"

Jacinta shook her head. "I don't think so. At least, not for a while. He's got a lot to deal with cleaning up after the Shadowdancers."

"Poor Dirk. I keep trying to imagine what it must have cost him to do what he did. He never shared his plans with anyone, you know. Not even me. Not even when I asked him to. He was too afraid I'd get caught up in the backlash if he failed. It couldn't have been easy for him to find himself facing Kirsh across a battlefield, either."

"I wouldn't lose too much sleep over how Dirk is coping," Jacinta advised. "He was doing just fine when I saw him last."

Alenor stared at her cousin, wondering at her tone. "Didn't you like him, Jacinta?"

Jacinta shrugged. "I liked him well enough."

"But..."

"But nothing. He's doing just fine, Alenor. Don't worry about Dirk. Think about how you're going to propose to Alexin instead."

"What?" she gasped in shock.

"You are going to marry him, aren't you? Goddess, Allie, I didn't spend all that effort covering up for you two with the dreaded Lady Dorra just so you can toss him aside as soon as you're a free woman!"

"But I never..."

"You never what? For pity's sake, girl, Kirsh has been dead for close on a month! What have you been doing?"

"But it's only been...Oh, Jacinta! Even if I wanted to... well, no, that's not what I mean, of course I *want* to...it's just... well, it's been such a short time. It's indecent!"

"Well, yes, I can see how it would be indecent for you to marry the man who was publicly condemned to die for the crime of being your lover less than a month after your husband murdered his mistress and then threw himself on a blade to avoid facing the consequences of starting a civil war."

The queen frowned at her cousin disapprovingly. "You make it sound so...tacky, Jacinta."

"Well, it is rather," Jacinta agreed. Then she smiled brightly. "But I'd not worry about it too much, if I were you, your majesty. Give it a few months for the fuss to die down and the bards will be singing about you and Alexin as if it was one of the great love affairs of history."

"What will they say about Kirsh and Marqel, I wonder?"

"The less said about those two, the better," Jacinta suggested with a grimace.

"And what of you, Jacinta? Will they sing great ballads about you and Raban Seranov, someday?"

"Only if I don't murder him in our bed some night when I tire of his snoring. Or maybe they *will* sing about me *because* I murdered him in our bed one night when I finally tired of his snoring."

Alenor studied Jacinta curiously. "You're making jokes again."

"Am I?" she shrugged. "Strange. I don't feel like laughing."

"I wish I could help you, Jacinta. You helped me find the

only moments of happiness I've had in the last few years. But I'm barely dealing with *my* mother. I don't think I have the strength to take on yours at the same time."

"That's all right, Allie," Jacinta assured her. "There is a whole new world waiting for us out there. You're going to rule a free Dhevyn. I'm going to start a dynasty. Neither of us is going to have the time to worry about how happy we are."

Alenor wondered, for a moment, why she wasn't feeling more afraid. She should be. She was young, untried and untested. Her mother thought her far too inexperienced to handle the job. Her people probably thought the same. But Alenor had a network of contacts her mother had never had access to. The new Lion of Senet was like a big brother to her and the Lord of the Suns was one of her best friends. The Baenlanders were no longer a problem, which meant their shipping would no longer be raided and for that matter, with the Lady Lexie's help, she might even have a chance of reining in the Brotherhood and doing something to rid Dhevyn of the corruption that had spread throughout its bureaucracy while Senet was in charge.

She could do this.

"You're right, Jacinta," she said, giving her cousin's hand a reassuring squeeze. "There *is* a whole new world waiting for us out there."

Alenor rose to her feet and picked up her crown. In her heart, Alenor knew it. She could rule Dhevyn and rule it well.

And she was going to.

Starting now.

Chapter 92

Tia had never seen the Lord of the Suns' palace and she was quite taken aback by its beauty when her carriage trundled through the gateway. The ancient building was a relic of a time that seemed more elegant, less brutal, than the world they lived in now. Seeing the palace helped her appreciate Dirk's fascination with learning as much as he could about the long forgotten people who had constructed it.

She was welcomed into the palace like an honored guest, although Tia still hadn't gotten used to people bowing and curtsying wherever she went. She wanted to put a stop to it, but Misha wouldn't let her. It was all part of the game, he claimed. Anyway, she had as much right to the claim of highborn as anyone did, he reminded her. Tia didn't actually think having Lady Ella Geon as a mother was anything to be terribly proud of, but she understood what he was trying to say.

Dirk was down by the lake. He was standing on the shore staring out over the water, his hands thrust deeply into the pockets of his trousers. He turned at the sound of her footsteps. He didn't look surprised to see her.

"They told me I'd find you out here."

"And here I am ..." He studied her for a moment and then looked away, as if he couldn't bear her scrutiny.

"You look well," she said, thinking if she'd tried harder, she could have thought of something even more banal to say.

"So do you."

"I have to say I'm a little disappointed, though. You know ... Lord of the Shadows, Lord of the Suns and all that ... here in the very seat of your power, I thought you'd be dressed like a monk or something."

The briefest of smiles flickered across his face. "One of the advantages of being the boss. I get to set the dress code."

"I saw Eryk up at the house. He seems a little ... unhappy."

"He's still trying to figure out what happened in Omaxin. And if he had something to do with Kirsh dying. We've gone to some pains to keep it from him that he was the one who delivered the poison to Antonov."

"Poor Eryk."

"He'll be all right eventually, and Caterina will help him through it. He just needs time."

She studied him curiously for a moment. "You don't need a hostage anymore, Dirk. The Brotherhood contract on you has long been called off."

"Caterina doesn't want to leave."

"Really?"

He frowned at what she was implying. "It's not what you think, Tia. She actually suggested she marry Eryk."

"You're kidding! Why?"

"From her point of view, it's an excellent match, I suppose. Eryk adores her and she gets to live in a palace. If she returns to Tolace, she'll end up married to a sailor or a Brotherhood man and spend the rest of her life cooking and cleaning and making babies. She's quite a pragmatist, our Caterina."

"Or an opportunist."

"If they're both happy with the arrangement, does it really matter?"

"I suppose not," she agreed uncertainly. "But are you really going to allow it?"

"Not right away," Dirk assured her. "For one thing, they're both far too young and naive to know what they want. Eryk certainly is, at any rate. Besides, it's a little too glib a solution for my liking. I'm sure Caterina means what she says now, but I don't want Eryk getting hurt the first time she spies some handsome fellow who takes a shine to her and she realizes how much better she could do. I told her I'd think about it. And that she could stay until I made up my mind."

"Isn't that just making it harder on her if you eventually refuse her?"

"It won't hurt Caterina to have her mettle tested a little."

Tia nodded in agreement, thinking they'd all had their mettle tested recently.

"How's Misha?"

"He's got a lot of work ahead of him," she said. "But he's stronger than people give him credit. He'll manage. Landfall was rather trying. But we got through it." She began to walk along the shoreline. Dirk fell into step beside her as they headed away from the palace. "Have you seen Alenor?"

Dirk shook his head. "Not since she went back to Kalarada."

"She's married to Alexin now. I was in Kalarada for the wedding. It was quite a party. I expected you to be there."

"I was in Elcast. Anyway, Alenor doesn't need me around to rule Dhevyn. She's more than capable of doing it on her own."

"Did you know she gave Lady Lexie the Duchy of Elcast?"

Dirk nodded. "We corresponded a good deal about it. Alenor thought I might want it."

"You didn't?" she asked curiously.

"Not even when I thought I was Wallin's son."

"Then it was you who suggested Oscon of Damita adopt Rees's son as his heir?"

"No. That was Alenor's idea. Faralan wasn't capable of ruling Elcast on her own. She'll be much happier in Damita. Her baby is Oscon's great-grandson and with Baston dead, he needed an heir. It seemed the best solution all round."

"And it saves Alenor from having to deal with a disinherited heir someday, bent on reclaiming his father's estates," Tia observed.

"As I said, she's more than capable of ruling Dhevyn on her own."

"Did you hear Alenor made Mellie her heir until she has a child of her own?" Tia asked, feeling a bit like a slave delivering a summary of the local gossip she'd heard around the village well.

"Then the next Queen of Dhevyn will be Melliandra Thorn," Dirk predicted. "After what Marqel did to her, Alenor will probably never bear another child."

They walked along the shore for a way in silence.

"Did you know Ella is dead?" she ventured carefully.

"Yes." There was no emotion in his voice.

"She was poisoned. With ergot, Misha says. It wasn't very pleasant, by all accounts."

"Not an undeserved fate, when all is said and done," he remarked.

"Was it you?"

Dirk stopped at looked her. "Do you really want me to answer that?"

She thought about it for a moment, and then shook her head. "I'm sorry. I had no right to ask..."

"You still think I'm a cold-blooded killer, don't you?"

"Well, you see, that's the problem, Dirk," she sighed. "I don't know what you are."

He looked away, but when he looked back at her, his steel-gray eyes were just as unreadable, just as hard to fathom, as they had ever been. "I'm sorry for the pain I caused you, Tia. I'm sorry I hurt anyone. But I couldn't stand by and do nothing. And the battle isn't over yet. It's going to take years to undo the damage Belagren and Antonov did."

She nodded, knowing he spoke the truth. "I thought about it, you know. I thought about how much I love Misha. I thought about how much good I could do as the wife of the Lion of Senet. It all seems a little too perfect."

"What's wrong with that?"

"I'm not sure. I suppose I don't want to finish up like your father."

"You mean with my knife buried up to the hilt in your throat?" he asked, with more than a little bitterness.

"That's not what I meant."

"Then what did you mean?"

She shrugged, not sure how to put her thoughts into words. "Lexie told me once I'd never understand what Morna and Johan shared unless I experienced it for myself."

"Is that why you're here?" he asked, looking a little alarmed at the notion. "To rekindle what you think we had?"

"No. Lust brought on by isolation isn't love, Dirk. I had to meet Misha before I truly understood that, though."

"Does he know you're here?"

"He suggested it. He's concerned about what will happen in the future if you and I can't get along."

"You told him about us, didn't you?"

She nodded and then smiled, feeling a little foolish. "I think the day I found myself pouring my heart out to Misha about what a cad you were was the day it occurred to me who I really loved."

Dirk didn't reply. They kept walking along the shore with nothing but the distant honking of an aggravated swan disturbing the silence.

"Misha's right, I suppose. I guess that's why I said I'd come. To clear the air. I don't know how you did it, Dirk, not really. I mean I understand *what* you did, I even think I know why, but how you could do all those terrible things and never let on to anyone, never share it..." She shrugged. "I'm not sure I'm saying this right."

"I think I understand."

Tia hesitated, not sure what else to say. "Perhaps we'll see you in Avacas for the coronation? Misha would like it if you came."

"I think my presence is required. The Lord of the Suns is supposed to crown the Lion of Senet, I believe. I have to return to Avacas for the trial, in any case. Ella's dead, but Madalan and Yuri still need to be dealt with."

She suddenly couldn't meet his eyes. "You'll understand if you're not invited to the wedding, won't you? I mean, it's only going to be a small affair. Misha hates making a fuss."

"It's all right. I won't be offended."

He didn't sound offended, but there was no way of telling if he meant it or not. She looked at him uncertainly. "Look...I just wanted to say one more thing...when I first learned you were Johan's son...when I found out who you were...it wasn't easy for me...for any of us. You're so like him in some ways, and other ways you're so different. I wanted...Oh, damn...I'm not making any sense. I wanted you to be like him, I suppose. I so badly wanted you to be proud, and honorable, and noble...all the things I thought Johan was."

"And I wasn't?"

"Johan's pride cost him Dhevyn, Dirk. You got it back for him. You got it back in a way Johan was incapable of even imagining."

"Is that a compliment or a condemnation?" he asked with a wry smile. "And I truly don't deserve any credit for freeing Dhevyn. That was your doing, Tia, not mine."

"What I'm trying to say, Dirk," she said, "is that I think Johan would have been proud of you." She smiled then, and realized it was probably going to be all right between them. "Your methods probably would have given him apoplexy..."

"My lord?"

Dirk turned to the servant who had hailed him. "Yes?"

"There is *another* new acolyte waiting to see you, my lord. This one is very insistent."

"Tell him I'll be right there," Dirk ordered, before turning back to Tia. "I'm sorry. I really have to go."

"A new acolyte?"

"We've been flooded with them recently. It's suddenly fashionable to be a Sundancer again."

She nodded. "Then I shouldn't keep you any longer. Goodbye, Dirk."

"Good-bye, Tia."

"Dirk!" she called after him.

He stopped to look at her over his shoulder.

"Do you remember the day we arrived in Omaxin? You told me one day I'd have to admit you were on my side."

Dirk nodded slowly. "I also remember you telling me I'd have to do something fairly spectacular to convince you."

"You certainly did that."

He smiled at her. "Misha's a lucky man, Tia. You can tell him I said so, if you want."

"I will," she promised.

Dirk walked back toward the palace without looking back. Tia watched him leave with an odd feeling it took her a little while to define. She smiled to herself when she realized it wasn't so much what she was feeling, but what she *wasn't* feeling.

For the first time she could remember, she wasn't angry at Dirk Provin.

Chapter 93

The new acolyte was waiting for Dirk in the morning room, looking out over the gardens toward the lake. She was wearing a dark blue riding habit and had obviously not even waited to change before demanding to see him. She turned when she heard him enter.

"Jacinta?"

"Please don't say my name like that. You sound like my mother."

"What are you doing here? Is something wrong?"

"Nothing more than usual," she shrugged. "Was that who I think it was just now with you on the lawn?"

"Tia Veran," he confirmed. "Although she'll be Princess Tia Latanya soon."

"I'm a little surprised to find her seeking an audience with the Lord of the Suns," Jacinta remarked with a raised brow. "I got the distinct impression you two didn't get along."

"We had a few loose ends that needed to be settled." Dirk walked across the room and stopped a few paces from her. "Did Alenor send you?"

"No."

The thought she had come here of her own volition filled him with a strange sense of anticipation. "Then what are you doing here? I thought you'd be married to Raban Seranov by now."

She laughed. "Like *that* was ever going to happen while I still had breath in my body."

"Your mother called off the wedding?"

"I called it off," she told him defiantly.

"So you've run away again," he concluded with a smile.

"Running away is something children do, Dirk. I happen to feel I have a higher calling than making babies to perpetuate the Seranov line."

"A *higher* calling?"

"Actually, it was my mother who gave me the idea. You see, I discovered it was far easier to be a dutiful daughter of Dhevyn hundreds of miles away in Omaxin than when actually confronted with Raban Seranov in person. In one of our many rather heated discussions, my mother threatened to pack me off to a temple somewhere if I didn't toe the line." She smiled airily. "It suddenly occurred to me I wanted nothing more than to serve the Goddess."

"*You* want to join the Sundancers?" he asked skeptically. "What about that noble speech you gave me about the stability of Dhevyn requiring the union of the Seranov and D'Orlon houses?"

"Alenor married Alexin," she shrugged. "With the Queen of Dhevyn married to the Duke of Grannon Rock's second son, I didn't really think my contribution would make that much difference, do you?"

"We don't just accept anybody into the Sundancers, my lady," he said.

"Well, you'd better let me in or there'll be hell to pay," she threatened. "I didn't come all this way to have you refuse me. Anyway, changing the world's not a thing you can tackle on your own, Dirk. Even someone like you is going to need a hand from time to time."

"And if I did need a hand, what makes you think I'd ask you?"

"I'm the only one who understands you."

"Is that so?"

"Well, maybe not the only one. I think Misha understands you better than you'd like. He worked out what you were up to long before anyone else did."

"You've seen him recently?"

She nodded. "At Alenor's wedding. He's a good man. Tia

is a very lucky girl. If he wasn't already taken, I might have made a play for him myself. Come to think of it, I did ask him to marry me once."

"I thought you weren't interested in finding a husband?"

"I'm willing to make an exception for someone exceptional."

"How exceptional, exactly?"

She smiled coyly. "Are you flirting with me?"

"Are *you* flirting with me, would be more to the point." He reached out and took her hand. "Why did you really come?" he asked, drawing her closer.

"You *need* my help, Dirk. We still need to study all those notes from Omaxin. We need to finish dismantling the Shadowdancers. We need to find out when the next Age of Shadows is due..."

"No, we don't."

"You don't *want* to know when the next Age of Shadows is due?"

"Well...actually...I already know," he said. "Neris told me before I left Mil."

Jacinta stared at him, open-mouthed.

"But that means..." She was too shocked to finish the sentence. It took her a moment to recover and then she swore in a very unladylike manner. "You've known all along?"

"The knowledge is useless, Jacinta. That was the reason Neris refused to tell anybody. He figured he was better off keeping Belagren in the dark than letting her discover she didn't have anything to worry about. He destroyed the murals in Omaxin that would give it away, built the traps in the Labyrinth and faked his death...all of it, just to prevent the Shadowdancers from learning they really had nothing to fear."

Jacinta appeared too shocked to be angry at him. "So why did he tell you?"

"He had to tell someone, I suppose."

"But...I mean...*damn* it, Dirk! Why didn't you *say* something? Why go through all of this? And what do you mean, the information is useless? We have to make plans! We have to prepare!"

"There's no point."

"That's the *whole* point, Dirk!"

"The next Age of Shadows is about fifteen hundred years away, Jacinta."

He'd never seen her lost for words before. She was almost too stunned to speak.

"So...so you went to Omaxin and pretended to look for the answers in the ruins. You made up that whole eclipse thing...you drove Antonov insane..." she spluttered. "You even went to war over it. You're unbelievable! Does anybody else know?"

He shook his head. "Not yet. That's one of the challenges ahead of us. To find a way to *make* it known so that fifteen hundred years from now people will be ready for it and another Belagren doesn't appear on the scene claiming it's a divine event and repeat the whole damn sorry business." He grinned suddenly. "Maybe we'll rewrite the *Book of Ranadon* and make it compulsory reading in every school. There's a certain irony in that, don't you think?"

Jacinta shook her head, still having difficulty accepting Dirk had known the most valuable secret on Ranadon and not breathed a word of it to anyone. Then as if something else had just occurred to her, she looked up at him, searching his face. "You said *we*."

"Well, if you insist on helping..." he said, raising her hand to his lips.

She snatched her hand from his. "Isn't the Lord of the Suns supposed to take a vow of celibacy or something?"

"Not required. I checked."

"You did? Why?"

He smiled. "Because a certain very well-bred lady asked me once to do her a favor. I couldn't, in all conscience, let the matter go without checking to see if the next time she asked me to make mad, unbridled, passionate love to her, I was in a position to refuse."

Jacinta scowled at him. "I don't know if I *want* anything to do with you after hearing you've known all along when the Age of Shadows was due. No wonder Tia never trusted you. What else are you plotting, Dirk Provin? What other terrible plans and secrets are lurking in that strange and devious mind of yours?"

"Don't worry. I plan to lead a very long and boring life from now on. I've done most of the terrible things I had to do."

"Only *most* of them? You single-handedly changed the face of Ranadon, Dirk. Dear Goddess! What else is there *left* to do?"

"I want to find out if lions are real," he said.

CHARACTER LIST

ALENOR D'ORLON—Queen of Dhevyn. Rainan's daughter. Wife of Kirshov.

ALEXIN SERANOV—Second son of the current Duke of Grannon Rock. Reithan's cousin.

ANALEE LATANYA—Deceased. Princess of Damita. Wife of Antonov. Mother of Misha, Kirshov and Gunta.

ANTONOV LATANYA—The Lion of Senet. Father of Misha, Kirshov and Gunta. Husband of Analee of Damita.

BALONAN—Seneschal of Elcast castle.

BARIN WELACIN—Prefect of Avacas.

BELAGREN—Deceased. High Priestess of the Shadowdancers.

BLARENOV—Member of the Brotherhood based in Paislee.

BRAHM HALYN—Sundancer living on Elcast. Brother of Paige Halyn, the Lord of the Suns.

CALLA—Mil's blacksmith.

CASPONA TAKARNOV—Deceased. Shadowdancer in training with Marqel.

CATERINA FARLO—Dirk's hostage. Daughter of Brotherhood members.

CLEGG—Captain of the *Calliope*.

DAL FALSTOV—Captain of the *Orlando*.

DARGIN OTMAR—Master-at-arms in the Queen's Guard.

DIRK PROVIN—Second son of Duke Wallin of Elcast and Princess Morna of Damita. Illegitimate son of Johan Thorn.

DROGAN SERANOV—Deceased. Duke of Grannon Rock until the War of Shadows. Killed fighting with Johan against Senet. Father of Reithan. Husband of Lexie.

ELESKA ARROWSMITH—Baenlander. Daughter of Novin Arrowsmith. Mellie Thorn's best friend.

ELLA GEON—Shadowdancer and physician. Expert in herbs and drugs. Tia's mother.

ERYK—Orphan from Elcast. Dirk's servant.

FARALAN—Daughter of the Duke of Ionan. Duchess of Elcast. Married to Rees Provin

FREDRAK D'ORLON—Deceased. Duke of Bryton. Killed in a hunting accident not long after his wife, Rainan Thorn, assumed the throne of Dhevyn. Alenor's father.

FRENA—Servant in Elcast Castle. The baker Welma's daughter.

GAVEN GREYBROOK—Pirate on Johan's ship. Killed in the tidal wave that hit Elcast.

GUNTA LATANYA—Deceased. Youngest son of Antonov Latanya and Analee of Damita. Sacrificed as a baby to ensure the return of the second sun.

HARI—Pirate captured in Paislee. Sacrificed on Elcast during the Landfall Festival.

HAURITZ—Butcher living in Elcast Town.

HELGIN—Physician and tutor at Elcast.

JACINTA D'ORLON—Cousin and lady-in-waiting to Alenor.

JOHAN THORN— Deceased. Pirate. Exiled King of Dhevyn.

KALLEEN—Leader of Kalleen's acrobat troupe.

KIRSHOV LATANYA—Second son of the Prince of Senet. Regent of Dhevyn. Husband of Alenor.

LANATYNE—Member of Kalleen's acrobats.

LANON RILL—Second son of Tovin Rill, Governor of Elcast.

LEXIE SERANOV THORN—Wife of Johan Thorn. First husband was the Duke of Grannon Rock. Mother of Reithan Seranov and Mellie Thorn.

LILA BAYSTOKE—Herb woman from Elcast.

LILE DROGANOV—Pirate based in Mil.

LINEL—Pirate captured in Paislee. Sacrificed on Elcast during the Landfall Festival.

MADALAN TIROV—Shadowdancer and aide to the High Priestess Belagren.

MARQEL—Also known as Marqel the Magnificent. Landfall bastard. Performs as an acrobat in Kalleen's troupe until she is taken into the Shadowdancers.

MASTER KEDRON—Elcast master-at-arms.

MELLIE THORN—Daughter of Johan Thorn and Lexie Seranov.

MISHA LATANYA—Eldest son of Antonov, the Lion of Senet. Also known as the Crippled Prince.

MORNA PROVIN—Deceased. Duchess of Elcast. Princess of Damita. Daughter of Prince Oscon. Sister of Analee. Married to Wallin Provin. Mother of Rees and Dirk.

MURRY—Member of Mistress Kalleen's acrobats.

NERIS VERAN—Sundancer and mathematical genius. Believed to be dead.

NOVIN ARROWSMITH—Pirate living in Mil.

OLENA BORNE—Deceased. Shadowdancer attached to Prince Antonov's court.

OSCON—Exiled ruler of Damita. Father of Analee and Morna.

PAIGE HALYN—Lord of the Suns.

PARON SHOEBROOK—Cobbler's son on Elcast.

PELLA—Baker in Mil.

PORL ISINGRIN—Pirate. Captain of the *Makuan*. Based in Mil.

RAINAN D'ORLON—Née Thorn. Former queen of Dhevyn. Mother of Alenor. Johan Thorn's younger sister.

REES PROVIN—Duke of Elcast. Dirk's brother.

REZO—Sailor on the *Calliope*.

ROVE ELAN—Lord Marshal of Dhevyn.

REITHAN SERANOV—Son of the late Duke of Grannon Rock and Lexie Seranov. Johan's stepson.

SABAN SERANOV—Duke of Grannon Rock. Father of Alexin and Raban.

SERGEY—Captain of the Avacas Palace Guard in Senet.

SOOTER—Member of Mistress Kalleen's acrobats.

TABOR ISINGRIN—Son of Porl Isingrin.

TIA VERAN—Daughter of Neris Veran and Ella Geon.

TOVIN RILL—Governor of Elcast.

VARIAN—Nurse to the sons of Elcast.

VIDEON LUKANOV—Head of the Brotherhood in Dhevyn.

VONRIL—Juggler. Son of Kalleen.

WALLIN PROVIN—Deceased Duke of Elcast.

WELMA—The master baker at Elcast Castle.

WILIM—Officer in the Queen's Guard.

YORNE—Apprentice baker. Welma's son.

YURI DARANSKI—Physician in the palace at Avacas.

ABOUT THE AUTHOR

JENNIFER FALLON lives in Alice Springs, Australia, and writes anywhere she can get her hands on a computer. She works in sales, marketing and training in the IT industry and changes jobs so often that even she isn't sure where she works these days.